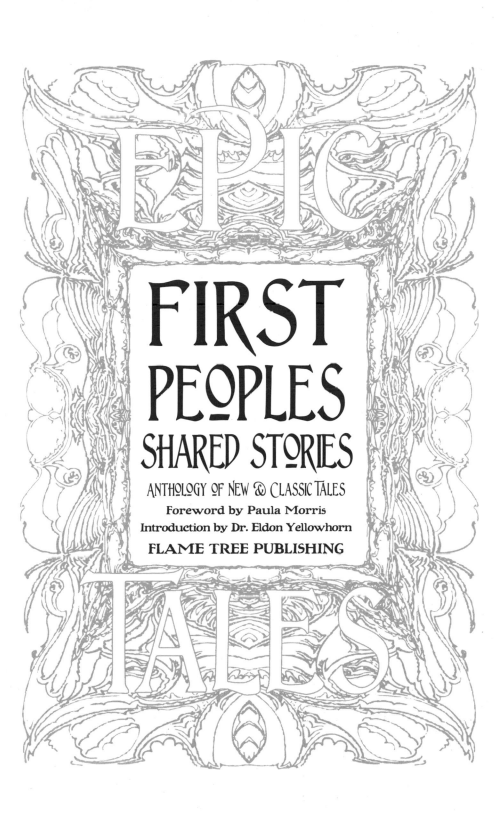

EPIC

FIRST PEOPLES

SHARED STORIES

ANTHOLOGY OF NEW & CLASSIC TALES

Foreword by Paula Morris

Introduction by Dr. Eldon Yellowhorn

FLAME TREE PUBLISHING

TALES

This is a FLAME TREE Book

Publisher & Creative Director: Nick Wells
Editorial Director: Catherine Taylor
Editorial Board: Catherine Taylor, Gillian Whitaker and Taylor Bentley
Associate Editor: Dr. Marc André Fortin

Special Thanks to Tiffany Morris, Hinahina Gray and Salt & Sage Books

FLAME TREE PUBLISHING
6 Melbray Mews, Fulham,
London SW6 3NS, United Kingdom
www.flametreepublishing.com

First published 2022
Copyright © 2022 Flame Tree Publishing Ltd

22 24 26 25 23
1 3 5 7 9 10 8 6 4 2

ISBN: 978-1-83964-942-4
Special ISBN: 978-1-80417-323-7

The cover image is created by Flame Tree Studio
based on artwork courtesy of Shutterstock.com/Rocket400 Studio.

'Confusion of Tongue', 'The Gherawhar (Goana)', 'Whowie', 'Why All the
Animals Peck At the Selfish Owl: The Coming of the Light', 'The Water Rat who
Discovered the Secret of Fire and How it was Taken from Him by the Eagle
Hawk', 'A Wonderful Bun Bar Rang (Lizard)', are reproduced, with permission,
from David Unaipon's *Legendary Tales of the Australian Aborigines*, Melbourne
University Press, Carlton, 2001.

'Māui Tames The Sun', 'Creation', 'The Coming of Kūmara', 'Patupaiarehe',
'Taniwha', 'Denizens of the Sea' are reproduced, with permission, from A.W. Reed,
Māori Myth and Legend, Raupo, Auckland, NZ, 2011.

Incidental motif images courtesy of Shutterstock.com/Karlionau.

A copy of the CIP data for this book is available from the British Library.

Printed and bound in China

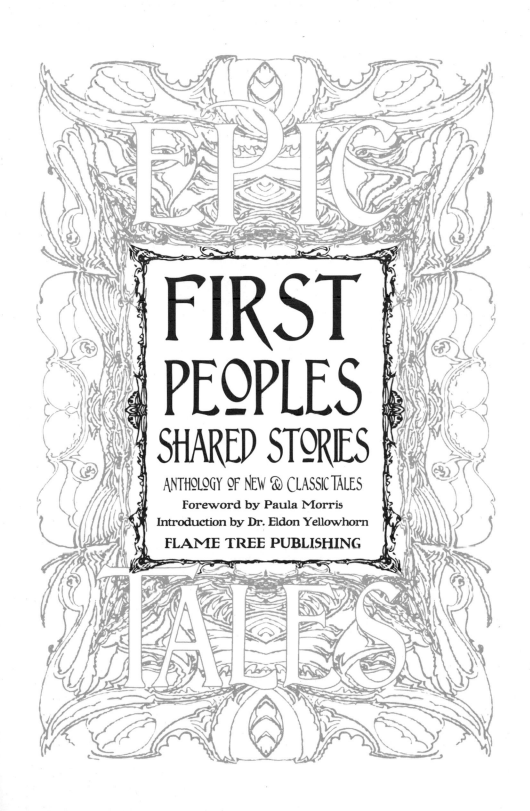

EPIC

FIRST PEOPLES

SHARED STORIES

ANTHOLOGY OF NEW & CLASSIC TALES

Foreword by Paula Morris

Introduction by Dr. Eldon Yellowhorn

FLAME TREE PUBLISHING

TALES

Contents

CONTENTS

EPIC

FIRST PEOPLES
SHARED STORIES
ANTHOLOGY OF NEW & CLASSIC TALES
Foreword by Paula Morris
Introduction by Dr. Eldon Yellowhorn
FLAME TREE PUBLISHING

TALES

Foreword

SHARING STORIES suggests an opportunity: to encounter, revisit or place in a broader context the narratives that make up the cultural inheritance of the world's First Peoples. This English-language anthology explores both the classic and contemporary, revealing both the potent richness of story traditions and inevitable tensions around the teller and the tale.

For many First Peoples, growing up in colonised countries, classic stories were part of what Pacific writer Albert Wendt – in his memoir *Out of the Vaipe, the Deadwater* – called 'banned knowledge'. This was rejected as pagan and primitive, or no longer relevant in the context of an imposed new national identity. The pressure to assimilate resulted in losses of languages, traditions, values, connections, and ways of seeing, all of which are expressed in the stories we told. Colonising cultures may frame their own narratives as history and those of the colonised as superstition or whimsy.

The written word has proven to be particularly important in recording oral testimonies and traditions, even if those writing down the stories often lacked sufficient language skills, cultural knowledge, and local context. However well-intentioned, they made mistakes – sometimes misinterpreting or mistranslating. In addition, what keepers of knowledge chose to share with explorers, missionaries, anthropologists, and other foreign investigators was often partial, and sometimes an intentional misdirection. Not all stories could and would be shared.

Some stories endure, to be rediscovered by new generations, but what remains has its own complex terrain. The chronicling of stories from oral traditions may have been designed for an outside audience, serving as an 'exotic' or ersatz souvenir. Some narratives have been appropriated or cited to demean past beliefs and practices. The act of recording may present the story as a static object, fixed both in content and interpretation, rather than fluid. In fact, stories could take different forms and directions depending on storytellers, their communities, their regions, and language groups. There is no one version that is authoritative.

In Māori tradition, the baskets of knowledge were retrieved after a perilous quest through the heavens. In different versions of this story, the protagonist changes, and the names and meaning of the baskets change as well. In one version, the god Tāne returned with three baskets; in another, the demi-god Tāwhaki returned with four. In another, the fourth basket was left behind in the heavens: its knowledge remains out of reach, representing everything people can never know. The whole story can never be told: it's always beyond our grasp.

In this anthology, classic stories from one part of the world may resonate with those from another, testimony to the shared humanity of our narrative impulses, as well as to old – and often forgotten – patterns of migration, settlement, trade, and travel. But there are disconnections as well, among the partial or conflicting accounts, and the leap from the past into the present.

The contemporary stories in the anthology suggest the range of contradictions in the lives of First Peoples today. These stories negotiate the fault lines between past and the present, rural and urban, the community and the individual, ancient and modern belief systems. From subject matter to style, from setting to idiom, the contemporary work here diverges from expected paths. Above the vast, often invisible roots of heritage grow soaring trees. Sometimes they twist or buckle, cross-pollinating in ways not conceivable – or possible – for our ancestors. But they're nourished by the same soil, fed by unbroken lines that run deep into our shared world.

Paula Morris

Publisher's Note

INSPIRED BY the tales of first peoples across the world, this collection brings together stories new and old. Ancient stories rooted in oral tradition sit alongside new fiction from indigenous writers, which draw on their culture while exploring a wide range of themes, from folklore and colonisation to futurism and science fiction.

This collection seeks to at once highlight the enduring and shared spirit of humanity, while also bringing new perspectives and attention to the legacy of First Nations, of Indigenous Peoples, of First Peoples. Yet, it must also be acknowledged that many of the older stories reproduced here were collected and translated by Western writers, and are therefore positioned from a Western perspective. The process of recording, translating and printing a story of course removes it from its original context, and in this case also inherently imbues them with preconceived notions about indigenous peoples. With this in mind, we have endeavoured to be selective in our choices, and not reproduce stories we found to be especially harmful or problematic in their retelling.

In these instances, our goal has been to decolonize these stories and return them to their owners, which is reflected by first crediting them to their culture of origin. Nonetheless, we do ask that the reader keep in mind that these tales, decontextualized from their original oral forms, have been filtered through a colonial lens. While informative, they should not be viewed as coming from the voices of the peoples from which they originate. As in our other anthologies, variances in spelling due to differing geographical origins have been retained in order to reflect the authors' voices, including in the introduction and foreword. Aboriginal and Torres Straight Island readers are also asked to please note that some of the tales within contain representations and words of First Peoples who have passed away.

These older stories are also balanced by an array of incredible submissions from modern indigenous voices, which remain sorely underrepresented in the publishing world and beyond. Fresh and inventive while also rooted in tradition, we are sure readers will enjoy this selection of tales from a talented group of writers.

Introduction

AS AN UNDERGRADUATE enrolled in an Anthropology course studying cultures native to North America, one of my assignments was to select a topic that reflected the traditions of a particular people. My choice was easy considering my Piikani heritage. While researching the folklore of my ancestors for that term report I came upon the publication *Mythology of the Blackfoot Indians* (1908) by Clark Wissler and D.C. Duvall. As I pored over the myths recorded by an early modern anthropologist who interviewed members of the last generation to witness the old buffalo days, I was taken aback to read the same stories that I had heard as a child. Although presented in English, they still contained the same outlines as the ones I remembered. Perhaps the most enduring impression the written versions made on me was how sterile and dull they were compared to when I heard them in the Blackfoot oral tradition. Wissler also came to shallow conclusions that reduced the narratives to inconsequential anecdotes.

The Problematic Filter of Ethnology

Wissler's treatment was hardly unique since the origin story of ethnology is the study of ethnic folks as the Other. When scholars such as Albert Gallatin brought the European Enlightenment to America, secularism had not yet emerged; thus, the tales told by pagan and heathen folk became the nemesis of rationalism. These scholars' staunchly Christian perspective also skewed their regard for the Indigenous people they encountered and entrenched the belief of inferiority.

Ethnographers throughout the nineteenth century, and even into the twentieth century, never unburdened themselves of that cultural superiority complex, and so their studies of mythology continued to reflect that belief. None of the writers composing classic ethnographies, such as *Blackfoot Lodge Tales* (1892) by George Bird Grinnell, *My Life as an Indian* (1907) by Willard Schultz, *The Old North Trail* (1908) by Walter McClintock and *The Blackfeet: Raiders of the Northwestern Plains* (1958) by John C. Ewers, were Blackfoot. Although they came from different traditions the ethnographers and their informants converged around the same motives. Blackfoot people experienced unrelenting violence from the settler population such that they could feel the stresses on their customs. Anthropologists of the late nineteenth and early twentieth century, for their part, thought that Indigenous people constituted a 'vanishing race'. Therefore, these chroniclers were not literary personalities composing original stories with graceful prose. Rather, they were translators preserving the essence of Blackfoot stories and storytelling by adhering clumsily to a word-for-word interpretation. Their transcribed legends eschewed amusement since there was no room for quirkiness in their salvage-collecting of Blackfoot oral narratives. Nor did they write for Indigenous people, most of whom could not read or appreciate English texts. Theirs was a serious calling for other academics who would refer to these myths in comparative studies. Humour and quirkiness were filtered from the preserves of intellectual artifacts of a people doomed to extinction. As a result, anthropological treatments of old Blackfoot stories lack the entertainment quality that instilled them with much levity. Moreover, the audience ethnographers wrote for did not exist in the realm of popular culture. Whereas the spoken works were lively and engaging, ethnography extracted whimsy and spontaneity from the composition. For Indigenous students of anthropology, like myself, reading these volumes today is like drinking flat soda pop: while the flavour is there, the fizz is missing – and that is what makes the beverage extraordinary.

Well over a century ago, John Wesley Powell pronounced in the *First Annual Report of the Bureau of Ethnology* (1881): 'Mythology is primitive philosophy.' He discouraged his colleagues from taking oral narratives too seriously, saying, 'It is vain to search for truth in mythologic philosophy but it is important to search for veritable philosophies, that they may be properly compared and that the products of the human mind in its various stages of culture may be known.' He explained the purpose of researching old stories as follows: 'The objective or scientific method of studying a mythology is to collect and collate its phenomena simply as it is stated and understood by the people to whom it belongs. In tracing back the threads of its historical development the student should expect to find it more simple and childlike in every stage of his progress.' His bias served to crystallize anthropological discourse against mythology and to infantilize Indigenous people in the minds of his peers. George Bird Grinnell wrote in *Blackfoot Lodge Tales*, 'The Indian is a man, not very different from his white brother, except that he is undeveloped.' He merely echoed the perspective of the leading scholars of his time.

A belief in the absence of veracity in the narratives was a stance widely shared by later cohorts of white anthropologists who studied these stories. Denialism is a thread that leads directly back to the original days of anthropology. Even when researchers empathized with the plight of their subjects, like their progenitors they still saw no history in mythology. Their focus turned instead to the symbolism contained in the narrative. What binds these ethnographers is their cultural distance from Indigenous people, and so they have no vested interest in searching for reality behind the allegory. As I progressed in my studies, I learned more about the position of mythology within the discipline and the outside influences that directed anthropological thought. Mythology gave meaning to the everyday lives of ordinary people, so its true purpose was to put our minds in balance with the world out there. Therefore, this psychological device was set against the vast sweep of antiquity, but the general estimation was that myths contained no history.

Before I started my research, the prevailing thought was that old stories offered only symbolic chronicles about a mythic past, but not actual history. Initially that was something I, too, accepted as fact. Now, however, my purpose in studying mythology as an archaeologist is to consider the antiquity of oral narratives my ancestors told around the fires of their tipis during those long-ago prairie nights and determine when these stories became part of Blackfoot culture. My advantage is that I have access to analytical methods through my studies in anthropology and archaeology that earlier generations did not. I use them to extract new insights from old stories. I can now refute the long-held notion that myths exist in a state of timelessness that eludes our efforts for establishing chronologies. The following stories are the fruits of my labour and the discoveries I have made from my research.

Oral Traditions and History

Tracing Indigenous oral narratives back beyond the written word might seem impossible at first glance, except for the fact that archaeologists routinely educe history from unwritten sources. Archaeology offers a bundle of methods that help us delve into antiquity without the requirement of writing. Walter McClintock, in his ethnography *The Old North Trail* (1910), related a story about the origin of tobacco as a Blackfoot custom and how it brought the sacred Beaver medicine bundle into our religious life. In this beaver tale, two brothers were in love with the same woman. However, she bestowed her affections on the younger one. In his jealousy, the older brother decided to eliminate his rival. His scheme had he and his brother go on a hunting trip to an island in the middle of a large lake as the summer waned. His deceitful plan meant sneaking off with their raft and stranding his brother there. With no provisions for the winter, he would surely suffer before succumbing to the cold season.

Fate brought salvation for the young man because the island was the home of the Chief of the Beavers and his family. They discovered this forlorn young man and invited him to spend that winter in their lodge. The Beaver Chief transformed him into a beaver, and the whole family took care of him throughout the winter. As spring approached a young beaver saw the unscrupulous sibling return to find the trophy of his criminal adventure. The rodent patriarch advised his adopted human son on an equally deceptive manoeuvre to get his revenge. As the young man prepared to leave and return to his people, his surrogate father gifted him with a small bag of tobacco seeds and the beaver medicine bundle and instructed him on the songs and prayers to perform. He and his adopted beaver brother went to live with the humans long enough to teach them to sow, cultivate and harvest tobacco.

At first glance, the gift of tobacco from the mythical beaver clan resembles the kind of folklore that has no parallel in secular reality. However, deconstructing the story yields the clues to the antiquity of this custom in Blackfoot culture. The Beaver Chief gave tobacco seeds to the young man, who then brought them home. The humans accept this gift because smoking a mixture of bearberry and the inner cambium of red osier dogwood was already a well-established tradition. They merely added tobacco to their repertoire of smoking products. Determining the source of tobacco is the key issue from this story. It had to come from the south because it is not a native plant on the northern plains, where it only grows due to human intervention. So, tobacco products, such as seeds and phytoliths, are the signature and proxy for this story.

Archaeologists working at earth-lodge villages constructed by Indigenous farmers along the Missouri River have collected tobacco seeds from these hearths where smokers discarded the contents of their pipes. Using the trusty method of radiocarbon dating helped determine the antiquity of organ material discovered during excavations and surveys. This technique produced results that showed tobacco appearing among the farming cultures of the Middle Missouri River circa 700 CE. Since the customary homeland of the Piikani people, who are the southernmost branch of the Blackfoot Confederacy, includes the Upper Missouri River, they must have been the ones who brought tobacco cultivation to its northern limit in the Saskatchewan River basin. The botanical transfer that inspired the story about the Beaver Chief occurred during a climatic event called the Medieval Warm Spell. Drawing a conclusion around these factors yields a conservative estimate of 900 CE as the era when the story of tobacco first entered Blackfoot mythology and when the beaver medicine bundle became a central feature of our religious life.

Gardening was not a Blackfoot custom before that time, and the success of a tobacco crop depended on favourable environmental conditions. Moreover, the plant had to fit into their customary lifestyle of moving regularly to harvest the country foods they needed, such as berries and other vegetation. Thus, they could not camp by their gardens all through the summer to tend their crops. By cutting down the vegetation, burning it, and tilling the ash into the soil before planting their tobacco seeds, Blackfoot gardeners mimicked the natural habitat of a plant that colonizes disturbed lands. Centralizing beavers in this story was deliberate as proximity to the habitat created by beaver dams was ideal for tobacco gardens. The riverine forest around the reservoir offered protection for the seedlings from cooler air temperatures in the spring, and the impounded waters meant the roots of the plant had a source of soil moisture. This strategy worked even as the climate deteriorated with the onset of the Little Ice Age when the North American fur trade started. By the time Anthony Henday became the first Hudson's Bay Company trader to reach the northern plains in 1754, tobacco cultivation was a thriving custom for Blackfoot gardeners.

Star Lore and History: The Celestial Marriage Tale and the Precession of the Equinoxes

Star lore is a large motif in old stories that my ancestors kept; so much so that Wissler and Duvall dedicated a whole section to it in their survey of Blackfoot mythology. One story that has attracted much interest for over a century concerns the woman who married Morningstar. Many ethnographers collected this narrative, and such anthropological luminaries as Franz Boas and Claude Lévi-Strauss have offered up their interpretations on its meaning. The focus of these analyses always centres on the symbolic or psychological situation and never on the historical occurrence.

While the details may vary, this celestial marriage tale is common to many cultures across western North America. In the Blackfoot version, two young women sleeping on the open prairie awake in the pre-dawn time and see Morningstar shining bright. One of them states that he is her choice for a husband. Hearing this declaration, Morningstar travels to the earth in his search for a wife. When they meet, he brings her back to the sky country where they marry. While resident there, the human woman becomes pregnant and has a baby boy, who they call Okiinaa. Shortly thereafter she incurs the anger of her heavenly in-laws when she uproots a large holy turnip. This creates a hole in the sky, and through it she sees her former home and her family, which cause her to become nostalgic. Fearing the wrath of his father, Sun, Morningstar sends his wife back to earth with their son. He warns her that Okiinaa should not touch the ground until Morningstar's mother, Moon, has grown full and starts to wane. Otherwise, Sun would take him back to the sky country and put him in that hole she created when she pulled up the holy turnip. She resumes her life back on earth and one day she leaves baby Okiinaa in the care of her mother while she goes to collect wood. Okiinaa's grandmother gets distracted and does not notice when he crawls onto the ground. When she realizes what has happened, she quickly lifts him up and cradles him until he falls asleep. She places him on a buffalo robe and covers him with a blanket. When Okiinaa's mother returns she inquires about her son and learns he is asleep. When she lifts the blanket, she is horrified to find only a puffball mushroom where Okiinaa should be. That night when she looked to the sky country there was a new star at the centre of the sky. She knew it was her baby Okiinaa sitting in the hole she created when she uprooted that holy turnip.

Archaeoastronomy is the study of how ancient people observed celestial bodies and organized the stars and constellations they observed in the night sky. It is one of the more esoteric branches of archaeology, but it is key to understanding this story and the metaphors embedded therein. Okiinaa, who is the grandchild of Sun and Moon, is the Blackfoot equivalent of Polaris, the pole star. In this story of the woman who married Morningstar, the metaphor of childbirth is the central theme. It tells us that until that marriage, there was no star at the centre of the sky, and then a star was born. That is true! Polaris only became the pole star around 500 CE, and prior to that there was no pole star. So, the historical event related in this folktale represents the moment when naked-eye astronomers on the plains first realized that there was a star at the centre of the sky country that never moved, and all the other stars circled it. Their observation is real because of the astronomical phenomenon known as the precession of the equinoxes, which is a function of the earth's axis being tilted 23.4 degrees off the plane of the ecliptic. One revolution of the axis itself takes approximately twenty-six thousand years to complete. This causes the illusion that the entire vault of heaven is moving, but in fact our planet's axis is changing position relative to the stars in the sky. Indeed, the astronomical phenomenon tells us that the story of the Star Husband entered Blackfoot culture circa 500 CE. The story explains why there is a stationary star where earlier generations did not see one.

Star Lore and History: The Lost Boys and the Rise of Large-Scale Communal Hunting

Archaeoastronomy and the precession of the equinoxes also explain another story in the mental library of Blackfoot storytellers. Decorating the smoke flaps of Blackfoot tipis are a cluster of circles that depict the constellation we call the Lost Boys, and which western astronomers label the Pleiades. This story begins with a hapless hunter, his delinquent sons and their spiteful friends. It ends with the ancestors of the Blackfoot people inventing the large-scale communal hunting technique called the buffalo jump. It also recounts how the Sundance, which we call the Ookaan in our language and which has nothing to do with the sun, became the centre of our religious life.

Immediately after the Ice Age, when the continental glaciers retreated from the Northern Plains, our ancient, remote ancestors occupied the newly revealed country and made it their homeland. Their mobile, hunting lifestyle suited the grasslands, which teemed with herding mammals that they learned to stalk, track, trail and prey upon with their spears. Communal hunting meant a small group of men cooperating to ambush a handful of their quarry. In this manner local bands of hunters supported their needs for food, hides and tools. While this method stood the test of time, a big change occurred around two thousand five hundred years ago when a new culture emerged that revolutionized the meaning of communal hunting by coordinating the efforts of hundreds of people from across a broad region. Since archaeologists found the first traces of it in the Besant Valley of southern Saskatchewan, the persistent question remained: How did this Besant culture assemble a crowd large enough to conduct their hunts? During winter small bands were dispersed across the landscape. Yet when spring arrived, they had to gather at a specific place and time for one of their buffalo hunts.

The answer is told in the Blackfoot story of the Lost Boys and how they became denizens of the sky country. Back in the old Dog Days, before our ancestors got horses, there lived a family with several boys. Since there were so many of them, their father struggled to provide enough of everything for them. He went hunting nearly every day, and though he always brought back meat, it would only last for one or two meals. His sons would request clothing made from the soft, supple hides of newborn calves. The next thing they knew their mother was sewing clothes for them made from the tough hides of the old cows. They felt resentful because when they met their relatives the other children teased them about their clothing. Finally, the boys decided that they could not live with the taunts anymore. They agreed that if they did not get the clothes they wanted, they would run away. Now, the eldest boy was old enough to have gone on a vision quest. A spirit had come to him and given him a medicine song that had the power to lift them upwards. He told his brothers that by singing it they could all reach the sky country together.

One day they attended a large encampment with their parents. When they went to mingle with some other children, they heard the familiar mockery about their clothes that always followed them. There was too much derision hurled in their direction, so they decided the time was right to leave their stingy parents and go live in the sky country. They stripped down until they were naked and threw their clothes in a pile, preparing to sing their brother's medicine song. Thinking that their idle threats would amount to nothing, the people in the camp began to laugh and make jokes about them. Their parents begged them to get dressed and not make a scene. The oldest boy responded by saying, 'In the spring when the buffalo calves have their yellow robes, we will leave the sky country to remind you of your stinginess.' Then they began singing the medicine song, which caused them to start rising. Their relatives were astounded as they went higher and higher, until they lost sight of them.

When the boys reached the sky country they were surprised with their success. They were also chilly, so they huddled together to keep warm. Just then Moon came walking by and found them sitting there naked. She asked them why they were in such a state. They related their tale of woe and asked her if they could live with her. Moon then asked her husband, Sun, if the boys could live in the sky. Sun agreed to give them refuge and make them star people. Then the boys asked

Sun if he would punish their stingy parents and mean-spirited relatives and take all the water away. Thereafter when Sun went out to cross the sky, he was extra hot.

Back on the ground the people, the dogs and all the other animals began to suffer because of the heat. After seven days, all the rivers had run dry. Even the springs no longer gave water. The chief of the dogs had his own medicine, and he suspected the lost boys were behind the calamity. He called a meeting of the pack out on a butte not too far from the camp. He related his suspicion to the other dogs and told them if they all howled together, they could make a big, loud wail that would reach the sky country. They explained to Moon that their pups were hurting for lack of water and too much heat. They told her that the people had learned their lesson and they would be kind to their children.

Up in the sky country, Moon heard the dogs' plaintive yowls. She approached Sun and told him what the dogs bayed to her. Therefore, he no longer had to punish the people. Sun was not so hot anymore. Water returned to the rivers and the springs began to flow again. Everyone was happy, especially the dogs because people started to treat them a little bit better.

Both Walter McClintock and Clark Wissler included this story in their respective ethnographies but neither of them could make much sense of it. In fact, Clark Wissler only concluded that it answered for the Blackfoot people the age-old question: Why do dogs howl at the moon?

Even today Blackfoot people still tell this story, but the main takeaway is advice for young parents to be mindful of their children. Beyond this shallow understanding of it there is another explanation that eludes people because the context in which it makes sense no longer exists.

Observers of the Lost Boys constellation see it in the eastern sky after sunset in the autumn. Throughout the winter it appears when night closes in, but it is also in motion as the season progresses. By the spring equinox, when the days are getting longer, this cluster of stars appears only briefly in the western sky before it sets too. In the story, Moon finds the Lost Boys, but that is another way of saying these two celestial objects are in conjunction. The crescent moon and the constellation only share the sky once, and that is around the spring equinox, which is also the beginning of summer in the Blackfoot calendar.

When the boys leave for the sky country, their parting words are that they want to remind their relatives of their stinginess. However, another way of interpreting this message is that the disappearance of the Pleiades from the evening sky is an accurate predictor of the buffalo calving season. Indeed, their message is a mnemonic device announcing the time to gather for the spring buffalo hunt. For people who were isolated in their winter camps across the landscape, this discovery was a scheduling breakthrough. Thus, the Besant culture succeeded because they had found an effective stellar calendar that they used to coordinate the movement of hunters to reach the place where, before dispersing for the winter season, they had agreed to gather for the spring buffalo jump.

This occurred when it did, circa 2500 years ago, because that is when the earth's axis reached the point where this constellation appeared to move into that part of the sky where its apparent motion coincided with the buffalo calving season. However, that is not the end of the story. There is another feature of the Lost Boys story that has to do with the Ookaan, or Sundance, which had nothing to do with sun worship and everything to do with celebrating the covenant between the hunters and their prey. After the star cluster leaves the evening sky, it reappears in the night sky around the summer solstice except that it rises shortly before dawn. Then the sun rises and obliterates the stars. I contend that this heliacal rising was the signal to the Blackfoot people to perform the Ookaan ceremony.

Opening Dialogue and Reassessing Collected Stories

White, male anthropologists enjoyed a centuries-long soliloquy about the mythologies of Indigenous people that energized poetry, literature and music. Examples such as the 'Song of Hiawatha' by H.W. Longfellow, *The Last of the Mohicans* by J.F. Cooper or the Symphony No. 9, *From the New World* by Antonin Dvořák are the nineteenth-century progenitors of twentieth-century mythologic theorists such a Claude Lévi-Strauss and Joseph Campbell. Like Franz Boas, they looked to Freud and Jung for inspiration in psychoanalysing the cultures of Indigenous people while overlooking the environmental messages or astronomical observations contained in old stories.

This volume of traditional narratives replaces that soliloquy with dialogue. The Indigene speaks back to the scholars who possessed a mythologic monopoly. It invites the reader to reconsider the written versions of the oral stories. To reimagine their meaning within the medium of presentation, taking into account advances in research methods that change our understanding of their original provenance.

My research into Blackfoot mythology puts to rest the idea that myths occupy a timeless region in our imagination. I argue that there are rational messages contained in these stories that we can interpret by deploying the methods of archaeology and archaeoastronomy. Far from being the irrational fables that early modern anthropologists supposed they were, these old stories tell us about the environment in which our ancestors thrived.

Cultures that had no writing tradition had only the narrative device to preserve their knowledge. Therefore, humans across the world love their stories, storytellers and storytelling because they give us our humanity. They help us imagine our lives outside of ourselves.

Shared Stories Across Continents

Mythologies, irrespective of their provenance, do exhibit common themes. Origin stories, for example, exist in all oral traditions because people must account for their existence and self-awareness. Although the lived experience of our ancestors inspired the broad outline of these narratives, there is always a Creator: a supernatural being who possesses the power to create the world, animate people and share the spirits of blood, breath and speech. All the elements that nurture the human condition are endowments from this universal architect. Thus, the phrase 'In the beginning' represents the first words uttered because they introduce us and our world to ourselves. What follows are the stories that explain our world to the existential questions we ask in our internal dialogue.

Just as origin stories proliferate to explain our existence, so, too, do prophecies that portend the end of the world, since that Creator can just as easily be the Destroyer. Like the contemporary Doomsday Clock that foreshadows the end of history, ancient people believed the end of creation to be inevitable. Whether we refer to nuclear apocalypse, Judgement Day or cosmic cataclysms like the one that wiped out the dinosaurs, all good stories must come to an end. Somehow, we accept that humanity's tenure on this earth is as temporary as a storm upon our land. If there is one takeaway message from archaeological investigations, it is that the world is always ending for somebody. We are drawn to this conclusion because antiquity is littered with the ruins of failed civilizations. Cultures everywhere have a habit of personifying natural forces, such as the great flood or the great earthquake or the devastating volcano, because geological catastrophes are life-changing, traumatic events that have long affected the lived experience of our ancestors. The power they exhibit made them plausible agents of termination in eras past. Our modern anxiety is fueled by the fear of nuclear holocaust due to its potential for global eradication. Narratives of demise may foretell our destruction, but our reaction is to our lives with purpose and to do our best to avoid the last spoken verse of our existence.

Thus, between the day of creation and the night of annihilation appear all the elements of the human condition. Like the stories in this volume, when we tell tales of beauty that invokes anger, siblings who conspire against each other, the hero's journey or the lovers' quarrel that incites war, we recount the hard-earned lessons that make us the people we are. Yet some of our myths also include elements that fall within the realm of history. We can appreciate old stories for their entertainment value, for their psychological fulfillment, or for their explanation of the nature of things, but we can also discern in them the roots of our cultures' histories.

Dr. Eldon Yellowhorn

An Unwanted Two-Spirit

Chukwu Sunday Abel, Nigeria

WHEN A SNAKE *sloughs its skin, it doesn't lose its dreadfulness with its old skin.*

You came to us with good news of salvation, we accepted it. You came through our land borders uninvited and handed to us your books of alphabets, we embraced them even at the expense of our own tongue(s). You told us to discard our flourishing authorities, they were primitive and unpopular – we accepted your acclaimed error-free rule by majority. Thereafter, you tethered on our necks your strange supreme books to guide our indulgences – we didn't rebel even as the sleeping eyes of our ancestors glowered angrily at us . You told our children to slough their God-given soot through the help of your hot anti-melanin oil, and we turned blind-eyed, but the silent voices of our sleeping ancestors warned us, told us of their wrath, called us unworthy sons. However, we never questioned you, we didn't complain, we gobbled them gluttonously so as not to offend this our nonreciprocal bromance.

Now, you came with this gospel of self-determination, gospel of free-choice. You told our women to stand and pee, to climb our palm trees, to become sons, to become husbands; and our men, you told to become wives, to bear children. Aru! Were snakes to lose their dreadfulness, women would use them to bind their hair.

* * *

There was no place like home, one's home, one's ancestral home, especially when one's first name was *Echezona*, "do not forget". Don't forget your root, perhaps. "Don't forget where you come from", a maxim from my father before his death.

Google told me: "Nigeria, an African country on the Gulf of Guinea, has many natural landmarks and wildlife reserves…"

Then, "Anambra is a state in the southeastern part of Nigeria…" Nothing was said about culture and tradition, nothing about ajoagwo nor Ngenebaka – "they were predominantly Christians and spoke Igbo", Google said. My father before his death told me nothing about Ajoagwo; nor did my mother who died before him.

When our flight touched down on Muritala Muhammed International Airport, Lagos, I knew that I had not only made myself happy but made my father proud. Lagos was the most populated state of the 36; was soiled by numerous carcasses of woebegone nylon bags, discarded empty plastic cans, bagged refuses, and human faeces in black nylon bags. Perhaps, in the absence of a well-structured waste disposal system, the residents of the bellicose but accommodating city that emerged from collective unpremeditated floridness from the past and present residents, the reason for its longstanding apothegm, *shine your eyes*, resorted to littering the face of their unsmiling city with their dumps; maybe in protest of incessant failed governments or as evidence of deficiency in the midst of sufficiency.

They drove competitively and recklessly on the road in a bid to overtake whomever, whatever was in their front. Nobody waited for another. Patience was time-wasting. It was unsafe to adhere to the traffic regulations. Whoever wanted obeying religiously the traffic rules ate his dinner on the road or passed the night on the Lagos roads. But Google didn't tell me this; nor did my father.

Lagos to Anambra was about 480 km by road and would take about nine hours. By flight, it would take less than an hour. But I was on expedition, having a better view of the countryside would be to go by road. It was the longest of the road trips I had ever made. But it wouldn't have been as time-taking as it was if not for the military and police checkpoints that punctuated the flow. The checkpoints were notable as much as they were characteristic: woebegone concrete filled drums, coated yellow paint with uneven black stripes that punctuated its overall shade of yellow, stood tactfully on the road in such a way that only a single vehicle would be able to move slowly in between the drums in a zigzag. Atop the drums were tires sprinkled with green leaves of weeds struggling for sunlight. The policemen (for police checkpoints) or soldiers (military checkpoints) stood side by side on the road, with longstanding Russian AK-47 held menacingly in their hands. They pervaded anxiety in the air as they smiled this time and frowned in the next second leaving passengers numb. They conspired in low tones and yelled spitefully in a coerce pitch at unyielding bus drivers. Many changed their route at their sight, to avert a possible extortion or mistreatment. Sometimes, buses sped off, tried maneuvering the policemen who would wave conspiratorially at the drivers to stop. The drivers would decelerate and then jam on the brake. One of the policemen would handshake the bus-driver looking into the passengers' faces to know if there were any potential threat, a perceived stumbling block to his handshake with the driver. He would then shake his head and hail the driver – a sign that he has been passed. Same thing he did with other commercial buses coming after and after until the day ended and another came. Shaking hands and head or pointing at the side of the road with the shout of park well if the driver refused to shake hands with him; he would be delayed for so many hours over particulars, loads on board, licence, etc., after which the bus would be taken to the police station for a crime that would have been overlooked with a mere handshake (bribe) with one of the policemen. This was the core task of policing in this part of the world that Google didn't tell me.

The historic Niger bridge that lay over Mungo Park-discovered Niger River (Mr. Mungo Park must have dug-up the river from the bowel of the earth) was the gateway to the southeastern part of the country and to my destination, Anambra state.

Amerikanah nno, welcome, they said one after the other – men and women, boys and girls. One thing was peculiar in their looks, their skin stood out, nitid in its unusual whiteness. Scurfy, parched, harmattan-whited. Their lips were caked by that same harmattan, some of them trickled out blood which was usually licked cursorily. The people visited, then the totem of the land – they moved pridefully as if they owned the land, fearless, territorial and arrogant. The closest I had come with snakes was during my college days at Messiah College, Mechanicsburg. They said whenever a visitor entered the community, these arrogant snakes came to welcome them.

It was in the middle of the night when I was jolted by rope-like creature descending on to the bed I lay in from the room window. The room was starkly dark, the power holding company was not aware of the existence of Umunri community, also, the water corporation. I switched on my torchlight and the nine-foot variegated (brown, black, white) python was bared to my petrified eyes. My spinal cord shivered. I scurried to my feet, directed the ray of the torchlight at its head, its eyes flickered. The thought of the Singaporean woman swallowed by a python haunted me as much as the one before me. Then you realized that you were in a different, strange-yet-familiar environment in which 911 was useless and in which there was no replica. Then, the situation was: kill or be killed.

* * *

The day you strolled into this our land, the atmosphere smelt differently. It was a Christmas period, dry season but the heavens heralded the misfortune you would bring upon our land. The bright and dry heavens bellowed, unleashed its fangs on us – lightning paralyzed the *Udala* tree at the village square. The *Udala* tree, one of the remaining monuments of our ancestors, where we had our gatherings. The unusual downpour disrupted our festivities, the cloudburst, as thick as hailstorm, pelted our bodies. They said you had returned from a land that knew no lack – where fallen crumbs could be picked up in their garbage-dumps and eaten. They said it was a land of no-lack except for mosquitoes and roaches and rats, unless one wanted to see them in places where they were preserved. They said where you came from lacked darkness also, it must as well lack culture and manners.

They said that you were born in this our land by a man from this our land and a woman from this land. How then did a leopard change its skin? How did coyotes and wolves become allies? Nobody knew who you were even though we knew that you were the only child of Mazi Okonkwo, who went missing so many years ago. It was said that he left with the whitemen that brought message of salvation to us. We knew when you were born but now, you have been reborn. We saw you as a woman from your looped hair touching your torso, your pendulous legs, your glowing sun-untainted skin, fake mascaraed antenna-like eyelashes, rouged pinkish cheeks – until you were caught climbing Mazi Uchendu palm tree. Thereafter, you told us you were not a woman. You showed us at the village square what made you a man. You said you were a man. You agreed to be part of our village gatherings, to obey our traditions and culture, you drank from the cup we drank from – because you called yourself a son of the soil. No sooner had we done these, than you went to the sacred river of our deity, *Mmiri Ngenebaka* and swam in it. You told our youths to kill the sacred fishes of the *Ngenebaka* river, to hunt the crocodiles – to ridicule us, what made us. As if the killing of the fishers was not enough, your massacred the sacred bride of *Ajoagwo Arusi*, our sacred peaceful pythons. Were you not told that our forefathers met these sacred pythons in this land? Were you not told that one who killed our python died? Not only did you kill these pythons, you told our youths to disbelieve that the pythons had protected them, prospered them and kept our farmlands fertile from the time of our ancestors.

As if the wrath of the gods you had brought upon yourself were not enough, you did that which the tongue had never spoken in our land – that which no ear has ever heard of, which no heart has ever conceived, in our land. That which was capable of making the gods open up the earth to swallow us. That which made our farmlands weep and produce no crops, which caused our streams dry off.

Without fear for the gods and your *chi*, under the split crimson moon of the night, and at the paralyzed *Udala* tree, you were caught soiling the chastity of a bearded man like you. *Aru*! He said you gave him a cigar that made his head woozy, his legs wobbly and his organ stiff. He said that you told him that where you came from, the land that knew no lack, that a man was free to go in with a man, a woman free to go in with another woman. When the *Ikoro*, gong of war went, summoned everyone at the village square over your act, the strangest and rarest in our land. You told the elders and chiefs, children and adults, men and women of Umunri that there was no wrong in your wrongdoing. You said, though you were a man, you were also a woman. *Amerikanah* Wonder! As you offended the land, the gods, the land in turn unleashed on you its venom for killing our sacred pythons, desecrating the sacred river of our deity, and for soiling our land by your unspeakable alien culture.

* * *

The Ikoro gong of war plumbed sonorously in the night, throughout the three clans that comprised the seven villages in Umunri. From strategic locations in each clan, sharing same message. The night became extremely uncommunicative, noiseless, aside the chirps of some unconcerned crickets. Even owls which usually relished the blissful night breeze, observed silence. The moon withdrew into its shell stealthily, making darkness incomprehensibly thicker. Kerosene lanterns displaying yellowish tongues of fire, and smoke puffing into the air from its perforated cork, were the only source of luminance. Everywhere seemed to be bearing hovering evil spirits as if the gods had already unleashed their expected fangs. Something urgent must be done to avert that. Shrubs appeared like humans when sighted from distance, leaving the viewer terrific with head as if swollen. That *Ikoro, gong of war* sounded was to parade a nocturnal unusual rapist, and to officially announce the end of strange foreign practices. A nocturnal rapist who despoiled the longstanding values of the land.

* * *

Echezona now called Amerikanah by Umunri people, continued his staggering, his sagged scrotum slapping against his thighs. His penis shrink, maybe catching cold, but it wouldn't be catching cold in that dire condition. Not when he already received uncountable strokes of canes in addition to his *agbara* infested body. The youths steered him to the village square where bigger crowd had gathered, awaiting the arrival of the miscreant. His partner in their alien act, walked beside him. On their heads were crowns of abomination, woven from tender yellowish fronds. Their waists too, were wreathed with same fronds. Their bodies, from head to toe, gleamed with ashes. The culture and tradition of Umunri was clear and direct on this – as it was unpardonable. In Umunri, the sacred pythons of Ngenebaka were indeed inviolable in acts and in words. They were gods in disguise. They were tamed by the gods, toothed and venomous yet harmless. Must be reverenced, praised by the lips of the women, eulogized and thanked by that of the men. When it lay in your bed at night before you, the gods needed it, you were to sleep on the bare floor or enjoy its warmth and poking in your bed. Whoever killed any must carry out a burial rite for it. The type of burial rite and ritual so befitting to a chief who had collected so many titles before his death. The chiefs with the red conic cap with two white *ugo* feathers by the side. A number of goats must be slaughtered to accompany the murdered god, python to its meticulously dug grave. Numerous spotless fowls must be sacrificed to the gods as to appease them; to restore the purity of the land and ward off the evil spirits that might come in consequence. These rituals and rites were required to wash off the curse of the gods, to wash untimely death off whomever killed the inviolable python, and to restore his progress.

Every child of Umunri knew why the sacred pythons, *ajoagwo arusi* were inviolable, why the fishes in the sacred *Ngenebaka* river were sacred, why the river itself wouldn't be swam both by intent and in an error. The story of why these must not happen had been told in hoarse voices, clear voices, in day's light and in the night's darkness.

The ancestral father of Umunri, Nwanri had migrated from Nri with his three sons, also his daughters, wives and the wives of his sons, to settle in the southern part of Ngenebaka river. His daughters and wives were constantly abducted by neighbouring villages, sold into slavery or offered as sacrifices to the gods of their abductors. Nwanri and his household could not match his enemies militarily, as a result, he offered one of his virgin daughters as a sacrifice to the goddess of Ngenebaka river by burying her alive at the bank of Ngenebaka river; he pledged his loyalty to the Ngenebaka's river-goddess, demanding protection and prosperity from her. The river-goddess prospered him and protected him from his enemies. She fought for him physically with her pythons and spiritually as well. That came about the sacredness of ajaogwo deity.

But the previous cases in Umunri were either the killing of the sacred python, or the killing of the fishes in the Ngenebaka river. There hadn't been a case of blatant disregard for the culture of the people as was in this. Or a case in the time past involving the three offence committed by one person. Or a case of a man doing that that could only be done with a woman with his fellow man.

When they arrived at the square, the crescendo of Umu-ada chants thundered into their mulish ears, piercing his heart and clouding his mind. His mind in which he thought why human life would be ranked below that of a python in this part of the world and in this 21st century. This part of the world in which one's sexuality could sully the land and invoke the wrath of the gods. This part of the world in which the right to self-determination was neglected.

Among the irate youths, some said their blood should be used to purge the land of their sins, some said they should be ostracized, some said they should be castrated, but none said they should be forgiven. The gods were angry and must be appeased. "Was it limited to killing of the sacred pythons and swimming in the mmiri Ngenebaka, Amerikanah will be treated with mercy, but considering the magnitude of the last of the offence: sodomy, it's unpardonable", one of the gyrating youths said.

Echezona stood before the unrepentant Umunri people, naked, body sprinkled ashes, his hair scraped – those were the inevitable recipes required to appease the gods of the land in such occasion. The culprit must be paraded naked with chants from the youths that relate with the abominable act, after which the final judgement would be passed by the Ndi-ichie – Chiefs-in-council. He stood feebly on his wobbly legs, awaiting the Ndi-ichie's pronouncement – his fate.

In Umunri community, whoever killed the sacred python and refused carrying out the rituals and rites, died. In Umunri, from time immemorial, whoever was caught having sex with an animal, was ostracized. Whoever was caught having sex with his or her blood relative, was sent out of the community with the partner and never to return. But there hadn't been a case of a man sleeping with another – the gravest, rarest crime in the land.

The Man Who Lost Himself

Chukwu Sunday Abel, Nigeria

LIKE EVERY MORTAL – *life begins in the womb and ends in the tomb. Death is an assault on humanity against which we have no defence; an end we can't escape and indeed, a part of human situation into which every being enters. For death, every one of us lives in an unfortified city. The You-in-you shall die.*

You want me to tell you what you shall become? You want me to tell you your end (destiny)? A man who knows his *end*, lives in an unending illusion till his end (death). You insist I tell you your destiny? Your destiny on earth is that the *you-in-you* shall die. You shall lose *yourself*. I don't mean that you will die but the *you-in-you* shall die. So, the you-in-you will die and the manner in which the *you* will die and what *you* will die for, are also what you want to know. I commend you for your bold-step, because to resign to fate, is to be crippled fast. A man who has not discovered what he will die for, is not worth living.

Now listen, prepare your heart to know your *destiny*, prepare your ears to hear how the you-in-you shall die. To know your end, do you remember your beginning? Do you remember who you are? Do you know the son of whom you are? Do you know the land you live in? Do you know how many years your ancestors occupied this land? Now, you stare at me dazedly, you breath so fast as if your lungs are demanding so much air than usual. You refuse to answer the questions as if an invisible string tethered on mount *Kilimanjaro*, holds your tongue. Your glaring eyes seem to be glowering abstractedly at your tomorrow which holds your end. *Did you just ask me if your end, the end of you will come tomorrow?* Yes, your end shall come tomorrow, but note, tomorrow is endless.

In this land where your ancestors lived-in, this land where you live-in and your descendants shall live. This land you have tilled with your hands, grew crops on, the rivers you have fished in, the mountains you have hunted on. This your land, a woman, a queen will come-into from a faraway land. But before she comes into this land where you live, her emissaries shall forerun her. These forerunners will come into your land, this land your ancestors lived-in, this land you live-in. These forerunners will come with books on their right-hands, swords on their left-hands, crystal crucifixes on their chests, and in their hearts, is your end, the end of *you*. You grimace at the impossibility of this revelation, because you think you have fought many battles and won in all, you think you have hunted so many wild animals and conquered them all. You say you have wrestled so many aliens to the ground in defence of your land, this land that is free of cold, that defines *you*. You say you have fought so many enemies who later became your slaves. I know that in your land as well as other surrounding towns, you are not just known as a king but also as the strongest man of war. Your name instills fear in your enemies whenever it is said that you will physically take part in or lead a war. Your exploits in previous wars gave you the pseudonym, '*Agaba*' which means 'let's go' when translated. But this involves people that you who are feared by your enemies, will be afraid to fight. Your war song: *Nzogdu-Nzogbu,enyimba-enyi* that symbolizes your unrivaled military might, the strength of your youthful soldiers and the fearlessness they carry, your soldiers will be so afraid to sing at the sight of the sword of the queen. You say you are invincible. *Ti ye mma gi n' obo*, sheath your sword. Prepare yourself for the end. Prepare your land for your end.

You ask me how your end shall come?

These forerunners, you shall take for gods, for you have never seen their type before. What they will come with, you have never seen before. What they will say to you, you have never heard of before. Their glowing sun-colour-like skin, untainted by sun which shines fervently but gratuitously in your land, you shall baffle at. Their green-pigmented spic-and-span eyes which contrast your shaded eyes, you shall be afraid to look into. Their teeth, glistering white, unlike yours blighted by age and nuts, you shall stare ceaselessly at. Their soft Caucasian palms by which your end shall come, will embrace your black, scaly, hard and jagged palm in a specious hospitality.

They will influx your land like hymenopterous insects whose habitat has been shattered by a trespassing hunter. They will come into your land through your land borders. They will tell the world that they discovered the rivers you fished in, that they discovered you, as if you had strayed out of the earth, as if they unearthed your rivers from the bowel of the earth. You shall resent them, go into spiritual battles with them, to dislodge them out of your land which they will occupy. You shall consult the gods but the gods will be silent. You shall compel your chief-priests to strike them with thunder and brimstone, but *Amadioha* will be latent, *Ogun* will be slumbering, *Sango* will be on recess, all in a tacit betrayal. Out of desperation, your blacksmiths will live in their furnaces as to furnish more weapons for the armoury of your land. Thereafter, you shall mobilize your foot soldiers against these invaders but they will fear mosquitoes more than your soldiers. Your *Ikoro*, gong of war, will reverberate rotundly in the nights, throughout the three clans that comprise the seven villages that make up your land. From strategic locations in each clan, sharing same message of the imminent war and the preparations thereof. Your nights will become extremely uncommunicative, noiseless, aside the imaginative stamping approaching feet of the emissaries of the queen in your heads. Even owls which usually relish the blissful night breeze, will observe silence. As your deities betrayed you, the moon will also betray your nights. It will withdraw into its shell stealthily making darkness incomprehensibly thicker. Everywhere will seem to be bearing hovering evil spirits. Shrubs will appear like humans when sighted from distance, leaving your people terrific with heads as if swollen. The hearts of your people will be pounding from the fear infixed in them by the message of war and imaginary images of clanging machete, flaring arrows and gushing blood of subdued warriors of war, appearing hauntingly. But this is not a war of swords, bow, spears and sticks. The emissaries of the queen will come with what is more than that – rare puissant weapons.

I see your hands twitching as if your anxiety wants to escape through them. I told you to sheath your sword. Sheath your sword because your end is not by their swords, even if not so, your swords stand no chance against the queen. Strength they say, wanes, gut, diminishes, health, fails, providence, disappoints. The mouth is to be blamed for not saying what the eyes saw but not for the ears that heard but refused to follow through. A wise learns from the mistakes of others, a fool lives to experience the mistakes of others. Learn from the fate of Jubo Jubogha (Amanyababo). Learn from him. Is your sword mightier than that of Jubo? Didn't your father seek his military assistance when your land was invaded? Didn't your people worship him like a god? Was it not the queen that humiliated him before the very eyes of his people, tore his kingdom into shreds, raised his people against him? Was it not the powerful, invincible hand of the queen that forced him out of his kingdom? Did you not hear the story ? The story of how his heroical sword by which he founded the Opobo kingdom, built an unassailable fortress, was so anaemic in preventing the emissaries of the queen from invading his land, the emissaries of the queen who are born for war, whose names instill fear in the hearts of their enemies. Tell me, is your land more fortified than that of Opobo? Are your army mightier than the defeated Opobo army? You stand no chance against the queen. Also, did you not hear how king Badu Bonsu II of Ahanta went? The mighty king of great feats, who died though not by the hands of the queen but by that of Prince of Orange. Learn from the fate of Badu who was hanged to death in his land before the eyes of his sleeping ancestors, his royal head severed from his body, confiscated and taken hostage by the Prince of Orange in a foreign land, the land of the Prince of Orange. Learn from the fate of Oba Ovoranwen Nogaisi whose love for his kingdom was questioned by the emissaries of the queen. Did you not hear that he raised his sword against the emissaries of the queen and was ignominiously humilliated before his people, removed from his throne and forced to take refuge in another land, across the river. Learn from them and quieten your twitching hands, vitiate your rage and wait for your end, the end of you. *Ukpana opkoko gburu, bu nti chiri ye.*

Now listen. Your soldiers will be subdued effortlessly before your very eyes with powerful exceptional weapons you have never seen or heard of. After your army have been trounced, then will you sue for peace. Consequently, early morning cock crow in your land will put fear in the lives of your people that they will always wish it were forever nightfall. Sorrowful songs will be sung in all corners of your land. You will plead for the belligerent hands of the emissaries of the queen to allow you live in your land, this land your ancestors lived-in. You shall beg the queen not to give you Judo's treatment. Not to force you out of your land as was with Judo. The queen will listen to you. The queen will allow you live in your land but will give you a new name – just like she did to Judo whose name her emissaries could not pronounce correctly because they spoke through their noses. The proceeds of your farms will be taxed heavily by the queen. Your women will walk massively in one heart, starkly naked, singing in clamour and resentment against the queen, against her heavy taxes.

You remember they will come with sword. The sword has served its purpose, its end – to defeat you and your people in your land and to subjugate you and subject you and your people to the queen in a faraway land.

You remember I also told you that your end is not by the sword.

Now, the second weapon they will come with, the books on their right-hands, will be deployed against you and your people after you have been subjugated. These books are of two kinds – the first will be used to teach your people the language of the queen in a faraway land. This book will imbibe in your people new tongue other than your longstanding language, the one through which your people commune with your gods, which *defines you and them*, which tells the *you-in-you*, which your ancestors told you never to discard. This book will make your people speak through their noses, in the manner the queen and her emissaries who will overrun your land in readiness for her arrival, do.

Do not ask me if your end is by this book, for the book antecedes your end, the end of you.

Now listen to what the second book will do to you and your people – the second book will be tethered on your necks to dictate and guide your daily indulgence. It will be used to divide your people against you, to depose your chiefs and install illegitimate chiefs in place. The chiefs will slough their beings and wear the unfitting identity of the queen in a faraway land. Do not forget, the queen's skin is sun-colour-like unlike yours sooted by invisible smoke of the sun. These queen-installed chiefs shall execute the orders of the queen through her emissaries.

By these books, your people will lose their true selves. They will become strangers to their original selves as the presence of their original being in them wanes.

Your mien tells your rage, and your heaving heart shows your desperation, but remain calm, for the enemy is an insurmountable one.

The third of the weapons they will come with, the crystal crucifixes, will be deployed against you and your people. These crucifixes will wrestle the grotesque and before-feared-and-reverenced *Amadioha* to the ground and take its position in the hearts of your people. Do not ask me if *Amadioha* will still be in latency when the contest will happen. This same crucifix will displace the slumbering highly spirited *Ogun* from the hearts of your people. The historic feats of *Sango* will be wiped out of the hearts of your people by this crucifix. Your worship places shall be desecrated. Your people will worship another God, the God the crucifix represents, the God of the queen in a faraway land, instead of your gods which truly define you, the you-in-you.

Now listen attentively for all of these I have mentioned are the preamble to your end, the end of you. You shall run out of this land, this land your ancestor lived-in. You shall run to a faraway land, the land of the queen whose emissaries will overrun your land. Your end is near but not in the land of the queen. Your end lies sedately in this land which you shall return-to after some years in the land of the queen. In the faraway land, you shall learn to speak proficiently through your nose like the queen whose land you live-in. You shall speak her language, learn her ways and understand her books – the one tethered on the necks of your people and the one which teaches them the language and ways of the queen. You shall eat the food of the queen, wear the clothes of the queen, while you live in her land.

When you return to your land, this land you live-in, your people will celebrate your return. They will admire your new self, self laced by the ways of the queen. They will admire the strangeness of your looks, the strangeness associated with your newly acquired language, the language of the queen; the strangeness of your new self. You shall flout your new acquisitions, speak through your nose like the emissaries of the queen, to fascinate them. They will envy you but celebrate you. You will become their hope, their mouthpiece, and their future.

At your return, this land you live-in will be reborn. Some of your ancestral monuments will be razed down. A new name will be given to this your land. So many places will be renamed by the tongues of the emissaries of the queen. Some of these places will be named after the emissaries of the queen. Your rivers and mountains will have new names. But you will not be bothered about this, nor bothered about the looting of your land. Your return will bring hope to your people. You shall try to demystify the emissaries of the queen to your people. You will tell them that they are not gods. You will tell them that they are mortal, that they have blood in their veins. You shall rant verbosely and gingerly at the gathering of your people, in your market places, at your festival of new yam, festival of age-grade, demanding the queen removes her hand from your reborn land. Your voice will thunder so loud into the mulish ears of the queen as you demand she ease the tendon of the book tethered on your necks.

Now, your end is nearer than ever. As you clamour for the end of the queen's presence in your land, the queen will visit your land, your reborn land. She will shake your hand softened by years away from your land, with her gloved palms. You shall always smile even though in your belly, you have no genuine instinct to. The queen will wave her gloved hands in the air, at your sun-pelted people. Like the queen, you shall wave tirelessly at them.

The queen will agree to your request – she will withdraw her powerful domineering hand from your land. It is a win for you, you shall think, and a loss for the queen. I won't say. It is left for you to conclude.

You shall now rule over yourselves by your own hands and not by the queen's hand. It will be celebrated across your land by all and sundry. The old book will be unfastened from your necks but another one, written conspicuously by the hand of the queen, will be handed to you.

After you have ousted the domineering hand of the queen, shall you meet with your end. As you celebrate the departure of the queen, you ignorantly celebrate the end of you, the end of the you-in-you. Your ancestors will stand-up against you. Their tongues will lather you. Their tongues will ridicule your new names, your new monuments of the queen. Your ancestors will scorn you, for you have lost the real you, the you which you will call primitive, which you will call barbaric. Your ancestors will pounce on you, an unworthy son who abandoned his tongue for that of a woman in a faraway land, who desecrated the sacred deities of his land to please the queen in a faraway land, who tarnished his melanin to align with the queen in a faraway land.

The angry stinger of your ancestors will inject into your laced body, the fangs of perennial ruefulness. You shall try to restore the lost you – you shall try to restore the dignity of your deities, the pride in the supposed-primitive ways of your ancestors, to rename your mountains, rivers and monuments, but you shall not be able. Now, you have lost the you-in-you – your end, your destiny.

The Creation Story of the Four Suns

Aztec

TONACATECUTLI AND TONACACIUATL dwelt from the beginning in the thirteenth heaven. To them were born, as to an elder generation, four gods – the ruddy Camaxtli (chief divinity of the Tlascalans); the black Tezcatlipoca, wizard of the night; Quetzalcoatl, the wind-god; and the grim Huitzilopochtli, of whom it was said that he was born without flesh, a skeleton.

For six hundred years these deities lived in idleness; then the four brethren assembled, creating first the fire (hearth of the universe) and afterward a half-sun. They formed also Oxomoco and Cipactonal, the first man and first woman, commanding that the former should till the ground, and the latter spin and weave; while to the woman they gave powers of divination and grains of maize that she might work cures. They also divided time into days and inaugurated a year of eighteen twenty-day periods, or three hundred and sixty days. Mictlantecutli and Mictlanciuatl they created to be Lord and Lady of Hell, and they formed the heavens that are below the thirteenth storey of the celestial regions, and the waters of the sea, making in the sea a monster Cipactli, from which they shaped the earth. The gods of the waters, Tlaloctecutli and his wife Chalchiuhtlicue, they created, giving them dominion over the Quarters.

The son of the first pair married a woman formed from a hair of the goddess Xochiquetzal; and the gods, noticing how little was the light given forth by the half-sun, resolved to make another half-sun, whereupon Tezcatlipoca became the sun-bearer – for what we behold traversing the daily heavens is not the sun itself, but only its brightness; the true sun is invisible. The other gods created huge giants, who could uproot trees by brute force, and whose food was acorns. For thirteen times fifty-two years, altogether six hundred and seventy-six, this period lasted – as long as its Sun endured; and it is from this first Sun that time began to be counted, for during the six hundred years of the idleness of the gods, while Huitzilopochtli was in his bones, time was not reckoned.

This Sun came to an end when Quetzalcoatl struck down Tezcatlipoca and became Sun in his place. Tezcatlipoca was metamorphosed into a jaguar (Ursa Major) which is seen by night in the skies wheeling down into the waters whither Quetzalcoatl cast him; and this jaguar devoured the giants of that period.

At the end of six hundred and seventy-six years Quetzalcoatl was treated by his brothers as he had treated Tezcatlipoca, and his Sun came to an end with a great wind which carried away most of the people of that time or transformed them into monkeys.

Then for seven times fifty-two years Tlaloc was Sun; but at the end of this three hundred and sixty-four years Quetzalcoatl rained fire from heaven and made Chalchiuhtlicue Sun in place of her husband, a dignity which she held for three hundred and twelve years (six times fifty-two); and it was in these days that maize began to be used.

Now two thousand six hundred and twenty-eight years had passed since the birth of the gods, and in this year it rained so heavily that the heavens themselves fell, while the people of that time were transformed into fish. When the gods saw this, they created four men, with whose aid Tezcatlipoca and Quetzalcoatl again upreared the heavens, even as they are today; and these two gods becoming lords of the heavens and of the stars, walked therein.

After the deluge and the restoration of the heavens, Tezcatlipoca discovered the art of making fire from sticks and of drawing it from the heart of flint. The first man, Piltzintecutli, and his wife, who had been made of a hair of Xochiquetzal, did not perish in the flood, because they were divine. A son was born to them, and the gods created other people just as they had formerly existed.

But since, except for the fires, all was in darkness, the gods resolved to create a new Sun. This was done by Quetzalcoatl, who cast his own son, by Chalchiuhtlicue, into a great fire, whence he issued as the Sun of our own time; Tlaloc hurled his son into the cinders of the fire, and thence rose the Moon, ever following after the Sun. This Sun, said the gods, should eat hearts and drink blood, and so they established wars that there might be sacrifices of captives to nourish the orbs of light.

Collected by Hartley Burr Alexander

Xolotl Creates the Parents of Mankind

Aztec

ALL PROVINCES WERE AGREED that in heaven were a god and goddess, Citlallatonac and Citlalicue, and that the goddess gave birth to a stone knife (*tecpatl*), to the amazement and horror of her other sons which were in heaven. The stone hurled forth by these outraged sons and falling to Chicomoxtoc ('Seven Caves'), was shattered, and from its fragments arose sixteen hundred earth-godlings. These sent Tlotli, the Hawk, heavenward to demand of their mother the privilege of creating men to be their servants; and she replied that they should send to Mictlantecutli, Lord of Hell, for a bone or ashes of the dead, from which a man and woman would be born.

Xolotl was dispatched as messenger, secured the bone, and fled with it; but being pursued by the Lord of Hell, he stumbled, and the bone broke. With such fragments as he could secure he reached the earth, and the bones, placed in a vessel, were sprinkled with blood drawn from the bodies of the gods. On the fourth day a boy emerged from the mixture; on the eighth, a girl; and these were reared by Xolotl to become parents of mankind. Men differ in size because the bone broke into unequal fragments; and as human beings multiplied, they were assigned as servants to the several gods.

Now, the Sun had not been shining for a long time, and the deities assembled at Teotiuacan to consider the matter. Having built a great fire, they announced that that one among their devotees who should first hurl himself into it should have the honour of becoming the Sun, and when one had courageously entered the flames, they awaited the sunrise, wagering as to the quarter in which he would appear; but they guessed wrong, and for this they were condemned to be sacrificed, as they were soon to learn.

When the Sun appeared, he remained ominously motionless; and although Tlotli was sent to demand that he continue his journey, he refused, saying that he should remain where he was until they were all destroyed. Citli ('Hare') in anger shot the Sun with an arrow, but the latter hurled it back, piercing the forehead of his antagonist. The gods then recognized their inferiority and allowed themselves to be sacrificed, their hearts being torn out by Xolotl, who slew himself last of all. Before departing, however, each divinity gave to his followers, as a sacred bundle, his vesture wrapped about a green gem which was to serve as a heart. Tezcatlipoca was one of the departed deities, but one day he appeared to a mourning follower whom he commanded to journey to the House of the Sun beyond the waters and to bring thence singers and musical instruments to make a feast for him. This the messenger did, singing as he went. The Sun warned his people not to harken to the stranger, but the music was irresistible, and some of them were lured to follow him back to earth, where they instituted the musical rites.

Collected by Hartley Burr Alexander

Manco Capac Founds Cuzco

Inca

WE ARE TOLD THAT TAMPU-TOCCO was a house on a hill, provided with three windows, named Maras, Sutic, and Capac. Through the first of these came the Maras tribe, through Sutic came the Tampu tribe, and through Capac, the regal window, came four Ayars with their four wives – Ayar Manco and Mama Ocllo; Ayar Auca (the 'joyous', or 'fighting', Ayar) and Mama Huaco (the 'warlike'); Ayar Cachi (the 'Salt' Ayar) and Mama Ipacura (the 'Elder Aunt'); Ayar Uchu (the 'Pepper' Ayar) and Mama Raua.

The four pairs knew no father nor mother, beyond the story they told that they came out of the said window by order of Ticci Viracocha; and they declared that Viracocha created them to be lords; but it was believed that by the counsel of the fierce Mama Huaco they decided to go forth and subjugate peoples and lands. Besides the Maras and Tampu peoples, eight other tribes were associated with the Ayars, as vassals, when they began their quest, taking with them their goods and their families. Manco Capac carrying with him, as a palladium, a falcon, called Indi, or Inti – the name of the Sun-god – bore also a golden rod which was to sink into the land at the site where they were to abide; and Salcamayhua says that, in setting out, the hero was wreathed in rainbows, this being regarded as an omen of success.

The journey was leisurely, and in course of it Sinchi Rocca, who was to be the second Inca, was born to Mama Ocllo and Manco Capac; but then came a series of magic transformations by which the three brothers disappeared, leaving the elder without a rival. Ayar Cachi, who had such great power that, with stones hurled from his sling, he split the hills and hurled them up to the clouds, was the first to excite the envy of his brothers; and on the pretext that certain royal treasures had been forgotten in a cave of Tampu-Tocco, he was sent back to secure them, accompanied by a follower who had secret instructions from the brothers to immure him in the cave, once he was inside. This was done, and though Ayar Cachi made the earth shake in his efforts to break through, he could not do so. Nevertheless, he appeared to his brothers, coming in the air with great wings of coloured feathers; and despite their terror, he commanded them to go on to their destiny, found Cuzco, and establish the empire. "I shall remain in the form and fashion that ye shall see on a hill not distant from here; and it will be for your descendants a place of sanctity and worship, and its name shall be Huanacauri. And in return for the good things that ye will have received from me, I pray that ye will always adore me as god and in that place will set up altars whereat to offer sacrifices. If ye do this, ye shall receive help from me in war; and as a sign that from henceforth ye are to be esteemed, honoured, and feared, your ears shall be bored in the manner that ye now behold mine." (It was from this custom of boring and enlarging the ears that the Spaniards called the ruling caste *Orejones* ('Big-Ears'); and it was at the hill of Huanacauri that the Ayar instructed the Incas in the rites by which they initiated youths into the warrior caste. At this mount, which became one of the great Inca shrines, both the Salt and the Pepper Ayars were reputed to have been transformed into stones, or idols, and it was here that the rainbow sign of promise was given.)

As they approached the hill, they saw near the rainbow what appeared to be a man-shaped idol; and Ayar Uchu offered himself to go to it, for they said that he was very like it. He did so, sat upon the stone, and himself became stone, crying: "O Brothers, an evil work ye have wrought for me. It was for your sakes that I came where I must remain forever, apart from your company. Go! go! happy brethren, I announce to you that ye shall be great lords. I therefore pray that, in recognition of the desire I have always had to please you, ye shall honour and venerate me in all your festivals and ceremonies, and that I shall be the first to whom ye make offerings, since I remain here for your sakes. When ye celebrate the *huarochico* (the arming of the sons as knights), ye shall adore me as their father, for I shall remain here forever."

Finally Manco Capac's staff sank into the ground and from their camp the hero pointed to a heap of stones on the site of Cuzco. Showing this to his brother, Ayar Auca, he said, "Brother! thou rememberest how it was arranged between us that thou shouldst go to take possession of the land where we are to settle. Well! behold that stone." Pointing it out, he continued, "Go thither flying," for they say that Ayar Auca had developed some wings; "and seating thyself there, take possession of the land seen from that heap of rocks. We will presently come and settle and reside." When Ayar Auca heard the words of his brother, opening his wings, he flew to that place which Manco Capac had pointed out; and seating himself there, he was presently turned into stone, being made the stone of possession. In the ancient language of this valley the heap was called *cozco*, whence the site has had the name of Cuzco to this day.

Collected by Hartley Burr Alexander

Anansi, the World, and the Stories

Laura Barker, Akan/Caribbean/Black British

IT WAS STILL DARK. The Sky God was eating an early breakfast of devilled goat when Anansi knocked at his door. The Sky God knew Anansi's knock and he did not wonder how the trickster spider skittered his way past the doorman and into the Sky God's private conservatory where light beamed in through fourteen huge ornate windows. "Good morning," said the Sky God, pressing a napkin to his oily lips.

Anansi bowed deeply. "I have come," he said, "to collect the stories that you promised me last week when you were drunk."

The Sky God chuckled. Every week or so Anansi would try to persuade the Sky God to part with all the stories in the world, which he was keeping in his vast library. Last week Anansi had prostrated himself on the ground, begging the Sky God, saying that he could not live without the stories. The doorman had to drag him out. The week before he offered a lifelong supply of spider silk, and a box of mangos. Usually the Sky God dismissed Anansi immediately, but today's approach amused the Sky God and he commended Anansi for his boldness.

Anansi bowed deeply again and asked when he might have the stories. "It is most urgent," he said. "The poor people of earth are unable to gossip, for example. Imagine. They can see two people arguing in the street but they cannot speculate about what the upset is. They can see two children being unusually polite but they cannot tell that a rich grandparent has just arrived from out of town and that they are vying for gifts. They can see a man in the tavern hiding his face in his own arms in humiliation but they cannot come to each other and talk about how this man's wife has betrayed him."

"Let me see," said the Sky God. "Bring me Onini the python, Osebo the leopard, Mmoatia the fairy, and Mmoboro the hornet. Then we will see about the stories."

Capturing Mmoboro the hornet was so easy it was almost unenjoyable. Anansi went to her nest and shook her tree violently, spilling water out of his water gourd. Mmoboro clung to her nest, thinking there was a storm. "Come," Anansi told her, pointing out a dry calabash. "Let us shelter from this storm together. Ladies first."

As soon as Mmoboro was inside the calabash Anansi wove his web over the opening. He brought the calabash home and put it in his bedroom for safe keeping.

Anansi had never met Mmoatia, the bad-tempered fast-moving fairy, but he knew vaguely what she looked like, and he decorated a doll to look like her. He put a sign saying 'I am the real Mmoatia, accept no substitutes' around her neck and placed her outside Mmoatia's apartment. Then he painted the doll with the strongest construction-grade epoxy resin he could find. When the fairy flew out of her apartment, she saw the doll at once, and went up for a closer look. Anansi watched her put a finger on the doll. When it stuck, she used her other hand to try to pull herself off, and then she used a foot, and then another foot. When she was well and truly stuck to the doll, Anansi snuck up behind her and wrapped her in his web, taking her home and depositing her in his bedroom along with Mmoboro.

For the leopard, Anansi dug a hole in the ground and waited for the leopard to fall in. Sometimes, simple plans were the best ones. "I'll help you out," Anansi said to Osebo, when the inevitable fall came, "with my web." When Osebo was completely bound in spider silk, Anansi and his wife Aso carried him back to their house.

"I'm worried because I don't know how to get the python," Anansi told his wife at dinner, after they put Osebo in Anansi's bedroom. "So much is resting on this. It's a lot of pressure." Anansi pushed his green banana to the side of his plate and sighed.

"Don't worry my love, I know just the thing for Onini," said Aso. "He's a lonely man, so we must lure him to our house under the pretence of meeting a woman. Let's say it's my sister."

Aso didn't have a sister, but she wrote a letter from an imaginary woman called Soso who offered long descriptions of things that a spider woman could do with a snake. Anansi read the letter and found himself hot with a sort of jealousy mixed with a sort of excitement. "How come you've never offered to do any of this stuff to me?" he asked his wife.

Aso shrugged. "You're not a snake," she said.

Anansi called on Onini and explained that his wife's sister Soso had seen him last week at the market and was overcome with lust.

"Your wife doesn't have a sister," said Onini. He was suspicious until he read the letter. Then he said, "Well Anansi, now, I don't mind telling you that a famously strong python such as myself, well, I get letters from adoring women all the time. However. This letter is really something." He read out some choice phrases.

"Yes, yes," said Anansi. "Very nice. Anyway, she wants to meet you."

"Of course," said Onini. "Have her call round at my house."

"Not at all," said Anansi, "My wife would never let her call round at your house, you must come to ours to meet her."

"Absolutely not," said Onini. "I will not be chaperoned." He closed the door in Anansi's face.

"Don't worry," said Aso, when Anansi explained the situation. "I have just the thing." She went to her lingerie drawer and picked out a lightweight black lace garment which covered the entire body save for some choice gaps, and put it in an envelope alongside another note.

Anansi took the undergarment out of the envelope and held it up to the light. "How come you've never worn these for me?" he said.

Aso shrugged. "What are you bringing to the table?" she said. "Where are all the special garments that you are wearing for me?"

"I come to bed wearing silk," he told her.

She laughed at him. "You're a spider," she said. "That's like me saying I come to bed with my own spit in my mouth."

"You don't like my silk anymore?"

"I love your silk Anansi, but I have silk of my own too. It's not like it's anything new is it?"

He read the note she had written for Onini. "Take out that bit about the split tongue," he told her. "It's obscene."

"Don't be ridiculous. He will never come around here if we don't lure him. Don't be so old-fashioned."

Anansi went to Onini. Onini read the note. When he saw the undergarment, Onini's tail stuck right up in the air. "Alright," he said, when he had recovered a little. "I will come round for dinner. I hope your wife makes the soup with the boiled eggs, that's my favourite."

"I will be cooking," said Anansi, "And it's green bananas and stew."

Anansi returned home and asked his wife the next step of the plan.

"You and me have to attend to an emergency," she said. "And we pretend to leave. There is a note on the table from my sister to Onini explaining that she made the emergency up to get us out of the house so the two of them can proceed with some intimate couplings uninterrupted. The note says she is upstairs getting changed and that she would like him to tie himself up in the kitchen with some rope so that when she comes downstairs, she can pleasure him."

Anansi read the note. "Surely nobody actually uses this sexual position?" he said to his wife, of one of the drawings accompanying the note.

Aso looked over his shoulder. "Oh yes," she said, "That one is particularly popular with pythons."

"Why," said Anansi, "have you never come to me in this position?"

"Maybe I will one day," said Aso. "And maybe one day you will come to me in special positions too."

"Hmm," said Anansi. "Well, I don't think this plan will work. For one thing, we don't have rope."

"We're using your silk. That way we make sure it sticks to him. Get spinning. I will get started with dinner. I'm going to make him soup with boiled eggs."

"How do you know that's his favourite?"

"He's a python, Anansi, all snakes love eggs." She started cooking. Anansi spun silk while Aso stewed millet leaves with the beans and pounded her own chillies and soaked rice.

"Why are you going to so much trouble?" said Anansi, watching her whip noodles around her silk. "For me, you use the chillies that comes in the jar. And I've never seen you cook with millet leaves."

"Yes but Onini is my guest," she said. "I wouldn't use jarred chillies for a guest. It must look authentic or he will realise we are up to something and it will spoil our plan."

"Why don't you ever make this meal for me?"

"Why would I? You've never cared that much for boiled eggs. And what is this? Why should I make special meals for you? Where are all the special meals that you are making for me?"

"Hmm," said Anansi. Aso boiled twelve eggs.

"Twelve," said Anansi. "That's a bit much."

"He's a python Anansi, he's not a grass snake."

When Onini arrived, Aso said, "Please accept our apologies – Anansi and I have been called out on an emergency. My sister is upstairs changing, she will be downstairs to entertain you shortly, she has left a note on the table. Please, make yourself at home and my sister will be down presently to serve you soup with boiled eggs."

Onini managed to hide his excitement and apologised to his hosts regarding their emergency. Aso and Anansi went outside. Aso wandered around but Anansi put his face to the window and stared at Onini reading the note. When Onini's tail stuck straight up in the air, he started tying it to the chair like the note instructed. When he looked like he was thoroughly stuck, Anansi barged in and bound the python completely to the chair with more of his silk. "Good," said Aso, who came in behind him.

Anansi put all the captured creatures in a wheeled trolley and took them to the Sky God's house.

"I have what you asked," said Anansi. He presented the creatures who were all tied up in his silk.

The Sky God was impressed. "Well done, my friend," he said. "You may have all the world's stories."

The stories were released. And immediately, or so it seemed to Anansi, everyone on earth was chatting about his wife and the python. How she had given him a pair of her undergarments, how she had told him lewd stories involving his split tongue and the place in her body that silk came out of, how his tail stood straight up just at the mention of her name. How she tied him up in her web and weaved herself around him like the spider woman that she was, how he used the tip of his tail to great effect, how the leopard let them use his apartment, how the hornet gifted Aso one of her stings so Aso could use it to tickle the python's back, how Mmoatia the bad tempered fairy lent them a doll of her likeness for use in one of their many bedroom games.

Later that week, when Aso came to him in a sexual position she mentioned in her note, wearing undergarments similar to the ones that had gone in Onini's envelope, Anansi wept. He left his house and went to the tavern where he put his head in his arms and cried.

"Ah," said the bartender, offering him a gourd of palm wine on the house. "My friend. It is tough, always tough, when your woman betrays you. But it is so much tougher when your woman betrays you for the most famous python on the planet."

"Who told you that?" said Anansi.

"My dear spider. The whole world is talking about it."

Musoke the Moon-Boy

Uganda

YEARS AND YEARS AGO in Uganda there was a woman whose banana garden bordered the high road, and every night the travellers who passed by stole fruit and vegetables out of her garden, and this made her very angry. So she took counsel with her old nurse, who lived with her, and they dug a ditch, and covered it with sticks, and branches, and earth, and leaves, and said to each other:

"The next thief who comes at night will tumble in."

The next evening the herdsman of the Chief was driving his cows home to the kraal, when one of them strayed into the woman's garden, and fell into the ditch trap and broke its leg. The cowherd was very angry and told the Chief, and the Chief sent for the woman, and said, "Why did you set a trap for my cow?"

When the poor woman explained what she had done the Chief was still more angry, and said:

"You meant to kill my people. You are a wicked woman." And he ordered her to be beaten. The woman implored the Chief to have mercy on her, and he said:

"Well, you may go home now, I will not beat you, but the next child you have shall be mine. If it is a boy I will kill him, if it is a girl you may keep her until she is twelve years old, and then she shall be my slave."

Very soon afterwards the woman had a child, and it was a most beautiful baby boy. She cried very much when she thought that her dear little baby would be killed; so she sent her old nurse to the Chief to say that it was a girl. The Chief said, "Bring the child here that I may see it."

When the nurse came back and told the woman, she cried more than ever; but just then a stranger passed down the road and turned into the garden to ask for a drink of water. She had a little baby tied on her back and she carried a roll of mats on her head. The nurse gave her a drink of water and said, "We are two women in great trouble." And then she told the stranger the story.

The stranger said, "I will lend you my little girl baby; go and show her to the Chief and save the life of your little boy."

So .the nurse went again to the Chief's house, and when he saw the baby he said, "Tell the mother to bring this child to me when she is twelve years old."

Nobody suspected anything, and when the old nurse got home she packed up all their things, and at dawn the next morning they set out for Singo with the stranger who had been so kind to them.

The years passed, and they all lived happily in Singo, and the baby grew into a beautiful boy, and they called him Musoke, which means Rainbow. Every day Musoke took his goats on to the hillside and played on a reed pipe as he walked, and the goats skipped about and jumped, but some were staid old things, and walked sedately. This was the song Musoke sang in the morning when he took the goats out before the sun was hot.

Little black kids,
Little. white kids,
Speckled and striped and brown, I love them all
And they all love me,

Our life is happy and gay and free;
Eat and sleep, and sing and play,
That is our life of every day.
Out to the, hills when the sun is low
What we talk of who can know?
Home to rest when the sun is high
What do we dream of; they and I?
Little black kids,
Little white kids, etc. etc., etc.

In the evening, when he brought his goats home, he sang another song to them on his reed pipe.

Come home, come home, little Brothers,
The shadows are soft and long.
Come home, come home, little Brothers,
And I'll sing you a slumber song.
For the plantains are peeled in the kitchen
And over the fire they steam,
And the housewife has saved the peelings for you
As luscious and cool and green as they grew.
Come home, come home, little Brothers, etc., etc.

One day a messenger arrived from the Chief, who said, "Your little girl must be twelve years old now. The Chief has sent for her." The mother was very sad. She sent the old nurse out to the hills where Musoke was herding the goats, and said:

"Tell my child to come home by the back way and to sit in the kitchen hut till I have told him what to do."

Then she cooked food for the messenger, and said, "When you have eaten you shall see the little girl and take her away with you."

She dressed Musoke in a little barkcloth and put bracelets on his hands, and as she did so she told him the story of his birth, and said, "I have saved your life up till today, I can do no more. You must use your wisdom"; and she told him a Luganda proverb, "It is no use asking the gods to help you if you don't mean to run fast." Then she led Musoke to the messenger, and said, "Here is my little girl, take her to the Chief." And she gave Musoke a present to take, a big hen, and some sem-sem seed in a packet of banana fibre – and the old nurse went with them carrying their roll of mats.

The Chief was very pleased with the little girl and the present she brought, and he gave the old nurse a hut, and said, "Take great care of this beautiful child, and see that she learns how I like my meals cooked, that in time she may be useful to me."

At first Musoke was very careful what he did, but he grew careless, and one day he saw a reed pipe on the ground, and in a moment he forgot everything and began to play his old goat song:

Little black kids,
Little white kids,
Speckled and striped and brown.

The people heard him in amazement. "Do girls play reed pipes?" they cried. "Who is this child?"

Musoke was frightened and ran home, and for some time he was very careful; but he soon forgot again, and one day he found some boys throwing stones into a wild plum tree. And he took the stones and threw them further and higher than any of the others. And the boys were amazed, and said:

"Can a girl throw? How did you learn to throw stones?"

Then Musoke was frightened and ran home; but the boys told their parents, and everybody began to talk about it, and at last it reached the ears of the Chief that there was something queer about the little girl who had come from Singo. And he sent to the old nurse and said:

"Come to the Council House tomorrow with the little girl and I will question you about the strange things she does."

When the nurse heard this she said to Musoke, "What have you done, my child? Now the Chief will find that we have been deceiving him, and he will kill us."

That night Musoke lay awake wondering what he should say when they questioned him in the Council House next day. And then he saw the moonlight shining through the chinks of the reed door, and he slipped softly out into the courtyard and sat down by a great stone. Everything was beautiful and peaceful round him. The hut threw a deep shadow across the courtyard, and behind it the wind sighed and the banana trees threw long flickering shadows which reached him now and then, and all round him the crickets were chirping, but no wise thoughts came to the poor boy. He sat huddled up in his little barkcloth against the big stone, and wondered what he should say in the Council House next morning.

A big fluffy owl flew past him and stopped in surprise. "Why are you not in bed, little girl?" he said.

"I am not a little girl," said Musoke; and he told his story to the owl.

"Ask the Moon to help you," said the owl, and flew away.

Musoke looked up at the Moon, but she seemed so far away and so cold and still.

A black bat flew squeaking past him and startled him a little. "What are you doing out of doors at night, little girl?" he said.

"I am not a little girl," said Musoke, and told the bat his story.

"Ask the Moon to help you," said the bat, and flew on.

Musoke looked up again at the Moon; but she seemed still further away, and colder and stiller than ever.

A big cricket hopped on to the stone by his side and gave such a loud chirp that Musoke quite jumped.

"Why don't you ask the Moon?" he said; "only the Moon can help you. But you must stand up, and shut your eyes, and stretch your arms high above your head when you speak to her."

So Musoke stood up and shut his eyes and stretched his arms high above his head; and then he laughed, for he felt his muscles swelling and was glad that he was a boy.

"Oh, dear Moon, have pity on me, and tell me what to do, and how to answer the Chiefs in the Council House tomorrow!"

Then from far away came a gentle voice. "Little boy, I have watched you for many years and I love you dearly. If you go to the Council House tomorrow and the Chiefs question you, nothing can save you – will you come and live with me in the Cloud Land? Once I had a little boy of my own, but he fell out of his cradle into the Great Lake and became an island, and since then I have been very lonely, for the stars are far away and never talk to me."

Musoke said, "How can I come to you right up in the sky?" And the Moon answered, "I will send a shower of rain and make a rainbow and you must climb up on that."

In a few minutes Musoke felt the rain beginning to fall and soon a beautiful rainbow appeared, and he said to the cricket:

"Tell my old nurse where I have gone, and give my greetings to my mother and tell them I am quite safe: I could not play at being a girl any more." Then he climbed up on the rainbow, and the Moon took him in her arms and laid him in the lovely pearl cradle where her own little boy used to lie, and told him not to lean out too far. In the morning no one knew where he had gone, and they never found him. But if you look up at the Moon you will see something like a cloud lying across it, and in England they call that the 'Man in the Moon', but it is really Musoke the Moon-Boy in his cradle.

Perhaps some day you may see a moon rainbow. You may have to watch for many nights, for it is very rarely seen.

Some people have never seen one at all.

Collected by Rosetta Gage Harvey Baskerville

The Story of Nsangi and the Apes

Uganda

ONCE UPON A TIME, far away upon the mountains, there was a village in which the people were very unhappy, for some huge apes came every day and stole little children. There was one poor widow woman who had three little girls, and she hid them away in her house and never let them go out for fear the apes might see them. But every day her fears grew that she might lose her children, as other people in the village had lost theirs, and the little girls were growing weak and thin, because they never went outside their dark house, and never got any fresh air or sunshine.

At last the woman went to an old wise tortoise and asked him, "Tell me what I can do to save my children from the apes." And the tortoise said, "Apes never take children who are over twelve years old. If you can hide your little girls till then no apes will touch them, but I should advise you to take them away to a cave in the mountain side where they will get fresh air and room to run about."

So the tortoise showed the woman a cave. It was big and airy, and had a little entrance which could be closed by a stone inside and could not be opened from the outside, and there the woman took her three little girls and showed them how to close the entrance when she had gone, and she told them *not* to open the door to *any one* except herself. "I will come every day with a basket of food," she said, "and I will sing a song as I come so that you will know it is me. If any one comes to the door who does not sing my song do not open it."

The next day the woman brought a basket of food and she sang this song as she climbed up the mountain path:

> *Three in a cave,*
> *Three in a cave,*
> *Only three in a cave.*
> *All day long while the sun is shining,*
> *All night long while the moon is shining,*
> *Only three in a cave,*
> *Only three in a cave.*

When the eldest girl was twelve years old the woman took her home and the two younger ones longed for the years to pass when they might leave the cave too (for they had no play mates but the lizards), but it was not safe till they were twelve years old, and the only glimpse they got of the outside world was when they opened the door for their mother, who now sang as she came:

> *Two in a cave,*
> *Two in a cave,*
> *Only two in a cave.*
> *All day long while the sun is shining,*
> *All night long while the moon is shining,*
> *Only two in a cave,*
> *Only two in a cave.*

Then the day came when the second girl was twelve years old, and only the little one, whose name was Nsangi, was left in the cave. She was lonely and cried very much, for now she had no one but the lizards to play with; but her mother said, "I will come earlier and stay longer with you every day, for now your sisters are at home and can do the work there.

Now, there was one old ape who saw the two little girls digging in their garden and wondered where they had come from, for he had never seen children in that house, and he watched and saw the woman go up the mountain path with a basket of food and as she climbed she sang:

> *One in a cave,*
> *One in a cave,*
> *Only one in a cave.*
> *All day long while the sun is shining,*
> *All night long while the moon is shining,*
> *Only one in a cave,*
> *Only one in a cave.*

When she arrived at the cave Nsangi ran out to meet her, and the old ape hid behind a rock quite near. For several days he listened to the woman singing, and when he thought he had learnt the song he went to the cave door and sang it; but Nsangi heard it inside the cave and was terrified, for the ape's voice was like a hoarse old crow, and her mother's voice was like a bird's. The old ape was very angry, but he went away into the forest and found a young cousin of his who was a great mimic and could copy people's voices. Together they hid behind the rock and listened while the woman sang. Nsangi ran out to meet her mother, and begged her to take her home, for the ape had been to the cave. The woman was very distressed, but she said, "I must go home and tell your sisters, and I will stay with you till you are twelve years old. Your sisters can bring us a basket of food every day. I must go now and make arrangements."

When she had gone the apes went after her, sprinkling sharp thorns on the path, and then they hurried to the cave, and the young one sang, copying the woman's voice. Perhaps it was not *exactly* right, but Nsangi was too frightened to notice little mistakes. She was so glad that her mother had returned so quickly that she opened the door at once. The apes caught her and carried her away, right into the middle of the forest. She cried all the way, and wherever her tears fell little white flowers sprang into blossom. Meanwhile her mother had made all arrangements at home and was returning to the cave, but every now and then she had to stop to take a thorn out of her foot, and this delayed her. At last she reached the cave and found it empty, and the lizards told her what had happened and they told her to follow the trail of the little white flowers which were Nsangi's tears.

The poor woman hurried back to the village and told the people what had happened, and the men came out with spears and knives to hunt the apes and they followed the trail of little white flowers right into the middle of the forest, and here they found a big tree which was the King Ape's Palace. Up this tree the apes had carried Nsangi, but as they dragged her up, her foot was cut on a sharp branch and the blood dropped down on to a creeper with thick green leaves, and wherever a drop of blood fell a beautiful crimson flower blossomed, like a convolvulus, only with thick soft petals. The men prepared to make a big fire round the tree, and when the apes saw that their King's palace was going to be burnt they all collected to defend it, and there was a great battle and all the apes were killed, and Nsangi climbed down the big tree and then the men lighted a fire and burnt it to the ground. That was the end of the King Ape's Palace.

And since that day apes have been afraid to go near villages, or steal children, for their mothers always tell them what happened to the King Ape's Palace.

But the birds and bees carried the seeds of the little white flowers all over the country and the old people call them 'Nsangi's tears', and you can still see the crimson creeper with flowers like a convolvulus, only with thick soft petals, but you must search for it in the deep forests. Some people have never seen it, but there are some people who never see anything.

Collected by Rosetta Gage Harvey Baskerville

Goso, the Teacher

Zanzibar, Tanzanian Coast

ONCE THERE WAS A MAN named Go'so, who taught children to read, not in a schoolhouse, but under a calabash tree. One evening, while Goso was sitting under the tree deep in the study of the next day's lessons, Paa, the gazelle, climbed up the tree very quietly to steal some fruit, and in so doing shook off a calabash, which, in falling, struck the teacher on the head and killed him.

When his scholars came in the morning and found their teacher lying dead, they were filled with grief; so, after giving him a decent burial, they agreed among themselves to find the one who had killed Goso, and put him to death.

After talking the matter over they came to the conclusion that the south wind was the offender.

So they caught the south wind and beat it.

But the south wind cried: "Here! I am Koosee, the south wind. Why are you beating me? What have I done?"

And they said: "Yes, we know you are Koosee; it was you who threw down the calabash that struck our teacher Goso. You should not have done it."

But Koosee said, "If I were so powerful would I be stopped by a mud wall?"

So they went to the mud wall and beat it.

But the mud wall cried: "Here! I am Keeyambaaza, the mud wall. Why are you beating me? What have I done?"

And they said: "Yes, we know you are Keeyambaaza; it was you who stopped Koosee, the south wind; and Koosee, the south wind, threw down the calabash that struck our teacher Goso. You should not have done it."

But Keeyambaaza said, "If I were so powerful would I be bored through by the rat?"

So they went and caught the rat and beat it.

But the rat cried: "Here! I am Paanya, the rat. Why are you beating me? What have I done?"

And they said: "Yes, we know you are Paanya; it was you who bored through Keeyambaaza, the mud wall; which stopped Koosee, the south wind; and Koosee, the south wind, threw down the calabash that struck our teacher Goso. You should not have done it."

But Paanya said, "If I were so powerful would I be eaten by a cat?"

So they hunted for the cat, caught it, and beat it.

But the cat cried: "Here! I am Paaka, the cat. Why do you beat me? What have I done?" And they said: "Yes, we know you are Paaka; it is you that eats Paanya, the rat; who bores through Keeyambaaza, the mud wall; which stopped Koosee, the south wind; and Koosee, the south wind, threw down the calabash that struck our teacher Goso. You should not have done it."

But Paaka said, "If I were so powerful would I be tied by a rope?"

So they took the rope and beat it.

But the rope cried: "Here! I am Kaamba, the rope. Why do you beat me? What have I done?"

And they said: "Yes, we know you are Kaamba; it is you that ties Paaka, the cat; who eats

Paanya, the rat; who bores through Keeyambaaza, the mud wall; which stopped Koosee, the south wind; and Koosee, the south wind, threw down the calabash that struck our teacher Goso. You should not have done it."

But Kaamba said, "If I were so powerful would I be cut by a knife?"

So they took the knife and beat it

But the knife cried: "Here! I am Keesoo, the knife. Why do you beat me? What have I done?"

And they said: "Yes, we know you are Keesoo; you cut Kaamba, the rope; that ties Paaka, the cat; who eats Paanya, the rat; who bores through Keeyambaaza, the mud wall; which stopped Koosee, the south wind; and Koosee, the south wind, threw down the calabash that struck our teacher Goso. You should not have done it."

But Keesoo said, "If I were so powerful would I be burned by the fire?"

And they went and beat the fire.

But the fire cried: "Here! I am Moto, the fire. Why do you beat me? What have I done?" And they said: "Yes, we know you are Moto; you burn Keesoo, the knife; that cuts Kaamba, the rope; that ties Paaka, the cat; who eats Paanya, the rat; who bores through Keeyambaaza, the mud wall; which stopped Koosee, the south wind; and Koosee, the south wind, threw down the calabash that struck our teacher Goso. You should not have done it."

But Moto said, "If I were so powerful would I be put out by water?"

And they went to the water and beat it.

But the water cried: "Here! I am Maajee, the water. Why do you beat me? What have I done?"

And they said: "Yes, we know you are Maajee; you put out Moto, the fire; that burns Keesoo, the knife; that cuts Kaamba, the rope; that ties Paaka, the cat; who eats Paanya, the rat; who bores through Keeyambaaza, the mud wall; which stopped Koosee, the south wind; and Koosee, the south wind, threw down the calabash that struck our teacher Goso. You should not have done it."

But Maajee said, "If I were so powerful would I be drunk by the ox?"

And they went to the ox and beat it.

But the ox cried: "Here! I am Ngombay, the ox. Why do you beat me? What have I done?" And they said: "Yes, we know you are Ngombay; you drink Maajee, the water; that puts out Moto, the fire; that burns Keesoo, the knife; that cuts Kaamba, the rope; that ties Paaka, the cat; who eats Paanya, the rat; who bores through Keeyambaaza, the mud wall; which stopped Koosee, the south wind; and Koosee, the south wind, threw down the calabash that struck our teacher Goso. You should not have done it."

But Ngombay said, "If I were so powerful would I be tormented by the fly?"

And they caught a fly and beat it.

But the fly cried: "Here! I am Eenzee, the fly. Why do you beat me? What have I done?" And they said: "Yes, we know you are Eenzee; you torment Ngombay, the ox; who drinks Maajee, the water; that puts out Moto, the fire; that burns Keesoo, the knife; that cuts Kaamba, the rope; that ties Paaka, the cat; who eats Paanya, the rat; who bores through Keeyambaaza, the mud wall; which stopped Koosee, the south wind; and Koosee, the south wind, threw down the calabash that struck our teacher Goso. You should not have done it."

But Eenzee said, "If I were so powerful would I be eaten by the gazelle?"

And they searched for the gazelle, and when they found it they beat it.

But the gazelle said: "Here! I am Paa, the gazelle. Why do you beat me? What have I done?"

And they said: "Yes, we know you are Paa; you eat Eenzee, the fly; that torments

Ng"ombay, the ox; who drinks Maajee, the water; that puts out Moto, the fire; that burns Keesoo, the knife; that cuts Kaamba, the rope; that ties Paaka, the cat; who eats Paanya, the rat; who bores through Keeyambaaza, the mud wall; which stopped Koosee, the south wind; and Koosee, the south wind, threw down the calabash that struck our teacher Goso. You should not have done it."

The gazelle, through surprise at being found out and fear of the consequences of his accidental killing of the teacher, while engaged in stealing, was struck dumb.

Then the scholars said: "Ah! he hasn't a word to say for himself. This is the fellow who threw down the calabash that struck our teacher Goso. We will kill him."

So they killed Paa, the gazelle, and avenged the death of their teacher.

Translated by George W. Bateman

Potter's Field

Shelley Burne-Field, Māori (Ngāti Mutunga)

*Old Yew, which graspest at the stones
That name the under-lying dead,
Thy fibres net the dreamless head,
Thy roots are wrapt about the bones.*
– Tennyson

THE ONCOLOGIST STOPPED TERRY'S CHEMO halfway through Covid but when things opened up again, Terry convinced the cancer team to give him one more shot to save his rotting liver. Lounging in the hospital armchair he told the nurse, who was my mum, "Get it right up there, Dawn." Then he made a joke about getting a chill beside the 'crack of Dawn,' and apparently Mum had giggled, despite the fact they both knew Terry was done for.

I liked Terry a lot, and not in a sex way. He was a nice old koro (grandpa) type, who looked like a vagabond with thin, messy hair. His face used to be pale, like his Irish ancestors, but since I'd met him a year ago, his cheeks had tightened and turned wasp-yellow. I think he saw me as a mokopuna (grandkid) type, and one day he started talking to me about dying of liver cancer.

"My pot o' gold's running out, Arai, girl," he mused one day. "I'm a gonner."

After the worst of Covid, life got back to kind of normal, and Terry carried on carrying on. We were both members of The Heavenly Art Centre which was an old Girl Guide hall that had grass growing out of the guttering, and a crooked rainbow painted on the side. I joined six months before Terry started turning yellow.

The centre President, Leslie, who looked like the Vicar of Dibley and fluttered her eyes just the same, decided that art classes were now essential – thank the Lord. She painted 'the floor is lava' signs, and stuck strips of tape to the hall's bouncy wooden floorboards, and we were open for business. There was no chance of coronavirus cross-contamination on account of Leslie's fat two-metre tape measure. We also had to bring our own cups, teaspoons, hand sanitiser, coconut buns and ginger nuts. Leslie provided the rest: budget tea bags (the best kind), green tea-leaves plus a cast-iron teapot, cardboard box milk (the worst kind), and raw sugar, because raw sugar was more healthy, because it was raw.

I knew Leslie from work and she'd twisted my arm to sign up as an art member. She was also connected, politically, and she'd twisted whoever's arm to get the Girl Guide hall at a $1.00 peppercorn lease. Awesome. At the time I was going through the *'everyone-I-know-is-on-their-OE-because-they-have-a-relative-in-London-they-can-stay-with-and-I'm-stuck-in-this-shit-hole-kiwi-town-because-I'm-broke'* phase so I needed something else to take my mind off the fat question of 'colonisation'. I suppose since our land was stolen over a hundred years ago, there have been generations of my whānau who have always been in a broke phase. Colonisers, meh.

To explain a not-too-distant example, take my final end of Year 13 school trip. I didn't get to tick the expensive option to go skiing in Queenstown, or the ultra expensive option to tour classical Rome (I shit you not – a dozen rich kids got to go to freaking Rome!). *My* group of local disenfranchisees got to tick the local option – staying at our local whānau marae. I've stayed at our marae literally six hundred and ninety-five times. It's our home place. I know it inside and out. My Aunties and Uncles and Koro and Nannies – our tūpuna – are all in photographs on the walls. Their bodies are buried in the paddock next door in the urupa. It's a great marae. And, yeah, I've heard the lectures about Korean and German tourists paying mega dollars to stay at our authentic local place to learn all about Māori blah blah blah, but that didn't make the final Year 13 hurrah any less stink.

The only art class members who'd returned after Covid were Leslie, Terry, me and Lamatau. Nothing much had changed for us during lockdown. Even though some of our hours were shortened, all of us had worked right through, except Terry. He'd been let go from his electrician's job months before. No sick leave left. No insurance. His superannuation had been used up just to live.

He was already a long-time member when I joined, and he supplied clay for the pottery wheels and sculpting. Even through everything, illness, no job, he was there each weekend, turning up, but this particular Saturday, he seemed more tired than ever.

"I found a new spot, lass," he wheezed… "but I need a hand to dig it up – help out, eh?"

So we went clay-hunting, making a point of not breathing on each other. Terry usually looked for clay in low mossy drains, deposits in the river, or road cuttings. I reckon he had one of those divining rods, but for clay. My Nanny told me that Terry was a decent pākehā because at least he was respectful and didn't disturb any sacred sites. The spot he'd found was in a damp corner of railway land at the edge of town. The sun baked my raven-blue bob. It was my 'Poe' look, and Terry got it straight away. "Nevermore," he squawked.

We walked the length of the railway track along one boundary. At the end of the paddock, the grass flowed into trampled paths. I instantly saw why: cut stalks of watercress lined the drain in the southern corner. Close by, a wire fence drooped, pulled down by climbing feet. We weren't the only ones gathering veggies here. A quince tree perched in one corner. It had lost some of its puckered fruit orbs. I felt sorry for whoever had stolen the quinces. Yuck. I remembered Nan's crystallised quince jam that crunched in between my teeth and tasted like perfume. When there was nothing else, Mum made me spread it on brown bread for school lunches. I don't know how anyone could eat that stuff.

Beside the drain opened Terry's clay diggings; precise and tidy holes. Another paddock away, a stand of macrocarpa trees swept the dirt with their curled branches, and the smell of turpentine rode the breeze. A dragonfly thrummed past my ear. The town clock gonged.

"No manu flying around today?" I asked, leaning on my shovel.

"Birds know things," said Terry, looking past the explosion of blackberry bramble. "It's nice here. Peaceful."

He would process the raw dirt into clay over a week: drying it, crumbing it, mixing it with water, screening it twice, leaving it to mud, evaporating the moisture again, slow and measured; then he would massage it on to a plaster board until it transformed into workable gold. The next week, Terry, struggling to keep his shorts above his hips, carried in a different looking slab, as big as a wedding cake, and dumped it on the bench. The clay was pale like mustard mixed with cream.

My pre-Covid clay sculptures were simple. I created koru spirals with a green glaze; garden name plaques with a sunflower motif; and coffee cups shaped as breasts or dicks (best-sellers). When my fingers touched the new clay, I could feel the silkiness, the richness and something else. My first piece turned into a male bust with a hellish, gaping and twisted mouth, complete with uvula. I entitled it 'The Scream' until Terry informed me about the famous painting. I changed the title to 'Surprise!' and left it at that. It sold at the Sunday market, along with three dick coffee cups.

And so I helped Terry dig and cart the clay, and I made pieces for the winter exhibition, all the while watching his face get thinner, his lips drier, his eyes the colour of saffron. My Nanny said karakia for Terry each night and I took him pork bone and watercress broth.

Our art class was a mix alright. Terry, practical and a doer. Leslie worked as a supervisor at the wastewater ponds, and Lamatau supervised the deli at the local Food Fresh. I worked at the local council and was constantly supervised by someone who looked like Nana Mouskouri. I was too young to know who Nana M was, but Leslie reckoned my supervisor's upper lip and brow gave it away.

In our new after-Covid phase, we were missing three others: Dianne, our lipstick-chewing floral artist, who had holed up at her Acacia Bay mansion, as had six of her mah-jong group. We'd heard that Dianne's local bar, which also happened to be the local fish and chip shop, had stayed open right through lockdown and never been caught.

"Ess-holes," snorted Lamatau. None, and I mean *none* of us were impressed with Dianne's access to battered crabsticks.

Missing art member number two was Roland, a retired lawyer. He wasn't answering his emails, but Leslie had heard through a friend of a friend that through lockdown he'd been buying boxes of wagyu beef and farmer's market eggs through a third party (Leslie's dad's cleaner's niece).

Missing art member number three was Bazza, our Queensland car sales executive who had moved back to Rockhampton. Actually, I was disappointed Bazza hadn't returned. He was 23 and rocked washboard abs. Before Bazza fled, he crocheted 233 beautiful garnet poppies to deliver to both the pensioner flats and the kaumātua houses on ANZAC day. He was a mix of simple talents.

The annual exhibition was coming up fast, and I was excited we were getting together most weekends to make art. I hadn't felt so happy since the pandemic struck, though Terry looked terrible.

"Arai, the sculptor," Terry said to me, his breath warm with the tang of morphine. He ambled past, eyeing my newest work: a body reclined on a board, the legs stretched out grotesquely long, ending in block feet; the handless arms rested across the figure's chest; the mouth covered with a mask, and deep holes for eyes made from the point of Lamatau's number ten brush. He ambled past again.

I palmed my chapped lips and mumbled, "Stay out of my breath zone, man!"

Terry danced away on bare feet, bowing to tip his tea-cosy hat low enough to sweep the paint splatters from the floor, but he tripped over Leslie's mandala carry-all, teetered, and snatched at her easel for balance. It collapsed, one leg splintering and another snapping completely in half. Her latest project, an acrylic painted hand-saw, fell and clanged. I jumped.

"For fuck's sake Terry!" Leslie squealed. "We're meant to be social distancing! Now you're breathing the fuck all over me. Jesus." She stepped off the stool, paintbrush held high in one hand, the other hand untangling her long skirt caught behind her calves. Terry picked up the saw. The picture on the metal showed a kune kune pig in a paddock, surrounded by a red picket fence. A violent green smudge ran off the toothy edge.

"Shit, sorry Les," he mumbled. "I fucked your pig."

Leslie's top lip arched, then she looked to the ceiling beams and bellowed like a donkey; a laugh we hadn't heard in months. It echoed off empty walls, and brightened the sun rays seeping through the milky windows.

Lamatau screamed, "Ah, Derry! You trying to turn Leslie's kune kune into a Kandinsky?" She whipped up her paintbrush like a conductor, and left a turquoise smear on the black hair donut perched on top of her head. "Awww, dumb," Lamatau moaned when she realised she'd painted herself.

"Oh my," gasped Leslie. "Cuppa time, honey buns?"

I was laughing and weeping. "Āe, āe." I nodded, sniffing back the tears. It was so nice to feel normal again. Even Terry wore a grin under his whiskers while he picked up the mess.

We sat outside with coffee, the four of us.

"Guess what peeps?" Leslie began, not waiting for us in the slightest. She lifted her skirt up to her thighs, and offered her bulging, pale legs to the sun. "I've started an online course. I'm going to become a death historian."

I sat crossed legged on the edge of the camp chair. Death historian? Lamatau and I raised eyebrows and nodded into our coffee.

"Yes indeedy," said Leslie. "Now, take for example the Christchurch earthquake." Her eyes lit up. "When I get my Diploma, I can tell you exactly how many people died, where people are buried, cemeteries or urupa, or private graveyards, or cremation etcetera, how the hospitals coped, or didn't, orphans, all that, and then I can squeeze out the cultural juice about how society viewed death *at that time*." Leslie stopped. "Oh shit, Terry. Sorry! I didn't mean to talk about, you know, the big D." Leslie's cheeks glazed ruby.

"Aw, don't even worry bout it." Terry waved her away. His eyes flickered, and there was no more white left on the eyeballs; they were as yellow as wasps crawling on a yellow dandelion, squashed under his yellow feet. A question lolled off my tongue before I could stop it.

"Have you bought your plot yet?" I asked Terry. Lamatau looked at me in horror.

The conversation dried up, and so did the spit coating my teeth. I opened my mouth, then snapped it shut, and sucked on the end of my long sleeve to get some moisture flowing. Ant lines marched through the grass.

"Oh right. How much is a plot, like?" Terry asked gently, as though my question had stolen his breath away.

"Terry, I'm so sorry," I began, and then Leslie came to the rescue for all of us.

"Well I've just thought about it, and actually, everyone has to face up to the big D I suppose; everyone." Leslie leaned back further into her camp chair, thigh dimples bulging through the sides. "Terry," she instructed, "where are you going to be buried?"

Terry shrugged. He simply didn't know. He hadn't thought that far ahead. I sat up, trying to figure out how someone couldn't know where they were going to be buried. We had our ancient urupa – where all of us who belonged to the marae would be laid to rest. How awful not to belong? Then I had a thought: I could help, maybe? I dealt with people every day who bought their plots ahead of time. What did he want to know? Had he thought about which cemetery? There were seven cemeteries in the district, did he know? Three were full, two were private, and two, the largest ones, had plots available for the next 100 years, for a price. Lamatau stared into her coffee. Leslie looked at me admiringly.

"Hun, you could be a death historian yourself!"

I thanked her, but I was more interested in Terry's expression. It was haunted by his two wasp-flower yellow eyes, that were close to broke. I knew that desperate look, the money part of it anyway.

"How much?" he asked again, quietly.

I told him the price of a standard plot that Council charged, his eyebrows shot up. Next, the price of a family garden plot, then the price for a space for cremations with a plaque on the ground. Then the price of a slot in a cremation wall. He pursed his lips and now he looked terrified. Was he a veteran? No. Insurance? No. Rich family? No. Any family? No. Family trust? No. Welfare subsidy? Yes. Maybe. There was a debt.

"Well, fuck," said Leslie, while I sucked so hard on my sleeve, that a piece of cotton shredded off for good.

* * *

I worked at the Council on Mondays, except today I had a sniffle, and a sore throat. I text my supervisor that I wouldn't be in. She was a bit of an ice-pick, racist too, chipping at me for not taking out the recycling, or leaving thirty seconds too early. "Bloody Māoris" I heard her hiss more than a few times. A few months ago, I would have worried about her response to me being sick, but the virus had changed everything; some things for the better, like taking sick leave, and telling bosses to go grind themselves. I am staying home and saving lives, including my own, so suck it.

I self-isolated for two weeks at Mum's house. Nanny was home most days too, knitting and playing poker online. Mum had been so busy at the hospital. I worried for her, but she was one of the lucky ones. She'd offered herself up as a guinea pig for a new vaccine, and was still cooking me kawa kawa and bone broth, and saying karakia every night with Nanny – even crossing their hearts. I was still sick as a dog. Leslie brought spicy Thai pumpkin soup to the doorstep, but I'd lost all my taste and smell. Lamatau dropped off pork chop suey with rice noodles and shovels of garlic. Nanny made lemon, kohukohu, and olive leaf tincture and I sniffed clear for the first time in days.

One wet morning, Terry dropped off a smaller clay block to my house. He was hanging on to dear life and dodging Covid like I don't know how. The exhibition was coming up soon. I waved to him through the glass door. He was barefooted as usual, in shorts. His shinbones stretched the skin into white ridges down both legs. He waved back, and his wrists were so pinched, I thought his hand might fall off.

It gave me an idea for my next sculpture: a baby's hand reaching out of a glazed vagina holding a manaia – an angel. I worked on the clay, and lathered the labia in exquisite oxidised Shino and a spec kof iron. I fired it and called it 'Grasp the future.' My Covid test came back positive.

Mum's garage was lined with ply and maroon Axminster carpet that smelled like cat pee. I threw the clay on a pottery board and started building up blobs on blobs, then added snake coils rolled up between my palms, and bits or plugs to form shapes. The trunk of a tree formed. My fingers moulded roots that became winding and gnarled. I squashed the ends. My thumbs rubbed back and forth, smoothing. The clay seemed liquid and then stodgy. I squeezed the clay into branches with twigs that were bare of leaves. No, that was wrong, this tree should grow leaves. Lots of leaves, sucking up the energy from the whenua, the land. I scrunched it all up and started again.

A new tree formed in my hands. Mum had told me once that yew trees grew in cemeteries in England. Then I remembered the big kōwhai tree in the paddock by the marae, covered in golden flowers shaped like Christmas bells. I blinked and pulled up my hoodie. This sculpture that was forming was a yew tree, definitely. It didn't feel Māori. Or did it? My breath misted. My teeth chattered. A bird crashed into the louvre window, cracking one of the panes. My fingers whirred over the clay, and soon each root of the tree ended up in the sculpted mouths of three human corpses. I stood back from the wheel and licked my lips. This was gonna be a great piece! I named it on the spot: 'Forget Yew'. Done.

My second test came back negative, and I went back to work the following Monday. Winter had set in, and the days of Leslie sunbathing at the art centre were long gone. The river was in flood, and she was flat out dealing with overflowing sewage. I sat behind the counter in my duck-egg blouse waiting for ratepayers. At 11:13am, Terry stumbled through the automatic doors, into the foyer, and made a bee-line for me. God, he looked unreal. Like a zombie doppelgänger version of himself, dragging his foot behind him with every step. In any movie, he would be gummy Zombie #1, first to get munted by a cricket bat. His skin had turned more orange than yellow. Later, Lamatau would describe the shade as 'Mister Drump orange'.

"Hey, Arai."

"Hey, Terry. The clay's been amazing this week, thank you."

He smiled and mmm'd. There were words behind his lips that needed to be released.

"I've been thinking about what happens if someone can't afford a plot?" he said and scratched his whiskers. "It might be me soon, Arai. I'm not too worried about that. But, what about other people who can't afford it?" Terry's eyes stung mine. "I can't sleep thinking about it."

"Welfare gives people a couple of grand," I explained. "If it's an accident, ACC gives more cash. Aotearoa isn't like, you know, New York.' My voice lowered to a whisper. "Councils or hospitals have to help find a person a grave, even if you're poor."

"Ah," he said, nodding slowly. "There's the rub," he sighed. The rub? I blinked and rubbed my fingers under the desk.

"Where could they end up?" he asked, like a child waiting for his father's fist. That little word told me everything. *Where* mattered.

Would the sun shine on his grave? Would there be friends or family around him? Was it a pretty place? With flowers and visitors? Would it be comfy? Like laying down in a bed with your own pillow? A soothing spot? Somewhere that could be found, if somebody wanted to find him? Again, I thought about my place at the urupa, with my whānau and my ancient tūpuna all around me.

"Terry," I said quietly. "Most of the cemeteries have spaces available. I mean, I s'pose they're not the primo spots or anything, but, you know, they'd be fine, I think."

I frantically searched on the screen for any plots that flashed green for go, but my vision blurred and I scrolled, jerkily, like a discount shopper. This wasn't happening. Not to my friend. How could they leave him alone? What sort of people did that? Then my eyes widened. I had an idea.

"How about at our urupa?" I squeaked. "I mean I could ask Nanny?"

"Oh no, no," he said quietly. "That's family land. No, it's okay, love. Thank you so much for even thinking of it."

"I'm so sorry, I can't see." I turned away and wiped my eyes. Why was *I* crying? Terry was the one who was dying! My cheeks felt like they'd been slapped red. I couldn't give Terry what he and I both wanted.

"It's all good, Arai. You're doing great. It'll sort itself for me." Terry took a deep breath, blinked in slow motion, and smiled. I swore his eyelids were buzzing. "I wonder what we could do for those others?" he murmured. "The ones who have nothing?" I could smell his sickness, even from behind the thick plastic screen that caught our spit on either side. "See you on Saturday?" he asked.

"Yep, see you there," I stuttered. "I've got some new pieces ready for the exhibition. Have you been painting?" I asked.

"I like running my fingers through the paint now," he said and grinned. "Like you feel the clay in your hands?"

I nodded and tried to smile my best smile ever. I hoped it didn't look like a grimace.

* * *

Terry hadn't arrived at the exhibition. Leslie had filled the electric jug, switched it on, and set up the easels. Lamatau dragged inside a box of knitted pom-poms hats and crocheted blankets to give out in town later that night. She was rugged up herself, wearing a thick crocheted cape.

"Brrrr! Air-contitioner, Arai?" she asked, eyebrows arching up to the ceiling. I fiddled with the buttons on the remote to find the sun setting. In between shifts, Mum had knitted a bagful of fingerless gloves. I wore mine, black.

Leslie's lavender scarf hung down her back. "It's a peasant cowl," she explained, wrapping it around her.

"Isn't a peasant cowl like Red Riding Hood, with a bow?" I asked, but Leslie shrugged, laughing, then her eyes opened wide. "I've just got my first research assignment! About the 1918 influenza pandemic."

I sat at the potter's table. It was empty and I drummed my fingers on my knees. Terry wasn't here yet. I struggled to listen as Leslie ran through her new info.

"It's heinous, really." Leslie glanced around as though she was telling a dirty joke. "About 9000 people died in Aotearoa in two months! There were even mass graves. One big one in Auckland with 444 people, and others that have been forgotten." Her voice was hushed in the quiet room. "There's a monument to the 1918 dead up at the hill cemetery in town. Those are the acknowledged deaths, anyway. You don't even want to know what happened to indigenous Māori – shocking." She shook her head, slowly, gauging our reaction.

My stomach lurched. I was suddenly frightened and fidgety, and I didn't know why. "Wow, that's amazing." My breath hitched. "Where's Terry?" Leslie's talk of death and unmarked graves sat on my chest and pressed me into my chair.

"You okay, Arai?" asked Lamatau. I shook my head, trying to clear a haze that had gathered around me like, like clay. Like somebody was shovelling clay on my head and into my ears, and my mouth.

"What is it, ma honey?"

I woke up with my head in Leslie's cleavage, and Lamatau wiping my forehead with a warm tea towel. I drove back home and collapsed into Nanny's arms. She fed me, soothed me and I started another clay piece. This time, it took shape into an empty rectangular hole. Yep, it was a grave. When Leslie rang later to tell me that she'd found Terry dead in his bed, it wasn't really a surprise. I scrunched up the clay grave and cried.

* * *

It turned out that councils *do* bury poor white people, like Terry. But to say I was pissed off about the shit welfare burial deal, would not be true. I was beyond livid. Like, batshit crazy angry. I stormed into the finance office and let rip.

"An *unmarked* grave?" I screamed. "You've got to be joking?"

"Whoa, Arai. Take a chill pill," shushed Nana-M, my supervisor. I paced in front of her desk, my gaze locked on to a magenta coin purse that lay half open at the corner of her blotter pad. The hint of silver spilled out. "Settle. Settle," said Nana-M, miming with her palms.

"Why are you doing that with your hands?"

"Why are *you* here, Arai?"

I took a deep breath that caught at the top of my lungs, just under my collarbone, and started again. "I can't believe this place is going to bury my friend in an unmarked grave, with no headstone allowed, and people will just walk all over the top of him without even knowing he's there! We would never do that!" My voice began low, but ended in a rising shriek.

"I suggest you go home," stuttered Nana M. "I'm not putting up with this, this abuse any longer."

That was the limit of my dealings with authority. I'm not that hero. I didn't go home. I stayed at my desk and frantically searched for any free plot, any patch of grass that Terry could claim as his own. That maybe we could pay for? I called Nanny.

"We'll have him, darling," soothed Nanny. "It'll be okay, kare."

I took a deep breath. It would work – but what about anyone else? As Terry said, what about those who had nothing? Not just poor, but no whānau, no friends? In our world, everyone was taken in, helped, shown manaaki – but this world? Then Leslie called and everything fell into place.

"Hi Leslie," I whispered, still at my desk. "Nanny said Terry can be buried at the marae. It'll be okay, but I still worry about others? You know, how Terry wanted a place for others too… Oh *Alright*, sorry, I'm listening. Wait what? Really? Here in town? …*really*? A burial place? Where? Where? Oh shit. *Where* did you say?"

I looked at the phone and blinked. The printer went ballistic in the background, and a fluorescent light buzzed on and stayed on above me. That light had flickered for a thousand years.

Leslie had called with *historical* news. There was a place.

A place for Terry.

Leslie had discovered that Terry's clay paddock wasn't railway land after all, but it had belonged to the old Hospital Board, and then was transferred to the Council in the 1970s. Our clay field was a mass grave from the 1918 pandemic.

"It has room, hun," she'd told me on the phone, excitedly. "Room for new burials. We could do it up, for Terry? And for anyone else who can't afford it?"

My eyes watered and my heart squeezed. Terry's face loomed in front of me. It would work. Leslie's dad played golf with the Mayor up the coast, and soon Leslie had wheedled another $1.00 a year lease for the paddock/burial ground. I could imagine Leslie munching on the Mayor's conscience like a mastiff with a beef knuckle. She could chew those bones, man. I hung up and left the office.

I met Leslie and Lamatau at the clay paddock fence. I knew it was the right place for our friend. A potter's field. It had beckoned to me all along. Through my fingers. Through my thumbs. Through Terry.

Charcoal clouds rolled above, while the emerald grass glistened below. I imagined laying down in it, as comfy as my own pillow. Lamatau's tears dripped off her chin as she draped garlands of flowers over the gate. Leslie took photos to start the process for Terry's burial and vowed to put up a new sign, honouring those past and present. We would make it colourful, with rainbows and art and sculptures. A place of manaaki and love. I marked a spot to plant a yew tree for Terry. Another spot to plant a kōwhai tree to watch over everyone and keep them safe.

This place could be found, if somebody wanted to visit. A place, peaceful and known. A place under clay sunflower plaques, with a name on it, to be remembered with aroha.

For Glenn

Sunset on Mars

Gina Cole, Fiji

VITI SAT WITH CAPTAIN THEODORA AND SOCHETNA, the thief. She contemplated the fiery ball dropping in slow motion towards Mars horizon. A light blue glow washed over her colleagues' gawping faces, open-mouthed like indigo children watching distant fireworks explode in the sky.

"Beautiful," said Theo, pushing back her Captain's hat.

Reconstituted chicken and wild rice lay cold and congealed on Viti's abandoned plate. Replicator food sickened her. She craved her bubu's dalo and palusami.

In the seat next to Viti, Sochetna's rotund cheeks plumped out in profile. Her fuzzy red hair smudged together with blue sunlight, gave her a purple halo. These dreamlike Martian vistas did nothing to relieve Viti's claustrophobia. She detested her trapped existence inside the oppressive lifepod. Elliptical walls closed in on her, there was no escape. She tried to find respite whenever she left the lifepod's close confines to take spacewalks for research or repair. She loved walking away from everything, wandering into the red desert. When she looked back at the lifepod it loomed over barren Martian plains, a gigantic silvery egg perched on four stout fold-out legs – propped up against the imposing backdrop of Olympus Mons. Lasertrips provided her some relief although they were too short and they took place in the living imaginary, the playtime netherworld. A skewed reality.

Viti leaned over, tossed her plate into the recycling conduit, curled her full lips. "This food is ash."

"Such a waste," said Sochetna.

The smirk on Sochetna's face bothered Viti. She turned her head to gaze at the sapphire sunset. "You are a fine one to talk about waste."

Sochetna heard the mumbled comment, jumped from her chair, kicked it across the room. Her unruly black hair bounced around her face with the sudden movement.

"I didn't steal your stupid lasertime," she said, eyes ablaze.

Viti's heartrate increased. She lifted her chin, rose from the seat, moved with cat-like stealth towards Sochetna, fists clenched.

"Let me take your next lasertrip then … to check," she said, eyeing Sochetna, challenging her to refuse.

Sochetna backed away, blinked fast, wished she'd kept her big mouth shut. She threw her arms in the air, defeated.

"Fine. I have nothing to hide. And once you realize the truth you will owe me double lasertime in return," said Sochetna.

Viti's eyes narrowed as she considered Sochetna's offer. Double lasertime, a big sacrifice. She just needed more proof. This wager would put the whole saga to bed once and for all.

"Okay, double it is," said Viti.

She remembered when physicists first discovered the mem-branes. Her grandmother had foreseen big trouble.

"Those spacemen need to be very careful when they throw themselves into the music of the vā," Bubu had warned. "There are many pathways in the great unknown, and they are not always in harmony with each other."

Nobody knew for sure what caused the branes or where they'd come from. Huge time and space vortices whirling in the cosmos, passageways between different existences. When they were first discovered many people disappeared into the branes and never returned. A group of dedicated physicists figured out how to travel inside them using laser tec. The branes still presented a deep unknowable mystery. But they provided amusement for the bored survivors living on the Moon and on Mars – with no other place to go. Viti heeded Bubu's warnings and didn't use the lasertrips – until after her death. At first, she'd taken just one lasertrip back in time, to see Bubu before she died, so they could talk. Viti didn't think Bubu would've disagreed with such a visit. After that trip Viti was hooked. Much like a drug becomes addictive after the first hit. Although the initial glorious onslaught is never quite replicated in its full splendour.

Viti circled Sochetna, who side stepped, bobbed, held her hands in a loose block against her face.

"You'll be sorry," said Sochetna.

They hadn't come to blows yet, but it might happen tonight. Captain Theo jumped in between them, her hands held up, fingers spread wide like the branches of a vesi tree. This lasertrip conflict between her two science officers had to stop.

"Break it up, you two. I am sick of your bickering. We're all stuck here, and this bad atmosphere doesn't help."

She hoped her intervention would calm the dispute – at least for a while. Viti unclenched her fists, took a long breath. Sochetna slumped, scowled.

"You are witness to our agreement, Captain," said Sochetna.

"Yes, yes, Viti will owe you double time on the lasertrip. If you are right," said Captain Theo. She sighed, scraped her hands through wavy dark hair.

"Alright. I'll program it for you," said Sochetna. She backed away into the dim blue light at the edge of the room.

"Great," said Viti, her resolve exhausted. She gazed out once more through an oval porthole, searched the shifting red sands sweeping across the Martian plains to gather in huge dunes at the foothills. There was always mystery hiding in Martian sands – grand shapes, variegated colours, beauty.

Captain Theo slouched into a cushioned rib chair. "She's not herself you know. Her research has come to a complete halt since this feud started up between you."

"She stole my lasertime," said Viti.

The sun disappeared below the horizon, turning the sky dark blue with a collar of stars rising above the mountains as true night began to fall.

"Have you double-checked the logs?"

Viti remained tight-lipped. She didn't want to debate the issue with Captain Theo. Sochetna appeared from the south corridor, arms held stiff at her sides, her lips in a pout.

"I've lined up the laserpod for you," she said.

Viti eyed her. "I ran the logs. I know you took my five sols."

"Well, the logs are wrong," said Sochetna. She twisted her mouth. "Go and see for yourself. I'm telling you. You'll regret this."

Viti pushed past her, strode out of the room. Sochetna and Captain Theo followed close behind. Viti didn't know how Sochetna had done it, but computer logs don't lie. The numbers were clear as a sunny day on Earth.

* * *

Their dispute arose after Viti's last lasertrip when she'd stayed overnight on Luna Base and caught the laserport to Shadow Earth the following morning. She spent four wonderful Earth days in the summer of 2330 at Te Werahi beach with her wife Shell and their dog, a frisky Jack Russell named Haki who ran after the wind. They took long walks to the curve in the beach where Motuopao Island rose from the sea, and a lighthouse ruin lay on the headland in a rocky heap. They swam in the ocean, ate fish and chips cooked on hot coals, and talked into the night. On their final evening, the sky filled with glittering stars. They built a bonfire on the sand, huddled together under a blanket to watch meteors fall into the horizon to the west of Te Rerenga Wairua. But, on their lasertrip home – via Luna Base – Viti was yanked out of the trip and laserported to Mars lifepod, five sols early. She tried to laserport back to Shell and Haki, but the remaining five sols of her trip had disappeared from the pod logs. Sochetna flew out on the very next lasertrip from Mars lifepod. Somehow, she had tagged on five extra sols to her trip. There was no doubt in Viti's mind that Sochetna had stolen her last five sols with Shell and Haki, and she wanted to get them back.

* * *

One single-pod laserporter lay like a fat grey slug in the transport bay. A control console flickered in the opposite corner. Viti stepped into the laserporter and lowered herself into the oval seat. Standing at the console, Sochetna sent the lasertrip co-ordinates for Luna Base into the pod. Captain Theo stood with arms folded. Her legs shook back and forth, her forehead contorted into a frown.

"I am not convinced this is going to change anything," said Captain Theo. "The time passage to Shadow Earth is blocked. There are no more lasertrips left on Luna Base. They'll be annoyed you even tried."

The more Captain Theo thought about it, the more nervous she became. There was disharmony in this lasertrip, a sense of something off balance with the vā, the great space. She had no stomach for the fight between Viti and Sochetna, but she wished there were another way to resolve the impasse.

"I have a right to my five sols. They can't stop me," said Viti.

"You won't find what you're looking for," said Sochetna.

"I'm going to see Shell and Haki. You talk in riddles," said Viti. She tried to slam the hatch door shut but failed when the hydraulics kicked in and the hatch closed in slow motion.

"See you in a minute," said Captain Theo, as the pod door clicked shut.

Viti locked the interior latch and waved awkwardly at Captain Theo through the porthole, her ears burning red. The instrument-panel inside the laserpod blinked – red, black, red, black. She pushed the green 'Go' button and the laserpod whisked her in a disorienting mind-transport to Sochetna's pre-programmed destination inside the living imaginary.

Sochetna monitored Viti's life signs from the console, transferred her holographic image to the viewer above the instrument panel.

"She's holding steady, Captain."

"Go ahead, ignite," said Theo. She watched Viti's image elongate into the fourth dimension, before morphing into the fifth dimension, where it became a convex cylinder, and disappeared into a point.

* * *

Viti stumbled from the laserpod, fell on to a smooth floor, edged into a smoky haze. The smell of burnt leaves filled the air. Scraping noises echoed nearby.

"Hello?"

She groped along a wall, found a dip, a door, stepped into a wide passageway, inhaled clean air. Why hadn't she arrived in the lasertrip entry-bay at Luna Base? How did Sochetna bypass Luna Base and bring her here – wherever here was? Her wrist-pad read 20 May 2450, Tāmaki Makaurau, Aotearoa. She ran down the hall searching for a way out – opened and closed doors into small rooms – until she found a wooden staircase curling in a bizarre descent to an atrium where a huge door carved with ornate designs opened on to a yellow verandah. Concrete steps led to a lawn, and out to a tree-lined street. A large oak tree grew next to a wrought iron fence, branches waving in the wind, leaves casting dappled sunlight over the lawn. Viti took the steps in two bounds, turned to face a yellow three-storey house with a grey roof.

"Finally! You took your time."

Viti recognized the mocking tone. She peered up at the porch where the voice had come from. At the end of the verandah sat Sochetna, rocking to and fro on a swing seat. She held what appeared to be a glass of red wine.

"What the hell… Sochetna?"

"Yeah, it's me. I've been trapped in this place for bloody ages. Help yourself to the grog and food in the fridge," she said, and raised her glass.

Viti inhaled, braced herself, walked up the path on to the porch, leaned on the wooden railing for support.

"But I just saw you in Mars lifepod. What are you doing here in my lasertrip? Where are we?"

"Don't ask me. After I arrived, I somehow split in two. And I met myself, or a split off part of myself. Anyway, there are two of me now, and the other me, she stole my laserpod, took off, and left me stranded. Believe me, it's her in Mars lifepod."

"You're kidding! There's two of you?" asked Viti.

"Yep. But the *me* on Mars, is not me. It's her," said Sochetna.

"Well, which one is the real you?" asked Viti.

"We're both real. We live on separate planes. I think I must have travelled through a brane at the exact same instant that she did. What are the odds? But I'm the true one. It is me who lives in Mars lifepod with you, and *she* lives in this place. She did a switcheroo on me and I need to switch her right back."

Viti's breath hitched in her throat. She tried to take in what Sochetna had just said. Her thoughts swam and darted in all directions.

"So, you reckon we're on a different plane?"

"Are you stupid? That's what lasertripping is. Travel to a different plane."

Viti threw her hands in the air. "I know that, you idiot. But we've only ever lasertripped to Shadow Earth. Where in the universe is this place?"

"I dunno," said Sochetna. Her eyes widened as the wind picked up.

"I'm supposed to be on Shadow Earth, not … here," said Viti.

She now regretted taking this lasertrip and wanted more than anything to go home to Mars lifepod. She laughed to herself. So, Mars lifepod had become home now – how ironic.

"Is this … Earth?"

"You're nuts. How long is it till we can make a safe trip back to Earth?" asked Sochetna.

Viti crossed her arms. "One hundred and ninety-six Earth years, give or take a few months. But we can lasertrip to Shadow Earth. You know that."

"Ha! Well, forget about Earth. She's a goner. And you can't live on Shadow Earth. And Luna Base is full up. Mars lifepod is our home now," said Sochetna.

Viti's face brightened. "Wait a minute. Why did this lasertrip land here? Why aren't we on Luna Base?"

"Not sure. Something to do with the black hole upstairs," said Sochetna.

"The smoked-up room?"

Sochetna nodded. "Yep. That room has already taken the cat and the family I had – she had – in this plane."

"You met other people? Where are they?"

"The hole sucked them all in," said Sochetna.

Viti didn't trust her. Something had gone terribly wrong here and it was all Sochetna's doing.

"Why are you still here? How do I know you aren't the phony Sochetna, and the real one is back on Mars?"

Sochetna jumped off the swing seat. The glass dropped from her hand spilling red wine down the front of her grey uniform and smashing on the deck as she grabbed at Viti's jacket. Viti wrenched Sochetna's wine-soaked hands from her clothing and retreated. She sure had the same bad temper.

"I am the real Sochetna. You've got to believe me." Her lower lip quivered as she spoke. She swiped tears off her cheeks, tried to hide her face.

"Okay. Tell me what we fight about on Mars lifepod," said Viti.

Sochetna laughed through her tears. "Oh, too easy. Everything. Okay, we fight about the five sols you reckon I stole from your lasertrip to 2330. Well, I suppose I did steal them, but for good reason."

Viti slapped her thighs, shook her head.

"So, you admit it!"

Sochetna curled her arms over her head, tried to hide her face again as words rushed from her mouth.

"I figured out how to reverse-program my laserpod to give me five sols from your account on Mars."

Tears welled in Viti's eyes. "You laserlifted me from my holiday with my wife."

"I'm sorry. I needed to get your attention. I knew you'd be pissed off and I hoped you'd come to investigate. And look, here you are. It worked."

They lapsed into silence, glared at each other. The oak tree rustled in the wind; orange leaves floated to the lawn in effortless arcs.

"I answered your question. Do you believe me now?" asked Sochetna.

Viti planted her hands on her hips. "How did this happen?"

Sochetna pointed up. "I told you … the black hole."

Viti sneered. "The black hole."

Sochetna paced the yellow porch. She'd had enough chit chat.

"This place is disintegrating. We've got to get out. I have a plan."

She rushed past Viti. Pungent red wine fumes swirled in her wake. She stopped at the huge front door and beckoned to Viti.

"Hurry."

Viti checked her wrist-pad readings. The co-ordinates were still correct. She followed Sochetna's shaky form into the house. As they made their way up the staircase to the smoke-filled room the house creaked and swayed like a space barge. The doorknob crackled. Sparks flew when Sochetna took hold of it. She fell to the floor screaming and cradling her hand. The door flew open, hit the wall with a resounding 'thwack!'

"What happened?" asked Viti. She reached down to help Sochetna to her feet.

"Electric plasma. The room charge has increased since you arrived. We've got to move fast," said Sochetna. She tried to shake the throbbing pain from her hand.

Viti flapped her arms to sweep away the haze gathering around her. "I've never seen smoke like this in any lasertrip."

"It's the fraud's fault. She left in my laserpod a few hours ago. Her departure fired up the black hole. I only just managed to drag your pod out."

"So, what next?" asked Viti.

"I reverse-programmed my laserpod to get your five sols. I reckon we do the same thing with your pod, reprogram it to reverse and laserjump back to Mars via the black hole. I reckon the pretender figured it out. If she can do it, so can I."

Viti raised her eyebrows. She had no better plan. Sochetna dropped to the floor, crawled on her belly into the smoky room. Viti followed, sweeping her wrist-pad torchlight from side to side as white smoke engulfed them. She coughed until her lungs hurt.

"Be careful, the hole is right in front of us," said Sochetna.

The smoke evaporated and there it was, a black hole filled with stars, swirling in the middle of the floor. Viti recoiled as a floorboard dislodged beneath her feet and sailed into the vortex.

"This is our way out. Help me get your laserpod," said Sochetna. She skittered sideways into the smoke like a crab.

Viti followed her to the neighbouring room. They dragged the pod close to the brink of the whirling black hole.

"Get in, quick," said Sochetna.

Viti squeezed on to the seat. Sochetna lay to one side, balanced on the rim. Viti pulled the hatch shut.

"So, what now?"

"We enter the co-ordinates for Mars lifepod into the instrument-panel and hope for the best."

Sochetna typed a sequence into the console. They waited, helpless, as the black hole widened. Floorboards creaked and broke apart, plank after plank, until the floor gave way beneath them and the laserpod whirled into the vortex.

"We're moving," said Viti.

"I feel sick," said Sochetna.

"Can you see out the window?"

Sochetna lifted her head, peeked through the porthole.

"It's all black. Wait, I see white lines, curved white lines."

Sochetna's words slurred together. She passed out. Her skull lolled on the headrest; her tongue drooped from her mouth like a sleeping dog. The pod span faster and faster. Viti watched the stars elongate into the curved lines Sochetna had observed. There were no steering discs to control the pod in the vortex. Viti stared into the vā, her mind blank. Pods were built for lasertrips into the living imaginary, not for controlled flight. Trapped in the tiny vessel with no pilot control as it hurtled around the vortex, Viti struggled with claustrophobia. She had never remained conscious during a lasertrip, even though a usual transport lasted only a minute. At the five-minute mark as the pod rotated she fought nausea, gritted her teeth, tried to stay alert. At the six-minute mark she passed out.

When she came to, smoke eddied outside the laserpod porthole. Sochetna moaned and flapped her arms.

"Wake up. We've stopped," said Viti. She held her elbows up to protect herself from Sochetna's flailing.

"Aarrrggh … let me outta here," said Sochetna.

Viti shoved her away. "The console's gone dark."

Sochetna kicked at the roof. "We're going to die."

"Calm down. We *will* die if you don't pull it together," said Viti. She pushed Sochetna's legs to one side.

At that moment, someone – or something – unfastened the outside hatch clip. Viti unclipped the inner lock and the hatch door opened in a smoky puff. Sochetna lurched from the pod, jumped into the vapour. Viti followed, stepped down from the laserpod. Sochetna's laugh echoed nearby. The fog cleared and there – across the room at the console – stood Captain Theo and Sochetna, staring – slack-jawed. Viti gasped, turned. Next to her, with a smirk on her face, stood another, identical Sochetna in a wine-stained uniform. Viti looked back and forth between wine-stained-Sochetna now laughing next to her, and control-desk-Sochetna, gawping, and white-knuckling the console.

"Me! I am the one and only," said wine-stained-Sochetna. "You are an imposter."

Control-desk-Sochetna shrank, babbled incoherently.

"I'm not going back there," she said.

* * *

Five sols later, Viti gazed out of the huge western porthole.

"Glorious…" she said, her eyes fixated on the dim cobalt sky.

She abandoned a plate of cold porridge, flopped into a canvas chair. Sochetna-One – the 'original', as she liked to call herself – moved a metal seat next to Viti and Captain Theo and faced the blue Mars sundown. She lazed in the metal chair, dipped her fingers into a bag filled with dehydrated carrot chips. This had become the crew ritual every evening, to watch the radiant blue twilight play out its iridescent drama. This night was no different except for an incoming transmission from Luna Base which interrupted their quiet reverie.

"Come in, Mars lifepod. This is Luna Base. Over."

Viti dragged herself away from the dramatic azure nightfall to answer the Luna Base transmission, clicked open the receiver. "Mars lifepod, over."

The comfeed hissed and crackled into their peaceful atmosphere.

"Just checking on you. How's the new arrival, Mars?"

Sochetna-One laughed and threw her head back, almost fell off her chair.

"She's settling in. We've decided not to put her into stasis. There's enough room for us all in the lifepod," said Viti. "Any news on the laserport malfunction?"

"We're still working on it. All lasertrips remain suspended until further notice. Your guest will have to stay with you for the foreseeable future, Mars."

"Copy that, Luna Base. Mars out," said Viti.

The comfeed ended. A metallic echo rang in the silence as Sochetna-Two – the visitor from the black hole – walked into their midst holding a packet of dehydrated apple slices. Her face flickered orange at the edges as she flumped into a chair next to Sochetna-One. Viti often saw her profile smudge, disintegrate, like a faulty holograph. It only happened at sundown. She had dismissed it as a trick of the blue light bouncing off red dust suspended in the Martian sky.

"Wow," said Sochetna-Two. She gawked like a child at the blue glow spreading along the Martian horizon.

Both Sochetnas looked to Viti, their faces serious.

"Sorry, I can't give you back your five sols," they said, in unison.

They turned to each other, open-mouthed. This kept happening – where they uttered the same words at the same time – and neither of them liked it.

Viti laughed. "Guess I don't owe you double lasertime."

Sochetna-Two struggled to open the food packet in her hands.

"Look at you, you idiot," said Sochetna-One. She pointed with her chin at Sochetna-Two, ripped the bag from her hands. "Give it to me." Sochetna-Two snarled at her.

"What a beautiful blue infinity," said Captain Theo.

Captain Theo's large bluish feet rested on a metal box; her strange hairy arms stretched along the back of the sofa. Her edges blurred into the azure night sky.

Viti ignored her increasing unease as the Martian sunset bathed their faces in dark blue wonder.

Mythology of Mindanao

The Philippines

A LONG, LONG TIME AGO Mindanao was covered with water, and the sea extended over all the lowlands so that nothing could be seen but mountains. Then there were many people living in the country, and all the highlands were dotted with villages and settlements. For many years the people prospered, living in peace and contentment. Suddenly there appeared in the land four horrible monsters which, in a short time, had devoured every human being they could find.

Kurita, a terrible creature with many limbs, lived partly on land and partly in the sea, but its favourite haunt was the mountain where the rattan grew; and here it brought utter destruction on every living thing. The second monster, Tarabusaw, an ugly creature in the form of a man, lived on Mt. Matutun, and far and wide from that place he devoured the people, laying waste the land. The third, an enormous bird called Pah, was so large that when on the wing it covered the sun and brought darkness to the earth. Its egg was as large as a house. Mt. Bita was its haunt, and there the only people who escaped its voracity were those who hid in caves in the mountains. The fourth monster was a dreadful bird also, having seven heads and the power to see in all directions at the same time. Mt. Gurayn was its home and like the others it wrought havoc in its region.

So great was the death and destruction caused by these terrible animals that at length the news spread even to the most distant lands, and all nations were grieved to hear of the sad fate of Mindanao.

Now far across the sea in the land of the golden sunset was a city so great that to look at its many people would injure the eyes of man. When tidings of these great disasters reached this distant city, the heart of the king Indarapatra was filled with compassion, and he called his brother, Sulayman, begging him to save the land of Mindanao from the monsters.

Sulayman listened to the story, and as he heard he was moved with pity.

"I will go," said he, zeal and enthusiasm adding to his strength, "and the land shall be avenged."

King Indarapatra, proud of his brother's courage, gave him a ring and a sword as he wished him success and safety. Then he placed a young sapling by his window and said to Sulayman:

"By this tree I shall know your fate from the time you depart from here, for if you live, it will live; but if you die, it will die also."

So Sulayman departed for Mindanao, and he neither walked nor used a boat, but he went through the air and landed on the mountain where the rattan grew. There he stood on the summit and gazed about on all sides. He looked on the land and the villages, but he could see no living thing. And he was very sorrowful and cried out:

"Alas, how pitiful and dreadful is this devastation!"

No sooner had Sulayman uttered these words than the whole mountain began to move, and then shook. Suddenly out of the ground came the horrible creature, Kurita. It sprang at the man and sank its claws into his flesh. But Sulayman, knowing at once that this was the scourge of the land, drew his sword and cut the Kurita to pieces.

Encouraged by his first success, Sulayman went on to Mt. Matutun where conditions were even worse. As he stood on the heights viewing the great devastation there was a noise in the forest and a movement in the trees. With a loud yell, forth leaped Tarabusaw. For a moment they looked at each other, neither showing any fear. Then Tarabusaw threatened to devour the man, and Sulayman declared that he would kill the monster. At that the animal broke large branches off the trees and began striking at Sulayman who, in turn, fought back. For a long time the battle continued until at last the monster fell exhausted to the ground and then Sulayman killed him with his sword.

The next place visited by Sulayman was Mt. Bita. Here havoc was present everywhere, and though he passed by many homes, not a single soul was left. As he walked along, growing sadder at each moment, a sudden darkness which startled him fell over the land. As he looked toward the sky he beheld a great bird descending upon him. Immediately he struck at it, cutting off its wing with his sword, and the bird fell dead at his feet; but the wing fell on Sulayman, and he was crushed.

Now at this very time King Indarapatra was sitting at his window, and looking out he saw the little tree wither and dry up.

"Alas!" he cried, "my brother is dead"; and he wept bitterly.

Then although he was very sad, he was filled with a desire for revenge, and putting on his sword and belt he started for Mindanao in search of his brother.

He, too, travelled through the air with great speed until he came to the mountain where the rattan grew. There he looked about, awed at the great destruction, and when he saw the bones of Kurita he knew that his brother had been there and gone. He went on till he came to Matutun, and when he saw the bones of Tarabusaw he knew that this, too, was the work of Sulayman.

Still searching for his brother, he arrived at Mt. Bita where the dead bird lay on the ground, and as he lifted the severed wing he beheld the bones of Sulayman with his sword by his side. His grief now so overwhelmed Indarapatra that he wept for some time. Upon looking up he beheld a small jar of water by his side. This he knew had been sent from heaven, and he poured the water over the bones, and Sulayman came to life again. They greeted each other and talked long together. Sulayman declared that he had not been dead but asleep, and their hearts were full of joy.

After some time Sulayman returned to his distant home, but Indarapatra continued his journey to Mt. Gurayn where he killed the dreadful bird with the seven heads. After these monsters had all been destroyed and peace and safety had been restored to the land, Indarapatra began searching everywhere to see if some of the people might not be hidden in the earth still alive.

One day during his search he caught sight of a beautiful woman at a distance. When he hastened toward her she disappeared through a hole in the ground where she was standing. Disappointed and tired, he sat down on a rock to rest, when, looking about, he saw near him a pot of uncooked rice with a big fire on the ground in front of it. This revived him and he proceeded to cook the rice. As he did so, however, he heard someone laugh near by, and turning he beheld an old woman watching him. As he greeted her, she drew near and talked with him while he ate the rice.

Of all the people in the land, the old woman told him, only a very few were still alive, and they hid in a cave in the ground from whence they never ventured. As for herself and her old husband, she went on, they had hidden in a hollow tree, and this they had never dared leave until after Sulayman killed the voracious bird, Pah.

At Indarapatra's earnest request, the old woman led him to the cave where he found the headman with his family and some of his people. They all gathered about the stranger, asking many questions, for this was the first they had heard about the death of the monsters. When they found what Indarapatra had done for them, they were filled with gratitude, and to show their appreciation the headman gave his daughter to him in marriage, and she proved to be the beautiful girl whom Indarapatra had seen at the mouth of the cave.

Then the people all came out of their hiding-place and returned to their homes where they lived in peace and happiness. And the sea withdrew from the land and gave the lowlands to the people.

Collected by Mabel Cook Cole

Legend and Song of the Daughter and the Slave

The Ndau Tribe of Eastern Zimbabwe,

Mozambique and Malawi

A MAN HAD THREE WIVES, one of whom he loved far more than the other two. She was his favourite, the wife beloved.

One day he went trapping and caught a guinea-fowl which he brought back and gave to the favourite wife, that she might cook it for him. Now such signs of favour often arouse jealousy among the wives; so one of them, ill-humoured, stole the guinea-fowl. Next morning, though all searched, no one could find the bird, nor could they discover who had taken it. So it was decided to reveal the guilty one by an ordeal. A cord was suspended over the Buji river like a bridge; the two jealous wives must cross the river, treading upon the cord, and the one who was guilty would fall in.

Now the woman who stole the fowl had two daughters. The elder daughter, who was named Mwa′li, had been married long ago and lived far away; the younger lived at home. The guilty wife knew that with the ordeal she would fall into the river and be drowned. So she called her young daughter and said, "When I am dead, go and live with your married sister and take with you your slave maid." (Slaves are often war-captives taken from the enemy; young boys and girls were brought home from the wars as booty.)

Next morning, at the trial, each wife, as she crossed the river must sing,

Lusi′nga, lusinga,   *Cord, Cord,*
Da′ndali! Kuti′ ndilini,   *Da′ndali! If I am guilty*
Da′ndali! Nda ka be ga′nga,   *Da′ndali! And stole the treasure*
Da′ndali! Ganga′ la chi′de,   *Da′ndali! Of the beloved,*
Da′ndali! Lusinga′, daru′ka,   *Da′ndali! Then, cord, break*
     with me,
Da′ndali! Ndi wile mwa Buji,   *Da′ndali! Into the Buji*
Da′ndali! Ndi zo fila′ mwo.   *Da′ndali! I'll fall and perish.*

The first of the jealous wives, who was innocent, sang this song and crossed safely. The second, who was guilty, sang the song also, talking to the cord; when she was midway across the stream the cord broke, she fell into the water and was drowned.

The daughter then set out for the home of her married sister, Mwa′li. Now Mwa′li had not seen her younger sister for so many years that it was as if she had never looked upon her. Nor had she ever seen the slave-maid. But the slave knew the way to Mwa′li's home and she led the little sister through the forests and along the narrow paths. As they were nearing the kraal where Mwa′li lived they came to a pond and laid off their clothing and bathed, for they were heated and tired. The little sister was richly dressed and carried no bundles, the slave was scantily clad and bore the basket. When they came out of the water the slave said, "Let us change garments! Let us see how I would look in your clothes, and you take my basket – just for a little while; then we will change back again." So the slave wore her mistress's rich clothing and the little mistress carried the basket. They started walking, but after they had gone a short distance the little sister said, "Let us stop!" for they were nearing Mwa´li's home and could already see the kraal. "Give me my clothes," she said, "for we are almost there!"

But the slave urged, "Let us walk just a *little* further; then we will change back to our own clothes again." And so they went on till the little sister cried again, "O, give me my clothes! We are almost there." But once more the slave persuaded her to go "a little further"; so she kept saying until they were at the very entrance to the kraal. And here was Mwa´li, coming forth to meet them! The little sister wept, for Mwa´li took her to be a slave, and treated the slave like a sister. She tried to explain, but the slave interrupted her proudly, crying, "No! Do not listen to her. She is nothing but a lying slave. I am your sister." And so Mwa´li was deceived.

Now the little sister was sent each day to the gardens to watch the crops and keep the birds from eating them. Early every morning she set out, and late each evening she returned. Thus was she made to work, treated as a slave and poorly fed. But each morning, early, when she came to the gardens, she sang this song:

Mai va-i-le´ram,	*Mother, she was saying*
(Linde´, linde´!)	*(O watch, O watch!)*
Ku´ fa kwa´n gu pa´no,	*When I die, my daughter,*
(Linde´, linde´!)	*(O watch, O watch!)*
E´nda ku muku´lu	*Go to elder sister.*
(Linde´, linde´!)	*(O watch, O watch!)*
Mukulu´ ndi ya´ni?	*Who is elder sister?*
(Linde´, linde´!)	*(O watch, O watch!)*
Mukulu´ ndi Mwa´li.	*Elder sister, Mwali.*
(Linde´, linde´!)	*(O watch, O watch!)*
Mwa´li wa-ndi la´sha,	*Mwali , she hath spurned me,*
(Linde´, linde´!)	*(O watch, O watch!)*
Ngo kuda´ mula´nda.	*For to love the slave-girl.*
(Linde´, linde´!)	*(O watch, O watch!)*

Then the spirit of the dead mother would come and brush the dirt from her daughter and clothe her in rich garments – and each night the girl went back dressed as she used to be at home. Then the real slave, when she saw the little sister coming, would cry out and exclaim, "Look how the slave comes so richly clad!" and she would take the clothes from the little sister and beat her. Now this is often the way with poor people: when they suddenly reach a rich estate they are cruel to those beneath them. So this slave in her new-found power beat and abused her former mistress.

But each day in the garden the spirit of the dead mother comforted the girl and cried out in compassion, "How can Mwa´li treat you thus! How wrong this is!" And again the mother would dress the girl in fine garments and give her good food. But every night the slave came and took the clothes away.

At last Mwa´li's husband noticed how the supposed slave came back every evening richly dressed and went forth in the morning again dressed as a slave. He determined to find out where she got those fine garments! So he followed to the garden and hid, and heard the voice of the mother's spirit saying, "Oh! That Mwa´li should treat you thus!" And he saw the girl decked again with beautiful clothes. He was convinced that this was Mwa´li's real sister.

So he came home and told his wife what he had seen. And then they heated a pot of boiling water, and dug a pit and spread a mat over it and called the slave who was pretending to be the sister and bade her sit down. The slave did so, the mat gave way and she fell into the pit. Then they poured boiling water over her and killed her for her lies.

This story proves the constancy of a Mother's love, which even after death will still protect its child.

Recorded from the singing and the sayings of C. Kamba Simango, Ndau Tribe, Portuguese East Africa, and Madika Cele, Zulu Tribe, Natal, Zululand, South Africa by Natalie Curtis

The Winning of Halai Auna at the House of Tuina

Yana People, Native American

OLD PUL MIAUNA HAD A SON, Pun Miaupa, a wife, and two daughters.

Pun Miaupa had a quarrel with his father and made up his mind to leave him. "I am going away," said he to his father and mother one day.

"I am tired of living here."

The mother began to cry.

"Which way are you going?" asked the father.

Pun Miaupa gave no answer; wouldn't tell his father where he was going. The father stood up and walked out of the house. The mother stopped crying and said:

"I want you to go straight to my brother, your uncle Igupa Topa. Tell him where you are going. Do not go without seeing him."

Pun Miaupa left his mother, went to his uncle's, stood on the roof of the sweat-house. The old man was very busy throwing out grass that day. A great many people had gambled at his house a day earlier; they had left much grass in it.

"Uncle, are you alive?" asked Pun Miaupa.

The old uncle looked up and saw his nephew, who said:

"Uncle, I am full grown. I am going on a very long journey, I am going far away. My mother told me to come here and see you."

"Where are you going, my nephew?"

"To the north."

"I thought so," said the old man, who knew that his nephew would go to get Wakara's youngest daughter.

Wakara took all his daughter's suitors to Tuina's sweat-house, and they were killed there. Igupa Topa knew this and said, "Wait a little, nephew, I will go with you."

"Uncle," said Pun Miaupa, "you are too old. I don't want you to go; the journey would kill you. I want to travel very fast on this journey."

"I will go at my own pace, I will go as I like," said the uncle.

"Well, come with me if you can go fast."

Igupa Topa dressed, took a staff, and looked very old. "Go on, I am ready," said he.

Pun Miaupa started. He turned around to look at his uncle, and saw the old man; saw him fall while coming out of the sweat-house. Pun Miaupa stopped, held down his head, and thought, "He will not go, even as far as Wajami."

The uncle rose and followed on.

"You are too old, uncle; you cannot walk well. Stay at home; that is better for you."

"Go ahead," said the old man; "walk fast. I will come as I can."

Pun Miaupa went on; his uncle followed. Igupa Topa stumbled every few steps, fell, hurt himself, tore his skin. Pun Miaupa looked back very often. The uncle was always tumbling. "He must be bruised and broken from these falls," thought the nephew.

Pun Miaupa was on a hill beyond Chichipana. He sat down and smoked. His uncle came up while he was sitting there.

"Let me smoke; then I want to see you jump to that mountain over there," said the old man, pointing to it.

"I shall leave you behind if I do that."

"Leave me to myself," said the old man.

Pun Miaupa put on deerskin leggings and a beaded shirt – a splendid dress. He went then with one spring to the top of the opposite mountain and looked back to see his uncle; but old Igupa Topa had jumped too. He was just passing Pun Miaupa and went far beyond him.

"I thought you were too old to jump," said Pun Miaupa, coming up to him.

They jumped again, jumped to a second mountain, and the uncle was ahead the second time. After that they walked on. The old man fell very often, but Pun Miaupa did not pity him any longer; he laughed when his uncle fell. They travelled a good while, travelled fast, and when both reached Wajami Mountain, they sat down to rest there.

"I want Wakara to send out his youngest daughter for wood," said Pun Miaupa in his mind; and the next minute Wakara, who was far away in his own sweat-house, told his youngest daughter to take a basket and go for wood. This daughter was Halai Auna.

At that moment, too, Wakara's wife, Ochul Marimi, said to the girl: "Why do you lie asleep all the time and not help me? I want you to get me leaves for acorn bread."

Halai Auna took the basket and went upon the mountain side to find wood and leaves. Pun Miaupa saw the girl filling her basket.

"That is Wakara's daughter," said he to his uncle.

"Stop! Be careful!" said Igupa Topa.

The uncle put himself into his nephew's heart now to strengthen him. There was only one person to be seen. Igupa Topa went into his nephew, went in because he knew that Tuina killed all men who tried to get Halai Auna, and he wished to save his sister's son, Pun Miaupa.

When the girl had her basket full and turned to place it on her back, she saw Pun Miaupa behind her; she could not move, she was so frightened.

"Why are you afraid? Am I so ugly?" asked Pun Miaupa.

He pleased her; but she said not a word, just ran, hurried home with the basket, and threw it down at the door.

"What is your trouble?" asked the mother. "You don't like to work, I think."

"What is the matter?" asked Wakara. "You are frightened."

"I saw a man on the mountain, a man with woodpecker scalps on his head."

"The southern people wear woodpecker scalps," said Wakara; "that must be one of the southern people."

Pun Miaupa sprang through the air, came down in front of Wakara's sweat-house, went in and sat near Halai Auna on a bear-skin. Nice food was brought for all, and when they had finished eating, Wakara said:

"Now, my daughters, and you, my wife, Ochul Marima, make ready; let us go. I wish to see my brother, Tuina, and hear what he says of Halai Auna's new husband."

They dressed, put on beads, and put red paint on their faces. Halai Auna said nothing. She sat with her head down; she was sorry; she liked Pun Miaupa, she felt sure that they would kill him.

When all were ready, Wakara took his wife's hand and danced around the fire with her. He had two unmarried daughters besides Halai Auna; one of these took her father's hand, the other took Halai Auna's, and all danced around the fire and circled about Pun Miaupa. They put him in the middle and danced in a circle; they began to sing, and rose in the air then and danced right up out of the sweat-house, went through the smoke-hole and moved westward, singing as they went:

"I-nó, i-nó, i-nó, no-má
I-nó, i-nó, i-nó, no-má."

They moved faster as they went, and danced all the time. It was dark when they danced up through the roof of the sweat-house; no one saw them, though there were many people round about. Old Wakara's sons-in-law lived in that place; all the stars were his daughters, and his daughters were married, except Halai Auna and the two who danced around the fire. Wakara went without being seen. He would let no one have Halai Auna unless one whom Tuina could not kill.

Now, a little before daylight they reached Tuina's house. Wakara stood on the roof of the sweat-house and called, "My brother, I want you to spring out of bed."

Tuina was asleep in the sweat-house. He had three daughters and no son. The daughters were called Wediko, and his wife was Utjamhji. Wakara went down into the sweat-house and sat at the side of Tuina. Tuina took a bear-skin and put it down at his other hand, and told Halai Auna and her husband to sit on it. Tuina took up a big sack of tobacco and a large pipe cut out of maple wood. The tobacco was made of his own hair, rolled and cut fine. He put this in the pipe and gave it to Pun Miaupa. Wakara and Tuina watched now, and looked at him. The young man smoked all the tobacco and gave back the pipe.

Tuina filled the pipe now with a different, a stronger tobacco. He used to rub his skin often, and what he rubbed off he dried and made fine. This was his tobacco of the second kind. He had a sackful of this stored away, and he filled his pipe now with it.

Pun Miaupa smoked, seemed to swallow the smoke. It was not he who was smoking, though, but the uncle in his heart. He emptied the pipe and returned it. Tuina took now tobacco of a third kind – his own flesh dried and rubbed fine. He filled the pipe, gave it to Pun Miaupa, and waited to see him fall dead at the second if not at the first whiff.

The country outside the sweat-house was full of dead people, all killed by Tuina's tobacco. Some of the bodies were fresh, others decayed; some were sound skeletons, others a few old bones.

Pun Miaupa smoked out this pipe, gave it back empty. Tuina handed him a fourth pipe. The tobacco was made of his own brains, dried and rubbed fine. Pun Miaupa smoked this and gave the empty pipe back to Tuina.

Tuina now tried the fifth pipe. He filled it with marrow from his own bones, gave it to Halai Auna's husband. Wakara, and Tuina watched now, waiting to see him fall. Pun Miaupa swallowed all and gave the pipe back.

Tuina had no other kind of tobacco and could do no more. He dropped his head. "I don't know what kind of person this is," thought he. All at once he remembered old Igupa Topa, and thought:

"This may be a young one of that kind. I can do nothing with him, he has beaten me."

Halai Auna was very glad to have such a husband. This was the first man of all who had come to see her who had not been killed by Tuina. She laughed all this time in her mind.

Pun Miaupa went out, killed five deer, and brought them in. The women cooked a great deal that day. Wakara and Tuina sat in the house, talked and ate Pun Miaupa's fresh venison. The next night all slept. Igupa Topa went out of Pun Miaupa's heart, went about midnight, and sat north of the pillar in the side of the house, sat without saying a word. He had a white-feather in his head, and looked very angry and greatly dissatisfied.

Early next morning Tuina and Wakara were up and saw the old man sitting there with that big feather in his head, and they looked at him.

"Oh," said Tuina. "I know now why Halai Auna's husband can smoke my tobacco. I know that old Igupa Topa this long time. I know what that old fellow can do."

They put plenty of food before Igupa Topa, but he would eat none of it. Pun Miaupa killed five deer that morning and brought them in. The two old men were glad to see such nice venison, and see so much of it. Igupa Topa sat by himself, and ate nothing.

"Uncle, why do you not eat?" asked Pun Miaupa.

He made no answer, but watched till all were asleep; then he stood up and ate, ate the whole night through, ate all the acorn bread, all the roots, ate all that there was in the house, except venison. That was not his kind of food; he would not touch it. He sat down on the north side of the central pillar when he had finished eating.

"You must work hard to cook food enough," said Tuina next morning to the women. "Some one in this house must be very hungry."

The women worked hard all that day; in the evening the house was full of good food again. Pun Miaupa's uncle would not eat a morsel placed before him, but when night came he ate everything there was except venison.

"There must be some one in this house who is very hungry," said Tuina, when he rose the next morning. "Make ready more food today, work hard, my daughters."

"We will not work today; that nasty old fellow eats everything in the night time. We will not carry wood and water all day and have nothing to eat the next morning."

"I don't like him, either," said Tuina; "he will go very soon, I hope."

Igupa Topa heard these words and remembered them. Tuina's wife and Wakara's wife, both old women, had to work that day without assistance. In the middle of the forenoon a great cloud rose in the south. Pun Miaupa's uncle raised it. "Let rain come, thick heavy rain," said he in his mind. "I want darkness, I want a big storm and cold rain."

The cloud was black; it covered all the sky; every one came in, and soon the rain began. It rained in streams, in rivers; it filled the valleys, filled all places. The water reached Tuina's sweat-house, rushed in, and filled the whole place; all had to stand in water; and the rain was very cold.

Old Tuina and Wakara were shivering; their teeth knocked together; their wives and daughters were crying. Igupa Topa had taken his nephew and Halai Auna up to his place on the north side, near the roof of his sweat-house, where they were dry.

The sweat-house was nearly full of water. All were crying now. Some time before daylight one of Tuina's daughters was drowned, and then the other two, and Wakara's two daughters. About dawn Tuina and Wakara with their two wives were drowned. All were dead in the sweat-house except Igupa Topa, his nephew, and Halai Auna. At daylight the rain stopped, the water began to go down, and all the bodies floated out through the doorway. The place was dry. Pun Miaupa made a fire. Halai Auna came to the fire and began to cry for her father, her mother and sisters.

"You must not cry," said Pun Miaupa; "my uncle did this. He will bring all to life again quickly."

But Halai Auna was afraid, and she cried for some time.

Just after midday Igupa Topa went outside, saw the dead bodies, and said: "Why sleep all day? It is time to be up, you two old men and you five young girls!"

Tuina and Wakara sprang up, went to the creek, and swam. "No one but Igupa Topa could have done this to us," said they.

All the women rose up as if they had been only sleeping.

"My brother, I shall go home tomorrow," said Wakara. "It is time for me."

Very early next morning Wakara and his wife began to dance, then the two daughters, then Halai Auna and her husband. They danced out by the smoke-hole, rose through the air, sang, and danced themselves home.

Wakara had been five days away, and all his daughters' husbands were saying: "Where is our father-in-law? He may have been killed." All were very glad when they saw old Wakara in the sweat-house next morning.

Before leaving Tuina's sweat-house Igupa Topa had gone into his nephew's heart again. When Wakara came home, he took his new son-in-law to try a sport which he had. The old man had made a great pole out of deer sinews. This pole was fixed in the ground and was taller than the highest tree. Wakara played in this way: A man climbed the pole, a second bent it down and brought the top as near the foot as possible. He let the top go then, and it shot into the air. If the man on the pole held firmly, he was safe; if he lost his grip he was hurled up high, then fell and was killed.

"Come, my son-in-law," said Wakara one day, "I will show you the place where I play sometimes pleasantly."

They went to the place. The old man climbed first, grasped the pole near the top. Pun Miaupa pulled it down; his uncle was in his heart, and he was very strong. He brought the top toward the ground, did not draw very hard, and let the pole fly back again. It sprang into the air. Wakara was not hurled away; he held firmly. Pun Miaupa brought down the pole a second time, he brought it down rather softly, and let it go. Wakara held his place yet. He tried a third time. Wakara was unshaken.

"That will do for me," said Wakara. "Go up now; it is your time."

Pun Miaupa went on the pole and held with his uncle's power. It was not he who held the pole, but Igupa Topa. "I will end you this time," thought Wakara. He bent the pole close to the ground and let go. Wakara looked sharply to see his son-in-law shoot through the air – looked a good while, did not see him. "My son-in-law has gone very high," thought he. He looked a while yet in the sky; at last he looked at the pole, and there was his son-in-law.

He bent the pole a second time, bent it lower than before; then let it fly. This time Wakara looked at the pole, and Pun Miaupa was on the top of it.

Wakara was angry. He bent the pole to the ground, bent angrily, and let it go. "He will fly away this time, surely," thought he, and looked to the sky to see Pun Miaupa, did not see him; looked at the pole, he was on it. "What kind of person is my son-in-law?" thought Wakara.

It was Wakara's turn now to go on the pole, and he climbed it. Pun Miaupa gave his father-in-law a harder pull this time, but he held his place. The second time Pun Miaupa spoke to Wakara in his own mind: "You don't like me, I don't like you; you want to kill me. I will send you high now."

He bent the pole, brought the top almost to the foot of it, and let it fly. He looked to the top, Wakara was gone. He had been hurled up to the sky, and he stayed there.

Pun Miaupa laughed. "Now, my father-in-law," said he, "you will never come down here to live again; you will stay where you are now forever, you will become small and die, then you will come to life and grow large. You will be that way always, growing old and becoming young again."

Pun Miaupa went home alone.

Wakara's daughters waited for their father, and when he didn't come back they began to cry. At last, when it was dark and they saw their father far up in the sky, they cried very bitterly.

Next morning Pun Miaupa took Halai Auna, his wife, and his uncle, and went to his father's house.

Chuhna, the greatest spinner in the world, lived among Wakara's daughters. All day those women cried and lamented.

"What shall we do?" said they; "we want to go and live near our father. Who can take us up to him?"

"I will take you up to him," said Chuhna, the spinner, who had a great rope fastened to the sky.

Chuhna made an immense basket, put in all the daughters with their husbands, and drew them up till they reached the sky; and Wakara's daughters, the stars, are there on the sky yet.

Collected by Jeremiah Curtin

The Finding of Fire

Yana People, Native American

IN THE BEGINNING Au Mujaupa had fire very far down south on the other side of a big river. The people in this country had no real fire; they had a kind of fire, but it wasn't good. It just warmed a little; it wouldn't cook like the fire which we have now. People killed deer and fished, but they had to eat fish and venison raw.

In the west people had fire, but it wouldn't cook. In the north there were many people, and in the east; but they had no fire that would cook.

"There must be fire in some place," said the people at Pawi; "how can we find it?"

"I will go out tonight to look," said Ahalamila.

That night he went to look for fire. He went to the top of Wahkanopa, looked east and west, saw no fire in either place. Next he looked north; no fire in the north. He looked south; saw no fire anywhere.

Ahalamila came home and talked to the chief and people. "I saw no fire," said he; "I could not see any, but I will go to a better place the next time and take some one with me. I will go tomorrow night to the top of Wahkalu. Who here has a good head, who a sharp eye to see fire? I want to look for fire tomorrow night from the top of Wahkalu; from that place I will look all around the whole world to find fire."

"We have a man here," said the chief, "who can see through a tree, who can see down through the earth to bed rock, who can see through a mountain. You can take him tomorrow night with you. He is Siwegi."

Ahalamila went to Siwegi. "Will you go tomorrow night to look for fire?" asked he.

"I will go if the way is not too long."

"Oh," said Ahalamila, "it will not be long. I will shorten it."

Siwegi agreed to go; and when the time came, they started. Ahalamila doubled up the trail and made it short; in an hour they were on the top of Wahkalu, both ready now to look for fire. The night is very dark; they can see the smallest fire easily.

They look to the east, look with great care, look a good while, see no fire; they look to the north in the same way, see no fire; they look to the west, no fire there. Now Ahalamila looks south, looks a long time, and sees nothing: he looks half an hour to the south, sees a little glimmer like a light very far away.

"Siwegi," said he, "I see a small light down south; it seems like fire far away. I think it is fire."

"Look again," said Siwegi, "look sharply." Maybe it is fire."

"I have looked enough, I think it is fire," said Ahalamila; "but I want you to see it, I want you to look now.'"

Siwegi looked a little while. "Yes, that is fire," said he.

"Well," said Ahalamila, "we see fire, we know that it is far off in the south."

Ahalamila made the road short, and they were back at Pawi in an hour. "We have found fire," said Ahalamila to the chief and the people. "We know where fire is, we can have fire now."

"We must have that fire," said the people.

There is no way to get the fire but to go for it," said Ahalamila.

"Well," said the chief, "since Ahalamila saw the fire he will go for it; but the road is long. Who will go and help him? Who will go for fire with Ahalamila?"

About fifty men offered to go, and they started next morning. The journey was long and very hard. Soon two or three men were tired and went home; not long after more were tired and when they had gone far down to a great river, just north of where the fire was, of the fifty who started only three were left, – Ahalamila. Metsi, and old Shushu Marima.

Just south of the great river Au Mujaupa had a very big village, and in the village a large sweat-house.

In that house he kept the fire, and had a great crowd of people living in the country outside who served him, and kept every one in the world from stealing his fire. These people were Patcha, Chil Wareko, Chil Daiauna, Sabil Keyu, Juhauju, Juwaju, Jukami, Jukilauju.

The three, Ahalamila, Metsi, and old Shushu Marimi, were at the northern end of the bridge, and sat there watching till all at the sweat house was quiet. The bridge was very narrow and slippery; so Ahalamila put pitch on his feet and hands, and on Metsi's and Shushu's feet and hands. All three crossed without slipping, and found every one asleep in the sweat-house.

The old chief, Au Mujaupa, had covered the fire well with ashes. All was silent within and without. Ahalamila, Metsi, and Shushu crept onto the sweat-house quietly, and looked in. All were asleep.

"I will go down first," said Metsi.

"No, I will go first," said Ahalamila. "I will get the fire and reach it to you; you take it and run very fast."

Ahalamila slipped down. Metsi and Shushu remained on the roof. Ahalamila opened the fire carefully, took out a good piece and handed it to the old woman. She put it in her ear. He handed her another; she put it in her other ear, slipped down from the top of the sweat-house, ran across the bridge, and hurried away.

Ahalamila gave Metsi two pieces. He put them in his two ears and started. Ahalamila filled his own ears and followed.

The three had run over two mountains when Au Mujaupa woke up and saw that the ashes had been opened, and that fire had been taken, that a coal had fallen near the central pillar. He sprang up, went to the top of the sweat-house, shouted, called to all his people, –

"Fire has been stolen! Fire has been stolen! Go, you, and follow!"

Now Patcha, Chil Wareko, Chil Daiauna, Sabil Keyu, and all the wind people rose up and followed, raced and stormed in every direction. So much rain came that the whole country was covered with water.

Now Juwaju was ahead of all Au Mujaupa's people chasing the three robbers. Chil Wareko, came too, and fell upon the three furiously; he drenched and chilled them. Next came Jukami and Patcha, who nearly froze them.

Metsi was almost dead; the fire went out in both his ears. Ahalamila lost his fire, too. Chil Wareko, Juwaju, and Patcha quenched it, and then he let it fall.

Old Shushu was behind a good way, but she ran all the time. She kept her hand on one ear as she ran. She lost the fire out of her other ear, and when the piece fell out it broke in two and fell apart. Chil Wareko picked up the fire and took it back; he found six pieces, thought that he had all. He and the others stopped following.

Ahalamila and Metsi ran ahead, left old Shushu to get on the best she could, and reached home first. They were wet, very cold, and tired.

"Where is your fire?" asked the chief.

"I have none; Chil Wareko took my fire," said Ahalamila.

"Where is your fire?" asked the chief.

"Chil Wareko took it," said Metsi.

The chief was very sorry, and all the people were sorry. The old woman did not come, and the people said, "She must be frozen dead."

At sundown old Shushu came back; she came very slowly, was terribly tired, but courageous. She reached the sweat-house, came in, said nothing, lay down wet and cold.

"Where is the fire?" asked she; "did not Ahalamila and Metsi bring fire? They are young and strong, and had plenty of fire."

After a while she stood up, drew some wood-dust together, then sat down, opened her ear and held it over the dust; a big piece of fire came out. Wood was brought quickly, and soon the whole sweat-house was warm. The people who were cold before were warm now and glad.

"Bring meat and we will try how it tastes when it is roasted," said the chief.

He cut some venison and roasted it. One and another tasted the meat. "It is very good," said they; a third one said, "I'll try it," and Gagi took a taste. "Oh, it is sweet, very good," said Gagi.

Each one roasted meat and ate heartily. Next day all went to hunt, and had a great feast in the evening. A chief from another place came to the feast and got fire, took it home with him. Soon all people had fire; every one had fire in all parts of the country.

Collected by Jeremiah Curtin

The Boy Hunter Who Never Sacrificed to the Deer He Had Slain, or The Origin of the Society of Rattlesnakes

Zuni People, Native American

IN VERY ANCIENT TIMES, there lived at Tâ'ia,' below the Zuñi Mountains, an old *shiwani* or priest-chief, who had a young son named Héasailuhtiwa ('Metal-hand'), famed throughout the land of the Zuñis for his success in hunting.

When very young, this lad had said to his parents: "My old ones, let me go away from the home of my fathers and dwell by myself."

"Why do you, a young boy, wish to go and dwell by yourself, my son? Know you not that you would fare but badly, for you are careless and forgetful? No, no! remain with us, that we may care for you."

But the boy answered: "Why should I fare badly? Can I not hunt my own game and roast the meat over the fire? It is because you never care to have me go forth alone that I wish to live by myself, for I long to travel far and hunt deer in the mountains of many countries: yet whenever I start forth you call me back, and it is painful to my longing thoughts thus to be held back when I would go forward."

It was not until the lad had spoken thus again and again, and once more, that the parents sadly yielded to his wish. They insisted, however, much to the boy's displeasure, that his younger sister, Waíasialuhtitsa, should go with him, only to look after his house, and to remind him here and there, at times, of his forgetfulness. So the brother and sister chose the lofty rooms of a high house in the upper part of the pueblo and lived there.

The boy each day went out hunting and failed not each time to bring in slain animals, while the sister cooked for him and looked after the house. Yet, although the boy was a great hunter, he never sacrificed to the Deer he had slain, nor to the Gods of Prey who delight in aiding the hunter who renews them; for the lad was forgetful and careless of all things.

One day he went forth over the mountain toward the north, until he came to the Waters of the Bear. There he started up a huge Buck, and, finding the trail, followed it far toward the northward. Yet, although swift of foot, the youth could not overtake the running Deer, and thus it happened that he went on and on, past mesas, valleys, and mountains, until he came to the brink of a great river which flows westwardly from the north. On the banks of this great river grew forests of cottonwood, and into the thickets of these forests led the trail, straight toward the river bank. just as the young man was about to follow the track to the bank, he thought he saw under a large tree in the midst of the thickets the form of the Deer, so, bending very low, he ran around close to the bank, and came up between the river and the thicket.

As he guardedly approached the tree, his eyes now following the track, now glancing up, he discovered a richly dressed, handsome young man, who called out to him: "How art thou these days, and whither art thou going?"

The young man straightened up, and quickly drawing his breath, replied: "I am hunting a Deer whose tracks I have followed all the way from the Waters of the Deer."

"Indeed!" exclaimed the stranger, "and where has thy Deer gone?"

"I know not," replied the youth, "for here are his tracks." Then he observed that they led to the place where the stranger was sitting, and the latter at the same time remarked:

"I am the Deer, and it was as I would have it that I enticed thee hither."

"*Hai-í!*" exclaimed the young man.

"Aye," continued the stranger. "Alas! alas! thou forgetful one! Thou hast day after day chased my children over the plains and slain them; thou hast made thyself happy of their flesh, and of their flesh added unto thine own meat and that of thy kindred; but, alas! thou hast been forgetful and careless, and not once hast thou given unto their souls the comfort of that which they yearn for and need. Yet hast thou had good fortune in the chase. At last the Sun-father has listened to the supplications of my children and commanded that I bring thee here, and here have I brought thee. Listen! The Sun-father commands that thou shalt visit him in his house at the western end of the world, and these are his instructions."

"Indeed! Well, I suppose it must be, and it is well!" exclaimed the young man.

"And," continued the Deer-being, "thou must hasten home and call thy father. Tell him to summon his *Pithlan Shíwani* (Priest of the Bow, or Warrior) and command him that he shall instruct his children to repair to the rooms of sacred things and prepare plumed prayer-sticks for the Sun-father, the Moon-mother, and the Great Ocean, and red plumes of sacrifice for the Beings of Prey; that fully they must prepare everything, for thou, their child and father, shalt visit the home of the Sun-father, and in payment for thy forgetfulness and carelessness shalt render him, and the Moon-mother, and the Beings of the Great Ocean, plumes of sacrifice. Hasten home, and tell thy father these things. Then tell thy sister to prepare sweetened meal of parched corn to serve as the food of thy journey, and pollen of the flowers of corn; and ask thy mother to prepare great quantities of new cotton, and, making all these things into bundles, thou must summon some of thy relatives, and come to this tree on the fourth day from this day. Make haste, for thou art swift of foot, and tell all these things to thy father; he, will understand thee, for is he not a priest-chief? Hast thou knives of flint?"

"Yes," said the young man, "my father has many."

"Select from them two," said the Deer-being – "a large one and a smaller one; and when thou hast returned to this place, cut down with the larger knife yonder great tree, and with the smaller knife hollow it out. Leave the large end entire, and for the smaller end thou must make a round door, and around the inside of the smaller end cut a notch that shall be like a terrace toward the outside, but shall slope from within that thou mayest close it from the inside with the round door; then pad the inside with cotton, and make in the bottom a padding thicker than the rest; but leave space that thou mayest lie thy length, or sit up and eat. And in the top cut a hole larger inside than out, that thou mayest close it from the inside with a plug of wood. Then when thou hast placed the sweetened meal of parched corn inside, and the plumed prayer-sticks and the sacred pollen of corn-flowers, then enter thyself and close the door in the end and the hole in the top that thy people may roll thee into the river. Thou wilt meet strange beings on thy way. Choose from amongst them whom thou shalt have as a companion, and proceed, as thy companion shall direct, to the great mountain where the Sun enters. Haste and tell thy father these things." And ere the youth could say, "Be it well," and, "I will," the Deer-being had vanished, and he lifted up his face and started swiftly for the home of his fathers.

At sunset the sister looked forth from her high house-top, but nowhere could she see her brother coming. She turned at last to enter, thinking and saying to her breast: "Alas! what did we not think and guess of his carelessness." But just as the country was growing dim in the darkness, the young man ran breathlessly in, and, greeting his sister, sat down in the doorway.

The sister wondered that he had no deer or other game, but placed a meal before him, and, when he had done, herself ate. But the young man remained silent until she had finished, then he said: "Younger sister, I am weary and would sit here; do you go and call father, for I would speak to him of many things."

So the sister cleared away the food and ran to summon the father. Soon she returned with the old man, who, sighing, "*Ha hua*!" from the effort of climbing, greeted his son and sat down, looking all about the room for the fresh deer-meat; but, seeing none, he asked: "What and wherefore hast thou summoned me, my son?"

"It is this," replied the son, and he related all that had been told him by the Deer-being, describing the magnificent dress, the turquoise and shell ear-rings, necklaces, and wristlets of the handsome stranger.

"Certainly," replied the father. "It is well; for as the Sun-father hath directed the Deer-being, thus must it be done."

Then he forthwith went away and commanded his Priest of the Bow, who, mounting to the topmost house, directed the elders and priests of the tribe, saying:

> *Ye, our children, listen!*
> *Ye I will this day inform,*
> *Our child, our father,*
> *He of the strong hand,*
> *He who so hunts the Deer,*
> *Goes unto the Sunset world,*
> *Goes, our Sun-father to greet*
> *Gather at the sacred houses,*
> *Bring thy prayer-sticks, twines, and feathers,*
> *And prepare for him,*
> *For the Sun-father,*
> *For the Moon-mother,*
> *For the Great Ocean,*
> *For the Prey-beings, plumes and treasures.*
> *Hasten, hasten, ye our children, in the morning!"*

So the people gathered in the *kiwetsiwe* and sacred houses next morning and began to make prayer-plumes, while the sister of the young man and her relatives made sweet parched cornmeal and gathered pollen. Toward evening all was completed. The young man summoned his relatives, and chose his four uncles to accompany him. Then he spread enough cotton-wool out to cover the floor, and, gathering it up, made it into a small bundle. The sweet meal filled a large sack of buckskin, and he took also a little sack of sacred red paint and the black warrior paint with little shining particles in it. Then he bade farewell to his lamenting people and rested for the evening journey.

Next morning, escorted by priests, the young man, arrayed in garments of embroidered white cotton and carrying his plumes in his arms, started out of the town, and, accompanied only by his four uncles, set out over the mountains. On the third day they reached the forest on the bank of the great river and encamped.

Then the young man left the camp of his uncles and went alone into the forest, and, choosing the greatest tree he could find, hacked midway through it with his great flint knife. The next day he cut the other half and felled it, when he found it partly hollow. So with his little knife he began to cut it as he had been directed, and made the round door for it and the hole through the top. With his bundle of cotton he padded it everywhere inside until it was thickly coated and soft, and he made a bed on the bottom as thick as himself.

When all was ready and he had placed his food and plumes inside, he called his uncles and showed them the hollow log. "In this," said he, "I am to journey to the western home of our Sun-father. When I have entered and closed the round door tightly and put the plug into the upper hole securely, do ye, never thinking of me, roll the log over and over to the high brink of the river, and, never regarding consequences, push it into the water."

Then it was that the uncles all lamented and tried to dissuade him; but he persisted, and they bade him "Go," as forever, "for," said they, "could one think of journeying even to the end of the earth and across the waters that embrace the world without perishing?"

Then, hastily embracing each of them, the young man entered his log, and, securely fastening the door from the inside, and the plug, called out (they heard but faintly), "*Kesi!*" which means "All is ready."

Sorrowfully and gently they rolled the log over and over to the high river bank, and, hesitating a moment, pushed it off with anxious eyes and closed mouths into the river. Eagerly they watched it as it tumbled end-over-end and down into the water with a great splash, and disappeared under the waves, which rolled one after another across to the opposite banks of the river. But for a long time they saw nothing of it. After a while, far off, speeding on toward the Western Waters of the World, they saw the log rocking along on the rushing waters until it passed out of sight, and they sadly turned toward their homes under the Mountains of the South.

When the log had ceased rocking and plunging, the young man cautiously drew out the plug, and, finding that no water flowed in, peered out. A ray of sunlight slanted in, and by that he knew it was not yet midday, and he could see a round piece of sky and clouds through the hole. By-and-by the ray of sunlight came straight down, and then after a while slanted the other way, and finally toward evening it ceased to shine in, and then the youth took out some of his meal and ate his supper. When after a while he could see the stars, and later the Hanging Lines [the sword-belt of Orion], he knew it was time to rest, so he lay down to sleep.

Thus, day after day, he travelled until he knew he was out on the Great Waters of the World, for no longer did his log strike against anything or whirl around, nor could he see, through the chink, leaves of overhanging trees, nor rocks and banks of earth. On the tenth morning, when he looked up through the hole, he saw that the clouds did not move, and wondering at this, kicked at his log, but it would not move. Then he peered out as far as he could and saw rocks and trees. When he tried to rock his log, it remained firm, so he determined to open the door at the end.

Now, in reality, his log had been cast high up on the shore of a great mountain that rose out of the waters; and this mountain was the home of the Rattlesnakes. A Rattlesnake maiden was roaming along the shore just as the young man was about to open the door of his log. She espied the curious vessel, and said to herself in thought: "What may this be? Ah, yes, and who? Ah, yes, the mortal who was to come; it must be he!" Whereupon she hastened to the shore and tapped on the log.

"Art thou come?" she asked.

"Aye," replied the youth. "Who may you be, and where am I?"

"You are landed on the Island of the Rattlesnakes, and I am one of them. The other side of the mountain here is where our village is. Come out and go with me, for my old ones have expected you long."

"Is it dry, surely?" asked the young man.

"Why, yes! Here you are high above the waters."

Thereupon the young man opened from the inside his door, and peered out. Surely enough, there he was high among the rocks and sands. Then he looked at the Rattlesnake maiden, and scarcely believed she was what she called herself, for she was a most beautiful young woman, and like a daughter of men. Yet around her waist – she was dressed in cotton mantles – was girt a rattlesnake-skin which was open at the breast and on the crown of the head.

"Come with me," said the maiden; and she led the way over the mountain and across to a deep valley, where terrible Serpents writhed and gleamed in the sunlight so thickly that they seemed, with their hissing and rattling, like a dry mat shaken by the wind. The youth drew back in horror, but the maiden said: "Fear not; they will neither harm you nor frighten you more, for they are my people." Whereupon she commanded them to fall back and make a pathway for the young man and herself; and they tamely obeyed her commands. Through the opening thus made they passed down to a cavern, on entering which they found a great room. There were great numbers of Rattlesnake people, old and young, gathered in council, for they knew of the coming of the young man. Around the walls of their houses were many pegs and racks with serpent skins hanging on them – skins like the one the young girl wore as a girdle. The elders arose and greeted the youth, saying: "Our child and our father, comest thou, comest thou happily these many days?"

"Aye, happily," replied the youth.

And after a feast of strange food had been placed before the young man, and he had eaten a little, the elders said to him: "Knowest thou whither thou goest, that the way is long and fearful, and to mortals unknown, and that it will be but to meet with poverty that thou journeyest alone? Therefore have we assembled to await thy coming and in order that thou shouldst journey preciously, we have decided to ask thee to choose from amongst us whom thou shalt have for a companion."

"It is well, my fathers," said the young man, and, casting his eyes about the council to find which face should be kindest to him, he chose the maiden, and said: "Let it be this one, for she found me and loved me in that she gently and without fear brought me into your presence."

And the girl said: "It is well, and I will go."

Instantly the grave and dignified elders, the happy-faced youths and maidens, the kind-eyed matrons, all reached up for their serpent skins, and, passing them over their persons, – lo! in the time of the telling of it, the whole place was filled with writhing and hissing Serpents and the din of their rattles. In horror the young man stood against the wall like a hollow stalk, and the Serpent maiden, going to each of the members of the council, extracted from each a single fang, which she wrapped together in a piece of fabric, until she had a great bundle. Then she passed her hand over her person, and lo! she became a beautiful human maiden again, holding in her hand a rattlesnake skin. Then taking up the bundle of fangs, she said to the young man: "Come, for I know the way and will guide you," – and the young man followed her to the shore where his log lay.

"Now," said she, "wait while I fix this log anew, that it may be well," and she bored many little holes all over the log, and into these holes she inserted the crooked fangs, so that they all stood slanting toward the rear, like the spines on the back of a porcupine.

When she had done this, she said: "First I will enter, for there may not be room for two, and in order that I may make myself like the space I enter, I will lay on my dress again. Do you, when I have entered, enter also, and with your feet kick the log down to the shore waters, when you must quickly close the door and the waters will take us abroad upon themselves."

In an instant she had passed into her serpent form again and crawled into the log. The young man did as he was bidden, and as he closed the door a wave bore them gently out upon the waters. Then, as the young man turned to look upon his companion coiled so near him, he drew back in horror.

"Why do you fear?" asked the Rattlesnake.

"I know not, but I fear you; perhaps, though you speak gently, you will, when I sleep, bite me and devour my flesh, and it is with thoughts of this that I have fear."

"Ah, no!" replied the maiden, "but, that you may not fear, I will change myself." And so saying, she took off her skin, and, opening the upper part of the door, hung the skin on the fangs outside.

Finally, toward noon-time, the youth prepared his meal food, and placing some before the maiden, asked her to eat.

"Ah, no! alas, I know not the food of mortals. Have you not with you the yellow dust of the corn-flower?"

"Aye, that I have," said the young man, and producing a bag, opened it and asked the girl: "How shall I feed it to you?"

"Scatter it upon the cotton, and by my knowledge I will gather it."

Then the young man scattered a great quantity on the cotton, wondering how the girl would gather it up. But the maiden opened the door, and taking down the skin changed herself to a serpent, and passing to and fro over the pollen, received it all within her scales. Then she resumed her human form again and hung the skin up as before.

Thus they floated until they came to the great forks of the Mighty Waters of the World, and their floating log was guided into the southern branch. And on they floated toward the westward for four months from the time when the uncles had thrown him into the river.

One day the maiden said to the youth: "We are nearing our journey's end, and, as I know the way, I will guide you. Hold yourself hard and ready, for the waters will cast our house high upon the shores of the mountain wherein the Sun enters, and these shores are inaccessible because so smooth."

Then the log was cast high above the slippery bank, and when the waters receded there it remained, for the fangs grappled it fast.

Then said the maiden: "Let us now go out. Fear not for your craft, for the fangs will hold it fast; it matters little how high the waves may roll, or how steep and slippery the bank."

Then, taking in his arms the sacred plumes which his people had prepared for him, he followed the girl far up to the doorway in the Mountain of the Sea. Out of it grew a great ladder of giant rushes, by the side of which stood an enormous basket-tray. Very fast approached the Sun, and soon the Sun-father descended the ladder, and the two voyagers followed down. They were gently greeted by a kind old woman, the grandmother of the Sun, and were given seats at one side of a great and wonderfully beautiful room.

Then the Sun-father approached some pegs in the wall and from them suspended his bow and quiver, and his bright sun-shield, and his wonderful travelling dress. Behold! there stood, kindly smiling before the youth and maiden, the most magnificent and gentle of beings in the world- the Sun-father.

Then the Sun-father greeted them, and, turning to a great package which he had brought in, opened it and disclosed thousands of shell beads, red and white, and thousands more of brilliant turquoises. These he poured into the great tray at the door-side, and gave them to the grandmother, who forthwith began to sort them with great rapidity. But, ere she had done, the Sun-father took them from her; part of them he took out with unerring judgement and cast them abroad into the great waters as we cast sacred prayer-meal. The others he brought below and gave them to the grandmother for safe-keeping.

Then he turned once more to the youth and the maiden, and said to the former: "So thou hast come, my child, even as I commanded. It is well, and I am thankful." Then, in a stern and louder voice, which yet sounded like the voice of a father, he asked: "Hast thou brought with thee that whereby we are made happy with our children?"

And the young man said: "Aye, I have."

"It is well; and if it be well, then shalt thou precious be; for knowest thou not that I recognize the really good from the evil, – even of the thoughts of men, – and that I know the prayer and sacrifice that is meant, from the words and treasures of those who do but lie in addressing them to me, and speak and act as children in a joke? Behold the treasure which I brought with me from the cities of mankind today! Some of them I cherished preciously, for they are the gifts to me of good hearts and I treasure them that I may return them in good fortune and blessing to those who gave them. But some thou sawest I cast abroad into the great waters that they may again be gathered up and presented to me; for they were the gifts of double and foolish hearts, and as such cannot be treasured by me nor returned unto those who gave them. Bring forth, my child, the plumes and gifts thou hast brought. Thy mother dwelleth in the next room, and when she appeareth in this, thou shalt with thine own hand present to her thy sacrifice."

So the youth, bowing his head, unwrapped his bundle and laid before the Sun-father the plumes he had brought. And the Sun-father took them and breathed upon them and upon the youth, and said: "Thanks, this day. Thou hast straightened thy crooked thoughts."

And when the beautiful Mother of Men, the Moon-mother – the wife of the Sun-father – appeared, the boy placed before her the plumes he had brought, and she, too, breathed upon them, and said: "Thanks, this day," even as the Sun-father had.

Then the Sun-father turned to the youth and said: "Thou shalt join me in my journey round the world, that thou mayest see the towns and nations of mankind – my children; that thou mayest realize how many are my children. Four days shalt thou join me in my journeyings, and then shalt thou return to the home of thy fathers."

And the young man said: "It is well!" but he turned his eyes to the maiden.

"Fear not, my child," added the Father, "she shall sit preciously in my house until we have returned."

And after they had feasted, the Sun-father again enrobed himself, and the youth he dressed in appearance as he himself was dressed. Then, taking the sun-dress from the wall, he led the way down through the four great apartments of the world, and came out into the Lower Country of the Earth.

Behold! as they entered that great world, it was filled with snow and cold below, and the tracks of men led out over great white plains, and as they passed the cities of these nether countries people strange to see were clearing away the snow from their housetops and doorways.

And so they journeyed to the other House of the Sun, and, passing up through the four great rooms, entered the home of the aunts of the Sun-father; and here, too, the young man presented plumes of prayer and sacrifice to the inmates, and received their thanks and blessings.

Again they started together on their journey; and behold! as they came out into the World of Daylight, the skies below them were filled with the rain of summer-time.

Across the great world they journeyed, and they saw city after city of men, and many tribes of strange peoples. Here they were engaged in wars and in wasting the lives of one another; there they were dying of famine and disease; and more of misery and poverty than of happiness saw the young man among the nations of men. "For," said the Sun-father, "these be, alas! my children, who waste their lives in foolishness, or slay one another in useless anger; yet they are brothers to one another, and I am the father of all."

Thus journeyed they four days; and each evening when they returned to the home where the Sun father entered, he gave to his grandmother the great package of treasure which his children among men had sacrificed to him, and each day he cast the treasures of the bad and double-hearted into the great waters.

On the fourth day, when they had entered the western home of the Sun-father, said the latter to the youth: "Thy task is meted out and finished; thou shalt now return unto the home of thy fathers – my children below the mountains of Shíwina. How many days, thinkest thou, shalt thou journey?"

"Many days more than ten," replied the youth with a sigh.

"Ah! no, my child," said the Sun-father. "Listen; thou shalt in one day reach the banks of the river whence thou camest. Listen! Thou shalt take this, my shaft of strong lightning; thou shalt grasp its neck with firm hands, and as thou extendest it, it will stretch out far to thy front and draw thee more swiftly than the arrow's flight through the water. Take with thee this quiver of unerring arrows, and this strong bow, that by their will thou mayest seek life; but forget not thy sacrifices nor that they are to be made with true word and a faithful heart. Take also with thee thy guide and companion, the Rattlesnake maiden. When thou hast arrived at the shore of the country of her people, let go the lightning, and it will land thee high. On the morrow I will journey slowly, that ere I be done rising thou mayest reach the home of the maiden. There thou must stop but briefly, for thy fathers, the Rattle-tailed Serpents, will instruct thee, and to their counsel thou must pay strict heed, for thus only will it be well. Thou shalt present to them the plumes of the Prey-beings thou bringest, and when thou hast presented these, thou must continue thy journey. Rest thou until the morrow, and early as the light speed hence toward the home of thy fathers. May all days find ye, children, happy." With this, the Sun-father, scarce listening to the prayers and thanks of the youth and maiden, vanished below.

Thus, when morning approached, the youth and the maiden entered the hollow house and closed it. Scarce did the youth grasp the lightning when, drawn by the bright shaft, the log shot far out into the great waters and was skimming, too fast to be seen, toward the home of the Rattle-tailed Serpents.

And the Sun had but just climbed above the mountains of this world of daylight when the little tube was thrown high above the banks of the great island whither they were journeying.

Then the youth and the maiden again entered the council of the Rattlesnakes, and when they saw the shining black paint on his face they asked that they too might paint their faces like his own; but they painted their cheeks awkwardly, as to this day may be seen; for all rattlesnakes are painted unevenly in the face. Then the young man presented to each the plumes he had brought, and told the elders that he would return with their maiden to the home of his father.

"Be it well, that it may be well," they replied; and they thanked him with delight for the treasure-plumes he had bestowed upon them.

"Go ye happily all days," said the elders. "Listen, child, and father, to our words of advice. But a little while, and thou wilt reach the bank whence thou started. Let go the shaft of lightning, and, behold, the tube thou hast journeyed with will plunge far down into the river. Then shalt thou journey with this our maiden three days. Care not to embrace her, for if thou doest this, it will not be well. journey ye preciously, our children, and may ye be happy one with the other."

So again they entered their hollow log and, before entering, the maiden placed her rattlesnake skin as before on the fangs. With incredible swiftness the lightning drew them up the great surging river to the banks where the cottonwood forests grow, and when the lad pressed the shaft it landed them high among the forest trees above the steep bank. Then the youth pressed the lightning-shaft with all his might, and the log was dashed into the great river. While yet he gazed at the bounding log, behold! the fangs which the maiden had fixed into it turned to living serpents; hence today, throughout the whole great world, from the Land of Summer to the Waters of Sunset, are found the Rattlesnakes and their children.

Then the young man journeyed with the maiden southward; and on the way, with the bow and arrows the Sun-father had given him, he killed game, that they might have meat to eat. Nor did he forget the commandments of his Sun-father. At night he built a fire in a forest of piñons, and made a bower for the maiden near to it; but she could not sit there, for she feared the fire, and its light pained her eyes. Nor could she eat at first of the food he cooked for her, but only tasted a few mouthfuls of it. Then the young man made a bed for her under the trees, and told her to rest peacefully, for he would guard her through the night.

And thus they journeyed and rested until the fourth day, when at evening they entered the town under the mountains of Shíwina and were happily welcomed by the father, sister, and relatives of the young man. Blessed by the old priest-chief, the youth and the maiden dwelt with the younger sister Waíasialuhtitsa, in the high house of the upper part of the town. And the boy was as before a mighty hunter, and the maiden at last grew used to the food and ways of mortals.

After they had thus lived together for a long time, there were born of the maiden two children, twins.

Wonderful to relate, these children grew to the power of wandering, in a single day and night; and hence, when they appeared suddenly on the housetops and in the plazas, people said to one another:

"Who are these strange people, and whence came they?" – and talked much after the manner of our foolish people. And the other little children in the town beat them and quarrelled with them, as strange children are apt to do with strange children. And when the twins ran in to their mother, crying and complaining, the poor young woman was saddened; so she said to the father when he returned from hunting in the evening:

"Ah!, 'their father,' it is not well that we remain longer here. No, alas! I must return to the country of my fathers, and take with me these little ones," and, although the father prayed her not, she said only: "It must be," and he was forced to consent.

Then for four days the Rattlesnake woman instructed him in the prayers and chants of her people, and she took him forth and showed him the medicines whereby the bite of her fathers might be assuaged, and how to prepare them. Again and again the young man urged her not to leave him, saying: "The way is long and filled with dangers. How, alas! will you reach it in safety?"

"Fear not," said she: "go with me only to the shore of the great river, and my fathers will come to meet me and take me home."

Sadly, on the last morning, the father accompanied his wife and children to the forests of the great river. There she said he must not follow but as he embraced them he cried out:

"Ah, alas! my beautiful wife, my beloved children, flesh of my flesh, how shall I not follow ye?"

Then his wife answered: "Fear not, nor trouble thyself with sad thoughts. Whither we go thou canst not follow, for thou eatest cooked food (thou art a mortal); but soon thy fathers and mine will come for thee, and thou wilt follow us, never to return." Then she turned from him with the little children and was seen no more, and the young man silently returned to his home below the mountains of Shíwina.

It happened here and there in time that young men of his tribe were bitten by rattlesnakes; but the young man had only to suck their wounds, and apply his medicines, and sing his incantations and prayers, to cure them. Whenever this happened, he breathed the sacred breath upon them, and enjoined them to secrecy of the rituals and chants he taught them, save only to such as they should choose and teach the practice of their prayers.

Thus he had cured and taught eight, when one day he ascended the mountains for wood. There, alone in the forest, he was met and bitten by his fathers. Although he slowly and painfully crawled home, long ere he reached his town he was so swollen that the eight whom he had instructed tried in vain to cure him, and, bidding them cherish as a precious gift the knowledge of his beloved wife, he died.

Immediately his fathers met his breath and being and took them to the home of the Maiden of the Rattlesnakes and of his lost children. Need we ask why he was not cured by his disciples?

Thus it was in the days of the ancients, and hence today we have fathers amongst us to whom the dread bite of the rattlesnake need cause no sad thoughts, – the *Tchi Kialikwe* (Society of the Rattlesnakes).

Thus much and thus shortened is my story.

Collected by Frank Hamilton Cushing

Of the Pretty Girl and the Seven Jealous Women

Southern Nigeria

THERE WAS ONCE a very beautiful girl called Akim. She was a native of Ibibio, and the name was given to her on account of her good looks, as she was born in the spring-time. She was an only daughter, and her parents were extremely fond of her. The people of the town, and more particularly the young girls, were so jealous of Akim's good looks and beautiful form – for she was perfectly made, very strong, and her carriage, bearing, and manners were most graceful – that her parents would not allow her to join the young girls' society in the town, as is customary for all young people to do, both boys and girls belonging to a company according to their age; a company consisting, as a rule, of all the boys or girls born in the same year.

Akim's parents were rather poor, but she was a good daughter, and gave them no trouble, so they had a happy home. One day as Akim was on her way to draw water from the spring she met the company of seven girls, to which in an ordinary way she would have belonged, if her parents had not forbidden her. These girls told her that they were going to hold a play in the town in three days' time, and asked her to join them. She said she was very sorry, but that her parents were poor, and only had herself to work for them, she therefore had no time to spare for dancing and plays. She then left them and went home.

In the evening the seven girls met together, and as they were very envious of Akim, they discussed how they should be revenged upon her for refusing to join their company, and they talked for a long time as to how they could get Akim into danger or punish her in some way.

At last one of the girls suggested that they should all go to Akim's house every day and help her with her work, so that when they had made friends with her they would be able to entice her away and take their revenge upon her for being more beautiful than themselves. Although they went every day and helped Akim and her parents with their work, the parents knew that they were jealous of their daughter, and repeatedly warned her not on any account to go with them, as they were not to be trusted.

At the end of the year there was going to be a big play, called the new yam play, to which Akim's parents had been invited. The play was going to be held at a town about two hours' march from where they lived. Akim was very anxious to go and take part in the dance, but her parents gave her plenty of work to do before they started, thinking that this would surely prevent her going, as she was a very obedient daughter, and always did her work properly.

On the morning of the play the jealous seven came to Akim and asked her to go with them, but she pointed to all the water pots she had to fill, and showed them where her parents had told her to polish the walls with a stone and make the floor good; and after that was finished she had to pull up all the weeds round the house and clean up all round. She therefore said it was impossible for her to leave the house until all the work was finished. When the girls heard this they took up the water pots, went to the spring, and quickly returned with them full; they placed them in a row, and then they got stones, and very soon had the walls polished and the floor made good; after that they did the weeding outside and the cleaning up, and when everything was completed they said to Akim, "Now then, come along; you have no excuse to remain behind, as all the work is done."

Akim really wanted to go to the play; so as all the work was done which her parents had told her to do, she finally consented to go. About half-way to the town, where the new yam play was being held, there was a small river, about five feet deep, which had to be crossed by wading, as there was no bridge. In this river there was a powerful Ju Ju, whose law was that whenever anyone crossed the river and returned the same way on the return journey, whoever it was, had to give some food to the Ju Ju. If they did not make the proper sacrifice the Ju Ju dragged them down and took them to his home, and kept them there to work for him. The seven jealous girls knew all about this Ju Ju, having often crossed the river before, as they walked about all over the country, and had plenty of friends in the different towns. Akim, however, who was a good girl, and never went anywhere, knew nothing about this Ju Ju, which her companions had found out.

When the work was finished they all started off together, and crossed the river without any trouble. When they had gone a small distance on the other side they saw a small bird, perched on a high tree, who admired Akim very much, and sang in praise of her beauty, much to the annoyance of the seven girls; but they walked on without saying anything, and eventually arrived at the town where the play was being held. Akim had not taken the trouble to change her clothes, but when she arrived at the town, although her companions had on all their best beads and their finest clothes, the young men and people admired Akim far more than the other girls, and she was declared to be the finest and most beautiful woman at the dance. They gave her plenty of palm wine, foo-foo, and everything she wanted, so that the seven girls became more angry and jealous than before. The people danced and sang all that night, but Akim managed to keep out of the sight of her parents until the following morning, when they asked her how it was that she had disobeyed them and neglected her work; so Akim told them that the work had all been done by her friends, and they had enticed her to come to the play with them. Her mother then told her to return home at once, and that she was not to remain in the town any longer.

When Akim told her friends this they said, "Very well, we are just going to have some small meal, and then we will return with you." They all then sat down together and had their food, but each of the seven jealous girls hid a small quantity of foo-foo and fish in her clothes for the Water Ju Ju. However Akim, who knew nothing about this, as her parents had forgotten to tell her about the Ju Ju, never thinking for one moment that their daughter would cross the river, did not take any food as a sacrifice to the Ju Ju with her.

When they arrived at the river Akim saw the girls making their small sacrifices, and begged them to give her a small share so that she could do the same, but they refused, and all walked across the river safely. Then when it was Akim's turn to cross, when she arrived in the middle of the river, the Water Ju Ju caught hold of her and dragged her underneath the water, so that she immediately disappeared from sight. The seven girls had been watching for this, and when they saw that she had gone they went on their way, very pleased at the success of their scheme, and said to one another, "Now Akim is gone forever, and we shall hear no more about her being better-looking than we are."

As there was no one to be seen at the time when Akim disappeared they naturally thought that their cruel action had escaped detection, so they went home rejoicing; but they never noticed the little bird high up in the tree who had sung of Akim's beauty when they were on their way to the play. The little bird was very sorry for Akim, and made up his mind that, when the proper time came, he would tell her parents what he had seen, so that perhaps they would be able to save her. The bird had heard Akim asking for a small portion of the food to make a sacrifice with, and had heard all the girls refusing to give her any.

The following morning, when Akim's parents returned home, they were much surprised to find that the door was fastened, and that there was no sign of their daughter anywhere about the place, so they inquired of their neighbours, but no one was able to give them any information about her. They then went to the seven girls, and asked them what had become of Akim. They replied that they did not know what had become of her, but that she had reached their town safely with them, and then said she was going home. The father then went to his Ju Ju man, who, by casting lots, discovered what had happened, and told him that on her way back from the play Akim had crossed the river without making the customary sacrifice to the Water Ju Ju, and that, as the Ju Ju was angry, he had seized Akim and taken her to his home. He therefore told Akim's father to take one goat, one basketful of eggs, and one piece of white cloth to the river in the morning, and to offer them as a sacrifice to the Water Ju Ju; then Akim would be thrown out of the water seven times, but that if her father failed to catch her on the seventh time, she would disappear forever.

Akim's father then returned home, and, when he arrived there, the little bird who had seen Akim taken by the Water Ju Ju, told him everything that had happened, confirming the Ju Ju's words. He also said that it was entirely the fault of the seven girls, who had refused to give Akim any food to make the sacrifice with.

Early the following morning the parents went to the river, and made the sacrifice as advised by the Ju Ju. Immediately they had done so, the Water Ju Ju threw Akim up from the middle of the river. Her father caught her at once, and returned home very thankfully.

He never told anyone, however, that he had recovered his daughter, but made up his mind to punish the seven jealous girls, so he dug a deep pit in the middle of his house, and placed dried palm leaves and sharp stakes in the bottom of the pit. He then covered the top of the pit with new mats, and sent out word for all people to come and hold a play to rejoice with him, as he had recovered his daughter from the spirit land. Many people came, and danced and sang all the day and night, but the seven jealous girls did not appear, as they were frightened. However, as they were told that everything had gone well on the previous day, and that there had been no trouble, they went to the house the following morning and mixed with the dancers; but they were ashamed to look Akim in the face, who was sitting down in the middle of the dancing ring.

When Akim's father saw the seven girls he pretended to welcome them as his daughter's friends, and presented each of them with a brass rod, which he placed round their necks. He also gave them tombo to drink.

He then picked them out, and told them to go and sit on mats on the other side of the pit he had prepared for them. When they walked over the mats which hid the pit they all fell in, and Akim's father immediately got some red-hot ashes from the fire and threw them in on top of the screaming girls, who were in great pain. At once the dried palm leaves caught fire, killing all the girls at once.

When the people heard the cries and saw the smoke, they all ran back to the town.

The next day the parents of the dead girls went to the head chief, and complained that Akim's father had killed their daughters, so the chief called him before him, and asked him for an explanation.

Akim's father went at once to the chief, taking the Ju Ju man, whom everybody relied upon, and the small bird, as his witnesses.

When the chief had heard the whole case, he told Akim's father that he should only have killed one girl to avenge his daughter, and not seven. So he told the father to bring Akim before him.

When she arrived, the head chief, seeing how beautiful she was, said that her father was justified in killing all the seven girls on her behalf, so he dismissed the case, and told the parents of the dead girls to go away and mourn for their daughters, who had been wicked and jealous women, and had been properly punished for their cruel behaviour to Akim.

Moral: Never kill a man or a woman because you are envious of their beauty, as if you do, you will surely be punished.

Collected by Elphinstone Dayrell

The Fate of Essido and His Evil Companions

Southern Nigeria

CHIEF OBORRI lived at a town called Adiagor, which is on the right bank of the Calabar River. He was a wealthy chief, and belonged to the Egbo Society. He had many large canoes, and plenty of slaves to paddle them. These canoes he used to fill up with new yams – each canoe being under one head slave and containing eight paddles; the canoes were capable of holding three puncheons of palm oil, and cost eight hundred rods each. When they were full, about ten of them used to start off together and paddle to Rio del Rey. They went through creeks all the way, which run through mangrove swamps, with palm oil trees here and there. Sometimes in the tornado season it was very dangerous crossing the creeks, as the canoes were so heavily laden, having only a few inches above the water, that quite a small wave would fill the canoe and cause it to sink to the bottom. Although most of the boys could swim, it often happened that some of them were lost, as there are many large alligators in these waters. After four days' hard paddling they would arrive at Rio del Rey, where they had very little difficulty in exchanging their new yams for bags of dried shrimps and sticks with smoked fish on them.

Chief Oborri had two sons, named Eyo I. and Essido. Their mother having died when they were babies, the children were brought up by their father. As they grew up, they developed entirely different characters. The eldest was very hard-working and led a solitary life; but the younger son was fond of gaiety and was very lazy, in fact, he spent most of his time in the neighbouring towns playing and dancing. When the two boys arrived at the respective ages of eighteen and twenty their father died, and they were left to look after themselves. According to native custom, the elder son, Eyo I., was entitled to the whole of his father's estate; but being very fond of his younger brother, he gave him a large number of rods and some land with a house. Immediately Essido became possessed of the money he became wilder than ever, gave big feasts to his companions, and always had his house full of women, upon whom he spent large sums. Although the amount his brother had given him on his father's death was very large, in the course of a few years Essido had spent it all. He then sold his house and effects, and spent the proceeds on feasting.

While he had been living this gay and unprofitable life, Eyo I. had been working harder than ever at his father's old trade, and had made many trips to Rio del Rey himself. Almost every week he had canoes laden with yams going down river and returning after about twelve days with shrimps and fish, which Eyo I. himself disposed of in the neighbouring markets, and he very rapidly became a rich man. At intervals he remonstrated with Essido on his extravagance, but his warnings had no effect; if anything, his brother became worse. At last the time arrived when all his money was spent, so Essido went to his brother and asked him to lend him two thousand rods, but Eyo refused, and told Essido that he would not help him in any way to continue his present life of debauchery, but that if he liked to work on the farm and trade, he would give him a fair share of the profits. This Essido indignantly refused, and went back to the town and consulted some of the very few friends he had left as to what was the best thing to do.

The men he spoke to were thoroughly bad men, and had been living upon Essido for a long time. They suggested to him that he should go round the town and borrow money from the people he had entertained, and then they would run away to Akpabryos town, which was about four days' march from Calabar. This Essido did, and managed to borrow a lot of money, although many people refused to lend him anything. Then at night he set off with his evil companions, who carried his money, as they had not been able to borrow any themselves, being so well known. When they arrived at Akpabryos town they found many beautiful women and graceful dancers. They then started the same life again, until after a few weeks most of the money had gone. They then met and consulted together how to get more money, and advised Essido to return to his rich brother, pretending that he was going to work and give up his old life; he should then get poison from a man they knew of, and place it in his brother's food, so that he would die, and then Essido would become possessed of all his brother's wealth, and they would be able to live in the same way as they had formerly. Essido, who had sunk very low, agreed to this plan, and they left Akpabryos town the next morning. After marching for two days, they arrived at a small hut in the bush where a man who was an expert poisoner lived, called Okponesip. He was the head Ju Ju man of the country, and when they had bribed him with eight hundred rods he swore them to secrecy, and gave Essido a small parcel containing a deadly poison which he said would kill his brother in three months. All he had to do was to place the poison in his brother's food.

When Essido returned to his brother's house he pretended to be very sorry for his former mode of living, and said that for the future he was going to work. Eyo I. was very glad when he heard this, and at once asked his brother in, and gave him new clothes and plenty to eat.

In the evening, when supper was being prepared, Essido went into the kitchen, pretending he wanted to get a light from the fire for his pipe. The cook being absent and no one about, he put the poison in the soup, and then returned to the living-room. He then asked for some tombo, which was brought, and when he had finished it, he said he did not want any supper, and went to sleep. His brother, Eyo I., had supper by himself and consumed all the soup. In a week's time he began to feel very ill, and as the days passed he became worse, so he sent for his Ju Ju man.

When Essido saw him coming, he quietly left the house; but the Ju Ju man, by casting lots, very soon discovered that it was Essido who had given poison to his brother. When he told Eyo I. this, he would not believe it, and sent him away. However, when Essido returned, his elder brother told him what the Ju Ju man had said, but that he did not believe him for one moment, and had sent him away. Essido was much relieved when he heard this, but as he was anxious that no suspicion of the crime should be attached to him, he went to the Household Ju Ju, and having first sworn that he had never administered poison to his brother, he drank out of the pot.

Three months after he had taken the poison Eyo I. died, much to the grief of everyone who knew him, as he was much respected, not only on account of his great wealth, but because he was also an upright and honest man, who never did harm to anyone.

Essido kept his brother's funeral according to the usual custom, and there was much playing and dancing, which was kept up for a long time. Then Essido paid off his old creditors in order to make himself popular, and kept open house, entertaining most lavishly, and spending his money in many foolish ways. All the bad women about collected at his house, and his old evil companions went on as they had done before.

Things got so bad that none of the respectable people would have anything to do with him, and at last the chiefs of the country, seeing the way Essido was squandering his late brother's estate, assembled together, and eventually came to the conclusion that he was a witch man, and had poisoned his brother in order to acquire his position. The chiefs, who were all friends of the late Eyo, and who were very sorry at the death, as they knew that if he had lived he would have become a great and powerful chief, made up their minds to give Essido the Ekpawor Ju Ju, which is a very strong medicine, and gets into men's heads, so that when they have drunk it they are compelled to speak the truth, and if they have done wrong they die very shortly. Essido was then told to dress himself and attend the meeting at the palaver house, and when he arrived the chiefs charged him with having killed his brother by witchcraft. Essido denied having done so, but the chiefs told him that if he were innocent he must prove it by drinking the bowl of Ekpawor medicine which was placed before him. As he could not refuse to drink, he drank the bowl off in great fear and trembling, and very soon the Ju Ju having got hold of him, he confessed that he had poisoned his brother, but that his friends had advised him to do so. About two hours after drinking the Ekpawor, Essido died in great pain.

The friends were then brought to the meeting and tied up to posts, and questioned as to the part they had taken in the death of Eyo. As they were too frightened to answer, the chiefs told them that they knew from Essido that they had induced him to poison his brother. They were then taken to the place where Eyo was buried, the grave having been dug open, and their heads were cut off and fell into the grave, and their bodies were thrown in after them as a sacrifice for the wrong they had done. The grave was then filled up again.

Ever since that time, whenever anyone is suspected of being a witch, he is tried by the Ekpawor Ju Ju.

Collected by Elphinstone Dayrell

Finding Home

Kylie Fennell, Gumbaynggirr People

THE KEEPER SITS AT HER DESK flanked by towers of overflowing filing cabinets. Manila folders and scraps of paper burst from overstuffed drawers. The contents represent echoes of her past. Breadcrumbs of stories untold. Stories yet to unfold.

She clings to any fragments of information she can find, collecting them like a bowerbird. Faded photographs with torn edges. Copies of documents that once lived on microfilm or were buried in dusty government archives. Rare records and oral histories she's hunted down over the years. Each of them a clue. A piece of a puzzle she needs to solve so everything makes sense.

It's up to her to put all the pieces together. The pieces that anchor her to the community, culture and Country lost to her for so many years.

She is the Keeper of knowledge and preserver of storylines, past, present and future.

* * *

The Musician's ears pop as they descend the mountain range, jolting her attention away from her phone.

She's been reading the same reviews over and over. Words like *'disappointing'*, *'forced'* and *'annoyingly angsty'* weave a knot in her mind.

"You're not reading those bloody reviews again?" her boyfriend, and manager, asks.

"They're right. The songs have no heart."

Her boyfriend cups his hand over hers. "The album's great. You're a brilliant artist."

Dusty, the blue heeler she inherited from her grandmother, barks from the back seat.

"See, even Dusty agrees."

She forces a laugh.

They're driving from Tamworth to play at a private party on a property near Grafton on the north coast of New South Wales. After the success of her first album she'd been performing at major country festivals and venues that hold thousands. A far cry from performing for some rich property owner and his mates.

Her debut album was a soundtrack to her personal grief and heartbreak, her lyrics and music as raw as her pain.

The critics and fans loved it. Everyone assumed she was singing about bad break-ups and ex-boyfriends but the songs are about something more powerful than that. They're about the death of her grandmother. The woman who practically raised her while her single mum worked three jobs. She was the Musician's compass. Her rock. Her confidante.

By the time the Musician started her second album she was spent. Lost. She'd resorted to emulating others and imagined heartbreaks. The reviews shouldn't come as a surprise.

Her boyfriend says this weekend's gig is a chance to reset and reconnect to her music without any pressure. Maybe he's right.

The road straightens as they reach the bottom of the range. Grey-green hills mark a landscape dotted with cattle and the occasional farmhouse.

"Didn't your grandmother originally come from down this way?"

"I think so but she never really spoke about it." Her stomach growls. "How much further to a shop?"

"There's a service station up ahead. Whoa!"

Her boyfriend slams on the brakes as they round a bend to find a herd of cattle blocking the highway. A farmer approaches the driver window and takes his Akubra from his head to wipe his brow.

"Sorry, mate, but these gals won't budge. You'll have to go back and take Cangai Bridge Road. Go over the bridge then follow the road back out to the highway."

The Musician's boyfriend shrugs suggesting that it might be the 'scenic route'. The Musician is less optimistic when they find the detour is a dirt road.

She changes her opinion though when the road emerges alongside a blue-green river, its shore a blanket of pebbles. Here and there white water skips over rocks that jut out from the surface. The Musician can almost hear the water gurgling. Singing to her.

They get to the bridge but she doesn't want to cross it. She wants to stay and hear the music of this place. She tells her boyfriend to pull over and they get out of the car.

She breathes in the crisp air and laughs as a willie wagtail appears and starts dive-bombing Dusty.

Dusty snaps at the bird but misses each time. The willie wagtail lands on Dusty's back and lifts its beak in challenge before launching itself into the air and flying across the bridge.

In the blink of an eye Dusty is off, chasing the bird, and the Musician chases Dusty.

* * *

The Keeper was nine years old when her mother and father separated. She can only recall little things from that time like the timber cottage with a giant river red gum beside it, a gully and a creek behind. The constant thrum of cicadas and insects. The sounds of bird calls. The trickle of a river in the distance.

She remembers her father saying goodbye. He'd wiped away the fat tears that rolled down her cheek, saying he'd see her soon. His face crinkled into a reassuring smile. He told her it wasn't anyone's fault.

"Some things aren't meant to be forever. Your mum and me – our time has passed."

His voice had cracked as he'd spoken. Or maybe it was the sound of his heart breaking.

A bird broke into song in the red gum.

"Do you hear that?" her father asked, squeezing her hand. "That's the willie wagtail. It's our messenger bird. When you see or hear a willie wagtail, you'll know it's me sending you a message."

Her father died a few months later.

Remembering her father's words, the Keeper never blamed anyone. It wasn't the same for her siblings.

The Keeper was what they called a 'change-of-life' baby. Her brother and sister had already left home by the time she was born and were strangers to her.

They'd come to their father's funeral but didn't speak to their mother.

She'd contacted them when the dementia overtook their mother and she had to be moved to a nursing home. Her siblings never visited their mother or came to her funeral.

The brother and sister couldn't forgive their mother for their father's death.

The Keeper couldn't forgive *them*.

After they left her father, the Keeper lived with her mother and grandparents on the Mid North Coast.

Not long after the move some official-looking types turned up at school and took a boy away.

The Keeper overheard some teachers talking about it. They used the words 'mixed race' and some other terms she didn't know but she could tell by the way they said them – screwing up their face like they'd just sucked a lemon – that they weren't good words.

Another day, a kid at school asked her if she was Aboriginal.

The Keeper said she didn't know and asked her mum when she got home.

Her mother got angry before a scared look came across her face. "You aren't Aboriginal. Your great-grandparents were Italian. Your father's grandparents came from South America." She bent down to eye level and put her hands on the girl's shoulders. Her tone serious. "That's what you tell people, okay?"

The Keeper came to understand that being Aboriginal was synonymous with shame and fear.

Many years later she felt a greater shame – a shame borne of denial.

The Keeper married and moved to Grafton with her husband. They didn't have any children and she had no family to speak of. But her life was comfortable. She should have been content. She shouldn't have felt anchorless. Adrift at sea. Alone.

One day in the main street an older Aboriginal woman approached her.

"*Baarrii*? Is that you?" she cried. "It's gotta be! You're the spittin' image of ya mother."

She wrapped her arms around the Keeper sobbing the word '*baarri*'.

The woman turned out to be her father's sister. Later she learned that '*baarri*' meant niece.

The Keeper's journey to reclaim her culture began that day. Over time she was introduced to the Elders. She listened. She listened more. She learned the old ways. The bush ways. How to read the land and seasons.

She learned how her people would wait for the blossoming of a particular shrub or vine that would signal the coming of fish up the river, or the best time to eat a specific animal or plant.

She learned how the old people would rub bunches of a poisonous weed together in the water to stun fish to make it easier to spear.

She learned about a certain spot across the river, high up on a hill, where her ancestors danced and performed a ceremony when someone died. The spirit of the dead would see the dancing and know they weren't forgotten.

The Keeper made her connection to Country and now must help others do the same.

* * *

The Artist wonders if he can in fact call himself an artist after one good painting and a series of mediocre ones.

He's really a lawyer. A profession his father approves of yet gives him little pleasure.

While the pay is good, the hours are ridiculous. In the little spare time he has, he sketches. Landscapes featuring exotic places he's been. Italy's Amalfi Coast. Scotland's rolling hills. Kyoto's temples dusted in snow.

He loves painting but it's not a 'real' job.

* * *

The Artist is helping his daughter with a family history assignment when he finds the photo of his grandfather. It's faded but the way his grandfather's dark eyes twinkle back at him and the cheeky grin on the man's face immediately transport him back to his childhood.

He remembers a time when he was about twelve and his grandfather came to visit. He'd taken him for fish and chips by the Brisbane River.

The old man lit up a rollie and watched the CityCats and yachts snake their way up and down the mud-coloured river that resembled a brown snake, the city's concrete towers standing to attention on the other side.

The Artist's grandfather made a sound that was halfway between a sigh and 'hmph'.

He spoke about a different river. His river. The river where he swam with his mates and caught turtles for dinner. "Gumbaynggirr Country," he said.

The Artist's grandfather went back regularly to his river. He'd camp there for weeks at a time.

His grandfather had asked whether he could take the Artist with him but the Artist's dad refused. "Maybe when you're old enough to take care of yourself."

That time never came.

His grandfather passed away on one of those trips. *Peacefully*, they'd been told.

He'd taken a nap under an old red gum and had never woken up.

The Artist tried to find his grandfather's river but it was harder than it sounded. His dad knew nothing about the place and didn't care to help.

Gumbaynggirr Country extends all the way from Grafton down to Nambucca and rivers are plentiful in that part of the world. Over time the Artist's need to feel connected to his grandfather was pushed into the background. Until he found the photo.

* * *

The Artist's brushes dance across the canvas as if they have a mind of their own. He paints like a man possessed, until a faithful representation of his grandfather smiles back at him.

On a whim he enters the Brisbane Portrait Prize. He doesn't win, but he's one of the finalists.

His success spurs him on but nothing else he paints fills him with the same sense of completeness.

He persists and paints his landscapes.

He holds an exhibition. At the end of the night an older woman he hadn't noticed earlier zeroes in on him.

"You've been some fancy places," she says.

She points to a landscape of Bacharach in Germany with a river in the background. "What about this place? That river there?"

"The Rhine. Perhaps the most beautiful river in the world."

She makes a 'hmph' sound that the Artist finds eerily familiar.

"You have a different opinion?"

"For me," her dark eyes sparkle, "the most beautiful river is at Cangai. Gumbaynggirr Country."

At that moment the gallery owner delivers the disappointing news that none of the Artist's paintings have sold. When he turns back to quiz the woman further, she's gone.

The Artist can't stop thinking about the encounter with the woman and what she'd said about the river in Gumbaynggirr Country. The next day he quits his job and tells his wife he wants to go to Cangai.

His wife holds the fort at home for two weeks so he can go and paint.

The Artist camps by the river at a spot between the bridge and a gully that leads to a creek.

The landscape and river are as beautiful as the woman said. There aren't any grand landmarks or features. The beauty comes from its simplicity. Its restraint. None of which translates on to the canvas.

It's the end of the two weeks and the Artist has resigned himself to giving up his artistic ambitions. He's going home to get a job. He packs up his brushes.

"Get back here," someone cries.

The Artist looks up to see a young woman running across the bridge. She's chasing a blue heeler. The dog's chasing … a willie wagtail!

The dog runs right past him towards the gully and the Artist gives chase.

* * *

The Keeper goes to the place where the house once was. She sits under the red gum and waits. Her months of planning are coming to fruition. She could have told them who she was and invited them here, but they had to find their own way. Even if they needed a little help.

She had seen the portrait of her brother in a newspaper. He was much older than she remembered but still recognisable. She tracked down the Artist and planted the necessary seed at his exhibition.

The Keeper had seen an interview with the Musician talking about her grandmother and how the dog goes everywhere with her.

She just needed a couple of favours from her friends. The farmer whose cattle had 'strayed' on to the road and the property owner who'd booked the Musician for his party.

Then it was up to the willie wagtail to deliver its message and the land itself to speak to them.

The willie wagtail flutters back to her, landing on her shoulder. The dog arrives and greets her like an old friend.

The Artist appears and does a double take.

"You're the woman from my exhibition."

The Musician arrives puffing, her face flushed. Her gaze falls on the dog nuzzling the Keeper's hand.

"He doesn't normally like strangers," she says.

The Keeper speaks.

"*Ngayu yaam gurriji yilaa Gumbaynggirr guuyu jurruy biin. Darruyay yilaami ngiyambandi jagunda Gumbaynggida.*"

"That is a Welcome to Country. A welcome to your Country."

"Who are you?" the Artist and Musician ask in unison.

"You can call me Aunty. Not because that's what everyone calls me but because I *am* your aunt. Your great-aunt."

The Artist and Musician exchange a confused look.

"Let me tell you a story…"

The Fable of the Origin of the People of Peru

Pedro Sarmient de Gamboa, Inca

IN THE BEGINNING, and before this world was created, there was a being called Viracocha. He created a dark world without sun, moon or stars. Owing to this creation he was named Viracocha Pachayachachi, which means 'Creator of all things'.

And when he had created the world he formed a race of giants of disproportioned greatness painted and sculptured, to see whether it would be well to make real men of that size. He then created men in his likeness as they are now; and they lived in darkness.

Viracocha ordered these people that they should live without quarrelling, and that they should know and serve him. He gave them a certain precept which they were to observe on pain of being confounded if they should break it. They kept this precept for some time, but it is not mentioned what it was. But as there arose among them the vices of pride and covetousness, they transgressed the precept of Viracocha Pachayachachi and falling, through this sin, under his indignation, he confounded and cursed them. Then some were turned into stones, others into other things, some were swallowed up by the earth, others by the sea, and over all there came a general flood which they call *uñu pachacuti*, which means 'water that overturns the land'. They say that it rained 60 days and nights, that it drowned all created things, and that there alone remained some vestiges of those who were turned into stones, as a memorial of the event, and as an example to posterity, in the édifices of Pucara, which are 60 leagues from Cuzco.

After the Flood

It must now be known that Viracocha Pachayachachi, when he destroyed that land as has been already recounted, preserved three men, one of them named Taguapaca, that they might serve and help him in the creation of new people who had to be made in the second age after the deluge, which was done in this manner. The flood being passed and the land dry, Viracocha determined to people it a second time, and, to make it more perfect, he decided upon creating luminaries to give it light. With this object he went, with his servants, to a great lake in the Collao, in which there is an island called Titicaca, the meaning being 'the rock of lead', of which we shall treat in the first part. Viracocha went to this island, and presently ordered that the sun, moon, and stars should come forth, and be set in the heavens to give light to the world, and it was so. They say that the moon was created brighter than the sun, which made the sun jealous at the time when they rose into the sky. So the sun threw over the moon's face a handful of ashes, which gave it the shaded colour it now presents. This frontier lake of Chucuito, in the territory of the Collao, is 57 leagues to the south of Cuzco. Viracocha gave various orders to his servants, but Taguapaca disobeyed the commands of Viracocha. So Viracocha was enraged against Taguapaca, and ordered the other two servants to take him, tie him hands and feet, and launch him in a *balsa* on the lake. This was done. Taguapaca was blaspheming against Viracocha for the way he was treated, and threatening that he would return and take vengeance, when he was carried by the water down the drain of the same lake, and was not seen again for a long time. This done, Viracocha made a sacred idol in that place, as a place for worship and as a sign of what he had there created.

Leaving the island, he passed by the lake to the main land, taking with him the two servants who survived. He went to a place now called Tiahuanacu in the province of Colla-suyu, and in this place he sculptured and designed on a great piece of stone, all the nations that he intended to create. This done, he ordered his two servants to charge their memories with the names of all tribes that he had depicted, and of the valleys and provinces where they were to come forth, which were those of the whole land. He ordered that each one should go by a different road, naming the tribes, and ordering them all to go forth and people the country. His servants, obeying the command of Viracocha, set out on their journey and work. One went by the mountain range or chain which they call the heights over the plains on the South Sea. The other went by the heights which overlook the wonderful mountain ranges which we call the Andes, situated to the east of the said sea. By these roads they went, saying with a loud voice "Oh you tribes and nations, hear and obey the order of Ticci Viracocha Pachayachachi, which commands you to go forth, and multiply and settle the land." Viracocha himself did the same along the road between those taken by his two servants, naming all the tribes and places by which he passed. At the sound of his voice every place obeyed, and people came forth, some from lakes, others from fountains, valleys, caves, trees, rocks and hills, spreading over the land and multiplying to form the nations which are today in Peru.

Translated by Sir Clements Markham K.C.B.

Sinking Cities

Sophie Garcia, Nahua Nation, Atlixco Pueblo of Mexico

"IT'S TIME FOR ME TO COME BACK," *a golden figure in the corner says. "I've lived in California for many lifetimes, and even more away. But now it is time for me to come back."*

He sits up from his chair and his face becomes visible – "Dad?"

"Si, mija."

Vibrant lights flood the room. Both acutely aware of the situation at hand, their meeting spot fades away and with it their connection – but the message demands to be remembered, clinging to the memory membrane as the mind becomes blinded by light and brilliant notes of flutes and violins.

"Olivia, turn off the alarm," Citlali says.

"I did not get that – please restate your command." [Mago Del Oz Plays]

"Olivia, turn off the alarm."

"Alarm off. Anything else I can do for you Citlali?"

"No,thank you" she groans putting on her slippers.

As if by a miracle, she arrives only six minutes past clock-in time with three beverages on her person and music blaring out of her dangling earrings which form a wired spiral into her eardrum – the stimulation from which is not nearly enough to match the hustle and bustle of Chinatown, still as protected as ever from monopolization. Every business is owned by a different family with generational ties to the neighborhood. *I wonder what that feels like.* At last, the bank. The glass doors automatically open with her presence, and the elevator promptly brings her to a well-lit hallway on the secret top floor. Suddenly overwhelmed with a brilliant understanding of how much light she brings to this place, not just here at Toltech but the world, she breathes in and out, twirling around the sleeve of her flannel whose painted backside reads 'The Time is Now and it Always Has Been'. As satisfying as the 180 degree view of the bridge is, her fellow apprentices spinning in their chairs in front of the glass paneling is what fills her heart with elation. "Hi, Citlali! We'll be starting in a minute, feel free to grab some snacks." her supervisor says.

"Okay. Thanks!" she whispers, rushing over to the table with baskets of fruit, from her co-worker's Itzel's garden, no doubt.

* * *

"Okay y'all, please start making your way over here for our check-in, we have a bunch of really exciting announcements to make." A lunar crescent forms as people take their seats around an empty rectangular stand. The supervisor incidentally taps somewhere in the air between the stand's two vertical poles and a small loading symbol resembling a staircase in Mesoamerican pyramids materializes. Each of the three steps appear individually, their assembly synced to a silent beat only to begin again. The anticipation has reached its peak as an image of a model wearing green visors and a flowy white tunic with pixelated patterns forming a saint emerges in 3D from the screen. "As you all know, Toltech has partnered with LA fashion house Xola to create our own anti-surveillance fashion line targeting the algorithms used by border patrol across Anahuak," he taps the screen,

"They just sent the latest prototypes. We'll be testing them this week at our downtown warehouse, so let's make sure that our camera systems are up to date with the BP algorithms for a successful first walk. In other great news we have secured more funding to send out teams to install our wi-fi routers in pueblos. Those of you with direct relationships with your tribal nations can expect an email on next steps but it's safe to say some of you, should you choose to – will visit home! And finally, our youth programs, especially Coding with Ancestral Mathematics need more students so please let me know if you know of folks who would be a good fit at the program as former students yourselves. Tlazocamati."

* * *

When they disperse, Citlali gets a vibration signal from her phone – a voice message from her dad. Pinching her thumb and index finger, she stretches open the voice-box as if opening a small music box containing extremely delicate petals and melodic notes, "Hi Beba. How are you? I can't wait for you to come visit. I was thinking a lot about what you said the other day and it makes me happy. I'd love to live in California with you – just please make sure everything's good on your end first, because it might take me a while to find work. I know how bad the housing situation is up there and I don't want to cause you any problems. Call me when you can." Her phone vibrates again – this time reminding her of an upcoming appointment.

* * *

Citlali knocks on the window of a metallic van made to look like a submarine with a painted sign that says 'Feels on Wheels'. Once inside, she takes a seat on a black leather couch. The driver greets her and asks, "Shall we take a drive or a walk?"

"I'm really not trying to walk right now, let's drive up to Twin Peaks."

They drive up a long, winding road called Diamond into beautiful stretches of forest remarkably conserved and tucked away at the highest point in the city. The fog is so lusciously thick it results in a dream-like haze. As they exit the vehicle and walk towards the bench, they notice a man dancing. Citlali sits down before him and breathes in deeply. "How have you been doing?" he asks.

She breathes out. " I'm really tired. I've got so much going on right now I can't even list out what's new for me this week."

"I hear that" he affirms, "Why don't you try?"

"I am trying. That's the problem actually. I'm trying so hard to be the best that I can at all times, to win a victory in the war that is survival and it never ends."

Her therapist stares at her embarrassedly, unaware that his display of discomfort was not unnoticed.

"Thank you for speaking to that and I apologize for my wording. It sounds like you're doing all the things you're supposed to do and need a well-deserved break. How have you been making space for rest?"

"That's okay. I've been sleeping well with homemade tea blends and I am going on vacation soon. But I think I want to take more than a break from my position at Atom."

"I'm glad to hear that you're making time for rest. As far as stepping back from Atom – I want you to know that because of my employment contract with them, if you did decide to quit we'd no longer be able to meet. Which is okay – but I'm curious as to what you mean by that."

"This opportunity has been great for my career, I just know I was meant for more."

"With all due respect, Atom is the number one tech company in the world. I don't think it gets any better than this. Why don't we meet again after your vacation?"

After getting dropped off in front of Atom HQ, Citlali crosses the quiet street, sat down on the steps of a rotting hollow Victorian and rolled up a blend of tobacco and flowers she got from her friend Gruta's campo in Oaxaca. The warm scent signatures relax her mind. Looking across the street she sees two men. One of them is Keith, a coworker that she'd been meaning to reach out to for a meeting. She had noticed something strange in the backend. The algorithms tailoring ads and other user experiences to a local demographic of users were littered with wormholes. There were gaps in the code that would swallow the nearest line or two only to replace it with foreign code. She wondered what would cause such a thing, and why they hadn't received any complaints about it.

* * *

Saying goodbye to the man he was talking to, Keith walks away. Once inside Atom, he scans his thumb at the turnstile and makes a left for the bathroom. In the lobby, there's a framed newspaper. It bears a photo of Citlali smiling with other Toltech members under the words: 'Powering Indigenous Science and Tech For a Sustainable World: How Atom's New Recruits Are Making Waves'. Keith exits the bathroom and types in a negative number on a blue screen in the hallway, once he hit enter – the wall opens to reveal an elevator. It descends past the server room into a basement. There's no one in there but him, he hits a switch and multiple screens light up, automatically updating seed libraries, where coders can borrow self-improving algorithms, run it, and upload their optimized version. One of the algorithms, the one Keith is interested in, is seeking to replicate a piece of an ancient technological artifact discovered in Tenochtitlan. According to the dark web forums he frequented, this artifact was an earpiece that ancient Mesoamerican governmental figures used to communicate with extraterrestrials. By inserting it into their ears, they would be able to listen to alien communications and respond by focusing on and broadcasting their thoughts without the burden of language, only with complex emotions and visual symbols, which was common practice in pre-Columbian times. Keith had been experimenting with it as the head tech-grunt of the marketing department. He chose to target those living in the nearby shelters not only because they made his life hell and he would have a silent vengeance to savor as he walked through the lawless streets of San Francisco each morning but because they likely already possess weird hallucinations and spending habits – all of which he could monitor from the comfort of his office. While Atom was in a race with global competitors to be the first to put advertisements in dreams, the way Keith saw things was he was simply going to change the world.

* * *

Citlali gets off the bus at the beach and looks to the deep night sky. Without the light pollution she can spot a few fixed stars and planets she studied as an astrology-obsessed teen. The Sunset wasn't the neighborhood she grew up in but it was now her sanctuary. On one of the concrete staircases leading down to the sand there's an altar with a forty ounce, candied flowers, and photos. Surely another overdose. Since the mass squats, a government manufactured-drug hit the streets, turning up laced in just about everything. It was an unofficial way of "cleaning up the city" and making way for new development. The city was small and overcrowded so very few neighborhoods had permanent housing available. Citlali had been lucky. With her two jobs, she was making a quarter below the median income, the sweet spot to earn a ticket, and after praying every night for months she had won the lottery. The lottery-system was the only way families could find private, affordable housing. They either occupied the same house for generations or just left town. If you were single, you could rent a pod in a co-living space and maybe even meet someone to start a family with – was what the Mayor told everyone. Citlali was not a single woman.

* * *

Saturn was a gardener and a chef. He had created a closed circle of growing, eating, and composting from the same plot of earth. While there were many urban farms in the cities – Saturn got his special ingredients elsewhere. He was half Ohlone and, as a federally-recognized Native, he'd been bestowed access to a land trust. There was a board of his elders in charge of the park, farm, and commune. While some land had been formally returned to First Nations as part of a global climate emergency plan – many nations were still running things bureaucratically instead of with their traditional governing structures. Saturn denounced this injustice at every opportunity while working at the farm. But Saturn's true life was in cuisine. Customers paid good money to learn and feast with him. He had a hundred thousand followers on his channel who'd drop everything to attend his cookouts, classes, even markets he'd vend at. They saw him as a selfless leader in the food justice community offering overflowing plates and an abundance of free recipes amidst the culinary renaissance that came with #LandBack. But he saw himself as a selfish man because he loved seeing others enjoy his meals. To exclaim, get up and dance, praise god, and kiss the air all because of *his* creations which he was never hungry enough to eat after making. Citlali had been his favorite person to feed since they met. She was the one who inspired him to start his channel, taking care of all the editing and search engine optimization while letting him do what he did best. After damning software for crashing with her entire chest, she'd lie down and ask him to crush her because Saturn's weight calmed her down. With each other life felt easy.

* * *

After their fire-roasted dinner, Citlali can't stop overthinking about a friendship she felt was over, but had a prior commitment to meet soon. "I'm not sure if I should still take her. I don't even remember how long it was since she started spiraling and falling out with everyone. All I know now is that she's living in a shelter and posts about mind-control. Will she even make it to the airport?"

"She definitely needs this, with more reason. Didn't she tell you about how she's dying to go to Mexico at the last market before the squats?"

"Yeah, but that's literally what every displaced Native says. I get chest pains from the fact that I don't live there on a weekly basis."

"Well if she makes it you'll have a lot more fun than if you were to go there alone," Saturn points out.

"That's true. I'll miss you," Citlali wooes.

"I'll miss you too."

* * *

Dolores awoke this morning feeling groggy and aware of her bones. As she reaches below the bed for a glass of water and takes a sip, stills of the night terrors frame her day consciousness. Someone trying to force-feed her grapes made in laboratories and eyes peeping out of camera sockets. The weighted blanket covering her legs far from thick enough to evade the multitude of gazes on her body. She brings her glass of water over to the window, the sky is white. As classic as this might feel to tourists, it's rare to see fog in the Mission – as the favorite place for Tonatiuh to beam his rays of warmth in the

7x7 square mile radius that is San Francisco. Still, the moment is just right – early enough for the street vendors setting up on Mission and 16th and late enough to miss the buzzing conglomerates of techies entering and exiting the BART station. The robberies have been getting extreme lately so they've been suggested by the mayor to travel in groups of twelve. Most do so until reaching their individual pods at their coliving bases. Dolores hates taking BART, because during her route, and especially inside the underwater tunnel beneath the Bay Bridge, she can perceive whispers encompassed by high-pitched industrial whistling and make out howls between the violent metal clashes on the train tracks.

* * *

She checks her phone for notifications. Scrolling through she sees that her package was received by a receptionist downstairs and that today is Ye Coatl on the Tonalpohualli calendar, *three-snake hub*? She sees a message from Citlali asking if she was still coming on the trip. *Yes, of course*. She hastily pulls up her digital wallet to find her ticket. It's empty. She rotates it from all angles to be sure, maybe even to find the receipt – only for it to crash. Upon her phone's third crash/restart cycle, she remembers a detail from her nightmare – someone uttering a threat to ransom her phone – holding a digital version of herself hostage in a blue nucleus. Her arms weaken at the memory of feeling like a pawn. Her hands start to sense a radioactive heat pulsing through her phone, spiking up into her joints making her drop her phone. Ashamed, she picks it up and hurriedly replies to Citlali, *I'll meet you there*.

It took a conversation with the airline, a five hour flight, and long showers but they made it to the Centro in Mexico City. On the plane, sharing music and reading – they both discovered that nothing had changed between them. Upon hearing Dolores over-explain herself, Citlali could gather why Dolores might have pushed her away. But feeling was not enough for Dolores, who had a hard time differentiating between her intuition and her imagination, she questioned Citlali as if performing a sneak attack with three words that cleared all doubt from her mind, "Are we good?"

* * *

They stroll down to the Zocalo following the white strands of kopalli smoke that keenly resemble the hair on a little abuelita's head, much like the hair of the brujos and curanderas lined up along the sidewalk, offering their services to pedestrians. They're on their way to the entrance to the plaza where Citlali's dad, Kiahuitl, is. One of his many repeated stories was the one of why he chose that spot. Before the invasion of the Spanish colonizers, there existed the Templo Mayor for the Federation of Tenochtitlan. There were ceremonies performed according to the Tonalpohualli calendar, none of which actually had human sacrifice that was all harmful Spanish propaganda. It was demolished and a cathedral built over its west side, but over the years, archaeologists excavated the ruins and mapped it out. It is above the entrance of the Templo Mayor that her dad chose to stand as a gate-guardian, appearing as nothing more than the left corner of the west side entrance to the average Zocalo visitor.

* * *

Passing the assembly of healers, a woman with teased hair facing them in the distance looks at them with wide, concerned eyes. Dolores becomes hyper-aware of her appearance wondering if that is what's causing the fear in this woman's wrinkled face. When they reach her, Dolores asks if she's okay. The woman says, "You have a shadow cast over you. There is a person who wants to see you in bondage, in addiction. His shadow is rushing to be two steps ahead of you. He thinks he knows you intimately, but he doesn't."

Dolores is nodding thankful to be seen on a spiritual level, which is her primary mode of existence. "Is that why you looked at me like that?" she asked innocently.

"Yes. I can't see his face clearly but I know he's white."

Dolores confesses, "Tengo un chingo de miedo."

The woman smiles then laughs, "You don't have anything to fear. Look, just get a limpia from me and ask your dead for protection. I can see they gave you the gift, remember evil is no match for good." Dolores hugs her, shocked at their mutual familiarity and ease. Citlali lets her know she'll be down the block with her dad. She nods, as the doña blows the conch shell to begin the limpia. Her spirit slowly heeds the call back to her body as the curandera begins to blow smoke through the shell. She feels her nervous system restore as she gets slapped with plants to the beat of a chant.

* * *

After thanking the woman for her kindness, Dolores walks over to find Citlali sitting next to a man wearing a blue Baja hoodie. She approaches and hugs him. When she sits down the three share their reunion in the sun, long overdue. That night, the girls planned to go to a dark-wave renegade in an abandoned church. Kiahuitl agreed to stay in the city at their rented house to stay close with them, saving himself the long metro ride home. He lived in what locals called *Ecatepunk*, a peripheral city with a large indigenous population, past a mural that read 'No Pigs Allowed Beyond This Point.'

* * *

Dolores had a friend in the Federal District – Lorena the nun. They had met as teenagers during Dolores's brief exile to a Mexican convent and Lorena immediately took her under wing, teaching her everything there was to know about escapades. Dolores had gotten expelled after getting caught climbing over the vined wall, but Lorena had managed to keep her double life undiscovered. They were all to meet at Lorena's church at nine. Waiting outside of the church and running her hand across the cobblestone, Dolores admitted to Citlali that it was grounding for her "because you know who built these walls." Lorena opened the creaky, wooden church doors and ushered them to the garden. They took shots of the mezcal they brought as an offering to the night. After a few rounds, Lorena giggled, "I can't wait for you two to meet my girlfriend. She's DJing tonight."

* * *

Instead of taking the metro, they take a shortcut designed to protect the safety of nuns centuries ago – a system of underground staircased tunnels leading from one church to another avoiding the metropolis that was so dangerous for women traveling alone, and still is in many ways. The three descend into darkness by Lorena's candlelight; carvings in the walls soon become visible, but hardly understandable to Citlali's frustration. The further they go, the duller the air and stronger the pressure. By now, they were surely underwater since Mexico City was built on top of a lake and every year without fault – it sank another twenty inches into the primordial waters. Drunk with the trust that came with being intoxicated with her two closest friends in a subterranean passageway Dolores asked, "Can you hear spirits?"

"More so I can feel their presence." replies Lorena.

"Ta bien heavy in here, no?" Citlali murmurs, "Sometimes I think I see them."

No longer listening, Dolores attempts to balance herself by stretching her arms as far as she could in the narrow walls. She props herself up and jumps over the last two steps. In mid-air, her ears pop and become permeated by a rattling sound breaking the dense silence from a moment before. The other two look back at Dolores. "What is that?" Citlali asks. Lorena points her candle at the floor and holds up a metal knob of sorts for all to see.

"That thing came out of my ear," Dolores states in shock.

"What? Let me see," Citlali urges, "Um, it looks like an earphone mic or a battery of some sort. I can ask the Toltech lab to run it when we get home. Are you okay?"

Dolores doesn't reply, dizzied by an orchestra of whispers louder and clearer than they've ever been until she closes her eyes to visualize a protective orb of purple light surrounding her, drowning out all but one, maternal voice – *Don't be afraid, child*.

Grass Dancer

Owl Goingback, Native American

Charlie's coming.

Roger Thunder Horse poked his head above the sandbags and sighted along the barrel of his M-16 rifle. He focused his attention at the forest beyond the perimeter wire, searching for a line too straight, an angle that didn't belong, something out of the ordinary. He knew the enemy was out there. Somewhere. Everything was just too damn quiet. Too still. Like the calm before a storm. Things always got that way right before they got hit. Even the tiny green tree frogs had hushed their shrill cries. Like Roger, they also waited.

The men of 3rd Battalion 26 Marines, K Company, knew what it was like to engage the enemy, and to face death. Their tiny outpost, stationed on top of a mountain known to them only as Hill 861, came under rocket and mortar attack nearly every night. Located in the province of Quang Tri, Hill 861 was just below the Demilitarized Zone, near the border of Laos, in the godforsaken country of Vietnam.

Two miles southeast of Hill 861 was the Khe Sanh Combat Base, home for a little over six thousand U.S. and South Vietnamese soldiers. Khe Sanh was a regular city compared to Hill 861. The base had an airstrip, twenty-four howitzers and half a dozen tanks. A couple of miles south of the base was the village it was named for. Several other U.S. Marine outposts were scattered around the base, in an effort to keep the North Vietnamese from moving south across the border.

Neither the combat base nor the surrounding outposts had much of a deterring effect upon the North Vietnamese. Intelligence reports complied during the past two months showed that Charlie was moving massive amounts of troops and firepower below the DMZ in preparation for something big. North Vietnamese Army divisions 325 C, 324 and 370, along with a regiment of the 304th – an elite home guard from Hanoi – were already entrenched in the area, with more units moving in every day. According to the latest estimates, there were somewhere between thirty and forty thousand North Vietnamese Army regulars in the surrounding countryside, compared with an allied force totaling less than seven thousand men.

Early yesterday morning, Company I from Hill 881 had made contact with a battalion of North Vietnamese Army regulars dug in between Hill 881 South and Hill 881 North. The tropical forest covering the mountains was so thick, they hadn't seen the enemy until they were right on top of them. Twenty marines were killed, and another thirty wounded, in the first two minutes of the firefight.

Less than an hour after the ambush, a NVA defector had appeared at the Khe Sanh airstrip waving a white flag. The defector, a 1st Lt. La Than Tonc, informed the base commander that North Vietnamese troops were preparing to overrun the base in an effort to sweep across two northern provinces to seize the city of Hue.

Charlie's coming.

Hearing the news, Roger and his fellow marines had dug their trenches deeper, added more sandbags to the bunkers, and reinforced the perimeter with additional claymore mines, triple coils of barbed wire, German razor tape, and trip flares. They had done all they could do to protect themselves. Now it was just a matter of waiting to be hit.

The waiting was the hardest part. To pass the time, most of them played cards, smoked pot, sang, or shot rats. There were a lot of rats in the bunkers and trenches of Hill 861. A few, usually the new guys, would stare at the jungle for hours until they developed a blank look in their eyes known as the thousand-yard stare.

Roger wiped a hand across his face. He watched the sun as it slowly sank behind the hills to the west. Darkness was coming, and with it would come the enemy. Shadows already gathered in the valley below. To the south, a haze of bluish smoke marked the location of the village of Khe Sanh – or what was left of it. The Viet Cong had attacked Khe Sanh earlier in the day. They didn't like it that the villagers were friendly toward the Americans, trading fresh vegetables for canned rations, cigarettes, and candy.

He had seen what the VC did to civilians who were friendly to Americans. Children with their limbs hacked off. Women with their vaginas cut out. Old people gut-shot and left to die. In the six months he had been in Vietnam, Roger had seen enough horrors to last him a lifetime. Maybe two.

Six months. Six months till I can get out of this hell hole. Six months till I can go home.

Going home was all he ever thought about. Day and night. Night and day. The war had lost all meaning for him. He no longer cared who won. Survival was the only thing that mattered anymore. He was just putting in his time, keeping his head down, trying not to get shot before he rotated out.

Less than a year had passed since he left the Kiowa Reservation in Oklahoma, but it seemed like a lifetime. He longed for the wide-open spaces where a man could feel the wind on his face and sleep under the stars without worrying about mortar attacks or snipers. He missed driving into town on a Saturday night to catch a movie. He missed ice-cream cones. But most of all he missed his aunt, Ruth, and his brother, Jimmy. He still remembered how upset they had been when he told them he was leaving.

"What's that?" Jimmy had asked as Roger entered the kitchen. He'd noticed the envelope in Roger's shirt pocket. Aunt Ruth turned away from the stove, where she was cooking scrambled eggs and sausages.

"Bad news?" she had asked, eyeing the envelope suspiciously. Aunt Ruth may have been well into her sixties, but she was still as sharp as ever. She didn't miss much. Roger had hoped to wait until after breakfast before discussing the contents of the letter, but he'd just have to go ahead and break the news to them.

"I'm afraid it is, Aunt Ruth," Roger said, standing beside Jimmy. "It's from Washington. I've been drafted."

Aunt Ruth put a hand on the counter to steady herself. She recovered quickly and grabbed a towel to wipe her hands off.

"Here, let me see that." She crossed the room and held her hand out. Roger handed her the envelope. Aunt Ruth read the letter twice before giving it back to him.

"So, what are you going to do?" she asked.

Roger shrugged. "What else can I do? It's not like I have a choice."

"There's always a choice to any situation." She walked back to the stove to stir her eggs. "You could go to Canada till the war's over."

Roger thought about it a moment, then shook his head. "No, that would be running away. People would say I was a coward then. I wouldn't be able to call myself a warrior, or much of a man for that matter. No, Aunt Ruth, I can't run."

She turned and looked at him, a sadness in her eyes. He really didn't have a choice. A lot of young men were moving to Canada to avoid the draft, but they weren't Indians. Roger was full-blooded Kiowa. In his veins flowed the blood of his ancestors. The blood of warriors. If he ran, he would bring disgrace on the entire tribe.

"When do you leave?" she asked.

"I have to report for my physical first thing Monday morning."

"Do you have to go away?" Jimmy asked, tears forming.

"Yeah, I have to," Roger said, squatting down beside his brother's wheelchair.

Jimmy, who was eleven, suffered from a painful spinal disease that curved his backbone and made it nearly impossible for him to walk. If nothing else, the military would provide a steady paycheck. With enough money, they might be able to find a doctor who could fix Jimmy's back. Ever since their parents had been killed in a car wreck, and they had moved in with their Aunt Ruth, there was barely enough money to buy food, let alone pay expensive doctor bills.

Roger stood up. "I almost forgot. I've got a favor to ask."

He crossed the kitchen and walked back into his bedroom. When he returned, he carried his dance regalia, which consisted of buckskin leggings, moccasins, a ribbon shirt, porcupine hair roach, bells, dance stick and fan, and an eagle-feather bustle.

"I need you to take care of this stuff until I get back," Roger said as he laid the regalia in Jimmy's lap.

Jimmy started to protest, but changed his mind and remained silent. He knew what an important responsibility he was being given. An honor. Not only was Roger one of the best traditional dancers in the state, but the forty-three golden eagle feathers used in the regalia had been passed down for generations, from one Thunder Horse to the next. Roger had used thirty-six feathers to make the bustle and the other seven for the fan.

Jimmy ran his fingers gently over the feather bustle. "It makes my hand tingle."

Roger smiled. "It's supposed to. That bustle is a medicine piece. What you're feeling is its power... its energy. Not only are those eagle feathers sacred, they're medicine feathers. The spirits of your ancestors are in those feathers, Jimmy. I guess a little bit of my spirit is in them too. They'll protect you while I'm gone, keep you safe till I get back."

Jimmy looked down at the bustle, then back up. "What if you don't come back?"

"Then the regalia is yours, all of it," Roger said, a sadness coming over him. It would be the first time he and Jimmy had ever been apart.

"You know I can't dance," Jimmy said.

Roger laid his hand on Jimmy's shoulder. "You can do anything you put your mind to. Anything at all."

He turned away and went back into his room to pack. Vietnam was a long way away.

* * *

Whump!

The first mortar shell landed about fifty yards away. Dirt and rocks rained down like tiny hailstones all around him.

Whump! Whump! Whump!

Three more rounds landed in the same area as the North Vietnamese walked a line of fire from east to west.

"Incoming!" someone yelled, but by then everyone already knew they were under attack.

Roger hunched lower and searched for something to shoot at. The sun was down and night had come. The shadows along the perimeter were as deep as those in the valley below. He thought he saw movement along the fence line but couldn't be sure. A few seconds later someone set off a trip flare.

The flare streaked into the sky and exploded, splattering the area into a metallic brilliance as it drifted gently in the air, swinging slowly back and forth. Roger saw several dozen men in black clothing,

VC guerrillas, scurry along the fence line. As the flare revealed their position, the VC opened fire with machine guns and rifles. Roger returned fire.

Charlie's here.

Slapping a fresh clip into his M-16, Roger hit the bolt release and chambered a round. He held his breath to steady his hands and squeezed off a short burst. There seemed to be no end to the number of enemy soldiers swarming up the hill. A company of NVA regulars, about two hundred strong, had joined the VC at the fence. Using bamboo ladders, they had already breached the outer perimeter in two places. Those in the lead used satchel charges to clear a path through the claymores. Once past the minefield, there were only two more fences between them and the base.

The area between the fences was lit up like a carnival as explosions, flares, and tracer rounds split the night. The noise was a deafening blend of detonations, shots, screams, and curses. From somewhere near the outer perimeter a bugle sounded, its shrill notes like that of a wailing demon. Roger would have loved to throttle the neck of the person blowing it, for each piercing note caused his flesh to crawl.

As Roger raised up to fire off another burst, he felt a hand upon his left shoulder. He turned and saw 1st Lt. Chris McGee standing next to him.

"I wouldn't poke your head up too far," the lieutenant warned. Roger looked up and saw a stream of blue-green tracer rounds pass like fireflies above his head. The North Vietnamese had opened up on their position with a heavy machine gun. Roger nodded and hunkered lower in the trench.

Lt. McGee, an artillery officer, kneeled down and placed a radio on the ground before him.

"What happened to your radio operator?" Roger asked. He had to yell to be heard.

"He took a round between the eyes," McGee yelled back. He picked up the radio's receiver and called the artillery unit at Khe Sanh.

"Oh-eight to Marine Artillery Jacksonville. We have enemy troops inside the wire. Request H and E shells, fire number five."

"Jacksonville to Oh-eight," came the reply. "What kind of fuses?"

McGee looked at Roger, who shrugged. He thumbed the button to talk. "Oh, hell, mixed quick and delay, I guess."

"Roger, Oh-eight." The radio hissed.

Twenty seconds later, Roger ducked as a single artillery shell whistled over their heads, sounding as loud as a freight train roaring through a narrow canyon. The shell exploded just beyond the outer fence. Two more quickly followed.

McGee thumbed the receiver again and shouted above the noise. "Oh-eight to Jacksonville. Mixed shells H and E, and WP. Air burst twenty meters. Keep it working up and down the road." He turned to Roger and motioned for him to take cover.

Roger dove to the bottom of the trench as a salvo of artillery shells sailed over their position. The shells, both high explosive and white phosphorous, detonated along the edge of the forest. Night became day and the earth trembled as burning phosphorous and white-hot steel slammed into the ground. Trees exploded, bushes burned, and soldiers were ripped apart, their screams of agony drowned out by the shells bursting above their heads. Roger stood up and watched as NVA soldiers endured the hellfire of the howitzers.

But though the artillery shells rained death down upon them, the North Vietnamese hadn't been stopped. Nor had they given up. As those in the front died, others crawled forward to take their place. Like an army of spiders, they kept coming.

"Out of my way!" someone yelled.

Roger leaped to the side as James Smith – Smitty to everyone – slid into the trench. Smitty, a muscular black man from southern Alabama, was a machine gunner in the same squad as Roger. Back in the States he had been an amateur boxer. In Vietnam he was a professional killer. Pushing between the lieutenant and Roger, Smitty rested the barrel of his M-60 machine gun on the stack of sandbags in front of him.

"I figured you could use some help, Geronimo," he said as he fed an ammo belt into the gun.

"Hell, the lieutenant and I were planning on winning this war by ourselves," Roger answered.

Smitty grinned, cocked the M-60, aimed, and commenced killing the enemy. Roger turned his attention back toward the fence line and proceeded to do the same.

* * *

Jimmy Thunder Horse sat up with a start, his heart pounding. At first he wasn't sure where he was, the darkness was so complete. But gradually his eyes adjusted and he could make out the familiar shapes in his bedroom. The nightstand beside his bed. His dresser. His desk. He listened carefully and was further reassured that all was well by the gentle snoring of Aunt Ruth from down the hall.

"Just a dream," he whispered. "It was just a bad dream."

Bad dream nothing. He had just had the worst nightmare of his life. Jimmy had been in a deep forest, fleeing from something he couldn't see. Though it was nighttime, the sky was lit with explosions of colors. Red. Yellow. White. Like the Fourth of July. He wasn't alone. Dead things ran with him. Half-naked men with no arms, or parts of their faces missing, lumbered along beside him. He tried to outrun them, but the ground was slick with blood. He slipped and fell and the men were upon him. All of them had the same face. They were all Roger.

Jimmy leaned over and turned on the lamp on his nightstand. His hands still shook as he opened the nightstand's drawer and took out a stack of letters. The letters, fifteen in all, were from Roger. He opened the first envelope and removed a photograph.

The picture of Roger had been taken a little over two months ago. He was standing on top of a building made out of sandbags. There were similar buildings in the background, with narrow trenches between them. Roger wore green fatigue pants and dusty combat boots. He was shirtless, which showed how thin he'd become in the last six months. Around his neck hung a pair of dog tags and his medicine pouch. In his right hand he held a M-16. In his left he held a dead rat. Roger was smiling in the picture.

Jimmy had stared at the picture for hours, studying every little detail of it. Maybe, he thought, if he stared at the photograph long enough, he could make Roger climb out of it and come home. The letter that came with it portrayed a different side of the war than what was shown on the evening news. Roger talked about humorous things, like rat races, mud football and burning shit on latrine duty. For the life of him, Jimmy could not understand what was so funny about burning shit.

All of the letters Roger sent to Jimmy were lighthearted. But there were others, sent to Aunt Ruth, that told a different story about Vietnam. Jimmy wasn't supposed to have seen the letters, but he found them in the kitchen closet, tucked behind his aunt's jar of sassafras roots. The letters spoke of horrors unimaginable to an eleven-year-old boy. They told about firefights and land mines, body counts and mutilations. One thing for sure, despite how cheerful he seemed in the letters he sent to Jimmy, Roger was scared. He had sent extra money home in his last letter to Aunt Ruth, with a request that it be used to purchase a special prayer song at the next powwow.

He put the letters back, threw off his covers, and swung his legs over the side of the bed. He lowered himself carefully into his wheelchair and rolled across the room to the far wall. Roger's dance bustle hung from a nail on the wall, low enough that Jimmy could take it down whenever he wanted. He slipped the bustle off the nail and laid it in his lap.

His hand tingled as he gently touched the eagle feathers. The bustle had lost none of its power. As he stroked the feathers, an image of Roger came to mind. Jimmy saw his brother step proudly as he entered the dance arena during the grand entrance, his face painted, his head held high. He saw him challenge the other dancers in the sneak-up dance, dropping to one knee to search for the enemy's trail, only to rise again to charge the drum. Roger never missed a beat when he danced, never failed to turn toward the drum when an honoring beat sounded. People always said that Roger's medicine was strong, that the Great Spirit came upon him when he danced.

A tear ran down Jimmy's cheek. It fell upon one of the eagle feathers. Jimmy quickly wiped it off. "Please, Roger, come home. Come home and dance for me."

* * *

Everything went white. The blast was so bright, it left its image etched on the inside of Roger's eyelids. The heat singed his hair and the force knocked him to the bottom of the trench.

Artillery round. Didn't hear it coming. Was it ours, or one of theirs?

He sat up and shook his head to clear his vision, but his left eye refused to clear. Wiping a hand across his face, he discovered that he had been wounded. Roger stared in disbelief at the blood smeared on his palm.

Further examination with his fingertips showed the wound to be a minor one. A small cut ran across his forehead, directly above his left eyebrow. At the most, it might require a couple of stitches to mend.

He was lucky. The artillery round had come close to being a direct hit. Fortunately, his flak jacket and helmet had taken most of the shrapnel. Roger started to get back up when he noticed Lt. McGee lying in the bottom of the trench with him.

Roger felt for a pulse in McGee's neck, but his fingers slipped into a bloody gash. He fumbled a pack of matches out of his shirt pocket and lit one. The tiny flame showed that the artillery blast had ripped away the right side of McGee's neck and a good portion of his face. Roger shuddered and extinguished the match.

He pushed himself away from Lt. McGee's body and stood up. Smitty still fired away with his M-60, apparently unaware they'd even been hit. But as Roger stepped beside him, he noticed that Smitty operated the gun with his left hand. His right arm hung useless at his side. Bone showed where shrapnel had torn away the upper third of Smitty's bicep.

"Hell of a blast, eh, Chief?" Smitty grinned.

"Jesus!" Roger said. He took off his belt and tied it around Smitty's right arm to stop the flow of blood. "You stupid idiot. You want to bleed to death?"

"Don't much matter one way or another," Smitty answered. "We're all gonna die anyway." He nodded toward the fence line. Roger looked, and felt his stomach knot in terror.

The North Vietnamese had already reached the last barricade. In a few seconds they would be over it and down in the trenches. There were hundreds of them. Too many to fight.

"We've got to get out of here!" Roger grabbed Smitty by his shirt and tried to pull him back.

"Ain't going nowhere," Smitty said, tearing free from Roger's grasp. He turned back to his M-60 and fired away.

"We're going hand-to-hand. You can't fight with that arm!"

Smitty ignored him.

"You'll be killed!" Roger shouted as he scrambled along the trench to take up a new position farther back. He wasn't sure if Smitty heard him. Seconds later, a grenade exploded where the big man stood. Roger turned away and didn't look back.

As he hurried along the trench, Roger realized that there was nowhere to run. The North Vietnamese had broken through the defenses and were about to overrun the base. Everywhere he looked, he saw the enemy. In the trenches along the south side of the base, the marines had thrown away their guns and fought with bayonets and knives.

Movement to his left caught his attention. Roger turned and saw a VC toss a satchel charge into a bunker. Before the VC could get clear of the blast, Roger cut him in half with a burst of automatic fire. No sooner had he killed the Viet Cong than two NVA regulars jumped into the trench in front of him, weapons firing.

He threw himself to the ground. The deadly spray of bullets kicked up dirt all around him. Roger shot back. One soldier went down, the top of his head blown off. The other, though wounded, continued to fire his weapon.

Roger rolled to his right to get out of the way. A pain ripped through his left thigh.

I'm hit!

He emptied his clip into the enemy soldier, skimming the bullets along the ground. He tried to stand up, but his leg crumpled beneath him like an accordion.

Get up! Get up! Get up!

Though Roger's brain screamed the command, his body refused to listen. He looked at his left leg and saw that he had taken several rounds in the thigh. Blood spurted from the wound.

Oh, God. He hit an artery.

Roger knew he would bleed to death if he didn't get medical attention right away. He would put a tourniquet on his leg, but he had used his belt to put one on Smitty's arm. Unless…

He pushed himself up on his elbows and looked around. His M-16 was only a few feet away from him. The rifle was equipped with a sling that could be used as a tourniquet.

Got to get to it. It's my only chance.

He gritted his teeth, rolled over on his stomach and crawled toward the rifle. He only had a few feet to crawl, but it seemed like a mile. His body broke out in a cold sweat as pain shot through his left leg. He stopped and took several deep breaths.

Come on. Come on. You can do it.

Roger reached out and grabbed the M-16 and dragged it to him. He unhooked the sling and tied it tight around his leg. The effort made him dizzy and it was all he could do to keep from passing out. He had just gotten the tourniquet tied when he heard voices approaching him. They were not speaking English.

Panic flared through him. He fumbled to get the empty clip out of the magazine and replace it with a full one. As he slipped a full clip into the rifle, three North Vietnamese soldiers came around a corner ahead of him. All three of them were armed with AK-47s. Seeing Roger, they raised their weapons and fired. Roger did the same. It was a good day to die.

* * *

Pain danced down Jimmy's spine as he pulled himself out of the wheelchair. He held onto the car door for support and used the outside rearview mirror to look at his face. Aunt Ruth had braided his hair for him before they left the house, tying a hawk feather to the left braid. His request had surprised her, for he had never bothered to fix his hair for a powwow before. With a steady hand, he drew a line across his cheeks with a stick of red greasepaint. A line of black went just below the red.

Whey they arrived at the fairgrounds, Jimmy had waited until after his aunt went to speak with the head singer before returning to the car. He had left the back door unlocked so he wouldn't have to ask her for the key. She hadn't noticed the items hidden beneath the blanket on the back floorboard.

The leggings and breechcloth had been a pain to put on by himself, but he finally managed to get everything tied in place. The leggings were too long and had to be pinned up, and he had to stuff the moccasins with newspaper to keep them from falling off his feet. The ribbon shirt went on easily, though it was two sizes too big, and the porcupine hair roach was only cocked a little to the left. He also had to struggle to get the bells on, but he was able to bend over far enough to tie them just above his calves. Wiping his fingers off on a paper napkin, Jimmy reached into the car for the final piece of regalia.

He leaned his weight against the car door and tied the leather thongs around his waist. Once they were tied, he adjusted the bustle so that it hung in the small of his back. He had to hurry. It was almost time. He could hear the arena announcer call for everyone's attention. Aunt Ruth would be with the announcer. In her purse was the letter that had arrived at the house the day before.

Jimmy double checked to make sure the bustle was secure. Satisfied, he picked up the eagle-feather fan and dance stick in his right hand. He held his breath as he let go of the door long enough to slip a crutch off the back seat and under his left arm. A crutch was sheer agony to use, but this was one time when a wheelchair just wouldn't do. Closing the car door, he made his way slowly toward the arena.

The crowd around the arena stood, many with their heads bowed. Jimmy moved carefully so as not to make his bells jingle too loudly. He didn't want to be noticed. Not yet anyway.

The drum was set up in the center of the dance arena. A dozen or so singers sat around it on folding metal chairs. Jimmy noticed that several of the singers held their hands in front of their eyes, as if to hold back tears, as they listened to what was being said. The arena announcer stood and faced the audience, his left arm around Aunt Ruth's waist. His voice echoed across the fairgrounds as he spoke into the microphone.

"Roger Thunder Horse was known by many of you. He was a fine young man, a skilled dancer, a loving son, nephew and brother. When the government called on Roger, he didn't run away, like a lot of young men have done. He went to serve his country, the best he could, in that far-off place called Vietnam.

"A month ago Roger wrote to his aunt, Ruth, telling her how bad things were over there. He wanted her to ask the drum to sing a special song for him so that he might come home safely. Roger sent Ruth some money to lay on the drum to pay for the song, which she did.

"Well, this is the first powwow since Roger's letter and the drum was going to sing that song for him." The announcer paused and swallowed hard, trying to control the quiver in his voice.

"Yesterday, Ruth got a letter from the United States Government. Roger Thunder Horse died in combat while defending his base from the Viet Cong."

A heavy silence fell over the grounds.

"At this time the drum asks that you remain standing as we sing a special veteran's song for Roger Thunder Horse. We also sing it for all the young men and women still serving their country in Vietnam. May they come home safely."

The head singer struck the drum with his drumstick. His voice lifted in song. The other men seated around the drum joined in.

As the song began, the head man dancer moved away from the bench to lead the dance. The other dancers – those who were veterans – waited until he passed where they stood and then followed him. The head lady dancer took Ruth by the arm and led her around the arena so that she, too, could dance to honor her nephew.

Jimmy pushed his way through the crowd and positioned himself at the eastern entrance to the arena. The regalia he wore had belonged to one of the finest dancers in the state. Wearing the regalia was one way of paying tribute to Roger's memory. Dancing in it was another.

As the head man dancer passed in front of where he stood, Jimmy took an agonizing step forward. He stepped again, leaned his weight on the crutch, rolled his hips, and dragged his back leg. He bit his lower lip to keep from crying out in pain. He would not cry out. His brother had been a warrior. He would be one too.

As he moved out into the arena, Jimmy saw an image of Roger in his mind – proud, dancing like the wind – and knew that his brother's spirit went with him. A few more steps brought him into plain view of everyone.

One of the singers looked up and saw him, a surprised expression on his face. He nudged the singer seated next to him, who also looked up. Just then the head singer – a large, powerful man named Henry Strong Bear – spotted Jimmy in the arena. Henry smiled, raised his drumstick high into the air and struck the drum a powerful blow.

The drum, like a heartbeat – God's heartbeat – echoed across the land. The vibrations entered Jimmy, filled him. For the first time he felt what Roger had felt, knew what it was like to dance. The feeling took his breath, made tears roll down his face. He threw his head back and yelled. The other dancers yelled too, answering his war cry.

Jimmy threw his crutch away in anger. He expected to fall, but didn't. If anything, as he shuffled along, his steps grew stronger.

He turned his head and moved his body, imitating the movements he had seen Roger do so many times before. He screamed again, in pain this time, as the bones in his spine straightened and realigned themselves. The drum sounded an honoring beat. Jimmy turned toward it and raised his eagle fan high.

Louder beat the drum. Louder sang the singers. Their voices lifted up to the heavens. Jimmy's body burned like it was on fire, but he felt strength and flexibility he had never known before. He twisted and turned, lifted his legs high, and brought his foot down with each beat of the drum. He circled the dance arena once. Twice. Three times. As he did, a strange and wonderful thing happened.

Where Jimmy stepped on the bare earth, grass suddenly appeared. The tiny blades of grass sprouted from the ground and grew several inches in a single heartbeat. They appeared in the shape of a footprint, but quickly spread to form a thick carpet of green.

The other dancers stopped and stared in amazement at what was happening beneath Jimmy's feet. A hush fell over the spectators as they, too, noticed. Some pointed. Others prayed. And then the crowd cheered as they realized that what they were witnessing could only be a miracle.

Jimmy danced faster. Gone was the pain that had crippled his body. His back straight, his head held proud, he danced like no one had ever seen before. And with each step he took, more grass sprang up. Thick. Green. Alive. The arena, once bare dirt, was soon covered with grass. New life to replace the life that was lost.

The song changed from a veteran's song to a sneak-up dance. Jimmy dropped to one knee and shielded his eyes, searching for an imaginary enemy as he had often seen Roger do. He shook his bustle and rolled his shoulders, rising to charge the drum when the tempo picked up.

Singers from the audience ran to join those already in the arena. Leaping over benches and folding chairs, they raced each other to the drum. Thirty. Forty. Maybe even fifty. They stood eight rows deep. Their voices echoed across the fairgrounds.

And in the arena, Jimmy danced alone. Sweat poured off his tiny body as he twisted and turned. He saw neither the singers nor those who watched him. He saw only Roger.

Basked in a brilliant white light, Jimmy's brother danced beside him in full regalia. Roger smiled as he challenged him, tried to outdo him, pushed him to dance even harder. Together they circled the arena. Side by side they danced the war dances, the sneak-ups and the crow hop. Together they moved. Side by side. As one.

The songs finally came to an end. The last drumbeat fell. Jimmy stopped and closed his eyes. He felt the pounding of his heart, and the wetness of tears on his cheeks. He didn't want to open his eyes again, afraid of what he would see, but knew he had to. Finally, he opened his eyes and looked up. He was alone. Roger was gone.

"Bye, Roger. I love you."

He turned and saw the singers by the drum, and the crowd outside the arena. He also saw the blades of grass stirring gently in the wind and knew that something special had happened. Last, he looked down at his legs and realized that not only had he walked, he had danced.

Jimmy's body trembled as he lifted his face toward the sky and said a prayer of thanks. As he finished his prayer, someone touched his arm. He turned. Aunt Ruth stood beside him.

"Are you okay?" she asked. She wiped the tears from his cheeks with a damp handkerchief. She had also been crying.

Jimmy nodded. He took a deep breath and swallowed, choking back a sob. He didn't want Aunt Ruth to see him cry. Crying was for children. He was the man of the house now. He had to be a warrior, like his brother.

"He was here, you know," Jimmy said. "Roger. He danced with me. Did you see him?"

Ruth nodded. "Yes, Jimmy, I saw him. We all saw him. He was in the wind… in the grass."

She looked into his eyes, and smiled. "And he was in you, Jimmy. I saw Roger's spirit in you when you danced. In your movements, in the way you held your head. They were the same. His spirit will be with you always…"

"It's in the regalia," Jimmy whispered. "His spirit is in the bustle."

"Not just in the bustle," Ruth corrected. She placed her hand on his chest. "Roger's spirit is here. In your heart. It will always be here. Forever."

She took Jimmy's hand and led him slowly out of the arena. The dancing was over for now. Behind them the grass continued to grow.

The First Tui Tonga

Tonga

THERE FIRST APPEARED on the earth the human offspring of a worm or grub, and the head of the worm became Tui Tonga. His name was Kohai and he was the first Tui Tonga in the world. The descendants of the worm became very numerous.

A large casuarina tree grew on the island of Toonangakava, between the islands of Mataaho and Talakite in the lagoon of Tongatabu. This great casuarina tree reached to the sky, and a god came down from the sky by this great tree. This god was Tangaloa Eitumatupua.

When he came down there was a woman fishing. Her name was Ilaheva and also Vaepopua. The god from the sky came to her and caught her, and they cohabited. Their sleeping place was called Mohenga.

The god ascended to the sky by the big casuarina, but again returned to the woman. They went and slept on the island of Talakite. They overslept and the day dawned. There flew by a tern, called tala, and found them. The tern cried and the god Eitumatupua awoke. He called the woman Ilaheva: "Wake! it is day. The tern has seen us, because we overslept. Wake! It is day." So that island was called Talakite (Tern-saw) in commemoration of the tern finding them. Another island was called Mataaho (Eye-of-day).

The god returned to the sky, but came back to the woman and they co-habited. The woman Ilaheva became pregnant and gave birth to a male child. The woman tended the child on earth, but the god dwelt in the sky. After a time the god returned and asked the woman about their child.

"Ilaheva, what is our child?" Ilaheva answered: "A male child." Then said the god: "His name shall be Ahoeitu (Day-has-dawned). Moreover," the god asked the woman: "Is the soil of your land clay or sand?" The woman replied: "My place is sandy." Then said the god: "Wait until I throw down a piece of clay from the sky, to make a garden for the boy Ahoeitu, and also a yam for the garden of our child."

So the god poured down the mount (near Maufanga, Tongatabu) called Holohiufi (Pour-the-yam), and brought down the yam from the sky. The name of the yam was *heketala* (slip-tern). That was the garden he brought down.

The god returned to the sky, while the woman and child remained on earth, on their land called Popua (the land to the east of Maufanga in Tongatabu, on which rises the hill Holohiufi). The mother and son lived together until the child Ahoeitu was big. Ahoeitu asked his mother: "Vaepopua, who is my father? Tell me so that I may go some time and see him." And the mother told him that his father was in the sky. "What is his name?" the boy asked. "It is Eitumatupua," replied the mother.

The boy grew big and one day he told his mother: "I want to go to the sky, so that I can see my father, but there is nothing for me to go in." His mother instructed him: "Go and climb the great casuarina, for that is the road to the sky; and see you father." She gave him a *tapa* loin cloth and anointed his head with oil. When he was ready, he asked: "How will I know my father, as I am not acquainted with his dwelling place in the sky?" His mother replied: "You will go to the sky and proceed along the big wide road. You will see you father catching pigeons on the mound by the road."

Ahoeitu climbed the great casuarina tree and reached the sky. He went along the road as his mother had directed, found the mound, and saw his father catching pigeons. When his father saw him approaching, he sat down because he was overpowered at seeing his son. Ahoeitu spoke when he saw his father sit down, as if paying respect to him, his own son. That is why he spoke at once to his father, saying: "Lord, stand up. Do not sit down."

The lad went to his father and they pressed noses and cried. Then the father asked him: "Where have you come from?" "I have come from earth, sent by Ilaheva, my mother, to seek you, my father Eitumatupua." His father responded: "Here am I," and he put forth his hand and drew his son's head to him and again they pressed noses and cried. The god was overpowered at the realization that here was his son. Leaving the pigeon catching, they went to Eitumatupua's residence, to the house of Ahoeitu's father. There they had kava and food.

That day the celestial sons of Eitumatupua were having an entertainment. They were playing the game called *sikaulutoa* (played with a reed throwing-stick with a head of toa or casuarina wood). The god sent Ahoeitu to his brothers, saying: "You had better go to the entertainment of your brothers, which they are having on the road in the green (*malae*). So Ahoeitu went and looked on at the game of throwing reeds at the casuarina trunk. The people saw the lad and all gazed at him with one accord. They liked him, because he was very handsome and well formed. All of the people at the entertainment wondered who he was and whence he had come. His brothers were immediately jealous of him.

Some of the people said that they knew that he was the son of Eituma-tupua, who has just come to the sky from the earth. Then all the people of the entertainment knew, and also his brothers knew that this lad was their brother. The brothers were very angry and jealous that it should be said that this strange lad was the son of their father. They, therefore, sprang upon and tore him to pieces, then cooked and ate him. (Some accounts say his flesh was eaten uncooked.) His head was left over, so they threw it among the plants called *hoi*. This caused one kind of *hoi* to become bitter. There is another kind that is sweet. The bitter kind became so because Ahoeitu's head was thrown into it. That kind of *hoi* is not eaten, because it is poisonous.

After a little while Ahoeitu's father, Eitumatupua, said to a woman: "Go, woman, and seek the lad at the entertainment, so that he may eat, lest he become hungry." The woman went at once to the entertainment and asked: "Where is Ahoeitu? The lad is wanted to come and eat." The people answered: "He was here walking around and observing the *sika* game." They searched, but could not find him at the entertainment. So the woman returned to Eitumatupua and reported: "The lad is not to be found."

Eitumatupua suspected that Ahoeitu's brothers had killed the lad. Therefore, he sent a message for them to come. He asked them: "Where is the lad?" and they lied, saying: "We do not know." Then their father said: "Come and vomit." A big wooden bowl was brought. They were told to tickle their throats, so that they would vomit up the flesh of the lad and also the blood; in fact, all the parts they had eaten. They all had their throats tickled and they vomited, filling the wooden bowl.

They were then asked: "Where is his head?" The murderers replied: "We threw it into the bush, into the *hoi* bush." Then the god Eitumatupua sent a messenger to seek the head of Ahoeitu. They also collected his bones and put them together with his head into the bowl and poured water on to the flesh and blood. Then were plucked and brought the leaves of the *nonufiafia* tree. The leaves of this tree placed on a sick person possess the virtue of bringing immediate recovery, even if the person is nigh unto death. So the *nonufiafia*, or the Malay apple (*Eugenia malaccensis*), leaves were covered over the remains of Ahoeitu, and the bowl containing them was taken and put behind the house. They visited the bowl continually and, after a time, poured out the water. The flesh of his body had become compact. They visited the bowl again and again and at last found him sitting up in it.

Then they told Eitumatupua that Ahoeitu was alive, for he was sitting up. They were told to bring him into the house, into the presence of his father. Then Eitumatupua spoke, ordering that the brothers of Ahoeitu, who ate him, be brought. Their father then addressed them.

"You have killed Ahoeitu. He shall descend as the ruler of Tonga, while you, his brothers, remain here." But the brothers loved Ahoeitu, as they had just realized that he was their real brother and had one father with them. Therefore, they pleaded with their father to be allowed to accompany Ahoeitu, a plea which was finally granted.

Ahoeitu returned to earth and became Tui Tonga, the first (divine) Tui Tonga of the world. The Tui Tonga who originated from the offspring of the worm were displaced.

Ahoeitu's brothers followed and joined him. They were Talafale, Matakehe, Maliepo, Tui Loloko, and Tui Folaha. Eitumatupua told Talafale that he was to go to the earth, but that he would not be Tui Tonga, as he was a murderer. He was, however, to be called Tui Faleua. Eitumatupua said that Maliepo and Matakehe were to go to guard the Tui Tonga. Tui Loloko and Tui Folaha were to govern. Should a Tui Tonga die, they were to have charge of all funerary arrangements, just as though it were the funeral of the Tui Langi (King of the Sky), Eitumatupua.

It is the descendants of Ahoeitu, he who was murdered in the sky, who have successively been Tui Tonga. The descendants of Talafale are the Tui Pelehake. The descendants of Matakehe are not known, having become extinct. The descendants of Maliepo are called Lauaki. The descendants of Tui Loloko are still called Tui Loloko.

The Tui Tonga and their families are of the highest rank, because Ahoeitu came originally from the sky. He was the first chief appointed from the sky, the Tui Tonga of all the world of brown people as far as Uea (Wallis island), the ruler of the world. His divine origin makes his descendants real chiefs. In fact, it became customary to ask of one who is proud or thinks himself a chief: "Is he a chief? Did he descend from the sky?"

The son of Ahoeitu was Lolofakangalo, and he became Tui Tonga when Ahoeitu died; and the son of Lolofakangalo was Fangaoneone and he became the third Tui Tonga. The son of Fangaoneone was Lihau, and he was the fourth Tui Tonga. The son of Lihau was Kofutu; he was the fifth Tui Tonga. Kaloa, the son of Kofutu, was the sixth Tui Tonga. His son Mau-hau was the seventh Tui Tonga. Then followed Apuanea, Afulunga, Momo, and Tuitatui. It was Tuitatui who erected the Haamonga-a-Maui, or Burden-of-Maui (the well-known trilithon of Tongatabu).

The following account concerns the Tui Tonga Tuitatui and what he did on the raised platform house (*fale fatataki*). His sister went to him. Her name was Latutama and she was female Tui Tonga. Her attendant followed her to Tuitatui's house. After his sister arrived Tuitatui ascended to his platform and then he began his lies, for, behold, he had desire for his sister to go up to the platform, so that they might have sexual intercourse. From above he said to his sister below: "Here is a vessel coming, a vessel from Haapai very likely; a very large vessel."

And Latutama answered: "Oh, it is your lies." 'It is not my lies,' retorted Tuitatui. "Come up and see the vessel yourself." Then his sister climbed up and sat with him on the platform, while her attendant remained below, and Tuitatui and his sister had sexual intercourse. That was the way of that Tui Tonga, and it was known to the attendant.

They dwelt together at their place of abode in Hahake (eastern Tonga–tabu), the name of which was Heketa (near the modern village of Niutoua). The trilithon called the Burden-of-Maui and Tuitatui's terraced stone tomb are situated there. There was also there the Olotele (or dwelling-place of the Tui Tonga) and the course for the game played by the Tui Tonga with the sikaulutoa (a reed throwing-stick with a head of toa, or casuarina wood).

The sons of Tuitatui were Talaatama and Talaihaapepe. When Tuitatui died, his son Talaatama succeeded him.

Then Talaatama spoke to his brother Talaihaapepe concerning the undesirability of Heketa as a place of residence. Said he: "Let us move and leave this dwelling place, because of our love for our two vessels; lest here they go aground and be broken to pieces, for this is a very bad anchorage."

His brother Talaihaapepe replied: "It is true, but where will we go?" And Talaatama answered: "To Fangalongonoa (*fanga*, shore; *longonoa*, quiet), lest our vessels get wrecked." That is the reason why they moved their vessels to Fangalongonoa and made their dwelling near by. The place where they dwelt was called Mua. They took their two vessels with them. The name of one vessel was 'Akiheuho,' and the name of the other vessel was 'Tongafuesia.'

That is the reason why Laufilitonga dwells at Mua. It is the dwelling place prepared by Talaatama and Talaihaapepe. It was they who first moved from Hahake (referring to Heketa on the northeast coast of Tong-atabu) and it was they who prepared Mua. And all of the Tui Tonga who have succeeded them have dwelt there, even unto Laufilitonga, the present Tui Tonga.

When Talaatama died, he was succeeded by Tui Tonga Nui Tama Tou. This was not a person, but a piece of tou (*Cordia aspera*) wood which Talai-haapepe caused to be set up as Tui Tonga, for he did not himself wish to become Tui Tonga immediately after his brother Talaatama. It being Talaihaapepe's desire that a dummy Tui Tonga be enthroned, the piece of tou wood was dressed in *tapa* and fine mats and duly appointed. A royal wife (*moheofo*), too, was appointed for the Tama Tou. After it had been three years Tui Tonga, the vault stones were cut for the tomb and the Tama Tou was buried in the vault. Then it was pretended that his wife was pregnant, so that she might give birth to a Tui Tonga. The fictitious child was none other than the wily Talaihaapepe, the brother of Talaatama, who was then proclaimed Tui Tonga. A proclamation was made to the people of the land that the Tui Tonga's wife (the moheofo) had given birth to a son whose father was the recently deceased Tui Tonga Tama Tou. The truth of the matter was that it was really Talaihaapepe, who was at once proclaimed Tui Tonga.

These are the things that those three Tui Tonga, Tuitatui, Talaatama and Talaihaapepe, did.

Then followed in succession the Tui Tonga Talakaifaiki, Talafapite, Tui Tonga Maakatoe, Tui Tonga i Puipui, and Havea.

Havea was assassinated. He died and his body was cut in two and his head and chest floated on shore. He was murdered while having his bath, and the name of the expanse of water where he bathed is Tolopona. It is by the roadside at a place called Alakifonua (modern village of Alaki, Tongatabu island). After his head and chest floated on shore, a gallinule (*Porphyrio vitiensis*) called *kalae* came and pecked the face of the dead chief. In consequence that beach was called Houmakalae. When Lufe, the chief of the dead Tui Tonga's mother's family, learned of the king's death, he said: "The Tui Tonga is dead. He has died a bad death, for he is cut in two. Come and kill me and join my buttocks and legs to the Tui Tonga's trunk, so that the corpse may be complete." His relatives obeyed him. They slew him to make the Tui Tonga's body complete and then buried the remains. Thus it was done for the Tui Tonga Havea who was slain.

Another Tui Tonga was Tatafueikimeimua; another was Lomiaetupua; another Tui Tonga was Havea (II.), who was shot by a Fijian man called Tuluvota; he was shot through the head and he died.

Another Tui Tonga was Takalaua. His wife was a woman called Vae. When she was born, she had a head like a pigeon's head, and her parents deserted her. Her father's name was Leasinga and her mother's name was Leamata. They left her at the island of Ata (near Tongatabu), while they sailed to Haapai.

Ahe, the chief of the island of Ata, went down to look at the place where the boat had been beached, and he said, "Perhaps the canoe went last night." He walked about near the place where the canoe landed, and he saw something moving. It was covered with a piece of *tapa*. Behold, a woman had given birth to a girl child and deserted her, because she and her husband disliked the infant and were afraid of their child. Her parents were Leasinga and Leamata. Because she had a head like a pigeon's, they decided to abandon her. The chief of Ata went and unwrapped the moving bundle, and said: "It is a girl with a pigeon's head."

He took her, did the chief of the island, and fed and cared for her, and adopted her as his daughter, and called her Vae. She lived and grew big, and the beak of the bird was shed, and her head, like a pigeon's, was changed. She grew very beautiful, and she was brought to Mua as a wife for the Tui Tonga Takalaua. The woman who was born with the pigeon's head bore children to Takalaua, the Tui Tonga. Her first son was Kauulufonuafekai, and her second son was Moungamotua, and the third was Melinoatonga, and the fourth was Lotauai, and the fifth was Latutoevave; that child talked from his mother's womb. Those were all Vaelaveamata s children to the Tui Tonga Takalaua.

Vae had five male children, some were grown up and some were still young when their father Takalaua the Tui Tonga was murdered. His children, Kauulufonuafekai, Moungamotua, and his other sons, were very angry over their father's murder, and they said: "Let us go and seek the two murderers."

They made war on Tongatabu and conquered it, and the two murderers fled to Eua. And Kauulufonuafekai and his people entered a vessel and pursued the two murderers, whose names were Tamasia and Malofafa, to Eua. They fought the people of Eua, and conquered them, and the two fugitives fled to Haapai. Kauulufonuafekai and his brothers sailed in pursuit to Haapai. Haapai was waiting ready for war with the avengers, and they fought and Haapai was conquered. The two murderers then fled to Vavau, and Kauulufonuafekai pursued, and conquered Vavau. Again the two murderers fled, this time to Niuatoputapu. Kauulufonuafekai pursued, and fought and conquered Niuatoputapu. Thence the two murderers fled to Niuafoou. Still they were pursued. Kauulufonuafekai fought and conquered Niuafoou also. The two murderers again fled, but whither? Kauulufonuafekai went to Futuna to seek them, and fought and conquered Futuna.

Kauulufonuafekai had spoken in the vessel to his brothers and warriors: "Do you think my bravery is my own, or is it a god (*faahikehe*) that blesses me and makes me brave?" And his brothers, warriors, and people in the vessel all answered: "What man in the world is strong in his own body, and brave in his own mind, if not blessed by a god? You are brave and strong, because a god blesses you. That is the reason why you are strong and brave." Kauulufonuafekai replied: "I am not brave because of the help of a god. My bravery is the bravery of a man." Then his brothers said to him: "It is not. You are brave and strong from a god." Kauulufonuafekai replied: "I will divide my body into two parts when we go and fight at Futuna. I will leave my back for the god to bless and protect, while I guard my front myself, and if I am wounded in front, it will be a sign that I am brave and strong because a god blesses me; but should I be wounded in my back, it will be a sign that it is my own bravery, and that a god has nothing to do with it."

They went and fought the Futunans, who attempted to drive the Tongan vessel away. Then the Tongans in turn chased the Futunans on the sea and drove their warriors inland. But they were fighting for nothing, for the murderers were not at Futuna; they were at Uea. Thus Futuna was fought for nought, as it was thought that the murderers were there. They fought Futuna and the warriors from the vessel of Kauulufonuafekai, chased the people of Futuna, and caused them to flee. Kauulufonuafekai ran up the road in pursuit. A man in ambush speared Kauulufonuafekai through his back into his chest. The chief turned and clubbed the man who had speared him. And Kauulufonuafekai, returning, said: "I told you. Don't you say that I am brave through a god. Here I am wounded in the place that was left for the god to guard. I am not wounded from my front. My wound came from my back, which I left for him to guard; therefore I am not brave and strong from any god. It is my own bravery and the strength of this world. Come and we will go on board the vessel."

They went on board and sailed, but one of their brothers, Lotauai, was left behind at Futuna, for the people of Futuna had captured him. They did not kill him, but they let him live.

The vessel of Kauulufonuafekai sailed, and after voyaging for five days Kauulufonuafekai said: "Let us return to Futuna, because I have love for my brother, who is detained there; and my wound is itching, because it wants to fight." So they returned and Futuna saw the vessel coming, and the

Futunans spoke to the lad, the brother of the chief, whom they had taken and they called his name: "Lotauai! the vessel is returning; the brave chief is coming again." And Lotauai, the lad that they held, said: "I told you that the chief would return with his warriors. It is for love of me, because you hold me prisoner. Had the chief and his warriors come for love of me, and come and found me dead, you having killed me, Futuna would indeed have died (been exterminated). But I am alive, so no one will be killed and you will not he punished."

Then the people of Futuna said to the lad: "Lotauai, what can we do to live!" They were afraid that the chief would come and kill them.

The chief's brother said: "Come and put on fine mats (*ngafingafi*), and pluck leaves from the chestnut (*ifi*) tree and put them round your neck. That is the thing to do to live, for it is the recognized Tongan way of begging mercy. Come and sit with bowed head at my back, while I sit in front, so that the chief that you are afraid of will see that I am still alive. That is the means by which you will live. Also prepare for his reception; cook food, and bring kava. After we have pacified the chief by sueing for mercy, then bring the kava and food, then we (Tongans) will drink it and g-o away." The vessel arrived and the people of the land came with loin mats (*ngafingafi*) round them, and chestnut leaves around their necks. And came the brave chief, and found his young brother still alive. And his young brother told the chief: "The people of the land are sueing for mercy, to live, because they are afraid." Kauulufonuafekai replied: "They live, and I am thankful that my brother still lives."

Then the kava and food were brought by the people of Futuna. They had kava with the chief and made friends. Then Kauulufonuafekai gave a Tongan boat to the people of Futuna, and said: "I have no wealth (*tapa* and mats) to give you, but here is a present for you, that I give you: Any vessel coming from Tonga is yours, but do not kill its people. All goods that are brought in it from Tonga are to be your present. That is my payment to you, because you allowed my brother, whom you took, to live, and I received a wound from you in the fight. That is why I give you the goods from the Tongan vessels." Hence comes the meaning of the expression: 'Vete fakafutuna, to seize like the Futunans.'

Then the vessel left to go and seek the murderers in Fiji. Kauulufonuafekai went and fought the different islands of Fiji, but the two murderers were not found in Fiji. They returned from Fiji and went to Uea, and fought and conquered Uea.

The two murderers were not able to flee from Uea, but were overtaken there, for they were prisoners held for sacrifice. When the Uea people came to sue for mercy, after they were conquered in the fight, the two murderers came with them. Kauulufonuafekai did not know the faces of the two murderers, but he knew their names. When the Uea people came to sue for pardon they all had long hair; but the two murderers, wlho came with them, had short hair which was just beginning to grow, their heads having been shaven. The chief knew them by their short hair, as all the Ueans had long hair. The chief called: "Tamasia!" for that was the name of one. He answered: "I am here." Then the chief called out the name of the other one: "Malofafa!" and he answered: "I am here." The chief then said: "What a long time you have been. Thanks to the god that you fled and that you are still alive. Come, you two Tongan men, we will sail for Tonga."

The vessel conveyed the two men to Tonga. There Kauulufonuafekai commanded that the two murderers should be brought and cut up alive as food for Takalaua's funeral kava. They were brought and cut up, and after they were cut up, their pieces were collected and burned in the fire.

It is said that Kauulufonuafekai had had their teeth pulled out at Uea, and then he had thrown them a string of dry kava, that he had worn round his neck most of the time since he had left Tonga. Upon throwing the dry kava to them, he told them to chew it. They tried to chew, with their bleeding gums, but were not able in the least to chew. After a very long, long time of thus giving them pain, from the morning of one day to the next day, Kauulufonuafekai told them to enter the vessel for them to leave for Tonga.

Takalaua, the Tui Tonga that was murdered, was buried, and Kauulufonuafekai was appointed Tui Tonga. He, the child of the woman with the pigeon's head, was Tui Tonga. The brother of Kauulufonuafekai, Moungamotua, was appointed Tui Haatakalaua (tui, king; haa, family; Takalaua, his father's name) and he went and lived at 'Kauhalalalo' in Fonuamotu near Loamanu (at Mua, Tongatabu), in order to rule from there the land. And he was to be called Tui Haatakalaua. Moungamotua was the first Tui Haatakalaua, the brother of Kauulufonuafekai, the Tui Tonga.

Kauulufonuafekai was the first to arrange that the apaapa, or master of ceremonies in the kava ring, should sit at a distance, not near to him, because he was afraid of being murdered, as his father, the Tui Tonga Takalaua, was murdered. Therefore the kava ring was formed so that the people in it sat at a distance from the chief. He instructed some of his brothers to sit at his back to guard him lest he should be murdered. The name given to those brothers that sat behind him, was huhueiki (huhu, to suspect; eiki, chief).

Another Tui Tonga was Vakafuhu; another was Puipuifatu; another was called Kauulufonua; another Tui Tonga was Tapuosi I., and another Tui Tonga was Uluakimata I., (Telea). His vessel was called Lomipeau (lomi, keep under; peau, waves). That was the ship that often went to Uea to cut and load stones for the terraces (paepae) of the royal tombs. Paepae o Telea is the name of the graveyard of the Tui Tonga Telea. Fatafehi he was the son of Telea; his mother was Mataukipa. Another Tui Tonga was Tapuosi II., and another Tui Tonga was Uluakimata II. His sons were the Tui Tonga Tui Pulotu I. and his brother, Tokemoana. The latter was appointed Tui Haauluakimata (tui, ruler; haa, family; Uluaki-mata, his father's name). Their sister Sinaitakala, was the female Tui Tonga; Fatani was their brother, also Faleafu, all of one father.

The son of Tui Pulotu was Fakanaanaa and he was Tui Tonga; another Tui Tonga was Tui Pulotu II.; and another Tui Tonga was Maulupekotofa. The son of Pau was Fatafehi Fuanunuiava, and the son of Fuanu-nuiava was Laufilitonga, the Tui Tonga that is alive in the world. That is the end of the Tui Tonga. The old Tui Tonga, the offspring of the Worm, are gone. The list of female Tui Tonga is not given, but only the list of the male Tui Tonga.

Here are their names in order: (1) Ahoeitu, (2) Lolofakangalo, (3) Fangaoneone, (4) Lihau, (5) Kofutu, (6) Kaloa, (7) Mauhau, (8) Apuanea, (9) Afulunga, (10) Momo, (11) Tuitatui, (12) Talaatama, (13) Tui Tonga Nui Tama Tou, (14) Talaihaapepe, (15) Talakaifaiki, (16) Talafapite, (17) Tui Tonga Maakatoe, (18) Tui Tonga i Puipui, (19) Havea I., (20) Tatafueikimeimua, (21) Lomiaetupua, (22) Havea II., (23) Takalaua, (24) Kauulufonuafekai, (25) Vakafuhu, (26) Puipuifatu, (27) Kauulufonua, (28) Tapuosi I., (29) Uluakimata I. (Telea), (30) Fatafehi, (31) Tapuosi II., (32) Uluakimata II., (33) Tui Pulotu I., (34) Fakanaanaa, (35) Tui Pulotu II., (36), Pau, (37) Maulupekotofa, (38) Fatafehi Fuanunuiava, (39) Laufilitonga.

The Tui Tonga Uluakimata, he who was called Telea, had many wives. One of his wives was Talafaiva. She was said, by the people of Mua who saw her, to be the most beautiful of women, for there was not another woman in the world so beautiful as she – she was unsurpassed. She was also a very great chief, for both her parents were chiefs. There was not another woman of such high rank, or so beautiful, or so well formed. She was the only woman called by all the world fakatouato (chief by both parents). Talafaiva brought fifty other wives (fokonofo) to Telea. The second wife of Telea was Nanasilapaha, and she brought fifty other wives to Telea. The third wife of Telea was Mataukipa and she brought one hundred other wives to Telea.

Mataukipa was the wife that always received the tail of the fish, and rump of the pig every day. "Why is the head of the fish, and the head of the pig, and the middle cut of the fish, and back of the pig always taken to Talafaiva and Nanasilapaha?" This was the question which troubled Mataukipa, so she decided to confer with her father. "I will go to my father, Kauulufonuahuo (head-of-the-land-cultivators), and ask him if it is good or bad this thing that the Tui Tonga is doing to me." So she carried her child on her back and went to the place called Mataliku, where Kauulufonuahuo dwelt. He was an industrious gardener, growing yams, bananas, *kape* (a root like the taro), taro, *ufilei* (a small sweet yam), *hoi* (fruit tree), and large bread fruit trees.

Her father saw his daughter coming, and went to greet her. "You have come. Who is with you?" His daughter, Mataukipa, answered: "Only we two." Then the father asked: "Why was there no one to come with you? Why only you two? Are you angry?" and Mataukipa replied: "No!" Her father said: "You stay here while I go and prepare some food, then I will take you back to Mua."

They had their kava prepared twice. Then the people went and prepared the oven and baked yams and a pig. Afterwards the daughter spoke to her father: "Why are the Tui Tonga's wishes like that?" she asked, and her father inquired: "How?" His daughter replied: "When our fish and pig is brought, the two women always eat the head and back of the pig, and the head and middle part of the fish, and I always get the tail of the fish and the rump of the pig."

The father of the woman laughed, and made this reply to the woman: "And are you grieved at it?" The woman answered: "I am grieved at it."

The father replied to the woman: "Don't be grieved. Your portion is the rump of the pig and the tail of the fish, because the land will come eventually to your children. They will be rulers."

The woman's mind was at peace after her father's explanation as to why she always was given the tail of the fish and rump of the pig, but before that she was jealous of the two women, and thought: "The chief loves the two women more than me." Consequently she was jealous.

They returned to her place and the woman was content, because of the explanation of her father, and they all lived together. When the Tui Tonga Telea died, the woman Mataukipa had a son called Fatafehi, and a daughter called Sinaitakala-i-langi-leka. Fatafehi was appointed Tui Tonga and Sinaitakala became female Tui Tonga. Thus what Mataukipa's father had told her came true; her son became Tui Tonga and her daughter female Tui Tonga and her descendants were Tui Tonga, the last being Laufili-tonga.

The Tui Tonga Telea dwelt in the bush, because he preferred it, and was more at home there, especially on the weather shore of Vavau. Each of his dwelling places and sleeping places at the weather shore of Vavau has a name, and each place is named after the thing he did at that place.

Telea and his wife Talafaiva came and dwelt on the island of Euakafa. Their house was built on the top of the mountain, and a reed fence was erected round the place. There was a big tree called *foui* growing there, and Talafaiva told Telea: "It is not a nice tree. You had better have it cut down." But Telea answered: "Oh, leave it. It is all right."

They had dwelt there for some time, when a man called Lolomanaia came from a place called Makave (in Vavau island). His vessel landed at the place where Telea dwelt, because Lolomanaia was in love with Talafaiva. He ascended and waited till it was dark. When it was dark he went to the place of Telea. He pushed the gate to see if it was closed or open. When he pushed it he found that it was closed, and he tried and tried to find some way to get inside the fence. He went round outside of the fence and found the big tree that Talafaiva had told Telea to cut down. He climbed the tree and thereby gained access to the enclosure. He slept with the woman Talafaiva, the wife of Tui Tonga Telea. After they had slept he tattooed a black mark on her abdomen, to annoy Telea, for him (Telea) to know that he (Lolomanaia) had committed adultery with his wife.

Telea slept with Talafaiva in the day, and he saw what had been done to his wife's abdomen. Telea asked her: "Who, Talafaiva, has tattooed your stomach?" Talafaiva replied: "It is true! Chief, will you pardon me? It was Lolomanaia, who came to me. Don't you be angry, because you know I told you, on the day that the fence was made for our enclosure, to cut down the big foui tree, because the tree was badly placed, and you said to leave it. The man climbed up it and came to me. His name was Lolomanaia." Telea was very wroth and arose and went out. He called his man servant by name. "Uka! come here, for me to tell you. Go and beat Talafaiva. She has had intercourse with a man."

Uka took a club, and went with it to her. Telea did not know that he was really going to kill Talafaiva. He only meant that he should beat her. After Telea's wrath cooled, he found that Uka had really killed Talafaiva, and that she was dead. The beautiful and well formed woman was dead. Uka came to report to Telea, and Telea asked: "Have you beaten Tala-faiva?" and Uka, the man servant, answered: "I have beaten her." The chief asked: "And how is she?" Uka replied: "She is dead," and Telea asked: "Is she quite dead?" and Uka replied: "She is quite dead." Again Telea asked: "Is she quite dead, my wife Talafaiva?" and Uka made reply: "She is quite dead."

Telea was grief stricken: "Oh! oh! my misplaced confidence! I did not mean that you should really go and kill her. I only meant for you to beat her a little because I was angry. I really loved my wife, whom you have killed. You are an old fool!" Telea went and wept over Talafaiva, who was really dead, for a night and a day.

Then Telea the Tui Tonga said: "We will go and cut stones for a vault for Talafaiva." So they went and cut the stones for the vault, and made the vault. Then Talafaiva was buried in the vault. The grave yard with the vault standing in it is on Euakafa island. The big casuarina tree at the graveyard is called Talafaiva. That is all about Talafaiva, the wife of Telea, about her ways and the meaning of what we hear about her. After Talafaiva's death Telea went to Tonga (Tongatabu) and lived there and died there.

The stones for the vault of this Tui Tonga Telea were cut at Uea, and the terrace stones were cut there also. This is the Tui Tonga that owned the vessel called Lomipeau, and this is the vessel that brought the stones for his vault and the terrace round it.

Collected by Edward Winslow Gifford

The Origin of the Magellan Clouds

Tonga

ONCE UPON A TIME there was living at Vaini, in Tongatabu, a great chief called Maafu, whose descendants are living to this day. It was Maafu's habit to bathe every evening in a water hole known as Tufatakale, so called because close by there lived at one time a man and a woman whose names were Tufa and Kale. Maafu, being a cleanly person, used to take a piece of coconut husk with him as a sort of scrubbing brush. After he had finished with it, he always threw it on a flat stone at the side of the water hole.

Living in the immediate vicinity was a huge female lizard, who, after Maafu's evening bath, always came and swallowed the piece of coconut husk. Time went on and a most astonishing thing occurred. The lizard gave birth to twins – not lizards – but to all appearance, shape, and size, human beings. She called them Maafu Toka and Maafu Lele.

Years rolled by and the two boys had almost reached manhood, when one day they went to their mother and said: "We are tired of living here by ourselves. Tell us who our father is and we will go to him and live with him." The old lizard realized that it was of no use trying to keep hidden any longer two such fine, healthy, and happy youths. So with a sad heart she rubbed them all over with scented oil, dressed their hair and hung sweet smelling garlands of flowers and leaves round their necks. Her directions were that they were to take a certain road and at the end of it, where it opened out into the town, they would see a large house, outside of which a number of people would be sitting drinking kava. They were not to go up at once, but were to watch and see to whom the greatest respect was being paid. Then, after the kava drinking was over, they were to approach the person to whom the greatest respect had been shown. That person would be Maafu, their father.

The boys bade their mother farewell. By carrying out her instructions they soon found the house and saw the kava drinking ceremony. It did not take them long to recognize their father, but they waited at a little distance until the kava-drinking was finished. Then they approached the party. While they were drawing near, the people turned to each other and asked who the two young men of such handsome appearance were. But none knew them and then conjectures were made as to whether a canoe had arrived from Haapai or Vavau.

The two lads went straight to where Maafu was sitting and when close to him, sat down cross-legged on the ground in a respectful manner and waited for him to take notice of them. After an interval Maafu addressed them: "Young men, we do not know who you are, nor whence you have come. Please inform us." Their only reply was that he was their father. He did not dispute the fact; indeed, he did not even ask who was their mother, because he was afraid that she would want to come and live with them too.

So the boys grew up to manhood with Maafu, but, owing to their unnatural origin, they were the very incarnation of mischief. Besides they were fleeter of foot than ordinary mortals and excelled in all athletic exercises, especially spear throwing. Although on one occasion they broke the leg of one of Maafu's nephews, this did not worry Maafu so much as the fact that they used him (Maafu) as a target for their spear throwing, each endeavoring to throw his spear as close as possible without hitting the old man. Maafu at last determined to get rid of the two youths, but in such a manner that he did not appear to be the perpetrator of the deed.

With this end in view Maafu called the lads to him one morning and explained that he wanted them to get him some water from a certain water hole called Atavahea, which was far away. They were to get the water at high noon, as it was sweetest then. He did not tell them, however, that there was a huge duck living there and that persons going to get water at high noon had never returned.

It was just noon when the boys reached their destination. One stood on the bank, while the other waded into the pond with the empty coconut shells. Hardly had he reached the middle, when the sky became overcast and a rushing sound like a roaring wind was heard. Glancing up, the lad in the water saw a huge duck making straight for him. With admirable quickness he ducked and, as the bird passed over him, his fist shot out with lightning rapidity and with such force as to break the duck's wing. Then the lad seized the duck by the neck and held it up to his brother's view, calling out: "Here is a fine duck for Maafu." The boys filled the coconut shells with water and returned to Vaini. It was in no pleasant frame of mind that old Maafu witnessed their return. Nevertheless, he hid his feelings and thanked them for the water and the bird.

Next morning Maafu sent the boys to another water hole called Muihatafa, which lay in an opposite direction to Atavahea, and from which they were to bring him water. The water, however, must be obtained from the bottom of the pond, as water from that part of the pond had an especially fine flavor. Maafu did not tell the lads that in this water hole there lurked a huge parrot fish. Straightway the lads went and on their arrival at the water hole, one waded in and dived down to the bottom of the pond. Hardly had he reached the bottom when he saw an enormous parrot fish (*humu*) rushing at him with gaping jaws. Without a moment's hesitation, he thrust his arm down its throat. Rising to the surface he held it up to his brother's view, exclaiming: "Here is a fine fish for Maafu."

The two young men returned to Vaini with the water and the fish. When Maafu saw them approaching he lost all patience and said angrily to them: "I am tired and disgusted with the way you have been behaving yourselves. You have been most mischievous, breaking my nephew's leg' and endangering my life on several occasions. I have come to the conclusion to give you each a plantation (*api*) far from this town, so that you will not be able to worry us any further."

The lads, realizing what Maafu's feelings were, replied: "Do not trouble to do that. We will go of our own accord and so far away that you cannot reach us. We will take our duck and our fish and go up to the sky and live there. Should you want to see us, you will only have to look up on a dark night, and if we want to see you, we will only have to look down." So the lads went to the sky and are there to this day. Navigators know that should they steer their course by the stars Maafu Toka and Maafu Lele, it will bring them to Vaini. These stars are known to astronomy as the Magellan clouds.

Collected by Edward Winslow Gifford

Scarface

Blackfeet Nation, Native American

Origin of the Medicine Lodge

1

IN THE EARLIEST TIMES there was no war. All the tribes were at peace. In those days there was a man who had a daughter, a very beautiful girl. Many young men wanted to marry her, but every time she was asked, she only shook her head and said she did not want a husband.

"How is this?" asked her father. "Some of these young men are rich, handsome, and brave."

"Why should I marry?" replied the girl. "I have a rich father and mother. Our lodge is good. The parfleches are never empty. There are plenty of tanned robes and soft furs for winter. Why worry me, then?"

The Raven Bearers held a dance; they all dressed carefully and wore their ornaments, and each one tried to dance the best. Afterwards some of them asked for this girl, but still she said no. Then the Bulls, the Kit-foxes, and others of the *I-kun-uh'-kah-tsi* held their dances, and all those who were rich, many great warriors, asked this man for his daughter, but to every one of them she said no. Then her father was angry, and said: "Why, now, this way? All the best men have asked for you, and still you say no. I believe you have a secret lover."

"Ah!" said her mother. "What shame for us should a child be born and our daughter still unmarried!" "Father! mother!" replied the girl, "pity me. I have no secret lover, but now hear the truth. That Above Person, the Sun, told me, 'Do not marry any of those men, for you are mine; thus you shall be happy, and live to great age'; and again he said, 'Take heed. You must not marry. You are mine.'"

"Ah!" replied her father. "It must always be as he says." And they talked no more about it.

There was a poor young man, very poor. His father, mother, all his relations, had gone to the Sand Hills. He had no lodge, no wife to tan his robes or sew his moccasins. He stopped in one lodge today, and tomorrow he ate and slept in another; thus he lived. He was a good-looking young man, except that on his cheek he had a scar, and his clothes were always old and poor.

After those dances some of the young men met this poor Scarface, and they laughed at him, and said: "Why don't you ask that girl to marry you? You are so rich and handsome!" Scarface did not laugh; he replied: "Ah! I will do as you say. I will go and ask her." All the young men thought this was funny. They laughed a great deal. But Scarface went down by the river. He waited by the river, where the women came to get water, and by and by the girl came along. "Girl," he said, "wait. I want to speak with you. Not as a designing person do I ask you, but openly where the Sun looks down, and all may see."

"Speak then," said the girl.

"I have seen the days," continued the young man "You have refused those who are young, and rich, and brave. Now, today, they laughed and said to me, 'Why do you not ask her?' I am poor, very poor. I have no lodge, no food, no clothes, no robes and warm furs. I have no relations; all have gone to the Sand Hills; yet, now, today, I ask you, take pity, be my wife."

The girl hid her face in her robe and brushed the ground with the point of her moccasin, back and forth, back and forth; for she was thinking. After a time she said: "True. I have refused all those rich young men, yet now the poor one asks me, and I am glad. I will be your wife, and my people will be happy. You are poor, but it does not matter. My father will give you dogs. My mother will make us a lodge. My people will give us robes and furs. You will be poor no longer."

Then the young man was happy, and he started to kiss her, but she held him back, and said: "Wait! The Sun has spoken to me. He says I may not marry; that I belong to him. He says if I listen to him, I shall live to great age. But now I say: Go to the Sun. Tell him, 'She whom you spoke with heeds your words. She has never done wrong, but now she wants to marry. I want her for my wife.' Ask him to take that scar from your face. That will be his sign. I will know he is pleased. But if he refuses, or if you fail to find his lodge, then do not return to me."

"Oh!" cried the young man, "at first your words were good. I was glad. But now it is dark. My heart is dead. Where is that far-off lodge? where the trail, which no one yet has travelled?"

"Take courage, take courage!" said the girl; and she went to her lodge.

II

Scarface was very sad. He sat down and covered his head with his robe and tried to think what to do. After a while he got up, and went to an old woman who had been kind to him. "Pity me," he said. "I am very poor. I am going away now on a long journey. Make me some moccasins."

"Where are you going?" asked the old woman. "There is no war; we are very peaceful here."

"I do not know where I shall go," replied Scarface. "I am in trouble, but I cannot tell you now what it is."

So the old woman made him some moccasins, seven pairs, with parfleche soles, and also she gave him a sack of food, — pemmican of berries, pounded meat, and dried back fat; for this old woman had a good heart. She liked the young man.

All alone, and with a sad heart, he climbed the bluffs and stopped to take a last look at the camp. He wondered if he would ever see his sweetheart and the people again. "*Hai'-yu!* Pity me, O Sun," he prayed, and turning, he started to find the trail.

For many days he travelled on, over great prairies, along timbered rivers and among the mountains, and every day his sack of food grew lighter; but he saved it as much as he could, and ate berries, and roots, and sometimes he killed an animal of some kind. One night he stopped by the home of a wolf. "*Hai-yah!*" said that one; "what is my brother doing so far from home?"

"Ah!" replied Scarface, "I seek the place where the Sun lives; I am sent to speak with him."

"I have travelled far," said the wolf. "I know all the prairies, the valleys, and the mountains, but I have never seen the Sun's home. Wait; I know one who is very wise. Ask the bear. He may tell you."

The next day the man travelled on again, stopping now and then to pick a few berries, and when night came he arrived at the bear's lodge.

"Where is your home?" asked the bear. "Why are you travelling alone, my brother?"

"Help me! Pity me!" replied the young man; "because of her words I seek the Sun. I go to ask him for her."

"I know not where he stops," replied the bear. "I have travelled by many rivers, and I know the mountains, yet I have never seen his lodge. There is some one beyond, that striped-face, who is very smart. Go and ask him."

The badger was in his hole. Stooping over, the young man shouted: "Oh, cunning striped-face! Oh, generous animal! I wish to speak with you."

"What do you want?" said the badger, poking his head out of the hole.

"I want to find the Sun's home," replied Scarface. "I want to speak with him."

"I do not know where he lives," replied the badger. "I never travel very far. Over there in the timber is a wolverine. He is always travelling around, and is of much knowledge. Maybe he can tell you."

Then Scarface went to the woods and looked all around for the wolverine, but could not find him. So he sat down to rest *"Hai'-yu! Hai'-yu!"* he cried. "Wolverine, take pity on me. My food is gone, my moccasins worn out. Now I must die."

"What is it, my brother?" he heard, and looking around, he saw the animal sitting near.

"She whom I would marry," said Scarface, "belongs to the Sun; I am trying to find where he lives, to ask him for her."

"Ah!" said the wolverine. "I know where he lives. Wait; it is nearly night. Tomorrow I will show you the trail to the big water. He lives on the other side of it."

Early in the morning, the wolverine showed him the trail, and Scarface followed it until he came to the water's edge. He looked out over it, and his heart almost stopped. Never before had any one seen such a big water. The other side could not be seen, and there was no end to it. Scarface sat down on the shore. His food was all gone, his moccasins worn out. His heart was sick. "I cannot cross this big water," he said. "I cannot return to the people. Here, by this water, I shall die."

Not so. His Helpers were there. Two swans came swimming up to the shore. "Why have you come here?" they asked him. "What are you doing? It is very far to the place where your people live."

"I am here," replied Scarface, "to die. Far away, in my country, is a beautiful girl. I want to marry her, but she belongs to the Sun. So I started to find him and ask for her. I have travelled many days. My food is gone. I cannot go back. I cannot cross this big water, so I am going to die."

"No," said the swans; "it shall not be so. Across this water is the home of that Above Person. Get on our backs, and we will take you there."

Scarface quickly arose. He felt strong again. He waded out into the water and lay down on the swans' backs, and they started off. Very deep and black is that fearful water. Strange people live there, mighty animals which often seize and drown a person. The swans carried him safely, and took him to the other side. Here was a broad hard trail leading back from the water's edge.

"Kyi" said the swans. "You are now close to the Sun's lodge. Follow that trail, and you will soon see it."

III

Scarface started up the trail, and pretty soon he came to some beautiful things, lying in it. There was a war shirt, a shield, and a bow and arrows. He had never seen such pretty weapons; but he did not touch them. He walked carefully around them, and travelled on. A little way further on, he met a young man, the handsomest person he had ever seen. His hair was very long, and he wore clothing made of strange skins. His moccasins were sewn with bright coloured feathers. The young man said to him, "Did you see some weapons lying on the trail?"

"Yes," replied Scarface; "I saw them."

"But did you not touch them?" asked the young man.

"No; I thought some one had left them there, so I did not take them."

"You are not a thief," said the young man. "What is your name?"

"Scarface."

"Where are you going?"

"To the Sun."

"My name," said the young man, "is A-pi-su'-ahts. The Sun is my father; come, I will take you to our lodge. My father is not now at home, but he will come in at night."

Soon they came to the lodge. It was very large and handsome; strange medicine animals were painted on it. Behind, on a tripod, were strange weapons and beautiful clothes – the Sun's. Scarface was ashamed to go in, but Morning Star said, "Do not be afraid, my friend; we are glad you have come."

They entered. One person was sitting there, Ko-ko-mik'-e-is, the Sun's wife, Morning Star's mother. She spoke to Scarface kindly, and gave him something to eat. "Why have you come so far from your people?" she asked.

Then Scarface told her about the beautiful girl he wanted to marry. "She belongs to the Sun," he said. "I have come to ask him for her."

When it was time for the Sun to come home, the Moon hid Scarface under a pile of robes. As soon as the Sun got to the doorway, he stopped, and said, "I smell a person."

"Yes, father," said Morning Star; "a good young man has come to see you. I know he is good, for he found some of my things on the trail and did not touch them."

Then Scarface came out from under the robes, and the Sun entered and sat down. "I am glad you have come to our lodge," he said. "Stay with us as long as you think best. My son is lonesome sometimes; be his friend."

The next day the Moon called Scarface out of the lodge, and said to him: "Go with Morning Star where you please, but never hunt near that big water; do not let him go there. It is the home of great birds which have long sharp bills; they kill people. I have had many sons, but these birds have killed them all. Morning Star is the only one left."

So Scarface stayed there a long time and hunted with Morning Star. One day they came near the water, and saw the big birds.

"Come," said Morning Star; "let us go and kill those birds."

"No, no!" replied Scarface; "we must not go there. Those are very terrible birds; they will kill us."

Morning Star would not listen. He ran towards the water, and Scarface followed. He knew that he must kill the birds and save the boy. If not, the Sun would be angry and might kill him. He ran ahead and met the birds, which were coming towards him to fight, and killed every one of them with his spear: not one was left. Then the young men cut off their heads, and carried them home. Morning Star's mother was glad when they told her what they had done, and showed her the birds' heads. She cried, and called Scarface "my son." When the Sun came home at night, she told him about it, and he too was glad. "My son," he said to Scarface, "I will not forget what you have this day done for me. Tell me now, what can I do for you?"

"*Hai'-yu*" replied Scarface. "*Hai'-yu*, pity me. I am here to ask you for that girl. I want to marry her. I asked her, and she was glad; but she says you own her, that you told her not to marry."

"What you say is true," said the Sun. "I have watched the days, so I know it. Now, then, I give her to you; she is yours. I am glad she has been wise. I know she has never done wrong. The Sun pities good women. They shall live a long time. So shall their husbands and children. Now you will soon go home. Let me tell you something. Be wise and listen: I am the only chief. Everything is mine. I made the earth, the mountains, prairies, rivers, and forests. I made the people and all the animals. This is why I say I alone am the chief. I can never die. True, the winter makes me old and weak, but every summer I grow young again."

Then said the Sun: "What one of all animals is smartest? The raven is, for he always finds food. He is never hungry. Which one of all the animals is most *Nat-o'-ye*? The buffalo is. Of all animals, I like him best. He is for the people. He is your food and your shelter. What part of his body is sacred? The tongue is. That is mine. What else is sacred? Berries are. They are mine too. Come with me and see the world." He took Scarface to the edge of the sky, and they looked down and saw it. It is round and flat, and all around the edge is the jumping-off place [or walls straight down]. Then said the Sun: "When any man is sick or in danger, his wife may promise to build me a lodge, if he recovers. If the woman is pure and true, then I will be pleased and help the man. But if she is bad, if she lies, then I will be angry. You shall build the lodge like the world, round, with walls, but first you must build a sweat house of a hundred sticks. It shall be like the sky [a hemisphere], and half of it shall be painted red. That is me. The other half you will paint black. That is the night."

Further said the Sun: "Which is the best, the heart or the brain? The brain is. The heart often lies, the brain never." Then he told Scarface everything about making the Medicine Lodge, and when he had finished, he rubbed a powerful medicine on his face, and the scar disappeared. Then he gave him two raven feathers, saying: "These are the sign for the girl, that I give her to you. They must always be worn by the husband of the woman who builds a Medicine Lodge."

The young man was now ready to return home. Morning Star and the Sun gave him many beautiful presents. The Moon cried and kissed him, and called him "my son." Then the Sun showed him the short trail. It was the Wolf Road [Milky Way]. He followed it, and soon reached the ground.

IV

It was a very hot day. All the lodge skins were raised, and the people sat in the shade. There was a chief, a very generous man, and all day long people kept coming to his lodge to feast and smoke with him. Early in the morning this chief saw a person sitting out on a butte near by, close wrapped in his robe. The chief's friends came and went, the sun reached the middle, and passed on, down towards the mountains. Still this person did not move. When it was almost night, the chief said: "Why does that person sit there so long? The heat has been strong, but he has never eaten nor drunk. He may be a stranger; go and ask him in."

So some young men went up to him, and said: "Why do you sit here in the great heat all day? Come to the shade of the lodges. The chief asks you to feast with him."

Then the person arose and threw off his robe, and they were surprised. He wore beautiful clothes. His bow, shield, and other weapons were of strange make. But they knew his face, although the scar was gone, and they ran ahead, shouting, "The scarface poor young man has come. He is poor no longer. The scar on his face is gone."

All the people rushed out to see him. "Where have you been?" they asked. "Where did you get all these pretty things?" He did not answer. There in the crowd stood that young woman; and taking the two raven feathers from his head, he gave them to her, and said: "The trail was very long, and I nearly died, but by those Helpers, I found his lodge. He is glad. He sends these feathers to you. They are the sign."

Great was her gladness then. They were married, and made the first Medicine Lodge, as the Sun had said. The Sun was glad. He gave them great age. They were never sick. When they were very old, one morning, their children said: "Awake! Rise and eat." They did not move. In the night, in sleep, without pain, their shadows had departed for the Sand Hills.

Collected by George Bird Grinnell

Origin of the Medicine Pipe

Blackfeet Nation, Native American

THUNDER – YOU HAVE HEARD HIM, he is everywhere. He roars in the mountains, he shouts far out on the prairie. He strikes the high rocks, and they fall to pieces. He hits a tree, and it is broken in slivers. He strikes the people, and they die. He is bad. He does not like the towering cliff, the standing tree, or living man. He likes to strike and crush them to the ground. Yes! yes! Of all he is most powerful; he is the one most strong. But I have not told you the worst: he sometimes steals women.

Long ago, almost in the beginning, a man and his wife were sitting in their lodge, when Thunder came and struck them. The man was not killed. At first he was as if dead, but after a while he lived again, and rising looked about him. His wife was not there. "Oh, well," he thought, "she has gone to get some water or wood," and he sat a while; but when the sun had under-disappeared, he went out and inquired about her of the people. No one had seen her. He searched throughout the camp, but did not find her. Then he knew that Thunder had stolen her, and he went out on the hills alone and mourned.

When morning came, he rose and wandered far away, and he asked all the animals he met if they knew where Thunder lived. They laughed, and would not answer. The Wolf said: "Do you think we would seek the home of the only one we fear? He is our only danger. From all others we can run away; but from him there is no running. He strikes, and there we lie. Turn back! go home! Do not look for the dwelling-place of that dreadful one." But the man kept on, and travelled far away. Now he came to a lodge, – a queer lodge, for it was made of stone; just like any other lodge, only it was made of stone. Here lived the Raven chief. The man entered.

"Welcome, my friend," said the chief of Ravens. "Sit down, sit down." And food was placed before him. Then, when he had finished eating, the Raven said, "Why have you come?"

"Thunder has stolen my wife," replied the man. "I seek his dwelling-place that I may find her."

"Would you dare enter the lodge of that dreadful person?" asked the Raven. "He lives close by here. His lodge is of stone, like this; and hanging there, within, are eyes, – the eyes of those he has killed or stolen. He has taken out their eyes and hung them in his lodge. Now, then, dare you enter there?"

"No," replied the man. "I am afraid. What man could look at such dreadful things and live?"

"No person can," said the Raven. "There is but one old Thunder fears. There is but one he cannot kill. It is I, it is the Ravens. Now I will give you medicine, and he shall not harm you. You shall enter there, and seek among those eyes your wife's; and if you find them, tell that Thunder why you came, and make him give them to you. Here, now, is a raven's wing. Just point it at him, and he will start back quick; but if that fail, take this. It is an arrow, and the shaft is made of elk-horn. Take this, I say, and shoot it through the lodge."

"Why make a fool of me?" the poor man asked. "My heart is sad. I am crying." And he covered his head with his robe, and wept.

"Oh," said the Raven, "you do not believe me. Come out, come out, and I will make you believe." When they stood outside, the Raven asked, "Is the home of your people far?"

"A great distance," said the man.

"Can you tell how many days you have travelled?"

"No," he replied, "my heart is sad. I did not count the days. The berries have grown and ripened since I left."

"Can you see your camp from here?" asked the Raven.

The man did not speak. Then the Raven rubbed some medicine on his eyes and said, "Look!" The man looked, and saw the camp. It was close. He saw the people. He saw the smoke rising from the lodges.

"Now you will believe," said the Raven. "Take now the arrow and the wing, and go and get your wife."

So the man took these things, and went to the Thunder's lodge. He entered and sat down by the door-way. The Thunder sat within and looked at him with awful eyes. But the man looked above, and saw those many pairs of eyes. Among them were those of his wife.

"Why have you come?" said the Thunder in a fearful voice.

"I seek my wife," the man replied, "whom you have stolen. There hang her eyes."

"No man can enter my lodge and live," said the Thunder; and he rose to strike him. Then the man pointed the raven wing at the Thunder, and he fell back on his couch and shivered. But he soon recovered, and rose again. Then the man fitted the elk-horn arrow to his bow, and shot it through the lodge of rock; right through that lodge of rock it pierced a jagged hole, and let the sunlight in.

"Hold," said the Thunder. "Stop; you are the stronger. Yours the great medicine. You shall have your wife. Take down her eyes." Then the man cut the string that held them, and immediately his wife stood beside him.

"Now," said the Thunder, "you know me. I am of great power. I live here in summer, but when winter comes, I go far south. I go south with the birds. Here is my pipe. It is medicine. Take it, and keep it. Now, when I first come in the spring, you shall fill and light this pipe, and you shall pray to me, you and the people. For I bring the rain which makes the berries large and ripe. I bring the rain which makes all things grow, and for this you shall pray to me, you and all the people."

Thus the people got the first medicine pipe. It was long ago.

Collected by George Bird Grinnell

Imitate

Shane Hawk, Cheyenne and
Arapaho Tribes, Native American

"MAYBE I OUGHTA stop reading you these creepy stories before bed," I said as I tousled Tate's bowl cut. "You get too scared." His eyes glistened with anxious anticipation.

"But Dad, I think there really is something down there!" Tate held his red Pendleton blanket close to his chubby cheeks. His room was small, about ten by ten, and decorated by all his favorite things: action heroes, baseball players, comic books, you name it.

He was at that age that still demanded bedtime stories, but he was getting more curious about my knack for horror. For the past two weeks I'd read him stories that scared me as a kid. They scared me, but also excited me, made my mind race and create different worlds.

"Okay, okay. I'll check for you. You say it's under the bed?" I asked, chewing on my last bit of beef jerky. My arthritic knees were not forgiving as I made my way down to the laminate wood floor. I knocked over my reusable water bottle like the clumsy fool I am. Luckily, the cap was tight and none of the cucumber and electrolyte water mixture spilled out on to Tate's bedroom floor. That would've been yet another headache.

Shoes, missing socks, and toys riddled the space beneath his bed. I already knew I wouldn't find anything, so I pushed his stuff aside and acted like I was searching. "Nope, I don't see a soul!" I exclaimed as I held on to his bed to lift myself up to see Tate. My lower back was aching, but I didn't want to take any more of those damned pain meds.

"Dad, you barely checked! Can't you look longer and really check for the monster under my bed?" Tate asked with puppy-dog eyes. A heavy sigh left my lips, and my shoulders sank.

"Sure, Tatey. Why not? I'll check again. Extra-good this time." Went back to my hands and knees, but this time I lay out on to my stomach. It had been a while since my last pushup and getting down quickly like that felt like a doozy. I was still facing the floor and noticed a board where the laminate was peeling. Crap, I knew I shouldn't have been a cheapskate with the goddamned flooring. The wife would never let me hear the end of it.

Looking up, I saw something new beneath the bed, some lump of mass. What in the world? A red blanket with the same patterns as Tate's blanket covered the thing. I lay there frozen as it rolled my way and unwrapped itself. It was my son. Almost a replica except his eyes; they were two smoldering charcoal briquettes with ash falling away. My own eyes must've resembled two harvest moons and my open jaw a cavern. I couldn't move. The boy was frightened and bit his lip the same way Tate had just a moment ago. He then moved his lips, but the words formed inside of my head. He told me something scary was above his mattress.

"Did you find anything?" Tate asked from atop his bed.

"Um, I don't kn—" I tried to say as I crept back up to look at my son, but he and his blanket vanished. What the fuck? I immediately shot back down to look beneath Tate's bed. Nothing.

"Goodnight, Daddy," Tate said from the doorway, holding his red blanket and sucking on his thumb. He then closed the door. I scrambled to reach my feet, knees and lower back cracking as if I had driftwood for bones. Yelling, I swung the door open, but a dark, peaceful home said nothing back.

"Honey?" My wife, Meli, called out in confused worry. She jolted toward me and asked if everything was alright. The words wouldn't come out. I yanked her arm toward Tate's bedroom. Flicked the light switch. Tate was fast asleep.

"There was a clone, or something, of Tate underneath his bed just now!" I said, wiping sweat beads from my forehead. "He told me to look under his bed for a monster, you know, the scary bedtime stories. I knelt and a carbon copy of Tate was under his bed, saying there was a monster on top of his bed." I realized I must've sounded like a goddamn madman after seeing the look on my wife's face.

"You using cactus again?" She asked as she leaned into me to examine my eyes. "Mm, dilated pupils, bloodshot whites. Please don't tell me—"

"No, no. I haven't in years. Scout's honor." My tongue-in-cheek mention of Boy Scouts didn't fit the tone of this conversation. I hated the Boy Scouts and their Order of the Arrow. Wasn't enough to steal our land, but the WASPs also tried to imitate our ceremonies, our regalia, and call it their own. My aging brain reminded me to return from my stupid mental tangent. My body tensed as I crossed my arms.

My wife raised an eyebrow, cocked her head, and rubbed her arm absently.

"If you say so. I assume you didn't get much sleep on the couch last night. Hopefully you get more shuteye tonight. I'm going to bed, Dak."

I opened my mouth to say something, but my tongue wouldn't cooperate. All I could do was watch her walk to our bedroom and click the door shut behind her. The couch would be my bed for the third night in a row. Before crashing, I peeked again into Tate's room. There he was, sound asleep beneath the glow-in-the-dark stars strewn across his ceiling.

* * *

The sunrise peeked through the back patio door and filled the living room with its warm, soothing light. Well, soothing when you want to be awake. I regretted not sleeping on the other end to face west.

My wife was already off to work and didn't leave a note for the third morning. Couldn't blame her. I acknowledged my misstep, my mistake. Regret filled the crater in my chest, spilling off the sides, and I'd have to work extra hard to bandaid the situation. As soon as it could fade and be in our rearview, the sooner we could be a solid family again.

My unshaven face and unkempt hair glared back at me in the mirror next to the fridge. A reminder of how fucked I felt. Another wrinkle here, another gray hair there. More salt than pepper. I wondered what my dad would think of my choice of haircut. Wow, Dakota. Trying to imitate the white man? My hair was down to my ribs until my forties. After a while, I cut it all off to be more modern. But what was 'modern?' Was it erasing the richness of the past for the dullness of the future? A past filled with beautiful ornaments, character, and belonging traded for a future filled with grayscale details, imitations, and a different belonging? The thought of growing my hair out again became a serious consideration.

Grabbing the milk and Froot Loops, I made Tate some of his typical breakfast. Yes, he could have done it himself, but I was already awake.

"Tate, breakfast! Come get it while it's hot!" I thought it was funny to make him think I slaved over some eggs, bacon, and toast when I just tossed some sugar-coated circles into a bowl of sugar-coated liquid.

Rubbing his eyes, Tate entered the kitchen in his Ninja Turtle pajamas, and offered a gigantic yawn. He then walked up to the counter and looked at the bowl of cereal.

"I don't like cereal, Dad."

My expression was incredulous.

"You always eat this stuff, don't you?" I asked, rubbing my stubbled chin.

"I don't want Froot Loops. Can I have some of that?" Tate asked with his finger pointed in the coffee pot's direction.

"Coffee? You're nine!"

"Dad, I'm ten. I wanna try some coffee," Tate said as he pushed the cereal bowl toward me and crossed his arms.

Math calculations came into my brain. Sure, I was the idiot.

"Yeah, ten, I knew that. Just messing with you, son," I said as I ate a spoonful of Toucan Sam's colorful rings. "I mean, yeah, I could let you try a cup. It'll stunt your growth, though. Don't you wanna be tall like me someday?"

Heck, I needed some caffeine myself. My headache felt like someone was slowly turning a corkscrew between my eyes.

Water, grounds, flipped the switch.

If the caffeine made Tate crazy, that would be his teachers' problem. My wife changed her work schedule a week prior. She worked earlier to get home in time for Tate to come home on the bus. This meant I barely saw her as my shifts for Adam's Pest Control were from noon until around eight o'clock.

Poured the coffee into two mugs and slid one over to Tate.

"Cream, sugar?" I asked.

"No, Daddy. Just black."

It took me years to enjoy a fresh cup of joe with nothing added. This was too weird. I offered Tate a fake smile and narrowed my eyes as he sipped from his mug. After the first few test sips, he gulped the entire mug.

This is way too hot, even for me. What is wrong with this kid? I thought as only a half-ounce of the scalding liquid entered my mouth at a time.

"That was good. So tasty. Can I have another cup, Dad?" Tate asked as he jingled his mug about as if asking for spare change downtown.

"Erm. Glad you liked it, Tate. But one cup is enough for a boy your size. And your age."

"Okay, fine. Do we have any peanut butter in the cupboard, Daddy?" Tate asked, a smile slowly stretching across his face.

My chest tingled, and I wondered if my lack of sleep was affecting my senses, molding the world before me into something unrecognizable.

"I'm sorry, Tate. Dad hasn't been sleeping too good. Did you say you wanted peanut butter?" I asked, rubbing the sleep from my eyes.

Beep, beep. Tate's school bus arrived. The microwave's green digital clock agreed with the time the bus driver, Mr. Delphan, arrived each morning. Time had passed like a flash. I could've sworn the clock read 5:33AM when I first entered the kitchen.

Shook my damn head as if to knock something loose and told Tate to run and put on his school uniform. My wallet was on the floor beside the couch, and I grabbed a five-dollar bill from it for Tate's lunch. As I looked up with the lunch money in hand, Tate was at the door, fully dressed and with combed hair. How could he have done that? I kissed the top of his head, handed him the bill, and walked him outside.

"Have a great day, son. I'll see ya tonight!" Mr. Delphan shifted into drive despite Tate still walking back to an open seat. We exchanged our final waves goodbye.

I turned around and stared into the grass parallel to the cracked sidewalk while scratching my stubbled cheek. Tate was allergic to peanut butter.

* * *

Was I losing it? Does excessive use of cactus have long-term effects on the brain? I assumed the hallucinations were only temporary. The eeriness sent daddy longlegs down my arms. I spread my hands out on the kitchen's island as I leaned downward and concentrated on my breath. Dr. Langston showed me these exercises for when my world was crushing inward.

Dakota, my tribe. Became my name, too. Always hated the Anglo name my mom gave me, Jabin. Supposed to mean "perceptive" or something. Assumed my dad always hated it too because he loved calling me Dak. I think he loved me more when I drank, but not too sure.

Spiced rum and peyote riddled my past. The drink I took up from my father and enjoyed it as early as my second year of high school. Well, until I dropped out the following year. I joined a small group of Dakota men who suffered from sauce addiction and wanted to go on spiritual journeys to find themselves again, their purpose. Peyote was a Native's hallucinogen of choice. It was used to obtain 'enlightenment,' or have life-changing experiences with what they called greater spirits, entities.

My cucumber water went almost everywhere with me. Yeah, it was bitter, but I wanted to work on my health and fix a decade of dehydration. Work on it for Meli, for us. I drank rum like it was a fountain soda. Staying hydrated made me feel better overall, and I kicked the bottle down the stairway to hell. An actual battle won by an Indian? Something to celebrate.

However, it had been years since my last dosing of cactus. I still couldn't grasp how I tripped enough the previous night to visualize two Tates, or at least one imitation. The hallucination was so vivid, so real. Sure, I was sleep deprived. The couch had annoying, firm bars in between each cushion to keep its structure. Didn't help my chronic back pain. And I saw things in the past when I lacked sleep, but this?

And what the hell was up with Tate that next morning? Froot Loops were his favorite cereal. Coffee? Peanut butter? Maybe it was a subconscious rebellion against me and Meli's doomed marriage. Maybe he knew what I did and was acting out.

* * *

"They call it a mischief," Rogers said. Sweat beads were crowding his hairless upper lip.

"Call what a mischief?" I asked as I covered my mouth with my forearm.

"A damned group of rats. You know, like a group of crows is a 'murder,' an army of frogs, a gaggle of geese," he responded with an appropriate air of intelligence. "Say, are you cool to handle this one yourself? We got double booked, and I've gotta get to the Henderson residence for squirrels in their attic. They said they'd tip me big under the table if I get it done fast."

"No problem, bud." I raised my hand toward his work truck to hint for him to leave. We often worked in teams, but it was okay. The job seemed easy. "Have fun with that," I chuckled, remembering the Hendersons as a crazy family. The head of the household had a screw or two loose. He offered me a half-ass salute, which made me laugh even more. Rogers was in the U.S. Army for some time, and I suspected his sense of decorum faded along with his respect for war. As he walked away, the large red and yellow logo for Adam's Pest Control on his coveralls bounced with each step.

I swigged my cucumber water and the back of my tongue picked up more bitterness than usual. Blegh.

Maybe the rat nest's musky stench in the air penetrated my taste buds at that exact moment. The rats smelled like death despite the piss and shit I assumed lined the entire crawlspace.

After an initial inspection, I discovered two backfills and three burrows. I filled them with soil from the homeowner's failed garden. To remove the breeding nests, I first had to scare the rats with bright light because they're nocturnal. I twisted two high-beam lamps and threw them into the crawlspace. Nothing skittered. No sign of rats scurrying away.

Went back to my truck to place heavy-duty welding gloves on both of my hands. I figured if I crawled under that house and got ambushed by rats, they'd have a hard time biting through the gloves. Slung my work sack over my shoulder, which carried traps, bait, and thick plastic baggies for critter corpses.

With body aches from my feet through my torso and up to my neck, I knelt to enter the crawlspace. If I'd still been drinking, there's no way I'd be able to fit into that skinny stretch under the house with my gut. By this time, I'd sloughed off all excess weight.

For my protection, I also put on some safety glasses and a head covering. Cobwebs, random nails, and loosened splinters populated these tight spaces. Didn't want my coveralls to get too jacked up, so I used a small tarp under my chest to separate me from the grime.

My eyes caught small spirals swirling in the home's foundation. At that moment, I figured the heat was getting to me and I regretted not taking an extra swig of my cucumber water before crawling inward to avoid any dehydration. I also should have worn something to protect my nose from the awful smells. The stench was overwhelming and forced me to gag only minutes into the crawlspace.

An echoing screech pierced my ears and didn't sound too far off. The screech was atypical for the rats I'd exterminated in the past. Imaginary spiders once again crawled up my arms.

The lamps I tossed into the crawlspace covered much of the area but left some corners dark. Those corners radiated the type of darkness so black your eyes see patterns and figures that aren't really there. Or were they? I saw more of those tiny spirals in one particular corner. Some spirals emitted a faint green light that grew stronger with my every movement.

With my limited space, I moved on to my back and fumbled in my pocket for my mini flashlight. Clicked the flashlight and tilted my head backward. My gaped mouth let out a shrill scream. I flipped back on to my stomach.

Convulsing. Bubbling. Popping. There were seven, maybe eight, rats all melted together. Their mouths opened in unison and another deep-toned screech infiltrated my eardrums. All three of my lights went out and a resonant humming filled my head. My body didn't thrash about, and I didn't make for the exit. I lay there on my stomach in an all-consuming stupor.

The melted pile of half-dead rats gave off a fetid stench of death which strong-armed my nostrils. I dealt with rat carcasses often, but the stinging scent was overpowering. Remnants of my breakfast shot out of my throat with little effort. With bile coating my lips, a forced smile grew, and my eyes became lost in the shifting spirals of various colors.

There was a large movement at the center of the rat pile. It was pulsating much more than before but jutting out toward me. It wriggled and let out somber cries. A creature broke through the melted rats.

It was my son.

He was squeezing out of the sickly mess of rats. A jelly-like substance smeared across his face. Could only guess it was a mixture of the rats' innards. By the time he was halfway out of the rats, I scooted my body that much further to the exit. I wondered if my coworker sprayed chemical compounds in there before he left. Was I suffering brain damage and hallucinating? Dread flooded my veins and wormed its way into my brain, paralyzing me in a state pinned between fight or flight.

"Daddy. It hurts…" Tate said. Or the thing that looked like Tate. It was as if he was crawling through a glue trap I often set for rats. So slow. The colored spirals were dancing around him and, in an instant, fell away, vanished. Steam came off his body like the morning coffee pot we shared.

Then his skin.

It was as if his old skin got caught on a nail, stretched out, and reached its ultimate point of tension before ripping away.

I remembered seeing a time-lapse video showing a tarantula leaving its old skin behind for a new set of furry feelers. It was simultaneously captivating and revolting. But this, this was only revolting. Dry heaves developed into more vomiting up my breakfast. The Tate-thing crawled through it anyway.

With every move it made, I slid back an equal distance.

The new skin was an older Tate, a teenaged Tate. Still slim, but with long, dark hair and peach fuzz across his upper lip.

"Dad, just let me go. You can't save me." His voice was deeper, more pronounced. He coughed and black slime spilled from his mouth.

Quiet, angry curse words swam under my breath as I struggled to keep my distance and get the hell out of there.

I reached the entryway of the crawlspace and sprang to my feet, knee joints cracking like thunder. The moonless night startled me. I started this job around three o'clock. How long was I inside there? It felt like minutes. I watched the entryway for the Tate creature to follow. It didn't.

"Whoa, buddy! Easy there," Rogers warned as I spun around and almost knocked him over. "Did ya finish up the house?"

Though it was a brisk night, sweat seeped from my armpits and forehead. A quick swipe of my brow only got a small portion of it. I must have looked manic, though I attempted my best to keep it cool.

"Yeah, yep. Caught about seven or eight rats. Pretty beat. Ready to go home."

"Well, you've gotta get your lights and equipment all packed up." Rogers pointed toward the crawlspace illuminated by jaundiced light.

Thanked Rogers and waved him off to have a good night.

Frayed nerves. An empty stomach. A throbbing migraine. Was time to get the hell home and unwind. Eat dinner and erase the day with some rest.

* * *

"What do ya wanna drink?" I asked while face deep in the fridge.

"Apple juice," Tate said with marked enthusiasm.

"Apple ju—what?" I semi-closed the fridge door to question his choice. Was it happening again? Tate despised apple juice.

Our eyes met. He held a determined expression and gave a languid tilt to his head. There were those eyes again. Two burning discs of charcoal, this time twisting beneath creased brows. My neck hair stiffened as a chill swam up my spine.

"I said what I said, Daddy."

His articulate emphasis made me swallow a gulp of air. Down went reality and up came fantasy. This wasn't real. This wasn't real. This wasn't real.

"Say, Meli, what would you like to drink, honey?" I called out, eyes still staring into the Tate-thing's scorched black discs. An awkward silence stilted the air. As I repeated myself, her voice rang out.

"Already got my wine. Come on, you two. Let's go." There was a clear tone of irritation on her tongue.

My body resembled a marble statue as I gazed into the hypnotic green swirls floating around the Tate-thing's face.

"What's taking you so long?" Meli asked.

His eyes shifting interrupted the mesmeric reverie. Those beautiful brown halos I cherished since the day he was born returned to his face.

"Let's eat, Dad," Tate said as he pulled my hand, leading me away from the fridge and toward the dining room table.

At the table, forks and knives sawed through meat, scraping against the plates. We always put a good helping of greens on Tate's plate to entice him to like vegetables. It was always a battle to get him to enjoy anything with nutrition. Tonight, he was eating the steamed broccoli without a complaint or shoving it to the side far away from the venison.

"I'm impressed, baby. Normally, you hate broccoli!" Meli said with a smirk. She leaned in to tousle his hair and added, "My boy is growing up, he's changing."

Tate turned toward her and smiled while chewing. As Meli looked down at her plate for her next bite, Tate swung his head toward me. His innocent smile stretched out into a wide grin. The ends of his mouth almost reached the smoldering black circles, exposing his crooked baby teeth. A millipede poked out of his mouth, tiny legs churning about.

I slammed my palm on the table with so much force, my water bottle fell over.

"Goddammit! I'm sick of your shit!" Unchewed venison flung from my lips. "Who are you? What have you done with my son?" My heart was thumping, blood rushed through my arms and neck. The Tate-thing's eyes went back to normal, no millipede in sight. His face twisted into a shallow cry, then a wail.

"What the hell is wrong with you, Dak? Come here, honey." Meli reached out for the Tate-thing and it joined in her arms for a motherly embrace. She was hugging and consoling that... thing. Disgusting.

I opened and closed my mouth without a word. My fingers repeatedly curled into fists. With trembling hands, I rubbed the back of my neck as if trying to get a stain out of it.

"I'm taking him to bed. Dak, you need to calm the fuc—Sorry, baby. Mommy doesn't mean to curse. Come on." As she got up to leave, the Tate-thing looked to me. It lifted its chin and covered its mouth to conceal a giggle. Its eyes were black holes, two collapsed stars pulling me into its event horizon. At that moment, all hope escaped me. The only thing I could sense was an impending doom. After I had shut it out for so long, the darkness was creeping back in again.

* * *

Yard work was always tiring. Hated digging ditches. Used to on the rez for pennies on the dollar. Thank the Wakan deities I escaped that place and settled down here in Anoka. The smell of moist earth comforted me. Reminded me of my mom. She'd make pottery from clay. Made beaded jewelry by hand, too, and sold it at the powwows. The monotony of yard work often drove my mind into those distant memories. Those ghosts.

The darkness bled back in, and thoughts of her dying of diabetes plagued my mind. Those deep regrets of not visiting her, not calling. Was old enough to be out on my own, have my own problems. She always rubbed that worry stone for me, but I never returned the favor. I was a shit son. A shit husband.

Knew Meli went to her sister's house when I read her note that next morning. She didn't spell it out, but I knew. Said she couldn't handle me now, especially with everything involving that blonde woman. What we did. What I did. Was like carrying around a bison on my shoulders, the guilt.

My back could only break so much. Had weak knees and all. If a coroner splayed me open, right here, right now, he'd find minimal connective tissue. Where's all the sinew? You got bone against bone here, my friend. Yeah, yeah. Should've been healthier, should've stayed fit. All of life's 'should haves' and 'could haves' filling that guilt bison strapped to my shoulders.

My drifting mind allowed me to dig deeper and deeper and ignore all the energy I was using up. Swigged my water bottle; the electrolytes coated my esophagus and spread out to my limbs. A rejuvenation. I aimed for six feet.

* * *

First the birdshot, then the slug. Could fit more shells in there, but I only wanted two. Pumped my Mossberg to load the birdshot shell. Was the dangling dreamcatcher charm on my shotgun corny? Probably, yeah. But I knew my boomstick sent whatever was on the receiving end to a dream state somewhere. Most of the time it was a deer.

Oh, yeah, it was squirming alright. That was no son of mine. It cried and cried. I drove four stakes into the earth, one for each limb. Tied each down with a Palomar knot. Learned that one from the Scouts.

Wasn't in the mood to have perfect trigger discipline. Held the barrel between the thing's eyes, slid it down to its throat, then its torso. My finger teased us both by twitching.

Do it. Do it. Do it.

Big, black saucer eyes stared up at me. It writhed in anger as the shotgun barrel explored its alien body.

Planted my feet, firmed my shoulder, and released.

The tiny lead balls tore holes across its chest and face. The craters revealed a stringy black interior. The substance that made up its body composition was akin to a black, melted mozzarella. A collective of minuscule, sticky strands created a strong individual entity.

Those green spirals danced around its head. It was putting on a show. It was trying to distract me from what I set out to do.

Next was the slug shell.

The thing immediately went slack, all taut muscle fibers released.

I created a cavity within its chest cavity. It was beautiful. There was no heart, no vital organs blown to smithereens. Just a black mucus, thick as molasses. It oozed out of the hollowed basin. This was not desecration. This creation was far from holy, far from sacred. It was unknowable. An altered version of my son, Tate. It was demonic, or something of the sort.

Ripped out the stakes, which held it down to the loam soil, and tossed the knotted ropes aside. Does it deserve a proper burial like us? It was not of this world, yet here I was giving it a proper burial. Was I burying the idea of my son? This monster took him over and killed him. Was it my duty to remove him from this planet? To throw him into that hole and salt the earth? I'd banish this evil entity from my life.

Packed the earth down, a mixture of wet, heavy clay, and light topsoil. Threw in shovelfuls of deadened leaves from the black maples for good measure.

Sudden emotion inundated me like a monstrous tidal wave. I was heaving. Then I was whimpering. Then I leapt in anger and smashed the shovel on the burial mound. Smashed and smashed until my back gave out and rolled over sobbing.

Why? Why did it take my son? Fatherhood kept me going. It was one of the few things that made me get out of bed, to not wish for that darkness to take me.

The back patio door creaked.

Wiped my tears and the snot trailing down my nose.

It was Tate.

And he had those awful, black eyes.

"Killed the real son?" it asked.

The darkness emitting from his eyes drew me in. Swallowed me.

Whole

Somto Ihezue, Igbo

FIRST, WAS ISI.

In the forests of the Jardim, the scent of jasmines wafting on a breeze, wrapping the air in a sweetness. The rosemary, the basil, the sage, a cascade of fragrance so sharp, it cuts into the morning dew. That was Isi. She was the warm smell of your mother's house, of freshly baked bread, fir trees, and the fields where the goats once grazed. She was the places you hid as a child, the wardrobes, a tang of tobacco and old smoke trapped in the shelves. And she was more. The colliding aroma of salt and stone as the oceans met the mountains, the stench of bodies stacked after a war. The catching of it all, bold, consuming, lightning in your nostrils, that was her. Isi was the first breath drawn ... she was the last, and Abali murdered her like she was nothing.

He had stormed the Jardim, burning it to the ground. The rabbits, their fur ash with soot, had braved the flames to huddle alongside the antelopes in the Tembe river. With Isi guiding them, some of the forest creatures made it out of the carnage, the same could not be said for the trees. Crackling in the fire, the moisture in their leaves resisted for a while; in the end, they too became ash. The smell of burning bark drowning her, Isi watched as columns of thick grey smoke blotted the sky, the forest – her home, a charred memory, and all she had left was fury. With each breath, it raged.

Face to face with Abali, she found a figure draped in shadows. It pooled on the earth where he stood, warping and twisting about him. Brandishing our father's ax, its steel glistening in the fire, Isi broke through the smoke, at him. In tendrils, the shadows lunged from around Abali, moving like phantom fingers and materializing into solid dark spears. Dodging and weaving through the mass of sharp-edged blackness, Isi edged forward. When a spear flew too close, slicing her arm, she did not stop, she moved, on a journey, like rain. Leaping into the air, she brought her ax down on Abali, and as through a ghost, it phased past him, striking earth. Isi looked up and two figures wearing Abali's form stared down at her. From the two came four, and from the four, a hundred. Abali multiplied on, a legion strong. Unbowed, Isi conjured a fetor; toxic as it was putrid, and she struck, the wretched smell ripping the clones from the inside out. Yet, the more she slew, the more they grew. One spirit against an army of darkness, Isi fell.

"Where are the others?" As his spawns collected back into him, Abali's voice, which had started as a hundred storms, ended, a wind caught in the trees.

"How – how are you here?" Isi made to stand and collapsed back into the dirt. Racing across her skin, the lacerations from the spears weren't healing. Imbued with dark energy, they festered. "You were bound for all eternity – how —"

"Where are they?"

Pain seething through her, Isi picked herself up, and this time, she stood.

"You will fail." She searched the shadows for the eyes lurking within, and when she found them, she held them. "You failed before… you will fail again."

"Tell me." Abali streamed his hands through her braids. "What memory do you have of me?"

Eyes shut like in prayer, Isi whispered to the skies, "Uda, brother, night gathers."

As the words left her lips, Abali took hold of her, dangling her off the floor. Reaching into her face, he peeled off her nose. In his hand, Isi became incense and scattered to the wind.

* * *

We did not remember, but we knew. Of Abali, who sought to cloak the world in shadows. For our father's light stood in the way, Abali waged war on him. In a battle spanning lifetimes, our father, Nkpuru Obi, aided by The First Ones, imprisoned Abali, his shackles fortified by the very life force of The First. With others like Abali waxing ever stronger and bent on destroying him, our father split his soul, and we were born – the five, the one. But this we did not know, as their worship trickled, their temples turned to rubble, The First Ones crept into the earth and slept. In their slumber, Abali broke free.

* * *

I willed my eyes open. Unstirring, my body stayed, like a boulder had rolled over it. I could see the moon and her craters, the other worlds dancing around the sun. The stars, billions of miles away, came into focus. They weren't twinkles anymore. Trembling fingers grazed my skin and I heaved, remembering to breathe, my limbs remembering how to move. I turned to find Uda staring at me, and I remembered.

"Isi," I said, "I dreamt – I saw her —"

"I heard her." Uda looked away, into the horizon. "Night gathers."

Squeezing into each other, we sat in the cold. In all the centuries we had walked earths, we never knew death, and loss was a distant thing. The feeling in my chest, like my heart was cast in bronze, I did not understand it. And there was something, a wave, washing over me, and when I tried to stand, it came for me, again and again. A tear ran down my face and Uda caught it, bringing his forehead to mine. On his face, I saw all he wanted to say – but couldn't. So we sat, in the night, in the shards of what could only be our grief.

We had not seen Isi, not in a while. Father's soul-splitting demanded we stayed apart, ensuring we were never destroyed all at once. For as long as one of us endured, we all did. Isi may have perished, but she'd return, perhaps in a millennium, a different life. We weren't certain, but the roses still held their fragrance. We knew we'd see her again. And in that knowledge, we knew Abali wouldn't stop until he killed us all.

Despite what the splitting insisted, we lived together, Uda and I. Centuries ago, he had called to me, his voice an ailing song, pain etched into words. I followed it to the spirit city of Nnewi – our birthplace. Uda had been its keeper. From the city gates to the streets, up to the Temple of Names, bodies littered the grounds, blood tracing down their ears.

Hidden in the old crypts, I found my brother.

"Anya – I – I didn't mean to – they wouldn't stop – the voices – they wouldn't stop," he cried, hands clasped over his ears. "Anya, make it stop – please – make it go away."

A thunderbolt. When you were eight and the rains poured for a month. Your nana's singing, a spell putting you to sleep. The hush after the rains fell their last. Dawn, calling. Your brother's laughter as he swung from an udara branch. A flutter of sparrows. The snap of the branch. A silence. Your father's unheard prayers, then he went to war and died screaming. Your child's first words, their last. Hearing it all, was to hear my brother, it was hearing Uda.

I had taken him with me, back to my home in the Manjero valley. The voices followed – of the living, the dying, the gone. They came in his sleep, in his every waking moment. But this time, he had me.

The illusions I planted in his mind gave him glimpses of peace and, while the façade eventually faded, for those fleeting quiet moments, Uda was grateful.

Only a matter of time before Abali found us, we fled the valley. I could not see him, not entirely. Abali blended into the dark corners of existence like a shadow on an ill-lit street. Our sister, Mmetuta, had become keeper of Nnewi in Uda's stead. Though abandoned, the energy from our birth still lived in its trees, in the rocks, in the places where the rivers tore. Mmetuta had taken up the mantle of preserving it. To her, we headed. She would have been the first to know of Isi, she would have felt it, the death, and all the suffering that came with it, like a spider on her skin. Miles and miles apart, I could feel her hand in mine, knowing, comforting.

The last of us, Detu-ire, was to join us in Nnewi and there we'd take our stand against the darkness. Banding together made finding and eradicating us easier. But we were without a choice. Alone, none of us could rival Abali.

The road to Nnewi was daunting on Uda. Journeying through cities and villages, the noise, the people – hives of bees nesting in his head. So we moved under the cover of night. It calmed Uda, but it slowed us. It calmed me too. I wasn't as precarious as Uda, but I could see everything, everyone. Their souls, their yesterday and fragments of their tomorrow. I could see the tiniest ant in the deepest burrow, the sun like it was blazing right before me. And before a raindrop hit the earth, I saw it. It took its toll on all of us, what we carried within. As one, as our father, we had been stronger. Apart, our strength also became our weakness. For Uda, it wasn't just a weakness anymore, it was torture.

We all gathered at the end of each century. It was unwise, us being together, but on that day, the pain and the loneliness faded away. And Uda would sing, like a bird that found the wind. His voice, the soothing of a babbling stream, strong, like racing chariots. With Isi, Mmetuta, Detu-ire, and I, all of us, together, Uda came alive. Camping around a fire, the stories would fill what little space was between us: stories of the mortals, some erratic sprite Detu-ire had fallen for; up until they tried to kill him. Mmetuta and all her wars, Isi… and her forests. Reclused in the valley, Uda and I never had much to tell, so we listened, we laughed and we were content. Now, we were gathering again, to battle, and without Isi.

Halfway across the shallow pass of Nkata, trudging behind me, Uda let out a gasp. It was a silent thing, and it shook the hills. Hands over his ears, he caved to his knees, head bobbing to and fro. I ran to him.

"Anya." Uda folded into me. "Detu-ire, he screams…" He tightened his hands around his ears, any tighter and he'd crush in his skull.

My sight traveling through miles of cities, oceans, and wastelands, I went to Detu-ire. When I found him, I found shaded hands clamped on his jaw, forcing his mouth open. Detu-ire flailed, and he tore, and it wasn't enough. Reaching into his mouth, the hands ripped out my brother's tongue. They let go of him, and Detu-ire clanged to the ground, a steel corpse, mouth ajar.

"No!"

Abali heard me. Out of the shadows writhing around him, he stepped into the light. I had seen a thousand lifetimes, watched the first of men crawl out the mud. I had seen all facets of existence, all things mighty and small. Never had I seen a thing like Abali. His skin, a starless night, his hair, locs of clouds sprawling to the floor; and in his eyes, fire was catching. With the texts of the dark religion spiraled in ethereal whorls across his body, Abali was a myth burning alive. We retained not a sliver of father's memories, so we had never seen him, his true form. And without the memories, the words spoken to mold us were lost to the ages, and without the words, we could never merge back into one. All we knew of our past life, The First Ones told us. Still entrapped by his being, Abali lunged at me and I scampered back, my sight racing fast into me as I fell into Uda's arms.

"Detu-ire?" Uda asked, a sadness shrouding him. He knew.

"We must hurry." I stood, gazing into the void. "I see – I see him now."

It was worse. I not only saw Abali, he saw me. Every pebble, color, and path I saw, he saw too, like he was carved into me. With him watching us through my eyes, the journey to Nnewi became a nightmare. And there was Detu-ire. Isi's death had come in a dream, his I had seen. I relived it, over and over, my mind coming undone. Detu-ire was good. He was kind. He had dwelled amongst mortals, not as god, but as friend. Their corn he gave the taste of sunlight, and the wine, an emotion brewing on the tongue. Detu-ire was the sting of salt and the burn of pepper. When famines ravaged, he sweetened the bitter kola and turned the grimness of the cacti broth to the savor of egusi soup. It was the only way the children could keep it down. The waterfall flowing into our home in the Manjero valley, he made to taste of peace, a gift to Uda.

Like I had been for him, Uda became my anchor. Pulling me up when the visions were drowning me, leading the way when all I saw was Abali. At long last, we got to Nnewi, Abali half a day behind us.

"He is coming." I slumped into Mmetuta's outstretched arms.

"Let him come."

* * *

On the stones of our birth, we stood, Mmetuta, Uda, and I. We stood, we waited, and Abali came.

"There is death in this place." His words drifted into the temple. "Can you hear it?"

Like in response, Uda screamed, a shrill piercing scream.

"What is it?" Mmetuta asked, wild-eyed. In her hand, a diamond orb hung from a chain, her armor, forged from a star.

"He is not alone." The clattering of Uda's teeth rang across the halls like the clapping of school children. "He brought them – he brought – all of them."

Abali had seen Uda's torment through me, and he wielded it against us. Pulling the strings of death on the very grounds where my brother had wiped out the clans of Nnewi, he resurrected their voices, their suffering, and Uda could hear it all.

"Murderer! Murderer!" Uda clawed at himself, cracks zipping across the temple pillars as his cries pulsated louder.

Mmetuta knelt, taking his face in her hands, "Nwanna'm dere du, be still brother, feel no more." With that, Uda went quiet, a lake. "It's just us now." Mmetuta turned to me, swinging her chain till the orb at the end became a blur. "Come, take vengeance with me."

When a horde of shadows charged into the temple, Mmetuta muttered into her weapon, a curse, and she charged back. Unlike with Isi, the shadows she slew didn't multiply, they faded into nothing. She badgered on, a mammoth through fields of grass. Mmetuta was formidable. While we had lived in solitude, she had scoured the realms, hunting those who posed a threat to us. They said father had been revered. Mmetuta? Mmetuta was feared.

A second horde came ramming through the southern temple gate. Light building in my hands, I rose to the ceiling. The light was but a glowing ball, but to Abali, it was ten thousand suns. Scorching his many shadows, it banished them, until Abali was all that remained. Mmetuta attacked. Wherever he went, her orb followed. Every step he took, she took, destroying his dark spears before they could form, the light I carried, overwhelming him.

"Enough!" Abali caught the orb in his fist. Liquefying it, the molten metal poured out from between his fingers. "Ignorant things, you know nothing of —"

Mmetuta reached forward and grabbed him.

A dagger's tip on your neck. The scalding flames that took half your village. Sahara's burn and the frostbites of the Antarctic. The blisters when you walked six miles to fetch drinking water. Childbirth.

The rush of a lover's kiss, prick of a rose thorn, the rough of bark. Slipping into a spring you found buried in the woods. Warm sand between your toes, ocean wind in your clothes. Your nana's hands weaving your hair. Your thumb squeezed in the palm of your little girl. Mmetuta.

When her touch met Abali's skin, she damned him with the pain of a hundred men burning at the stake, leaving him bare and screaming.

"Anya!" She called to me, fastening her grip unto him. Black veins branched from her hands to her neck, up to her face. "End it!"

The light in my hand lengthening into a javelin of pure starlight, I flew to her, the tip aimed at Abali's heart – if he had one. Piercing the base of his chest, his flesh cracking open, I stopped. In Abali's eyes, someone was staring back at me.

"Who – what are you —"

It happened in a heartbeat. Spears emerged from Abali like spikes on a porcupine, stabbing holes into Mmetuta. I cowered back. Pushing her off him, he ripped off Mmetuta's skin and, as her bones rattled to the ground, Abali rose. He bridged what little distance separated us, and I just stood there, my body ashiver. When he grabbed me, his fingers going to my eyes, there came a muttering, like glass being scraped on stone.

"I – am – death – in – this – place."

Abali spun around to find Uda, aquiver, frothing at the mouth.

"Hear!" Into Abali's face, Uda shrieked with the longing of all those who spoke, shredding him to pieces. "Run," he said to me, collapsing to the ground, as the high walls and the pillars began to crumble and fall. "There is no defeating him." He pointed to the sable pieces of Abali latching back unto each other.

"No – no – I'm not leaving without you." I hoisted him up.

Pressing his hand into mine, he drew a long, worn, breath. "I am spent."

"I can't, I can't —"

"It's alright." He smiled, something I had not seen in forever. "It's alright."

Through the falling rubble, past Mmetuta's bones, out the temple, and into the empty city, I fled. I looked back at the caving building, at the granite, and the statues of The First Ones tumbling to the ground, and I cried.

Dim and fey, a shadow kindled from the wreckage. Abali. Cradled in his arms, my brother. I had watched Abali put an end to three of my siblings, I could not do it again. So I ran, and I flew, and I swam and, in a stolen place where dawn met dusk, I rid myself of sight, severing my tie to Abali. If I couldn't see, he could not see through me.

* * *

"And is Abali still searching for Anya?" The girl asked.

"Yes."

"These stories, who told them to you?"

"My... my brother."

"Where is he?"

"...Dead."

"Oh."

"It was a long time ago."

"Well, I haven't heard of these people, Abali, Uda, Mme – Mma —" I imagined she was itching her head. "Mmatata?"

"Mmetuta."

"Mmetuta," the girl repeated. "My nana says you're not human."

"Does she?"

"Yes, and so does the entire village."

"Hm."

"I should go." I listened to the scuttle of her feet as she stood. "Will you be here tomorrow?"

"We'll see."

The girl would return tomorrow, and she wouldn't find me. I was never long in a place. After the battle of Nnewi, I roamed worlds, hiding, hemming into crowds. From traveling with the Fulani through the grasslands of Niger to climbing the Taurus mountains with the Sarikeçililer, I waned, bits of me, memories, wilting away. I told the stories to remember. But it wasn't enough. Without my abilities, in time, I'd be a husk, wandering till infinity. A steep price, one I was willing to pay.

Decades into my self exile, moving with a caravan in the Kalahari, mind half-lost, I heard it:

"Anya, Nwanna'm – Child of my father.
My skin has morphed from brass to gravel to glass.
In darkness, I am bound,
in echoes, I wither.
Nwanna'm, do not forget my name,
do not forget the black of my hair,
or the brown of my eyes
For in this melody, I may fall."

In the desert storm, wind and sand thrashing at me, I still picked out the voice. Uda. But he had perished, I saw it, I saw it. I needed to know, and so I reached…

Brown of dunes. Azure wings of hummingbirds deep in The Congo. Mint jades daring to bloom. Winter's frosting melting off grass, emerald grasshoppers chirping on and off. The burning radiance of autumn leaves. Crystal ponds, and the speckled trouts at their bottom. Spring and her rainbows dousing the Binibi peaks in coloured fire. Northern lights. Rings of Saturn. They all flooded in, and I let it consume me. I remembered Uda and the rhythms that lived on his lips; Isi, her hair the smell of plants growing; Detu-ire, and the goodness that was his soul; Mmetuta, fierce and true. I remembered them all. Eyes scouring, I found my brother deep in the holds of Zanabu. He was a pale thing, like death lived in the lining of his skin. A million souls poured around him, singing, screaming, whispering, laughing, wailing.

"I will not stop," Abali said, latching once again on to my vision. "In anguish, I will keep him, till time eternal. "Come and see."

To Zanabu, I went to see. Marching into its strongholds, its demons crawled out, screeching. A glare and they scattered into their pits. When I came before Abali in the tombs of the forgotten, it wasn't victory I found in his eyes. Again, like in Nnewi all those years ago, something, someone else was looking at me.

"Where is my brother?"

His shadows gave way, and from within himself, Abali spat out Uda, and I caught him, letting him fall into me. There we sat, in each other, as we did in the valley.

"What has he done to you?" Seeing Uda the way he was, broke me.

"I am sorry I called." Uda's voice was leaving him. "They wouldn't let me sleep."

"It's alright." I kissed his cheek. "You can rest now."

My body wracking with sobs, I removed his ears, and in my arms, Uda's body broke into a hymn, and he was gone.

"Here's your trophy." I threw the ears at Abali.

"Your turn." His hand went to my face, and I held it.

"This is not the end of us."

He moved the braids that had fallen over my face. "You have his eyes," he said, and he gouged them out.

* * *

We awoke. Isi, Mmetuta, Detu-ire, Uda, and I. We awoke, panting, afraid, and one. Behind the intricacy of the old texts on his face, behind the cowries spotting the silver of his hair, we saw him, eyes fogged with tears. "Abali."

"Obi'm – beat of my heart." He knelt to the slab where we lay, his head on ours. "Forgive me, for the pain I caused. You did not remember me…"

We remembered now. Two souls, pure energy given form. The First Ones, unsure of what our combined might would unleash, imprisoned one, the other, us, they ripped apart, and fed lies.

"They will awaken, The First Ones, they will come for us."

"And when they do, we will be here."

Abali's lips touched ours and from the ends of our hair to the soles of our feet, we felt it, electricity. We tasted it, seawater and guava seeds. His heart, a gentle thudding against ours, we inhaled his skin; burning coal. Parting his lips from ours, in his eyes, we found love staring back at us.

"We want to see you, all of you."

Into the moon, we soared. In its glow, we saw him, the one we had loved since the dawning of time. We saw him, and we were whole.

The Mother of the World

Native American

IN THE FROZEN REGIONS OF THE NORTH, beyond the lands which are now the hunting-grounds of the Snakes and Coppermines, there lived, when no other being but herself was, a woman who became the mother of the world. She was a little woman, our fathers told us, not taller than the shoulders of a young maiden of our nation, but she was very beautiful and very wise. Whether she was good-tempered or cross, I cannot tell, for she had no husband, and so there was nothing to vex her, or to try her patience. She had not, as the women of our nation now have, to pound corn, or to fetch home heavy loads of buffalo flesh, or to make snow-sledges, or to wade into the icy rivers to spear salmon, or basket kepling, or to lie concealed among the wet marsh grass and wild rice to snare pelicans, and cranes, and goosanders, while her lazy, good-for-nothing husband lay at home, smoking his pipe, and drinking the pleasant juice of the Nishcaminnick by the warm fire in his cabin. She had only to procure her own food, and this was the berries, and hips, and sorrel, and rock-moss, which, being found plentifully near her cave, were plucked with little trouble. Of these she gathered, in their season, when the sun beamed on the earth like a maiden that loves and is beloved, a great deal to serve her for food when the snows hid the earth from her sight, and the cold winds from the fields of eternal frost obliged her to remain in her rude cavern. Though alone, she was happy. In the summer it was her amusement to watch the juniper and the alders, as they put forth, first their leaves, and then their buds, and when the latter became blossoms, promising to supply the fruit she loved, her observation became more curious and her feelings more interested; then would her heart beat with the rapture of a young mother, whose gaze is fixed on her sleeping child, and her eyes glisten with the dew of joy which wets the cheeks of those who meet long parted friends. Then she would wander forth to search for the little berry whose flower is yellow, and which requires keen eyes to find it in its hiding-place in the grass, and the larger which our white brother eats with his buffalo-meat; and their progress, from the putting forth of the leaf to the ripening of the fruit, was watched by her with eager joy. When tired of gazing upon the pine and stunted poplar, she would lie down in the shade of the creeping birch and dwarf willow, and sink to rest, and dream dreams which were not tinged with the darkness of evil. The sighing of the wind through the branches of the trees, and the murmur of little streams through the thicket, were her music. Throughout the land there was nothing to hurt her, or make her afraid, for there was nothing in it that had life, save herself and the little flower which blooms among thorns. And these two dwelt together like sisters.

One day, when the mother of the world was out gathering berries, and watching the growth of a young pine, which had sprung up near her friend the flower, and threatened, as the flower said, "to take away the beams of the sun from it," she was scared by the sight of a strange creature, which ran upon four legs, and to all her questions answered nothing but "Bow, wow, wow." To every question our mother asked, the creature made the same answer, "bow, wow, wow." So she left off asking him questions, for they were sure to be replied to in three words of a language she could not understand. Did he ask for berries? No, for she offered him a handful of the largest and juiciest which grew in the valley, and he neither took them nor thanked her, unless 'bow' meant 'thank you.' Was he admiring the tall young pines, or the beautiful blossoms of the cranberry, or the graceful bend of the willow, and asking her to join him in his admiration? She knew not, and leaving him to his thoughts, and to utter his strange words with none to reply, she returned to her cave.

Scarcely was she seated on her bed of dried leaves when he came in, and, wagging his tail, and muttering as before, lay down at her feet. Occasionally he would look up into her face very kindly, and then drop his head upon his paws. By and by he was fast asleep, and our mother, who had done no evil action, the remembrance of which should keep her awake, who never stole a beaver-trap, or told a lie, or laughed at a priest, was very soon in the same condition. Then the Manitou of Dreams came to her, and she saw strange things in her sleep. She dreamed that it was night, and the sun had sunk behind the high and broken hills which lay beyond the valley of her dwelling, that the dwarf willow bowed its graceful head still lower with the weight of its tears, which are the evening dew, and the dandelion again imprisoned its leaves within its veil of brown. So far her dreams so closely resembled the reality, that for a time she thought she was awake, and that it was her own world – her cave, her berries, and her flowers, which were before her vision. But an object speedily came to inform her that she dwelt in the paradise of dreams – in the land of departed ideas. At the foot of her couch of leaves, in the place of the dog which she had left there when she slept, stood a being somewhat resembling that she had beheld in the warm season, when bending over the river to lave her bosom with the cooling fluid. It was taller than herself, and there was something on its brow which proclaimed it to be fiercer and bolder, formed to wrestle with rough winds, and to laugh at the coming tempests. For the first time since she was, she turned away to tremble, her soul filled with a new and undefinable feeling, for which she could not account. After shading her eyes a moment from the vision, she looked again, and though her trembling increased, and her brain became giddy, she did not wish the being away, nor did she motion it to go. Why should she? There was a smile upon its lip and brow, and a softness diffused over every feature, which gradually restored her confidence, and gave her the assurance that it would not harm her. She dreamed that the creature came to her arms, and she thought that it passed the season of darkness with its cheek laid on her bosom. To her imagination, the breath which it breathed on her lips was balmy as the juice of the Sweet Gum Tree, or the dew from her little neighbour, the flower. When it spoke, though she could not understand its language, her heart heaved more tumultuously, she knew not why, and when it ceased speaking, her sighs came thick till it spoke again. When she awoke it was gone, the beams of the star of day shone through the fissures of her cavern, and, in the place of the beautiful and loved being lay the strange creature, with the four legs and the old 'bow, wow, wow.'

Four moons passed, and brought no change of scene to the mother of the world. By night, her dreams were ever the same: there was always the same dear and beloved being, each day dearer and more beloved, coming with the shades, and departing with the sun, folding her in its arms, breathing balm on her lips, and pressing her bosom with its downy cheek. By day, the dog was always at her side, whether she went to gather berries or cresses, or to lave her limbs in the stream. Whenever the dog was there, the more beloved being was not; when night came, the dog as surely disappeared, and the other, seen in dreams, supplied his place. But she herself became changed. She took no more joy in the scenes which once pleased her. The pines she had planted throve unnoticed; the creeping birch stifled the willow and the juniper, and she heeded it not; the sweetest berries grew tasteless – she even forgot to visit her pretty sister, the rose. Yet she knew not the cause of her sudden change, nor of the anxiety and apprehension which filled her mind. Why tears bedewed her cheeks till her eyes became blind, why she trembled at times, and grew sick, and feinted, and fell to the earth, she knew not. Her feelings told her of a change, but the relation of its cause, the naming to her startled ear of the mystery of 'the dog by day, and the man by night,' was reserved for a being, who was to prepare the world for the reception of the mighty numbers which were to be the progeny of its mother.

She had wandered forth to a lonely valley – lonely where all was lonely – to weep and sigh over her lost peace, and to think of the dear being with which that loss seemed to her to be in some way connected, when suddenly the sky became darkened, and she saw the form of a being shaped like that which visited her in her sleep, but of immense proportions, coming towards her from the east. The clouds wreathed themselves around his head, his hair swept the mists from the mountain-tops, his eyes were larger than the rising sun when he wears the red flush of anger in the Frog-Moon, and his voice, when he gave it full tone, was louder than the thunder of the Spirit's Bay of Lake Huron. But to the woman he spoke in soft whispers; his terrific accents were reserved for the dog, who quailed beneath them in evident terror, not daring even to utter his only words, 'bow, wow.' The mother of the world related to him her dreams, and asked him why, since she had had them, she was so changed – why she now found no joy in the scenes which once pleased her, but rather wished that she no longer was, her dreams being now all that she loved. The mighty being told her that they were not dreams, but a reality; that the dog which now stood by her side was invested by the Master of Life with power to quit, at the coming in of the shades, the shape of a dog, and to take that of Man, a being who was the counterpart of herself, but formed with strength and resolution, to counteract, by wisdom and sagacity, and to overcome, by strength and valour, the rough difficulties and embarrassments which were to spring up in the path of human life; that he was to be fierce and bold, and she gentle and afraid. He told her that the change she complained of, and which had given her so much grief, wetted her cheek with tears, and filled her bosom with sighs, was the natural result of the intimate connection of two such beings, and was the mode of perpetuating the human race, which had been decreed by the Master of Life; that before the buds now forming should be matured to fruit, she would give birth to two helpless little beings, whom she must feed with her milk, and rear with tender care, for from them would the world be peopled. He had been sent, he said, by the Good Spirit to level and prepare the earth for the reception of the race who were to inhabit it.

Hitherto the world had lain a rude and shapeless mass – the great, man now reduced it to order. He threw the rough and stony crags into the deep valleys – he moved the frozen mountain to fill up the boiling chasm. When he had levelled the earth, which before was a thing without form, he marked out with his great walking-staff the lakes, ponds, and rivers, and caused them to be filled with water from the interior of the earth, bidding them to be replenished from the rains and melted snows which should fall from the skies, till they should be no more.

When he had prepared the earth for the residence of the beings who were to people it, he caught the dog, and, notwithstanding the cries of the mother of the world, and her entreaties to him to spare its life, he tore it in pieces, and distributed it over the earth, and the water, and into air. The entrails he threw into the lakes, ponds, and rivers, commanding them to become fish, and they became fish. These waters, in which no living creature before moved, were now filled with salmon, trout, pike, tittymeg, methy, barble, turbot, and tench, while along the curling waves of the Great Lake the mighty black and white whale, the more sluggish porpoise, and many other finny creatures, sported their gambols. The flesh he dispersed over the land, commanding it to become different kinds of beasts and land-animals, and it obeyed his commands. The heavy moose, and the stupid we-was-kish, came to drink in the Coppermine with the musk-ox, and the deer, and the buffalo. The quiquehatch, and his younger brother, the black bear, and the wolf, that cooks his meat without fire, and the cunning fox, and the wild cat, and the wolverine, were all from the flesh of the dog. The otter was the tail of the dog, the wejack was one of his fore-paws, and the horned horse, and the walrus, were his nose.

Nor did the great man omit to make the skin furnish its proportion of the tribes of living beings. He tore it into many small pieces, and threw it into the air, commanding it to become the different tribes of fowls and birds, and it became the different tribes of fowls and birds. Then first was seen the mighty bird which builds its nest on trees which none can climb, and in the crevices of inaccessible rocks – the eagle, which furnishes the Indians with feathers to their arrows, and steals away the musk-rat and the young beaver as his recompense. Then was the sacred falcon first seen winging his way to the land of long winters; and the bird of alarm, the cunning old owl, and his sister's little son, the cob-a-de-cooch, and the ho-ho. All the birds which skim through the air, or plunge into the water, were formed from the skin of the dog.

When the great man had thus filled the earth with living creatures, he called the mother of the world to him, and gave to her and her offspring the things which he had created, with full power to kill, eat, and never to spare, telling her that he had commanded them to multiply for her use in abundance. When he had finished speaking, he returned to the place whence he came, and has never been heard of since. In due time, the mother of the world was delivered of two children, a son and a daughter, both having the dark visage of the Indian race, and from them proceeded the Dog-ribs, and all the other nations of the earth. The white men were from the same source, but the father of them, having once upon a time been caught stealing a beaver-trap, he become so terrified that he lost his original colour and never regained it, and his children remain with the same pale cheeks to this day.

Brothers, I have told you no lie.

Collected by James Athearn Jones

The Wahconda's Son

Native American

BROTHERS, I AM AN OTTO, and a chief. I am a man of courage and truth. I have been a warrior, and a hunter of the bear and wolf ever since the great meeting of aged counsellors and brave-warriors pronounced me a man. I never fled from a foe; and none ever saw me afraid. Who will say that the Guard of the Red Arrows was ever other than a man in his heart? When the Padoucas bound him to the stake, and kindled fires around him; when they thrust sharp, heated stones into his flesh, and tore off his nails with fiery pincers, did they force a cry from him? Did they see his cheek wear the badge of a woman's weakness? No, I am a man. Brother, I will tell you a tale. While the nation of the Ottoes had their hunting-grounds in the shade of the Mountains of the Great Being, they were led in war to battle – in peace were advised in council by a brave and warlike chief, who was called Wasabajinga, or the Little Black Bear. He was the head chief of the nation, and its greatest warrior. His martial exploits and daring deeds were the theme of all the tribes who roamed through the vast woods between the Mississippi and the Mountains of the Setting Sun, the Missouri, and the Lake of the Woods. All had heard of his great deeds; and many had seen and felt his prowess. He was stronger than the bear, he was swifter than the deer, he was nimbler than the mountain-cat or the panther. Who was so expert at stealing horses as Wasabajinga? By his cabin-door stood the best in all the land; and they had belonged to the Konzas, the Pawnees, the Omawhaws, the Puncas, the Sioux, and other tribes whose eyes were sharp and arrows long, but neither so sharp nor so long as those of the Otto warrior. He had entered alone the camp of the Missouries, at the time when the stars are the sole torches of night, and had brought thence many scalps; he had crept to the lodge of an Arrowauk, and taken the beloved maiden. He had struck dead bodies of all the nations around – Osages, Padoucas, Bald-heads, Ietans, Sauxs, Foxes, and Ioways. And who had such eyes for the trail and the chase as he? He could show you where the snake had crawled through the hazel leaves; he could trace the buck by his nipping of the young buds; he could spring to the top of the tallest pine with the ease of the squirrel, and from thence point out unerringly where lay the hunting-lodges and grounds of all the tribes of the land; he could endure as much fasting as the land-tortoise, or the bear of the frozen north, and march as long as the eagle could fly; never hungry till food was placed before him; never tired when there was more glory to be won. Strong, healthy and nimble, Wasabajinga lived to learn that there was no one in the wilds able to cope with him in battle, and to have his wisdom as loudly applauded as his valour.

At home it was the good fortune of this famous chief to be equally prosperous and happy. He had nine wives, all beautiful as the path of the Master of Life – all good and amiable. Though they all lived in the same cabin, ate out of the same bowl, warmed themselves at the same fire, and slept on the same skins, there was a fair sky among them – it never thundered and lightened in the cabin of the Otto warrior. One nursed another's child as kindly as if it were her own; one performed the field-tasks allotted to another, who in return prepared the bison meat for the fire, and drew home the fuel from the woods. There was peace, and the calmness of a summer day, in the cabin of Wasabajinga – he lived the happiest of his nation.

His children were many – ten sons were in their father's cabin; each could bend his father's bow, each poise his father's spear, and each wield his father's war-club. Daughters he had but one, who grew up the most beautiful of all the maidens of the land. She had a skin much whiter than that of Indian maidens generally; her teeth were white and even; her hair long, black, and glossy, as the feathers of the raven; her eyes mild as the dove's in the season of its mating; and her step was that of a deer who is scared a little. And she was good as she was beautiful. No one ever saw her cross or sulky like other women; nothing made her angry. Though she was beloved by her parents, and a great favourite with all the wives of her father, yet she never claimed exemption from the duties which belong to Indian females. Willingly would her little hands have laid hold of the faggot, and her small feet have travelled forth with her mother to the labours of the field of maize; but the fond affection of all around her, and their belief that she was something more than mortal, protected her from a call to share in their labours. She was allowed no part in the cutting-up of the bison; she was not permitted to pound the corn, or winnow the wild rice, or bring firing from the woods. It was the pride of the youthful part of the tribe to prepare ornaments for her person. The young maidens (for she was envied by none) wove wampum, and made beads for her; the young men passed half their time in hunting the red and blue heron for the gay tuft upon his crown, and the Spirit Bird for his train of yellow, green, and scarlet, that her hair might vie in colours with the beautiful bow that rests upon the mountains after the rains. They made her bracelets for her wrists, and anklets for her legs, of the teeth of the fish with shining scales, and pendants for her ears of the bones of the birds of night and music. Thus lived Mekaia, or the Star-flower, which was the name of the beautiful Otto, till she had reached her seventeenth summer.

It was a little before sunset upon a pleasant day in the month of green-corn, that a young man riding upon a noble white horse was seen entering the great village of the Ottoes. He appeared to be very young, but he was tall and straight as the hickory-tree. He was clothed as our brother is clothed, only his garments were scarlet, and our brother's are black. His hair, which was not so dark as that of the Indians, was smooth and sleek as the hair on the head of a child, or the feathers on the breast of the humming-bird. His head was encircled with a chaplet made of the feathers of the song-sparrow and the red-headed-woodpecker. He rode slowly through the village without stopping till he came to the lodge of Wasabajinga, when he alighted, leaving his good horse to feed upon the grass which grew around the cabin. He entered the lodge of the chief. The stern old warrior, without rising from his bed of skins, asked him who he was, and whence he came. He answered that he was the son of the great Wahconda, and had come from the lodge of his father, which lay among the high mountains towards the setting-sun.

"Have you killed any buffaloes on your journey?" demanded Wasabajinga.

"No," answered the young god.

"Then you must be very hungry," said the chief.

The young man answered that the son of the Wahconda had his food from the skies, because the flesh of the animals which lived on the earth was too gross for him. He lived, he said, upon the flesh of spirit beasts, and fishes, and birds, roasted in the great fire-place of the lightnings, and sent him by the hands of the Manitous of the air. His drink was the rain-drops purified in the clouds.

The chief asked him if he had come on a message from the Wahconda to the Little Black Bear of the Ottoes.

The young man answered that he had. He said his father had shown him from the high mountains of the west the beautiful daughter of the Otto chief – had told him she was good as she was beautiful, and bidden him come and ask her for his wife. His father, he said, bade him tell the Bear of the Ottoes, that, though his daughter must now leave her father, and mother, and nation, and accompany his son into the regions of ever-bright suns, and balmy winds, yet, in a few seasons more, when the knees of the chief had become feeble, and his eyes dim with the mists of age, and his time had come to die, that he should rejoin his daughter and tend her little ones, and be as joyful as the bird of morning on the banks of the rapid river that glided through the valley of departed souls.

"How shall I know that the Wahconda has said this?" asked the chief.

"I will do these things for a sign," answered the boy-god. "Tomorrow, when the sun first rises from his slumbers behind the hills of the east, he shall show himself in a cloudless sky. In the space of a breath, darkness shall cover the face of the heavens, the thunder, which is the voice of my father, shall roll awfully, but the lightnings, which are the glances of his eye, shall be spared. Before the Indians shall have time to raise themselves from the earth, upon whose cold bosom, in their terror, they will prostrate themselves, the darkness shall be recalled from the earth and shut up in the cave of night. The moment the thunders cease, the lightnings, which are the glances of his eye, shall commence their terrific play over the face of the cloudless sky. By these signs ye shall know that I am the Wahconda's son."

"If these things shall be done," said the chief, "the maiden shall be yours."

It was soon told in the village, that the Wahconda's son had come from his father's lodge among the mountains, to ask the beautiful Star-flower for his wife. And it was also told, that with the rising of the sun on the next morning, he would convince the Little Black Bear, that he had not a forked tongue, nor spoke with the lips of a mocking-bird. There was little sleep that night in the Otto village. Our nation awaited with great dread and much trembling the coming of the morning, fearing danger to themselves and the very earth on which they dwelt, from the threatened waking of the Wahconda's voice, and the glancing of his eye.

The nation had assembled beside the cabin of the warrior, when the sun came out from behind the mountains. The young man kept his promise. When the sun first came in view, there was not a cloud on the face of the sky. In the space of a breath, thick darkness overspread the earth, rendering it as dark as the darkest night, and the thunders rolled so awfully, that the very earth seemed to reel like a man who has drunken twice of the fire-eater, which the brothers of our friend sell us in the Village of the High Rock. But what astonished our people most was, that no lightning accompanied the thunder. In a few minutes the darkness was driven away by the same mighty hand which called it forth; the thunder became as mute as the sleep of a child which is filled with its mother's milk, and the sun shone out full and clear as before the Wahconda had shut his mouth. Then succeeded most terrific lightnings; lightnings which rent the solid trees, and clove asunder the flinty rocks. A moment, and they too were called back; the Great Being had closed his eyes, and the lightnings were imprisoned between their lids. The Indians stood for a moment aghast, and then fell on their faces in worship of the Being who could command all things so promptly to do his bidding, and who kept his mouth shut, and his eyes closed, in mercy to the poor creatures of the earth.

When they had recovered from their fright, they rose to an upright posture, and paid their obeisance to the stranger, now proved to be the Wahconda's son by signs that no one would dare dispute. He showed his love for them by the kind look he gave them. Turning to the Little Black Bear, he said, "Has the Wahconda's son proved himself worthy to have the beautiful daughter of the Otto chief to be his wife?"

Wasabajinga answered, "The Wahconda's son has proved himself worthy to have for his wife the daughter of the head chief of the Ottoes. The chief gives her to him, in the presence of all his nation."

The chief went into his lodge, and brought out his daughter. The son of the Wahconda then went up to the beautiful maiden, and fondly pressing her in his arms, called her his wife, and told her that, moved by her beauty and goodness, he had left the pleasant skies of his dwelling, to come into the cold and misty region where the Ottoes had their lodges. She wept, but the tears came not from her heart, and smiles beamed through them, as the stars of night shine through mist, or the sun of a spring morning looks, through a cloud of vapour. Then the beautiful couple went through the Indian form of marriage. When this was ended, the tribe gathered to the feast in the cabin of the chief. Rich and juicy was the bear's meat, set out on the buffalo robe, and ripe were the berries, and sweet was the roasted corn, which the women brought to feed the guests. They sung, and danced, and recounted their warlike exploits in the ears of the listening boy. They told of their hostile visits to the countries of the Padoucas and Bald-heads; they mimicked the cry of terror which burst from the Ietans when a painted man of the Ottoes crept with an uplifted hatchet into their camp by midnight, and took five scalps as they slept. Then one arose and sung a song of marriage. Brothers, this was the song he sung:

> *"Who is that?*
> *Oh, it is the Master's fair-haired son,*
> *Come to wed the warrior's beauteous daughter.*
> *Tall and manly is his form;*
> *Beautiful and fair is she;*
> *See his step how light,*
> *See his eyes how bright with love and joy;*
> *How glad he looks:*
> *So turns his eyes the husband-dove*
> *Upon its gentle little wife.*
> *He came and caught the maiden in his arms,*
> *He pressed her to his bosom as a mother*
> *Presses her infant.*
> *She was pleased, and wept,*
> *But her's were tears of joy;*
> *Hung her head, and hid her beauteous face,*
> *Yet was she not ashamed.*
> *Her's was maiden bashfulness.*
> *Blushes she to be so caught in love?*
> *See her stolen glances! sunlit glances! see!*
> *She doth not altogether hate the youth.*
> *Why dost thou weep, mother of the bride?*
> *Weepst thou to be parted from thy daughter?*
> *Weep no more.*
> *What is life?*
> *A reed beat down by every wind that stirs,*
> *A flower nipt by the first autumnal blast,*
> *A deer that perishes by prick of thorn,*
> *Here at morning,*
> *Gone at evening.*
> *Weep not, tender mother of the bride;*
> *Soon thou'lt meet her in the happy vales*
> *Beyond the setting sun:*
> *Ask the lover, he will tell thee so."*

When the feast was concluded, the songs and dances, and sacrifices, finished, the Wahconda's son prepared to take his departure to the mountains where his father dwelt. The tribe attended him to the edge of the forest, which had been the hunting-grounds of the Ottoes ever since the rivers ran, and there they left him to pursue his journey with his beautiful and happy wife to the abodes of spirits, and great warriors, and just men. But before the chief parted from his daughter, he made her husband a long speech, and prayed that peace might ever be between them and their people. He told him he had given him his all – his dearly beloved daughter, to whom he must be kind and affectionate. He must not put heavy burdens upon her; he must not send her to cut wood, nor bring home the bison's flesh, nor pound the corn, for her hands had never been hardened in tasks like these, nor her shoulders bowed in her father's house to the labours of the field, or forest, or cabin. "She had been," he said, "the darling of her father's household, and knew not labour but by name."

The Wahconda's son smiled at the words of the old chief, and told him "that services, like those he had mentioned, were never required of women in the Wahconda's dwelling. The people of the happy vales and the spirits of the mountains fed not," he said, "upon bison's meat, nor pounded corn; and the sun, which was the same at all seasons, beamed so warm, that they kept no fires. It was a lovely land, far pleasanter than that which the Ottoes abode in, nor was it subject to those dreadful storms and tempests which terrified and annoyed those who dwelt upon the banks of the Great River." And then, mounting his noble horse, and taking his little wife behind him, he again bade them farewell and rode away.

He had been gone two moons – the third was in its wane, and the parents had become consoled for the loss of their daughter. It was upon a clear and beautiful evening in the Moon of Harvest, when the forest was losing its robe of green, and putting on its garment of brown and scarlet, and cool and steady winds were succeeding to the hot and parching breezes of summer, that the Ottoes assembled to dance and feast in the cabin of their chief. It was one of the most beautiful nights ever beheld. Nothing was heard to break the stillness of the hour, save the rustling of the branches of the cedar and pine, the slight music of a little rivulet, and the mournful singing of the wekolis, perched in the low branches of the willow. The feast was prepared, the Master was propitiated, and they were sitting down to partake of the good things of the land and water, when suddenly the earth began to move like the waters of lake Huron, when agitated by winds from the regions of the frozen star. Upon every side of them, above them, and beneath them, the earth thundered, with a rattling sound. In vain did the Ottoes attempt to leave the cabin; they rolled about like a canoe launched upon a stormy river, or a ball tossed upon frozen water. The rocking of the earth continued throughout the hours of darkness. When light came, it was frightful to behold the disfigured face of the earth. In some places lakes were scooped out, and mountains piled up on their brink. Trees were rooted up and broken; little streams had disappeared, even large rivers had ceased to be. The tall magnolia lay broken in many pieces, the larch tree had been snapped like a rotten reed. The flowers of the meadows were scorched and seared, the deer in the thicket lay mangled and bruised, the birds sat timid and shy on the broken bough. The people called their priests together, and demanded why these things were. The priests answered, "Because the Master of Life was angry, but with whom they knew not. Yet soon should they learn, for there was one coming hither who would be able to tell them."

Three suns had passed, and the knowledge of the cause still remained hidden from them. On the morning of the fourth day, when the chief went out of his lodge, he found his beloved daughter weeping by the door of the cabin. Oh! how changed was the beautiful Mekaia – she was no longer a Star-flower. The brightness of her eye had departed, as the beauty of the green fields and leafy forests is driven hence by the chills of winter, her cheek was sunken and hollow, her long black locks lay uncombed upon her shoulders, and the joy and cheerfulness which once warmed her heart, and made her foot lighter than the antelope's, were no more. She, whose feet were fleeter than the deer's, now walked feebly, and rested oft; she, whose tongue out-chirped the merriest birds of the grove, and warbled sweeter music than the song-sparrow, now spoke in strains as gloomy and sad as the bittern that cries in the swamps when night is coming on, or the solitary bird of wisdom perched among the leaves of the oak. The father sat down by her, and asked her whence she came.

"From the valley upon this side of the mountains," she answered.

"Where is thy husband?" demanded Wasabajinga.

"Dead," answered the Starflower, and wept afresh.

"Wah!" exclaimed the warrior, and hid his face with his hands. When he had sat thus awhile, he inquired the manner of his death. She told him, that, before they reached the mountains of the Wahconda, they saw a pale man coming towards them, mounted on a low, black horse. When he came up them, he asked her husband if he would buy blankets, and beads, and the fire-eater. That the Wahconda's son answered, "No"; and told him it was very – very bad in him to carry the fire-eater, to destroy the poor misguided Indians. The man upon the black horse answered, "That he was a better man than the Wahconda's son, for he was no heathen, but lived where men worshipped a greater Wahconda than his father in a beautiful house built with hands, and not beneath the shade of the cypress and the oak." Upon this, her husband did but smile, when the pale man elevated the spear he carried in his hand, and, with the bolts which issued from it, struck him to the earth, from which he never rose again. Then there came a cry of mourning from the cabin of the Little Black Bear. The women rushed out, and tore their hair, and cut their flesh with sharp stones, through grief for the death of the husband of their beloved Starflower. And they sung a melancholy lament, for the youth who had perished in the morning of life, while the down was yet upon his cheek, and his heart had never felt the shaft of sorrow. They sung how happy the lovers were, ere the malice and cruelty of white men destroyed their joys; ere their sacrilegious hands had laid one low in the dust, and left the other to pine under the bereavement, till death would be a blessing. They painted the anger and grief of the great Wahconda when he found the darling of his house numbered with the slain. They sung that, exasperated with the children of earth for the murder of his beloved son, he called upon his earthquakes to deface and lay waste their country. They bade the eye note how well these ministers of his wrath had performed his dread commands. So they sung – "For many a weary day's journey upon the banks of the Mighty River, for many a long encamping in the direction of the setting sun, the land lies in ruins. The bough is broken, and the solid trunk is rent. The flower lies bleeding, and the voice of the dove is hushed. But see, he has bidden the marks of havoc be effaced from the country of the Ottoes, because it is the native land of the beautiful woman who had become the wife of his son."

Long was the mourning continued, and deep the grief, which for many a moon pervaded the cabins and camp of the Ottoes. The Great Wahconda did not permit the Starflower to remain long upon the earth, but soon called her away to be re-united to his beloved son in the land of spirits. Yet she often returns to look upon the place of her birth, to breathe on the things she loved, and to sit beneath the shade of the trees she planted. In the season of flowers, she is often seen by moonlight, binding together the choicest which grow on the prairie, and her voice is often heard in the sighs of the breeze in spring. The Wahconda's son never comes with her, for he fears the treachery and violence of the pale faces.

Collected by James Athearn Jones

The Origin of Women

Native American

THERE WAS A TIME, when, throughout the Island, neither on land nor in the water, in field or forest, was there a woman to be found. Vain things were plenty – there was the turkey, and the swan, and the blue jay, and the wood-duck, and the wakon bird; and noisy, chattering, singing creatures, such as the daw, and the thrush, and the rook, and the prairie-dog, abounded – indeed there were more of each than was pleasing to the ear – but of women, vain, noisy, laughing, chattering women, there were none. It was, indeed, quite a still world to what it is now. Whether it is better and happier, will depend much upon the opinion men entertain of those, who have changed its character from calm and peaceable to boisterous and noisy. Some will think it is much improved by the circumstance which deprived the Kickapoos of their tails – while others will greatly deplore its occurrence.

At the time of which I am telling my brother, the Kickapoos, and indeed all men, wherever found – were furnished with long tails like horses and buffaloes. It was very handy to have these appendages in a country where flies were numerous and troublesome, as they were in the land of the Kickapoos – tails being much more sudden in their movements than hands, and more conveniently situated, as every body must see, for whisking off the flies which light upon the back. Then they were very beautiful things, these long tails, especially when handsomely painted and ornamented, as their owners used to ornament them, with beads, and shells, and wampum – and being intended as a natural decoration to the creature, the depriving him of it may well have produced, as it did, a great deal of sport and merriment among the other animals, who were not compelled to submit to the deprivation. The fox, who is rather impudent, for a long time after they were chopped off, sent to the Kickapoos every day to enquire "how their tails were;" and the bear shook his fat sides with laughter at the joke, which he thought a very good one, of sending one of his cubs with a request for a "dozen spare tails."

I have said, that throughout the land there were no women. There were men – a plenty, the land was thronged with them – not born, but created of clay – and left to bake in the sun till they received life – and these men were very contented and happy. Wars were very few then, for no one need be told that half the wars which have arisen have grown out of quarrels on account of love of women, and the other half on account of their maintenance. There was universal peace and harmony throughout the land. The Kickapoos ate their deer's flesh with the Potowatomies, hunted the otter with the Osages, and the beaver with the Hurons; and the fierce Iroquois, instead of waking the wild shout of war, went to the land of the Sauks and Ioways to buy wampum, wherewith to decorate their tails. Happy would it have been for the men if they were still furnished with these appendages, and wanted those which have been supplied in their place – women!

But the consequence which usually attends prosperity happened to the Indians. They became very proud and vain, and forgot their creator and preserver. They no more offered the fattest and choicest of their game upon the memahoppa, or altar-stone, nor evinced any gratitude, nor sung, nor danced in his praise, when he sent his rains to cleanse the earth and his lightnings to cool and purify the air. When their corn grew ripe and tall, they imputed it to their own good conduct and management; when their hunt was successful, to their own skill and perseverance. Reckoning not, as in times past, of the superintendence of the Great Spirit over all things, they banished him altogether from their proud and haughty hearts, teaching them to forget that there was aught greater or more powerful than himself.

Though slow to anger, and waiting long before he remembers the provocations he has received, the Great Spirit, in the end, and when no atonement is made, always inflicts an adequate punishment for every offence. Seeing how wicked the Indians had become, he said to his Manitous: "It is time that the Kickapoos and other men were punished. They laugh at my thunders, they make mock of my lightnings and hurricanes, they use my bounties without thanking me for them. When their corn grows ripe and tall, instead of imputing its luxuriance to my warm suns and reviving showers, they say, 'We have managed it well;' when their hunt is successful, they place it to account of their own skill and perseverance. Reckoning not, as in times past, of my superintendence over all things, they have banished me altogether from their haughty hearts, and taught themselves to forget that there is aught greater and more powerful than the Indian."

So saying, he bade his chief Manitou repair to the dwelling-places of the men, and, to punish them for their wickedness, deprive them of that which they most valued, and bestow upon them a scourge and affliction adequate to their offences. The Spirit obeyed his master, and descended to the earth, lighting down upon the lands occupied by the Kickapoos. It was not long before he discovered what it was which that people and the other Indians most valued. He saw, from the pains they took in decorating their tails with gay paints, and beads, and shells, and wampum, that they prized them above every other possession. Calling together all the men, he acquainted them with the will of his master, and demanded the instant sacrifice of the article upon which they set so much value. It is impossible to describe the sorrow and compunction which filled their bosoms, when they found that the forfeit for their wickedness was to be that beautiful and beloved appendage. But their prayers and entreaties, to be spared the humiliation and sacrifice, were in vain. The Spirit was inexorable, and they were compelled to place their tails on the block and to behold them amputated.

The punishment being in part performed, the Spirit next bethought himself of a gift which should prove to them "a scourge and affliction adequate to their offences." It was to convert the tails thus lopped off into vain, noisy, chattering, laughing creatures, whose faces should he like the sky in the Moon of Plants, and whose hearts should be treacherous, fickle, and inconstant; yet, strange to relate, who should be loved above all other things on the earth or in the skies. For them should life often be hazarded – reputation, fame, and virtue, often forfeited – pain and ignominy incurred. They were to be as a burden placed on the shoulders of an already overloaded man; and yet, a burden he would rather strive to carry than abandon. He further appointed that they should retain the frisky nature of the material from which they were made, and they have retained it to this day.

The Great Spirit, deeming that the trouble wherewith he had provided man would not sufficiently vex and punish him, determined to add another infliction, whose sting, though not so potent and irksome, should be without any alleviation whatever. He sent great swarms of mosquitoes. Deprived of tails, by which flies could be brushed away at the pleasure of the wearers, the Indians dragged out for a long time a miserable existence. The mosquitoes stung them, and their tails teased them. The little insects worried them continually, and their frisky companions, the women, were any thing but a cup of composing drink. At length the Great Spirit, seeing how the poor Indians were afflicted, mercifully withdrew the greater part of the mosquitoes, leaving a few as a memorial of the pest which had formerly annoyed them. The Kickapoos petitioned that the women should also be taken away from them, and their old appendages returned – but the Great Spirit answered, that women were a necessary evil, and must remain.

Collected by James Athearn Jones

Hua, King of Hana

His Hawaiian Majesty Kalakaua, Hawaii

The Legend of the Great Famine of the Twelfth Century

I

WITH THE REIGN OF HUA, an ancient king of Hana, or eastern Maui, is connected a legendary recital of one of the most terrible visitations of the wrath of the gods anywhere brought down by Hawaiian tradition. It is more than probable that the extent of the calamities following Hua's defiant and barbarous treatment of his high-priest and prophet was greatly colored and exaggerated in turn by the pious historians who received and passed the *moooelo* down the centuries; but the details of the story have been preserved with harrowing conciseness, and for more than six hundred years were recited as a solemn warning against wanton trespass upon the prerogatives of the priesthood or disregard of the power and sanctity of the gods.

In some of the genealogies Hua is represented as having been the great-grandfather of Paumakua, of Maui. This record, if accepted, would remove him altogether from the Hawaiian group, since Paumakua himself was undoubtedly an immigrant from Tahiti or some other of the southern islands. As he was contemporaneous with the distinguished priest and prophet Naula, who is said to have accompanied Laa-mai-kahiki from Raiatea, he must have appeared two or three generations later than Paumakua, and probably belonged to a collateral branch of the great Hua family from which Paumakua drew his strain.

It may therefore be assumed that as early as AD 1170 Hua was the *alii-nui*, or virtual sovereign, of eastern Maui. He is referred to as the king of Maui, but it is hardly probable that his sway extended over the western division of the island, as it was not until the reign of Piilani, nearly three centuries later, that the people of Maui became finally united under one government. Previous to that time, except at intervals of temporary conquest or occupation, eastern and western Maui were ruled by distinct and frequently hostile lines of kings. Hence the sovereignty of Hua could scarcely have reached beyond the districts of Koolau, Hana, Kipahulu and Kaupo, while the remainder of the island must have recognized the authority either of Palena, the grandson of Paumakua, or of Hanalaa, the distinguished son and successor of Palena, since the later *mois* of Maui traced their genealogies uninterruptedly through this branch of the Paumakua family.

But, from whatever source Hua may have derived his rank and authority, he was a reckless, independent and warlike chief. Having access to the largest and finest timber in the group, his war-canoes were abundant and formidable, and when not engaged in harassing his neighbouring frontiers he was employed in plundering expeditions to the coasts of Hawaii and Molokai. Tradition makes him the aggressor in the earliest remembered war between Maui and Hawaii. Although the name of the war (*Kanuioohio*) has been preserved, it probably did not reach beyond the limit of a powerful marauding excursion to the coast of Hilo, Hawaii, resulting in the defeat of the chiefs of that district by Hua, but in nothing more than a temporary seizure and occupation of their lands; for at that time Kanipahu was the *moi* of Hawaii, and would scarcely have permitted a permanent hostile lodgment in Hilo, whose chiefs acknowledged his suzerainty and were therefore entitled to his protection.

The high-priest of Hua was Luahoomoe. He claimed to be an *iku-pau* – that is, a direct descendant from *Kane* – and as such was strict in claiming respect for his person and sacred prerogatives. He did not approve of many of Hua's marauding acts, advising him instead to lead his people in happier and more peaceful pursuits, and not provoke either the retaliation of his enemies or the anger of the gods. This opposition to his aggressive methods exasperated Hua, and a feeling of suspicion and ill-will gradually grew up between him and the priesthood. He began to attribute his occasional failures in arms to deliberately-neglected prayers and sacrifices by Luahoomoe, and on one occasion, after having returned from an unsuccessful expedition to Molokai, he placed his *tabu* on a spring of water set apart for the use of the *heiau*, and on another wantonly speared a *puaa-hiwa*, or black *tabued* hog, sacred to sacrifice. When expostulated with for thus inviting the wrath of the gods, he threatened the high-priest with similar treatment.

Hua resided principally at Hana, where he constructed one of the largest royal mansions in the group, and all the leisure spared from his warlike pastimes was given to revelry. He had a hundred *hula* dancers, exclusive of musicians and drummers, and his monthly feasts were prolonged into days and nights of debauchery and unbridled license. Drunk with *awa*, an intoxicating drink made from a plant of that name, he kept the whole of Hana in an uproar during his frequent seasons of pleasure, and the attractive wives and daughters of his subjects were not unfrequently seized and given to his favourite companions.

The annual festival of *Lono* was approaching – an event marking the winter solstice, and which was always celebrated impressively on every island of the group. It was an occasion not only for manifesting respect for the nearest and most popular deity of the godhead, but for celebrating, as well, the ending of the old year and the beginning of the new. The ancient Hawaiians divided the year into twelve months of thirty days each. Each month and day of the month was named. They had two modes of measuring time – the lunar and sidereal. The lunar month began on the first day that the new moon appeared in the west, and regulated their monthly feasts and *tabu* days. Their sidereal month of thirty days marked one of the twelve divisions of the year; but as their two seasons of the year – the *Hooilo* (rainy) and *Kau* (dry) – were measured by the Pleiades, and their twelve months of thirty days each did not complete the sidereal year, they intercalated five days at the end of the year measured by months, in order to square that method of reckoning with the movements of the stars. This annual intercalation was made about the 20th of their month of *Welehu* (December), at the expiration of which the first day of the first month (*Makalii*) of the new year commenced. This was their *Makahiki*, or new-year day. The five intercalated days were a season of *tabu*, and dedicated to a grand yearly festival to *Lono*.

In preparation for this festival Hua had called for unusually large contributions from the people, and, in anticipation of another hostile expedition to Hawaii, had ordered quotas of warriors, canoes and provisions from his subject chiefs, to be reported at Hana immediately after the beginning of the new year. These exactions caused very general dissatisfaction, and the priesthood assisted in promoting rather than allaying the popular discontent. All this was reported to Hua, and he resolved to liberate himself at once and for the future from what he conceived to be an officious and unwarranted intermeddling of the priesthood with the affairs of state, by deposing or taking the life of Luahoomoe. In this desperate resolution he was sustained by Luuana, a priest who had charge of the *heiau* or chapel of the royal mansion, and who expected to succeed Luahoomoe as high-priest.

Hua sought in every way for a pretext for deposing or slaying Luahoomoe; but the priest was old in years, exemplary in his conduct, and moved among the people without reproach. Finally, at the instigation of Luuana, who assumed that the advice was a divine inspiration, Hua created a bungling and absurd pretence for an assault upon Luahoomoe. The dishonesty of the scheme was exposed, but it resulted, nevertheless, in the death of the unoffending priest.

As tradition tells the story, Hua found occasion in a public manner to order some *uwau*, or *uau*, to be brought to him from the mountains. The *uau* is a water bird, and seldom found in the uplands. As neither its flesh for eating nor its feathers for decorating could have reasonably been required, the object of despatching snarers in quest of it must have been a subject of comment; but kings then, as later, did not always deign to give reasons for their acts, and preparations were at once made by the household servants and retainers of the king to proceed upon the hunt.

"Be careful that the birds come from the mountains," said Hua, addressing the trusted *hoalii* in charge of the hunting party – "only from the mountains," he repeated; "I will have none from the sea."

"But can they be found in the mountains?" ventured the *hoalii*, looking inquiringly toward Luahoomoe, who was standing near and watching a flight of birds which seemed to be strangely confused and ominous of evil.

"Do you inquire of me?" said the priest, after a pause, and finding that the king did not answer.

"I inquire of any one who thinks he knows," returned the *hoalii*.

"Then the birds you seek will not be found in the mountains at this season of the year," returned the priest, "and you must set your snares by the sea-shore."

"Is it so that you would attempt to countermand my orders?" exclaimed Hua, in apparent anger. "I order my servants to go to the mountains for the *uau*, and you tell them to set their snares by the sea-shore!"

"I humbly ask the king to remember that I have given no orders," calmly replied the priest.

"But you have dared to interfere with mine!" retorted the king. "Now listen. My men shall go to the mountains in search of the birds I require. If they find them there I will have you slain as a false prophet and misleader of the people!"

With this savage threat the king walked away with his *hoalii*, while the priest stood in silence with his face bowed to the earth. He knew the import of Hua's words. They meant death to him and the destruction of his family. The bloody purpose of the king had been told to him at the sacrificial altar, had been seen by him in the clouds, had been whispered to him from the *anu* of the sanctuary.

"Since the gods so will it, I must submit to the sacrifice," was the pious resolution of the priest; "but woe to the hand that strikes, to the eyes that witness the blow, to the land that drinks the blood of the son of Laamakua!"

Luahoomoe had two sons, Kaakakai and Kaanahua. Both were connected with the priesthood, and Kaakakai had been instructed in all the mysteries of the order in anticipation of his succession, on the death of his father, to the position of high-priest. They were young men of intelligence, and their lives had been blameless. Knowing that they would not be spared, Luahoomoe advised them to leave Hana at once and secrete themselves in the mountains, and suggested Hanaula, an elevated spur of the mighty crater of Haleakala, as the place where they would be most likely to escape observation.

But a few weeks before Kaakakai had become the husband of the beautiful Oluolu, the daughter of a distinguished chief who had lost his life in Hua's first expedition against Hilo. Twice had she sought the *heiau* for protection against the emissaries of Hua, who had been ordered to seize and bring her to the royal mansion, and in both instances Luahoomoe had given her the shelter of the sacred enclosure. It was there that Kaakakai first met her, and, charmed no less by her beauty than her abhorrence of the lascivious intents of the king, he soon persuaded her to become his wife. But, even as his wife, Kaakakai did not deem her secure from the evil designs of the king, and had found an asylum for her in the humble home of a distant relative in a secluded valley four or five miles back of Hana, where he frequently visited her and cheered her with assurances of his love.

As the danger was imminent, Luahoomoe urged his sons to leave Hana without delay, promising Kaakakai that he would visit Oluolu the next day, and apprise her of her husband's flight and the place to which he had fled for concealment. But the old priest did not live to fulfil his promise, and Oluolu was left in ignorance of the fate of her husband.

Early next morning the bird-hunters returned, bringing with them a large number of birds, including the *uau* and *ulili*, all of which, they averred, had been caught in the mountains, when in reality they had been snared on the sea-shore.

Hua summoned the high-priest, and, pointing to the birds, said: "All these birds were snared in the mountains. You are therefore condemned to die as a false prophet who has been abandoned by his gods, and a deceiver of the people, who are entitled to the protection of their king."

Taking one of the birds in his hand, the priest calmly replied: "These birds did not come from the mountains; they are rank with the odour of the sea."

But the *hoalii* of the king steadfastly maintained that the birds had been snared in the mountains, and Hua declared the assurance of the hunters to be sufficient to outweigh the flimsy testimony of the priest.

Luahoomoe saw that he was doomed, and that the hunters had been schooled to sustain the lying assertion of the *hoalii*; yet he resolved to disconcert them all and make good his position, no matter what might be the result. He therefore asked permission to open a few of the birds, and the king sullenly granted it.

"Select them yourself," said the priest to the *hoalii*, and the latter took from the heap and handed to him three birds. The priest opened them, and the crops of all were found to be filled with small fish and bits of sea-weed.

"Behold my witness!" exclaimed the priest, pointing to the eviscerated birds, and turning toward the hoalii with a look of triumph.

Confounded and enraged at the development, Hua seized a javelin, and without a word savagely drove it into the breast of Luahoomoe, killing him on the spot. A shudder ran through the witnesses as the venerable victim fell to the earth, for violence to a high-priest was a crime almost beyond comprehension; but the king coolly handed the bloody weapon to an attendant, and, with a remorseless glance at the dying priest, leisurely walked away.

Sending for Luuana, he immediately elevated him to the dignity of high-priest, and ordered the body of Luahoomoe to be laid upon the altar of the *heiau*. The house of the dead priest was then burned, in accordance with ancient custom, and the king's executioners were despatched with attendants in search of the sons of Luahoomoe.

Proud of his newly-acquired honours, Luuana made preparations for extensive sacrifices, and then proceeded to the *heiau* with the body of Luahoomoe. As he approached the gate of the outer enclosure, the tall *pea*, or wooden cross indicative of the sanctity of the place, fell to the ground, and on reaching the inner court the earth began to quake, groans issued from the carved images of the gods, and the altar sank into the earth, leaving an opening from which issued fire and smoke. The attendants dropped the body of the priest and fled from the *heiau* in dismay, followed by the no less frightened Luuana.

The priests of the temple, who knew nothing of the death of Luahoomoe until they beheld his body about to be offered in sacrifice, stood for a moment awe-stricken at what was transpiring around them. They had been taught that the *heiau* was the only place of safety for them in a time of danger, and after the flight of Luuana and his attendants they tenderly conveyed the body of the high-priest to a hut within the enclosure to prepare it for burial.

Luuana repaired in haste to the *halealii* to report to the king what had occurred at the *heiau*. But his story excited but little surprise in Hua, for events quite as overwhelming were occurring all around them. The earth was affected with a slight but continuous tremor; a hot and almost suffocating wind had set in from the southward; strange murmurs were heard in the air; the skies were crimson, and drops of blood fell from the clouds; and finally reports came from all parts of Hana that the streams, wells and springs were no longer yielding water, and a general flight of the people to the mountains had commenced.

Such chiefs as could be found were hastily called together in council. Hua was completely subdued, and admitted that he had angered the gods by killing Luahoomoe. But what was to be done? Perhaps the sons of the martyred priest might be appealed to. But where were they? No one knew. It was suggested that a hundred human sacrifices be offered, but Luuana declined to appear again at the *heiau*, and resigned his office of high-priest. Another was appointed, and the sacrifices were ceremoniously offered. The *mu* had no difficulty in obtaining victims, for the people were desperate and offered themselves by scores. But the drought continued, and the general suffering increased from day to day. All other signs of the displeasure of the gods had passed away.

Other sacrifices were offered in great profusion, and an *imu-loa* was constructed, where human bodies were baked and in that form presented to the gods. But the springs and streams, remained dry, and the clouds dropped no rain.

The gods were redecorated, and the erection of a new *heiau* was commenced, but the people remaining in the district were too few and too weak to complete it; and a strict *tabu* was declared for a season of ten days, but the people were too desperate to observe it, and no attempt was made to punish those who disregarded it. Many drowned themselves, insane from thirst, and such as could procure the poisonous mixture died from the effects of *koheoheo* administered by their own hands.

The drought extended to the mountains, and the people fled beyond; but wherever they went the streams became dry and the rains ceased. The pestilence became known in western Maui, and the famishing refugees were driven back in attempting to enter that district.

After vainly attempting to stay the dreadful scourge, and seeing his kingdom nearly depopulated, Hua secretly embarked with a few of his attendants for Hawaii. He landed in the district of Kona; but the drought followed him. Wherever he went the fresh waters sank into the earth and the clouds yielded no rain. And so he journeyed on from place to place, carrying famine and misery with him, until in the course of his wanderings, occupying more than three years, he rendered almost one-half of the island of Hawaii a desolation. Finally he died, as the gods had decreed, of thirst and starvation – one legend says in a temple of Kohala – and his bones were left to dry in the sun; and the saying of 'rattling are the bones of Hua in the sun,' or 'dry are the bones of Hua in the sun,' has come down to the present as a significant reference to the fate of one high in power who defied the gods and persecuted the priesthood.

But rainless skies and drought did not mark alone the footsteps of Hua and his attendants. Wherever the despairing people of the district went the same affliction followed. Some of them sailed to Hawaii, others to Molokai and Oahu, and a few to Kauai; but nowhere could they find relief. Everywhere the drought kept pace with them, and famine and suffering were the result throughout the entire group. The diviners had discovered the cause of the scourge, but neither prayers nor sacrifices could avert or ameliorate it. And so it continued for nearly three and a half years.

II

DURING ALL the long years of famine and death what had befallen Oluolu, the young wife of Kaakakai, left in the secluded valley back of Hana? She saw the blight that suddenly fell upon the land; saw the springs and streams go dry around her humble home; saw the leaves of the banana wither and the grass turn yellow in the valley; saw famishing men, women and children madly searching for water, and tearing down cocoanuts for the little milk they afforded; and then by degrees she learned of all that had transpired and was still transpiring in Hana, including the sad story of the death of Luahoomoe and the flight of Kaakakai. But whither had he fled? No one could tell her; but, wherever he might be, she knew that, if alive, he would some day return to her, and therefore struggled on as best she could to live.

Her home was with Kaakao, whose wife was Mamulu. They had been blessed with three sons, all of whom had perished in Hua's useless wars, and now in their old age they were occupying a little *kuleana*, so far up the narrow valley winding into the hills that no land for cultivation was found above them. They had small patches of *taro* and potatoes, a score or two of cocoanut-trees of old growth, and plantains and bananas enough for their use. In the hills back of them were *ohias* and other wild fruits, and, with pigs and fowls in abundance, there was never any lack of food in the house of Kaakao.

But when the drought came, accompanied by the scorching south wind, Kaakao shared the fate of his neighbours. His pigs and fowls scattered in search of water, and did not return. The ripening plantains and bananas, together with a few bulbs of *taro*, were hastily gathered, and the food supply stored in the house was adequate to the wants of the occupants for some weeks to come; but fresh water was nowhere to be found, and the cocoanuts were stripped from the trees and laid away to meet, as far as possible, the terrible emergency.

Thus passed nearly half a month, during which time harrowing reports from the valleys below reached the *kuleana* through parties vainly searching everywhere among the hills for water. Then Kaakao saw that his supply of cocoanut-milk was nearly exhausted, and resolved to visit the sea-shore, where he knew of a spring in times past dripping from the rocks almost on a level with the waves. "Surely," he thought, "that spring cannot be dry, with all the water around it." And, swinging two water-calabashes over his shoulders, he started for the sea-shore. But he never returned. In passing to the coast he was seized, among others, and offered as a sacrifice in the *heiau*.

For two days his return was awaited at the *kuleana*. Then Mamulu solemnly said: "Kaakao is dead. We have no more water and but little food. Why suffer longer? Let us drink *koheoheo* and die."

"Not today, my good friend Mamulu," replied Oluolu, soothingly. "We will talk of it tomorrow. Last night in my dreams a whisper told me not to despair. Let us wait."

The next morning Oluolu rose at daylight. The last of the cocoanut-milk was gone, and the mouths of both were dry and feverish. There was a strangely cheerful light in Oluolu's eyes as she bent over the suffering but patient Mamulu, and, holding up a calabash, said: "I shall soon return with this filled with water! – think of it, Mamulu! – filled with pure, fresh water!"

"Poor child!" replied Mamulu, not doubting that her mind was wandering. "But where will you go for it?"

"Only a short walk – right up the valley!" returned Oluolu. "You know the little cavern among the rocks. The mouth is almost closed, but I can find it. The water is in the back part of the *ana*. It is running water, but it disappears in the darkness. Perhaps it comes from *Po*; but no matter – it is sweet and good. Luahoomoe came to me last night, with his long, white hair smeared with blood, and told me he had sent the water there. It is for us alone. If others know of it or taste it, it will disappear. So we must be careful, Mamulu, very careful."

Leaving the woman almost in a daze at the words thus spoken in rapid and excited sentences, Oluolu left the hut and started up the narrow valley. A walk of three or four minutes brought her to the entrance of an abrupt and chasm-like ravine gashing the hills on the right. To its almost precipitous sides clung overhanging masses of ragged volcanic rock, from the crevices of which a sturdy vegetation had taken root, and in time past gloomily shaded the narrow channel; but the interlacing branches of the trees were almost leafless, and all around were seen the footprints of death and desolation. Not a breath of wind cooled the sultry air, and no sound of living creature broke the silence of the heated hills. The mouth of the ravine was partially choked with huge boulders washed down by the freshets of centuries, and the ground was strewn with dead leaves and broken branches.

Casting her eyes around in every direction, to be sure that she was not observed, Oluolu quickly found a way over the boulders and ascended the ravine. Proceeding upward thirty or forty yards, and climbing a rocky bench, over which in seasons of rain had poured a little cascade, she stopped in front of an overhanging mass of vitreous rock, and the next moment disappeared in a stooping posture through a low opening almost concealed by decrepitations from above. The opening led to a cavern forty or fifty feet in depth, with an irregular width almost as great. The floor descended from the entrance, and was smooth and apparently water-worn. Two or three steps forward enabled her to stand upright; but all beyond was darkness, and for a moment she remained undecided which way to proceed. She heard a sound like that of a bare and cautious footstep on the smooth floor. She was startled, but suffering had made her desperate, and she listened again. The same sound continued, but it was mellowed into the soft murmur of waters somewhere back in the darkness, and with a swelling heart she groped her way toward the silvery voice, sweeter to her than the strains of the *ohe* or the songs of birds.

Closer and closer she approached, every step making more distinct the joyful music, until at last she felt the spatter of cool water upon her bare feet. Stretching out her hand, it came in contact with a little stream gushing from the back wall of the cavern, and instantly disappearing where it fell upon a layer of loose gravel washed down from the entrance. She hastily drank from her palm, and found that the water was cool and sweet. Then she held the mouth of the calabash under the stream, and, after wetting her head and drinking until prudence counseled her to stop, refilled the vessel, cautiously emerged from the opening, and hastened back to the hut.

Hesitating without the door, to satisfy herself that no one had arrived during her absence, Oluolu noiselessly entered, and, stealing to the *kapa-moe* upon which Mamulu was half-deliriously dreaming, poured a quantity of water upon her head, and, as she opened her eyes with a bewildered stare, dropped a swallow into her parched and open mouth.

Half-rising, Mamulu dreamily felt of her dripping hair, and then stared vacantly at Oluolu, who stood smilingly beside her with the calabash in her hand. In a moment she recalled all that had occurred before she dropped into the troubled sleep from which she had been so strangely aroused.

"Then it is not a dream!" she murmured, clasping her wasted hands upon her breast. "The gods have sent us water!" And she reached for the calabash.

"No," said Oluolu kindly, withdrawing the vessel. "We have plenty, but you are weak and would drink too much. Now lie down, with this roll of *kapa* under your head, and while I am giving you a swallow at a time I will tell you all about the water and how I found it."

And so, slowly feeding Mamulu with the precious fluid, and at the same time bathing her head and throat, Oluolu related to her everything that had occurred.

"But will the stream continue?" anxiously inquired Mamulu. "Would it not be well to fill all the calabashes in the house, and all we can procure, and so keep them, that we may not be left without water should the stream disappear?"

"I think it would not be well to anger the gods by doubting them," replied Oluolu. "The water was sent, not to prolong our sufferings, but to save our lives; and I am sure it will continue so long as we guard the secret and allow no others to use it."

Oluolu's faith was rewarded. Without any diminution in volume the little stream continued to flow and sink in the darkness of the cavern until the wrath of the gods was appeased and the rains finally came again. But Oluolu and her companion could not subsist on water alone. The parched earth produced no food; but they did not despair. Every day they cautiously watered a little patch of mountain *taro* in the ravine above the cavern, and at intervals of four or five days went to the sea-shore and returned with fish, crabs, limpets and edible sea-weed.

And so they managed to live without suffering, while the valleys became almost depopulated, and all others in Hana were stricken with famine. They seldom saw a human face in their journeys to and from the sea, and never in the valley where they lived, and the few they met avoided them, fearful, no doubt, that the miserable means of subsistence to which they resorted might become known to others.

III

IT WAS NEAR the end of the terrible scourge that the district of Ewa, on the island of Oahu, became its victim. It followed the appearance there of a Hana chief and a few of his retainers, who had been driven from Molokai. At that time there lived at Waimalu, in the district of Ewa, the celebrated priest and prophet Naula-a-Maihea. No one in the Hawaiian priesthood of the past was ever more feared or respected. It was thought by some that he had visited the shadowy realms of *Milu*, and from *Paliuli* had brought back the waters of life. He must have been well on in years, for, as already mentioned, he is credited with having been the priest of Laa-mai-kahiki on the romantic journey of that prince from the southern islands.

In evidence of the great sanctity of Naula, tradition relates that his canoe was upset during a journey from Waianae, Oahu, to Kauai. He was swallowed by a whale, in whose stomach he remained without inconvenience until the monster crossed the channel and vomited him up alive on the beach at Waialua, Kauai, the precise place of his destination. At another time, when crossing to Hawaii, and beset with adverse winds, two huge black sharks, sent by *Mooalii*, the shark-god of Molokai, towed him to Kohala so swiftly that the sea-birds could scarcely keep him company.

He built a *heiau* at Waimalu, the foundations of which may still be traced, and in the inner temple of the enclosure it is asserted that Lono conversed with him freely; and at his bidding the spirits of the living (*kahaoka*) as well as the shades of the dead (*unihipili*) made their appearance; for it was believed by the ancient Hawaiians that the spirits or souls of the living sometimes separated themselves from the body during slumber or while in a condition of trance, and became visible in distant places to priests of especial sanctity.

Consulting with the gods, Naula discovered the cause of the drought, and, becoming alarmed at the threatened destruction of the entire population of the group, undertook to stay the ravages of the spreading scourge. With a vision enlarged and intensified by sacrifice and prayer, he ascended the highest peak of the Waianae Mountains. Far as the eye could reach the skies were cloudless. He first looked toward Kaala, but discerned no sign of rain around its wooded summits. He turned toward Kauai, but not a cloud could be seen above the mountains of that island. Cloudless, also, were the mountains of Molokai. Finally, casting his eyes in the direction of Maui, he saw a small, dark spot like a rain-cloud hanging above the peak of Hanaula. "It may disappear," he thought; "I will wait." Midday came. He looked again, and the spot was still there. The sun grew red in the west. Again he looked and found that the cloud had neither disappeared nor moved. "Surely the sons of Luahoomoe are there," he said to himself. "I will go to them; they will listen to me, and the waters will come again."

Naula descended from the mountain, and the same night embarked alone in a canoe for Maui. He spread no sail, used no paddle, but all night his *waa* skimmed the waves with the speed of the wind, and at sunrise the next morning he landed at Makena, above which, a few miles inland, towered the peak of Hanaula, with the dark spot still hanging over it.

There, indeed, were the sons of Luahoomoe. Nurtured by the rains that had fallen alone on the peak of Hanaula, there they had remained unseen for three and a half years, waiting for the wrath of the gods to be appeased and for a summons to descend. A strange light accompanied the canoe of

Naula in the darkness. From their elevated retreat they noted it far out upon the ocean, and watched it growing brighter as it approached, until it went out on the beach at Makena. They knew it to be the signal of their deliverance, and hastened down the mountain to meet the messenger of the gods. One account says they met Naula at Kula; but the meeting occurred not far from the Makena landing, where the priest, inspired with a knowledge of their coming, awaited their arrival. As they approached, the venerable kahuna, his white hair and beard falling to his waist and a *tabu* staff in his hand, advanced to meet them. They bowed respectfully, and, returning the salutation, Naula said:

"I know you to be the sons of Luahoomoe, whose death by the hands of Hua, King of Hana, has been avenged by the gods upon the people of all the islands of Hawaii. The earth is still parched, and thousands are seeking in vain for food and water. Hua is dead; his bones lie unburied in the sun. Scattered or dead are the people of Hana; their lands are yellow, and their springs and streams yield nothing but dust and ashes. Great was the crime of Hua, and great has been the punishment. I am Naula-a-Maihea, the high-priest of Oahu, and have come to ask, with you, that the gods may be merciful and no longer scourge the people."

At the mention of his name the sons of Luahoomoe bowed low before the aged prophet of whose sanctity report had years before apprised them, and then Kaakakai replied:

"Great priest, willingly will we add our voices to your supplication to the gods, whose vengeance has indeed been terrible. But since our retreat was revealed to you and nothing seems to be hidden from your understanding, let me ask if you know aught of the fate of Oluolu. She was my wife, and I left her in a little valley in the mountains back of Hana. I loved her greatly, and am grieved with the fear that she is dead."

Without replying the priest seated himself upon the ground, and, unbinding the *kihei* from his shoulders, threw it over his head, shutting the light from his face. While one hand pressed the mantle closely to his breast, the other held to his forehead what seemed to be a talisman of stone suspended by a short cord from his neck. He remained motionless in that position for some minutes; then throwing off the *kihei* and rising to his feet, he turned to Kaakakai and said:

"I was not wrong in my thought. The presence here of the sons of Luahoomoe has sanctified the spot to communion with the spirits of the air. Oluolu, alone with a woman much her elder, still lives where you left her and hopefully awaits the coming of Kaakakai – for such I now know to be your name. The spirit of Luahoomoe has nourished and protected her."

"Great Naula, most favoured of the gods!" exclaimed Kaakakai, grasping the hand of the priest. "You have made my heart glad! Now ask of me what you will!"

On the very spot from which the priest had risen they proceeded to erect a rude altar of stones. When it was completed Naula brought from his canoe a combined image of the godhead – the *Oie* of the early priesthood – and a small enclosed calabash of holy water – *ka-wai-kapu-a-Kane*. Removing the *kapa* covering, the image was placed beside the altar, and while the priest recited the solemn *kaiokopeo*, or prayer of consecration, Kaakakai intoned the invocation and continued at intervals to sprinkle the altar with holy water.

The dedication ceremonies were at length concluded; but what was there to offer as a sacrifice? The hills were bare and parched. Far as the eye could reach the lands were deserted, and no living thing beside themselves was visible. Suddenly there appeared among the leafless shrubbery near them a large black hog sacred to sacrifice. The brothers exchanged looks of wonder, but the priest did not seem to be greatly surprised. The animal was immediately seized, killed and placed upon the altar, and sacrificial prayers were devoutly offered.

In the midst of these services a wind set in from the south. Black clouds began to gather, from which the answering voice of thunder came, and then a gentle rain began to fall upon the sere and hungry earth. Raising his face into the baptism, Naula with emotion exclaimed:

"The sacrifice is accepted! The gods are merciful, and the people are saved!"

And the rains continued, not there alone but all over the islands, until the grass grew green again and the banana put forth its shoots. Everywhere the rejoicing was great. The people returned to their deserted lands, and the valleys of Hana, even, blossomed as before. But Hua and his family had perished from the earth, and a new dynasty came into being to claim the sovereignty of eastern Maui.

The sons of the martyred Luahoomoe returned at once to Hana, and in the arms of Kaakakai the brave and faithful Oluolu recited the story of her sufferings and deliverance. With largely-augmented possessions Kaakakai became the high-priest under the new *régime,* and for generations his descendants continued to be among the most influential of the families of eastern Maui. Kaanahua became the god of the husbandman.

The political events immediately following the death of Hua are but vaguely referred to by tradition, and the few particulars known doubtless owe their preservation to the care taken by the priesthood – to which class the historians of the past usually belonged – to bring down, with all its terrible details, the fate of Hua, as a warning to succeeding sovereigns who might be disposed to trespass upon the sacred domain of the spiritual rulers who, in a measure, divided the allegiance of their subjects.

Kelea, the Surf-Rider of Maui

His Hawaiian Majesty Kalakaua, Hawaii

The Legend of Lo-Lale, the Eccentric Prince of Oahu

I

KELEA, OF WHOM IN THE PAST THE BARDS of Oahu and Maui loved to sing, was the beautiful but capricious sister of Kawao, king of Maui, who in about AD 1445, at the age of twenty-five, succeeded to the sovereignty of that island. Their royal father was Kahekili I, the son of Kakae, who, with his brother, Kakaalaneo, was the joint ruler of the little realm from about 1380 to 1415. Kakae was the rightful heir to the *moiship*, and, as such, his son Kahekili succeeded him; but as an accident in his youth had somewhat impaired his mental faculties, Kakaalaneo became, through the expressed will of the dying Kamaloohua, the joint ruler and virtual sovereign of the kingdom. He had sons and daughters of his own; but he loved his weak-minded brother, and respected the line of legitimate succession, and when the black *kapa* covered him, Kahekili became king of Maui and Lanai; for during that period the latter island was under the protection of the *mois* of Maui, while Molokai still maintained its independence.

Kakaalaneo was noted for his business energy and strict sense of justice. The court of the brothers was established at Lahaina – then known as Lele – and was one of the most respected in all the group. It was Kakaalaneo who introduced the bread-fruit there from Hawaii, and won the love of the people by continuous acts of mercy and benevolence. For some disrespect shown to his royal brother, whose mental weakness doubtless subjected him to unkind remarks, he banished his son Kaululaau to Lanai, which island, tradition avers, was at that time infested by powerful and malignant spirits. They killed pigs and fowls, uprooted cocoanut-trees and blighted *taro* patches, and a gigantic and mischievous gnome amused himself by gliding like a huge mole under the huts of his victims and almost upsetting them.

The priests tried in vain to quiet these malicious spirits. No sooner were they exorcised away from one locality than they appeared in another, and if they gave the *taro* patches a rest it was only to tear the unripe bananas from their stems, or rend the walls and embankments of artificial ponds, that their stores of fishes might escape to the sea. Aware of these grievances, Kaululaau took with him to Lanai a talisman of rare powers. It was the gift of his friend, the high-priest of his father, and consisted of a spear-point that had been dipped in the waters of *Po*, the land of death, and many generations before left by *Lono* on one of his altars.

Crowning a long spear with this sacred point, Kaululaau attacked the disturbing spirits, and in a short time succeeded either in bringing them to submission or driving them from the island. The gnome *Mooaleo* was the most difficult to vanquish. It avoided the prince, and for some time managed to keep beyond the influence of the charmed spear-point; but the monster was finally caught within the boundaries of a circular line scratched with the talisman upon the surface of the earth beneath which it was burrowing, and thereby brought to terms. It could not pass the line, no matter how far below the surface it essayed to do so. Heaving the earth in its strength and wrath, it chafed against the charmed restraint that held it captive, and finally plunged downward within the vertical walls of its prison. But there was no path of escape in that direction. It soon encountered a lake of fire, and was compelled to return to the surface, where it humbled itself before the prince, and promised, if liberated, to quit the island for ever. Kaululaau obliterated sixty paces of the line of imprisonment, to enable *Mooaleo* to pass to the sea, into which the hideous being plunged and disappeared, never to be seen again in Lanai.

In consideration of the great service of the exiled prince in restoring quiet and security to the island, his father permitted him to return to Maui, where he connected himself with the priesthood, and became noted for his supernatural powers. The charmed spear-point is referred to in later legends, and is thought to be still secreted with the bones of a high-priest in a mountain cave on the island of Maui, not far from the sacred burial-place of Iao.

But we have been straying two generations back of our story. The legendary accounts of the ruling families of the principal islands of the group are so threaded with romantic or fabulous incidents that, in referring to any of the prominent actors in the past, it is difficult to restrain the pen in its willingness to wander into the enchanted by-ways in which the *meles* of the period abound.

Having alluded to the immediate ancestors of Kelea, the sister of the young *moi* of Maui, we will now resume the thread of our legend by referring somewhat more particularly to the princess herself. Brought up in the royal court at Lahaina, with a brother only to divide the affections of her father, Kelea was humoured, petted and spoiled as a child, and courted and flattered beyond measure as she grew to womanhood. The *meles* describe her as a maiden of uncommon beauty; but she was wayward, volatile and capricious, as might have been expected of one so schooled and favoured, and no consideration of policy or persuasion of passion could move her to accept any one of the many high chiefs who sought her in marriage. She loved the water – possibly because she could see her fair face mirrored in it – and became the most graceful and daring surf-swimmer in the kingdom. Frequently, when the waters of Auau Channel surged wildly under the breath of the south wind, or *kona*, Kelea, laughing at the fears of her brother, would plunge into the sea with her *onini*, or surf-board, and so audaciously ride the waves that those who watched and applauded her were half-inclined to believe that she was the friend of some water-god, and could not be drowned.

No sport was to her so enticing as a battle with the waves, and when her brother spoke to her of marriage she gaily answered that the surf-board was her husband, and she would never embrace any other. The brother frowned at the answer, for he had hoped, by uniting his sister to the principal chief of Hana, to more thoroughly incorporate in his kingdom that portion of the island, then ruled by independent chiefs; but by other means during his reign, it may be remarked, the union of the two divisions was effected.

"Do not frown, Kawao," said Kelea, coaxingly; "a smile better becomes your handsome face. I may marry some day, just to please you; but remember what the voice said in the *anu* at the last feast of *Lono*."

"Yes, I remember," replied Kawao; "but I have sometimes believed that when the *kilo* declared that in riding the surf Kelea would find a husband, he was simply repeating an augury imparted to him by Kelea herself."

"You will anger the gods by speaking so lightly of their words," returned Kelea, reproachfully; and Kawao smiled as the princess took her leave with a dignity quite unusual with her.

Kawao loved his sister and was proud of her beauty; and while he was anxious to see her suitably married, and felt no little annoyance at the importunities of her suitors, he nevertheless recognized her right, as the daughter of a king, to a voice in the selection of a husband.

But the voice from the *anu* was prophetic, whatever may have inspired it; for while Kelea continued to ride the waves at Lahaina, a husband, of the family of Kalona-iki, of Oahu, was in search of her, and to that island we now request the reader to follow us.

There lived at that time at Lihue, in the district of Ewa, on the island of Oahu, a chief named Lo-Lale, son of Kalona-iki, and brother of Piliwale, the *alii-nui*, or nominal sovereign, of the island, whose court was established at Waialua. Kalona-iki had married Kikinui, and thus infused into the royal family the native and aristocratic blood of Maweke, of the ancient line of Nanaula.

Lo-Lale was an amiable and handsome prince, but for some cause had reached the age of thirty-five without marrying. The reason was traced to the death by drowning, some years before, of a chiefess of great beauty whom he was about to marry, and to whom he was greatly attached. As he was of a gentle and poetic nature, his disinclination to marriage may not be unreasonably attributed to that event, especially when supported by the relation that thereafter he abhorred the sea, and was content to remain at Lihue, beyond the sound of its ceaseless surges.

Piliwale had passed his fiftieth year, and, having but two daughters and no son, was more than ever desirous that his brother should marry, that the family authority might be strengthened and the line of Kalona perpetuated. And the friendly neighbouring chiefs were equally anxious that Lo-Lale should become the head of a family, and, to inspire him with a disposition to marry, described with enthusiasm the beauty of many maidens of distinguished rank whom they had met on the other islands of the group.

To these importunities Lo-Lale finally yielded; and as a suitable wife for so high a chief could not be found on Oahu, or, at least, one who would be personally acceptable to him, it was necessary to seek for her among the royal families of the other islands. Accordingly, a large *koa* canoe was fitted out at Waialua, and with trusty messengers of rank despatched to the windward islands in search of a wife for Lo-Lale. The messengers were instructed to quietly visit the several royal courts, and report upon the beauty, rank and eligibility of such marriageable chiefesses of distinguished families as they might be able to discover.

Among the chiefs selected for the delicate mission, and the one upon whose judgement the most reliance was placed, was Lo-Lale's cousin, Kalamakua, a noble of high rank, whose lands were on the coast of the Ewa district. He was bold, dashing and adventurous, and readily consented to assist in finding a wife for his royal and romantic relative.

Lo-Lale was at Waialua when the messengers embarked. He took an encouraging interest in the expedition, and when banteringly asked by his cousin if age would be any objection in a bride of unexceptional birth, replied that he had promised to take a wife solely to please his royal brother, and any age under eighty would answer. But he did not mean it.

"Not so," replied Piliwale, more than half in earnest. "I will not become the uncle of a family of monsters. The bride must be as worthy in person as in blood."

"Do you hear, Kalamakua?" said Lo-Lale, addressing his cousin, who was standing beside the canoe, ready for departure; "do you hear the words of Piliwale? She must be not only young but beautiful. If you bring or give promise to any other, she shall not live at Lihue!"

"Do not fear," replied the cousin, gaily. "Whomsoever she may be, we will keep her in the family; for if you refuse her, or she you, I will marry her myself!"

"Fairly spoken!" exclaimed the king; "and I will see that he keeps his promise, Lo-Lale."

Although the object of the voyage was known to but few, hundreds gathered at the beach to witness the departure, for the canoe was decorated, and the embarking chiefs appeared in feather capes and other ornaments of their rank. Turning to the high-priest, who was present, Piliwale asked him if he had observed the auguries.

"I have," replied the priest. "They are more than favourable." Then turning his face northward, he continued: "There is peace in the clouds, and the listless winging of yonder bird betokens favouring winds."

Amid a chorus of *alohas*! the canoe dashed through the breakers and out into the open sea, holding a course in the direction of Molokai. Reaching that island early the next day, the party landed at Kalaupapa. The *alii-nui* received them well, but inquiry led to nothing satisfactory, and, proceeding around the island, the party next landed on Lanai. It is probable that they were driven there by unfavourable winds, as Lanai was a dependency of Maui at that time, and none but subject chiefs resided on the island. However, they remained there but one day, and the next proceeded to Hana, Maui, with the intention of crossing over to Hawaii and visiting the court of Kiha at Waipio. Inquiring for the *moi*, they learned that Kawao had removed his court from Lahaina, for the season, to Hamakuapoko, to enjoy the cool breezes of that locality and indulge in the pleasures of surf-bathing. They were further informed that a large number of chiefs had accompanied the *moi* to that attractive resort, and that Kelea, sister of the king, and the most beautiful woman on the island as well as the most daring and accomplished surf-swimmer, was also there as one of the greatest ornaments of the court.

This was agreeable information, and the party re-embarked and arrived the next morning off Hamakuapoko, just as the fair Kelea and her attendants had gone down to the beach to indulge in a buffet with the surf. Swimming out beyond the breakers, and oblivious of everything but her own enjoyment, Kelea suddenly found herself within a few yards of the canoe of the Oahuan chiefs. Presuming that it contained her own people, she swam still closer, when she discovered, to her amazement, that all the faces in the canoe were strange to her. Perceiving her embarrassment, Kalamakua rose to his feet, and, addressing her in a courtly and respectful manner, invited her to a seat in the canoe, offering to ride the surf with it to the beach – an exciting and sometimes dangerous sport, in which great skill and coolness are required. The language of the chief was so gentle and suggestive of the manners of the court that the invitation was accepted, and the canoe mounted one of the great waves successively following two of lighter bulk and force, and was adroitly and safely beached. The achievement was greeted with applause on the shore, and when the proposal was made to repeat the performance Kelea willingly retained her seat. Again the canoe successfully rode the breakers ashore, and then, through her attendants, Kalamakua discovered that the fair and dashing swimmer was none other than Kelea, the sister of the *moi* of Maui.

With increased respect Kalamakua again invited his distinguished guest to join in the pleasure and excitement of a third ride over the breakers. She consented, and the canoe was once more pulled out beyond the surf, where it remained for a moment, awaiting a high, combing roller on which to be borne to the landing. One passed and was missed, and before another came a squall, or what was called a *mumuku*, suddenly struck the canoe, rendering it utterly unmanageable and driving it out upon the broad ocean.

When the canoe started Kelea would have leaped into the sea had she not been restrained; but Kalamakua spoke so kindly to her – assuring her that they would safely ride out the storm and return to Hamakuapoko – that she became calmer, and consented to curl down beside him in the boat to escape the fury of the winds. Her shapely limbs and shoulders were bare, and her hair, braided and bound loosely back, was still wet, and grew chilling in the wind where it fell. Kalamakua took from a covered calabash a handsome *kihei*, or mantle, and wrapped it around her shoulders, and then seated her in the shelter of his own burly form. She smiled her thanks for these delicate attentions, and the chief was compelled to admit to himself that the reports of her great beauty had not been exaggerated. He could recall no maiden on Oahu who was her equal in grace and comeliness, and felt that, could she be secured for his eccentric cousin, his search would be at an end. He even grew indignant at the thought that she might not prove acceptable, but smiled the next moment at his promise to marry the girl himself should she be refused by his cousin.

But the fierce mumuku afforded him but little time to indulge such dreams. The sea surged in fury, and like a cockleshell the canoe was tossed from one huge wave to another. The spray was almost blinding, and, while Kalamakua kept the little craft squarely before the wind as a measure of first importance, his companions were earnestly employed in alternately baling and trimming as emergency suggested.

On, on sped the canoe, farther and farther out into the open sea, tossed like a feather by the crested waves and pelted by the driving spray. The scene was fearful. The southern skies had grown black with wrath, and long streamers sent from the clouds shot northward as if to surround and cut off the retreat of the flying craft. All crouched in the bottom of the boat, intent only on keeping it before the wind and preventing it from filling. A frailer craft would have been stove to pieces; but it was hewn from the trunk of a sound *koa* tree, and gallantly rode out the storm.

But when the wind ceased and the skies cleared, late in the afternoon, the canoe was far out at sea and beyond the sight of land. It was turned and headed back; but as there was no wind to assist the paddles, and the waters were still rough and restless, slow progress toward land was made; and when the sun went down Kalamakua was undecided which way to proceed, as he was not certain that the storm had not carried them so far from the coast of Maui that some point on Molokai or Oahu might be more speedily and safely reached than the place from which they started. Their supply of *poi* had been lost during the gale by the breaking of the vessel containing it; but they had still left a small quantity of dried fish, raw potatoes and bananas, and a calabash of water, and ate their evening meal as cheerfully as if their supplies were exhaustless and the green hills of Waialua smiled upon them in the distance. Such was the Hawaiian of the past; such is the Hawaiian of today. His joys and griefs are centred in the present, and he broods but little over the past, and borrows no trouble from the future.

The stars came out, and a light wind began to steal down upon them from the northwest. It was quite chilly, and felt like the breath of the returning trade-winds, which start from the frozen shores of northwestern America, and gradually grow warmer as they sweep down through the tropic seas. These winds, continuing, with intervals of cessation, eight or nine months in the year, are what give life, beauty and an endurable climate to the Hawaiian group.

As the breeze freshened sails were raised, and then the course to be taken remained to be determined. Kalamakua expressed his doubts to Kelea, as if inviting a suggestion from her; but she was unable to offer any advice, declaring that she had not noticed the course of the wind that had driven them so far out upon the ocean.

"And I am equally in doubt," said the chief. "We may have been blown farther toward the rising of the sun than the headlands of Hana. If so, the course we are now sailing would take us to Hawaii, if not, indeed, beyond, while in following the evening star we might even pass Oahu. I therefore suggest a course between these two directions, which will certainly bring us to land some time tomorrow."

"Then, since we are all in doubt," replied Kelea, "and the winds are blowing landward, why not trust to the gods and follow them?"

"Your words are an inspiration," returned the chief, delighted that she had suggested a course that would enable him to make Oahu direct; for, as may be suspected, he was an accomplished navigator, and was really in little or no doubt concerning the direction of the several islands mentioned. "You have spoken wisely," he continued, as if yielding entirely to her judgement; "we will follow the winds that are now cooling the shores of Hamakuapoko."

Thus adroitly was Kelea made a consenting party to her own abduction. Kalamakua took the helm, slightly changing the course of the canoe, and his companions made themselves comfortable for the evening. Their wet rolls of kapa had been dried during the afternoon, and there was room enough to spare to arrange a couch for Kelea in the bottom of the boat. But she was too much excited over the strange events of the day to sleep, or even attempt to rest, and therefore sat near Kalamakua in the stern of the canoe until past midnight, watching the stars and listening to the story, with which he knew she must sooner or later become acquainted, of his romantic expedition in search of a wife for his cousin.

It is needless to say that Kalea was surprised and interested in the relation; and when Kalamakua referred to the high rank of his cousin, to his handsome person and large estates at Lihue, and begged her to regard with favour the proposal of marriage which he then made to her in behalf of Lo-Lale, she frankly replied that, if her royal brother did not object, she would give the proffer consideration.

As Kalamakua had concluded not to take the hazard of securing the consent of her brother, who doubtless had some other matrimonial project in view for her, he construed her answer into a modestly expressed willingness to become the wife of Lo-Lale, and the more resolutely bent his course toward Oahu. He watched the Pleiades – the great guide of the early Polynesian navigators – as they swept up into the heavens, and, bearing still farther to the northward to escape Molokai, announced that he would keep the steering-oar for the night, and advised his companions, now that the breeze was steady and the sea smoother, to betake themselves to rest. And Kelea at last curled down upon her couch of *kapa*, and Kalamakua was left alone with his thoughts to watch the wind and stars.

Although a long and steady run had been made during the night, no land was visible the next morning. Kelea scanned the horizon uneasily, and, without speaking, looked at Kalamakua for an explanation.

"Before the sun goes down we shall see land," said the chief.

"What land?" inquired Kelea.

"Oahu," was the reply, but the chief was not greeted with the look of surprise expected.

"I am not disappointed," returned the princess, quite indifferently. "You seem to have been sailing by the wandering stars last night, for before daylight I looked up and saw by *Kao* that your course was directly toward the place of sunset."

Five of the planets – Mercury, Mars, Venus, Jupiter and Saturn – were known to the ancient Hawaiians, and designated as *na hoku aea*, or wandering stars. The fixed stars were also grouped by them into constellations, and *Kao* was their name for Antares.

With a look of genuine surprise Kalamakua replied:

"I did not know before that so correct a knowledge of navigation was among the many accomplishments of the sister of Kawao."

"It required no great knowledge of the skies to discover last night that we were not bearing southward, and needs still less now to observe that we are sailing directly west," Kelea quietly remarked.

"I will not attempt to deceive one who seems to be able to instruct me in journeying over the blue waters," said Kalamakua, politely. "Your judgement is correct. We are sailing nearly westward, and the first land sighted will probably be the headlands of Kaawa."

"You have acted treacherously," resumed the princess, after a pause, as if suddenly struck with the propriety of protesting against the abduction.

"Possibly," was the brief reply.

"Yes," she continued, after another pause, "you have acted treacherously, and my brother will make war upon Oahu unless I am immediately returned to Hamakuapoko."

"He will find work for his spears," was the irritating response.

"Is it a habit with the chiefs of Oahu to steal their wives?" inquired Kelea, tauntingly.

"No," Kalamakua promptly replied; "but I would not eat from the same calabash with the chief who would throw back into the face of the generous winds the gift of the rarest flower that ever blossomed on Hawaiian soil!"

The pretty compliment of the chief moved Kelea to silence; yet he observed that there was a sparkle of pleasure in her eyes, and that the novelty and romance of the situation were not altogether distasteful to her.

Land was sighted late in the afternoon. It was Kaoio Point, on the western side of Oahu. Rounding it, they landed at Mahana, where they procured food and water and passed the night, and the next day had an easy voyage to Waialua.

Landing, Kalamakua at once communicated with Piliwale, giving the high rank of Kelea, as well as the strange circumstances under which she had been brought to Waialua. Queen Paakanilea promptly despatched attendants to the beach with appropriate apparel, and in due time the distinguished visitor was received at the royal mansion in a manner consistent with her rank.

The next day a message brought Lo-Lale from Lihue. He was dressed in his richest trappings, and brought with him, as an offering to Kelea, a rare necklace of shells and curiously-carved mother-of-pearl. He was conducted to the princess by Kalamakua.

They seemed to be mutually pleased with each other. In fact, Lo-Lale was completely charmed by the fair stranger, and in his enthusiasm offered to divide his estates with his cousin as an evidence of his gratitude.

Kalamakua had himself become very much interested in Kelea, and secretly hoped that his cousin might find something in her blood or bearing to object to, in which case he felt that she might be induced to regard his own suit with favour; but Lo-Lale declared her to be a model of perfection, and wooed her with so much earnestness that she finally consented to become his wife without waiting to hear from her brother.

Her rank was quite equal to that of Lo-Lale, and the king was so greatly pleased with the union that he added considerably to the estates of his brother at Lihue, and the nuptials were celebrated with games, feasting, dancing and the commencement of a new *heiau* near Waialua, which was in time completed and dedicated to *Lono*, with a large image of *Laamaomao*, the Hawaiian Æolus, at the inner entrance, in poetic commemoration of the winds that drove Kelea away from the coast of Maui.

At the conclusion of the festivities at Waialua, Kelea was borne all the way to Lihue in a richly-mounted *manele*, or native palanquin with four bearers. There were three hundred attendants in her train, exclusive of thirty-six chiefs as a guard of honour, wearing feather capes and helmets, and armed with javelins festooned with *leis* of flowers and tinted feathers. It was a right royal procession, and its entrance into Lihue was the beginning of another round of festivities continuing for many days. Portions of the *mele* recited by Lo-Lale in welcome of his wife to Lihue are still remembered and repeated, and the occasion was a popular theme of song and comment for a generation or more among the people of that district.

And thus Kelea, the beautiful sister of the *moi* of Maui, became the wife of Lo-Lale, brother of Piliwale, king of Oahu.

II

IT IS NOW IN order to return to Hamakuapoko, to note what transpired there on the sudden disappearance of Kelea before the strong breath of the mumuku. The king was profoundly grieved, and summoned the attendants of his sister to learn the particulars of the misfortune. To all of them it was manifest that the canoe had been blown out to sea in spite of the efforts of its occupants, and, as the gale continued to increase in violence during the day, it was feared that the entire party had perished. As to the strangers, no one seemed to know anything of them or of the island from which they came. They did not seem to belong to the *makaainana*, or common people, and one of them, it was believed from his bearing, was a high chief.

This was all the information the wailing attendants were able to give. One man, who had noticed the canoe as it came and went through the surf, thought it was from Hawaii, while another was equally certain that it was from Oahu; but as the general structure of canoes on the several islands of the group differed but little, their descriptions of the craft furnished no real clue to the mystery.

With the cessation of the storm, late in the afternoon, came a hope to Kawao that the missing canoe had safely ridden out the gale, and would seek the nearest land favoured by the changing winds. He therefore summoned the high-priest, and instructed him to put his diviners and magicians to the task of discovering what had become of the princess Kelea. Pigs and fowls were slain, prayers were said in the *heiau*, and late in the evening information came through supernatural agencies that Kelea was still living. But this was not satisfactory to the king. He demanded something more specific, and a *kaula* of great sanctity was prepared and placed in the *anu*, a wicker enclosure within the inner court, and in due time, in answer to the questions of the high-priest, announced that the canoe containing the princess was sailing in safety toward Oahu.

The words of the *kaula* were repeated to the king, and the next day he despatched a well-manned canoe, in charge of one of his plumed *halumanus*, or military aids, to find and bring back the lost Kelea. Owing to unfavourable winds or bad management the canoe did not reach Makapuu Point, Oahu, until the fourth day. Proceeding along the northeastern coast of the island, and landing wherever practicable to make inquiries, the easy-going messenger did not arrive at Waialua until two days after the departure of Kelea for Lihue.

Learning that the princess had become the wife of Lo-Lale, the disappointed *halumanu* did not deem it necessary to communicate with her, but briefly paid his respects to the king, to whom he made known the nature of his errand to Oahu, and his resolution to return at once to Maui and acquaint his royal master with the result of his mission.

Appreciating that, in his anxiety to see his brother properly mated, he had countenanced a proceeding sufficiently discourteous to the *moi* of Maui to warrant a hostile response, Piliwale treated the *halumanu* with marked kindness and consideration, and insisted upon sending an escort with him back to Maui, including the bearer of a friendly explanatory message from himself to Kawao. For this delicate service no one could be found so competent as the courtly Kalamakua, who was well versed in the genealogy of the Kalona family, and would be able to satisfactorily, if not quite truthfully, explain why it was that the canoe containing the princess, when driven out to sea, was headed for Oahu instead of Maui when the storm abated.

Kalamakua was accordingly despatched on the mission. Being a much better sailor than the *halumanu*, he found no difficulty either in parting company with him off the coast of eastern Maui or in reaching Hamakuapoko three or four hours in advance of the party he was courteously escorting thither. This enabled the wily Oahuan to secure an audience with the king, and deliver his message and explanation in full, before the halumanu could land and give his version of the story.

Kalamakua's explanation of the impossibility, after the storm, of reaching in safety any land other than Oahu or Molokai, seemed to be satisfactory; and when he dwelt upon the well-known high rank of Lo-Lale, as recognized by the *aha-alii*, and referred to his manly bearing, his amiable disposition and the amplitude of his estates, Kawao answered sadly:

"Then so let it be. It is perhaps the will of the gods. I would have had it otherwise; but be to Kelea and her husband, and to my royal brother the king of Oahu, my messenger of peace."

Thanking the *moi* for his kindly words, Kalamakua took his leave. As he was about to re-embark in the afternoon for Oahu, the discomfited *halumanu*, having but just then landed, passed him on the beach. Knowing that he had been outwitted, in his wrath he reached for the handle of his knife. But he did not draw it. Kalamakua stopped and promptly answered the challenge; but the *halumanu* passed on, and with a smile he stepped into his canoe, and a few minutes later was on his way to Oahu with Kawao's welcome messages of peace.

As the years came and went in their quiet home at Lihue, Lo-Lale lost none of his affection for Kelea. No wars distracted the group. Liloa, the son of Kiha and father of Umi, had become the peaceful sovereign of Hawaii; Kahakuma, the ancestor of some of the most distinguished families of the islands, held gentle and intelligent sway in Kauai; Kawao still ruled in Maui, and Piliwale in Oahu.

To gratify his wife, Lo-Lale surrounded her with every comfort. The choicest fruits of the island were at her command, and every day fresh fish and other delicacies of the sea were brought to her from the neighbouring coasts. In short, everything not *tabu* to the sex was provided without stint. Summer-houses were constructed for her in the cool recesses of the Waianae Mountains, and a *manele*, with relays of stout bearers, was always at her service for the briefest journeys. The people of the district were proud of her rank and beauty, and at seasons of *hookupu*, or gift-making, she was fairly deluged with rare and valuable offerings.

Yet, with all this affluence of comfort and affection, Kelea became more and more restless and unhappy. Nor did the presence of her children, of whom she had three, seem to render her more contented. She longed for the sea; for the bounding surf which had been the sport of her girlhood; for the white-maned steeds of ocean, which she had so often mounted and fearlessly ridden to the shore; for the thunder of the breakers against the cliffs; for the murmur of the reef-bound wavelets timidly crawling up the beach to kiss and cool her feet; and the more she yearned for her old-time pleasures, the greater became her dissatisfaction with the tamer life and surroundings of Lihue.

Knowing her love for the sea, Lo-Lale made occasional excursions with her to the coast, frequently remaining there for days together. Sometimes they visited the east and sometimes the south side of the island; but the place which seemed to please her above all others was Ewa, where Kalamakua made his home. He, too, loved the sea, and during her visits there afforded her every opportunity to indulge her passion for it. Together they had charming sails around the Puuloa (Pearl River) lagoon, and gallant rides over the surf at the entrance. There, and there only, did she seem to recover her spirits; there only did she seem to be happy.

This did not escape the notice of Lo-Lale, and a great grief filled his heart as he sometimes thought, in noting her brightened look in the presence of Kalamakua, that it was less the charms of the surf than of his cousin's handsome face that made the waters of Ewa so attractive to Kelea.

Life at Lihue finally became so irksome to her, and even the continued kindness of Lo-Lale so unwelcome, that she announced her determination to leave the home of her husband for ever. This resolution was not altogether unexpected by Lo-Lale, for he had not been blind to her growing restlessness and was prepared for the worst; and as the prerogatives of her high rank gave her the undoubted privilege of separation if she desired it, he reluctantly consented to the divorcement. When asked where it was her purpose to go, she answered: "Probably to Maui, to rejoin my brother."

"More probably not beyond Ewa," was Lo-Lale's significant reply. "But, no matter where you may go," he continued, with dignity, "take your departure from Lihue in a manner consistent with your rank. You were received here as became the sister of a king and the wife of the son of Kalona-iki. So would I have you depart. I reproach you with nothing, myself with nothing; therefore let us part in peace."

"We part in peace," was Kelea's only answer, and the next morning she quietly took her departure with four or five attendants. A chant expressive of Lo-Lale's grief at the separation was long after recited, but these lines are all of it that have been preserved:

> *"Farewell, my partner on the lowland plains,*
> *On the waters of Pohakeo,*
> *Above Kanehoa,*
> *On the dark mountain spur of Mauna-una!*
> *O Lihue, she is gone!*

Sniff the sweet scent of the grass,
The sweet scent of the wild vines
That are twisted by Waikoloa,
By the winds of Waiopua,
My flower!
As if a mote were in my eye,
The pupil of my eye is troubled;
Dimness covers my eyes. Woe is me!"

Leaving Lihue, Kelea descended to Ewa, and, skirting the head of the lagoon by way of Halawa, on the afternoon of the second day arrived at the entrance, immediately opposite Puualoa. There she found a large number of nobles and retainers of Kalamakua, the high chief of the district, amusing themselves in the surf. As she had not seen the salt water for some months, Kelea could not resist the temptation to indulge in her old pastime, and, borrowing a surf-board from one of the bathers, plunged into the sea, and soon joined the party of surf-riders beyond the breakers.

Soon a huge roller made its appearance, and all mounted it and started for the shore. The race was exciting, for the most expert swimmers in the district were among the contestants; but in grace, daring and skill Kelea very plainly excelled them all, and was loudly cheered as she touched the shore. Kalamakua was reposing in the shade, not far away, and, hearing the tumult of voices, inquired the cause. He was told that a beautiful woman from Lihue had beaten all the chiefs at surf-riding, and the people could not restrain their enthusiasm. Satisfied that there was but one Lihue woman who could perform such a feat, and that she must be Kelea, the wife of his cousin Lo-Lale, he proceeded to the beach just as a second trial had resulted in a triumph to the fair contestant quite as emphatic as the first. As she touched the shore Kalamakua threw his *kihei* (mantle) over her shoulders and respectfully greeted her. Kelea then informed him that she had formally separated from her husband and was about to embark for Maui.

"If that is the case," said Kalamakua, gently taking her by the arm, as if to restrain her, "you will go no farther than Ewa. When I went in search of a wife for Lo-Lale, I promised that if he objected to the woman I brought or recommended, or she to him, I would take her myself, if she so willed. You have objected to him. Is Kalamakua better to your liking?"

"I will remain at Ewa," was the satisfactory answer.

"Yes, and you should have gone there instead of to Lihue, when you landed at Waialua years ago," continued Kalamakua, earnestly.

"My thought is the same," was Kelea's frank avowal; and she beckoned to her attendants, and told Kalamakua that she was ready to follow him.

Did he expect her at the beach that morning? Tradition offers no direct answer to the question, but significantly mentions that Kalamakua spent one or two days at Lihue not long before, that houses were in readiness for her at Ewa, and that she was borne thither on a *manele*, escorted by the principal chiefs and nobles of the district.

Learning, not long after, that Kelea had become the wife of Kalamakua, the gentle-hearted Lo-Lale sent to her a present of fruits and a message of peace and forgiveness; but it was his request that they might never meet again, and he spent the remainder of his days in Lihue, caring for the welfare of his people and dreaming in the shadows of the hills of Kaala.

But little more need here be told. Kelea and Kalamakua lived happily together, and were blessed with a daughter, Laielohelohe, who inherited her mother's beauty, and became the wife of her cousin Piilani, son and successor of Kawao, *moi* of Maui; but it was not until after the betrothal of the cousins, which was agreed to in their childhood, that Kawao fully forgave his volatile sister for marrying a prince of Oahu without his consent.

Piikea, one of the daughters of Piilani and Laielohelohe, became in after-time the wife of the great Umi, of Hawaii, and through her great-grandson, I, the ancestress of Kalakaua, the present sovereign of the group. Lono-a-Pii, another of their children, succeeded his father as *moi* of Maui.

As a further example of the manner in which the blood of the reigning families of the several islands of the group was commingled in the early periods of their history, it may be mentioned that Kaholi, a son of Lo-Lale and Kelea, was united in marriage to Kohipa, one of the two daughters of Piliwale; while the other, Kukaniloko, who followed her father as sovereign of Oahu, became the wife of Luaia, grandson of Kakaalaneo, the joint ruler of Maui during the reign of the unfortunate Kakae.

Kaala, the Flower of Lanai

His Hawaiian Majesty Kalakaua, Hawaii

A Story of the Spouting Cave of Palikaholo

I

BENEATH ONE OF THE BOLDEST OF THE ROCKY BLUFFS against which dash the breakers of Kaumalapau Bay, on the little island of Lanai, is the *Puhio-Kaala*, or 'Spouting Cave of Kaala.' The only entrance to it is through the vortex of a whirlpool, which marks the place where, at intervals, the receding waters rise in a column of foam above the surface. Within, the floor of the cave gradually rises from the opening beneath the waters until a landing is reached above the level of the tides, and to the right and left, farther than the eye can penetrate by the dim light struggling through the surging waves, stretch dank and shelly shores, where crabs, polypii, sting-rays and other noisome creatures of the deep find protection against their larger enemies.

This cavern was once a favourite resort of *Mooalii*, the great lizard-god; but as the emissaries of *Ukanipo*, the shark-god, annoyed him greatly and threatened to imprison him within it by piling a mountain of rocks against the opening, he abandoned it and found a home in a cave near Kaulapapa, in the neighbouring island of Molokai, where many rude temples were erected to him by the fishermen.

Before the days of Kamehameha I resolute divers frequently visited the Spouting Cave, and on one occasion fire, enclosed in a small calabash, was taken down through the whirlpool, with the view of making a light and exploring its mysterious chambers; but the fire was scattered and extinguished by an unseen hand, and those who brought it hastily retreated to escape a shower of rocks sent down upon them from the roof of the cavern. The existence of the cave is still known, and the whirlpool and spouting column marking the entrance to it are pointed out; but longer and longer have grown the intervals between the visits of divers to its sunless depths, until the present generation can point to not more than one, perhaps, who has ventured to enter them.

Tradition has brought down the outlines of a number of supernatural and romantic stories connected with the Spouting Cave, but the nearest complete and most recent of these *mookaaos* is the legend of Kaala, the flower of Lanai, which is here given at considerably less length than native narration accords it.

It was during an interval of comparative quiet, if not of peace, in the stormy career of Kamehameha I, near the close of the last century, and after the battle of Maunalei, that he went with his court to the island of Lanai for a brief season of recreation. The visit was not made for the purpose of worshipping at the great *heiau* of *Kaunola*, which was then half in ruins, or at any of the lesser temples scattered here and there over the little island, and dedicated, in most instances, to fish-gods. He went to Kealia simply to enjoy a few days of rest away from the scenes of his many conflicts, and feast for a time upon the affluent fishing-grounds of that locality.

He made the journey with six double canoes, all striped with yellow, and his own bearing the royal ensign. He took with him his war-god, *Kaili*, and a small army of attendants, consisting of priests, *kahunas*, *kahili* and spittoon-bearers, stewards, cooks and other household servants, as well as a retinue of distinguished chiefs with their personal retainers in their own canoes, and a hundred warriors in the capacity of a royal guard.

Landing, the victorious chief was received with enthusiasm by the five or six thousand people then inhabiting the island. He took up his residence in the largest of the several cottages provided for him and his personal attendants. Provisions were brought in abundance, and flowers and sweet-scented herbs and vines were contributed without stint. The chief and his titled attendants were garlanded with them. They were strewn in his path, cast at his door and thrown upon his dwelling, until their fragrance seemed to fill all the air.

Among the many who brought offerings of flowers was the beautiful Kaala, 'the sweet-scented flower of Lanai,' as she was called. She was a girl of fifteen, and in grace and beauty had no peer on the island. She was the daughter of Oponui, a chief of one of the lower grades, and her admirers were counted by the hundreds. Of the many who sought her as a wife was Mailou, 'the bone-breaker.' He was a huge, muscular savage, capable of crushing almost any ordinary man in an angry embrace; and while Kaala hated, feared and took every occasion to avoid him, her father favoured his suit, doubtless pleased at the thought of securing in a son-in-law a friend and champion so distinguished for his strength and ferocity.

As Kaala scattered flowers before the chief her graceful movements and modesty were noted by Kaaialii, and when he saw her face he was enraptured with its beauty. Although young in years, he was one of Kamehameha's most valued lieutenants, and had distinguished himself in many battles. He was of chiefly blood and bearing, with sinewy limbs and a handsome face, and when he stopped to look into the eyes of Kaala and tell her that she was beautiful, she thought the words, although they had been frequently spoken to her by others, had never sounded so sweetly to her before. He asked her for a simple flower, and she twined a *lei* for his neck. He asked her for a smile, and she looked up into his face and gave him her heart.

They saw each other the next day, and the next, and then Kaaialii went to his chief and said:

"I love the beautiful Kaala, daughter of Oponui. Your will is law. Give her to me for a wife."

For a moment Kamehameha smiled without speaking, and then replied:

"The girl is not mine to give. We must be just. I will send for her father. Come tomorrow."

Kaaialii had hoped for a different answer; but neither protest nor further explanation was admissible, and all he could do was to thank the king and retire.

A messenger brought Oponui to the presence of Kamehameha. He was received kindly, and told that Kaaialii loved Kaala and desired to make her his wife. The information kindled the wrath of Oponui. He hated Kaaialii, but did not dare to exhibit his animosity before the king. He was in the battle of Maunalei, where he narrowly escaped death at the hands of Kaaialii, after his spear had found the heart of one of his dearest friends, and he felt that he would rather give his daughter to the sharks than to one who had sought his life and slain his friend. But he pretended to regard the proposal with favour, and, in answer to the king, expressed regret that he had promised his daughter to Mailou, the bone-breaker. "However," he continued, "in respect to the interest which it has pleased you, great chief, to take in the matter, I am content that the girl shall fall to the victor in a contest with bare hands between Mailou and Kaaialii."

The proposal seemed to be fair, and, not doubting that Kaaialii would promptly accept it, the king gave it his approval, and the contest was fixed for the day following. Oponui received the announcement with satisfaction, not doubting that Mailou would crush Kaaialii in his rugged embrace as easily as he had broken the bones of many an adversary.

News of the coming contest spread rapidly, and the next day thousands of persons assembled at Kealia to witness it. Kaala was in an agony of fear. The thought of becoming the wife of the bone-breaker almost distracted her, for it was said that he had had many wives, all of whom had disappeared one after another as he tired of them, and the whisper was that he had crushed and thrown them into the sea. And, besides, she loved Kaaialii, and deemed it scarcely possible that he should be able to meet and successfully combat the prodigious strength and ferocity of one who had never been subdued.

As Kaaialii was approaching the spot where the contest was to take place, in the presence of Kamehameha and his court and a large concourse of less distinguished spectators, Kaala sprang from the side of her father, and, seizing the young chief by the hand, exclaimed:

"You have indeed slain my people in war, but rescue me from the horrible embrace of the bone-breaker, and I will catch the squid and beat the *kapa* for you all my days!"

With a dark frown upon his face, Oponui tore the girl from her lover before he could reply. Kaaialii followed her with his eyes until she disappeared among the spectators, and then pressed forward through the crowd and stepped within the circle reserved for the combatants. Mailou was already there. He was indeed a muscular brute, with long arms, broad shoulders and mighty limbs tattooed with figures of sharks and birds of prey. He was naked to the loins, and, as Kaaialii approached, his fingers opened and closed, as if impatient to clutch and tear his adversary in pieces.

Although less bulky than the bone-breaker, Kaaialii was large and perfectly proportioned, with well-knit muscles and loins and shoulders suggestive of unusual strength. Nude, with the exception of a *maro*, he was a splendid specimen of vigorous manhood; but, in comparison with those of the bone-breaker, his limbs appeared to be frail and feminine, and a general expression of sympathy for the young chief was observed in the faces of the large assemblage as they turned from him to the sturdy giant he was about to encounter.

The contest was to be one of strength, courage, agility and skill combined. Blows with the clenched fist, grappling, strangling, tearing, breaking and every other injury which it was possible to inflict were permitted. In *hakoko* (wrestling) and *moko* (boxing) contests certain rules were usually observed, in order that fatal injuries might be avoided; but in the combat between Kaaialii and Mailou no rule or custom was to govern. It was to be a savage struggle to the death.

Taunt and boasting are the usual prelude to personal conflicts among the uncivilized; nor was it deemed unworthy the Saxon knight to meet his adversary with insult and bravado. The object was not more to unnerve his opponent than to steel his own courage. With the bone-breaker, however, there was little fear or doubt concerning the result. He knew the measure of his own prodigious strength, and, with a malignant smile that laid bare his shark-like teeth, he glared with satisfaction upon his rival.

"Ha! ha!" laughed the bone-breaker, taking a stride toward Kaaialii; "so you are the insane youth who has dared to meet Mailou in combat! Do you know who I am? I am the bone-breaker! In my hands the limbs of men are like tender cane. Come, and with one hand let me strangle you!"

"You will need both!" replied Kaaialii. "I know you. You are a breaker of the bones of women, not of men! You speak brave words, but have the heart of a coward. Let the word be given, and if you do not run from me to save your life, as I half-suspect you will, I will put my foot upon your broken neck before you find time to cry for mercy!"

Before Mailou could retort the word was given, and with an exclamation of rage he sprang at the throat of Kaaialii. Feigning as if to meet the shock, the latter waited until the hands of Mailou were almost at his throat, when with a quick movement he struck them up, swayed his body to the left, and with his right foot adroitly tripped his over-confident assailant. The momentum of Mailou was so great that he fell headlong to the earth. Springing upon him before he could rise, Kaaialii seized his right arm, and with a vigorous blow of the foot broke the bone below the elbow. Rising and finding his right arm useless, Mailou attempted to grapple his adversary with the left, but a well-delivered blow felled him again to the earth, and Kaaialii broke his left arm as he had broken the right. Regaining his feet, and unable to use either hand, with a wild howl of despair the bone-breaker rushed upon Kaaialii, with the view of dealing him a blow with his bent head; but the young chief again tripped him as he passed, and, seizing him by the hair as he fell, placed his knees against the back of his prostrate foe and broke his spine.

This, of course, ended the struggle, and Kaaialii was declared the victor, amidst the plaudits of the spectators and the congratulations of Kamehameha and the court. Breaking from her father, who was grievously disappointed at the unlooked-for result, and who sought to detain her, Kaala sprang through the crowd and threw herself into the arms of Kaaialii. Oponui would have protested, and asked that his daughter might be permitted to visit her mother before becoming the wife of Kaaialii; but the king put an end to his hopes by placing the hand of Kaala in that of the victorious chief, and saying to him:

"You have won her nobly. She is now your wife. Take her with you."

Although silenced by the voice of the king, and compelled to submit to the conditions of a contest which he had himself proposed, Oponui's hatred of Kaaialii knew no abatement, and all that day and the night following he sat alone by the sea-shore, devising a means by which Kaala and her husband might be separated. He finally settled upon a plan.

The morning after her marriage Oponui visited Kaala, as if he had just returned from Mahana, where her mother was supposed to be then living. He greeted her with apparent affection, and was profuse in his expressions of friendship for Kaaialii. He embraced them both, and said: "I now see that you love each other; my prayer is that you may live long and happily together." He then told Kaala that Kalani, her mother, was lying dangerously ill at Mahana, and, believing that she would not recover, desired to see and bless her daughter before she died. Kaala believed the story, for her father wept when he told it, and moaned as if for the dead, and beat his breast; and, with many protestations of love, Kaaialii allowed her to depart with Oponui, with the promise from both of them that she would speedily return to the arms of her husband.

With some misgivings, Kaaialii watched her from the top of the hill above Kealia until she descended into the valley of Palawai. There leaving the path that led to Mahana, they journeyed toward the bay of Kaumalapau. Satisfied that her father was for some purpose deceiving her, Kaala protested and was about to return, when he acknowledged that her mother was not ill at Mahana, as he had represented to Kaaialii in order to secure his consent to her departure, but at the sea-shore, where she had gathered crabs, shrimps, limpets and other delicacies, and prepared a feast in celebration of her marriage.

Reassured by the plausible story, and half-disposed to pardon the deception admitted by her father, Kaala proceeded with him to the sea-shore. She saw that her mother was not there, and heard no sound but the beating of the waves against the rocks. She looked up into the face of her father for an explanation; but his eyes were cold, and a cruel smile upon his lips told her better than words that she had been betrayed.

"Where is my mother?" she inquired; and then bitterly added: "I do not see her fire by the shore. Must we search for her among the sharks?"

Oponui no longer sought to disguise his real purpose. "Hear the truth!" he said, with a wild glare in his eyes that whitened the lips of Kaala. "The shark shall be your mate, but he will not harm you. You shall go to his home, but he will not devour you. Down among the gods of the sea I will leave you until Kaaialii, hated by me above all things that breathe, shall have left Lanai, and then I will bring you back to earth!"

Terrified at these words, Kaala screamed and sought to fly; but her heartless father seized her by the hand and dragged her along the shore until they reached a bench of the rocky bluff overlooking the opening to the Spouting Cave. Oponui was among the few who had entered the cavern through its gate of circling waters, and he did not for a moment doubt that within its gloomy walls, where he was about to place her, Kaala would remain securely hidden until such time as he might choose to restore her to the light.

Standing upon the narrow ledge above the entrance to the cave, marked by alternate whirlpool and receding column, Kaala divined the barbarous purpose of her father, and implored him to give her body to the sharks at once rather than leave her living in the damp and darkness of the Spouting Cave, to be tortured by the slimy and venomous creatures of the sea.

Deaf to her entreaties, Oponui watched until the settling column went down into the throat of the whirlpool, when he gathered the frantic and struggling girl in his arms and sprang into the circling abyss. Sinking a fathom or more below the surface, and impelled by a strong current setting toward the mouth of the cave, he soon found and was swept through the entrance, and in a few moments stood upon a rocky beach in the dim twilight of the cavern, with the half-unconscious Kaala clinging to his neck.

The only light penetrating the cave was the little refracted through the waters, and every object that was not too dark to be seen looked greenish and ghostly. Crabs, eels, sting-rays and other noisome creatures of the deep were crawling stealthily among the rocks, and the dull thunder of the battling waves was the only sound that could be distinguished.

Disengaging her arms, he placed her upon the beach above the reach of the waters, and then sat down beside her to recover his breath and wait for a retreating current to bear him to the surface. Reviving, Kaala looked around her with horror, and piteously implored her father not to leave her in that dreadful place beneath the waters.

For some time he made no reply, and then it was to tell her harshly that she might return with him if she would promise to accept the love of the chief of Olowalu, in the valley of Palawai, and allow Kaaialii to see her in the embrace of another. This she refused to do, declaring that she would perish in the cave, or the attempt to leave it, rather than be liberated on such monstrous conditions.

"Then here you will remain," said Oponui, savagely, "until I return, or the chief of Olowalu comes to bear you off to his home in Maui!" Then, rising to his feet, he continued hastily, as he noted a turn in the current at the opening: "You cannot escape without assistance. If you attempt it you will be dashed against the rocks and become the food of sharks."

With this warning Oponui turned and plunged into the water. Diving and passing with the current through the entrance, he was borne swiftly to the surface and to his full length up into the spouting column; but he coolly precipitated himself into the surrounding waters, and with a few strokes of the arms reached the shore.

II

KAAIALII WATCHED THE departure of Kaala and her father until they disappeared in the valley of Palawai, and then gloomily returned to his hut. His fears troubled him. He thought of his beautiful Kaala, and his heart ached for her warm embrace. Then he thought of the looks and words of Oponui, and recalled in both a suggestion of deceit. Thus harassed with his thoughts, he spent the day in roaming alone among the hills, and the following night in restless slumber, with dreams of death and torture. The portentous cry of an *alae* roused him from his *kapa-moe* before daylight, and until the sun rose he sat watching the stars. Then he climbed the hill overlooking the valley of Palawai to watch for the return of Kaala, and wonder what could have detained her so long. He watched until the sun was well up in the heavens, feeling neither thirst nor hunger, and at length saw a *pau* fluttering in the wind far down the valley.

A woman was rapidly approaching, and his heart beat with joy, for he thought she was Kaala. Nearer and nearer she came, and Kaaialii, still hopeful, ran down to the path to meet her. Her step was light and her air graceful, and it was not until he had opened his arms to receive her that he saw that the girl was not Kaala. She was Ua, the friend of Kaala, and almost her equal in beauty. They had been reared together, and in their love for each other were like sisters. They loved the same flowers, the same wild songs of the birds, the same paths among the hills, and, now that Kaala loved Kaaialii, Ua loved him also.

Recognizing Kaaialii as she approached, Ua stopped before him, and bent her eyes to the ground without speaking.

"Where is Kaala?" inquired Kaaialii, raising the face of Ua and staring eagerly into it. "Have you seen her? Has any ill come to her? Speak!"

"I have not seen her, and know of no ill that has befallen her," replied the girl; "but I have come to tell you that Kaala has not yet reached the hut of Kalani, her mother; and as Oponui, with a dark look in his face, was seen to lead her through the forest of Kumoku, it is feared that she has been betrayed and will not be allowed to return to Kealia."

"And that, too, has been my fear since the moment I lost sight of her in the valley of Palawai," said Kaaialii. "I should not have trusted her father, for I knew him to be treacherous and unforgiving. May the wrath of the gods follow him if harm has come to her through his cruelty! But I will find her if she is on the island! The gods have given her to me, and in life or death she shall be mine!"

Terrified at the wild looks and words of Kaaialii, Ua clasped her hands in silence.

"Hark!" he continued, bending his ear toward the valley. "It seems that I hear her calling for me now!" And with an exclamation of rage and despair Kaaialii started at a swift pace down the path taken by Kaala the day before. As he hurried onward, he saw, at intervals, the footprints of Kaala in the dust, and every imprint seemed to increase his speed.

Reaching the point where the Mahana path diverged from the somewhat broader *ala* of the valley, he followed it for some distance hoping that Ua had been misinformed, and that Kaala had really visited her mother and might be found with her; but when he looked for and failed to find the marks of her feet where in reason they should have been seen had she gone to Mahana with her father, he returned and continued his course down the valley.

Suddenly he stopped. The footprints for which he was watching had now disappeared from the Palawai path, and for a moment he stood looking irresolutely around, as if in doubt concerning the direction next to be pursued. In his uncertainty several plans of action presented themselves. One was, to see what information could be gathered from Kaala's mother at Mahana, another to follow the Palawai valley to the sea, and a third to return to Kealia and consult a *kaula*. While these various suggestions were being rapidly canvassed, and before any conclusion could be reached, the figure of a man was seen approaching from the valley below.

Kaaialii secreted himself behind a rock, where he could watch the path without being seen. The man drew nearer and nearer, until at last Kaaialii was enabled to distinguish the features of Oponui, of all men the one whom he most desired to meet. His muscles grew rigid with wrath, and his hot breath burned the rock behind which he was crouching. He buried his fingers in the earth to teach them patience, and clenched his teeth to keep down a struggling exclamation of vengeance. And so he waited until Oponui reached a curve in the path which brought him, in passing, within a few paces of the eyes that were savagely glaring upon him, and the next moment the two men stood facing each other.

Startled at the unexpected appearance of Kaaialii, Oponui betrayed his guilt at once by attempting to fly; but, with the cry of "Give me Kaala!" Kaaialii sprang forward and endeavoured to seize him by the throat.

A momentary struggle followed; but Oponui was scarcely less powerful than his adversary, and, his shoulders being bare, he succeeded in breaking from the grasp of Kaaialii and seeking safety in flight toward Kealia.

With a cry of disappointment, Kaaialii started in pursuit. Both were swift of foot, and the race was like that of a hungry shark following his prey. One was inspired by fear and the other with rage, and every muscle of the runners was strained. Leaving the valley path, Oponui struck for Kealia by a shorter course across the hills. He hoped the roughness of the route and his better knowledge of it would give him an advantage; but Kaaialii kept closely at his heels. On they sped, up and down hills, across ravines and along rocky ridges, until they reached Kealia, when Oponui suddenly turned to the left and made a dash for the temple and *puhonua* not far distant. Kaaialii divined his purpose, and with a last supreme effort sought to thwart it. Gaining ground with every step, he made a desperate grasp at the shoulder of Oponui just as the latter sprang through the entrance and dropped to the earth exhausted within the protecting walls of the *puhonua*. Kaaialii attempted to follow, but two priests promptly stepped into the portal and refused to allow him to pass.

"Stand out of the way, or I will strangle you both!" exclaimed Kaaialii, fiercely, as he threw himself against the guards.

"Are you insane?" said another long-haired priest, stepping forward with a *tabu* staff in his hand. "Do you not know that this is a *puhonua*, sacred to all who seek its protection? Would you bring down upon yourself the wrath of the gods by shedding blood within its walls?"

"If I may not enter, then drive him forth!" replied Kaaialii, pointing toward Oponui, who was lying upon the ground a few paces within, intently regarding the proceedings at the gate.

"That cannot be," returned the priest. "Should he will to leave, the way will not be closed to him; otherwise he may remain in safety."

"Coward!" cried Kaaialii, addressing Oponui in a taunting tone. "Is it thus that you seek protection from the anger of an unarmed man? A *pau* would better become you than a *maro*. You should twine *leis* and beat *kapa* with women, and think no more of the business of men. Come without the walls, if your trembling limbs will bear you, and I will serve you as I did your friend, the breaker of women's bones. Come, and I will tear from your throat the tongue that lied to Kaala, and feed it to the dogs!"

A malignant smile wrinkled the face of Oponui, as he thought of Kaala in her hiding-place under the sea, but he made no reply.

"Do you fear me?" continued Kaaialii. "Then arm yourself with spear and battle-axe, and with bare hands I will meet and strangle you!"

Oponui remained silent, and in a paroxysm of rage and disappointment Kaaialii threw himself upon the ground and cursed the *tabu* that barred him from his enemy.

His friends found and bore him to his hut, and Ua, with gentle arts and loving hands, sought to soothe and comfort him. But he would not be consoled. He talked and thought alone of Kaala, and, hastily partaking of food that he might retain his strength, started again in search of her. Pitying his distress, Ua followed him – not closely, but so that she might not lose sight of him altogether.

He travelled in every direction, stopping neither for food nor rest. Of every one he met he inquired for Kaala, and called her name in the deep valleys and on the hill-tops. Wandering near the sacred spring at the head of the waters of Kealia, he met a white-haired priest bearing from the fountain a calabash of water for ceremonial use in one of the temples. The priest knew and feared him, for his looks were wild, and humbly offered him water.

"I ask not for food or water, old man," said Kaaialii. "You are a priest – perhaps a *kaula*. Tell me where I can find Kaala, the daughter of Oponui, and I will pile your altars with sacrifices!"

"Son of the long spear," replied the priest, "I know you seek the sweet-smelling flower of Palawai. Her father alone knows of her hiding-place. But it is not here in the hills, nor is it in the valleys. Oponui loves and frequents the sea. He hunts for the squid in dark places, and dives for the great fish in deep waters. He knows of cliffs that are hollow, and of caves with entrances below the waves. He goes alone to the rocky shore, and sleeps with the fish-gods, who are his friends. He —"

"No more of him!" interrupted the chief, impatiently. "Tell me what has become of Kaala!"

"Be patient, and you shall hear," resumed the priest. "In one of the caverns of the sea, known to Oponui and others, has Kaala been hidden. So I see her now. The place is dark and her heart is full of terror. Hasten to her. Be vigilant, and you will find her; but sleep not, or she will be the food of the creatures of the sea."

Thanking the priest, Kaaialii started toward the bay of Kaumalapau, followed by the faithful Ua, and did not rest until he stood upon the bluff of Palikaholo, overlooking the sea. Wildly the waves beat against the rocks. Looking around, he could discern no hiding-place along the shore, and the thunder of the breakers and the screams of the sea-gulls were the only sounds to be heard. In despair he raised his voice and wildly exclaimed:

"Kaala! O Kaala! where are you? Do you sleep with the fish-gods, and must I seek you in their homes among the sunken shores?"

The bluff where he was standing overlooked and was immediately above the Spouting Cave, from the submerged entrance to which a column of water was rising above the surface and breaking into spray. In the mist of the upheaval he thought he saw the shadowy face and form of Kaala, and in the tumult of the rushing waters fancied that he heard her voice calling him to come to her.

"Kaala, I come!" he exclaimed, and with a wild leap sprang from the cliff to clasp the misty form of his bride.

He sank below the surface, and, as the column disappeared with him and he returned no more, Ua wailed upon the winds a requiem of love and grief in words like these:

"Oh! dead is Kaaialii, the young chief of Hawaii,
The chief of few years and many battles!
His limbs were strong and his heart was gentle;
His face was like the sun, and he was without fear.
Dead is the slayer of the bone-breaker;
Dead is the chief who crushed the bones of Mailou;
Dead is the lover of Kaala and the loved of Ua.
For his love he plunged into the deep waters;
For his love he gave his life. Who is like Kaaialii?
Kaala is hidden away, and I am lonely;
Kaaialii is dead, and the black kapa is over my heart:
Now let the gods take the life of Ua!"

With a last look at the spot where Kaaialii had disappeared, Ua hastened to Kealia, and at the feet of Kamehameha told of the rash act of the despairing husband of Kaala. The king was greatly grieved at the story of Ua, for he loved the young chief almost as if he had been his son. "It is useless to search for the body of Kaaialii," he said, "for the sharks have eaten it." Then, turning to one of his chiefs, he continued: "No pile can be raised over his bones. Send for Ualua, the poet, that a chant may be made in praise of Kaaialii."

Approaching nearer, Papakua, a priest, requested permission to speak. It was granted, and he said:

"Let me hope that my words may be of comfort. I have heard the story of Ua, and cannot believe that the young chief is dead. The spouting waters into which Kaaialii leaped mark the entrance to the cave of Palikaholo. Following downward the current, has he not been drawn into the cavern, where he has found Kaala, and may still be living? Such, at least, is my thought, great chief."

"A wild thought, indeed!" replied the king; "yet there is some comfort in it, and we will see how much of truth it may reveal."

Preparations were hastily made, and with four of his sturdiest oarsmen Kamehameha started around the shore for the Spouting Cave under the bluff of Palikaholo, preceded by Ua in a canoe with Keawe, her brother.

III

WHEN KAAIALII PLUNGED into the sea he had little thought of anything but death. Grasping at the spouting column as he descended, it seemed to sink with him to the surface, and even below it, and in a moment he felt himself being propelled downward and toward the cliff by a strong current. Recklessly yielding to the action of the waters, he soon discerned an opening in the submerged base of the bluff, and without an effort was drawn swiftly into it. The force of the current subsided, and to his surprise his head rose above the surface and he was able to breathe. His feet touched a rocky bottom, and he rose and looked around with a feeling of bewilderment. His first thought was that he was dead and had reached the dark shores of *Po*, where *Milu*, prince of death, sits enthroned in a grove of *kou* trees; but he smote his breast, and by the smart knew that he was living, and had been borne by the waters into a cave beneath the cliff from which he had leaped to grasp the misty form of Kaala.

Emerging from the water, Kaaialii found himself standing on the shore of a dimly-lighted cavern. The air was chilly, and slimy objects touched his feet, and others fell splashing into the water from the rocks. He wondered whether it would be possible for him to escape from the gloomy place, and began to watch the movements of the waters near the opening, when a low moan reached his ear.

It was the voice of Kaala. She was lying near him in the darkness on the slimy shore. Her limbs were bruised and lacerated with her fruitless attempts to leave the cave, and she no longer possessed the strength to repel the crabs and other loathsome creatures that were drinking her blood and feeding upon her quivering flesh.

"It is the wailing of the wind, or perhaps of some demon of the sea who makes this horrible place his home," thought Kaaialii.

He feared neither death nor its ministers; yet something like a shudder possessed him as he held his breath and listened, but he heard nothing but the thunder of the breakers against the cavern walls.

"Who speaks?" he exclaimed, advancing a pace or two back into the darkness.

A feeble moan, almost at his feet, was the response.

Stooping and peering intently before him, he distinguished what seemed to be the outlines of a human form. Approaching and bending over it, he caught the murmur of his own name.

"It is Kaala! Kaaialii is here!" he cried, as he tenderly folded her in his arms and bore her toward the opening. Seating himself in the dim light, he pushed back the hair from her cold face, and sought to revive her with caresses and words of endearment. She opened her eyes, and, nestling closer to his breast, whispered to the ear that was bent to her lips:

"I am dying, but I am happy, for you are here."

He sought to encourage her. He told her that he had come to save her; that the gods, who loved her and would not let her die, had told him where to find her; that he would take her to his home in Kohala, and always love her as he loved her then.

She made no response. There was a sad smile upon her cold lips. He placed his hand upon her heart, and found that it had ceased to beat. She was dead, but he still held the precious burden in his arms; and hour after hour he sat there on the gloomy shore of the cavern, seeing only the pallid face of Kaala, and feeling only that he was desolate.

At length he was aroused by the splashing of water within the cave. He looked up, and Ua, the gentle and unselfish friend of Kaala, stood before him, followed a moment after by Kamehameha. The method of entering and leaving the cave was known to Keawe, and he imparted the information to his sister. Ua first leaped into the whirlpool, and the dauntless Kamehameha did not hesitate in following.

As the king approached, Kaaialii rose to his feet and stood sadly before him. He uttered no word, but with bent head pointed to the body of Kaala.

"I see," said the king, softly; "the poor girl is dead. She could have no better burial-place. Come, Kaaialii, let us leave it."

Kaaialii did not move. It was the first time that he had ever hesitated in obeying the orders of his chief.

"What! would you remain here?" said the king. "Would you throw your life away for a girl? There are others as fair. Here is Ua; she shall be your wife, and I will give you the valley of Palawai. Come, let us leave here at once, lest some angry god close the entrance against us!"

"Great chief," replied Kaaialii, "you have always been kind and generous to me, and never more so than now. But hear me. My life and strength are gone. Kaala was my life, and she is dead. How can I live without her? You are my chief. You have asked me to leave this place and live. It is the first request of yours that I have ever disobeyed. It shall be the last!"

Then seizing a stone, with a swift, strong blow he crushed in brow and brain, and fell dead upon the body of Kaala.

A wail of anguish went up from Ua. Kamehameha spoke not, moved not. Long he gazed upon the bodies before him; and his eye was moist and his strong lip quivered as, turning away at last, he said: "He loved her indeed!"

Wrapped in *kapa*, the bodies were laid side by side and left in the cavern; and there today may be seen the bones of Kaala, the flower of Lanai, and of Kaaialii, her knightly lover, by such as dare to seek the passage to them through the whirlpool of Palikaholo.

Meles of the story of the tragedy were composed and chanted before Kamehameha and his court at Kealia, and since then the cavern has been known as Puhio-kaala, or 'Spouting Cave of Kaala.'

Little Pieces of Flint

D.K. Lawhorn, Monacan Indian Nation, Native American

CLOSE. So close now. Its static stench still lingers in the air. The hairs on the inside of my nostrils tingle with it. My ears twitch. I shut my eyes and hold my breath, pouring all my concentration into just listening. There. Far to the west. Down swells of air so vast it can only be the flapping of massive wings. No surprise here. A thunderbird can always be found traveling in one of the four cardinal directions. We Braves are taught this early on in our training.

I sprint westward.

An entire village slaughtered in a night. I knew them; went on many hunts for their elders. They were fine people: spiritual, generous. Not an ill thought or action existed among them. So, why then did a thunderbird come down and administer her justice upon them? Leave these good people – men, women, and children – as nothing more than charred husks where they slept? For as long as our people have existed, we have respected the thunderbirds' judgements. But no justice exists in what happened last night. I cannot let it pass. I am sure the Order of Bravery will agree with me after this is finished. But it is better to get it over with first, then go to them with deeds done. Just in case.

Our people knew this would be a risk when we rose our lands into the sky. The Creator never intended for us to live in the Upper-World. This plain above the clouds is meant for the Great Spirits and their guardian beasts, and those beasts were born and bred to protect their Great Spirit's territories with vigor. Tragedy loomed from the moment we arrived all those years ago. But we accepted the risk. Anything was better than the calamity awaiting us at the hands of those sea-faring white devils back down in our birthplace of the Mid-World.

And this accepted risk is why the elders who oversee our Floating Isle Confederation created the Order of Bravery. Monsters protect the Upper-World from humans. We Braves protect humans from monsters.

I finger each of the arrows in my hip quiver as I run, counting them more as a nervous tick than a double-check. One. Two. Three. Three. Two. One. Repeat. The first, second, and third steps in the plan concocted by this island's medicine woman and me. Little pieces of flint tip each arrow. Only, they are no longer flint, are they? The medicine woman blessed each stone this very morning before I set out in pursuit of the thunderbird. The flint's latent power brought forth from its core. I now wield three chips of the old Thunder Spirit, whom the Creator flung to the Mid-World after their attempted coup. Upon their impact with the earth, the old Thunder Spirit shattered into a million pieces. A million thunderstones. A single thunderstone can absorb the energy of a storm and clear the skies. The legends say three can capture a thunderbird. But these legends are untested, as far as we know.

Today, I do the testing.

I crest a hill and see the island's broad coastline. A precarious drop yawns before me, and the roiling ocean of bright white clouds stretches out far below. On the horizon, I can just make out the cliff shores of the next island over. That one is part of the territory assigned to me by the Order, unlike the island I currently stand on, which I only have personal connections to. Me being here means my island is without a Brave. Not defenseless, but close to it. None in my tribe are trained for combat outside of those who are sent to the Order of Bravery. And there, halfway between the islands, is the murderous thunderbird. She casts a dark shadow on the ever-moving Cloud Sea. Her course set directly for my island.

She is more beautiful than storytellers could ever hope to convey. When fully expanded, her wings stretch further than even the grandest of longhouses. The blue feathers covering her body shimmer with their own light as the air cuts through them. Her copper crown feathers stay completely still, as if they are made from the very metal they share a color with – some stories say they are. Her tail fans out behind her and flicks this way or that every so often, the barest movement dictating her flight path.

I drop to my knee and unsling my bow in a single motion. The thunderbird is pushing the longest range I have been able to reliably hit before. I can still stop her, but I must move fast. I will not be able to live with myself if I allow her to wreak her non-justice on another village. In the length of a deep breath, I notch a thunderstone arrow and draw the string back to my ear. The fluttering of her feathers and the movements of the Cloud Sea are my guides to the wind patterning. Above by three finger spans and to the right by four-and-a-half. As a child, when my tribe first gave me over to the Order of Bravery, I would have had to measure these out manually, but I know the distances by heart now.

I loose the arrow.

It cuts a clear arch across the sky, easy to see against the clear cerulean dome keeping the three Worlds bound together. One. Two. Three. Four.

The arrow disappears into the thunderbird's feathers. A bolt of lighting shoots out from the point of contact. The accompanying clap of thunder reaches me a moment later, strong enough to send me flying backward.

I turn the topple into a roll and somehow keep a grip on my bow. Teacher would have been proud of this if she were still alive to see me do it. Jaw tight and heart pounding, my free hand snaps down to my quiver. Tension releases. The arrows are still there. I rush back to the cliff's edge. The thunderbird has turned and is flying back toward me. Good. Her wings beat now, no longer just gliding, and continue to do so until she is moving at an unfathomable speed. Maybe not so good.

I knock another arrow, pull the fletching back until the sparrow feathers tickle my cheek, and study her rhythm. It seems erratic at first. But then I realize such a grand creature's dance will be equally as grand, and I am watching with the tiny, fallible eyes of a human. If I wish to take in the entirety of her dance, I must look with more. A deep breath, hold, and I put my whole being into attending the thunderbird's performance. My arms are shaking by the time I meet her on her own terms. She is doing a thunder dance; one I have seen fancy dancers do a hundred times at a hundred powwows. I am a fool for not having seen it immediately. My fingers release, relief floods into them, and the arrow thrums out.

At the same moment, the thunderbird, who has already closed the distance between us, rears back and flaps her wings hard in my direction. I expect a strong wind to buffet me. Instead, a wave of thunder sweeps over the cliff. I keep to my feet this time, but the ground beneath me quakes in uncertainty.

Then my arrow strikes home.

Lightning streaks out of the thunderbird's neck and strikes the cliff face somewhere below me, followed closely by yet another roll of thunder. The ground no longer just quakes but shifts. The thunderbird caws in recognition of the opportunity. Two more lightning bolts erupt from her golden eyes and slam into the rocky face below.

I go down with the edge of the cliff. Large mounds of earth jostle me back and forth. I lose sense of what is up, what is down. I feel a rib break as a large boulder slams into me. I prepare myself for the cold embrace of the Cloud Sea, but it never comes. The world has suddenly stopped moving, and I am lying with my face in a patch of grass.

I push myself up and see the final arrow lying beside me, broken in half.

A sapphire streak flashes in front of me as the thunderbird dives toward the Cloud Sea, her victory screech piercing the air. She thinks she has killed me. According to the stories, thunderbirds have terrible sight. Probably from all the lightning they shoot from their eyes.

No time to think about what comes next. The half of the arrow with the thunderstone head on it fits like a dagger in my palm. Perfect for what I must do. With a deep breath, I push myself over the edge and dive after the thunderbird.

The thunderbird rushes toward the Cloud Sea. The distance between us increases. I make myself into a human arrow. The air whips at my face, and I force my eyes to stay open. Still, the thunderbird pulls ahead.

I can see dozens of villages all over the Floating Isles meeting the same fate as the one last night did. Families, lovers, friends, all sent back to the Creator before their time by rogue judgement. Tragedy upon tragedy, repeating itself to no end, until the annihilation we escaped by rising above the clouds is dealt to us by a different force.

I would be undeserving of the title of Brave if I allowed this to happen.

To the air rushing past me, I whisper the true name of great Wind Spirit, trusting the air to deliver my summons to its master. A moment passes. The thunderbird has almost reached the clouds. Soon, she will pull up and launch forward, and I will have failed to protect my people. The spirits have been easier to call since we came to the Upper-World, opening many difficult paths of magic to those who know what names to speak. But they don't always respond to our calls, especially when they are as great as the Wind Spirit. I wish I could say I did not expect them to come to my aid, but that would be a lie. I am nothing if not prone to bouts of insane hope.

One moment my breath is there, still held strong in my lungs, then it is gone. I do not feel it go. The simplicity of the sudden absence keeps me from panicking. In fact, I am elated. Most Great Spirits require much more demanding offerings, but the Wind Spirit has always been eccentric. Plus, we have a long history of working together, and they have grown lenient with me.

The air stops moving by and starts to swirl around me. An invisible cloak of raging wind settles over my body, as it has many times before. I flex my free hand and point my toes straight back. My cloak whips out, and I shoot forward with the speed of ten thousand arrows combined.

Not even half a dozen spans above the clouds, the thunderbird spreads her wings and levels her body out with the sea. Only a fraction of a moment's delay before she will dart forward and out of my own flight path.

But it is enough.

I slam into her back at full speed and drive the broken arrow deep into her neck. My wind cloak shatters, voiding the area around me of all its air. My immediate want to suck in a breath to relieve my screaming lungs is impossible. I am glad for this, because a lightning bolt spears out from the wound I have just opened on the thunderbird's back, and there is no way taking a lung full of lightning would be good for me.

It is the following thunder that turns my vision black.

* * *

I wake up some time later. The clouds have washed me up on a sandy shore. The fist that held the broken arrow is charred black, but it doesn't hurt. I can just barely move it. My knuckles creak as I unfurl my hand. There, laying in the center of my palm, are two brilliant blue feathers and a perfect thunderstone. The stone is not black, as the ones that had tipped my arrows were. This one is the brilliant blue of the feathers with streaks of copper throughout and two flecks of gold right in the center.

First half of the plan completed. The second half would have to wait, just for a little while. After all, it is a long walk back to the medicine woman, and I am not even certain if my legs work right now.

I laugh and squeeze my blackened hand and its contents tight to my chest.

* * *

The canoe trip to the mountain takes twelve days in total. The medicine woman blessed both me and the canoe before I set out. In those twelve days, I fast and meditate, as is required by the Creator if this trip is to be completed. Finally, at the dawn of the twelfth day, the blue ridges of the mountain loom in the distance. This is the largest remaining chunk of the old Thunder Spirit's body, still housing their soul. It rebounded off the Mid-World and was suspended in the land between worlds for the rest of eternity for their trespasses against the Creator.

Also, the birthplace of the thunderbirds.

There they are now, hundreds flying around the peaks. I row the canoe only as close to the mountain as to be within shooting range of it. Then I pick up my bow, knock the only arrow I brought with me on this journey, and aim at the rocky face of the mountain. The blue feather fletching tickles my cheek. I take one last look at the thunderstone tied to the end of the arrow and admire its blue and copper and gold coloring, its perfect oval smoothness.

Then I let it go.

The elders who summoned me did so with the intention of having me kill the thunderbird who had destroyed one of their villages. But one does not kill a thunderbird. It's possible, but to do so would be an affront to the Spirits, Great and Small. Even the Creator herself would not sit well with such a transgression. Piety and respect of the natural world is a core tenet of the Order of Bravery. That was why the medicine woman and I came up with our own plan.

I lose sight of the arrow soon after I release it. The mountainside is dark, covered in deep blue shadows, and the thunderbirds swirling around it distract the eye. But the arrow's impact on the mountain is impossible to miss. A ball of lightning erupts and fingers upward into the rainbow-filled sky. Thunder shakes the clouds all the way out to where my canoe is floating. From the chaos, the thunderbird is released, finally back home where she belongs.

Her caw of release reaches my ears loud and clear even with vast distance between us. Then she joins the whirling mass of her sisters, and I lose sight of her.

I smile, lay my bow down, and turn the canoe around. I paddle for a bit until the bow of the canoe is cutting through the clouds at a decent clip. Then I grab the dried venison the medicine woman prepared for me, take a bite, chew for a long while, enjoying every flavor rolling over my tongue, finally swallow, and wake up back on the floor of the medicine woman's hut.

She is leaning over me, her beautiful brown eyes peering deep into mine.

"Wen'lei! You're back!" She takes me up into a tight embrace, so similar in feel to the countless embraces we have shared over innumerable nights, but much different in sentiment. "You haven't drawn a breath in twelve days. Even though I knew this is how it would go, I couldn't help but worry over you." To my disappointment, she suddenly jerks away from me and searches my face for some unfathomable mystery. "It's done?"

"It's done," I say.

And so it is.

The Story of the Creation

Pima People, Native American

IN THE BEGINNING there was no earth, no water – nothing. There was only a Person, Juh-wert-a-Mah-kai (The Doctor of the Earth).

He just floated, for there was no place for him to stand upon. There was no sun, no light, and he just floated about in the darkness, which was Darkness itself.

He wandered around in the nowhere till he thought he had wandered enough. Then he rubbed on his breast and rubbed out *moah-haht-tack*, that is perspiration, or greasy earth. This he rubbed out on the palm of his hand and held out. It tipped over three times, but the fourth, time it stayed straight in the middle of the air and there it remains now as the world.

The first bush he created was the greasewood bush.

And he made ants, little tiny ants, to live on that bush, on its gum which comes out of its stem.

But these little ants did not do any good, so he created white ants, and these worked and enlarged the earth; and they kept on increasing it, larger and larger, until at last it was big enough for himself to rest on.

Then he created a Person. He made him out of his eye, out of the shadow of his eyes, to assist him, to be like him, and to help him in creating trees and human beings and everything that was to be on the earth.

The name of this being was Nooee (the Buzzard).

Nooee was given all power, but he did not do the work he was created for. He did not care to help Juhwertamahkai, but let him go by himself.

And so the Doctor of the Earth himself created the mountains and everything that has seed and is good to eat. For if he had created human beings first they would have had nothing to live on.

But after making Nooee and before making the mountains and seed for food, Juhwertamahkai made the sun.

In order to make the sun he first made water, and this he placed in a hollow vessel, like an earthen dish (*hwas-hah-ah*) to harden into something like ice. And this hardened ball he placed in the sky. First he placed it in the North, but it did not work; then he placed it in the West, but it did not work; then he placed it in the South, but it did not work; then he placed it in the East and there it worked as he wanted it to.

And the moon he made in the same way and tried in the same places, with the same results.

But when he made the stars he took the water in his mouth and spurted it up into the sky. But the first night his stars did not give light enough. So he took the Doctor-stone (diamond), the *tone-dum-haw-teh*, and smashed it up, and took the pieces and threw them into the sky to mix with the water in the stars, and then there was light enough.

And now Juhwertamahkai, rubbed again on his breast, and from the substance he obtained there made two little dolls, and these he laid on the earth. And they were human beings, man and woman.

And now for a time the people increased till they filled the earth. For the first parents were perfect, and there was no sickness and no death. But when the earth was full, then there was nothing to eat, so they killed and ate each other.

But Juhwertamahkai did not like the way his people acted, to kill and eat each other, and so he let the sky fail to kill them. But when the sky dropped he, himself, took a staff and broke a hole thru, thru which he and Nooee emerged and escaped, leaving behind them all the people dead.

And Juhwertamahkai, being now on the top of this fallen sky, again made a man and a woman, in the same way as before. But this man and woman became grey when old, and their children became grey still younger, and their children became grey younger still, and so on till the babies were grey in their cradles.

And Juhwertamahkai, who had made a new earth and sky, just as there had been before, did not like his people becoming grey in their cradles, so he let the sky fall on them again, and again made a hole and escaped, with Nooee, as before.

And Juhwertamahkai, on top of this second sky, again made a new heaven and a new earth, just as he had done before, and new people.

But these new people made a vice of smoking. Before human beings had never smoked till they were old, but now they smoked younger, and each generation still younger, till the infants wanted to smoke in their cradles.

And Juhwertamahkai did not like this, and let the sky fall again, and created everything new again in the same way, and this time he created the earth as it is now.

But at first the whole slope of the world was westward, and tho there were peaks rising from this slope there were no true valleys, and all the water that fell ran away and there was no water for the people to drink. So Juhwertamahkai sent Nooee to fly around among the mountains, and over the earth, to cut valleys with his wings, so that the water could be caught and distributed and there might be enough for the people to drink.

Now the sun was male and the moon was female and they met once a month. And the moon became a mother and went to a mountain called Tahs-my-et-tahn Toe-ahk (sun striking mountain) and there was born her baby. But she had duties to attend to, to turn around and give light, so she made a place for the child by tramping down the weedy bushes and there left it. And the child, having no milk, was nourished on the earth.

And this child was the coyote, and as he grew he went out to walk and in his walk came to the house of Juhwertamahkai and Nooee, where they lived.

And when he came there Juhwertamahkai knew him and called him Toe-hahvs, because he was laid on the weedy bushes of that name.

But now out of the North came another powerful personage, who has two names, See-ur-huh and Ee-ee-toy.

Now Seeurhuh means older brother, and when this personage came to Juhwertamahkai, Nooee and Toehahvs he called them his younger brothers. But they claimed to have been here first, and to be older than he, and there was a dispute between them. But finally, because he insisted so strongly, and just to please him, they let him be called older brother.

Collected by J. William Lloyd

The Story of the Flood

Pima People, Native American

NOW SEEURHUH WAS VERY POWERFUL, like Juhwerta Mahkai, and as he took up his residence with them, as one of them, he did many wonderful things which pleased Juhwerta Mahkai, who liked to watch him.

And after doing many marvellous things he, too, made a man.

And to this man whom he had made, Seeurhuh (whose other name was Ee-ee-toy) gave a bow and arrows, and guarded his arm against the bow string by a piece of wild-cat skin, and pierced his ears and made ear-rings for him, like turquoises to look at, from the leaves of the weed called *quah-wool*. And this man was the most beautiful man yet made.

And Ee-ee-toy told this young man, who was just of marriageable age, to look around and see if he could find any young girl in the villages that would suit him and, if he found her, to see her relatives and see if they were willing he should marry her.

And the beautiful young man did this, and found a girl that pleased him, and told her family of his wish, and they accepted him, and he married her.

And the names of both these are now forgotten and unknown.

And when they were married Ee-ee-toy, foreseeing what would happen, went and gathered the gum of the greasewood tree.

Here the narrative states, with far too much plainness of circumstantial detail for popular reading, that this young man married a great many wives in rapid succession, abandoning the last one with each new one wedded, and had children with abnormal, even uncanny swiftness, for which the wives were blamed and for which suspicion they were thus heartlessly divorced. Because of this, Juhwerta Mahkai and Ee-ee-toy foresaw that nature would be convulsed and a great flood would come to cover the world. And then the narrative goes on to say:

Now there was a doctor who lived down toward the sunset whose name was Vahk-lohv Mahkai, or South Doctor, who had a beautiful daughter. And when his daughter heard of this young man and what had happened to his wives she was afraid and cried every day. And when her fatter saw her crying he asked her what was the matter? was she sick? And when she had told him what she was afraid of, for every one knew and was talking of this thing, he said yes, he knew it was true, but she ought not to be afraid, for there was happiness for a woman in marriage and the mothering of children.

And it took many years for the young man to marry all these wives, and have all these children, and all this time Ee-ee-toy was busy making a great vessel of the gum he had gathered from the grease bushes, a sort of *olla* which could be closed up, which would keep back water. And while he was making this he talked over the reasons for it with Juhwerta Mahkai, Nooee, and Toehahvs, that it was because there was a great flood coming.

And several birds heard them talking thus – the woodpecker, Hick-o-vick; the humming-bird, Vee-pis-mahl; a little bird named Gee-ee-sop, and another called Quota-veech.

Eeeetoy said he would escape the flood by getting into the vessel he was making from the gum of the grease bushes or *ser-quoy*.

And Juhwerta Mahkai said he would get into his staff, or walking stick, and float about.

And Toehahvs said he would get into a cane-tube.

And the little birds said the water would not reach the sky, so they would fly up there and hang on by their bills till it was over.

And Nooee, the buzzard, the powerful, said he did not care if the flood did reach the sky, for he could find a way to break thru.

Now Ee-ee-toy was envious, and anxious to get ahead of Juhwerta Mahkai and get more fame for his wonderful deeds, but Juhwerta Mahkai, though really the strongest, was generous and from kindness and for relationship sake let Ee-ee-toy have the best of it.

And the young girl, the doctor's daughter, kept on crying, fearing the young man, feeling him ever coming nearer, and her father kept on reassuring her, telling her it would be all right, but at last, out of pity for her fears and tears, he told her to go and get him the little tuft of the finest thorns on the top of the white cactus, the *haht-sahn-kahm*, and bring to him.

And her father took the cactus-tuft which she had brought him, and took hair from her head and wound about one end of it, and told her if she would wear this it would protect her. And she consented and wore the cactus-tuft.

And he told her to treat the young man right, when he came, and make him broth of corn. And if the young man should eat all the broth, then their plan would fail, but if he left any broth she was to eat that up and then their plan would succeed.

And he told her to be sure and have a bow and arrows above the door of the kee, so that he could take care of the young man.

And after her father had told her this, on that very evening the young man came, and the girl received him kindly, and took his bows and arrows, and put them over the door of the *kee*, as her father had told her, and made the young man broth of corn and gave it to him to eat.

And he ate only part of it and what was left she ate herself.

And before this her father had told her: "if the young man is wounded by the thorns you wear, in that moment he will become a woman and a mother and you will become a young man."

And in the night all this came to be, even so, and by day-break the child was crying.

And the old woman ran in and said: "Mossay!" which means an old woman's grandchild from a daughter.

And the daughter, that had been, said: "It is not your moss, it is your *cah-um-maht*," that is an old woman's grandchild from a son.

And then the old man ran in and said: "*Bah-ahm-ah-dah*!" that is an old man's grandchild from a daughter, but his daughter said: "It is not your *bah-ahm-maht*, but it is your *voss-ahm-maht*," which is an old man's grandchild from a son.

And early in the morning this young man (that had been, but who was now a woman and a mother) made a *wawl-kote*, a carrier, or cradle, for the baby and took the trail back home.

And Juhwerta Mahkai told his neighbours of what was coming, this young man who had changed into a woman and a mother and was bringing a baby born from himself, and that when he arrived wonderful things would happen and springs would gush forth from under every tree and on every mountain.

And the young man-woman came back and by the time of his return Ee-ee-toy had finished his vessel and had placed therein seeds and everything that is in the world.

And the young man-woman, when he came to his old home, placed his baby in the bushes and left it, going in without it, but Ee-ee-toy turned around and looked at him and knew him, for he did not wear a woman's dress, and said to him: "Where is my *Bahahmmaht*? Bring it to me. I want to see it. It is a joy for an old man to see his grandchild.

I have sat here in my house and watched your going, and all that has happened you, and foreseen some one would send you back in shame, although I did not like to think there was anyone more powerful than I. But never mind, he who has beaten us will see what will happen."

And when the young man-woman went to get his baby, Ee-ee-toy got into his vessel, and built a fire on the hearth he had placed therein, and sealed it up.

And the young man-woman found his baby crying, and the tears from it were all over the ground, around. And when he stooped over to pick up his child he turned into a sand-snipe, and the baby turned into a little teeter-snipe. And then that came true which Juhwerta Mahkai had said, that water would gush out from under every tree and on every mountain; and the people when they saw it, and knew that a flood was coming, ran to Juhwerta Mahkai; and he took his staff and made a hole in the earth and let all those thru who had come to him, but the rest were drowned.

Then Juhwerta Mahkai got into his walking stick and floated, and Toehahvs got into his tube of cane and floated, but Ee-ee-toy's vessel was heavy and big and remained until the flood was much deeper before it could float.

And the people who were left out fled to the mountains; to the mountains called Gah-kote-kih (Superstition Mts.) for they were living in the plains between Gahkotekih and Cheoffskawmack (Tall Gray Mountain.)

And there was a powerful man among these people, a doctor (*mahkai*), who set a mark on the mountain side and said the water would not rise above it.

And the people believed him and camped just beyond the mark; but the water came on and they had to go higher. And this happened four times.

And the *mahkai* did this to help his people, and also used power to raise the mountain, but at last he saw all was to be a failure. And he called the people and asked them all to come close together, and he took his doctor-stone (*mahkai-haw-teh*) which is called *Tonedumhawteh* or Stone-of-Light, and held it in the palm of his hand and struck it hard with his other hand, and it thundered so loud that all the people were frightened and they were all turned into stone.

And the little birds, the woodpecker, Hickovick; the humming bird, Veepismahl; the little bird named Ge-ee-sop, and the other called Quotaveech, all flew up to the sky and hung on by their bills, but Nooee still floated in the air and intended to keep on the wing unless the floods reached the heavens.

But Juhwerta Mahkai, Ee-ee-toy and Toehahvs floated around on the water and drifted to the west and did not know where they were.

And the flood rose higher until it reached the woodpecker's tail, and you can see the marks to this day.

And Quotaveech was cold and cried so loud that the other birds pulled off their feathers and built him a nest up there so he could keep warm. And when Quotaveech was warm he quit crying.

And then the little birds sang, for they had power to make the water go down by singing, and as they sang the waters gradually receded.

But the others still floated around.

When the land began to appear Juhwerta Mahkai and Toehahvs got out, but Ee-ee-toy had to wait for his house to warm up, for he had built a fire to warm his vessel enough for him to unseal it.

When it was warm enough he unsealed it, but when he looked out he saw the water still running and he got back and sealed himself in again.

And after waiting a while he unsealed his vessel again, and seeing dry land enough he got out.

And Juhwerta Mahkai went south and Toehahvs went west, and Ee-ee-toy went northward. And as they did not know where they were they missed each other, and passed each other unseen, but afterward saw each other's tracks, and then turned back and shouted, but wandered from the track, and again passed unseen. And this happened four times.

And the fourth time Juhwerta Mahkai and Ee-ee-toy met, but Toehahvs had passed already.

And when they met, Ee-ee-toy said to Juhwerta Mahkai "My younger brother!" but Juhwerta Mahkai greeted him as younger brother and claimed to have come out first. Then Ee-ee-toy said again: "I came out first and you can see the water marks on my body." But Juhwerta Mahkai replied: "I came out first and also have the water marks on my person to prove it."

But Ee-ee-toy so insisted that he was the eldest that Juhwerta Mahkai, just to please him, gave him his way and let him be considered the elder.

And then they turned westward and yelled to find Toehahvs, for they remembered to have seen his tracks, and they kept on yelling till he heard them. And when Toehahvs saw them he called them his younger brothers, and they called him younger brother. And this dispute continued till Ee-ee-toy again got the best of it, and although really the younger brother was admitted by the others to be *Seeurhuh*, or the elder.

And the birds came down from the sky and again there was a dispute about the relationship, but Ee-ee-toy again got the best of them all.

But Quotaveech staid up in the sky because he had a comfortable nest there, and they called him *Vee-ick-koss-kum Mahkai*, the Feather-Nest Doctor.

And they wanted to find the middle, the navel of the earth, and they sent Veeppismahl, the humming bird, to the west, and Hickovick, the woodpecker, to the east, and all the others stood and waited for them at the starting place. And Veepismahl and Hickovick were to go as far as they could, to the edge of the world, and then return to find the middle of the earth by their meeting. But Hickovick flew a little faster and got there first, and so when they met they found it was not the middle, and they parted and started again, but this time they changed places and Hickovick went westward and Veepismahl went east.

And this time Veepismahl was the faster, and Hickovick was late, and the judges thought their place of meeting was a little east of the centre so they all went a little way west. Ee-ee-toy, Juhwerta Mahkai and Toehahvs stood there and sent the birds out once more, and this time Hickovick went eastward again, and Veepismahl went west. And Hickovick flew faster and arrived there first. And they said: "This is not the middle. It is a little way west yet."

And so they moved a little way, and again the birds were sent forth, and this time Hickovick went west and Veepismahl went east. And when the birds returned they met where the others stood and all cried "This is the Hick, the Navel of the World!"

And they stood there because there was no dry place yet for them to sit down upon; and Ee-eetoy rubbed upon his breast and took from his bosom the smallest ants, the *O-auf-taw-ton*, and threw them upon the ground, and they worked there and threw up little hills; and this earth was dry. And so they sat down.

But the: water was still running in the valleys, and Ee-ee-toy took a hair from his head and made it into a snake – *Vuck-vahmuht*. And with this snake he pushed the waters south, but the head of the snake was left lying to the west and his tail to the east.

But there was more water, and Ee-ee-toy took another hair from his head and made another snake, and with this snake pushed the rest of the water north. And the head of this snake was left to the east and his tail to the west. So the head of each snake was left lying with the tail of the other.

And the snake that has his tail to the east, in the morning will shake up his tail to start the morning wind to wake the people and tell them to think of their dreams.

And the snake that has his tail to the west, in the evening will shake up his tail to start the cool wind to tell the people it is time to go in and make the fires and be comfortable.

And they said: "We will make dolls, but we will not let each other see them until they are finished."

And Ee-ee-toy sat facing the west, and Toehahvs facing the south, and Juhwerta Mahkai facing the east.

And the earth was still damp and they took clay and began to make dolls. And Ee-ee-toy made the best. But Juhwerta Mahkai did not make good ones, because he remembered some of his people had escaped the flood thru a hole in the earth, and he intended to visit them and he did not want to make anything better than they were to take the place of them. And Toehahvs made the poorest of all.

Then Ee-ee-toy asked them if they were ready, and they all said yes, and then they turned about and showed each other the dolls they had made.

And Ee-ee-toy asked Juhwerta Mahkai why he had made such queer dolls. "This one," he said, "is not right, for you have made him without any sitting-down parts, and how can he get rid of the waste of what he eats?"

But Juhwerta Mahkai said: "He will not need to eat, he can just smell the smell of what is cooked."

Then Ee-ee-toy asked again: "Why did you make this doll with only one leg – how can he run?" But Juhwerta Mahkai replied: "He will not need to run; he can just hop around."

Then Ee-ee-toy asked Toehahvs why he had made a doll with webs between his fingers and toes – "How can he point directions?" But Toehahvs said he had made these dolls so for good purpose, for if anybody gave them small seeds they would not slip between their fingers, and they could use the webs for dippers to drink with.

And Ee-ee-toy held up his dolls and said: "These are the best of all, and I want you to make more like them." And he took Toehahv's dolls and threw them into the water and they became ducks and beavers. And he took Juhwerta Mahkai's dolls and threw them away and they all broke to pieces and were nothing.

And Juhwerta Mahkai was angry at this and began to sink into the ground; and took his stick and hooked it into the sky and pulled the sky down while he was sinking. But Ee-ee-toy spread his hand over his dolls, and held up the sky, and seeing that Juhwerta Mahkai was sinking into the earth he sprang and tried to hold him and cried, "Man, what are you doing? Are you going to leave me and my people here alone?"

But Juhwerta Mahkai slipped through his hands, leaving in them only the waste and excretion of his skin. And that is how there is sickness and death among us.

And Ee-ee-toy, when Juhwerta Mahkai escaped him, went around swinging his hands & saying: "I never thought all this impurity would come upon my people!" and the swinging of his hands scattered disease over all the earth. And he washed himself in a pool or pond and the impurities remaining in the water are the source of the malarias and all the diseases of dampness.

And Ee-ee-toy and Toehahvs built a house for their dolls a little way off, and Ee-ee-toy sent Toehahvs to listen if they were yet talking. And the Aw-up, (the Apaches) were the first ones that talked. And Ee-ee-toy said: "I never meant to have those Apaches talk first, I would rather have had the Aw-Aw-Tam, the Good People, speak first. "

But he said: "It is all right. I will give them strength, that they stand the cold and all hardships." And all the different people that they had made talked, one after the other, but the Aw-Aw-Tam talked last.

And they all took to playing together, and in their play they kicked each other as the Maricopas do in sport to this day; but the Apaches got angry and said: "We will leave you and go into the mountains and eat what we can get, but we will dream good dreams and be just as happy as you with all your good things to eat."

And some of the people took up their residence on the Gila, and some went west to the Rio Colorado. And those who builded *vahahkkees*, or houses out of adobe and stones, lived in the valley of the Gila, between the mountains which are there now.

Collected by J. William Lloyd

The Call of Ancestors

Tsitsi Mapepa, Zimbabwe

Spring 1992

AT THE AGE of nine, Nyeredzi was trying to work out who she was as a human being. After a couple years of beautiful harvests, drought arrived to devour people and animals. It was as if the sky's brightest star was angry at them. As though they had done something wrong and were being punished for it.

One day in October, she set off with her mother for the Duva dam. The bush that was once green was now just dirt littered with beige plants. Twigs and dead leaves crunched under Nyeredzi and Zuva's sandals with every step they took. After walking about four kilometres, they stopped to rest under the fig tree. The gully that crisscrossed the land was a reminder of what was once there. The riverbed was dry.

Nyeredzi ran around picking up round pebbles scattered on the riverbed and throwing them in the air. When she grew tired, she returned to stand in the shade of the fig tree with her mother. A pigeon fell from a branch like a rock on to the dry ground, a reminder that the drought took many lives. Its chest heaved, pulsating with its final breaths. It was as if the weak were being weeded out. Nyeredzi bent down to touch it, but Zuva held her hand. Within seconds, another bird dropped from the tree, and that's when Zuva said they should leave. If the birds that flew close to the heavens were falling upon them like that, then it was a bad omen.

They walked under the hot sun, following the path that people used by the banks of the river as though they were looking for something on the riverbed. The reeds had withered, and some had dried on the parched soil. Zuva and Nyeredzi were not sweating anymore but their bodies were sticky. When Nyeredzi touched her skin, it burnt her.

'Mama, aren't we roasting under the sun that promised to give us light?' Nyeredzi asked. 'Why do we keep on digging the soil that soon buries us?'

Zuva turned to her daughter and looked in her eyes. 'Because we are searching for our ancestors and when they hear the sound of a hoe digging, they know we are searching for them. In return, they bless us with what you and I eat.'

'I thought that was God who does that,' Nyeredzi said.

'Isn't God your ancestor? Weren't you created from his image?'

Zuva kept on walking. They passed the carcasses of small dead animals along the edges of the pathway, insects crawling over them. The stench reminded Nyeredzi of a rotten rat she had smelled once.

Under the burning sky, she imagined they were paddling on a vast red ocean with their feet. When she licked her lips, they were as salty as the sea and parched. It was not the first time she had felt like this. There were times when Nyeredzi played outside with her friends, Hope and Marvellous, and they would stop to rest their hands on their knees trying to catch their breath; dry, hot air had sucked away their strength.

At the Duva dam, there was nothing but a small muddy puddle at the centre. All the fish were dead. Frogs blew bubbles and croaked underneath the shallow brown water. The sides of the dam looked iron-hard, cracked, like the landscape of a planet. An army of ants crawled through the gaps, marching towards the dead fish and back to the hole again to feed their queen.

Further away, the pine trees which surrounded the hill looked as though they were offering themselves before the sun. The buildings of Fertiliser Company were fenced with a grey Durawall. Its black corrugated roof rippled in the heat mirage. A few humming vehicles crossed over the bridge of High Glen road, disappearing from the Durawall fence. To her right, the Olivine company's cylindrical building stood tall, and then there was just the blue sky and the huge expanse of the bush with its rocks and dead trees.

Nyeredzi could see how concerned her mother was. It was as though their ancestors had forgotten about them and swallowed all of the saliva left above the earth. There was no need to dig the land that year. No need to search for those who came before them, as Zuva had described. They would not be heard anyway.

Nyeredzi and Zuva had come to see if there was any water in the dam. Food grew scarce and expensive. Zuva sent Edward and Dingani, who rented their cottage, to different places just looking for mealie meal. What they found was not white maize, but yellow mealie meal imported from other countries. Three meals became two meals. People learned to cope with that. Nyeredzi did too; Zuva had taught her to fast before. People were encouraged to stay indoors as the heat itself killed anything that breathed. They were encouraged to save water as much as they could but the Taha family were still forced to kill most of their chickens in a short time because they had started dying on their own.

Each day came slow and ended slow. In the evenings the family had a little energy to walk around. Mr and Mrs Manjo came to their house one night to visit.

'Mr and Mrs Manjo, please come in,' said Mwedzi. He got up to shake Mrs Manjo's hand, and then gave Mr Manjo a brief hug with a wide smile on his face.

Ruth, Abigail, and Hannah got up from the three-seater sofa and moved to the bench. Mr and Mrs Manjo sat down, looking surprised. Perhaps they were not expecting all of the girls to move seats. Nyeredzi hopped on to the sofa and sat next to Mr Manjo, looking at his face that was now starting to wrinkle.

'We have come because death is knocking on our doors,' he said.

'We do see that,' Zuva said.

'What do you suggest?' Mwedzi asked.

'The *Ndima-Ndima* dance,' Mrs Manjo responded. 'We need the ancestors to hear us.'

'All that bloodshed on the bush,' Zuva said, shaking her head.

'We better do it now, I think,' Mr Manjo said, looking at Zuva and Mwedzi for their approval. Nyeredzi was curious about what Zuva was going to do. In their community, if people had devoted their lives to being Christian, they should not be seen going back to their old traditional ways. Some people weren't bothered by being Christian and a traditional believer at the same time, but Zuva was a church leader.

'You know we can't get involved,' Zuva told him.

'We thought we should come to you first,' said Mrs Manjo.

'We do appreciate that,' Zuva said.

After Mr and Mrs Manjo left, Nyeredzi thought about what her mother had always told her. God was their ancestor; Nyeredzi was created from the image of God. But if everyone else was gathering for this dance, she wanted to be there, even if it was a clash between God and these old, different gods. Nyeredzi wanted to know what lay beneath what other people believed, whether she had been praying to the right God.

It would be the first time in her life witnessing a dance that called upon their ancestors, begging them to hear them. She had seen some dances at school but not as serious and important as the one their neighbours were planning.

In the following days, Mr and Mrs Manjo went from house to house, telling people about the *Ndima-Ndima* dance. From what Nyeredzi heard her parents say, a lot of them were on board, prepared to do anything that would save them from the drought – from death. Mr and Mrs Manjo often returned to ask Zuva questions. Where was it suitable to perform the dance? How many people would be appropriate to participate? Was food needed too? Were the children allowed to come along? They seemed to seek Zuva's approval, and Nyeredzi wasn't sure why. Perhaps, she thought, it was because her mother was a church leader.

People had chosen to perform the dance on a weekend when everyone was not occupied with work or other activities. It was to start at noon. Next to the curve of the riverbed, the ground was cleared, and *maponde,* mats weaved from reeds, were spread for people to sit under the *Msasa* tree. Its red leaves shimmered bright from afar. Some people said it was ancestors' blood rising from underneath, and that's why it was still alive. Others said that was where ancestors went when the land was dry. The tree was the communicator between the dead and living people, and it spat drops of water when people took shelter underneath it.

From their house, Nyeredzi saw people walking to the bush. Women had wrapped their heads in scarves, and around their waist they wore a large piece of fabric, *Zambia.* Some were patterned, others bore the words, *Madzitateguru edu tisunungurei,* set us free our ancestors. Nyeredzi wondered if people always had those things in their wardrobes. Not knowing made her feel like she was an outsider among her own neighbours.

'Mama, everyone is going – should we go too?' Nyeredzi asked, expecting her mother to say no.

'We are all going,' Zuva answered from her bedroom.

Nyeredzi was surprised because Zuva had told Mr and Mrs Manjo she couldn't get involved. Her sisters refused to join them, so Nyeredzi was the only one going with her parents. In her arms, Zuva held a *bonde,* a mat woven from reeds. Her father was holding a round clay pot filled with water. They walked towards the bush alongside other people, the streets quiet. No one was listening to the radio or watching TV that day. Nyeredzi noticed that, like her parents, people were carrying things related to their own cultures.

When they arrived at the prepared area, Mwedzi placed the clay pot he held in his hands under the *Msasa* tree. Zuva spread the mat on the ground nearby, in front of the tree, and they all sat on it. Nyeredzi admired the drawings on the clay pots: small figures of women carrying pails on their heads from the river, men hunting in the forest. She wanted to get up to touch the crushed leaves that floated in the pots circling the tree. She wanted to step on to the dancing area covered with mealie meal and sand – feel the coldness of the animal horns set aside in a *rutsero,* a round woven tray. She wanted to do everything and play the *Mbira,* the drums, and shakers placed next to the riverbed.

Many people were still arriving and Nyeredzi kept looking back until she saw her sisters approaching the dance place too.

'Mama look – they are coming,' Nyeredzi said, pulling Zuva's hand. Perhaps she would enjoy watching the dance with her sisters. Maybe they would start seeing things the way she did.

'Very well then,' Zuva said. She didn't seem surprised.

'Why do we have to start the dance after midday?'

'Because we do not want to wake the ancestors in the morning, and if we do it in the evening, we don't want to disturb their sleep.'

'Haven't they been sleeping all along?'

Zuva looked at her. 'You may think they are sleeping because when you put someone in the box, they will be in a sleeping position, but the soul rises. It's not sleeping anymore.'

'Like King Jesus did – he resurrected?'

'Exactly!'

Zuva folded her arms in front and looked out over the crowd. Mwedzi was talking to another man sitting next to him. Nyeredzi's sisters arrived and sat behind them on the *bonde.* They looked on with curiosity of the dance but pretended as though they weren't. Hundreds of people were waiting and Nyeredzi could see how anxious they were. Some ended up sitting on the dusty ground or on rocks because there weren't enough *maponde.* Others stood at the back.

One man wearing black shorts walked to the centre of the dance area. The crowd fell quiet. He had tribal drawings painted in white and red on his naked chest, arms, and around his eyes. *Zvuma*, necklaces, dangled on his neck. He knelt on the soil and raised his hands in the air.

'To our ancestors, your great-grandchildren are here today. We are here. You sacrifice a lot for us, and still, we break the rules. On behalf of my brothers who have killed on this land, forgive us?'

He stood up and walked over to the men holding shakers. Within seconds, the *Mbira* was on his lap, and his fingers moved swiftly. The rhythm drew everyone who was sitting on the ground and rocks. A group of men appeared from a dense bush, walking towards the drums and picking them up. They began to tap on the drums, the sound growing. Some of them grabbed the shakers and hummed with deep low voices. It raised hairs on Nyeredzi's skin. From that moment she knew she was not an outsider. The ancestors had arrived before they had been summoned, before Nyeredzi had devoted herself to them. They followed the line of the blood, and she knew that she had it inside her veins.

Two lines of men appeared from behind the shrubs dancing slowly towards the dance area. Their upper bodies were bare, and they wore black shorts underneath skirts of animal skins, made from patches of cheetah, leopard, zebra, impala and more. Around their necks dangled *zvuma* made from wooden beads; small arrows in the centre of them matched the bangles on their wrists. Their long headpieces were made of the African fish eagle feathers. Some of them had tattoos – their history dotted in darkened lines, and the images of animals seemed as though that's where their strength came from. Nyeredzi didn't know that some of her neighbours had these emblems on them.

She wondered why they had come to Zuva asking for her approval to go ahead with the traditional dance. It was clear everyone in the neighbourhood respected Zuva and Mwedzi, for who they were: Christians, down-to-earth people. Both of them had done a lot in the community and the Taha family prayed every day for everyone to be saved. And for the Taha family to be present on this occasion must be important for their neighbours, although Nyeredzi still wasn't sure why.

The men held spears in their hands like the warriors Nyeredzi had heard about in folk tales. These were the warriors who were fighting evil spirits. The people who had been killed on this land were moaning, haunting those who had taken their lives. Zuva had said it before to the girls: ghosts were haunting the murderers.

Before the men jumped up in the air in front of the drummers, they stomped on the ground and adjusted their headpieces so that they wouldn't fall. For the people sitting on the *maponde*, the land felt as though it was vibrating. It didn't take much time before the women who were wearing vivid colours of *zvuma* lifted clay pots on to their heads and joined the men. They swayed their hips in circles, the frills of their black skirts made from animal skin swooping up and down and sideways.

Their chests were covered in the manes of lions tied at the back. Bangles dangled on their wrists and *zvuma* on their necks. They all walked in a line and then knelt in front of the audience, placing the clay pots on the ground.

The women clapped their hands and began to ululate loudly, and other women in the crowd howled along with them. Nyeredzi wanted to do it too, but she was scared this was crossing the line. The women got up again, swaying their hips from side to side, fast, and jumped, throwing their hands in the air. They danced alongside the men, who sometimes moved to the front and threw their spears into the air. They looked serious, their bodies glistening with sweat.

Dust swirled in the air. The earth continued to vibrate, and their voices rang out, calling the ancestors.

Madzitateguru edu matikanganwa here	Our ancestors, have you forgotten about us
Dzokai muuye kuzotisunungura	Come back and set us free
vana venyu vafa nenzara, tinzwei woye	Your children are dying from famine, hear us

Haa hiya hoye, woye, woyeee,	*Haa hiya hoye, woye, woyeee,*
madzitateguru edu,	our ancestors,
vana vofa. Vakatadza vakadarika	children are dying. Those who sinned
vakawanda nedziro ramakavaka.	are hiding behind the wall you've built.
Regererai,	Forgive,
vana vofa vasati vakuzivai	children are dying before they know you
Haa hiya hoye, woye, woyeee,	*Haa hiya hoye, woye, woyeee,*
madzitateguru edu tinzwei…	our ancestors, hear us…

Some people sang along with the dancers. Shouldn't Nyeredzi join in too, to beg the ancestors to hear them? She did, clapping her hands, while her sisters looked at her as though she was doing something wrong. Zuva and Mwedzi did not say anything. Nyeredzi ululated with the rest of the women. The women who were dancing looked deep into her eyes. At that moment, Nyeredzi knew the ancestors had heard them.

She had a vision of being transported to a place she had never seen before. In this place old people sat on big rocks next to caves. Their bodies were covered in yellow fabric, like a rising sun. They held long brown walking sticks in their hands, earth in their palms, and red beads around their wrists and ankles, the blood of the ancestors. Grey-silver *zvuma* hung loose on their necks, like Mother moon and the stars that shined upon them in the dark times. They stomped on the ground with their sticks, summoning their great fathers and mothers. The women ululated and sang while men hummed in deep voices crouching on the ground.

One man with grey dreadlocks to his shoulders approached Nyeredzi and stretched his arm towards her. He opened his clenched fist and Nyeredzi saw a seed germinating in red soil. The old man gestured for Nyeredzi to take it. She hesitated then took the plant and dirt from his palm. Next an old woman with a clay pot filled with water approached. She dropped a seed into it and pushed the pot up to Nyeredzi's lips for her to drink. When Nyeredzi swallowed the seed, she felt full. Suddenly she found herself covered in a green fabric. The woman stared at Nyeredzi with a smile on her face.

'You, my daughter, you wear green. You are the wealth of this nation. What you bear in the future shall bring wealth in your palms. Your great grandfathers and mothers are there.' She pointed to the men and women in yellow. 'Gold, emerald, diamonds, whatever minerals you seek from them, they will give you.

She raised her hands in the air and water fell upon Nyeredzi, washing her whole body, as though she was being baptised or born again. Nyeredzi wiped water from her eyes and listened to the old lady's voice.

'I bathe you with holy water from our ancestors. Water shall pour on you whenever you call upon us, and if you ask, we will give you.'

The old woman touched Nyeredzi's shoulders with both hands. Her grip was firm but gentle at the same time, as though she didn't want to let go of Nyeredzi. Fear rushed in Nyeredzi's veins. The old woman's voice was thick, and she was not the kind of person Nyeredzi had ever met before.

Her right hand moved from Nyeredzi's shoulder to her left rib and said, 'This hand of mine on your chest is a red star of the aspiration I have seen in you. You have this endless burning flame in you no one can put out. You are like your mother who brings peace. She is the mother of this nation.'

The old woman pressed her lips together, stepping away and pointing. Nyeredzi took two steps backwards, looking where the woman was pointing – the vast land sprinkled with green vegetation, the sun above beaming on the leaves and the red earth, birds gliding. A breeze brushed Nyeredzi's face, and she realised that it came from the old woman's mouth, as though she was waking her from sleep.

'My daughter, an eagle will fly you to places you've never been, but when you get there, don't ever forget where you belong like your mother has not forgotten the trail of her bloodline. You were blessed before you were birthed.'

The old people were all looking at Nyeredzi, but because their eyes held a fierce intensity, she looked down as a sign of respect. When she raised her head again, they were gone. The caves were gone. Only the land was left. Nyeredzi had met the ancestors, and they had spoken to her. They had blessed her and foretold her future.

At that moment, the dancing women had moved close to her and her family. Dust formed a thick blanket in the atmosphere. Zuva turned to look at Nyeredzi, and whatever she saw made her touch Mwedzi's hand and squeezed it. He turned to look at Nyeredzi too. Both of them stared at her but didn't say a word. Her sisters were busy whispering, not paying attention to the dance.

'Fire is burning inside you like the *Msasa* leaves above us,' one of the dancers said to her. Nyeredzi had never met this woman before and didn't recognise her from their neighbourhood. 'They are burning, and they will keep burning.'

Most people were now singing along with the dancers. The women picked up the bowls of seeds and threw them in the air. They fell on people nearby, and one landed on Nyeredzi's head. She felt it at the core of her head and reached up, pinching it with her fingers. The women were still throwing seeds up into the air. Nyeredzi placed the seed on her tongue to swallow it. When the *Msasa* tree began to spit on them. That's when the dancers stopped. Sweat dribbled from them. Their bare feet were coated in dust. The men picked up the horns which they blew, sending people home. No one talked after that, even on their way home. It was as though everyone had been electrified by the ancestors' spirit.

* * *

Days after the *Ndima-Ndima* dance, the sky was still burning the earth. Animals were still dying. More impatient people began to say terrible things, complaining that they had wasted time going to participate in the dance. Nyeredzi kept the secret to herself that she had met the ancestors. Who could she have told? Why would the ancestors come to her? She was a child after all. How could she talk to her mother about it when Zuva was a church leader and against the old ways?

One afternoon Mr and Mrs Manjo came back to the Tahas' house.

'Please, come in Mr and Mrs Manjo,' Zuva said, gesturing for him to sit on the sofa. 'Would you like a glass of orange juice?'

'Yes, please. Thank you *Gogo*,' Mrs Manjo answered.

Zuva looked at Hannah, who got up and brought orange juice and a glass from the kitchen unit. Solid food was now rare to find, and it was only saved for the main meal like dinner. Mr Manjo picked up the full glass and held it for a while, his expression deep in contemplation. He took a sip and looked at Zuva.

'*Gogo*, I want to thank you and your family for coming to the *Ndima-Ndima* dance,' he said. 'It was an honour to have you all there.'

Nyeredzi, sitting on the *bonde*, smiled when she heard this.

'We were supposed to be there,' her mother told him. 'We were not guests, Mr Manjo.'

'I am aware of that, but one of the spirit mediums where we went last time said there is something important about your family,' he paused, and glanced at his wife, who nodded at him. 'It doesn't mean we've been looking into people's lives. It's just that the spirit medium said if you had not attended, the water would not fall on the ground and the ancestors would not hear us.'

Zuva looked shocked. 'Is that so?'

Mr Manjo turned his gaze to Nyeredzi, instinctively she hid behind the woven net of the armchair. She was scared that he might have seen the fire inside her eyes, just as the woman from the dance saw.

She was also afraid that her sisters were going to see it and then they wouldn't want to sleep in the same room as her anymore.

'How soon do you think it will rain?' Mrs Manjo asked Zuva.

'Be patient,' Zuva said in a soft voice. Mr and Mrs Manjo gulped down all the orange juice and left. Days came and passed, and soon the end of the year was approaching. The clouds formed in the sky, promising rain, but vanished as quickly as they had appeared. The sun burnt the clouds; it even burnt seeds under the ground.

Nyeredzi kept her distance from Hope and Marvellous, her friends. She didn't want them to see the fire that was now in her. This meant she felt lonely. Each time she stepped on the bare ground, it was as though something was pulling her from underneath, talking to her. The earth was trembling.

Quite often, she wandered off alone and hid behind the cottage under the water berry tree. She danced, thinking no one was there, until the day she realised that Zuva was standing right in front of her. Nyeredzi thought her mother was going to shout at her for performing the traditional dance. Instead, Zuva looked deep into her eyes. 'You have the fire I saw the day we went to the *Ndima-Ndima* dance under the *Msasa* tree,' she told Nyeredzi. 'Do not hide whatever you are feeling, my daughter. It's there to protect you.'

Zuva walked away without another word, and Nyeredzi resumed her dance. It was as if her mother had unlocked a gate, permitting Nyeredzi to follow her ancestors. The earth vibrated as she stomped on the ground. At the end of her dance, Nyeredzi asked the ancestors to cleanse her. That way, she would know there were no clashes between the two worlds of Christianity and of their ancestors. Where she came from, and where she was headed: these worlds to her were blended into one.

The answer Nyeredzi was waiting for took longer. When the skies turned dark and dense one day when she was walking alone in the bush from school, she felt scared. She lifted her legs in the air and began to dance again. Her tongue mimicked the words that were sung at the *Ndima-Ndima* dance, asking for forgiveness. She feared she might have had no right to ask the ancestors because her faith belonged somewhere.

Nyeredzi threw her satchel on the ground, unbuttoned the belt of her green uniform, and danced all the steps she saw being performed under the *Msasa* tree. Only later did she realise that this was what her ancestors had told her to do: *ask, and we will give.*

The clouds descended really low until the thunderheads swelled and blocked out the sun. The rain was finally here, and it was an enormous storm. At one point, Nyeredzi was frightened, thinking the ancestors had come to take her. The rain dampened the soil, penetrating the gaps of the cracked clay. It kept on coming down, hitting her body, the ground, the dead grass, and the thirsty trees that had wilted. Her green dress was now stuck to her body, as if she was born in it.

The fear that rushed in her veins somehow encouraged her to continue. This water that fell from the heavens revived her and gave her energy. She didn't know where it was coming from. She danced on alone in the bush, uncertain whether her great fathers and mothers had arrived to sing and dance along with her. To bless the land. Even with all the proof they had heard her, she didn't stop. Nyeredzi kept on calling upon them, not realising in that moment that the ancestors had come to cleanse her, just as she had asked.

Yeredzo River

Tsitsi Mapepa, Zimbabwe

Summer 1993

EVERYONE in Goho village knew that the waterfall was Selina's dwelling, but to them, it was also their source of water. Mother Earth's saliva poured from the cliff, forming the bridal veils that were divided by a horned rock twenty-five metres high. Sometimes the water flowed smooth as glass, and other times, depending on the weather, the deafening roar raged on people's faces and bodies if they were standing too close.

People said the horned rock was Selina's crown and that each day she lived was her wedding. Others called it the curtain divider, which allowed people to peer through, eager to see what was behind the water. They hoped that maybe one day they would see Selina herself lying on a bare rock within the cave. She had inherited this specific cave from her mother, Heroshina. It was wide, deep and curvy. And the rest of the area, where the water bumped on to the boulders and flowed along the meandering valley, was for the villagers and other creatures.

Women from the village of Goho came to fetch water from the river before the sun rose, and before it headed south, beyond the bald heads of their ancestors lying in the Earth. At that time of day, the water was still clean, untouched and undisturbed.

During the daytime, after the women had finished making food for their families, sent the children to school, cleaned their houses, and swept their yards with brooms, they brought their laundry to the Yeredzo river and washed it while sitting on the rocks. It was their meeting place. They knew the time: the sun never misled them. They knew the perfect spot that didn't have any algae, where the rocks weren't slippery, where their pre-schoolers could play in shallow waters and not drown. They gossiped about other people in the village and their love lives, all their secrets unfolding before the river.

It became their holy place, too, because they repented without realising it. This was where Mother Nature lifted the burdens that oppressed them and where their sins could be washed away with the water. This river invigorated them. It watched them come of age, sang to calm them down, cooled their bodies raging with hormones, washed away their blood, until they struggled to get up from where they sat.

Once the women were done with laundry, when all the clothes were laid out on the grassy patches and bushy trees to dry, the women and their children were cleansed. Each of them stayed close to their little ones, some carrying their babies on their backs. Though the river was special to them in many ways, safety was not guaranteed. Sometimes the long, slim creatures that slithered on their tummies appeared from nowhere, uninvited. The people of Goho were always cautious when it came to wild animals and sacred places, like Selina's dwelling.

Zuva was cautious as well, even after all this time away. She brought her daughters to the river, stepping into the shallow water feeling so much respect for Selina. Her daughters sank their feet in the soft sand alongside her. In her heart, she knew this visit home meant introducing her daughters to the values she had long held and telling them what was not accepted in their village. The lifestyle here was different and for her daughters to understand, Zuva had to tell them what happened to her sister, Maudie.

Maudie had broken so many rules in their village throughout her life and she seemed to have lost respect for their culture. Even though Zuva hadn't seen her for a long time, the rumours were already swimming through her ears. It proved that Maudie hadn't changed at all.

When they were still young, the freedom that ran in Maudie's blood made her lips loose. Once they had been at the river when Maudie shouted 'Heroshina's dwelling reeks.' At that time, Heroshina was already dead, but Selina was offended. Zuva told Maudie she had crossed the line and before her sister had finished bathing at the river, she was visited by a dangerous creature. Zuva had seen it coming, the green snake slithering between the gaps in the rocks, while Maudie stood on a flat rock, shaking her waist sideways, laughing.

Zuva whispered, 'Forgive.' Her friends and cousins screamed, trying to warn Maudie, but Zuva stood still, knowing in her heart that Selina would have heard her whisper, begging forgiveness for her sister. But Selina couldn't just forgive without warning Maudie of her wrongdoings. The snake circled her, and Maudie screamed in terror, dropping the towel and a bar of soap she was holding. As she ran away, she slipped and fell hard on to the rocks. Blood spilt from her mouth and by the time the river washed her tongue of her insensitive words, she was left with a chipped tooth.

When Zuva told her daughters the stories of her childhood, Selina was listening, enlivened by Zuva's presence. Zuva made a lot of people feel at peace when she was around them. It wasn't just Togara and Nyikadzino, it was also Selina, and the people of Goho. In the second Chimurenga war, she calmed injured people who in the end were swallowed by death. They didn't moan or scream: they fell asleep in her arms as if Zuva had put them to bed.

Later, as the sun began falling in the sky, Zuva walked out of the water and used the same dusty, narrow path she used years ago to walk home. Its edges had been washed away by rainfall. Her daughters followed. They passed by Goho Primary and High School which Zuva once attended. The long red-brick blocks of classrooms stood in small rows. The school ground was green, surrounded by gum and wild berry trees. She tried to point out her old classroom but too much had changed. The office was further away, now guarded by the black tarred car park, the assembly had a stage in front and the back section was an orchard.

Next to the padlocked wrought iron gate was a noticeboard. Zuva's gaze was drawn to Maudie's name on the board. With Maudie's success in education, she was now running a college in Harare. Though the villagers had honoured her for developing the school, she also wanted to change a lot of things in the village. This meant Maudie was a main topic at the river when women were bathing or doing laundry.

People would know Maudie was back by the way she revved the engine of her blue Range Rover as she raced home along the dusty road. They talked about how her feet were no longer touching the soil. Her Gucci wedge sandals defined her steps, lifting her butt in the air, walking as though she was on a seesaw. She seemed more unearthly, someone who thought they were superior to others. Zuva had witnessed this first-hand the afternoon they arrived from Harare, when the whole family sat outside for lunch together. Maudie was obsessed with her long, polished nails and she didn't want food stuck in her claws, so she used forks and knives even on the food that needed to be picked with bare hands.

Zuva walked away from the school noticeboard, her sister's behaviour gnawing at her thoughts. She talked and laughed with her daughters, but she was wondering how so many things had changed in her absence. How so many families were now visiting throughout the summer holidays to celebrate Christmas with their loved ones and how often they brought chaos.

Zuva's brother Garikai was the chief, so he and the elders held meetings once or twice a week to inform visitors about Selina's dwelling, but the young ones wanted to explore and know what lay beneath the deep curves of water, behind the thick veils. Curiosity kept knocking at the back of their skulls each day they walked past, on their way to and from herding cattle or weeding maize. The more curious they grew, the closer they got to Selina's dwelling, walking by as though it was not a sacred place.

During the Christmas season, it was hard for the elders to control everything that happened in the village. The young ones would be found diving into Selina's pool and none of them seemed to understand how serious this was because the lines had become blurred. They wondered if Selina really existed. Why they had never seen her sunbathing? Why had they only heard about her from other people? Why did the villagers claim she was there when none of them had ever come across her? All this stirred confusion within the village. People had always relied on the information they were told by their elders, just like Zuva's daughters. This included learning about the signs that warned them of Selina's emotions. The villagers knew what to do if something happened, but the Christmas visitors were ignorant.

When the water was bubbling around the curvy pool, it meant Selina was ready to sleep. It was forbidden to disturb her, even by diving from the edge of the cliff. Some mornings, when there was a fresh breeze, words would appear in the overlapping ripples on the water, and it meant Selina was in love; her body was craving a man but only the desired man would be able to read the letters.

When this happened, women of the village were afraid to lose their husbands to Selina. It was believed that some men were infatuated with her. Her breath whistled in their ears, echoing love songs. Others saw her in their dreams, her body beyond the definition of beauty. It melted their souls and drained all their strength into their groins.

The temptation was undeniable. A man would follow Selina into the cave where it seemed dark from the outside, but once he was in there, everything glittered. Her utensils, her clothes, the passages that took him to other rooms, even her body changed colours. She would ask three times if he really wanted to be hers. If he agreed, she would marry him. Quite often, when this took place, people would see flame lily flowers floating within her territory for a full month. It amazed everyone, how the flowers could remain fresh for that long. This honeymoon phase meant a man was never coming back, dead, or alive. If he chose not to stay with Selina, the man would wake with a fright from the dream and never remember what he saw in the cave.

When the thick bridal veils flowed violently from the cliff, Selina was in a vortex of despair, grieving for her long-lost mother, father, sister, brother and husbands. Her hormones swirled in and out of the river and the water was dirty for days. Dead leaves and branches would be scattered everywhere, frothy edges and boulders covered in Selina's green slime vomit. The water was unsafe for drinking, washing, or bathing. The chief and the mediums of the village would be called to ask Selina to calm down, and let the other creatures live in peace.

During Togara's time as a chief, it was unusual to see this happening. People behaved very well. Now that his son Garikai had taken over, a darkness had begun to grow. Corruption began the moment he bought the men of the village with his father's gold, so he could become the chief.

Years back, when Heroshina existed, there was a prediction that the villagers' disrespect towards Selina's dwelling would create havoc and bring death. But people had forgotten the warning. They thought it would never occur in their lifetime and for a long time, life was peaceful. Though the young ones sometimes trespassed on Selina's dwelling, she forgave them. She was more kind-hearted than her mother. Heroshina was impatient, and any obnoxious behaviour was punished ferociously.

But after so many decades, people were beginning to take Selina lightly. Their lifestyle had changed. The village had developed. The round huts with thatched roofs had been demolished to make way for brick houses with corrugated zinc or tiled roofs. Electricity lit their rooms at night, and the people no longer relied on Mother Moon and her children. Each roof in the village had a thin spiked horn to watch the moving pictures. They might think this horn resembled Selina's crown, but the worlds were far apart.

The village looked like a modern suburb. Now people went to the river for pleasure or to get away from the crowded houses. Women still enjoyed their meetings, though. Just because the villagers were moving along with the world didn't mean Yeredzo river had stopped flowing. Selina's dwelling was still there, and she watched the newer generation who came to bathe – the grandchildren of the elders who now used walking sticks to guide them as they walked.

* * *

A few days after Zuva and her family arrived, she was still waiting for the spirit mediums to go with the whole family to Togara and Nyikadzino's graves. There was to be a prayer to put her parents at rest and this was the only reason she'd come back.

Zuva had already taken her daughters to see where their grandparents lay. While they were waiting for the visit with the mediums, she encouraged the girls to bond with their cousins – Garikai's two sons, Revie and Taurai, and his daughters, Chenai and Mazvita.

She and Mwedzi were sleeping in her father's chamber. The very night they arrived, before supper, Melinda, her sister-in-law, came into the hut and knelt before Zuva.

'My sister, Zuva, I'm sorry for everything that has happened. You and I barely know each other, but I come to ask for forgiveness.' She touched Zuva's hands. 'Open your heart for my children and me. And please, when the right time comes, forgive Garikai and Maudie?'

Neither her brother nor her sister had come to apologise for their wrongdoings, so Zuva was surprised to hear Melinda say this. Clearly, no one had asked her to do that. It was time to make things right. Zuva lifted Melinda up and asked her to sit next to her.

'Melinda, my sister, I have never held anything against you. If anyone should apologise, it is me. I was hard on you when I arrived. I guess emotions were coiling inside me.'

'Please come and sleep in the house. We have more rooms.'

'The girls can come and sleep in there. Mwedzi and I will sleep in here but thank you for your kindness.'

'Anything you need, please let me know, I'm here,' said Melinda, and Zuva thanked her.

Zuva's daughters were already getting along with their cousins. And whenever they sat outside to chat, Maudie's children, Emmanuel, Lydia and Munya, joined them as well. While Zuva sat in her father's chamber during the day, she listened to their conversations. She was surprised that Maudie's children often talked about their fancy lifestyle. How they had travelled with their mother and father abroad to Europe and America and bought nice things that lasted longer. How they were planning to go and study there. Zuva's family was still living in an unfinished house that didn't have electricity, and yet here in a village, they flicked the plugs on and off as if they were in the city. Zuva wondered how Maudie and Fredrick had got so much money.

* * *

As the days passed, the temperature rose. It was hot. There were times when the children isolated into groups according to their ages. Some sat under the smelly berry fingerleaf tree to talk. Others spent most of their time in their bedrooms gossiping about dating. Zuva and Mwedzi often wandered off and ended up on the mountain at Togara and Nyikadzino's graves.

The young ones explored the village even under that heat. Nyeredzi and the other girls followed Munya, who was showing them around. Munya had participated in different sports at Peterhouse Boys'

School and promised to teach them to swim. Nyeredzi had seen the school several times when they lived in Marondera. It was a private school, and she dreamt that one day her parents would enrol her at one of those fancy schools.

At the river, Munya first swam out into the deep areas, showing the others how to float, but he grew bored quickly and started to climb up the cliffside.

'You can't go up there,' Nyeredzi shouted at Munya. 'Mama said so – it is forbidden.'

'What do you know?' he shouted back. 'You just came here a few days ago.'

'I know everything,' Mazvita said. 'I'll tell Papa you climbed there.'

'Boohoo.' Munya stuck his tongue out and kept climbing the rocky cliff while his cousins waited down by the curvy pool. At the top he strolled along the edge of the horned rock, then tucked his right hand behind his head as though he was posing for a photoshoot. He counted down from five and jumped, spinning his body twice in the air. When his body met the water, a big splash showered his cousins. His head rose above the water and they applauded. Munya's charms had made them forget the rules. Nyeredzi couldn't believe it.

'That was brilliant,' Chenai said, 'but don't do it again, unless you want to be Selina's husband.'

'Oh, chill. Nothing is going to happen to me. I can swim faster than Selina.' Munya wiped water from his face with his dry shirt. 'Just you wait – you haven't seen the best of me yet.'

'And what's that?' Abigail asked.

'I've got something better, something we can all enjoy.'

'I'm serious. You can't do that again,' Chenai said with a shaky voice.

Munya dashed off towards a little bush where he was hiding his stuff. He pulled out a bottle of cherry blossom body wash. 'It's my mother's. I suppose we can borrow it, just for now.' The cousins watched him twist the cap. His smile promised them it was going to be fun.

Nyeredzi shook her head, looking at her cousins, hoping they would say something, but they didn't. 'You know very well smelly things aren't allowed here, right?' she asked Munya.

Zuva had told her girls that soap and anything with a fragrance muddled with Selina, and people were encouraged to bathe far from her territory. Any dainty sip of spoiled water in Selina's mouth would mean severe consequences. There were stories of lives stolen, dead bodies floating down the river like leaves, veins popping out of their skin.

'Yeah–yeah!' Munya scoffed. 'Too many rules for one place. If you don't want to have a bubble bath with me, you are free to go. Anyway, you and Abigail have only been here for a few days, so I wouldn't expect much from you.'

Abigail and Chenai left, shaking their heads in disbelief, walking away into the valley of trees and grass. In the distance, birds chattered, and children could be heard crying from their houses. Nyeredzi wanted to go too, but she had to make sure Munya would get out of the pool safe and sound. She and Mazvita stood at a distance, both worried.

Munya held the body wash upside down and began pouring it in the pool. Bubbles formed, circulating the pool before flowing down the river. When the bottle was half empty, Munya placed it aside and jumped into the curvy pool. He began to swim slowly in circles and then increased his speed. Nyeredzi and Mazvita stood a metre away, watching him perform all kinds of somersaults as he circled along the edges of the pool. His feet flapped like a dolphin's tail, putting to use all he'd learned at his expensive school.

'Why won't you come in?' he asked them.

'We can't do what you are doing in there,' Mazvita said. 'You know the rules.'

'Well, your loss. Throw me the bottle – I might as well finish the body wash. I need more bubbles in here. They are all flowing down the river.'

'It's a river, not a tub,' Nyeredzi shouted. 'I am not handing you the bottle. Mama will be mad at me.'

'I can't believe people of Goho have spent all these years without even trying to do this. This is amazing. Hoo!' Munya reached for the bottle at the edge of the pool and poured the rest of the body wash into the water. He then swam back to the middle of the pool. 'And that Selina you always talk about, she doesn't exis…'

Munya didn't finish his sentence. In an instant his body was submerged, the force of the water tumbling him. Nyeredzi and Mazvita ran around the pool, calling his name and hoping they could grab Munya and pull him out. Fear rushed through the streams of Nyeredzi's blood, goosebumps rose on her skin, and the hair that was glistening in sweat before all stood at attention. The bubbles floating in the pool made it impossible to see Munya.

When the girls realised that Munya was really swallowed deep into the bowels of the Earth, Nyeredzi sent Mazvita back home to call the elders. She waited by the pool to see if Munya would rise again. It was evident Selina was angry. So, Nyeredzi stood there, next to her dwelling, hoping for a miracle, for Munya to show his face again. She hated herself for not listening to her mother and staying away.

Soon, the elders arrived. Nyeredzi stepped away to give the elders room to see but she was still in shock. She didn't know whether to apologise or do something else that would ease her guilty conscience.

The elders looked horrified, but Nyeredzi was sure they would be able to do something. Emmanuel, Maudie's oldest child, had taken diving lessons. He ran to the edge of the pool and said he could make out a blurry object that looked like a body deep underwater.

'He could be caught with roots or under a rock,' Emmanuel said.

'I can get him out,' Maudie responded, taking her shoes off so she could dive in.

'No, I'll go.' Emmanuel dived in. Everyone else knelt beside the pool, calling out to Munya. Within a few seconds, Emmanuel emerged from underneath the pool and shook his head. 'That's not Munya. I can't find him,' he said, his voice thick with worry.

He dived down again, and this time he took longer. Everyone was now only waiting for him. Maudie was trembling, Nyeredzi realised, and her uncle Garikai seemed lost. The ferocity he'd shown the past few days wasn't there anymore. Maudie climbed to the edge of the pool so she could dive in, but Garikai stopped her. It wasn't the time to show who could swim or not, this was serious. There was a protocol to follow, and they didn't have much time; the boys had been gone for too long.

'What should we do now?' she screamed at Garikai. 'I want my sons back!'

'We have to make an offering,' Garikai said, shivering.

Maudie lay by the edge of the pool. 'I beg you Selina, please return my sons,' she begged. 'I'll give you all I have, please.'

The commotion had drawn more of the villagers, and everyone seemed to feel for Maudie. To have a person, a child be taken – that hadn't happened in years. The fear of the unknown, the creature that lived under the water, terrified them to their bone marrow. Garikai stood there frozen, as though he'd forgotten the correct procedures. Finally, one of the village men asked if he could bring the offering to Selina, and Garikai nodded.

Garikai crouched down, clapping his hands, and looked up into the heavens. 'To the kings of this village, I ask from the core of my heart for you to rise from where you lie right now. Your blood has been pulled from the soil you have stepped on. Haah! I am stranded. Come and help me with this battle, the kings of this world, whose spirit lingers in the air.' He paused, clapped his hands three times, and let out a long sigh.

Nyeredzi wondered if something would happen. When the offering was brought to the river, the bubbles were still visible, the water was disturbed and murky. Maudie was still lying by the poolside, wailing, begging Mother Earth to hear her.

'Selina, I apologise for saying nasty things about your mother and for not believing that you exist,' Maudie cried. 'All I want are my sons back and alive. I beg you, Selina!'

Nyeredzi overheard a woman ask where Zuva and Mwedzi were. No one could tell her, so Nyeredzi whispered in her ear that her parents were working on the mountain, pulling weeds by her grandparents' graves. The woman ran off to fetch them, and Garikai made another speech. This time he offered Selina a basket tray, holding the flame lilies that Heroshina loved, a cup full of diamonds, two blocks of gold, five native fruits, and one bluestone. His hands trembled as he mumbled.

One of the mediums took the tray from him and slid it on to the water. They waited for Selina to swallow the offering. The skies had turned dark grey. A sandstorm spiralled towards them and blinded them. While they were trying to regain their vision, Selina returned the offering. When the dust cleared and everyone could see again, the offering was scattered on the ground – and all over Maudie.

Garikai collapsed. Nyeredzi didn't need one of the elders to explain what it meant. It had been rejected, but she didn't know the full story, that her uncle had snatched this position from Zuva, and just wanted to be a chief surrounded by people who knelt before him and brought him presents while he wore robes accessorised with gold and diamonds. He took his duties too lightly and left everything in the hands of village men whom he paid with his father's gold.

The wind howled amongst the trees and blew soil from the ground, slapping those gathered by the water. It blew dead leaves into the river and as the sky grew more oppressive, the clouds started spitting on them. In a deafening roar the veils washed away the bubbles of cherry blossom body wash. Everyone was cold and nobody knew what to do except beg for Selina's mercy.

* * *

Zuva and Mwedzi arrived.

'How long have they been under the water?' Zuva asked, looking at Nyeredzi.

'Too long, Mama. I am so sorry,' she said, shivering. 'I tried to help him, we all tried to stop him, but he didn't listen.'

Zuva touched Nyeredzi's shoulder before walking to the pool. Everyone was watching. Some people seemed shocked that Zuva had asked a young child instead of the elders. Even when she stepped close to the pool and dipped her hand in the water, they looked sceptical. How could she come and disrespect her brother by dipping her hand in the water when that was only done by the chief? But how could Garikai have known the procedure when he wasn't trained for it? This position he had snatched from Zuva wasn't easy.

'I demand you to come out, Selina,' Zuva said, her voice thick. 'For these people's sakes, so that tomorrow no one will disrespect you.'

People raised their eyebrows, looking at each other, but a voice echoed from the dark cave, Selina's voice. Zuva knew what would happen would shock everyone, but when she glimpsed at Nyeredzi she saw terror in her eyes.

'Ever since I was conceived, you all know what I do not like. Why would any of you disrespect me? Those who wrong me shall be punished.'

People waited, no one daring to speak, but Selina must have dived into the pool from her cave, because there, in the middle of the water, a svelte creature emerged. Long red dreadlocks swayed like kelp behind her. Perhaps that was why Heroshina liked the flame lilies so much. A large gold pendant hung loose around her brown neck. Everything else was flawless silver: it sparkled on her wrists, fingers, nails, and shimmered from her tail under the water.

Her movement lured everyone closer to the pool. They all gazed in awe. No one in the village had ever seen Selina before. But then, her long arms pushed Munya's body towards the surface and everyone watching gasped in horror. His lifeless body floated in the pool. Selina looked straight at Zuva.

Selina blew air on to the water's surface. 'I have so much respect for you, Mambokadzi,' she said. 'You've always protected me and my dwelling even though you were far away. I hear your prayers all the time. You begged the ancestors of this land to look after the villagers and me. In my heart, you never left.'

Mambokadzi meant Queen. Everyone around them stood with their mouths opened in shock. What they didn't know had come to light.

'It is my duty to protect every creature and this land that my father and mother left in my hands,' said Zuva.

'It's a shame it was your nephews today,' Selina told her. 'I don't want to make you unhappy but at the same time, I can't let people disrespect me.'

'Forgive them,' said Zuva.

'This is not the first time I've heard that word from you. It makes me feel bad whenever you ask me to do that, Mambokadzi.' Selina lowered her head. If Selina could bow down to Zuva like that, why did her own siblings disrespect her? Why did the villagers treat her as if she was not enough when she came back from war? They shamed and betrayed her before their own ancestors.

'Begging is not something one should be ashamed of and—'

'I'm so sorry for everything,' interrupted Maudie, looking at Selina, 'but please let me have my sons?'

'How dare you interrupt Mambokadzi when she is speaking?' Selina shouted. 'Wasn't stealing her husband enough?'

People gasped in shock.

'I have moved on from all that,' Zuva said. 'You shall not bring it up again.'

'I apologise, Mambokadzi,' Selina continued as she scowled at Maudie. 'Between you and Garikai, you took your father's stones that belong to Mambokadzi and used them for selfish reasons. Give them back to Mambokadzi or I'll destroy all of you.'

When Garikai heard this, he threw himself before Zuva. She looked away, but when Mwedzi knelt before Zuva too, and said, 'Mambokadzi,' the rest of the people there threw themselves on the ground as well. Nyeredzi stood with mouth agape, watching Selina inside the pool. Zuva glanced at Nyeredzi looking surprised, but someone pulled her down.

Zuva dipped her hand in the water again and whispered, 'Peace!'

Selina bowed her head and closed her eyes. It wasn't only peace Zuva brought to all creatures, it was also a deep understanding her siblings lacked: forgiveness, love, courage, and so many other things. Had all this not made Selina show herself for the first time?

'Your voice brings peace to my soul,' Selina said, 'and your hand brings warmth to my home. Something I haven't felt in such a long time. I am grateful for that. I will give Emmanuel back, but Munya will stay and shall become the protector of this place.'

'Selina,' Zuva asked, 'how can Munya become the protector of your place when you have killed him?'

'He is not dead. His body is getting ready to transform. I had to let you see him for the last time. For you to say the last words before he entered his new kingdom.'

'What about his mother?' Maudie was still lying on the ground, sobbing.

'A punishment must be given if one has broken so many rules.' Selina looked down the valley. Emmanuel's body lay on the riverbank. 'I will not keep the reminder of a bad deed. It shall make the mother know what she's done will never be erased. I could have killed him, but I saved him because I can't take much from you.'

Some people ran down the river towards Emmanuel, but Zuva remained in front of the pool. 'Give my brother another chance to make amends with my parents,' she said. 'My role will remain the same.

I will be ruling from where I now live, but Garikai will do the right thing by looking after the village, and its people.'

'Whatever you wish, Mambokadzi. We are only creatures that bow to you.'

'And you won't take any more lives.'

'As I have said,' Selina said, bowing her head, 'we live under your rules, Mambokadzi.'

Maudie crawled towards Zuva, as though she was no longer able to stand. 'What about Munya?' she asked. 'I want my son back. Please ask her to give Munya back?'

Zuva knelt next to Maudie and looked deep in her eyes. 'She could've taken both of them. We can't choose right now, so let's accept things as they are.' Maudie wept as Zuva wrapped her arms around her. 'I am sorry, my sister,' she said. This was the first time in years that Zuva had come close to Maudie or called her sister.

Selina blew air on the water's surface again and it rippled, turning Munya's body to face Zuva who mumbled words that no one else could make out. Everyone looked at Munya, who was now blinking with twinkling brown eyes dappled with golden spots. Shirtless, his lower body had changed, and his bronze tail flapped within the water, glowing. His body now resembled that of Selina.

Selina's own sparkling body had dissolved into the water, leaving a steady, swirling motion. Maudie stretched out her hand towards her son, who was swimming in circles, going deeper. Zuva stopped her sister because she understood what it meant. Munya would remain here, in Selina's realm, forever.

Morena-Y-A-Letsatsi, or the Sun Chief

Lesotho, Southern Africa

IN THE TIME OF THE GREAT FAMINE, when our fathers' fathers were young, there lived across the mountains, many days' journey, a great chief, who bore upon his breast the signs of the sun, the moon, and eleven stars. Greatly was he beloved, and marvellous was his power. When all around were starving, his people had plenty, and many journeyed to his village to implore his protection. Amongst others came two young girls, the daughters of one mother. Tall and lovely as a deep still river was the elder, gentle and timid as the wild deer, and her they called Siloane (the tear-drop.)

Of a different mould was her sister Mokete. Plump and round were her limbs, bright as the stars her eyes, like running water was the music of her voice, and she feared not man nor spirit. When the chief asked what they could do to repay him for helping them in their need, Mokete replied, "Lord, I can cook, I can grind corn, I can make 'leting', I can do all a woman's work."

Gravely the chief turned to Siloane – "And you," he asked, "what can you do?"

"Alas, lord!" Siloane replied, "what can I say, seeing that my sister has taken all words out of my mouth."

"It is enough," said the chief, "you shall be my wife. As for Mokete, since she is so clever, let her be your servant."

Now the heart of Mokete burned with black hate against her sister, and she vowed to humble her to the dust; but no one must see into her heart, so with a smiling face she embraced Siloane.

The next day the marriage feast took place, amidst great rejoicing, and continued for many days, as befitted the great Sun Chief. Many braves came from far to dance at the feast, and to delight the people with tales of the great deeds they had done in battle. Beautiful maidens were there, but none so beautiful as Siloane. How happy she was, how beloved! In the gladness of her heart she sang a song of praise to her lord – "Great is the sun in the heavens, and great are the moon and stars, but greater and more beautiful in the eyes of his handmaiden is my lord. Upon his breast are the signs of his greatness, and by their power I swear to love him with a love so strong, so true, that his son shall be in his image, and shall bear upon his breast the same tokens of the favour of the heavens."

Many moons came and went, and all was peace and joy in the hearts of the Sun Chief and his bride; but Mokete smiled darkly in her heart, for the time of her revenge approached. At length came the day, when Siloane should fulfil her vow, when the son should be born. The chief ordered that the child should be brought to him at once, that he might rejoice in the fulfilment of Siloane's vow. In the dark hut the young mother lay with great content, for had not Mokete assured her the child was his father's image, and upon his breast were the signs of the sun, the moon, and eleven stars?

Why then this angry frown on the chief's face, this look of triumph in the eyes of Mokete? What is this which she is holding covered with a skin? She turns back the covering, and, with a wicked laugh of triumph, shows the chief, not the beautiful son he had looked for, but an ugly, deformed child with the face of a baboon. "Here, my lord," she said, "is the long-desired son. See how well Siloane loves you, see how well she has kept her vow! Shall I tell her of your heart's content?"

"Woman," roared the disappointed chief, "speak not thus to me. Take from my sight both mother and child, and tell my headman it is my will that they be destroyed ere the sun hide his head in yonder mountains."

Sore at heart, angry and unhappy, the chief strode away into the lands, while Mokete hastened to the headman to bid him carry out his master's orders; but ere they could be obeyed, a messenger came from the chief to say the child alone was to be destroyed, but Siloane should become a servant, and on the morrow should witness his marriage to Mokete.

Bitter tears rolled down Siloane's cheeks. What evil thing had befallen her, that the babe she had borne, and whom she had felt in her arms, strong and straight, should have been so changed ere the eyes of his father had rested upon him? Not once did she doubt Mokete. Was she not her own sister? What reason would she have for casting the "Evil Eye" upon the child? It was hard to lose her child, hard indeed to lose the love of her lord; but he had not banished her altogether from his sight, and perhaps some day the spirits might be willing that she should once again find favour in his sight, and should bear him a child in his own image.

Meanwhile Mokete had taken the real baby to the pigs, hoping they would devour him, for each time she tried to kill him some unseen power held her hand; but the pigs took the babe and nourished him, and many weeks went by – weeks of triumph for Mokete, but of bitter sorrow for Siloane.

At length Mokete bethought her of the child, and wondered if the pigs had left any trace of him. When she reached the kraal, she started back in terror, for there, fat, healthy, and happy, lay the babe, while the young pigs played around him. What should she do? Had Siloane seen him? No, she hardly thought so, for the child was in every way the image of the chief. Siloane would at once have known who he was.

Hurriedly returning to her husband, Mokete begged him to get rid of all the pigs, and have their kraal burnt, as they were all ill of a terrible disease. So the chief gave orders to do as Mokete desired; but the spirits took the child to the elephant which lived in the great bush, and told it to guard him.

After this Mokete was at peace for many months, but no child came to gladden the heart of her lord, and to take away her reproach. In her anger and bitterness she longed to kill Siloane, but she was afraid.

One day she wandered far into the bush, and there she beheld the child, grown more beautiful than ever, playing with the elephant. Mad with rage, she returned home, and gave her lord no rest until he consented to burn the bush, which she told him was full of terrible wild beasts, which would one day devour the whole village if they were not destroyed. But the spirits took the child and gave him to the fishes in the great river, bidding them guard him safely.

Many moons passed, many crops were reaped and Mokete had almost forgotten about the child, when one day, as she walked by the river bank, she saw him, a beautiful youth, playing with the fishes. This was terrible. Would nothing kill him? In her rage she tore great rocks from their beds and rolled them into the water; but the spirits carried the youth to a mountain, where they gave him a wand. "This wand," said they, "will keep you safe. If danger threatens you from above, strike once with the wand upon the ground, and a path will be opened to you to the country beneath. If you wish to return to this upper world, strike twice with the wand, and the path will reopen."

So again they left him, and the youth, fearing the vengeance of his stepmother, struck once upon the ground with his wand. The earth opened, showing a long narrow passage. Down this the youth went, and, upon reaching the other end, found himself at the entrance to a large and very beautiful village. As he walked along, the people stood to gaze at him, and all, when they saw the signs upon his breast, fell down and worshipped him, saying, "Greetings, lord!" At length, he was informed that for many years these people had had no chief, but the spirits had told them that at the proper time a chief would appear who should bear strange signs upon his breast; him the people were to receive and to obey, for he would be the chosen one, and his name should be Tsepitso, or the promise.

From that day the youth bore the name of Tsepitso, and ruled over that land; but he never forgot his mother, and often wandered to the world above, to find how she fared and to watch over her. On these journeys he always clothed himself in old skins, and covered up his breast that none might behold the signs. One day, as he wandered, he found himself in a strange village, and as he passed the well, a maiden greeted him, saying, "Stranger, you look weary. Will you not rest and drink of this fountain?"

Tsepitso gazed into her eyes, and knew what love meant. Here, he felt, was the wife the spirits intended him to wed. He must not let her depart, so he sat down by the well and drank of the cool, delicious water, while he questioned the maid. She told him her name was Ma Thabo (mother of joy), and that her father was chief of that part of the country. Tsepitso told her he was a poor youth looking for work, whereupon she took him to her father, who consented to employ him.

One stipulation Tsepitso made, which was that for one hour every day before sunset he should be free from his duties. This was agreed to, and for several moons he worked for the old chief, and grew more and more in favour, both with him and with his daughter. The hour before sunset each day he spent amongst his own people, attending to their wants and giving judgement. At length he told Ma Thabo of his love, and read her answering love in her beautiful eyes. Together they sought the old chief, to whom Tsepitso told his story, and revealed his true self. The marriage was soon after celebrated, with much rejoicing, and Tsepitso bore his bride in triumph to his beautiful home in the world beneath, where she was received with every joy.

But amidst all his happiness Tsepitso did not forget his mother, and after the feasting and rejoicing were ended, he took Ma Thabo with him, for the time had at length come when he might free his mother forever from the power of Mokete.

When they approached his father's house, Mokete saw them, and, recognising Tsepitso, knew that her time had come. With a scream she fled to the hut, but Tsepitso followed her, and sternly demanded his mother. Mokete only moaned as she knelt at her lord's feet. The old chief arose, and said, "Young man, I know not who you are, nor who your mother is; but this woman is my wife, and I pray you speak to her not thus rudely."

Tsepitso replied, "Lord, I am thy son."

"Nay now, thou art a liar," said the old man sadly, "I have no son."

"Indeed, my father, I am thy son, and Siloane is my mother. Dost need proof of the truth of my words? Then look," and turning to the light, Tsepitso revealed to his father the signs upon his breast, and the old chief, with a great cry, threw himself upon his son's neck and wept. Siloane was soon called, and knew that indeed she had fulfilled her vow, that here before her stood in very truth the son she had borne, and a great content filled her heart. Tsepitso and Ma Thabo soon persuaded her to return with them, knowing full well that her life would no longer be safe were she to remain near Mokete; so, when the old chief was absent, in the dusk of the evening they departed to their own home.

When the Sun Chief discovered their flight, he determined to follow, and restore his beloved Siloane to her rightful place; but Mokete followed him, though many times he ordered her to return to the village, for that never again would she be wife of his, and that if she continued to follow him, he would kill her. At length he thought, "If I cut off her feet she will not be able to walk," so, turning round suddenly, he seized Mokete, and cut off her feet. "Now, wilt thou leave me in peace, woman? Take care nothing worse befall thee." So saying, he left her, and continued his journey.

But Mokete continued to follow him, till the sun was high in the heavens. Each time he saw her close behind him, he stopped and cut off more of her legs, till only her body was left; even then she was not conquered, but continued to roll after him. Thoroughly enraged, the Sun Chief seized her, and called down fire from the heavens to consume her, and a wind from the edge of the world to scatter her ashes.

When this was done, he went on his way rejoicing, for surely now she would trouble him no more. Then as he journeyed, a voice rose in the evening air, "I follow, I follow, to the edge of the world, yea, even beyond, shall I follow thee."

Placing his hands over his ears to shut out the voice, the Sun Chief ran with the fleetness of a young brave, until, at the hour when the spirits visit the abodes of men, he overtook Tsepitso and the two women, and with them entered the kingdom of his son.

How he won pardon from Siloane, and gained his son's love, and how it was arranged that he and Siloane should again be married, are old tales now in the country of Tsepitso. When the marriage feast was begun, a cloud of ashes dashed against the Sun Chief, and an angry voice was heard from the midst of the cloud, saying, "Nay, thou shalt not wed Siloane, for I have found thee, and I shall claim thee forever." Hastily the witch doctor was called to free the Sun Chief from the power of Mokete. As the old man approached the cloud, chanting a hymn to the gods, everyone gazed in silence. Raising his wand, the wizard made some mystic signs, the cloud vanished, and only a handful of ashes lay upon the ground.

Thus was the Evil Eye of Mokete stilled for evermore, and peace reigned in the hearts of the Sun Chief and his wife Siloane.

Collected by Minnie Martin

How Ah-Hā'-Le Stole the Sun for the Valley People

Native American

TO'-TO'-KAN-NO THE SANDHILL CRANE was chief of the Valley People and Ah-hā'-le, the Coyote-man lived with him. Their country was cold and dark and full of fog.

Ah-hā'-le was discontented and travelled all about, trying to find a better place for the people. After a while he came to the Foothills Country where it began to be light. He went on a little farther and for the first time in his life saw trees, and found the country dry and warm, and good to look at. Soon he saw the Foothills People and found their village. He was himself a magician or witch doctor, so he turned into one of the Foothills People and mingled with them to see what they had and what they were doing. He saw that they had fire, which made light and became Wut'-too the Sun. He saw also that there were both men and women, that the women pounded acorns and cooked acorn mush in baskets, and that everybody ate food. He ate with them and learned that food was good.

When his belly was full he went home and told the chief To-to'-kan-no that he had found a good place where there were people who had the sun and moon and stars, and women, and things to eat. He then asked To-to'-kan-no, "What are we going to do? Are we going to stay down here in the dark and never eat? The people up there have wives and children; the women make acorn soup and other things; the men have light and can see to hunt and kill deer. We live down here in the dark and have no women and nothing to eat. What are we going to do?"

Chief To-to'-kan-no answered; "Those things are not worth having. I don't want the Sun, nor the light, nor any of those things. Go back up there if you want to."

Ah-hā'-le went back to the foothills and did as he had done before, and liked the country and the people. Then he returned and told To-to'-kan-no what he had told him before, and again asked, "What are we going to do? Can't we buy the Sun? The people up there send the Sun away nights so they can sleep, and it comes back every day so they can see to hunt and get things to eat and have a good time. I like the Sun. Let us buy him."

To-to'-kan-no answered, "What is the matter with you? What would you do with the Sun; how would you use it?" But Ah-hā'-le was not satisfied. He went back to the Foothills People several times, and the more he saw of the Sun the more he wanted it. But To-to'-kan-no always said he did not want it. Finally however he told Ah-hā'-le that he might go and find out what it would cost.

Ah-hā'-le went and found that the people would not sell it; that if he got it he would have to steal it. And this would be very difficult, for Ah-wahn'-dah the Turtle, keeper of the Sun, was most watchful; he slept only a few minutes at a time and then stood up and looked around; besides, when he slept he always kept one eye open. If Ah-hā'-le moved his foot Ah-wahn'-dah would pick up his bow and arrow. Ah-hā'-le felt discouraged and did not know what to do. He feared that in order to get the Sun he would have to take Ah-wahn'-dah also.

But he decided to try once more, so he went again and turned into a man of the Foothills People. About four o'clock in the afternoon all the hunters went off to hunt deer. Then Ah-hā'-le turned into a big oak limb and fell down on the trail, and wished that Ah-wahn'-dah the Sun's keeper would come along first. And so it happened, for soon Ah-wahn'-dah came along the trail, saw the crooked limb, picked it up, carried it home on his shoulder, and threw it down on the ground. After supper he picked it up again and threw it against the fire, but it would not lay flat for it was very crooked and always turned up. Finally Ah-wahn'-dah threw it right into the middle of the fire. Then he looked all around, but could not see anybody. Ah-hā'-le who was now in the fire did not burn, but kept perfectly still and wished the keeper, Ah-wahn'-dah, would go to sleep.

Soon this happened and Ah-wahn'-dah fell fast asleep. Then Ah-hā'-le changed back into his own form and seized the Sun and ran quickly away with it.

Ah-wahn'-dah awoke and saw that the Sun was gone and called everybody to come quick and find it, but they could not for Ah-hā'-le had taken it down through the fog to the Valley People.

But when the Valley People saw it they were afraid and turned away from it, for it was too bright and hurt their eyes, and they said they could never sleep.

Ah-hā'-le took it to the chief, To-to'-kan-no, but To-to'-kan-no would not have it; he said he didn't understand it; that Ah-hā'-le must make it go, for he had seen how the Foothills People did it.

When To-to'-kan-no refused to have anything to do with the Sun, Ah-hā'-le was disappointed, for he had worked very hard to get it.

Still he said, "Well, I'll make it go."

So he carried the Sun west to the place where the sky comes down to the earth, and found the west hole in the sky, and told Wut'-too to go through the hole and down under the earth and come up on the east side and climb up through the east hole in the sky, and work in two places – to make light over the Foothills People first, then come on down and make light over the Valley People, and then go through the west hole again and back under the earth so the people could sleep, and to keep on doing this, traveling all the time.

Wut'-too the Sun did as he was told. Then To-to'-kan-no and all the Valley People were glad, because they could see to hunt, and the Foothills People were satisfied too, for they had the light in the daytime so they could see, and at night the Sun went away so all the people could sleep.

After this, when the Sun was in the sky as it is now, all the first people turned into animals.

Collected by C. Hart Merriam

The Birth of Wek'-Wek and the Creation of Man

Hool-poom'-ne, Native American

IN THE BEGINNING there was a huge bird of the vulture kind whose name was Mol'-luk, the California Condor. His home was on the mountain called Oo'-yum-bel'-le (Mount Diablo), whence he could look out over the world – westerly over San Francisco Bay and the great ocean; easterly over the tules and the broad flat Joaquin Valley.

Every morning Mol'-luk went off to hunt, and every evening he came back to roost on a large rock on the east side of the mountain. One morning he noticed that something was the matter with the rock, but did not know what the trouble was, or what to do for it. So he went off to consult the doctors. The doctors were brothers, two dark snipe-like little birds who lived on a small creek near the foot of the mountain. He told them his rock was sick and asked them to go with him, and led them to it. When they saw the rock they said, "The rock is your wife; she is going to give you a child"; and added, "we must make a big fire." Then all three set to work packing wood; they worked hard and brought a large quantity and made a big fire. Then they took hold of the rock, tore it loose, rolled it into the fire, and piled more wood around it. When the rock became hot, it burst open with a great noise, and from the inside out darted Wek'-wek the Falcon. As he came out he said "wek" and passed on swiftly without stopping. He flew over all the country – north, south, east, and west – to see what it was like.

At that time there were no people. And there were no elderberry trees except a single one far away to the east in the place where the Sun gets up. There, in a den of rattlesnakes on a round topped hill grew lah'-pah the elderberry tree. Its branches, as they swayed in the wind, made a sweet musical sound. The tree sang; it sang all the time, day and night, and the song was good to hear. Wek'-wek looked and listened and wished he could have the tree. Near by he saw two Hol-luk'-ki or Star-people, and as he looked he perceived that they were the Hul-luk mi-yum'-ko – the great and beautiful women-chiefs of the Star-people. One was the Morning Star, the other Pleiades Os-so-so'-li. They were watching and working close by the elderberry tree. Wek'-wek liked the music and asked the Star-women about it. They told him that the tree whistled songs that kept them awake all day and all night so they could work all the time and never grow sleepy. They had the rattlesnakes to keep the birds from carrying off the elderberries.

Then Wek'-wek returned to his home on Oo-yum-bel'-le (Mount Diablo) and told Mol'-luk his father what he had seen. He said he had seen the beautiful Star-women and had heard the soft whistling song of the elderberry tree that keeps one from feeling sleepy. He asked his father how they could get the music tree and have it at their home on Oo'-yum-bel'-le.

Mol'-luk answered, "My son, I do not know; I am not very wise; you will have to ask your grandfather; he knows everything."

"Where is my grandfather?" asked Wek'-wek.

"He is by the ocean," Mol'-luk replied.

"I never saw him," said Wek'-wek.

His father asked, "Didn't you see something like a stump bobbing in the water and making a noise as it went up and down?"

"Yes," said Wek'-wek, "I saw that."

"Well," replied Mol'-luk, "that is your grandfather."

"How can I get him?" asked Wek'-wek.

"You can't get all of him, but perhaps you can break off a little piece and in that way get him."

So Wek'-wek flew off to the ocean, found the stump bobbing in the water, and tore off a little piece and brought it home. When he awoke next morning the little piece had changed into O-let'-te, the Coyote-man, who was already living in a little house of his own on top of the mountain. O-let'-te told Wek'-wek that he was his grandfather.

Wek'-wek told Mol'-luk his father and added, "Now I've got my grandfather."

Mol'-luk replied, "Ask him what you want to know; he knows everything."

So Wek'-wek asked O-let'-te, "How are we going to get the elderberry music?"

"Ho-ho," answered O-let'-te, "that is very difficult; you might have bad luck and might be killed."

But Wek'-wek continued, "I want it."

Then the wise O-let'-te said: "All right, go and buy it, but mind what I tell you or you will be killed. You will find the Star-women pleasant and pretty. They will want you to stay and play with them. If you do so, you will die. Go and do as I tell you."

So Wek'-wek went. He flew fast and far – far away to the east, to the place where the Sun gets up. There he found Hul-luk mi-yum'-ko the Star-women and lah'-pah the elderberry tree. The Star-women were people of importance; both were chiefs. Wek'-wek had taken with him long strings of *haw'-wut*, the shell money, which as he flew streamed out behind. This he gave them for the elderberry music. The Star-women liked the *haw'-wut* and accepted it and led Wek'wek to the elderberry tree and told him to break off a little piece and take it home and he would have all. But when he reached the tree the rattlesnakes stood up all around and hissed at him to frighten him, for he was a stranger. The Star-women told him not to be afraid, they would drive the snakes away. So they scolded the snakes and sent them down into their holes. Then Wek'-wek took his *soo'-pe* [digging stick] and pried off a piece of the tree. The Star-women began to play with him and wanted him to stay with them, but remembering what O-let'-te his grandfather had told him, he paid no attention to them but took the piece of elderberry tree and carried it swiftly home to Oo-yum-bel'le.

When he arrived he said to O-let'-te, "Grandfather, I've brought the music-tree; what shall we do with it so we can have the music?"

O-let'-te laughed as he replied, "Do you really think you have it?"

"Yes," answered Wek'-wek, "here it is."

Then O-let'-te said, "We must put it in the ground over all the country to furnish music for the Mew'-ko [Indian people] we are going to make, for pretty soon we shall begin to make the people."

Wek'-wek answered "Yes," but thought he would wait and see who was the smarter, himself or O-let'-te-for he felt very proud because he had brought the music tree.

Then they went out and travelled over all the country and planted the elderberry tree so that by and by it would furnish music and food and medicine for the Indian people they were going to make. O-let'-te told Wek'-wek that the berries would make food, the roots and blossoms medicine, and the hollow branches music.

Collected by C. Hart Merriam

Buuts' Ka Luuk'

Arnoldo Millán Zubia, Mexico

EL CAPITÁN COSME VELASCO had become unhinged weeks prior to discovering the village. The lengthy list of sanguinary endeavors perpetrated by this reputedly civilized military official in the service of the Spanish Crown reads just the same as a record of crimes committed by the most cutthroat of pirate crews.

A nonviolent thought had not traversed the veteran conquistador's mind in months. And on this latest, seemingly endless invasion, the freedom to pillage, torture, rape and murder he enjoyed dwarfed that of all his previous missions combined. In this so-called New World, whose untouched lands were populated by those they hypocritically referred to as savages, he and his men knew themselves gods. They learned so as soon as they set their feet on its immaculate sandy beaches.

In the name of La Corona de Castilla, Velasco and his cruel conquistadors committed these and other merciless atrocities, without having to respond in any way to anybody for their exploits. Of this essential, liberating truth el Capitán had first become aware almost a decade back, when consigned to some other exploring errand, and had since not only relished, but thrived in it quite masterfully.

And so, when they chanced upon the village the squadron reveled, for it had been weeks of aimless wandering through the indomitable jungles of Chakán Putum and their yearning for blood and lustful satisfaction had built up to the point of being unbearable. As soon as they spotted the plume of smoke above the treetops, Velasco bolted in its direction. When his men caught up with him, they found him standing just beyond the tree line, gawking at the scene that was unfolding at the center of the tiny hamlet.

The natives – a group of no less than two dozen people of varying ages – were gathered around a towering bonfire while an elderly man disrobed before them. The wind carried a droning chant that the old man alone intoned. The indigenous tongue in which he crooned made the Spaniards' skin crawl. Then they all saw the old man raise his arms to his sides and slowly walk toward the flames. Even while standing inside the fire, his body wholly ablaze, his breaking voice was still clearly audible. He repeated a series of vocables over and over, which to Velasco sounded like *Ku Ku'j Ti' Ku Pu'uk Antal Wi'ij … Na'ajtal Wi'ij*. El Capitán knew some of the Mayan words uttered by the burning man, but failed to comprehend the full meaning of the phrase; something about God, or one of their false gods, more likely; a mountain, and … *some other heathen nonsense*, he decided.

The old man's voice blended smoothly with the cracks and pops of the lighted wood until it got completely lost in them. To the troop's bemusement, there were neither cries nor sobs from the onlookers when the old man's unmoving outline was finally consumed. And none of them averted their eyes from the grisly occurrence.

"Ni siquiera los niños," one of the soldiers muttered, as if they all shared in the same thought.

Then, unexpectedly, the dead man's voice was heard again, resonating over every other noise. A melody of swaying branches accompanied the spectral voice, and el Capitán envisaged seeing the man's scorched carcass rising from the ashes next. It took him a few seconds to catch sight of an old woman who was removing her already insufficient garments, and another brief moment to realize that it was her who now recited the same words the charred man had, and not him. Arms raised, she was about to step into the flames when Velasco decided he had seen enough and ordered his crew to disrupt the ritual.

"¡Ahora! ¡Atacad sin piedad, mis hombres!" el Capitán bellowed. No further instructions were needed. His men were savvy as to how to engage the naturals, for they had been doing it for a long time. The men were to be killed, the women captured, the children and elders spared and dismissed into the wilderness. But on that fateful afternoon, Velasco deviated from the usual proceedings when, in the midst of the fray, he barked a novel injunction that more than unsettled his typically devoted and stolid troop: "Habed muchos niños aquí. ¡Atrapádlos y traédmelos a todos, que os quiero para mí!"

His second-in-command gave him a long look of bewilderment. Velasco had declared that he wanted to keep the children. *For himself,* he specified. Whatever the ultimate purpose of their commanding officer was exactly, the men could not be sure of; they only knew they wanted no part of it. As licentious as they could be and had been towards the native women, el Capitán's underlings still kept a clear mind as to where the line of their depravity was drawn. Most of them had families back home on the old continent, and some even had children of their own; others, the younger ones, had siblings or cousins of that age group. Their interests lay chiefly in procuring riches for themselves, as the majority of them had been but simple sailors, shipwrights or seafaring merchants before enlisting as explorers for the New World venture.

Throughout the ruckus, Velasco caught some of his men urging the naturals to flee; he heard them beseech the infants and their mothers, in both Spanish and butchered Mayan, to run and save themselves. Strangely, the natives did not seem as scared of the Spanish steel swords, even when waved inches away from their faces, as much as they were concerned about their rite being cut short. They could be seen and heard arguing with their antagonists, gesturing and pointing and yelling indignantly, and doing all they could to try to make them understand whatever it was that was so important to them, regarding the botched ceremony. One of the renegade soldiers tried jostling an entire family beyond the tree line, to no avail. A sword pierced through his thorax from the back and out his chest: Velasco's.

Soon, el Capitán's rage, fed by the treachery of his underlings, evolved into an indomitable frenzy that concluded with the death of every individual present in the village. In the end only Velasco stood, fatigued, blood-soaked and mangled, among the piles of severed limbs and perforated bodies. Letting out a painful breath, he dropped to his knees and looked around at the reddened landscape. He felt as if he just awakened from a nightmare that he had no recollection of, unsure of the cause of the massacre that had evidently transpired. Had he really just slaughtered his men? All of them? Why would he murder those who had not brazenly opposed his commands? And the natives? Had he assumed the role of executioner toward the whole tribe, as well? Had his unquenchable thirst for blood truly reached such monstrous heights?

A foolish sense of pride crawled indecisively into his thoughts. As he reflected on it, he heard a twig snap to his right. He was surprised to find the old woman, completely nude still, staring intensely at him from the tree line. Her long gray hair flowed freely behind her, save for a single braid that fell to her navel, like a platinum furrow slicing across her leathery brown skin. She pointed a finger at the diminished fire – which had been smothered by the corpses of three Spaniards – then at him, all while declaring in her alien tongue something that sounded similar to what she and the old man had vocalized before, though not identical: *Ku Ku'j Ti' Ku Pu'uk Antal Jach Wi'ij.* She then laughed, shook her head and strolled away, letting herself get swallowed by the ubiquitous green backdrop.

Heavy nausea overpowered el Capitán. He tried standing but couldn't; his head spun wildly. After emptying his guts, the verdant world around him abruptly faded to black.

* * *

Night fell while Velasco slept. His indecent desires filled his dreams. As he was about to finish, he was awakened by the slain children he was fantasizing about. He found himself surrounded by numerous shining eyes, while tiny fingers poked him and tugged at his clothes and armor. Panic-stricken, he sat up as he let out a fierce shriek that made them retreat. He scrubbed the dried blood off his eyes with the back of his hand and realized that it was actually a troop of spider monkeys trying to make off with his helmet and weaponry. Clumsily, he got to his feet, attempting to retrieve his sword, but was met with a row of bared teeth and a chorus of deafening squeals. His hesitancy gave the monkeys enough time to scamper away with his things.

Dwindling embers, crushed and dispersed by the felled bodies of Velasco's victims, were the only source of illumination available. The sky seemed altogether devoid of its heavenly lanterns due to the abominable presence of an amassment of gloomy clouds. His body ached all over and the sole effort of putting his brain to use increased his lightheadedness.

The nearby hoot of a great horned owl caught el Capitán's attention. Searching for it, he witnessed something else take place: the mass of clouds above had made an opening through which the full moon shone down on a stone structure embedded in a small hill that was engulfed by dense tropical vegetation. Had that hill been there before? How could he have missed it? It was too close to go unnoticed. El Capitán grabbed a smoldering branch and walked over to the structure. It was a pyramid; a minor Mayan temple, he figured. He had seen his fair share of these type of monuments, but none quite like this one. It was minuscule; the smallest he had come across, like a scaled-down version of its counterparts. Moreover, it was buried too deep into the hill's earth, like it was inherently a part of it, a natural formation maybe, and yet at the same time it was evident that it was not. It had steps: fifty-two of them, by his count. In his weakened state, it was not easy climbing them but, when he reached the top, his pride renewed his vigor somewhat. He couldn't see the devastated village; the ubiquitous body of clouds continued fogging all celestial luminescence. Yet, he thought he made out movement below. Perhaps the old woman had returned, or a henchman of his still lived. He tried focusing his gaze but as much as he did, the dark clouds – which his new viewpoint made apparent they were not precisely that, but rather a strange, thick smoke – expanded until the entire atmosphere was overwhelmed. El Capitán recognized that the smoke leaked out the pyramid's entrance. He made a fist with his free hand and swallowed hard, anticipating the emergence of whoever dwelled inside the temple. Long after his arms stiffened, he relaxed. He resolved to fall back but the run of the steps seemed to have shrunk considerably; maybe he hadn't noticed it when going up but now he estimated they were no more than three or four inches deep. He decided that undertaking a descent in such darkness would be too dangerous, so instead he'd venture into the temple.

Velasco's torch was almost out, but he doubted a freshly lit one would serve for much among the turbid vapors. He couldn't see more than two feet ahead and, excluding his own steps, no sound was heard. It smelled of wet earth, just like outside. He trudged along the temple's cool interior until his torch died; he halted there and yelled out: "¡Salid, si habed alguien aquí dentro!" He waited, but no one came out. An utterly extrinsic, nearly forgotten feeling of fright suddenly crept up on him; it was the second time he had suffered it in too brief of an interval. He turned back, intent on fleeing, but was incapable of finding the exit. He started growing desperate and a suffocating sense of claustrophobia took hold of him. His shrieks echoed through the stone walls and, after a while, tears started flowing from their fleshy cages. Velasco had no doubt about having felt around the full perimeter of the pyramid's walls twice, if not three times. The exit was definitely gone and, when he accepted that as a fact, he flopped on to the ground, giving up all faith of getting out, and ultimately fell asleep.

When el Capitán awoke, he realized that nothing had changed; the smoke blinded him to his surroundings, still. Lying there, on the slick ground of that godforsaken Mayan man-trap, he cursed the turn of his luck, the intransigent benevolence of his men's hearts, and the ravenous avarice of the Spanish Crown. His head throbbed; he rubbed his nape and found a bleeding wound; he sighed and licked his fingers clean. New uncertainties flourished: had all that happened after the slaughter been just a trick of the mind? Could it all be but a vision caused by an untreated concussion sustained during the carriage? Even if these ruminations could be considered as unlikely possibilities, he was still forced to take action; waiting lethargically for things to develop by themselves could end with him starving to death inside the rocky prison.

Setting his mind on finding a way out, he rose, but before he began his rummage, the smoke around him shifted, opening up a path that led straight ahead. Although hesitant at first, Velasco advanced through the way that was shown to him. As if to further assist him, the smoke started giving off a faint light that glittered purplish for one second, greenish on the next. He reached the end of the lane. A tall and narrow portion of glossy rock wall was exposed before him. He thought himself a fool for letting hope build up inside him, and started laughing and mocking his own naivete. Then he was shocked by a glistening emitted by the smooth wall that persisted for a quarter of a minute. Velasco stepped back, blinded and filled with cold terror, covering his eyes with his fingers, but peeking between them. When the glint passed, an image appeared on the rocky surface: that of a cowardly man flinching at his own reflection. It took him a moment to grasp the nature of what he was seeing, but when he did, and that initial sense of awe subsided, Velasco was left feeling, yet again, embarrassed, although his pride quickly turned that sentiment into one of indignation as he recognized that he was being taunted by the deities that inhabited the temple. He was being ridiculed! Didn't these counterfeit idols know that Cosme Velasco wasn't a man to be trifled with? Not even in the feeble physical condition in which his reflection exhibited him! In it, he was a very old man, much older than he remembered being. He straightened his back and lifted his chin haughtily. He looked pathetic; a shadow of his former self. When did this happen? Had he slept for so long? It must have been years; decades, even! But then, his reflection started fading… No, it didn't vanish, but it did alter its picture… for the worse. He was still there, sprawled on the floor, still by himself and looking sickly, a lone breath away from death. Velasco felt it in his bones, that loneliness, that sickness. His heart was pounding in his chest. His head wound resumed its thunderous throbbing, forcing him to shut his eyes until the worst of the pain subsided. And when he opened them, he took a gander at the wall and found it bare again: nothing but smooth, solid rock in front of him. Just then, the heavy vapor spread out, cloaking the exposed spot, once more enveloping the chamber in its entirety. With nothing else transpiring, el Capitán was left to his thoughts.

⚬ ⚬ ⚬

The passing of time was a soporific affair; Velasco spent most of it dormant, and had not a clue as to how many hours or days had elapsed since he first entered the temple. Each time he woke, a smokeless path that led to the wall screen was made available for him. Sometimes he took it, and watched what was presented to him; other times he was too frightened and stayed in his place on the ground, until slumber overtook him. His pride was gone, his health waned dangerously, his sanity wavered, and looking at himself in that rock mirror did everything but help him. Every time he dared a glimpse, his reflection had been that same bleak portrayal of his ill-fated future: a worthless, frail, ancient man. But then, the variations started; they were slight at first, though still noticeable: a bit more mass on his muscles, his back a little less hunched and, consequently, his moribund reflection didn't look as close to death as it once had. It was particularly curious then, that he failed to perceive such rejuvenation taking place in his true self.

After an indefinite stretch of time went by, his reflection, at last, became that of the Cosme Velasco of old, even when in his real self he felt weaker and more decrepit than ever before. And so, he took that contradicting image like a new derision of the gods. Indubitably, he was naught but their puppet.

At some point he decided to look for loose stones that he could sharpen enough to slit his wrists with. His reflection appeared at that very moment with the apparent intent of distracting him from his task, for it did something it had never done before: it beckoned to him. Velasco froze. He tried to carry on his search of the ground around him with just his eyes, but the smoke seemed to thicken exceedingly as he did. For the first time he could smell it; he could taste it. The smoky substance had to belong to another world, as did the temple. He was convinced of these things now, just as he could not deny that he'd been called into the pyramid, shrine, tomb, or whatever it was, to function as nothing more than a perpetual laughingstock of the gods, if not for some other more degrading purpose than those his shriveled mind could conceive.

Even though he was forced to abandon his quest for loose stones, he refused to heed his reflection's call. Instead, he did what he was accustomed to doing and lay down, closed his eyes and forced them to remain shut until he managed to fall asleep, and dreamt; and the dreams his battered brain concocted were nothing but anxious visions of a titillating impossibility. He saw himself entering the monolithic mirror and coming out in a distant land on the other side of the rock wall, where he was greeted by his caller. In that faraway realm he was free of the temple's clutch and its sadistic gods' unwarranted vindictiveness. There, the heinous actions of his former self had not transpired, which meant he was at liberty to become a different man: the man he would have been if he hadn't joined the Crown's ranks.

With that image still fresh in his mind, he eventually roused and stood and scoured frantically about the surrounding smoke, but a path did not await him and, even after a while, it did not open up, as he had hoped. And so, like on the wretched day in which he entered the temple, he ran around patting the walls and tried uselessly to push the smoke away until all of his remaining energy was exerted and he had to stop to sit and rest.

He soon went back to sleep and again dreamt of crossing over into that alien world; and when the dream and his repose were over, he smiled and laughed ecstatically, for right there in front of him was the pathway cut between the smoke. His reflection was waiting for him inside the rock and waved and smiled back at him as he invited him over; its mineral eyes reiterating the promise of a better life on the other side of the rocky screen if he just trusted and joined him.

And he did.

El Capitán Cosme Velasco closed his eyes, took a deep breath and held it. Then he stepped forward, decisively, into the rock while the smoke enshrouded his entire body. Immediately afterwards, the temple commenced collecting its dark vapor, trembling violently as it sucked it through the ground. As the smoke cleared, the back of a complete skeletal frame could be seen lodged into the spot in which Velasco had crossed through; in fact, very few spaces free of an implanted human skeleton remained among the walls. When the last wisps of smoke were assimilated back into the earth, the temple and the small hill followed, for all three of them were one and the same ravening chthonic entity that would later on resurface in a different form and in another location, as it had done since the dawn of time.

Three Princesses

Paula Morris, Māori

THE PICTURE HANGING near the sliding glass door looked familiar. Fraser wondered if he'd seen the real thing in a museum somewhere else in Europe.

"It's not Estonian," the elfin hotel receptionist told him. "But I don't know who. It is a painting of three sisters. I can find out the artist's name for you."

She frowned at her computer screen, as though such information might be listed on the hotel's website.

It wasn't a real painting; it was a print in a gilt frame. Fraser supposed it was like the other pictures in the public areas of the hotel, chosen to make guests feel cosy and Baltic and medieval, despite the No Smoking signs and the shiny, spitting coffee machine. Tallinn had been a rich city once, the picture said, with merchants in fur robes and heavy gold chains who might have had blonde, smiling daughters like these ones. This part of the building would have been his warehouse, piled with amber and pelts, with sacks of flour or barrels of weapons. The merchant and his daughters would have lived upstairs, their windows looking out into the mist and the chimney smoke, gulls cawing from rooftops, snow flecking the thick glass.

This was how Fraser imagined Europe looked, once upon a time.

The women in the picture had bread for hair: burnished yellow strands braided, twisted and woven into rolls and pretzels. Fraser stepped closer. Their hair must have been very long; they must have had maids to help them plait and pile. Their scalps must have been pin cushions.

His own wife had short hair, which she described as low-maintenance, though it seemed to require an expensive cut and 're touching', whatever that was, every six weeks. She went to a salon, a word that Fraser thought affected and old-fashioned, on Jervois Road. He'd met her there once, when her car was being fixed, and he'd arrived too early. The place reeked of chemicals; his wife looked like a tin-foil hedgehog. The waiting-area chairs were fake leather, sticky with sweat when he tried to stand up. He'd been offered a coffee, and it arrived with a Hershey's chocolate kiss half-melted on the saucer. The stunted chocolate in its fussy packaging bothered him most of all, because it was American and too sweet, and not even the colour of chocolate. In a salon, surely they should serve bon-bons?

The hotel receptionist handed him his key, which was an actual key and not a plastic card, attached to a pale wooden doorstop.

"You should not take this out with you," she told him. Her hair was blonde but pale and wispy, unsuitable for competitive plaiting and weaving. "Leave it here at the desk whenever you go. Anyway, it is too heavy."

"Yes, it is," he said, feeling pleased at the sight of a real key, and the weight of it in his hand. He was pleased, too, to have to walk into an exposed cobbled courtyard to reach his room, and to step down two stone stairs, slick with rain, to unlock the door. The door stuck, and had to be rattled open; this pleased him as well. There was no point to Europe unless it was old and strange, creaky and quaint. Here it was fine for shops to be called salons. Here, men could wear pink jeans. Cars could be tiny enough to park sideways. Coffee could be served in tiny doll-cups. At the Christmas market down the road from his hotel, on a slanted square in the middle of the Old Town, people buying mulled wine could help themselves to a sprinkling of raisins, and take a sliver of biscuit to dunk.

In New Zealand all the biscuits would be gone in the first ten minutes. People would grab greedy handfuls of them as soon as they realised the biscuits were free. Larrikins would throw the raisins at loitering pigeons, and drink so much mulled wine they'd puke it up in the gutter. The streets around the Christmas market would be spiky with the fragments of smashed souvenir mugs, not handed back to the vendor as agreed, even though a deposit for their return had been paid.

The Three Princesses of Saxony. That was the name of the picture in the hotel lobby; the receptionist had told him when he was handing in his key en route to the Christmas market. Fraser was sure he had seen those princesses somewhere before, in some painting, in some museum, in some European city. There were so many museums in Europe, columned and echoing, built to resemble Greek temples. Castles would be better, he thought, swigging his mulled wine. Somewhere the three princesses might have lived.

The stench of the nearby pen, housing bales of hay and actual live reindeer – pale and indolent, lolling against the hay – was too much for him. In this oldest of old towns, he was a visiting merchant, and it was time to go shopping.

* * *

Once upon a time there were three princesses, beautiful and fair-haired. They were beautiful for a number of reasons. First of all, the rampant in-breeding among ruling European families was still far into the future, and afflictions like the Habsburg jaw were unknown horrors. Second, the general standards of beauty were more expansive and forgiving. If you didn't have bad teeth or a lazy eye, you could be considered a beauty. At various points in European history different notions of what was beauty surged and ebbed – sloping shoulders, long necks, small breasts, high foreheads, rosy cheeks. And if a girl was born into a wealthy family, then the sycophants, underlings, social climbers and alliance-seekers within her family's sphere of influence would all describe her as beautiful anyway.

These particular princesses were beautiful because they were young and well-fed and spent most of their time indoors, and because sugar cane was still growing in secret across the ocean, unknown to Europeans. So their complexions were soft and unlined, their teeth and gums were healthy, and they had a lot of time for preening, grooming and hair-brushing. Their skin wasn't scorched by the sun or lashed by the wind; they didn't have to subsist on boiled potatoes. Their faces weren't gaunt with malnutrition. Their hands weren't calloused or cut from work outside. Their backs weren't twisted from hauling pails of water or digging in a field. In winter they never risked frostbite or chilblains on their feet. They were never kicked in the face by a cow. It was much easier to be beautiful if you were rich.

The three princesses were fair-haired because they were born in northern Europe, surrounded by other fair-haired people and descended from other fair-haired people. The Mongols had yet to ride west; the Moors still lurked far to the south. Sometimes a person with brown hair would wander into their baronial hall or through their castle gates, but it's quite possible our princesses would live their entire lives without seeing someone with dark skin or black hair. They might have encounters with dwarves or witches, trolls or giants, but not with someone with brown skin and hair the colour of coal.

In any fairytale with multiple princesses, one princess is the most beautiful of all. Sometimes it's the oldest; sometimes it's the youngest. Declaring the fifth of twelve, say, the most beautiful is too confusing for the reader or listener. Sometimes, even though the youngest princess is the most beautiful, the knight or poor guy or old soldier or whoever the heroic challenger may be in that particular fairy tale chooses the oldest sister to marry. She is the top sister, whether she's the most beautiful or not. Or perhaps she would be offended if a more junior sister was chosen. Daughters should be married off in order, especially if they are all beautiful and fair-haired, and the oldest is not over forty.

Beautiful princesses are never over forty. By that stage in their lives, they should be queens, or dowagers, or dead. If their husbands happen to die first, the women must remarry and become stepmothers, seething with jealousy because they're forced to live with their new husband's beautiful daughters. To be over forty and no longer beautiful is a terrible thing; revenge must be taken. Nothing good comes from outlasting a husband, or outlasting your own beauty.

Our three princesses don't know this yet. They've never thought much beyond the happy-ever-after.

* * *

Fraser needed to find a present for his wife. He'd already bought her amber earrings and a scarf, but these weren't enough. She would suspect him of buying these items in the airport: he'd been rumbled before, betrayed by a duty-free receipt. Apparently this suggested neglect and panic-buying. It suggested a generic tourist-shop approach, a sense of obligation, the dwindling of passion and respect. His wife was, overall, an intelligent and reasonable woman, but buying presents for her was fraught with peril. There was too much implicit symbolism, a symbolism Fraser never grasped until the present was handed over and the damage done. The various gift-giving days each year – Valentine's Day, their wedding anniversary, Easter Sunday, Mother's Day, her birthday, Christmas, and the return from a big business trip like this one – were his Stations of the Cross.

He'd mentioned this to her once, and it seemed to make her happy rather than penitent.

"Feeling scourged, are you?" she asked him. Then she walked down the long passageway of their house, her head thrown back, cackling.

In the Christmas market he paced the narrow aisles of stalls, looking for something that would be symbolic in the right way. Too many of the stalls were selling things that would be useless in Auckland. Fraser couldn't go home with a furry hat or a giant pair of knitted mittens: these were not things his wife would wear down Jervois Road, not only because it was never cold enough. He couldn't buy her shot glasses featuring the Estonian flag – or, in fact, anything featuring the Estonian flag, though he thought she'd approve of the colours. She might refer to them as a colourway, which would annoy him, or a colour palette, which was almost as intolerable. When they were redecorating their bedroom, and Fraser was forced to show interest in swatches of fabric and paint shades with silly names like Mouse and Mushroom and Mist, his wife kept saying 'colourway' as though it were an actual thing, like the underpass at O'Hare airport with the rainbow-light installation.

He couldn't buy her anything made of beeswax, like candles or soap, because these would be confiscated at Auckland Airport as a bio-security threat, and he would end up appearing on *Border Patrol*, entrapped by a sniffer dog and denounced, on national television, by uniform-wearing functionaries and a satirical voiceover. The same applied to anything resembling Christmas wreathes, or reliant on dried flowers, sea shells and feathers. His wife had no idea how stressful it was to buy her a present overseas, even before the dark cloud of symbolism descended, obscuring all his good intentions.

One stall sold Christmas decorations, and Fraser spent some time there, staring so long at all the little faces looking back at him that the stallholder began handing him things, encouraging him to inspect the goods. Most of the decorations were small carved figures – trolls with dangling knitted legs, Vikings with axes, fair-haired girls in bright skirts and fabric floral wreaths. There were three different skirt patterns, three different 'colourways'. He could buy one of each – one for his wife, one each for his two daughters, although the decorations were fair-haired and his wife and daughters were dark. Fraser would tell them the tiny girls dangling from a shiny loop of thread reminded him of the girls in the hotel-lobby picture, *The Three Princesses of Saxony.*

* * *

Once upon a time there were three princesses, so beautiful and clever that their parents could not bear to part with them. No man in their kingdom was intelligent, handsome, brave, rich and/or important enough for them. No man was their equal. This is the fairy-tale part of this story, because in reality royal parents were unsentimental about daughters: daughters were expensive to clothe and house and tend, and their vocation was a strategic marriage followed by strategic children and then, hopefully, an early-ish death before they withered into harridans, shrews, witches, stepmothers, domineering dowagers or poison-savvy widows. Daughters were the pedigree puppies of the old world; their value lay in their sales potential.

The princesses were unhappy, because their doting parents kept them locked in a room high in the castle, hidden from the impertinences of inferior suitors. There they moped and muttered, and over-brushed each other's hair. They spent long hours devising elaborate hairstyles, braiding and pinning, twisting and piling, admiring each other's efforts. These were the pre-printing press days, so there were no books. Pianos were yet to be invented. There was only so much hand-sewing you could do, especially in winter when night drew in sometime in the middle of the afternoon, and the only illumination was the flicker of a candle and a smoke-spewing fireplace. The princesses wanted husbands and households of their own. Even the lowliest milkmaid in the realm had the chance to be seen and admired and kissed.

Their maid, who was brassy and over-familiar, kept them informed about social events at the castle, which mainly involved rowdy banquets in the big hall, but the princesses were never allowed to attend these. Lesser men might try to catch their eye, to make advances or proposals. The sight of these beautiful princesses might incite men to attempt a kidnap or start a war. Because they'd been hidden away so long, the princesses were more like mythical creatures; some people didn't believe they existed.

One winter morning the maid had breathless news to convey: a strange visitor had arrived at the castle late last night, not long after a heavy snow had begun to fall. He was tall and broad, with brown skin as warm as a piece of amber. Deep grooves were chiselled into his face – swirls and stripes and curls, somewhere between wound and pattern. He wore his long dark hair in a high bundle, pierced with a bone comb. Into his belt he'd tucked a white-tipped black feather, plucked from a bird no one at the castle had ever seen. He was a soldier and a traveller, born in a place far beyond the forest and the mountains, across many seas. He was on his way north, to look for a ship, and needed to rest his horse until the snow settled.

The three princesses were in an uproar. They wanted to see this dark-skinned stranger with his grooved face and magic feather, but they knew their parents would never permit it. So one of the princesses wrenched back the tapestry covering the open window, and the other two grabbed the maid. They dragged her to the stone sill and pushed her out so far that she was drowning in falling snow, moments away from plummeting to the slick white cobbles many floors below.

This is how they talked the maid into helping them.

That night, when the great hall was hazy with fire smoke and heaving with people, fresh reeds crunching underfoot, torches lit, drummers pounding, deer carcasses hissing on a long spit of lashed spears, the three princesses crept down the winding stone stairs to the kitchens. Each princess wore clothes the maid had procured for them – plain linen shifts and bright overskirts, kerchiefs tied over their heads to hide their elaborate, twisted piles of hair. The youngest sister wore a skirt patterned with

 246

pinks and yellows, the colours of spring; the middle sister wore a skirt patterned with blues and greens, the colours of summer; and the eldest sister wore a skirt patterned with russets and golds, the colours of autumn. The maid's face was white, the colour of winter, because she was afraid her collusion would be discovered and she would be put to death.

Hustled into a stone recess just beyond the hall, the three princesses waited for their moment. When the crowd fell silent, they stepped forward, though only as far as the threshold. The dark stranger had clambered onto a stool to address the assembly, and although he was standing at the far end of the hall, they could see him. He was taller than the tallest man they'd ever seen, and darker than the darkest man they'd ever seen. The white-tipped feather was tucked into his bundle of hair.

He was speaking in a language they didn't recognise, gesturing from one side of the great hall to the other. His words sounded like an incantation. The youngest princess wriggled forward, so she could see him better, and the others followed. Nobody noticed them, because everyone was looking at the dark man. His arms swept the room; his eyes swept the room. But he didn't appear to notice them either. The oldest sister, who was the most status-conscious, decided it was because they appeared too low-born and therefore unworthy of his interest. In the guise of maids, they would never attract his eye. And now she was down here, in the great hall, in the hot, throbbing heart of her father's fiefdom, she realised that it wasn't enough to look: she wanted to be seen as well.

Without saying a word to her sisters, the oldest of the princesses untied the kerchief entrapping her hair, and let it fall to the floor. Her hair was a golden city, woven with cobbled lanes and narrow paths, arched with bridges. In the light of the flaming torch on the wall, it gleamed.

It took just a moment for the dark stranger to fall silent, and look straight at her.

The middle sister wasn't having any of this. She had the best hair of all, a castle of butter, churned and moulded into turrets and gateways, encircled by a smooth yellow moat. There was no way she could stand cowering and simpering while her older sister got all the attention. She loosened the kerchief and let it fall.

The dark stranger's mouth fell open.

Privately, the youngest sister thought she had the prettiest hair, because it was the colour of buttercups, and just as soft. She tugged off her own kerchief and flung it onto the rushes underfoot. Her hair was a meadow, a field of undulating yellow, all gentle slopes and furrows. A draft caught the tendrils around her face and they shivered like flowers in a breeze.

Everyone was looking at them now, gazing at the three princesses few had ever seen.

Their father ordered them back to their room, and the dark stranger rode away the next morning. He didn't ask to marry any of the princesses, because he already had a wife at home, and she was demanding enough. He could have stayed here, he supposed, in this northerly place and never returned home at all, but it was too cold, the food was terrible, and bears, wolves and wild cats prowled the forests. Where he came from, there were only birds and fish, to be eaten rather than fought.

The maid was about to be put to death, so he asked for her instead, as a slave, though really he needed someone to guide him to a port. She rode with him on his horse, covered by the coarse wool of his cloak, whimpering with either fear or relief. Her hair was fair as a sand dune, fluffy like toi-toi. After she led him to the coast, he gave her six pieces of jade and let her go.

* * *

Back in the hotel, Fraser lay on his bed, watching ice hockey on TV because he could understand the match, if not the commentary. He admired the speed of it, and the slamming. The players wore bright armour and helmets, like knights built from Lego.

He missed his wife. She would have devised arch things to say about the youthful hotel staff and their cult-member smiles. She would have fed raisins to the reindeer in the market.

He hoped she and the girls liked the Christmas decorations he'd bought for them, the three fair-haired maidens dangling from shiny thread. One wore a skirt patterned with pinks and yellows, the colours of spring; one wore a skirt patterned with blues and greens, the colours of summer; and one wore a skirt patterned with russets and golds, the colours of autumn. They reminded him of the three princesses – not the ones in the picture hanging in the lobby, but a different three princesses he remembered seeing, through a haze of fire smoke, lit by a blazing torch. He'd almost forgotten them, but coming here had brought pieces of it back – just pieces, because it was so long ago, and too hard to re-assemble. So long ago, it felt like another life.

Red Christmas

Paula Morris, Māori

THE EVENING BEFORE the inorganic rubbish collection, the three McGregor kids walked to Uncle Suli's and asked to borrow his van.

Ani didn't like asking Uncle Suli for things. It seemed like they were always there, crowded onto his peeling doorstep, waiting for the familiar dark shape to appear behind the frosted glass of the front door. He never said no to anything, not to requests for a loan of a sleeping bag when Tama had school camp, or to half a loaf of bread when they'd run out of everything at home except tomato sauce and there was no money left in the tin under the sink.

He'd signed school reports for them, and handed over creased copies of Saturday's *Herald*. Sometimes there'd be something extra, unasked for – a calendar he'd got free at work, the occasional dollar coin for Henry. They always arrived with nothing and left with something. It was embarrassing.

"Getting late for the kiddies to be out," said Uncle Suli, scrabbling for the keys in his back pocket. He wore his usual summer weekend outfit: loose canvas shorts, and a polo shirt striped like a deck chair.

"We won't be long," said Ani.

He told them to try the streets on the harbour side of Te Atatu Road: they'd find a better class of rubbish there, though they were leaving it late, in his opinion.

"The Islanders start cruising before lunch," he said. "Soon as church's over. They'll have picked through the lot by now."

"I don't like going in daylight," said Ani, staring down at Uncle Suli's feet: his toenails looked like pickled onions. "People watching you going through their stuff."

"They don't want it, do they?" said Uncle Suli.

"I guess." Ani gripped the key ring tight, its feathery fuzz tickling her palm.

"Everything all right at home?"

She shrugged.

"Well, take care." He nodded towards the driveway and the dusty green van, the two boys smudged against its scuffed flank. Tama's eyes were closed, and Henry was rolling his tongue around inside of his mouth. "Don't want another accident."

"I don't have accidents."

"You don't have a license. Here." Uncle Suli leaned towards her, pressing something crisp and papery into her hand: she glimpsed the blue corner of a ten-dollar note. "Buy yourselves something to eat. And if you see anything like a toilet seat or a sink, chuck it in the back. I'm after a new bathroom."

"Thanks, Uncle Suli," said Ani, signalling the boys into the van with a jingle of the keys. They clambered into the passenger side, Tama hoisting Henry up by the shorts. Ani leaned against their door to close it. Uncle Suli stood in the doorway, gazing up at the streaky sky.

"Don't forget my Christmas present!" he called.

"Did he give you some money?" asked Tama, struggling with his seat belt.

"Maybe." Ani shoved the gear stick into reverse and backed out of the driveway in rapid jerks.

"Look," said Henry, who sat squashed in the middle, one scrawny leg pressed against the gear stick, jandals sliding off his feet. Uncle Suli was staggering towards the stumpy bushes of the front garden, miming a heart attack.

"He was the one who taught me how to drive," said Ani. She rammed the gear stick into first and drove away up the hill, eyes narrowed against the glare of the dipping sun.

* * *

Almost every house had a stack of rubbish, but Uncle Suli was right: most of it looked picked through, pieces of wood and machine parts and broken toasters separated from their original tidy piles and scattered across the mown grass verges. He was right, too, about the class of rubbish. The inorganic rubbish collection in their own neighbourhood, two weeks ago, had been a waste of time; much of the debris still leaned against letterboxes, unwanted – a hunk of concrete base from an uprooted washing line, or a car door torn from an old Holden.

On the quiet streets on the water-side of Te Atatu Road, the stacks were higher and looked more inviting. People threw away whole appliances, not just broken parts; they carried corrugated iron and decking planks into the street, pushed out lawnmowers and old wheelbarrows. They dumped all sorts of useful things, like wire coat hangers and galvanized buckets and pieces of carpet. Last year, someone Tama knew at school had found a bin bag filled with rolled-up sports socks, every pair perfect.

On a long curving street where the back gardens tumbled down to the mangroves of the creek, the McGregor kids passed another van, an elderly Asian man sitting behind the wheel. Two younger men angled a washing machine through the rear doors.

"Lucky," said Tama.

"It's probably broken," said Ani. "Seen anything, Eagle Eyes?"

Henry knelt on the seat, one hand on Ani's shoulder, peering around her towards the footpath. He was the best at spotting useful objects obscured in piles of scrap. So far this evening, he'd found them a rake with only one broken tine, a director's chair, and a bag of knitting needles.

Last December, he'd uncovered a ripped footstool and a box containing eighteen green glazed tiles. When they got home, their mother sat at the kitchen table fingering each tile as though it were a sea shell, arranging them into a perilous tower. They were too beautiful to use, she decided; she loved green, but they were too green. They reminded her of mussel shells, and of the sea at a place on the coast she visited as a child. They made her sad, she said, and Ani had to pack the tiles away and hide them in the carport.

"There's a lot of stuff there," Henry said, pointing down the street.

"Quick," said Tama. He looked over his shoulder, craning to see the other van. "Before they catch up."

Ani pulled up outside a dark brick house, its garden and driveway secured behind black wrought iron gates, a dog yelping from somewhere inside the house. Tama tore the pile apart, but careful Henry crouched with his back to the van, picking through the contents of a cardboard box. The house's cobbled driveway led to a grey garage door, a striped basketball hoop fixed on the wall above. It looked like the kind of house that might have good rubbish, but you could never tell: often the shabbiest houses threw away the most. The poor were too lazy to fix things, according to Uncle Suli; that's why they were poor.

Henry raced up, panting with excitement.

"Here," he said, shoving things at Ani through the open window. He'd found a power strip and a small metal box, the kind they used for money and raffle tickets at the school gala. Ani wriggled around in her seat to dump them in the back.

"Ani!" Tama slapped the side of the van. "Open up the big doors."

He sprang away, thudding off along the footpath to a house three doors down. By the time Ani swung the back doors open, Tama was weaving towards her like a drunkard to make her laugh, balancing a wooden step-ladder on his head.

"I saw it," Henry told her.

"Shut up," said Tama. He slid the step-ladder into the back of the van and pulled something out of his pocket. "Look at this."

Cradled in his hands was a bud vase, its narrow flute a mosaic of green glass.

"No chips or anything," he said. "Mum might like it."

Their mother might be up when they got home, staring out the back window and dripping cigarette ash into the kitchen sink, or she might still be in bed, her face turned to the wall, one fingernail picking at a spot in the wallpaper where she said the pattern made an ugly face.

"Shut the doors." Ani pulled herself up into the driver's seat.

"Move," said Tama, pushing Henry over. The van crawled away again, and he cradled the vase in his puddled sweatshirt on the floor.

"I'm surprised they threw it away," said Ani. "Maybe they'll change their minds."

"Too late."

"Feels a bit bad, though, stealing it."

"It's not stealing." Tama lifted his feet onto the dashboard. "And if we don't take it, the Chinks will."

"I guess," said Ani, slowing the van as they reached another half-toppled pile, in case Henry could make anything out in the mess.

* * *

The evening sky darkened to inky blue, splotched with stars. Ani drove the van down a long looping road, looking for the house they'd noticed last year. The rubbish wasn't great, but the boys liked the front garden.

The house itself was small and expressionless, the kind of plain-faced brick house that looked as though the owners were always away on holiday. Flower beds edged a path twisting towards the terrace; a bridge humped over a tiny pond rosy with orange fish. A plaster gnome was seated, fishing line dangling, at the water's edge. In their street, the gnome wouldn't have lasted a week.

Any rubbish left out had already disappeared. The boys stood a footstep shy of the wall, surveying the garden as though they were prospective buyers. Tama planted his feet far apart: they seemed too big for his body. He was nearly as tall as Ani already, built on a larger scale. His father had lived with them for almost a year, off and on: he was the kind of man who filled a room, their mother said, and that's how Ani remembered him – bulky and towering, wide as a doorway. He was nothing like her own father, who appeared slight, almost ill, in the one photograph she'd seen.

Henry looked more like her in some ways, lean and small for his age. Ani wasn't sure about Henry's father: Uncle Suli once called him a nasty piece of work, but that could have been any number of her mother's friends. Henry's skin was the darkest and Ani's was the lightest. She looked jaundiced, her mother said, like she'd been dipped in cat's piss. There was something of their mother in each of them, something around the eyes or the mouth that told strangers they were a family.

Behind the house, the harbour glinted beyond the dense mass of mangroves. The motorway was a string of lights stretching across the water towards the city. Ani hadn't been to town in months, not since a school trip to the art gallery. Every trip she took was local – a bus to the mall, a walk to the dairy. Even these suburban streets in Te Atatu South, only minutes away from home in the van, felt like a foreign country.

If she drove away now, she could be downtown in fifteen minutes. Ani had never seen the open-air cafés of the Viaduct at night: there'd be candles on every table, wine glasses, white plates. Downtown was like television, bright and glamorous, humming with conversation and music. And beyond that was the rest of the country, a blur of green in her mind, indistinct and unknown. She could follow the snaking line of the Southern motorway to where the city climbed into the Bombay hills.

She'd have to leave the boys, of course – leave them right here, staring at the pond and the fishing gnome. Perhaps the old people who lived here would take them in. Tama was a hard worker: he could weed the garden, and fix things around the house, and they could send Henry out at night to crush snails. He was good at that.

But Ani knew that nobody would take them in. The people who lived here wouldn't even invite them in for a mug of Milo; more likely they'd be calling the police to report two Māori kids messing up their neat front garden, trespassing on their front step. The boys wouldn't stick around, either. They'd chase the van up the street, calling her name. They wouldn't understand that they'd all be happier living somewhere else with new parents, a new school, a different name. They'd find their way back eventually to the scruffy blue house where the cracks in the driveway spewed weeds, where everything needed picking up or putting right, where their mother would be waiting.

And there was Uncle Suli's van, of course. He needed it because the buses, he said, were overpriced these days and, even worse, they were full of students, layabouts and foreigners.

Tama rapped on the glass and Ani wound down the window.

"Turn the van around quick," he said. "The big house back there, see? They're still putting stuff out."

Ani jammed the van into reverse: it surged like an old sewing machine up to a big brick house they'd passed earlier. The boys ran alongside, Henry tripping out of his jandals, Tama racing ahead. They'd never got their hands on fresh rubbish before.

From the open garage, a grey-haired man in sweatpants and a young woman dragged rattling boxes onto the sloping driveway. A teenaged boy, jeans sliding off his backside, climbed out of a silver Pajero parked on the front lawn. It was hard to believe such a big car ever fit in such a cluttered space. Some people had more stuff crammed into their garage than the McGregor kids had in their whole house.

Tama and Henry lingered in the shadow of the van waiting to pounce. The woman struggled up the driveway with a rusty pair of shears and a garden hose, its tail dragging along the concrete.

"Damian, you carry the particle board," she called back to the boy. "It's too heavy for Dad."

Her father dumped a box full of jangling parts on the verge. Tama and Henry conferred; Henry shook his head. Damian loped up with an armful of cork tiles, glancing up at the parked van and the huddling boys, flashing them a grin. Ani wound down her window.

"Get them," she hissed to Tama, and he dashed to the verge, scooping up the tiles. Damian returned with a giant square of particle board, leaning it against the front wall and hitching up his jeans.

"It's too big," Tama told her. "We'll never get it through the doors."

The boys made a few more quick raids, picking up a paint roller and tray, a tartan flask and a sagging shoebox packed with nuts and bolts. A car with a trailer had pulled up behind them and a man scuttled out, making for some lino off-cuts and the particle board. Tama scowled at him.

Damian lurched towards the verge, lowering a long folded screen with glass panels onto the ground.

"This is the last of it," he said, to nobody in particular, and loped back down the driveway.

Henry sprang forward and threw himself onto the screen, his arms spread wide, guarding it with his entire body. The man jamming the particle board onto his trailer looked over, suspicious.

"The doors," Tama told Ani. "Quick."

Ani slid from her seat and scampered to the back of the van, flinging the back doors wide open. Tama lugged the screen towards the van, Henry darting around him, protecting the flank. One of the panels swung free, revealing a brown plastic handle. It was a folding shower door.

"Well done," whispered Ani, helping Tama to slide the shower door in, leaned over to unfold it: each section was perfect, ridged brown plastic with slender panels of nobbled amber glass.

"Sure you want that?" asked the man with the trailer, pointing an accusing finger towards the dusty back window.

"Bugger off," said Tama, and they all scrambled back into the van.

"We got Uncle Suli's Christmas present," said Henry, drumming his heels against the bottom of the seat.

"It doesn't even look broken," said Tama. Last winter, he'd borrowed Uncle Suli's saw and cut down a broken desk the Tongans across the street were throwing away: now they had a coffee table. Ani had thought about re-covering a stool they'd found, but a month ago her mother got upset with Henry walking in front of the television when *Shortland Street* was on, and slung the stool through a window. One of the legs snapped when it hit the window frame. Henry got five stitches that night: Ani hurried him up to the Emergency Clinic on Lincoln Road, a pyjama jacket wrapped tight around his punctures. When Uncle Suli knocked on the door later that week, wanting to know about the shattered window and Henry's bandaged arm, she told him that Tama had been mucking about with a football.

"Anyone hungry?" Ani asked. "Who feels like pineapple fritters?"

She drove up the hill and turned left onto Te Atatu Road, driving faster now. If they hurried, they'd get to the fish and chip shop before it closed.

* * *

Uncle Suli's ten-dollar note bought two pineapple fritters from the fish shop, one for each of the boys, and a bag of chips to share, with money left over for a loaf of bread from the dairy.

"I'd rather have another bag of chips," said Henry, standing over the rubbish bin outside the dairy, nibbling the golden rim of his fritter.

"Where's everyone going?" asked Tama, his mouth full. The people in the cars parked either side of the van were hurrying off down Roberts Road.

"Maybe they've got good rubbish there," said Ani. She locked the van door and walked to the corner. Roberts Road was packed as a car park, groups of people strolling down the street towards a house burning with white lights, lit up like a stadium.

"I know what this is," said Henry, scampering ahead. "It's the Christmas house."

He danced a few steps away and then zig-zagged back to slam against Tama.

"Don't muck about." Ani pushed them both past stopped cars towards an empty patch of fence.

The house glimmered as though it were studded with diamonds. A gaudy giant Santa perched on the garage roof, his sleigh hanging off the guttering, the reindeers' antlers blinking candy stripes of red and white. Icing-sugar frost sprinkled the grass. The tiny front garden was mobbed with displays – an illuminated snowman, a waving penguin, a model train zipping around an ornamental pond. Even the Norfolk pine was festooned with giant red baubles and drooping lines of lights.

Ani had never seen a house covered in Christmas lights. She'd thought that only shops got decorations, holly and snowflakes spray-painted on their windows, artificial greenery swagged across their counters. The rest of the year, this place probably looked like any other suburban house – parched weatherboards and sandy tile roof, tight-lipped Venetians closed against the sun. But dressed up for Christmas, it looked like a palace.

"Wait till we tell Uncle Suli about this," said Henry.

"They must be made of money," growled Tama in Uncle Suli's voice, and they all laughed.

Some people were brazen, opening the gate and walking into the front garden to admire the decorations close up. A man clasping a pug dog leaned over the terrace railing to shake someone's hand.

The McGregor kids stayed on the other side of the fence, eating the last of the chips. A loudspeaker rigged to the garage door broadcast a tinny-sounding 'White Christmas.'

"In Iceland," Ani told the boys, "when it doesn't snow, they call it Red Christmas."

"Why?" Henry's mouth glistened with fritter grease.

"Not sure," she said. It was something she'd heard at school, from a geography teacher. He'd been to Iceland to look at their volcanoes and glaciers, because they were different, in some way, from the volcanoes and glaciers here. Ani knew what volcanoes looked like: ordinary green lumps, neutered and serene, lay all over the city. But she'd never seen a glacier. She'd never seen snow anywhere but on TV.

"Red Christmas," said Tama. "We have one of those every year. We don't need to go to Iceland."

"Come on," said Ani. She reached out a hand to stroke Tama's hair, but let it fall on his shoulder. "We better be getting the van back."

Tama nodded, but he didn't adjust his grip on the fence or on the ripped piece of newsprint, spotted with grease from the chips, still pinched between his fingers. His gaze followed the miniature train chugging along the circular track around the fish pond, its caboose painted a cheery yellow, a wisp of silver tinsel poking from the funnel.

"Can we stay a bit longer?" asked Henry.

"Two more minutes," she said.

Although Uncle Suli wouldn't be annoyed however late they arrived, she was suddenly eager to go, to pull the van into his driveway, to see the look on his face when they unloaded the shower door. And when they got back to their house, if they were lucky, their mother would be asleep. They could stow everything in the carport until morning. If she was asleep, it wouldn't be like the time they brought home the glass bowl. She wouldn't have the chance to smash it to pieces; she wouldn't slice Henry's fingers, or half-scalp Tama, or slash Ani's clothes – with Ani still in them, thin ribbons of blood lacing her like a corset. The vase could be hidden, maybe even till Christmas. None of the kids would breathe a word. They wouldn't tell a soul, not even Uncle Suli. All three of them were good at keeping secrets.

A Mother's Lament

Weyodi OldBear, Comanche Nation

I HAVE TO BE HONEST WITH MYSELF, even if none of us ever say the words out loud.

I miss the way the world was before.

It goes without saying that I can't remember my car without being moved to tears.

I can hardly stand to think about the internet.

I can't let myself miss my husband because if I did, I might never stop.

It's easiest if I pretend my children never existed.

I miss the days before I knew I was Nothing. That's what they call us now, Nothing.

They say it so much we even use it ourselves now. Nothings are what we've become. I miss the days before I had ever heard that word. I miss being a dentist at the urban IHS clinic. I miss vacations. God help me, I miss the TV. I wouldn't have the slightest qualm about trading what little self-respect I have left in order to sit and watch Stephen Colbert call Trump the Anti-Christ for a half hour, but I would happily settle for reruns of *Alf*. Who am I kidding? I would be overjoyed with the news in Dene, and I don't even speak the language, it's not my tribe.

No one really knows where they came from or how they got here. There are theories, though. Aren't there always?

Some people say it was a seance or some careless magical practice. Some say it was an 'Ancient Indian Curse.' Typical, really, when all else fails, blame the Natives. But somebody tell me what kind of Native would be stupid enough to send out a curse that would include themselves and their families, too? That's what I thought.

Some say it's because God has abandoned us.

Others say it's nothing like that, that the Beings are not magical at all but from somewhere in space or maybe another dimension. We only think they're magical because we are so primitive in comparison. These people think the Beings exist in our folklore because they have visited us before. They may be right, but it hardly matters. A difference that makes no difference is no difference.

The forms of the Beings are the embodiment of monsters from human stories, The Vampires, who suck not blood, but life from their Nothing victims, the SkinWalkers who turn from human to animal at will, the Witches who control the elements. They have come. And they have conquered us completely.

It's gone now, of course, everything that was before. Our masters have destroyed all Nothing technology, and refuse us anything more advanced than the harnessing of fire. It sounds like hyperbole. It isn't. We Nothings are not allowed to forge metals of any kind. We till and sow and harvest with tools of wood and sharpened animal horn. We are not encouraged to follow the presumptuous, for Nothings, habit of reading and writing. The good old days are here again and they are rotten.

We aren't allowed to leave the confines of our village without the permission of the sadistic Nothing-born Witch who rules over the locals. He was one of those who didn't fight the Beings but fell down and worshiped them on sight. His word is law here. He, in turn, bows and scrapes in the presence of the Beings.

There is no longer Jew or Christian or Muslim or Buddhist. We all worship the Beings, and they are jealous gods. They kill us Nothings as if we were ants invading walking in single file across their kitchen counter. From time to time they delight in tormenting us with the detached curiosity of a small boy with a magnifying glass.

Every new child born is tested for magical ability.

The Beings require us to throw any child displaying magical abilities into the fire. It burns green and never leaves the mother with so much as ash or bone.

My daughter, Justice, assures me, like the village witch assures the weeping mothers, that the child is not dead, only gone, but I can't bring myself to completely trust her. I can never forget she's one of them.

She was never like the rest of us. Not even before. My husband and I had four children. Justice was the oldest. Then Jordan, who was a year younger. Then the twins, Jason and Juniper. When Justice was a teenager, she went back to the rez to live with my grandmother. She studied, whatever it was she studied, with her. Old Ways, we said at the time.

My husband I both thought it was a little backwards, mostly of anthropological interest, but nice to continue the tradition for cultural reasons.

She is twenty-four, now, too old to go into the fire. She pretends she's a Nothing like the rest of the village. I say village because although Santa Fe used to be a city of 100,000, a village is all that's left. All her friends were killed in the war. They fought against the coming of The Beings. She believes she would be executed if she was found out. I find it hard to believe a teenaged girl was ever important enough to come to the attention of the Beings. All the grown up healers and witches in the world were not much more than a speed bump to them, after all. She's always thought she mattered more than she did. Her generation was spoiled.

She and I are all either one of us has left. If I loved her less, I might not mind the life she suffers now. If I loved her more, I might not be afraid of her. We never talk about the lives we lived before. We never talk about her days on the rez with my grandmother. We never talk about the future, for that matter. It's a life best lived not fully awake.

It's a life of terror. Other people appear to be happy. I sometimes wonder if we seem happy to them. Maybe Justice and I weren't cut out for life as peons. I used to be proud that she inherited my attitude, that she was a difficult woman. I used to be proud of her intellect. We both would have been better served by docile tempers and strong backs.

We were with the other women of the village doing our washing when it happened. Believe me, it sounds more idyllic than it was. Laundry is a dirty, sweaty, back-wrenching chore. Some of my most blissful memories now include dropping clothes at the dry cleaner.

We saw him there as we beat the clothes on the smooth stones. We didn't have to ask. We knew what he was. Even from across the stream, that thin silver chain on his left wrist that is the outward mark of the Great Lord of All Beings's favored ones shone like a halo. He could have raped her then and there if he wanted. Not one of us would have lifted a finger to stop him. I wouldn't have, that's for sure. Not that we could have stopped him if we tried. We're only Nothings, after all. The years since the war have taught us trying is useless.

If he had raped her, we would have told her what we always tell them – "You'll live," with the unspoken truth that if there was a baby it would go straight into the fire. I'm not sure if that's a blessing or a curse.

He didn't take her, though. What he wanted from my daughter turned out to be far worse than that.

He was tall and ugly. His nose was too big, and his face was too long. His hair could have used a good scrub. All the other Beings I have ever seen were immaculate. Of course, those were things I saw later. All I noticed at that first time was that he was tall and dark-haired. He wore a long black coat. I kept my head down just like the others. It's not strictly forbidden to look a Being in the eye. That doesn't make it a good idea.

He watched her, but he didn't move. At the time I cursed Justice for raising her head to look at him. In retrospect, I doubt it would have made a difference. Neither of them said a word.

He was waiting in our hovel when we returned. Justice tried to ignore him, walking past without a moment's pause. He spun her toward him, taking her chin between his thumb and forefinger.

"I was under the impression you were dead," he hissed. I have never heard a voice as silky or as terrifying.

She answered him as though he was just anyone. "I am dead."

I have no idea why, but I have always wanted to live; so I bowed low, pressing my face into the dirt floor.

"Does this Nothing know…" he asked, but my maniac of a daughter interrupted him.

"That she's harboring a fugitive witch?" she said.

"You're not wanted. For the record, you were never brought to the attention of The Beings when they captured the rest of your group of guerillas. No one is left who could identify you," he said, his entire body tense.

"Not even Biter?" Justice asked.

"Biter was executed almost immediately after our triumph. It seems he was a traitor passing information to Our Lord's enemies," he said, his voice tense with meaning; but I had no idea what the significance was. "A most fortunate discovery on my part."

Justice snorted "He was about to catch you so you turned him in, in your place."

"Why are you here, Miss Turning? " he asked.

"Where else would I be?" she answered.

"There is … There is a vacant place at my side," he said softly.

"What are you…?" her words trailed off into nothing. "Why?"

"Don't be stupid, Justice," he said bitterly.

I looked up, startled by the sound of my daughter's hysterical laughter, to see her shaking her head. He left without another word.

There was a storm that night. When I went to close the shutters, we have no glass these days, I saw him watching from the middle of the empty road, untouched by rain, his shape surrounded by a silvery glow.

In the morning, half the trees in the village were uprooted.

He never left her alone after that. He watched each day as she worked the fields. He remained distant. He remained silent, but he remained.

I became used to the lean figure in black scrutinizing Justice's every move. One day, as he followed at his usual distance, my daughter turned to stare back at him, and he did a peculiar thing. The Being knelt down and took a handful of dirt from her footprint.

Justice's breath caught in her throat. The Being in black opened his fist and blew Justice a kiss, sending dust flying everywhere. He smirked.

"What was that?" I whispered in her ear.

"Dirt from the intended's footprint can be used in … in a very effective love spell," she said anxiously. "It's his way of saying he wants me of my own free will."

"Who is he, Justice?" I asked. I couldn't hold myself back any longer. "How do you know him?"

"Stranger," she said, turning back towards the meadow.

Of course he was a stranger. What else would he be?

It didn't matter, she refused to answer any more questions about him, but he didn't go away.

Then on midsummer morning, we were sitting with some other women, gathering and weaving rushes, when he came closer than usual.

Justice stood, maybe to confront him, maybe to run; it doesn't matter, since he didn't give her the chance. In what seemed like a single stride, he pinned her against a tree. The other women and I did our best not to watch. We were all of a yard away from them.

Meanwhile, my daughter was snarling at a man with the power of life or death over us all.

"Go ahead, do it!" she shrieked.

"Oh, I intend to," he chuckled.

In a moment it became clear he was doing something to her, but rape wasn't it.

"Owww!" she squealed.

"Hold your head still, Turning, I need to do the other side," he chided.

"What was that for?" she asked irritably.

"To prevent this obscene little charade of yours from continuing any longer."

Delicate gold hoops now hung from Justice's ears. They had been empty so long the holes had closed up.

She moved to slap his face, but he caught her wrist easily. The Being dropped her hand and walked away laughing to himself. No Nothing was permitted iron, let alone gold. He had done it. He had marked Justice as a witch before the entire village. No, he had marked her as his witch.

She and I were alone more than ever after that. No Nothing with any sense of self-preservation associates with witches, or even suspected witches. As Justice's mother, I was automatically shunned as well. I don't blame them; if I was any one of them, I would have done the same.

For fourteen long days, Justice continued to rise and work alongside the rest of us. Still, he was everywhere, watching.

Humans are, essentially, what we are. Though the world was destroyed and remade in the Beings' image, the bar was more or less unchanged. At first it went silent at the sight of my child and I, but bit by bit we were forgotten, leaving Justice and I to disappear in the laughter and clamor around us. We enjoyed it until he appeared, leaning like some kind of cool guy from before in the doorway, arms folded across his chest. Once again, every eye turned to Justice.

"What do you want?" she snapped in his direction.

He said nothing, simply smiled a wolfish smile full of vicious crooked teeth. If I still had my practice, I could have done him a world of good.

Justice sat bolt upright in her chair and spoke, "We need to talk."

He ushered her through the door, almost smiling.

They stood in the middle of the road for half the night, keeping the villagers stranded in the bar, afraid to pass the two of them.

The Being seemed in turns predatory, solicitous, and condescending. I did not know what power she had over him. But Justice's stance conveyed nothing but rage. Of course, that was all guesswork on my part; I heard nothing they said.

When I asked, she didn't answer.

The next day, he politely asked her to accompany him on a walk. When she returned, there were love bites on her neck. I should have asked her what happened. She was my daughter, but I had no idea how to speak to her. I don't think I ever did.

Now that I have seen him up close, he is as ugly as sin. He has that puffiness about the face usually associated with alcoholics. Heavy creases frame his mouth and slash his forehead. His eyes are small and black and look straight through Nothings as if we aren't there at all. Those same eyes caress my last link to the world before like a pair of hands. I hate his filthy eyes. His hair is awful, and he has enough nose for three people. When Justice makes him angry, he can't talk without spitting, but he does nothing to hurt her. Even his tone changes when he speaks to her.

I hate him. I hate him, and my daughter loves him.

The Nothing-born village Witch nearly shits his pants at the sight of him, but Justice's face lights up the second he appears. Not that he gets the chance to appear much lately, since he hardly ever leaves her side. She no longer works the fields. She stinks of him. I know a few things about him now. He is a monster among monsters and they say he's part of the Great Lord of All Beings' inner circle; in service to the Lord since he was barely more than a boy. Born from an unholy union between a Vampire and Great Witch, unique even among Beings. None are more loyal, they say. Anything he wants is his. How can she love him?

Rules mean nothing to a Being who answers only to The Great Lord. I know his name now. I even have the power to say his name in my own mind, but it terrifies me. The truth is it might burn my mouth if I dared to even think his name too often. It goes without saying if the Being in the Black Coat wants a Nothing woman or even a Witch she is his.

I didn't raise my daughter to be a kept woman, but then I didn't spend twenty years in school to spend my days pounding clothes on a rock, either.

My Justice has become a whore. It is surprises me how easy it is to admit. I find it more difficult to swallow when I consider what she is prostituting herself to. I despise her when I think of her in the arms of that dirty son of a bitch. I wish she had died in the war with everyone else I ever loved. I wish she had never been born.

Three days ago, I woke up and she was gone. She left without saying good bye, she didn't even go through the trouble of leaving a note. Does she remember that I can read, even though they have taken away the books? I don't know where she is, but I know who she's with. I know that she is happy, but I wish that she was dead.

I know I shouldn't, but it doesn't make a difference.

We're all monsters now.

Biter's Tale

Weyodi OldBear, Comanche Nation

THE FIRST THING you should know about me is that I am beautiful in whatever form I take, it is my defining characteristic. The second thing is a few misguided souls have described me as a coward; I am not. I am a survivor. No matter what I survive. There is a difference.

The slowest of slow children knows a true name can be used as a powerful weapon against its owner. My true name is a private matter between me and the bitch who bore me. But since she has long since departed this plane of existence it should be enough to say I am called Biter and leave it at that.

I have known Stranger as long as I have known any of my own litter-mates. I knew him in the crowded smoke and darkness and chaos of the before time. Before the Lord of All Beings found a way to force open the portal to this green paradise and keep it open until the last of the Three Kinds had passed through.

No one knew why Stranger was made, whether it was perverted lust or curiosity, or on orders from The Lord of All Beings. Productive matings between different designations of Beings was not a done thing and yet … and yet a powerful Witch, the Nothing's name for those who had mastered control of solid matter, air, fire, and water both accepted and nourished the seed of one of those who live not by food but by sapping the life from others; commonly called Vampires. The fruit of this union came to be known as Stranger. The witch who bore him died as a result. It is said he has no true name, or if he has one he himself does not know what it is.

Either way this mixing of the species of Beings was not done again.

Stranger was always inscrutable.

Born with the ability to cast unlimited glamors, Stranger chose to inflict his natural face on those around him.

When the portal opened and the Beings of our world poured into this sweet smelling sphere of sunshine and green plants, most of us tumbled to Earth in the order we pushed our way through. That is to say elbow to elbow.

Not so Stranger and I. The Great Lord of All Beings sent the most powerful, most loyal, most disciplined Beings to the centers of strength where the puny Nothings might actually, almost amount to … not fully fledged Beings but almost … Somethings.

Side-by-side Stranger and I exterminated the vermin who were, it seemed to me, of a peculiarly pernicious strain. We worked hard at stamping them out. I thought we did. As it turned out I was doing most of the work.

A young Nothing-Witch of undetermined abilities presented herself to be a servant at the headquarters Stranger and I established for our operations against the Nothings. Her name was Justice.

We thought nothing of it at the time.

We didn't understand the people of this world, neither of us. Among the Three Kinds, the strongest ruled. This was the way of things since time immemorial. We did not question why a Nothing-Witch would wish to wait hand-and-foot on those who came to conquer her world. Instead we wondered why the rest of them did not.

For three years she served us. Cooked our meats. Poured our wine. Washed our dishes. Cleaned our blood and sulfur stained clothing. Combed our hair. Trimmed our nails. The relationship between master and servant is an intimate one. It would have been impossible not to notice her shiny black hair and rosy brown skin. She spent so much time either making, serving, or cleaning from our meals she constantly smelled of the fresh corn tortillas that accompanied our meats. It was intoxicating. I wanted to hump her right away.

"Down, Biter," Stranger said, his goblet still in his hand.

"Give me three reasons," I said blood warming my loins even as I tore into the meat the girl had laid before me. I could hump whatever I liked provided I ate it afterwards. Waste not, want not, as the bitch who bore me always said.

"Two should be sufficient. Firstly if you hump her and eat her we shall have to find a new servant and she is a very good cook," Stranger said swirling the wine in his glass. He did not, as far as I knew, need to eat, but he chose to eat because he enjoyed it. "And second of all if you do not eat her because she is some degree of witch and unless you feel you don't need the Great Lord's permission to whelp puppies on a Witch, even a Nothing-Witch…" he trailed off and let me finish the warning on my own. It went without saying a Nothing Witch was too primitive to be relied upon to inhibit conception. It felt like being doused with cold water.

I wasn't stupid so I left her alone.

Besides she treated both Stranger and I the same, and there was no point of being in possession of exquisite beauty if you're just going to squander it on some Witch who doesn't appreciate it.

Still it wouldn't be a mistake to assume we grew both grew fond of Justice as time went on. And yet the longer Justice was with us the more fault Stranger seemed to find with her in that pedantic, flea bite way of his. At the time I thought it was simply Stranger's unpleasant nature asserting itself.

One evening as she was serving our supper Justice had the misfortune to upend an entire bowl of soup in Stranger's lap.

Stranger bellowed like a wounded bull. The bowl flew shattering against the wall as he shoved Justice away from him.

In the pure stupid hot and cold flush of reflex I leapt between them. Surprised by the both of us.

"I should kill her now," he said gnashing his teeth, in retrospect seeming more anxious than angry.

Justice, as always, stood by impassively.

"Oh, come on, you can't kill Justice like she's a Nothing," I said in disbelief. "She's not a Being but she's hardly a Nothing, either."

Stranger sighed indulgently, hardly seeming upset any longer. "Very well, if it means that much to you, I won't kill her. Instead I will do something much more cruel: I will let her go."

If I had known anything about our enemy that would have been a sure sign my comrade was spending time with Nothings.

I had no idea what the words meant.

"Let her go where?" I asked, my heart still pounding.

"Release her. Justice will no longer be our servant. She will have to make her way without us," Stranger said.

"What will she do?" I asked wondering if she would simply find someone else to wait upon. I was jealous already.

"Not my concern," Stranger said cooly.

"What will we do?" I asked, the flush of action starting to subside.

"Get a new cook," Stranger said.

Then, within weeks, it happened.

The two of us stood alone in the presence of The Great Lord of All Beings.

"My Lord, I believe I have ferreted out the root of the resistance problem," Stranger said.

I was taken aback because this was the first I'd heard of any sort of getting to the root of anything. As far as I was concerned we were still caught up in the briars.

I was genuinely shocked when Stranger raised his left hand, white as marble, shot through with black veins, and a silver muzzle covered my face and muffled any threats I may have made. Silver chains followed immediately after.

"The reason the Nothings have been so successful is because they have had rather well-placed help, help from within our ranks," Stranger said in the sibilant hiss that is peculiar to him. "My own comrade, Biter."

The Great Lord of All Beings, his ancient skin as translucent as that of a newly hatched bird, responded with disgust but not surprise, picking his teeth with his long fingernails.

I was furious. My bonds burned at my wrists. The muzzle burned my pretty face. I did not know whether the rage or the pain was worse. I screamed into the muzzle but the only sounds that escaped were pitiful whines.

"See these resistors are stamped out, Stranger, every last one of them," The Great Lord of All Beings instructed in his piercingly high voice.

"As you wish, my Lord," Stranger said, his eyes averted, his head bowed, playing at deference like the virtuoso he was.

I tried to shout as much, to struggle through the burning pain to the tell The Great Lord of All Beings Stranger was a liar and a deceiver. We had all been deceived. But even to my own ears the sounds I made were meaningless and shrill.

"And get that dog out of here," The Great Lord of All Beings said dismissively, "he's giving me a headache."

For three days I was held in a windowless room in the depths of the Great Lord of All Beings' castle. Starved. Watered once a day like one of Justice's houseplants. Even that came through the silver muzzle.

Stranger must have been afraid I would tell someone, anyone, the truth.

The burning did not become more bearable, if anything it intensified moment by moment.

Somehow, the smell of my unwashed body served to make it all worse.

The execution was looming and I could not think clearly enough to imagine a plan of escape.

Then in the wee hours barely before I was due to be removed from my cell and incinerated until nothing was left but ash, two Nothings, bright-eyed-and-tender-fleshed, tumbled through the only door to my windowless cell.

"Shhhhhh," one whispered. "We're here to rescue you," brandishing what appeared to be a pair of giant overwrought metal scissors, "my name's Billy."

I wouldn't have asked why, even had I been able. If they had come to save me, who was I to argue? Honestly I wanted the muzzle removed. That was my only thought at the moment.

The instant I was relieved of the muzzle, thanks to the strange tool, I did have a few technical questions, however.

"How do you propose to avoid Stranger's hunters? One werewolf can track another to the ends of this world and into the next provided he's motivated," I felt it necessary to point out.

"The trick is to make them think you're already dead," so-called Billy said, "they can't find you if they don't track you in the first place."

My mouth may have fallen open when the younger of the two boys, barely across the threshold into sexual maturity, began to change before my eyes, into, well, a passable facsimile of myself. He may have been slack in places where I was muscular. He may have lacked some of my finely chiseled beauty, but he could pass for me. Especially after I'd spent a few days chained up in a windowless room.

Slowly the area where a muzzle would have covered his face became a mass of ooze and blood.

Was that what I looked like? Then I realized what this meant, what they meant to do.

"You mean to sacrifice one of your own to save my life?" I asked Billy, to be certain.

But it was my doppelganger who answered a simple breathy "Yes."

"We can't let them destroy what we're building," Billy said.

"They can kill any one of us at any time. Dying like this, to keep the fight alive, serves a purpose," my doppelganger said, and frankly it was unnerving because I couldn't bear to see myself being so agreeable in the face of my imminent demise.

It turned out Stranger had guarded his identity so well from the vermin he was secretly assisting they had no idea he was their true benefactor. And that was how I became the leader of a resistance I had no particular allegiance to, and yet … and yet survival is survival.

The ragged, clusters of resistors nursed my wounds for half a year without complaint.

If my only allies were Nothing vermin, so be it. They would become my vermin. If I had to lead their efforts against my former comrades in order to save my own neck … well it was better than being torn limb from limb. Granted, command was not half as glamorous as the literature would lead one to believe, but then few things are.

I grew a dashing, but neatly trimmed, goatee to cover the burns left by the muzzle.

A few years later rumors began to reach me, even in my little rat hole, that Stranger had risen to the Great Lord of All Beings' right hand. What was more he had taken for himself a Nothing-born Witch as a pet.

It surprised me. Stranger had always seemed uninterested in sex. Wouldn't give a bitch in heat a second sniff, you know the type.

But then again he had also always been an inscrutable bore.

Later I heard his pet was called Justice.

Justice I knew.

My betrayal began to take a logical shape in my mind, not just a move for power but sexual greed.

The reason we could not burn out the traitors was because Justice and Stranger were assisting them. Justice helped them because she was one of them, a spy sent to serve us. Stranger, the traitorous wretch, was a victim of her sexual thrall.

Unfortunately at that point in my life I was too busy avoiding Stranger's 'hunting parties' to give the rest of the puzzle the attention it deserved. The resistance was continually losing members to bloody evisceration but somehow it rarely seemed to be those I had much trust or respect for.

Stranger, as far as I knew, had no reason to suspect I might be alive. But even if he had, I doubt he would have had a spare thought about my wellbeing. Stranger was otherwise occupied.

Powerful forces were at work.

The Great Lord of All Beings had ruled over the Three Kinds since time out of memory. And in all that time day-in-day-out he had been served an elixir to stave off death by a witch called Beggar.

The trouble was, when the Great Lord of All Beings closed the portal to our nightmarish world he also closed the door to the potion that kept him alive.

Beggar was no fool.

When Beggar came through the portal she carried on her back an enormous bundle. Enough ingredients were in that bag to brew the Lord of All Beings' elixir for five years. She hoped to find the sources for each component in The Green World, as we called it then, within that time. To this end she sent out her slaves and lackeys scouring the globe for obscure and frankly grotesque potion ingredients.

But Beggar and her lackeys and slaves, try as they might, could not force the components of her terrible medicine to appear on a world where they did not exist.

I wasn't there but the witnesses all tell the same story.

One day, with trembling hand, Beggar presented The Great Lord of All Beings with an empty cup and a plea for mercy, more time, and a promise to do better in future.

He struck her dead, of course.

Lucky for him Stranger was there to step in and offer a new elixir, concocted from ingredients native to our new home.

For ten years, like Beggar, day-in-day-out Stranger stood at the Great Lord of All Beings' elbow and handed him a cup brimming with poison. Behind Stranger, and as unobtrusive as a shadow, stood Justice.

All the witnesses tell the same story.

One day, after downing his cup full of magical elixir in a single go, as was his habit, The Great Lord of All Beings began to strangle on his own rapidly blackening tongue. Stranger's elixir, brewed in truth not by Stranger but by the Witch Justice, had not strengthened the Great Lord of All Beings but rather hardened him to the point of brittleness and profound fragility.

The Formerly Great Lord of All Beings fell, his bones shattering as he hit the ground.

A red smoke began to issue from The Lord of All beings' mouth as his lips struggled to form a curse or perhaps a plea of his own. The entire court stood transfixed. Unable to move. Not a single Being in that room was able to move either for or against the Great Lord of All Beings. Even Stranger, who had calmly passed him the goblet, day after day and year after year, was paralyzed.

Everyone stood either unable or unwilling to move as the red smoke began to swirl around the ceiling of the Throne Room, chasing its own tail.

Everyone, that is, except for the Witch Justice, who took the Great Lord of All Beings' personal dagger in hand. It was more of a steak knife, really; he hadn't used it against anyone in a thousand years but he did like to show off, and keep everyone in line, by eating with it at dinner.

Justice took the jeweled dagger in her left hand and before the Great Lord could utter a curse against her she cut out his writhing tongue.

She followed with the swift removal of his eyes, lest he curse her with a look. The bleeding tongue and eyes she swallowed, struggling not to wretch as his ancient and horrible blood ran down her chin.

The red smoke began to billow in something like reverse but instead of returning to the Great Lord of All Beings the smoke streamed into the nostrils of The Witch Justice. She had taken the Great Lord of All Beings' power. Every bit of it.

We were never to know how powerful she was, or wasn't, before.

The Beings of the Inner Court fell down and worshiped Justice immediately. She had the strength to vanquish the Lord who reigned since time beyond memory, who were they to oppose her? In a matter of minutes she had become queen of the world.

Did Justice kill the Witch King who had caused so much suffering to her and her world?

No, she did not.

The first thing she did was to leave The Lord of All Beings' castle and pound a stake, tied with a black cloth, deep into the ground.

Then she turned her attention to the one who had been our absolute ruler.

Eyeless, tongueless, any extremity with which he might manage a curse cut away, she ordered he be shut away in a far corner of her castle, the castle that was once his own.

He is now cared for quite tenderly by an order of healers with no other duty. Ostensibly in perpetuity.

Perhaps the potion he took so long from Beggar's hand is what keeps him alive still. Perhaps it is some magic of Lady Justice. They say his wounds bleed without ceasing, a side effect of Stranger's poison, but the healers change his bandages like clockwork and with great gentleness. He's not locked away. Anyone who might wish to visit him is perfectly free to do so. Not that anyone does. Apart from the healers only Justice sees him now. The healers say she comes to him often, but no one knows what she says to him when they are alone. They say his hearing remains as sharp as ever.

Justice will not explain exactly what she did or how she did it. She says the ways of her magic are private, secret. Or perhaps the word is sacred. Either way she will not say.

With the ascension of Lady Justice the world changed overnight.

Nothings were suddenly allowed metal and a general amnesty declared.

The lives of Nothings were suddenly valued equal to any Beings'.

Though, by order of Lady Justice we call them 'people' now.

And I wonder, did I become a traitor only because Stranger named me one? I think not. I prefer to believe I would have rebelled quite on my own once I saw that if The Lord of All Beings had his way there would be precious little left worth ruling over, that the new world would soon be every bit as unlivable as the old. Stranger simply gave me a nudge in the right direction.

At times I resent the amnesty.

At other times it occurs to me, were all the marks of those horrid, dusty, years when standing pools of blood thickened in the streets, settled I cannot predict who would lie in whose debt, so perhaps it's best we leave the accounts untallied. The wounds have been burned clean and I do not mind the scars. Much.

It occurred to me soon after Justice came to power that I was a natural for a life at court. Imagine my chagrin when I realized the new Ruler of All had an inner circle consisting of one humorless sycophant who was as dull and bookish as she was.

Yes, of course, she had administrators and employees and functionaries of all kinds, but Lady Justice didn't have any hangers-on of note, no one whose job consisted of being pretty and wearing clothes well. Not even a wit, standing by with a handy quip.

It seems Lady Justice assigned to all of the old Lord of All Being's courtiers jobs of all things. I'm sure they found it preferable to the traditional fear of random death but still, one does shudder at the thought.

It was soon after she came to power that I began to realize she had not mercilessly hunted down the resistance so much as done a weeding among those who opposed The Great Lord of All Beings. Using a network of spies she captured and exposed all who risked the greater group of rebels with their foolhardiness or sheer stupidity, and also, I realized eventually, those who would have opposed her reign. These sacrifices served a double purpose, their prunings made the whole of the organization stronger while cementing Stranger's position and therefore her own.

By the time the coup came she had helped me to become their leader in my mind as much as those of my followers. Some might say carefully manipulated me into becoming their leader.

The irony no doubt appealed to her. Like all bitch goddesses she is a perverse cow at times. Of course I mean that with all due respect and a worshipful attitude. It takes a Bitch Goddess to mold a world worth having out of the smoldering ruins the Great Lord of All Beings left us. If he'd been given much longer the New World would have been as wrecked and wretched as the Old World.

I could say she was Stranger's puppet master as well as my own, but the truth may be more complex than that. I was not there at the time but I suspect she was more Stranger's spine. I sincerely doubt my old comrade would have had the temerity to do what he did to The Great Lord of All Beings without her at his elbow, whispering into his ear. Or twisting it as the situation called for.

Despite everything that had happened in the mayhem of the past I managed to get myself invited for dinner.

I walked past the Witch guards. Girls in brilliant livery with bayonets.

It seems they were expecting me.

They let me through at any rate.

"You'll have to open the door yourself," One said.

I did, making a point not to let on how heavy the door was.

I stood in the foyer of the castle, taken aback by the utter lack of servants. At the top of the stairs I saw Stranger and Justice, side-by-side. Justice seemed little changed. She stood there, unimpressed as always. Stranger shifted uncomfortably. There was a tense moment the first time my eyes met Stranger's. He always was an awkward bastard.

A shadow of anger and frustration passed over my heart. Last time we'd seen one another he'd framed me as a rebel, and yet it was on me to speak first. I won't even mention the chains and the muzzle. I sighed.

"Come here you miserable shit!" I shouted up the stairs holding out my arms for an embrace.

Stranger raced down the steps two at a time.

Lady Justice stayed where she was and threw back her head, laughing at the two of us.

At a dinner served by unseen hands I told raunchy jokes and made Stranger laugh until wine shot out his nose.

Remembering Lady Justice's garden at our headquarters so long ago I brought thoughtful gifts of seeds from all her favorite plants.

I called for more wine, repeatedly.

I managed to entice the Ruler of All and her love slave into a drunken sing-along of 'The Wily Wolves Were Wanting Wives', complete with hand motions, some of which were quite complex.

I intended to stay for a week. They put me to work. Admittedly it was interesting work that relied less on a strong back and more on a keen mind. I was flattered. I may have even enjoyed the daily problem-solving involved that is part and parcel of running a world.

There was never any plan for seduction. Not on my part, at least. It was a good world Justice was making. A fool could see that despite its peculiarities it was superior to the others that had come before. And it was very much a new world, so different it was from all else that had been known.

After half a year with the two of them, one night in their rooms, for discussion continued from morning 'til well past midnight about what should be done about various problems, halfway to dawn Lady Justice was slouched before her desk surrounded by papers and charts, pens strewn like fallen warriors when Stranger laid his hand on my shoulder.

In less time than the blink of an eye his intention was clear, his lips pressed to my ear. His whispered "Join us," was superfluous. It sounds far more innocuous coming from any lips but his.

That night was the beginning of all the endless variations of nights that can be conjured with three bodies. Stranger became something like a brother to me, all forgiven as we suckled her breasts side by side, and a lover of sorts as we spread her legs wide enough that we might lick her side by side, a kiss of sorts, our mouths meeting and sliding as we paid homage to our savior. There can be no pleasure greater than pleasure of our bodies on that mammoth bed of hers and the sea of sensation our coupling became, colliding and caressing until it was impossible to sort out who did what to whom. Impossible to care. It was animal and perfect.

It would be dishonest of me not to admit to myself above all others, that I had fallen in love with her as well. Not as Stranger loved her. No, I did not imagine her more than human, no matter how bright or beautiful or powerful she was. I love her because she is petty and demanding and egocentric alongside those things, her faults as well as her virtues writ large. It occurs to me now, with an understanding of power and its wielding that comes with having now worked under her governing for something close to three hundred years; all leaders, no matter what shiny face they show the world, are Dark Lords to one extent or another. Our Justice has remade all things. I suspect none has ever written their name across the history of this world so large before.

In truth I love her more each day. Not despite that fact that she is the greatest Dark Lord of all time but because of it.

It's not a bad world she's made. There are quibbles. Things I would change were it up to me, if I voice the wrong concerns she wrinkles her nose and forehead, kept smooth and young by the same magic through which Stranger and I remain as she prefers us.

"And that's why you're not in charge," she says.

It is not the world as it was before. I dare say it's quite a bit better, for the most part.

There is, of course, no pretending magic does not exist. Most villages of any respectable size still have Beings of some kind, Witches are most respected, but they have no special status unless they earn it by respect of the People. Respect from people isn't hard to come by, grant you. How could it be? Even a Vampire with their natural strength can do the work of a hundred people, and by spacing their feeding between a dozen people cause no harm. I imagine it's like a buffet. But the life of a single person is held by the courts as no less than the life of the greatest Witch, which, no matter what anyone says seems artificially high to me.

Because the people have metal again, even the meanest village has a smithee but technology of any sort which might release noxious fumes or foul the water or land is strictly forbidden. "It's for the best," she says. And why should the people bother now that they are aware of the advantage we hold and the things the Three Kinds can do?

The people are different now, as well, though I cannot put my finger on it. There is something fairy-like about the entire world. I wish Justice was a bit harsher with those who need it and more lenient with those of obvious superiority.

To which my beloved Dark Lord who keeps her enemies in deathless prisons of pain and impotence answers.

"And that's why you're not in charge."

Stranger laughs. That part goes without saying.

Property is even worse. Each does as he or she wishes according to desire and ability. She stamps out poverty, hunger, and disease wherever she finds them. I dare say there has never been less suffering among the meanest of peoples. And they treat her as divine.

The criminal part is, neither is there wealth to speak of. Our Dark Lady, who held steady at an appearance of thirty for close to eighty years but then for reasons known only to herself has spent the last two hundred with the visage of a sweet-faced and high-breasted sixteen year old, demands meaningful work from all and the fair distribution of goods.

There are markets everywhere, but the goods are available free of charge to everyone. There is no hunger or serious want. Even the Beings compete to see who can give away the finest wares. I personally find this degrading, but Justice says this is the old way. The way of her people. And since she's in charge it's the way of the world.

Human milk maids pull teats all day in satin gowns magicked to remain spotless and adorn their heads with jeweled crowns.

The world is a damn sight cleaner and better looking than it was before, but it is as if one awoke one day to find the meanings of once familiar words had changed.

Her castle, which was built by the demand The Lord of All Beings on the blood and tears and sweat of the enslaved is now more library than anything else. She demands a copy of all books brought to her as soon as they are printed.

The Lady Justice has established schools in every village and a magical university, the first of its kind, in the village of Santa Fe where she herself was born. Like judges, every teacher must meet rigorous standards designed by Our Lady herself.

Whatever else is true of her, that witch adores minutiae. If the devil is in the details and her name is Justice.

And yet she is a lovely devil, a captivating devil, a wise and fair and just devil which makes her all the more dangerous.

Only one name matters in all the Earth now and it is not mine and it is not Stranger's. Oh, we have power enough, both of us. Political power, and prestige, not to mention magic, yet the fact remains we are but her ornaments, like a matched set of lap dogs, one blonde the other black as night, one as radiant as the sun the other ugly as sin, to sit beside her throne and warm her bed on winter nights.

Not that I'm complaining, mind you.

That would be both ungrateful and unwise.

I dare not say any of this to Stranger. It would hurt his feelings. He's always been a tender hearted fool. He's always believed in each Lord he swore himself to, at least until they proved themselves willing to sacrifice him for the greater good. Stranger has a healthy regard for his own neck if nothing else. It's one of his more admirable qualities.

He fancies himself in love with our Dark Lady Justice. Our Unconquered Queen.

I will not deny that she has a high regard for him. If push came to shove I still find it hard to believe she wouldn't put one or both of us on the block. She'd do all she could to avoid it, but if she felt it was necessary to kill us I believe she would.

Neither will I deny that she is a Dark Lord in her own right. I have said as much to her face when he is absent. It seems to amuse her.

Life is long but so is memory. I recall the days when she used subterfuge, disguised as Stranger's loyal Nothing-born pet, to destroy all she saw as competition for Stranger's position of favor within The Lord of All Beings' ranks, while in fact winnowing out all who might feel enough loyalty to protect the madman, all so she could take power for herself.

Her deeds are great and so are her powers of deception.

This morning Lady Justice breakfasted on a porridge of grains with dried fruit. I sent a young Witch to control the river banks in a remote Witchless village in some place called O-Hi-O. I even gave him a map. Stranger looked over the new construction project schedule while our Lady of Perpetual Responsibility went over the resumes of proposed judges, if I recall correctly, or she may have done that after breakfast. She isn't really at her best in the morning; our beloved. Our Dark Lord. It is the least of her sins.

Goonur, the Woman-Doctor

Aboriginal and Torres Strait Islander Peoples

GOONUR WAS A CLEVER OLD WOMAN-DOCTOR, who lived with her son, Goonur, and his two wives. The wives were Guddah the red lizard, and Beereeun the small, prickly lizard. One day the two wives had done something to anger Goonur, their husband, and he gave them both a great beating. After their beating they went away by themselves. They said to each other that they could stand their present life no longer, and yet there was no escape unless they killed their husband. They decided they would do that. But how? That was the question. It must be by cunning.

At last they decided on a plan. They dug a big hole in the sand near the creek, filled it with water, and covered the hole over with boughs, leaves, and grass.

"Now we will go," they said, "and tell our husband that we have found a big bandicoot's nest."

Back they went to the camp, and told Goonur that they had seen a big nest of bandicoots near the creek; that if he sneaked up he would be able to surprise them and get the lot.

Off went Goonur in great haste. He sneaked up to within a couple of feet of the nest, then gave a spring on to the top of it. And only when he felt the bough top give in with him, and he sank down into water, did he realize that he had been tricked. Too late then to save himself, for he was drowning and could not escape. His wives had watched the success of their stratagem from a distance. When they were certain that they had effectually disposed of their hated husband, they went back to the camp. Goonur, the mother, soon missed her son, made inquiries of his wives, but gained no information from them. Two or three days passed, and yet Goonur, the son, returned not. Seriously alarmed at his long absence without having given her notice of his intention, the mother determined to follow his track. She took up his trail where she had last seen him leave the camp. This she followed until she reached the so-called bandicoot's nest. Here his tracks disappeared, and nowhere could she find a sign of his having returned from this place. She felt in the hole with her yarn stick, and soon felt that there was something large there in the water. She cut a forked stick and tried to raise the body and get it out, for she felt sure it must be her son. But she could not raise it; stick after stick broke in the effort. At last she cut a *midjee* stick and tried with that, and then she was successful. When she brought out the body she found it was indeed her son. She dragged the body to an ant bed, and watched intently to see if the stings of the ants brought any sign of returning life. Soon her hope was realized, and after a violent twitching of the muscles her son regained consciousness. As soon as he was able to do so, he told her of the trick his wives had played on him.

Goonur, the mother, was furious. "No more shall they have you as husband. You shall live hidden in my *dardurr*. When we get near the camp you can get into this long, big *comebee*, and I will take you in. When you want to go hunting I will take you from the camp in this *comebee*, and when we are out of sight you can get out and hunt as of old."

And thus they managed for some time to keep his return a secret; and little the wives knew that their husband was alive and in his mother's camp. But as day after day Goonur, the mother, returned from hunting loaded with spoils, they began to think she must have help from some one; for surely, they said, no old woman could be so successful in hunting. There was a mystery they were sure, and they were determined to find it out.

"See," they said, "she goes out alone. She is old, and yet she brings home more than we two do together, and we are young. Today she brought opossums, *piggiebillahs*, honey yams, *quatha*, and many things. We got little, yet we went far. We will watch her."

The next time old Goonur went out, carrying her big *comebee*, the wives watched her.

"Look," they said, " how slowly she goes. She could not climb trees for opossums – she is too old and weak; look how she staggers."

They went cautiously after her, and saw when she was some distance from the camp that she put down her *comebee*. And out of it, to their amazement, stepped Goonur, their husband.

"Ah," they said, "this is her secret. She must have found him, and, as she is a great doctor, she was able to bring him to life again. We must wait until she leaves him, and then go to him, and beg to know where he has been, and pretend joy that he is back, or else surely now he is alive again he will sometime kill us."

Accordingly, when Goonur was alone the two wives ran to him, and said:

"Why, Goonur, our husband, did you leave us? Where have you been all the time that we, your wives, have mourned for you? Long has the time been without you, and we, your wives, have been sad that you came no more to our *dardurr*."

Goonur, the husband, affected to believe their sorrow was genuine, and that they did not know when they directed him to the bandicoot's nest that it was a trap. Which trap, but for his mother, might have been his grave.

They all went hunting together, and when they had killed enough for food they returned to the camp. As they came near to the camp, Goonur, the mother, saw them coming, and cried out:

"Would you again be tricked by your wives? Did I save you from death only that you might again be killed? I spared them, but I would I had slain them, if again they are to have a chance of killing you, my son. Many are the wiles of women, and another time I might not be able to save you. Let them live if you will it so, my son, but not with you. They tried to lure you to death; you are no longer theirs, mine only now, for did I not bring you back from the dead? "

But Goonur the husband said, "In truth did you save me, my mother, and these my wives rejoice that you did. They too, as I was, were deceived by the bandicoot's nest, the work of an enemy yet to be found. See, my mother, do not the looks of love in their eyes, and words of love on their lips vouch for their truth? We will be as we have been, my mother, and live again in peace."

And thus craftily did Goonur the husband deceive his wives and make them believe he trusted them wholly, while in reality his mind was even then plotting vengeance. In a few days he had his plans ready. Having cut and pointed sharply two stakes, he stuck them firmly in the creek, then he placed two logs on the bank, in front of the sticks, which were underneath the water, and invisible. Having made his preparations, he invited his wives to come for a bathe. He said when they reached the creek:

"See those two logs on the bank, you jump in each from one and see which can dive the furthest. I will go first to see you as you come up." And in he jumped, carefully avoiding the pointed stakes. "Right," he called. "All is clear here, jump in."

Then the two wives ran down the bank each to a log and jumped from it. Well had Goonur calculated the distance, for both jumped right on to the stakes placed in the water to catch them, and which stuck firmly into them, holding them under the water.

"Well am I avenged," said Goonur. "No more will my wives lay traps to catch me." And he walked off to the camp.

His mother asked him where his wives were. "They left me," he said, "to get bees' nests."

But as day by day passed and the wives returned not, the old woman began to suspect that her son knew more than he said. She asked him no more, but quietly watched her opportunity, when her son was away hunting, and then followed the tracks of the wives. She tracked them to the creek, and as she saw no tracks of their return, she went into the creek, felt about, and there found the two bodies fast on the stakes. She managed to get them off and out of the creek, then she determined to try and restore them to life, for she was angry that her son had not told her what he had done, but had deceived her as well as his wives. She rubbed the women with some of her medicines, dressed the wounds made by the stakes, and then dragged them both on to ants' nests and watched their bodies as the ants crawled over them, biting them. She had not long to wait; soon they began to move and come to life again.

As soon as they were restored Goonur took them back to the camp and said to Goonur her son, "Now once did I use my knowledge to restore life to you, and again have I used it to restore life to your wives. You are all mine now, and I desire that you live in peace and never more deceive me, or never again shall I use my skill for you."

And they lived for a long while together, and when the Mother Doctor died there was a beautiful, dazzlingly bright falling star, followed by a sound as of a sharp clap of thunder, and all the tribes round when they saw and heard this said, "A great doctor must have died, for that is the sign." And when the wives died, they were taken up to the sky, where they are now known as Gwaibillah, the red star, so called from its bright red colour, owing, the legend says, to the red marks left by the stakes on the bodies of the two women, and which nothing could efface.

Collected by K. Langloh Parker

The Legend of the Pleiades

Aboriginal and Torres Strait Islander Peoples

AMONGST THE MUNGULKABULTU GROUP of the great Chepara tribe of Queensland there was once a king who ruled most severely over his people, but who was extraordinarily lenient with those of any neighbouring tribe or group.

There was a time when all the groups were so very friendly as to make the whole tribe accessible to one another, but the discipline was such that there could be no undue fraternizing and no trespasses. But now there was a laxness. People of the forbidden totems were received into each group, and forbidden marriages became somewhat common.

Yunguipan was the son of Paira the king, and he was an emu man.

He, according to the age-old laws should not have been permitted to look at an emu woman. We can see the wisdom of this rule.

Wakolo was the daughter of Kari, and Kari was also an emu woman.

Wakolo was about thirteen years of age and her sister had gone over to the camp of the marriageable maidens and the widows.

A great tribal fight had just taken place. The '*pukkan*' that led from the top of the mountain right down to the coast wound in places between great rocks, and was so overgrown in others that it was easy to leave it and wander far amongst the great towering Stenocarpus trees, and the eucalypti, and the ferns, before the traveller discovered that he was wrong.

Several men of the coast group had wandered lost in the jungle, and some had been speared by the Mungulkabultu people.

Then came a threat brought by a messenger with a message-stick, and it was answered by jeers.

The Mungulkabultus demanded many things of the men of the mountain and included in them was the girl Wakolo.

The coast people were of the same tribe as those of the mountain, but of a group that should have no dealings with them. Still they bore the same name.

Perhaps there would have been no trouble had the disciplining been as strict as it should have been.

Then after a time, there being no lasting decision in consequence of the fight, another king who was a strict king, ruled over the mountain people and he insisted that no more marriages take place between the groups except under special circumstances, and he was obeyed. In time they came to consider themselves a different people and they called themselves the Riste-burras. And another messenger picked his way amongst the thick undergrowth and the fallen brambles and between the giant trunks of gum-trees and the stems of palms. He was from the Riste-burras of the mountain and he came to the Mungulkabultus of the coast. Wakolo watched. She knew of that message and those demands of some years ago, and as yet she was not married.

This new messenger carried also demands. Wakolo was not specially mentioned, but women were demanded, and she thought that she would have to leave her people if there was a fight and her men were defeated. The Coast people were victorious and they returned to their lands carrying spoil and driving women before them. Wakolo was not amongst them. She returned to her camp and she found it broken and the women scattered about in the bush and the men standing apart.

272

Amongst them was Yunguipan. Paira the king was dead.

Suddenly Yunguipan spoke. He gave orders regarding the burial of his father and the disposal of his widows, and he ordered a march to another ridge and a camp to be fixed there. In this new camp Wakolo's sister went to the wurlies of the widows and those maidens that chose that place.

Yunguipan watched her go.

As was the custom several young men visited this camp in the evening, but not until some weeks had passed away since its formation.

Then the sister of Wakolo found a young man standing close to her wurlie, and as soon as she looked into his eyes he asked the question of a suitor.

"What do you eat, my girl?"

This question was put to find out for a certainty whether or not the two were of different totems and the suit might therefore be continued.

But it will be remembered that it was not a long time since the careless king had allowed the laxity.

Often an emu man of the now Riste-burras had been allowed to woo and win and take an emu girl, not only of the Mungulkabultus but even of the Riste-burras.

Wakolo's sister and the young man had spent some hours talking, and at several of the other wurlies, including some of the widows, were other young men talking in low tones.

And to this camp came, too, the young king.

He also looked at Wakolo's sister. He and Yunguipan often went to the same place.

One night as they sat talking Wakolo came up and without a word she entered the wurlie of her sister. The young king followed her in.

That night one of the old wise men – a councillor and a priest of the group – visited the king in his own camp. He instructed him in many things pertaining to the marriage rules and the married state. He told him that it was certainly wrong for an emu man to marry an emu woman, and he gave instances of the transgression of this law resulting in much harm to the whole tribe, and of course he ascribed the happening to magic.

It had no effect. Yunguipan still continued to visit Wakolo and her sister in the camp of the maidens.

Down on the coast the group were satisfied with that victory of many months before, and they were very quiet.

Now the priest who had advised the young king was very wroth upon seeing that his warnings had been disregarded, and he secretly visited the camp of the Riste-burras. He went as a messenger, pretending that he had a message from his king to the effect that a great ceremony was to be enacted the ceremony of the initiation of the young men.

But as he went from group to group showing his false message-stick he always found someone to whom he said that the young king of his group was breaking the marriage rules and that his transgressions would certainly result in some great disaster befalling the whole tribe now called the Chepara Tribe, and he advised the bringing of weapons to some secret place near the camp of the Mungulkabultus.

And so it was done, and the false messenger returned to his own people.

While the king was courting the sisters, Wakolo, and the other, the neighbouring groups were preparing, some to avenge the wrong done to the ancestors by young Yunguipan, and some in the belief that a special ceremony was to be performed to which they were invited as a very great favour.

But the false messenger had made one great mistake. He had listened in the Riste-burra group to a tale of woe told him by one captive woman, and her husband knew of it.

Therefore when all was ready for the attack upon the Mungulkabultus this man ran ahead and found Yunguipan.

He quickly told him of the treachery of the priest.

Yunguipan was both angry and afraid. He ran to the father of the girls and told him what he had heard. Kari, the mother, heard the tale, and she counselled her husband to advise the king to go to the place where the sacred rites of the men were performed, and there, perhaps, to find advice and a way out. She herself had never seen this place, but she fully believed that from it men returned with vigour and wisdom. Yunguipan believed this advice to be best.

Down amongst the tribes near the coast the preparations for a journey to the country of the Mungulkabultus were being hurried. The other people had been warned by the false messenger and were already marching to the country of the Riste-burras, or had gathered there. There was unusual secrecy about it all, for many men had sneaked away and had hidden weapons at places near the 'pukkan.'

When the day came it was very, very hot. The sun poured its dry rays out of a leaden sky, and the rocks of the sparsely-clad mountain side shed the intensified heat.

But down in the gullies the verdure was thick, and in a cool spot there, not far from the track, was the sacred spot that no woman was permitted to look upon.

Thither sped Yunguipan.

The false messenger had done his work well. Those people who believed that they were travelling to a big initiation ceremony were surprised to see a large number of men suddenly appear amongst them with all their weapons, and marking one another with the red ochre of war as they walked.

Soon the fury broke loose. Yunguipan was in the sacred grove. He heard the yells. He had just received communication from the spirits of his ancestors and he rushed to the camp of the widows and maidens. Wakolo and her sister he spied first. Throwing his cloak over them he picked them up in his arms and bore them away, and many others from that camp followed.

In his hurry and his excitement Yunguipan rushed without thinking of possible danger, to the sacred place. He reached it and found that he and the sisters were surrounded by others of the maidens' camp – both maidens and widows.

And now he realized that he had made a very great mistake. What would happen now?

He again called upon the spirits of his ancestors and his prayer was answered. He asked that he might be given something by which he could save the lives of himself and the sisters, and as he could not kill any of the others who came into the sacred place if he also did not kill Wakolo, he asked that they might be saved too.

The sounds of fighting came nearer. Several men of the Riste-burras came rushing through the bushes, and Yunguipan knew that they were being defeated. It was too dangerous for him to return to his people – more dangerous even than to be seen by the enemy. So he crept into a hollow log, taking several women with him, for there was not room for them all. The others found hollow logs also. There was room for all now.

Then the magical thing happened. Yunguipan felt himself changing. His skin went white and shrank until it was painful, for it was shrinking too fast for his flesh and bones. He made several incisions with the yam-stick of Wakolo around himself, and the surplus flesh and bones came out.

Bood fell upon the women and they had to do similarly, and at last each became a little white grub.

One of the other women came to the log of Yunguipan, and she too was stained with the blood, and when she returned she contaminated all the rest.

So the whole party became grubs, and in one log were Yunguipan and seven women, while how many of the others there were no one knows.

The men of the coast groups were utterly defeated. The sinning king was absent from the fighting, as I have told, and the rest were able to fight strongly, and before night the invaders of the mountain country were in full retreat, leaving some dead and many sorely wounded.

The victorious Mungulkabultus followed down the track and they came upon the waiting people, and, flushed as they were, they fell upon them and captured many prisoners whom they killed.

Then they returned and they asked one another what had become of Yunguipan and the women from the camp of the maidens.

No one knew.

They also asked why they had been attacked. The false messenger stood in fear and trembling. His agitation was noticed, and suspicion fell upon him and to escape for the while he went down to the sacred place. He saw there many signs that it had been visited by many people. He saw, too, the yam-sticks lying about. So he sat on a log – the very log in which Yunguipan and his seven followers had taken refuge and were now housed as white grubs all wrinkled over, and he wondered what he was to do and how he might escape the wrath that he knew was so likely to fall upon him.

Then another misfortune befell the people. The side of the mountain burst into flames.

Perhaps the hot sun shining down through the dry air so heated the mica or some other mineral in the rock that it set fire to a tiny wisp of moss or flower or grass and there was just enough breeze to fan it into flame.

From such tiny beginnings many conflagrations have been known to grow into huge destructive forest fires that have destroyed thousands of acres of good bush country and grass lands. The fire came down the mountain as rapidly as a waterfall comes over the rocks, and it swept into the gullies and mounted the tops of tall trees. It sent the heated and expanded air driving up into the heavens, and as the lower air rushed to the space thus caused about the flame a gale was made that drove the fire hither and thither leaving no spot unburned.

An advancing wave of flame sped to the camp.

The blacks ran to the nearest watercourse.

The man on the log at the sacred place saw the fire coming to him.

He was fairly safe, for the place was clear. Only a few very big logs lay about, and in two of them were the strange magic grubs.

The heat became terrific. Yunguipan and the women felt it and they began to wriggle and squirm. The man heard them, and in spite of his danger and in spite of the heat he probed into the log with one of the yam-sticks.

He found Wakolo and she uttered a scream. Immediately Yunguipan came out of his hole and he seized the hand that held the stick.

The fire died down.

Those who escaped it returned to the place of the camp.

New wurlies had to be built, but there was no place where young widows and maidens segregated themselves as was usual.

That there were many grubs in the logs of the sacred place was told by the priest who had hidden there, and permission was given to certain woman to go there and probe for them. This was another transgression of rules. Yunguipan came out from his log and he called to the others.

Wakolo was badly wounded. So Yunguipan spun two nets, into which he gathered all the women – himself and seven in one net, and the rest in another – and when the moon was full and it sent a long beam like a strip of carpet right down to the sacred place, with their legs through the meshes the two netfuls of grubs walked up and up until they reached the sky. The women down below probed the holes in the logs in vain, for there were no grubs to be got.

Bathing in the seas of the moon, Yunguipan and the women became stars, and they had to find a place amongst the other stars in the sky. They crossed the Milky Way, that *pukkan* of the departed spirits upon which they travel from the earth to heaven, and after wandering for many years they at last settled down.

Yunguipan is now Aldebaran, and the seven maidens are the visible Pleiades. One that seems to be broken is the wounded Wakolo. The other women are there, too, and they are the invisible members of the same group of stars. They are faintly visible when the night is clear with frost and there is no haze anywhere. The net can still be distinguished, and there is a long thread that connects the group of Aldebaran.

This story of the Pleiades is known, with just a little variation, to nearly all the tribes of Queensland, and even to the Kamilaroys in New South Wales.

Collected by C.W. Peck

A Mayan Story

Claudia Recinos Seldeen, Guatemala

HUNAHPU IS TELLING STORIES AGAIN. He knows he shouldn't be. His stories have no power. They can't change the shape of things. But, he reasons, his stories can paint a backdrop. They can tumble out of his mouth like fairy tales. At the very least, they can keep a little girl company in the darkest hours of night.

"Once upon a time…" Hunahpuh begins.

The little girl sighs. Her fingers grip the pink-patterned fabric of her blanket. But not in fear, Hunahpu is pleased to discover. Not in fear. This little girl is a lover of stories. She is rapt with excitement.

He leans forward with a smile.

The girl watches him draw closer. Her eyes widen. Her eyes never leave his. They pin him, giving him substance.

"Once upon a time," Hunahpu tells her, "there was a woman, and her name was Lady Blood Moon." Here, the little girl breathes a soft, "Oh."

It's a sound that feeds the god's soul, and he can't help the smile that tugs at his lips.

Lady Blood Moon.

The words are like tamarind in his mouth – sharp and sour, but also undeniably sweet. There's resentment there, and anger. But, like all children who must think about their mothers, there is also love.

"I like the moon," the little girl whispers. "I like the planets and the stars."

"Yes, but Lady Blood Moon didn't live up in the sky," Hunahpu reminds her. "She was a princess. A goddess. She was a conduit."

The girl's brow furrows. Hunahpu realizes she's already forgotten the word, though he was careful to explain it the last time he visited. He sighs. This is the trouble with gods telling stories. The narrative is like spun sugar, brittle and far too delicate.

He folds his hands together, resigned.

"A conduit," he says, "is like a bridge. Lady Blood Moon was a bridge between the Underworld – Xibalba – and the world we're in now. A link between life and death. Do you understand?"

The little girl nods, and Hunahpu is distracted, for a moment, by the way her dark curls spring and bounce. She is lovely, this child. He can sense life in her, bright and poised. For the span of a breath, Hunahpu is frightened. This is new territory for him. A new world. There are few stories of him here. He's a bit like a balloon bobbing at the end of a thread. He's afraid he'll be cut loose. And who would rescue him, then?

But the little girl is watching, her eyes dark as coal. Her gaze is an anchor, and Hunahpu's heart, which has been racing like a startled hare, begins to slow.

"A conduit," he repeats, trying to recover the threads of his story. He takes a deep breath, wipes the palms of his hands on his knees. "Lady Blood Moon was a conduit, and this made her very important, because the dead can't make new life. Do you see? The dead are simply dead, and must resign themselves to being so."

He is bungling the story. He can tell because the girl's mouth is puckering. He forces himself to slow down, to concentrate. He shakes his head and starts again.

"Lady Blood Moon was a princess in Xibalba, where souls go after they die."

"My mother's soul isn't in Xibalba," the little girl cuts in.

Hunahpu swallows. He must be careful here. If he cuts the strings that hold back the girl's grief, she will be lost to him. And so will the story. So he simply nods.

"The land where souls used to go after they died," he amends.

The little girl nods her approval, and Hunahpu's shoulders sag with relief.

"Lady Blood Moon was the daughter of the Lord of Death, who ruled over all of Xibalba. She grew up in the underworld. Her toys were the knucklebones of dead priests. Her playmates were the souls of lost children. Xibalba was all Lady Blood Moon knew, and so she thought she was happy."

The little girl is frowning deeply now, and Hunahpu knows he has to pause, or be interrupted.

"What is it?" he sighs.

"You said the dead can't make new life."

"That's right. The dead are simply dead."

"But, then, how could the Lord of Death have a daughter?"

Ah.

This is a new question. Hunahpu wonders if someone has taught her something in his absence. He shifts uncomfortably in his chair.

How to explain?

"The Lord of Death didn't make Lady Blood Moon. She simply was."

He looks to see if he's made himself understood, but he can tell by the dubious look on her face that he hasn't.

"It's like dominos," he tries. "You're given a certain number at the start of a game, and that's all you have to play with. You can't make any more."

She's still frowning, but she nods, willing to let it go, for now.

Hunahpu presses his lips together. Perhaps he'll explain, when she's older, about stories and their power. Perhaps he'll tell her about the Mayan myths burned in great fires by foreign priests. Interlopers from across the sea. Perhaps he'll tell her how her people's stories are like their temples. How they've been forgotten, swallowed up by the jungle. By the earth. By time.

But for now, he simply returns her nod, and continues.

"One day, Lady Blood Moon came upon a calabash tree."

"What's that?" the girl asks.

"It's a fruit tree," Hunahpu tells her.

"Like an apple tree?"

"Something like that. But this tree was special, because it housed the head of a brave god who'd been lured down into Xibalba and killed."

The little girl's eyes widen, though she's heard the story before. She has, in fact, recited it to her dolls when she thinks she's alone.

"The god's head called to Lady Blood Moon, asking her to free him. Lady Blood Moon was good-hearted, so she tried to do as the god asked. She reached up to untangle the calabash tree's branches, so he could be free. But, the god could not be freed. So, while Lady Blood Moon was busy with the branches, the god spit in her hand."

The little girl's nose wrinkles.

"Ew," she mutters.

Hunahpu covers his mouth with one hand to hide a chuckle.

"It was an act of magic," he explains. "It gave Lady Blood Moon a power that no one else in Xibalba had – the power to create life."

"I spit on Henry," the little girl confides.

Hunahpu straightens with a jolt.

"You what?"

"I spit on Henry. A boy in my class. I was trying to be a god. But I got in really big trouble."

Hunahpu can't help it this time. He laughs out loud, unrestrained and booming. His laughter fills the room, and he claps a hand over his mouth.

But he's too late. He's been heard. He has been incautious, and now their time has come to an end. He stands.

The disappointment is plain in the girl's face, but Hunahpu hardens his heart against it.

"Sleep, little one," he whispers.

The girl's eyes flutter closed at his command, and in a moment, she is asleep.

Hunahpu watches her for a while, his heart beating softly against his ribs. He loves this girl, there's no denying it. She carries the blood of his people. The ancient ones who worshipped him, centuries ago. The ones who told his stories, giving him life. He would like nothing more than to stay.

But there is stirring in the hallway.

Someone is coming.

Perhaps, he tells himself, he'll come back the following night. Perhaps he'll pick up the tale once more. Or, maybe, he'll tell her a new one. Surely, by now, she's old enough to hear about the Mayan temples. The Mayan ruins. The Mayan gods biding their time in the dark folds of the jungle, waiting for their stories to spark and catch.

The dead are dead, and must resign themselves to being so. But Hunahpu is not dead, and neither are his people. They live on, despite the conquerors and the invaders. Despite the priests and their fires.

Hunahpu is a god, and so his stories can't seed and root. He can't change the shape of things. But he can give one little girl a context. A backdrop. He can give her back a history as rich as her own soul.

Hunahpu slips into the shadows. He closes his eyes, closes his heart. He seals his lips, and like the tail-end of a story, he fades away. But only for a little while. Only until the next time. Stories, after all, can always be retold. Stories have a life that's all their own.

Māui Tames the Sun

Māori

Māui-nuka-rau – The Deceiver
Māui-whare-kino – The Evil House
Māui-tinihanga – The Many Devices
Māui-i-toa – The Brave
Māui-i-atamai – The Kind
Māui-moohio – The Wise
Māui-mata-waru – The Eight Eyes, The Supernatural.

THESE WERE some of the descriptive names applied to the whimsical, irresponsible demi-god of Polynesia. After a miraculous birth and upbringing he won the affection of his parents, taught useful arts to mankind, snared the sun, tamed fire, discovered new lands by pulling them up from the beds of the sea, and eventually met his death while attempting to kill the goddess of death, Hine-nui-te-poo. His malicious humour made his relatives highly suspicious of his motives, but his greatest deeds were of untold benefit to mankind – as when he snared and tamed the sun.

Te Rā, the sun, travelled swiftly across the sky. The hours of daylight were short. The nights were long and there was barely time to cook the morning and evening meals, no time to cultivate the plantation, to make war, to hunt, to fish, no time even to love.

"I'm going to capture the sun and force him to move more slowly!" Māui said to his brothers.

"Why?"

"It will make the days longer."

"Listen," they said earnestly, knowing how much trouble some of his experiments had caused. "No good can come of such foolishness. Leave the sun alone."

Māui laughed. "We shall do it together."

"We can never tame the sun," they protested. "He would burn us up before we could get near him."

"Not if you follow my plan," Māui said eagerly. "We'll plait strong ropes of flax. Early tomorrow morning we'll take them to where the sun rises. We can easily build shelters to shield us from the heat."

After some persuasion his brothers reluctantly set to work to plait ropes of flax fibre. As it was an unknown art, Māui had to teach them how to spin the fibre into flat, round and square ropes with three and five strands.

It was a long journey, but at last they reached Te Rua-o-te-Rā, the Cave of the Sun. When he rose above the horizon a coil of rope fell over his head and shoulders, and another and another.

"Pull hard," Māui shouted. "Don't let him get away."

Leaving his brothers to maintain the strain on the ropes, he ran towards the sun. From his girdle he pulled out his favourite weapon, the jawbone of his ancestor Muri-ranga-whenua, and belaboured the helpless sun until he cried for mercy. Māui chanted a powerful spell, known as a punga, to keep the sun from moving.

"Are you trying to kill Tama-nui-te-rā?" asked Tama in a weak voice, as he struggled to break the ropes. It was a significant remark, for it was the first time that the sacred name of the sun had ever been revealed.

"I have no wish to harm you. If you promise to travel more slowly in future, I'll let you go."

"No," said great Tama stubbornly. "Why should I change my habits on your account?"

"This is why," Māui said and battered the sun until he was weakened. When he was released he limped so slowly across the sky that men and women were able to cook their food, eat, work, play and make love at their leisure, while from his wounds came the bright rays we know as sunbeams.

After his long labour and the heat of the sun, Māui was thirsty. He called Tieke, the saddleback, to bring him a drink of water. The bird took no notice. Māui caught it in his hands and hurled it into the water. Where his hot hands touched Tieke's back the feathers were burned brown. He called Hihi, the stitchbird, but it also ignored the demi-god. Māui threw it into a fire that tinged its plumage with yellow. Ever afterwards the stitchbird was nervous and timid. Toutouwai, the robin, was equally uncooperative and was marked with a patch of white at the root of its bill "as a mark of incivility". It was Kōkako, the blue-wattled crow, who helped him. It flew to the water and brought back as much as it could carry in its ears. Māui rewarded it by pulling its legs so they were long and could move quickly.

* * *

There is another legend about Māui and the sun that refers to a period of perpetual daylight. The demi-god had become angered by the foolishness of mankind. They were so stupid that Māui felt the sunshine was being wasted on them. He held up his hands to stop the sunlight. It seems that he was unaware of the heat of the sun, for his hands were badly burned. He rushed to the sea to assuage the pain and for the first time the sun set and darkness rushed across the land.

Māui rushed after the fleeing sun and dragged it back. It escaped and fled to the west. Māui pulled it back a second time and tied a long rope to it, attaching the other end to the moon.

When the sun set the moon was dragged above the horizon, giving light to the world by night as the sun had done by day.

Māui experimented more cautiously this time and found that he could hide the moon behind his hand without burning himself. Since then he has continued to use his hand to control the appearances of the moon.

Collected by A.W. Reed

The Creation

Māori

Listen to the chants of creation

Lift, lift up the south land.
Upward, upward lift the south sky.
Put each in its own position
There to rest for ever.
Lift, lift up Rangi,
And with offering made to thee, O Rangi
We lift thee up!

Stand apart the skin,
Be divided the skin,
As the nettle to the skin,
As the tataramoa to the skin.
Do not grieve for your partner,
Do not cry for your husband.
Let the ocean be broken,

Let the ocean be far apart;
Be you united to the sea,
Yes, to the sea, O Earth;
Broken asunder are you two.
Do not grieve,
Do not continue your love,
Do not grieve for your partner.

IN THE BEGINNING was Te Kore, the Nothing, and from Te Kore came Te Pō, the Night. In that impenetrable darkness Rangi the Sky Father lay in the arms of Papa the Earth Mother.

The gods, who were their children, crawled through the narrow space between their clinging bodies. They longed for freedom, for wind blowing over sharp hilltops and deep valleys, and light to warm their pale bodies.

"What can we do?" they asked. "We need room to stretch our cramped limbs. We need light. We need space."

Then Tāne-mahuta, mighty father of the forest, father of all living things that love light and freedom, rose to his feet. For as long as a man can hold his breath Tāne stood, silent and unmoving, summoning all his strength. He pressed his hands against the body of his mother and turning upside-down he planted his feet firmly on his father. He straightened his back and pushed against Rangi.

The primal parents clung to each other. Tāne exerted all his strength, straining back and limbs, until at last the mighty bodies of earth and sky were forced apart.

"It was the fierce thrusting of Tāne that tore the heaven from the earth," was an ancient saying of the Māori people. "So they were sent apart, and darkness was made manifest, and so was the light."

Rangi was hurled far away while angry winds screamed through the space between earth and sky.

Tāne and his brothers looked at the soft curves of their mother. As the light crept across the land they saw a veil of silver mist that hung over her naked shoulders – the mist of grief for her lost husband. Tears dropped fast from Rangi's eyes. The showers of rain ran together in pools and streams across the body of Papa.

Although he had separated his parents so forcibly, Tāne loved them both. He set to work to clothe his mother in beauty that had not been dreamed of in the dark world. He brought his own children, the trees, and set them in the earth. But Tāne was like a child learning by trial and error the wisdom that had not yet been born. He planted the trees upside down. Their heads were buried in the soil, while the bare white roots remained stiff and unmoving in the breeze.

It was no place for his other children, the birds and the insects. He pulled up a giant kauri tree, shook the soil from its branches, set the roots firmly in the ground, and proudly surveyed the spreading crown set above the clean, straight trunk. The breeze played with the leaves, singing the song of a new world.

The earth lay still and beautiful, wrapped in a cloak of living green. The ocean lapped her body, the birds and the insects ran and fluttered in the fresh breeze. The brown-skinned gods frolicked under the leaves of the garden of Tāne. Each had a duty to perform. Rango-maa-tāne preserved the fertility of the growing things of earth. Haumia-tiketike tended the humble fernroot. Tū-matauenga was the god of war. Tangaroa controlled the restless waves. Only one of the seventy brothers left the placid shelter of his mother to follow his father. It was Tāwhiri-mātea, the god of all the winds that blow between earth and sky.

Tāne-mahuta raised his eyes to where Rangi lay, cold and grey and unlovely in the vast spaces above the earth and was sorry for the desolation of his father. He took the bright sun and placed it on Rangi's back with the silver moon in front. He travelled through the ten heavens until he found a garment of glowing red. After that he rested for seven days, and then spread the cloak across the sky from the east to west and north to south.

But Tāne was not satisfied. He decided that the gift was not worthy of his father and stripped it off. A small piece remained, a fragment of the garment men still see at the time of the setting sun.

"Great father," Tāne cried, "in the long dark nights before Marama the moon shines on your breast, all things sorrow. I will journey to the very ends of space to find adornment for you."

Somewhere in the silence he heard an answering sigh. He passed swiftly to the very end of the world, into the darkness, until he reached Maunganui, the Great Mountain, where the Shining Ones lived. They were children of Uru, Tāne-mahuta's brother. The two brothers watched them playing at the foot of the mountain.

Tāne begged Uru to give him some of the shining lights to fasten on the mantle of the sky. Uru rose to his feet and gave a great shout. The Shining Ones heard and came rolling up the slope to their father. Uru placed a basket in front of Tāne. He plunged his arms into the glowing mass of lights and piled the Shining Ones into the basket.

Tāne placed five glowing lights in the shape of a cross on the breast of Rangi and sprinkled the dark blue robe with the Children of Light. The basket he hung in the wide heavens. It is the basket of the Milky Way. Sometimes Uru's children tumble and fall swiftly towards the earth, but for the most part they remain like fireflies on the mantle of the night sky.

Collected by A.W. Reed

The Coming of Kūmara

Māori

IN VIEW OF the widespread cultivation of the succulent tuber known to the Māori as kūmara, in the North Island and in the more sheltered districts of the South Island, it is not surprising that a variety of myths were invented to explain its origin.

The kūmara was imported to New Zealand, which fact in turn necessitated a further series of legends to account for its arrival in the southern islands. There are several versions of the manner in which it was brought, one of them concerning Pou-rangahua who lived near the mouth of the Waipaoa River in the days when men lived on the products of lake, river, sea and forest. It was the craving of Pou's baby son for a mysterious, unknown food that sent the chief far across the Ocean of Kiwa, which we now call the Pacific, to try to satisfy his child's demands.

At Pari-nui-te-ra his quest succeeded, for there was the site of a famous kūmara plantation; but on landing his canoe was wrecked and he had no means of returning to his home. He was compensated for his loss by winning the friendship of the chief Tāne, who not only provided him with an abundant supply of kūmara but was also prepared to lend him one of his pet birds, feathered monsters so large and powerful that they were able to carry a grown man on their backs. Pou-rangahua slung two baskets of kūmara across the shoulders of one of the birds. It ran quickly along the sand, but under the double load was unable to lift itself from the beach. Tāne promptly led forth his favourite bird, the largest and strongest of all, and on its strong back Pou, with the baskets, at last began his flight back to Aotearoa. Skilfully avoiding all the perils of the journey, he arrived safely back at his home.

And so, according to the ancient legend, the kūmara came to Aotearoa, the gift from Hawaiki that revolutionised the diet of the Polynesians in this far-off land. But Pou-rangahua failed to heed the instructions of his generous host. Though he had been careful to avoid the clutches of Tama-i-waho, the ogre of Hikurangi, on his homeward journey, he was culpably careless of the welfare of Tāne's bird when he sent it back to its master.

"Pou returns," he said, "and closes the door for ever."

At Pari-nui-te-ra, the Polynesian chief waited in vain for the bird he loved. But, tired after its long flight and then exhausted by the further flight that Pou had demanded from landfall to home, it had fallen victim to the ogre of Hikurangi.

* * *

Other legends relate to a mythical origin, which influenced the elaborate ritual surrounding its cultivation and harvesting. Pani, or Pani-tinaku as she is sometimes known, was the "mother" or personification of the kūmara. She was the wife of Rongo-māui, a brother of Whānui; when the star Whānui rose above the horizon, the time had come, said the wise old tohunga, to lift the crop.

Many are the tales that are told of how Pani gave birth to the kūmara, tales of how the precious food was stolen from the gods by Rongo-māui and given to the sons of men. It was a heinous theft that robbed the atua of their food and, indeed, it was regarded as the origin of all theft. Whānui looked down at the men and women toiling like ants in their cultivations and in anger sent Anuhe, Toronu and

Moka to destroy the stolen fruits of the earth. It was so then and is still today, for these are the different kinds of caterpillar that feed on the foliage of the tubers.

According to a legend preserved by the tribes of Tūhoe, Pani cared for the five Māui brothers after the death of their parents. One day, when they returned from fishing, they complained to Rongo-māui that he was lazy because he never accompanied them on their fishing expeditions, and failed to help supply the family with food. Rongo resented the criticism. He made up his mind to give them a food supply that would prove he was a better provider that the foster-children of his wife. It was then that he climbed up to the realm of the gods and stole the essence of their food. Descending to earth he impregnated his wife with the seed, the life-spirit of the kūmara. When her time came, Rongo told her to go to the stream of Mona-ariki to give birth. As she stood in the sacred water she produced her young, the children who were named Nehu-tai, Pātea, Pio, Matatū, Pauarangi, and several others. These are the names of the varieties of kūmara provided by the ancestor as food for her descendants.

Then the sacred ovens were prepared, and so men learned the art of cooking food. Had it not been for Rongo-māui, men would be like birds and lizards that eat their food raw.

More than one canoe lays claims to the honour of introducing the kūmara to Aotearoa; but it is to Pani-tinaku and her husband Rongo-māui that we render homage for providing mankind with the food of the gods, and to Whānui, the star whose appearance reminds men it is time to harvest the fruits of their labour.

Collected by A.W. Reed

Patupaiarehe

Māori

PLEASANT IN ITS sun-dappled freshness, and in the cool depths where the sun seldom penetrated, prolific as a store house of bird life, the bush could in places harbour malevolent creatures that went by names such as patupaiarehe and maero. The latter were found more frequently in the rain forests of the South Island than in the sunnier North Island bush.

The patupaiarehe are usually described as fairies in English, but this description is misleading if we think of fairies as lovable "little people". The patupaiarehe were usually described as being taller than humans, fair-skinned, red-haired and dangerous to mortals. They were found in several parts of the North Island, but were most numerous in certain localities such as Ngongotahā, Pirongia and Moehau, where they were supposed to inhabit large fortified villages on the gloomy, mist-frequented heights of the mountains.

It has been suggested that they were a racial memory of fair-skinned people of distant countries. Another theory is that the earliest immigrants to Aotearoa, dispossessed of their lands by late arrivals, took refuge in the bush, building paa on the cloudy summits of the hills and descending from time to time in the concealing mist to abduct and ravish young women. The theory is supported by the belief that diggers of fernroot sometimes heard a mysterious voice that said, "You rejoice today, but my turn will come tomorrow." When the fernroot diggers heard it they set aside the first three roots as an offering to the original inhabitants of the land. Yet another belief was that wairua who had failed to reach the land of spirits were condemned to haunt the forest and hide themselves from the bright light of day. In this respect they had some affinity with kēhua, the ghosts who emerged at night to terrify anyone rash enough to venture into the darkness. There is a legend that relates their arrival in the *Tainui* canoe; another that says they were placed in their mountain retreats by the tohunga Ngā-toro-i-rangi who came in the *Arawa* canoe. Again it has been said that some patupaiarehe are descended from the atua Tama-o-hoi who divided Ruawāhia from Tarawera.

The various branches of the patupaiarehe had certain features and habits in common, though differing in other respects. The urukehu among the Māori, being light-haired with fair skin, were often regarded as descendants of the patupaiarehe through mixed marriages with mortal women. To a darker-skinned people, the untattooed, white-skinned beings were regarded as supernatural. They lived in pā made of the vines of the kareao (supplejack) and ventured far from their pā only on wet or misty days. The plaintive notes of their kōauau and pūtōrino exercised a fatal fascination on young women, who were lured to the homes of the patupaiarehe. Those who were abducted seldom returned, but lived in a permanently dazed condition amongst their captors.

Fortunately there were two methods of defence against the iwi atua, the supernatural tribe – cooked food and red ochre, which was freely used on tapu objects. The use of these deterrents is illustrated in the following two legends, from Ngongotahā and Pirongia.

Ruarangi and his young wife lived in the foothills of the Hākarimata Range. Tāwhaitū was gathering kūmara tubers when her neck was encircled by a strong white arm. She was swept off her feet and carried into the forest. Wet leaves brushed against her. The mist trailed damp fingers over her face. At the summit of Pirongia the patupaiarehe laid Tāwhaitū gently on a bed of moss in one of the whare of the ghostly pā. She lay in his arms throughout the long night listening to the plaintive music of the fairy people and the thin wailing of kōauau and pūtōrino while Whanawhana, her abductor and the chief of the hapū, told her of his love. Towards the morning she fell into a karakia-induced sleep.

When she woke she found herself lying in a forest clearing near her own home. Her husband Ruarangi was kneeling beside her, looking at her with an anxious expression. He had spent the night searching for her. Hiding her face in his breast she told him how she had been ravished by the dreaded patupaiarehe.

"Whanawhana has laid his evil spell on me," she sobbed. "When it is dark again I shall be drawn to him. I know he has taken my will. I shall not be able to resist his power."

In his distress Ruarangi consulted the tohunga. "There are ways to overcome the patupaiarehe," the tohunga advised him. "You must build a small wharau. Lay a heavy beam across the threshold and paint it with kōkōwhai (red ochre). You must also smear the kōkōwhai over your bodies and your garments.

"When this is done, dig a hole for an umu, light the fire, place food in it, and cover it well. If you do this in the late afternoon the smell of cooking food will last all night and protect your wife as she lies in the wharau."

That night the slowly steaming umu wafted a savoury smell round the wharau, guarding Ruarangi and Tāwhaitū from Whanawhana. Outside the hut stood the tohunga, naked, chanting karakia to repel the patupaiarehe.

Whanawhana and three companions appeared before the wharau. When they attempted to enter they were driven back by the priest's incantation and the smell of cooking food. Nor would they have dared to step over the painted beam laid across the doorway. Step by step they retreated slowly to the forest.

Tāwhaitū was not troubled again, although her union with Whanawhana proved fruitful and their descendants, who live by the Waipā River, are noted for the reddish tinge in their hair.

* * *

The best known of the fairy legends comes from the experiences of Iihenga, the great explorer and name-giver of the thermal region. In the course of his journeys he came to Rotorua – Rotorua-a-Iihenga, the second lake of Iihenga. Travelling around the shore, he reached the stream and mountain which we now know as Ngongotahā.

Iihenga was curious to know whether the plume that drifted lazily from the hilltop was smoke or mist. He climbed the slopes, undaunted by the plaintive songs he heard in the forests. From the corner of his eye he saw strange forms and movements that showed he was being followed.

A breath of wind tore the mist away from the peak, revealing the palisades of a pā and a tree blazing like a torch. He broke off a branch that was alive with flame. Pale forms rushed towards him. Iihenga swung the crackling branch in a fiery circle that caused the patupaiarehe to retreat. He plunged it into the bracken, filled the air with choking smoke and stinging sparks and fled back to his canoe.

Some time later he settled by the Waitetī Stream and tried to establish relations with the elusive white-skinned people whose music echoed eerily through the mist. One day he climbed up to the hilltop pā and called to the red-haired people of the mist. They ran towards him. He asked for water and a beautiful young woman offered him a drink from a calabash with a wooden mouthpiece. Iihenga drank deeply while the patupaiarehe crowded around and commented on his appearance. Iihenga named the mountain from this incident. Ngongo means "to drink" and is also the word for the mouthpiece of a tahā, or calabash.

The strange inhabitants of Te Tūāhu-a-te-atua, the sacred place of the god, plied him with questions and touched his body with ghostly fingers. Iihenga grew afraid. He slipped through the palisades and hurtled down the hillside.

The patupaiarehe streamed after him. Gradually he drew away from the shouting throng, but one of the fairy creatures kept close on his heels. It was the young woman who had offered him her calabash. She threw her garments away to leave her limbs unhampered. Iihenga knew that if she captured him she would rob him of his memory, and he would never see his wife again.

In the pocket of his belt there was a small fragment of kōkōwhai mixed with shark oil. Without faltering in his headlong flight he drew it out and smeared it over his body, for he remembered that the patupaiarehe were repelled by kōkōwhai and that the smell of food and oil was repugnant to them.

With a cry that had sadness and longing in it as well as frustration, the comely girl from the fairy pā stood still. Iihenga looked back and saw her motionless amongst the trees with arms stretched out in mute appeal to the mortal man who had escaped her clutches.

The experience of Ruru, the husband of Tangi-roa, was more painful. While on a tuna-catching (eel-catching) expedition, the young man was lost in the hills. Presently he stumbled into a clearing and was immediately surrounded by white, ghostly forms that caught him and carried him away to their pā. For a long time he was kept in the strange comatose state of mist captives of the patupaiarehe.

Attractive young women were usually loved and cared for by the male fairies, but Ruru was subjected to many indignities. They rubbed him with the palms of their hands and the soles of their feet until a strange moss or lichen began to grow from his skin and covered his body. The hair on his head fell out and he became completely bald.

After a time he was granted partial liberty. He was allowed to roam through the forest to search for berries and hunt for eels and birds; but as the patupaiarehe were unable to use fire in their damp retreat, the food was unpalatable.

Thinking that Ruru was dead, the aged tohunga Maringi-rangi sought to marry Tangi-roa, but was supplanted by a younger rival. The tohunga went to the seashore and wove spells of peculiar intensity, after which he lay down to sleep. When he woke he found a stranger sitting beside him. Maringi-rangi looked at him closely. The man was naked and covered with a peculiar moss-like growth in which the bald crown of his head lay like a polished boulder. The tohunga looked at him closely for a long time and then said, "You are Ruru! It is because of my magic that you have escaped from the patupaiarehe. Come with me."

He led Ruru along the beach and through the gates of the kaainga. A cry of horror rose from the women, who shouted, "A madman!"

"Don't be afraid," Maringi-rangi said. "This is our old companion Ruru. Call Tangi-roa. Tell her that her husband has come to claim her once again as his wife."

Tangi-roa ran towards them, but recoiled when she saw the bald-pated, lichen covered travesty of a man. Maringi-rangi led Ruru up to her and said with an evil smile, "Here is your reward, Tangi-roa. Welcome your lover and husband." The woman buried her face in her hands and wept bitterly. Looking down at her, the old tohunga's heart was touched. He remembered the passions and sorrows of his youth.

"Bring warm water quickly," he ordered.

Dipping his hands in the calabash, he repeated spells and incantations and rubbed the body of Ruru as the patupaiarehe had done when they had captured the young man. The kohukohu, or moss, came away freely and Ruru was restored to his wife – but to his dying day his skull remained as smooth as the water-worn boulder in the stream where he had hunted for tuna (eel) before he was caught by the fairy folk of the hills.

Collected by A.W. Reed

Taniwha

Māori

THE FOLKLORE OF Aotearoa is replete with tales of grisly monsters that inhabited dark caves and deep pools – a menace to travellers who were unaware of their presence. Monstrous in size as well as form, they were called taniwha. Although most were notorious man-eaters, many could be placated by gifts of food and the reciting of karakia and others were believed to be harmless except when tormented or neglected. The ocean-dwelling taniwha were known to have rescued the ship-wrecked parties, escorted sea-going canoes and even carried men on their backs. Such creatures were sometimes in the shape of sharks, sometimes whales.

More usually they were huge reptiles in form, with an insatiable desire for human flesh, even for whole canoe-loads of people. Interestingly there were no reptiles in Polynesia that could have given rise to the concept of crocodile-like monsters, and this has led to the speculation that they were a racial memory from tropical lands. Taniwha frequently resembled lizards (and were called by the same name – moko), of which the Māori had a superstitious fear, believing them to be the living representation of the powers that caused sickness and death.

Taniwha had a distinguished ancestry, having descended from the union of the great god Tāne and Hine-tūpari-maunga. Their daughter Pūtoto married Tāne's brother Taka-aho and gave birth to Tua-rangaranga, the progenitor of taniwha. Others, not in this direct line of descent, were believed to be ancestors; where taniwha had originally been human beings, or were inhabited by their wairua, they shared the immortality of the wairua.

Their habitat could vary. They frequently dwelt in water – salt or fresh – but some lived on land or could even fly. There were notable occasions when they lived and travelled underground and engaged in the earth-moving business, making considerable changes in the landscape.

From the thermal regions come the following three stories of taniwha.

* * *

MANY TRAVELLERS between Rotorua and Taupō had failed to reach their destination. It was suspected that they had been ambushed by some hostile tribe. A taua was sent out to find the enemy and destroy them. As the party travelled across the plain the scent of the men crept into the nostrils of Hotu-puku, who was lurking in a nearby cave.

The monster sprang out and rushed towards the unsuspecting men. The spines and excrescences on its back had the appearance of growths on some fabulous creature of the sea. Some of the men were trampled to death, others were seized in the cavernous mouth and swallowed whole. Those who escaped stumbled into the pā at Rotorua and told the tale of their misadventures.

Another war party was quickly assembled and took the trail to Hotu-puku's lair.

On the way they discussed their plans of campaign. On arrival at Kapenga, where the taniwha still lurked, they stripped leaves from tī-palms and plaited them into strong ropes.

They waited until the wind blew away from the cave and climbed down to it. They could hear the monster's stertorous breathing. It was sleeping soundly. The rope snares were arranged at some distance from the cave while the men drew close to the entrance. They were armed with cutting and thrusting weapons. Others held the ropes while a third party, composed of the youngest and boldest warriors, stood at the mouth of the cave to lure the taniwha into the open. They advanced cautiously as the ground shook and the huge form of Hotu-puku filled the dark mouth of the cave. It came forward at a run, its jaws distended, its long tongue darting from side to side. As the taniwha rushed out, the warriors retreated. Their ropes were lying on the ground, seemingly scattered at random, but in fact they had been placed with great care. The men took care not to disturb them.

A sudden shout startled the taniwha. The noose sprang from the ground as a score of hands tugged at the ropes. Hotu-puku's front legs were caught in a crushing grip. Like living things the other ropes circled its legs and body. They wove themselves round its neck and jaws, falling lightly and then biting into the scaly flesh. Only the tail was free. It lashed from side to side, sweeping men off their feet as the monster felt the bite of mere and taiaha, and the sting of cutting implements.

Maddened with pain, Hotu-puku strained against the ropes as the nooses were pulled tighter. The ropes were wound round the trunks of trees, pegging the taniwha down firmly until it lay lifeless in the ground.

Its appearance was that of a huhu grub, if one can imagine such an object swollen to the size of a young whale, or of a giant tuatete or tuatara, with scales and spiny ridges.

One of the chiefs suggested that they throw off their garments and cut the monster open to inspect the contents of its belly. There were many layers of fat to penetrate, but once these were stripped off the excited warriors exposed a grisly treasure trove. There were bodies of men and women who had recently been eaten and were still undigested. There were many greenstone mere, weapons such as kokiri and taiaha, weapons made from the bones of whales, sharks' teeth, mats, garments of dressed and undressed flax, and precious heirlooms.

The human remains were interred, after which the taniwha was dismembered and oil expressed from its fat. It was eaten by the warriors to express their contempt and to celebrate the victory over the enemy that had killed so many of their friends from Rotorua and Taupō moana.

One of the more well-disposed taniwha was Horomatangi. He had been brought from Hawaiki by the famous tohunga Ngā-toro-i-rangi. After Ngā-toro's arrival in Aotearoa his sister Kuiwai was grievously insulted in the homeland by her husband. Together with her sister Haungaroa she came to the new land across the sea in search of Ngā-toro to ask him to avenge the insult. The tohunga was unaware of their arrival but the watchful Horomatangi, who at that time was in the vicinity of White Island, saw them.

He then swam under the water until he reached the mainland, travelled underground, and came to the surface of Lake Taupō where he blew a column of water and pumice high into the air, creating a whirlpool some three or four kilometres south of Motutaiko at the Horomatangi Reef. From the lake he saw Kuiwai and Haungaroa in the distance. For some reason the taniwha was unable to reach the women and was forced to communicate with them by signs. Turning and twisting, Horomatangi travelled underground again. At Wairākei he exhaled violently. The earth shuddered as the steam of his breath broke through the ground, forming the Karapiti blow-hole. The white plume of condensing breath gushed high into the air and turned towards Ngā-toro's resting place at Maketū. Kuiwai saw the column of steam and interpreted the taniwha's sign correctly.

Exhausted by his labours, Horomatangi remained in the channel between Motutaiko, the little island at the southern end of Lake Taupō, and Wairākei, where he was transformed into a black rock. He sometimes assumes the form of a lizard and is then known as Ihu-maataotao.

On the nearby promontory of Motutere there once stood an extensive pā, and a church erected more than a hundred years ago. The church had a short length of life. Its early disintegration occurred when a missionary persuaded the inhabitants of the pā to make use of a sacred totara log that floated of its own volition in the neighborhood of the Horomatangi Reef. The log was either a taniwha or a tipua and may well have been the notable taniwha Horomatangi. When it was hauled ashore and used in the construction of the church its tapu was still potent. The men who cut it up suffered misfortune and the church was soon disused and fell into decay.

Horomatangi also enters into a legend that links Ōhinemutu by Late Rotorua with Rotoāira, the lake that nestles between Tongariro and Pīhanga. The taniwha Huru-kareao, who lived in the lake, was a relative of Horomatangi. He had taken the inhabitants of the lakeside pā under his protection and it is said that the men and women of that pā lived lives of such rectitude that Horomatangi was unable to find another hapū of equal reputation. The two taniwha entered into an arrangement to share responsibility for caring for these excellent people.

Having heard good reports of the pleasant springs of Ōhinemutu, Hineutu, a young woman who belonged to the Rotoāira hapū, decided to visit the pā by the lakeside at Rotorua. She travelled north and stayed there for a short time. The Arawa people of Ōhinemutu heaped indignities upon her, for they had little respect for the southern hapū. They had not heard of the favour with which her people were regarded by the taniwha of Taupō and Rotoāira.

Unable to endure the taunts of the young men and women of Ōhinemutu, Hineutu hurried back to her home and called for vengeance. The tohunga chanted incantations to summon Hurukareao to the pā. The taniwha in turn called his relative from Lake Taupō. When they heard Hineutu's tale their indignation rose to such a pitch that they threw themselves about in the lake, with disastrous results. The pā at Rotoāira was engulfed by the waves. At Tokaanu the surging waters changed the channel of the river and submerged another pā on its banks.

Through Taupō moana and over the hills and through the valleys the two taniwha sped northwards on their missions of vengeance. They were weary by the time they reached Ōhinemutu. They plunged into Lake Rotorua but only half of the village was submerged and many of the inhabitants escaped.

There are three springs, one at Rotoāira, one at Tokaanu, and another at Ōhinemutu, all of which are named Huru-kareao. At Motutaiko, Horomatangi lives in an underground cave. For many years he amused himself by upsetting passing canoes and satisfied his hunger by devouring their crews. Now he lies deep in his cave and contents himself with snapping harmlessly at the propellers of launches, the modern taniwha which prowl the lake today.

Collected by A.W. Reed

Denizens of the Sea

Māori

THE OCEAN AS well as the land was the bride of Rangi. In one account of the creation Rangi married Wainui-aatea, who gave birth to Moana-nui. (Moana means sea or ocean; wai means water.) The seas were personified in Hine-moana and Wainui. Not surprisingly Papa had little love for her rival. In characteristic style Elsdon Best once wrote: "The Ocean Maid is spoken of as constantly assailing the Earth Mother, ever she attacks her; all bays, gulfs, inlets we see are *'te ngaunga a Hinemoana'*, the result of the gnawing of Hine-moana, into the great body of Tuuaanuku, our universal mother. This aggression was noted by the Whānau-a-rangi (Offspring of Rangi), who appointed Rakahore, Hine-tū-ā-kirikiri, and Hine-one (personified forms of rock, gravel and sand) to protect the flanks of the Earth Mother from being swallowed by Hine-moana. When the serried battalions of the Ocean Maid roll in, rank behind rank, to assault the Earth Mother, gaunt Rakahore faces them fearlessly, and they break in fury around him. Still they rush on, in wavering array, to hurl themselves in vain against the rattling armour of the Gravel Maid, or upon the smooth but immovable form of the Sand Maid. They budge not, but ever stand between Papa the Parentless and the fury of Hine-moana."

The origin of the tides is ascribed to Parata, a taniwha that lived far out in the ocean, drawing water in and out of its mouth. By means of the incantations of Ngā-toro-i-rangi the *Arawa* canoe was nearly drawn into Te Waha-o-Parata (The Mouth of Parata) but escaped at the last moment.

Apart from whales and sharks, some of which have been described as taniwha, and have, on occasion, been well or ill-disposed to mankind, there was a weird creature called marakihau. The carvers of the Bay of Plenty represented it as a figure with human body and head, a fish's tail, and a long, tubular tongue termed a ngongo. The marakihau was of gigantic proportions, for the tongue was used to draw canoes into its capacious mouth.

Nearer to the land the ponaturi, a malevolent marine counterpart of the patupaiarehe, were feared by coast dwellers. The ponaturi were closely related to the patupaiarehe. They shared their aversion to the sunshine and strong daylight, but were creatures of the sea who came ashore only at night. One of the best known Māori legends is the account of how the cult hero Rātā rescued his father's bones from the ponaturi. In the following tale Kaumariki lost his friends and barely escaped with his life from these repellent creatures of the sea.

* * *

The bone fish-hook named Te Rama possessed the property of attracting fish from a great distance. It was coveted by Kaumariki who dared to violate its tapu. With the help of two friends, Tāwhai and Kupe, he stole the sacred fish-hook. Fearing the owner's revenge, they set sail in a canoe and did not stop until they reached a lonely island far across the sea. The water near the shore was teeming with fish.

"Look!" Kaumariki shouted. "Te Rama is already at work. The fish are leaping towards it."

They decided to wait until the following day. Kaumariki collected a heap of driftwood, but Tāwhai and Kupe decided to keep out the cold of the night by heaping sun-warmed sand over their bodies.

"The sand will grow cold long before dawn," Kaumariki warned. "A hot fire is the only way to drive out the demons of cold."

He dragged the firewood into a circle, set it alight and lay down in the centre. He was awakened by cries of terror. Looking across the dull embers of his fire he saw his friends imprisoned in their bed of sands fighting vainly against a horde of weird creatures. Their skins were a greenish-white that glowed with putrescent light. Their fingers terminated in long claws with which they were tearing the skin from the helpless men.

Kaumariki piled dry wood in the fire, driving back the bolder ones who were advancing towards him. As soon as the flames died down the creatures rushed to attack him, retreating only as the frantic man fed the flames.

At daybreak the sea creatures disappeared into the sea. Kaumariki stepped cautiously over the charred timbers and went to the trenches where the bodies had been lying. There was no trace of his friends. Skin, flesh, blood, bones and hair had all been devoured. Kaumariki dared not face another night alone on the haunted island. He dragged the canoe into the water and headed for home.

On arrival at the pā he gave Te Rama back to its owner and admitted his offence. In view of what he had suffered, his theft was pardoned.

"I must avenge the death of my friends," he said. "Who will come with me? I need at least a hundred warriors and one of our largest war canoes."

"How can you ever overcome the ponaturi?", he was asked. "The bravest fighter is no match for the endless multitudes of the sea devils."

"If you do as I tell you we shall overcome them," Kaumariki replied. "Let the women collect raupō leaves and manuka stakes. We shall use them to build a whare on the island. While they are doing this you must cut down many trees and fashion the trunks into the shape of men."

Kaumariki took four gourds. He packed them with fungus and filled them with shark oil, intending to use them as lamps. When they were finished he wrapped them in bark covers.

The next day the heavily laden crew set off on its journey of revenge. As soon as it reached the island, everyone helped to unload the canoe and build a large whare. When it was completed the wooden effigies, wrapped in cloaks, were placed on the floor.

The shadows deepened. Kaumariki posted a warrior in each corner of the building with a lighted lamp in his hands. The bark covers shielded the flame. In the subdued light it seemed as though many men were sleeping on the floor of the whare.

The remaining warriors sheltered inside a circle of fire that had been lit nearby. The hours passed slowly but everyone remained silent and alert. Towards midnight a whisper passed through the ranks of warriors. A dark shadow had appeared out of the water.

As it advanced up the beach the greenish-white skin of the ponaturi reflected the flames of the watchfire. It was joined by three more figures. The four ponaturi scouts, keeping well away from the fire, approached the whare. They peered through the open doorway, saw the motionless forms lying on the sandy floor and whispered, "Kei te moe! Asleep." Their leader turned and repeated loudly, "Kei te moe!"

Hundreds of ponaturi rushed up the beach, struggled through the doorway and fell on the cloaked forms. When they were all inside Kaumariki gave a shout. The four warriors who had been standing motionless in the corners of the whare pulled the shades from their lamps. The ponaturi were blinded by the light. Holding their hands over their eyes, they rushed blindly to and fro, searching for the door. In the confusion the four warriors slipped outside.

Kaumariki barred the door and signalled to the warriors to apply torches to the brushwood walls. A few terrified sea creatures managed to escape through the blazing walls. The rest were burned to death in a blaze of light and burning heat as the flames soared upwards, transforming the whare into a fiery revenge for the death of Tāwhai and Kupe.

* * *

Reference has been made several times to transformations and the difficulty of placing supernatural beings into specific categories. Such is true of Pānia and Moremore. Pānia was a young woman of the sea – not a ponaturi, but with the mind and appearance of mortal woman. There is no term by which she can be identified.

The land had already exercised a strange fascination for Pānia. Every evening she left her home in the sea and lay concealed among the flax bushes at the foot of the Hukarere cliff where Napier stands today, returning to her own people at dawn.

In the half-light of dusk Karitoki, a young chief from a neighbouring village, noticed her as he came to drink the water of a spring. He went over to her, took her by the hand and led her gently to his home. The door closed behind them. Pānia was content to remain with this man of the land until the stars grew dim before the dawn light. She left the arms of her sleeping husband, pressed her face gently against his tattooed cheek, and swam through the breakers back to her own people.

Each day as the light waned he waited her coming. Together they made their way past the flax bushes and the spring to their home. As the sea breeze dried her glistening body Karitoki felt the warmth of love welling up and reaching towards him in his strange sea bride.

A year went by. Pānia gave birth to a boy, a tiny bundle of humanity she named Moremore (Hairless). Each morning she left him with her husband. As the chief cared for his son during the day he began to fear that the child might inherit the characteristics of his sea ancestors. He went to the tohunga to ask how he could keep his wife and child with him permanently.

"It should not be difficult," the tohunga assured him. "Wait until they are both asleep. You must then place cooked food on their bodies. They will never return to the sea again."

It was perhaps understandable that the tohunga had assumed that Pānia was a ponaturi, or at least had some affinity with these supernatural creatures. The assumption was not correct. In trying to keep his loved ones with him Karitoki lost both son and wife. When she was touched by the tapu-dispelling food Pānia took her son in her arms and walked into the sea. She had no wish to leave her husband, but men and women of land and sea have different natures and different customs.

Pānia became a rock, which was often frequented by fishermen. In her left armpit the tāmure (snapper) swam, and between her thighs the hapuku (groper). Moremore, the hairless one, was transformed into a taniwha. In form he resembled a shark that made its home by the reef off the Hukarere shore and in the inner harbour by the mouth of the Ahuriri River.

In spite of the vast gulf that lies between men and women of alien cultures Pānia longed as desperately for her lover as Karitoki yearned for her. It is a sad story of lovers parted by conditions over which they had no control. At ebb tide Pānia could be seen below the reef with her arms stretched out vainly towards her lover.

Collected by A.W. Reed

A Short History, Purporting to Give the Origin of the Hausa Nation and the Story of Their Conversion to the Mohammedan Religion

Maalam Shaihuu, Hausa People, Nigeria

IN THE NAME OF ALLAH THE COMPASSIONATE, the Merciful, and may the peace of Allah be upon him, after whom there is no prophet. This is the history of the Hausa (nation). It has been familiar to every one from the time of their grandfathers and grandmothers, (and) is a thing which has been handed down from the *malamai* (learned men) and these elders. Any account other than this one is not authentic. If a questioner ask of you (saying) I Where did the Hausa people have their origin?' Say (to him) "Truly their origin was (from) the Barebari and Northerners." And this is the account of how this came to pass.

The king of Bornu had a horse with a golden horn. This horse did not neigh just at any time, but only on Fridays. If it neighed you would say it was a tornado. It was hidden away in a house. Now the king had a son. He (the son) continually gave him who looked after the horse money and robes in order that (he might persuade him) to bring his horse out, and they should come, and he should mate the horse with his mare. And it was always thus. (And) one day the man who was looking after the (king's) horse took (it) the horse out and brought it. The king's son too took his mare out. They went into the forest and the mare was covered.

Now the king has (had) previously said that whoever was seen (with) a foal from this horse at his house, he would have his throat cut. Things remained at this, (and) one day the mare gave birth, (and nothing happened) till the colt grew up, (when) one day the king's horse neighed, then the young horse answered. And the king said, "At whose ever house they see it let (that person) be killed (lit. be cut), and do not let him be brought before me." Then the councillors scattered (to make search) in the town. They were searching for the young horse.

And they came to the house of the king's son, and behold as it were the king's horse with its golden horn. Then the councillors said, "The king has said we must come with you." Then the king's son lifted his sword. He cut down two men, the remainder were scattered. Then he saddled up the young horse. He mounted. The king ordered he should be seized and brought (before him). The whole town mounted their horses (and) followed him. They did not come up with him. He has gone his way. The king, moreover, has given orders that his own horse is not to be mounted, and if not his horse, then there was not the horse to overtake him.

The king's son (rode) went on and (eventually) dismounted in the country of Daura. He saw the daughter of the king of Daura, she possessed the town. He stayed with her. And one day she said she wanted him in marriage and he too said he loved her. So they married. The king's daughter became with child. She bore a child, a son. She weaned it. She was again with child (and) bore a girl. And that was the origin of the Hausa nation.

The Barebari and Daura people were their ancestors. But the Mohammedan religion, as far as that is concerned, from Bornu it came. Hausas and Barebari and whatever race (you can name) in the West were at first in early times pagans. Then the *maalamai* (scribes) said that this is what happened.

There was a certain man away there at Bornu from among the children of their royal house, his name (was) Dalama. When he came to the throne he was called Mainadinama, the meaning of that is, 'a chief more powerful than any other.' After he had reigned for some months then he sent a messenger to the Caliph.

Now at this time Abubakari Sidiku, the blessing of Allah be upon him, he was Caliph. You have seen the beginning of his being sent, referring back to that man (Mainadinama), was that he was hearing about Mohammedanism before he succeeded to the kingdom. Behold the name of his envoy whom he sent, his name was Gujalo. At the time when the envoy came he found the Caliph's attention occupied with a war. He said nothing to the envoy. All he said was, "Remain here." Then he did not again remember his words because his mind was so occupied with words of the war of the father of the twins.

The messenger remained there till the messenger died. After three months and a few days then the Caliph Abubakari Sidiku he too died. After some months Umaru Ibunuhutabi was set up. He was the Caliph after Abubakari Asidiku. Then he called to mind the report of the envoy and his death. Then they held a consultation, they his friends who remained. They joined their heads about the question of sending an envoy to Bornu. Umaruasi was sent with manuscripts of the Koran. It was said the writing of Abdulahi the son of Umoru the Caliph, and turbans and a sword and spears and shields and the kingly fez and such things and plates; all these presents from the Caliph to Mainadinama.

When the envoy drew near he sent to them one to acquaint them of the news of his coming. The king of Bornu and his men mounted their horses and met him afar off. When he (the envoy) entered his town, then he bound the turban on him, he was established in his right to the kingdom, he was given the name of the king of Bornu, he (the king) gave him everything he was told to give him, because of the presents which he (the envoy) had been sent with for him. He lived among them. He was instructing them (the people of Bornu) in the creed of Allah and the names of His messengers, may the salvation and trust of Allah be assured to them.

They continued to honour him, to the extreme that honour could be carried. They sought a blessing (by eating) the remains of his meals and his food and from the spot (he) set his feet. Half of them were seeking blessing from the mucus from his nose and his spittle (by rubbing it on their persons). They were climbing the roofs in order to see him. They also sought blessing by touching his robes and his slippers and his whip, until it was even said they looked for a blessing from his beasts, and the remains of their fodder and their dung.

Now he wrote manuscripts for them in the writing of his own hand, the blessed one. He lived amid such works up to the very end of (his) sojourn (and this went on) till he was informed that, "Other owners of (another) land are behind you (and) are wishing for the Mohammedan religion, should they see you they would follow you."

He did not give (this report) credence until he had sent one to spy out (the land), his name is unknown. He (the spy) went and travelled over Hausa-land. He made secret inquiries, he heard they were praising the Mohammedan faith and that they wished for it. He returned and gave Umaru Ibunuasi the news. Umaru Ibunuasi told his people. He said they must go (and preach the Mohammedan religion). They agreed.

Then he made preparations. He sent Abdulkarimu-Mukaila to Kano. About 300 men, Arabs, followed him. When Abdulkarimu was near to them (the people of Kano) then he sent one to inform them. He (the messenger) came and said, "Tell them the envoy of the envoy has come."

When he came to them he told them what (message) he had been sent with. They believed him, they received the thing which he had brought. Now at this time Kano was an unenclosed town but not a walled town, the name of the men (man) at Kano (was) Muhamadu Dajakara at the time when Abdulkarimu alighted amongst them. He (Abdulkarimu) wrote them books in the writing of his own hand, the blessed one, because he had not come to them bringing books from Umaru Ibunu(I)asi.

And thus it has come to be reported that every one who wished to be able to write well let him set out towards Bornu and remain there (till he had learned to write) and then return (home). But Abdulkarimu continued to instruct them the laws of Allah and the commands of the law until they made inquiries about things which were not (to be found) in Arabia. He did not know what answer to give them. Then he said to them to leave the matter open till he returned (to Arabia).

Among the things they were asking about were panthers, and civet-cats, and rats, and servals, and tiger cats, and such like (whether clean or unclean). He lived with them (many) months (and) every day instructed them well in the Koran and the Traditions, till at length he was informed, "There is another town near this town, it is called Katsina, should the people of the town see you they would believe you and him who sent you." When he heard (them speak) thus, then he made ready, He set out himself to go to it (the town).

When they got news of his coming, then they met with him afar off. When he alighted among them he taught them about what (he had come) to instruct them in. He instructed one who was to write books for them. It was said, speaking of him, he did not write the Koran with his own hand, and because of this the Kano people surpass the Katsina in their knowledge of the Koran till today.

Then, after the completion of his work at Katsina, he went back, going to Kano, (and) remained there a short time. Then when he thought of returning to go to Bornu he said to them, "Shortly I shall return to you with the answer to what you were asking about." Then he rose up and went away.

But many among his people did not follow him, only a few among them followed him. The rest remained and continued to perform great deeds in Kano. Their descendants are found (and) known in Kano until today, till people called them seraphs, but surely they were not seraphs, they were just Arabs. Of a truth Abdulkarimu has set up a judge in Kano, and one to lead in prayers, and one to slaughter (live stock), and one who was to instruct the youths in the Koran, and one to call (them) to prayer.

He made lawful for them that which Allah had made lawful, and forbade that which Allah had forbidden. When he returned to go to Umaru Ibunulasi he gave him an account of what they had asked him about. And Umaru Ibunulasi was silent (on the subject) till he returned to go to the Caliph and then he sent an answer to it (the question) after six months had elapsed. He made lawful for them half of it, half he made unlawful. But Abdulkarimu did not return to Bornu after his return to their (his, Abdulkarimu's) town or to Kano. Thus (also) Umaru Ibunulasi, but he ruled over Egypt after his return home.

Now the remainder of the towns were coming in, half of them to Kano in order to know about the (new) religion, and half also to Katsina, until the creed filled all Hausa-land. Now the Kibi country, speaking of them, they refused (to adopt) the Mohammedan religion, they continued in their paganism. They persisted in it. Their kings, (these) were their names, Barbarma, Argoji, Tabariu, Zartai, Gobari, Dadafani, Katami, Bardo, Kudamdam, Sharia, Badoji, Karfa, Darka, Gunba, Katatar, Tamu. All these refused the Mohammedan creed after his advent into the land of the Hausas.

Then at the time when Zaidu came to the throne [then] he became a Mohammedan and those who were with him. The Kabi country became Mohammedan up to the time of Bata-Musa. These were the kings of Kabi under the Mohammedan régime. The first of them was Zaidu, (then) Muhamadu, Namakata, Sulaimana, Hisrikoma, Abdulabi, Dunbaki, Alia, Usmanu, Chisgari, Barbarmanaba, Muwashi, Muhamadu-Karfi, Bata-Musa.

After them Fumu ruled. He turned Mohammedanism into paganism. These were they who became pagans. The first of them (was) Fumu, (then) Kautai, Gunba, Sakana-Murtamu, Kanta, Rataini, Gaiwa, Gado, Masu, Chi-da-gora, Gaban-gari, Maikebe, Marshakold, Lazimu, Mashirana, Makata. These were they who all continued in paganism.

At the time when Kanta ruled he revived the Mohammedan religion (and) inquired of the learned men the contents of (their) books, He established the faith in his time and in that of them who followed him, till the whole of the Kabi country became Mohammedan. These were their names, Kantahu, Gofe, Dauda, Hamidu, Sulaimana, Mali, Ishaka, Muhamadu-Nashawi, Amuru, Muhamadu-Kabe, Kantanabaiwa, Muhamadu-Shifaya, Hamidu. All these continued in the Mohammedan faith.

When Barbarma, became king he changed the Mohammedan religion (and) became a pagan. Pagranism lasted up to the time of Hudu. He was the one Usmanu the son of Fodio made war against. He drove him out (and pursued him) till he slew him near to Kebi. Buhari the son of Abdu-Salimi, he it was who slew him. He was the king of Jega. His family are its kings till today.

It is finished. But as for Kano in (it) the faith continued after his, Abdulkarimu's, return (home). The faith continued to increase always with force and power. And it lasted on such footing for many years until the time of Mainamugabadi. It was he who changed the order of things Abdulkarimu had set up. He set at naught the law (of Mahomed), he made the kingship all powerful, he disregarded the Mohammedan faith, he exalted fetish worship, and was arrogant. He surpassed (all his predecessors in evil). Instructors endeavoured to instruct him, but their admonitions were of no avail against him, but he increased in pride. He was vainglorious. He continued thus till he died.

His brother Kunbari reigned in his stead and followed in his ways. He too continued in this (evil) till the time of Kunfa. He also spread paganism and evildoing – it was he who married 1,000 maidens. He instructed (people) to prostrate themselves and put earth on their heads before saluting him. He said, let not him whose name happened to be the same as that of his parents be called so, but (let him be called) by some sobriquet. He completely destroyed the creed, he sold free men, he built a palace, the one which the kings of Kano enter today. He did what he wished.

And it was so with all the people of Kano except a very few, speaking of them, they kept to the Mohammedan faith, they were not powerful, only the Kano people did not know how to make beer, except a few among them, men in outlying villages. Thus they did not eat any animal that had died a natural death. They removed the clitoris of their women, they covered their heads with a veil. They did nothing else but this.

They continued in such (conduct) until learned men were found in Kano, who had renounced the world, who feared Allah. (Of these learned men one) his name was Muhamadu-Zari. He stood up and preached. Rumfa paid no heed to whatever admonitions he admonished them. But they planned to kill him, till at last they did kill him in the night by slaying him from behind, in the road to the mosque, and he lay (there) murdered, cast aside, till dawn. He was buried about eight in the morning. His grave is known in Kano, it is visited and watched over, he was called 'the Kalgo man,' blessings are sought by prayers being made for him.

Then Abdulahi-Sako stood up (to proclaim the creed) after him. He was admonishing them but they paid no heed to him, except some people of no importance, but those in authority did not hear. And they frightened him so that he fled to the outlying towns in order to instruct the people of the lesser towns. Then the king sent one to seize him. They seized him, and continually flogged him till he was brought before (the king). He was (by this time) in and died after a few days. His grave is known, (it lies) behind the rock (known as) I the single rock, but it is not visited or watched over.

And so it came to pass that paganism existed till the time of Muhamadu-Alwali. It was he Usmanu, the son of Fodio, made war on, after he had ruled in the kingdom for seventeen years. He (Usmanu-dan-Fodio) drove him out and his men, he fled in the direction of the country on the right and none know where he settled till this day, (some) say Barnabarna (some) say it was not there. The learned men said that from the coming of Abdulkarimu till the coming of Usmanu, the son of Fodio, there were seventy-six kings. All their graves have remained in the town of Kano, but two of them, that of Bawa and Muharnadu-Alwali, are in Katsina.

The creed continued after the return of Abdulkarimu. The faith continued to grow always and took firm hold. Men from Gobir continued to come to Katsina and were adopting the Mohammedan faith with (in all) truth and earnestness, they embraced it, all together. The faith took hold among them also as it had taken hold in Katsina.

And so it was until the time of Agarga. He was the first who changed the state of things that Abdulkarimu had established in Katsina. Instructors (strove) to admonish him. He heard not. He remained in his heathenism till he died.

Kaura ruled the kingdom, and (then) his son; he followed the path his father had taken. Paganism continued till the time of Wari-mai-kworia. It was he who did evil and was most arrogant. He married 1,000 maidens. He embraced evil (and) did not cease. He sought for (a) medicine in order that he might go on living in the world and not die, till (at last) a certain wizard deceived him, saying he would never die, That doctor did for him what he did from (his knowledge of) medicines.

This king gave him much wealth, it was said 100 slaves, 100 female slaves, 100 horses, 100 black robes, and 100 cattle, cows and bulls a hundred, and 1,000 rams, and 1,000 goats. He gave him robes which could not be counted by reason of their number, and things of this description, Allah he know (what all).

In his reign two learned men made their appearance in Katsina, men who renounced the world (and) who feared Allah. The name of one was Muhamadu Ibnumusina, the name of the other also was Muhamadu Dunmurna. Each one among them gave instruction, (such) instruction as enters into the heart. He did not hear them. Then they made them afraid in order to dissuade them from preaching. They did not desist. The kings also did not pay any attention till these learned men died. In Katsina their graves are known till today, where young and old visit and guard, and at which blessings are sought by prayers for them.

Now Wari-mai-kworia, speaking of him, he lived eight years after he had had the medicine made for him to prevent his dying. He died the ninth year after (taking) it. When he died a quarrel about the kingdom arose among the king's sons. Half were slaying the other half until about 1,000 men were killed in the town of Katsina among both free men and slaves. Then the younger brother of Wari ruled after slaying the son of Wari.

He again continued in heathenism. (And) heathenism continued in Katsina till the reign of Bawa-Dungaimawa. It was he Usmanu, the son of Fodio, drove out of Katsina, he and his men, they went to Maradi, they settled there until today. His descendants continue to make war on the descendants of Usmanu, the son of Fodio, till today.

But the (men of) Gobir assembled together and continued in the faith and dwelt in it till the reign of Babari. He was the first who changed the true faith, it became lax, he exalted (and) set up paganism (and) was arrogant. The preachers (of the faith) preached to him but he would not receive (their instructions), but persisted in his heathenism till he died.

Bachira ruled over the kingdom, he did what his predecessor had done, he added to the evil he had done, and the harm, the foam from the wave of heathenism rose in the land of Gobir, its kings were proud. They sold free men, they acted as they wished until report had it that every king that ruled married one hundred maidens. But (the only redeeming point was) they did not know how to make beer, except a few among them, (and) they did not eat animals that had died a natural death, but when they greeted (their kings) they poured earth over their heads, they served idols.

(Some) who cleaved to the faith were (still) among them, at that time only a few (and) without power or influence among them. And they continued thus till the time of Bawajan-gwarzo. He went on (living) in heathenism. He was arrogant till a learned man was found in his reign, one who had fled from the world, one who served Allah. He was called Alhaji-jibrilu. It was said, speaking of him, he went from Gobir, he came to Mecca and performed the pilgrimage and resided (away) there twenty years. It was said he lived in Egypt eighteen years. He stayed in Mecca two years, and then returned to Gobir. He instructed them each new day and night, in secret and openly. They refused the thing (message) he brought and thought to kill him.

All the kings of Hausa(land) plotted to slay him. They could not. The malamai were in Kalawa at that time, but they could not speak from their (store) of knowledge for fear of the chiefs. Only Alhaji-Jibrilu, speaking of him, he stood (fast) in (his) preaching and strove openly (and) they were not able to kill him. He could not, however, prevent them (doing) the evil they dwelt in. And they continued in evildoing and heathenism in this reign.

(Then) Usmanu, the son of Fodio, was born at the time when Alhajijibrilu died. Usmanu, the son of Fodio, began to preach little by little till (the time when) Bawa-jan-gwarzo died. His brother Yaakubu reigned in his stead. Then Usmanu proclaimed (his) preaching openly till he did what (all the world knows) he did (and) finished. We have drawn the history to a close.

Allah, he is the one who knows all. It is finished.
The salvation and blessing of Allah
be upon
the prophet.
Amen.

Translated by R. Sutherland Rattray

How Brothers and Sisters First Came to Quarrel and Hate Each Other

Maalam Shaihua, Hausa People, Nigeria

THIS TALE IS ABOUT A MAIDEN. A certain man had three children, two boys and a girl, and it was the girl he loved. Then one day their big brother went with them to the forest, telling them to come for sticks. And when they had reached the forest, he seized the girl, climbed a tree with her, and tied her on to the tree, and came and said, "The maiden has been lost in the forest," and they said they did not see her, so they came home.

They were weeping. Then their father asked them what had happened, and they said, "Our young sister she was lost in the forest and we did not see her. We searched until we were tired, but we did not see her."

Then their father said, "It cannot be helped." Then one day traders came and were passing in the forest. The girl heard their voices and she sang, "You, you, you, who are carrying kola nuts, if you have come to the village on the hill, greet my big brother Hallabau, greet my big brother Tanka-baka, and greet my big brother Shadusa." When the traders heard this they said that birds were the cause of this singing. Then again she repeated the song. Then the leader of the caravan said he would go and see what it was that was singing thus.

So he went off and came across the maiden fastened to the tree. And he said, "Are you alive or dead?" The maiden said, "Alive, alive." So the leader of the caravan himself climbed up the tree and untied her. Now long ago the caravan leader had wished for offspring, but he was childless. Then he said, "Where is the maiden from?"

And the maiden said, "Our father begat us, we were three, two boys by one mother, I also alone, by my mother. Our father and mother loved me, but did not love my brothers. And because of that our big brother brought me here, deceiving me by saying we were going for sticks. He came with me here, tied me to a tree and left me. Our father is a wealthy man, and because of that, my brother did this to me." Then the leader of the caravan said, "As for me, you have become my daughter."

So the leader of the caravan took her home and nursed her till she recovered. She remained with him until she reached a marriageable age, and grew into a maid whose like was nowhere. And whenever she was heard of, people came to look on her, until a day when her elder brother reached manhood. He had not found a wife. Then he heard the report which said that a certain wealthy man had a daughter in such and such a village; in all the country there was not her like. Then he went to his father and said he had heard about the daughter of a certain wealthy man and it was her he wished to marry.

So his father gave him gifts, and he came to seek a wife in marriage. And Allah blessed his quest and he found what he sought, and the maid was wedded to him. They came home, but when he would consummate their union, she would not give herself to him; and it was always thus. Only, when they all went off to the farms she would lift her mortar and golden pestle which her father had given her, saying she was going to make 'fura' cakes. And she poured the grain into the mortar of gold and pounded and sung, "Pound, pound, mortar, father has become the father of my husband, alas for me! Mother has become the mother of my husband, alas, my mortar!" And so on till she had finished pounding. She was weeping and singing.

Now a certain old woman of the place heard what she was saying. It was always so, until one day she told the mother of the girl's husband, and she said, "When you are all about to go to the farm, do you, mother of the husband, come out, give her grain, and bid her pound 'fura,' as you are going to the farm. When you get outside steal away and come back, enter the house, and remain silent and hear what she says." So the mother of the man came out, their father came out, the boys and the woman all came out, and said they were off to the farm.

A little while after the man's mother came back and entered the hut and crouched down. Then the maiden lifted her mortar and golden pestle. She was singing and saying, "Pound, pound, my mortar, father has become my husband's father, alas, my mortar! Mother has become my husband's mother, alas for me!" She was singing thus and shedding tears, the mother also was in the room and was watching her until she had done all she had to do.

When the people of the house who had gone to the farms came back, the mother did not say anything. When night came, then she told her husband; she said, "Such and such the maid did." The father said, "Could it possibly be the maid who was lost?" Then they said, "But if it is she there is a certain mark on her back ever since she was an infant, she had been left in a house with a fire and it had burned her."

She was summoned. They adjured her by Allah and the Prophet and said, "This man who gave you in marriage, is he your father or were you given to him to be brought up only?" But the maiden refused to answer. Try as they could they could not get an answer. Then the father said, "Present your back that I may see."

She turned her back, and they saw the scar where the fire had burned her when she was an infant. Then they said, "Truly it is so. From the first when you came why did you refuse to tell us?" And they knew it was their daughter. And they sent to her foster father, the one who had found her, and he was told what had happened. And he said, "There is no harm done. I beg you give me the maiden. If I have found another I shall give her to the husband." But the girl's real father and mother refused to consent to this.

As for the husband, when he heard this he took his quiver and bow. He went into the forest and hanged himself. He died. And this was the beginning of hatred among the children of one father by different mothers.

Translated by R. Sutherland Rattray

Creation Story of the Mixtecs

Aztec

WHEN THE EARTH HAD ARISEN from the primeval waters, one day the deer-god, who bore the surname Puma-Snake, and the beautiful deer-goddess, or Jaguar-Snake, appeared. They had human form, and with their great knowledge (that is, with their magic) they raised a high cliff over the water, and built on it fine palaces for their dwelling. On the summit of this cliff they laid a copper axe with the edge upward, and on this edge the heavens rested. The palaces stood in Upper Mixteca, close to Apoala, and the cliff was called Place where the Heavens Stood. The gods lived happily together for many centuries, when it chanced that two little boys were born to them, beautiful of form and skilled and experienced in the arts. From the days of their birth they were named Wind-Nine-Snake (Viento de Neuve Culebras) and Wind-Nine-Cave (Viento de Neuve Cavernas). Much care was given to their education, and they possessed the knowledge of how to change themselves into an eagle or a snake, to make themselves invisible, and even to pass through solid bodies.

After a time these youthful gods decided to make an offering and a sacrifice to their ancestors. Taking incense vessels made of clay, they filled them with tobacco, to which they set fire, allowing it to smoulder. The smoke rose heavenward, and that was the first offering (to the gods). Then they made a garden with shrubs and flowers, trees and fruit-bearing plants, and sweet-scented herbs. Adjoining this they made a grass-grown level place (*un prado*), and equipped it with everything necessary for sacrifice. The pious brothers lived contentedly on this piece of ground, tilled it, burned tobacco, and with prayers, vows, and promises they supplicated their ancestors to let the light appear, to let the water collect in certain places and the earth be freed from its covering (water), for they had no more than that little garden for their subsistence. In order to strengthen their prayer they pierced their ears and their tongues with pointed knives of flint, and sprinkled the blood on the trees and plants with a brush of willow twigs.

The deer-gods had more sons and daughters, but there came a flood in which many of these perished. After the catastrophe was over the god who is called the Creator of All Things formed the heavens and the earth, and restored the human race.

Collected by Lewis Spence

The Mayan Creation Story

Maya

WE ARE TOLD THAT THE GOD HURAKAN, the mighty wind, a deity in whom we can discern a Kiche (Mayan from Guatemala) equivalent to Tezcatlipoca, passed over the universe, still wrapped in gloom. He called out "Earth," and the solid land appeared.

Then the chief gods took counsel among themselves as to what should next be made. These were Hurakan, Gucumatz or Quetzalcoatl, and Xpiyacoc and Xmucane, the mother and father gods. They agreed that animals should be created. This was accomplished, and they next turned their attention to the framing of man. They made a number of mannikins carved out of wood. But these were irreverent and angered the gods, who resolved to bring about their downfall.

Then Hurakan (The Heart of Heaven) caused the waters to be swollen, and a mighty flood came upon the mannikins. Also a thick resinous rain descended upon them. The bird Xecotcovach tore out their eyes, the bird Camulatz cut off their heads, the bird Cotzbalam devoured their flesh, the bird Tecumbalam broke their bones and sinews and ground them into powder. Then all sorts of beings, great and small, abused the mannikins. The household utensils and domestic animals jeered at them, and made game of them in their plight. The dogs and hens said: "Very badly have you treated us and you have bitten us. Now we bite you in turn." The millstones said: "Very much were we tormented by you, and daily, daily, night and day, it was squeak, screech, screech, holi, holi, huqi, huqi, for your sake. Now you shall feel our strength, and we shall grind your flesh and make meal of your bodies." And the dogs growled at the unhappy images because they had not been fed, and tore them with their teeth. The cups and platters said: "Pain and misery you gave us, smoking our tops and sides, cooking us over the fire, burning and hurting us as if we had no feeling. Now it is your turn, and you shall burn."

The unfortunate mannikins ran hither and thither in their despair. They mounted upon the roofs of the houses, but the houses crumbled beneath their feet; they tried to climb to the tops of the trees, but the trees hurled them down; they were even repulsed by the caves, which closed before them. Thus this ill-starred race was finally destroyed and overthrown, and the only vestiges of them which remain are certain of their progeny, the little monkeys which dwell in the woods.

Collected by Lewis Spence

The Myth of Huathiacuri

Inca

AFTER THE DELUGE the Indians chose the bravest and richest man as leader. This period they called Purunpacha (the time without a king). On a high mountain-top appeared five large eggs, from one of which Paricaca, father of Huathiacuri, later emerged. Huathiacuri, who was so poor that he had not means to cook his food properly, learned much wisdom from his father, and the following story shows how this assisted him.

A certain man had built a most curious house, the roof being made of yellow and red birds' feathers. He was very rich, possessing many llamas, and was greatly esteemed on account of his wealth. So proud did he become that he aspired to be the creator himself; but when he became very ill and could not cure himself his divinity seemed doubtful. Just at this time Huathiacuri was travelling about, and one day he saw two foxes meet and listened to their conversation. From this he heard about the rich man and learned the cause of his illness, and forthwith he determined to go on to find him. On arriving at the curious house he met a lovely young girl, one of the rich man's daughters. She told him about her father's illness, and Huathiacuri, charmed with her, said he would cure her father if she would only give him her love. He looked so ragged and dirty that she refused, but she took him to her father and informed him that Huathiacuri said he could cure him. Her father consented to give him an opportunity to do so. Huathiacuri began his cure by telling the sick man that his wife had been unfaithful, and that there were two serpents hovering above his house to devour it, and a toad with two heads under his grinding-stone. His wife at first indignantly denied the accusation, but on Huathiacuri reminding her of some details, and the serpents and toad being discovered, she confessed her guilt. The reptiles were killed, the man recovered, and the daughter was married to Huathiacuri.

Huathiacuri's poverty and raggedness displeased the girl's brother-in-law, who suggested to the bridegroom a contest in dancing and drinking. Huathiacuri went to seek his father's advice, and the old man told him to accept the challenge and return to him. Paricaca then sent him to a mountain, where he was changed into a dead llama. Next morning a fox and its vixen carrying a jar of *chicha* came, the fox having a flute of many pipes. When they saw the dead llama they laid down their things and went toward it to have a feast, but Huathiacuri then resumed his human form and gave a loud cry that frightened away the foxes, whereupon he took possession of the jar and flute. By the aid of these, which were magically endowed, he beat his brother-in-law in dancing and drinking.

Then the brother-in-law proposed a contest to prove who was the handsomer when dressed in festal attire. By the aid of Paricaca Huathiacuri found a red lion-skin, which gave him the appearance of having a rainbow round his head, and he again won.

The next trial was to see who could build a house the quickest and best. The brother-in-law got all his men to help, and had his house nearly finished before the other had his foundation laid. But here again Paricaca's wisdom proved of service, for Huathiacuri got animals and birds of all kinds to help him during the night, and by morning the building was finished except the roof. His brother-in-law got many llamas to come with straw for his roof, but Huathiacuri ordered an animal to stand where its loud screams frightened the llamas away, and the straw was lost. Once more Huathiacuri won the day. At last Paricaca advised Huathiacuri to end this conflict, and he asked his brother-in-law to see who could dance best in a blue shirt with white cotton round the loins. The rich man as usual appeared first, but when Huathiacuri came in he made a very loud noise and frightened him, and he began to run away. As he ran Huathiacuri turned him into a deer. His wife, who had followed him, was turned into a stone, with her head on the ground and her feet in the air, because she had given her husband such bad advice.

The four remaining eggs on the mountain-top then opened, and four falcons issued, which turned into four great warriors. These warriors performed many miracles, one of which consisted in raising a storm which swept away the rich Indian's house in a flood to the sea.

Collected by Lewis Spence

A Story of the Rise and Fall of the Toltecs

Aztec

THE TOLTECS, Ixtlilxochitl says, founded the magnificent city of Tollan in the year 566 of the Incarnation. This city, the site of which is now occupied by the modern town of Tula, was situated north-west of the mountains which bound the Mexican valley. Thither were the Toltecs guided by the powerful necromancer Hueymatzin (Great Hand), and under his direction they decided to build a city upon the site of what had been their place of bivouac.

For six years they toiled at the building of Tollan, and magnificent edifices, palaces, and temples arose, the whole forming a capital of a splendour unparalleled in the New World. The valley wherein it stood was known as the 'Place of Fruits', in allusion to its great fertility. The surrounding rivers teemed with fish, and the hills which encircled this delectable site sheltered large herds of game. But as yet the Toltecs were without a ruler, and in the seventh year of their occupation of the city the assembled chieftains took counsel together, and resolved to surrender their power into the hands of a monarch whom the people might elect. The choice fell upon Chalchiuh Tlatonac (Shining Precious Stone), who reigned for fifty-two years.

Legends of Toltec Artistry

HAPPILY SETTLED in their new country, and ruled over by a king whom they could regard with reverence, the Toltecs made rapid progress in the various arts, and their city began to be celebrated far and wide for the excellence of its craftsmen and the beauty of its architecture and pottery. The name of 'Toltec', in fact, came to be regarded by the surrounding peoples as synonymous with 'artist', and as a kind of hall-mark which guaranteed the superiority of any article of Toltec workmanship. Everything in and about the city was eloquent of the taste and artistry of its founders. The very walls were encrusted with rare stones, and their masonry was so beautifully chiselled and laid as to resemble the choicest mosaic. One of the edifices of which the inhabitants of Tollan were most justly proud was the temple wherein their high-priest officiated. This building was a very gem of architectural art and mural decoration. It contained four apartments. The walls of the first were inlaid with gold, the second with precious stones of every description, the third with beautiful sea-shells of all conceivable hues and of the most brilliant and tender shades encrusted in bricks of silver, which sparkled in the sun in such a manner as to dazzle the eyes of beholders. The fourth apartment was formed of a brilliant red stone, ornamented with shells.

The House of Feathers

STILL MORE FANTASTIC and weirdly beautiful was another edifice, 'The House of Feathers'. This also possessed four apartments, one decorated with feathers of a brilliant yellow, another with the radiant and sparkling hues of the Blue Bird. These were woven into a kind of tapestry, and placed against the walls in graceful hangings. An apartment described as of entrancing beauty was that in which the decorative scheme consisted of plumage of the purest and most dazzling white. The remaining chamber was hung with feathers of a brilliant red.

Huemac the Wicked

A SUCCESSION OF MORE or less able kings succeeded the founder of the Toltec monarchy, until in ad 994 Huemac II ascended the throne of Tollan. He ruled first with wisdom, and paid great attention to the duties of the state and religion. But later he fell from the high place he had made for himself in the regard of the people by his faithless deception of them and his intemperate and licentious habits. The provinces rose in revolt, and many signs and gloomy omens foretold the downfall of the city. Toveyo, a cunning sorcerer, collected a great concourse of people near Tollan, and by dint of beating upon a magic drum until the darkest hours of the night, forced them to dance to its sound until, exhausted by their efforts, they fell headlong over a dizzy precipice into a deep ravine, where they were turned into stone. Toveyo also maliciously destroyed a stone bridge, so that thousands of people fell into the river beneath and were drowned. The neighbouring volcanoes burst into eruption, presenting a frightful aspect, and grisly apparitions could be seen among the flames threatening the city with terrible gestures of menace.

The rulers of Tollan resolved to lose no time in placating the gods, whom they decided from the portents must have conceived the most violent wrath against their capital. They therefore ordained a great sacrifice of war-captives. But upon the first of the victims being placed upon the altar a still more terrible catastrophe occurred. In the method of sacrifice common to the Nahua race the breast of a youth was opened for the purpose of extracting the heart, but no such organ could the officiating priest perceive. Moreover the veins of the victim were bloodless. Such a deadly odour was exhaled from the corpse that a terrible pestilence arose, which caused the death of thousands of Toltecs. Huemac, the unrighteous monarch who had brought all this suffering upon his folk, was confronted in the forest by the Tlalocs, or gods of moisture, and humbly petitioned these deities to spare him, and not to take from him his wealth and rank. But the gods were disgusted at the callous selfishness displayed in his desires, and departed, threatening the Toltec race with six years of plagues.

The Plagues of the Toltecs

IN THE NEXT winter such a severe frost visited the land that all crops and plants were killed. A summer of torrid heat followed, so intense in its suffocating fierceness that the streams were dried up and the very rocks were melted. Then heavy rain-storms descended, which flooded the streets and ways, and terrible tempests swept through the land. Vast numbers of loathsome toads invaded the valley, consuming the refuse left by the destructive frost and heat, and entering the very houses of the people. In the following year a terrible drought caused the death of thousands from starvation, and the ensuing winter was again a marvel of severity. Locusts descended in cloud-like swarms, and hail- and thunder-storms completed the wreck. During these visitations nine-tenths of the people perished, and all artistic endeavour ceased because of the awful struggle for food.

King Acxitl

WITH THE CESSATION of these inflictions the wicked Huemac resolved upon a more upright course of life, and became most assiduous for the welfare and proper government of his people. But he had announced that Acxitl, his illegitimate son, should succeed him, and had further resolved to abdicate at once in favour of this youth. With the Toltecs, as with most primitive peoples, the early kings were regarded as divine, and the attempt to place on the throne one who was not of the royal blood was looked upon as a serious offence against the gods. A revolt ensued, but its two principal leaders were bought over by promises of preferment. Acxitl ascended the throne, and for a time ruled wisely. But he soon, like his father, gave way to a life of dissipation, and succeeded in setting a bad example to the members of his court and to the priesthood, the vicious spirit communicating itself to all classes of his subjects and permeating every rank of society. The iniquities of the people of the capital and the enormities practised by the royal favourites caused such scandal in the outlying provinces that at length they broke into open revolt, and Huehuetzin, chief of an eastern viceroyalty, joined to himself two other malcontent lords and marched upon the city of Tollan at the head of a strong force. Acxitl could not muster an army sufficiently powerful to repel the rebels, and was forced to resort to the expedient of buying them off with rich presents, thus patching up a truce. But the fate of Tollan was in the balance. Hordes of rude Chichimec savages, profiting by the civil broils in the Toltec state, invaded the lake region of Anahuac, or Mexico, and settled upon its fruitful soil. The end was in sight!

A Terrible Visitation

THE WRATH OF the gods increased instead of diminishing, and in order to appease them a great convention of the wise men of the realm met at Teotihuacan, the sacred city of the Toltecs. But during their deliberations a giant of immense proportions rushed into their midst, and, seizing upon them by scores with his bony hands, hurled them to the ground, dashing their brains out. In this manner he slew great numbers, and when the panic-stricken folk imagined themselves delivered from him he returned in a different guise and slew many more. Again the grisly monster appeared, this time taking the form of a beautiful child. The people, fascinated by its loveliness, ran to observe it more closely, only to discover that its head was a mass of corruption, the stench from which was so fatal that many were killed outright. The fiend who had thus plagued the Toltecs at length deigned to inform them that the gods would listen no longer to their prayers, but had fully resolved to destroy them root and branch, and he further counselled them to seek safety in flight.

Fall of the Toltec State

BY THIS TIME the principal families of Tollan had deserted the country, taking refuge in neighbouring states. Once more Huehuetzin menaced Tollan, and by dint of almost superhuman efforts old King Huemac, who had left his retirement, raised a force sufficient to face the enemy. Acxitl's mother enlisted the services of the women of the city, and formed them into a regiment of Amazons. At the head of all was Acxitl, who divided his forces, despatching one portion to the front under his commander-in-chief, and forming the other into a reserve under his own leadership. During three years the king defended Tollan against the combined forces of the rebels and the semi-savage Chichimecs. At length the Toltecs, almost decimated, fled after a final desperate battle into the marshes of Lake Tezcuco and the fastnesses of the mountains. Their other cities were given over to destruction, and the Toltec empire was at an end.

The Chichimec Exodus

MEANWHILE THE RUDE Chichimecs of the north, who had for many years carried on a constant warfare with the Toltecs, were surprised that their enemies sought their borders no more, a practice which they had engaged in principally for the purpose of obtaining captives for sacrifice. In order to discover the reason for this suspicious quiet they sent out spies into Toltec territory, who returned with the amazing news that the Toltec domain for a distance of six hundred miles from the Chichimec frontier was a desert, the towns ruined and empty and their inhabitants scattered. Xolotl, the Chichimec king, summoned his chieftains to his capital, and, acquainting them with what the spies had said, proposed an expedition for the purpose of annexing the abandoned land. No less than 3,202,000 people composed this migration, and only 1,600,000 remained in the Chichimec territory.

The Chichimecs occupied most of the ruined cities, many of which they rebuilt. Those Toltecs who remained became peaceful subjects, and through their knowledge of commerce and handicrafts amassed considerable wealth. A tribute was, however, demanded from them, which was peremptorily refused by Nauhyotl, the Toltec ruler of Colhuacan; but he was defeated and slain, and the Chichimec rule was at last supreme.

The Disappearance of the Toltecs

THE TRANSMITTERS of this legendary account give it as their belief, which is shared by some authorities of standing, that the Toltecs, fleeing from the civil broils of their city and the inroads of the Chichimecs, passed into Central America, where they became the founders of the civilization of that country, and the architects of the many wonderful cities the ruins of which now litter its plains and are encountered in its forests.

Collected by Lewis Spence

The Creation Story of The Third Book

Maya

THE OPENING OF THE THIRD BOOK of the *Popol Vuh* finds the gods once more deliberating as to the creation of man. Four men are evolved as the result of these deliberations. These beings were moulded from a paste of yellow and white maize, and were named Balam-Quitze (Tiger with the Sweet Smile), Balam-Agab (Tiger of the Night), Mahacutah (The Distinguished Name), and Iqi-Balam (Tiger of the Moon).

But the god Hurakan who had formed them was not overpleased with his handiwork, for these beings were too much like the gods themselves. The gods once more took counsel, and agreed that man must be less perfect and possess less knowledge than this new race. He must not become as a god. So Hurakan breathed a cloud over their eyes in order that they might only see a portion of the earth, whereas before they had been able to see the whole round sphere of the world. After this the four men were plunged into a deep sleep, and four women were created, who were given them as wives. These were Caha-Paluma (Falling Water), Choima (Beautiful Water), Tzununiha (House of the Water), and Cakixa (Water of Parrots, or Brilliant Water), who were espoused to the men in the respective order given above.

These eight persons were the ancestors of the Kiche only, after which were created the forerunners of the other peoples. At this time there was no sun, and comparative darkness lay over the face of the earth. Men knew not the art of worship, but blindly lifted their eyes to heaven and prayed the Creator to send them quiet lives and the light of day. But no sun came, and dispeace entered their hearts. So they journeyed to a place called Tulan-Zuiva (The Seven Caves) – practically the same as Chicomoztoc in the Aztec myth – and there gods were vouchsafed to them. The names of these were Tohil, whom Balam-Quitze received; Avilix, whom Balam-Agab received; and Hacavitz, granted to Mahacutah. Iqi-Balam received a god, but as he had no family his worship and knowledge died out.

The Granting of Fire

GRIEVOUSLY DID the Kiche feel the want of fire in the sunless world they inhabited, but this the god Tohil (The Rumbler, the Fire-god) quickly provided them with. However, a mighty rain descended and extinguished all the fires in the land. These, however, were always supplied again by the thunder-god Tohil, who had only to strike his feet together to produce fire.

The Kiche Babel

TULAN-ZUIVA WAS a place of great misfortune to the Kiche, for here the race suffered alienation in its different branches by reason of a confounding of their speech, which recalls the story of Babel. Owing to this the first four men were no longer able to comprehend each other, and determined to leave the place of their mischance and to seek the leadership of the god Tohil into another and more fortunate sphere. In this journey they met with innumerable hardships. They had to cross many lofty mountains, and on one occasion had to make a long *detour* across the bed of the ocean, the waters of which were miraculously divided to permit of their passage. At last they arrived at a mountain which they called Hacavitz, after one of their deities, and here they remained, for it had been foretold that here they should see the sun. At last the luminary appeared. Men and beasts went wild with delight, although his beams were by no means strong, and he appeared more like a reflection in a mirror than the strong sun of later days whose fiery beams speedily sucked up the blood of victims on the altar. As he showed his face the three tribal gods of the Kiche were turned into stone, as were the gods or totems connected with the wild animals. Then arose the first Kiche town, or permanent dwelling-place.

The Last Days of the First Men

TIME PASSED, and the first men of the Kiche race grew old. Visions came to them, in which they were exhorted by the gods to render human sacrifices, and in order to obey the divine injunctions they raided the neighbouring lands, the folk of which made a spirited resistance. But in a great battle the Kiche were miraculously assisted by a horde of wasps and hornets, which flew in the faces of their foes, stinging and blinding them, so that they could not wield weapon nor see to make any effective resistance. After this battle the surrounding races became tributary to them.

Death of the First Men

NOW THE first men felt that their death-day was nigh, and they called their kin and dependents around them to hear their dying words. In the grief of their souls they chanted the song 'Kamucu', the song 'We see', that they had sung so joyfully when they had first seen the light of day. Then they parted from their wives and sons one by one. And of a sudden they were not, and in their place was a great bundle, which was never opened. It was called the 'Majesty Enveloped'. So died the first men of the Kiche.

Collected by Lewis Spence

King Gumbi and His Lost Daughter

Manyema People of the Congo

IT WAS BELIEVED IN THE OLDEN TIME that if a king's daughter had the misfortune to be guilty of ten mistakes, she should suffer for half of them, and her father would be punished for the rest. Now, King Gumbi had lately married ten wives, and all at once this old belief of the elders about troubles with daughters came into his head, and he issued a command, which was to be obeyed upon pain of death, that if any female children should be born to him they should be thrown into the Lualaba, and drowned, for, said he, "the dead are beyond temptation to err, and I shall escape mischief."

To avoid the reproaches of his wives, on account of the cruel order, the king thought he would absent himself, and he took a large following with him and went to visit other towns of his country. Within a few days after his departure there were born to him five sons and five daughters. Four of the female infants were at once disposed of according to the king's command; but when the fifth daughter was born, she was so beautiful, and had such great eyes, and her colour was mellow, so like a ripe banana, that the chief nurse hesitated, and when the mother pleaded so hard for her child's life, she made up her mind that the little infant should be saved. When the mother was able to rise, the nurse hastened her away secretly by night. In the morning the queen found herself in a dark forest, and, being alone, she began to talk to herself, as people generally do, and a grey parrot with a beautiful red tail came flying along, and asked, "What is it you are saying to yourself, O Miami?"

She answered and said, "Ah, beautiful little parrot, I am thinking what I ought to do to save the life of my little child. Tell me how I can save her, for Gumbi wishes to destroy all his female children."

The parrot replied, "I grieve for you greatly, but I do not know. Ask the next parrot you see," and he flew away.

A second parrot still more beautiful came flying towards her, whistling and screeching merrily, and the queen lifted her voice and cried –

"Ah, little parrot, stop a bit, and tell me how I can save my sweet child's life; for cruel Gumbi, her father, wants to kill it."

"Ah, mistress, I may not tell; but there is one comes behind me who knows; ask him," and he also flew to his day's haunts.

Then the third parrot was seen to fly towards her, and he made the forest ring with his happy whistling, and Miami cried out again –

"Oh, stay, little parrot, and tell me in what way I can save my sweet child, for Gumbi, her father, vows he will kill it."

"Deliver it to me," answered the parrot. "But first let me put a small banana stalk and two pieces of sugar-cane with it, and then I shall carry it safely to its grandmamma."

The parrot relieved the queen of her child, and flew through the air, screeching merrier than before, and in a short time had laid the little princess, her banana stalk, and two pieces of sugar-cane in the lap of the grandmamma, who was sitting at the door of her house, and said –

"This bundle contains a gift from your daughter, wife of Gumbi. She bids you be careful of it, and let none out of your own family see it, lest she should be slain by the king. And to remember this day, she requests you to plant the banana stalk in your garden at one end, and at the other end the two pieces of sugar-cane, for you may need both."

"Your words are good and wise," answered granny, as she received the babe.

On opening the bundle the old woman discovered a female child, exceedingly pretty, plump, and yellow as a ripe banana, with large black eyes, and such smiles on its bright face that the grandmother's heart glowed with affection for it.

Many seasons came and went by. No stranger came round to ask questions. The banana flourished and grew into a grove, and each sprout marked the passage of a season, and the sugar-cane likewise throve prodigiously as year after year passed and the infant grew into girlhood. When the princess had bloomed into a beautiful maiden, the grandmother had become so old that the events of long ago appeared to her to be like so many dreams, but she still worshipped her child's child, cooked for her, waited upon her, wove new grass mats for her bed, and fine grass-cloths for her dress, and every night before she retired she washed her dainty feet.

Then one day, before her ears were quite closed by age, and her limbs had become too weak to bear her about, the parrot who brought the child to her, came and rested upon a branch near her door, and after piping and whistling its greeting, cried out, "The time has come. Gumbi's daughter must depart, and seek her father. Furnish her with a little drum, teach her a song to sing while she beats it, and send her forth."

Then granny purchased for her a tiny drum, and taught her a song, and when she had been fully instructed she prepared a new canoe with food – from the bananas in the grove, and the plot of sugar-cane, and she made cushions from grass-cloth bags stuffed with silk-cotton floss for her to rest upon. When all was ready she embraced her grand- daughter, and with many tears sent her away down the river, with four women servants.

Granny stood for a long time by the river bank, watching the little canoe disappear with the current, then she turned and entered the doorway, and sitting down closed her eyes, and began to think of the pleasant life she had enjoyed while serving Miami's child; and while so doing she was so pleased that she smiled, and as she smiled she slept, and never woke again.

But the princess, as she floated down and bathed her eyes, which had smarted with her grief, began to think of all that granny had taught her, and began to sing in a fluty voice, as she beat her tiny drum –

> "List, all you men,
> To the song I sing.
> I am Gumbi's child,
> Brought up in the wild;
> And home I return,
> As you all will learn,
> When this my little drum
> Tells Gumbi I have come, come, come."

The sound of her drum attracted the attention of the fishermen who were engaged with their nets, and seeing a strange canoe with only five women aboard floating down the river, they drew near to it, and when they saw how beautiful the princess was, and noted her graceful, lithe figure clad in robes of fine grass-cloths, they were inclined to lay their hands upon her. But she sang again –

> "I am Gumbi's child,
> Make way for me;
> I am homeward bound,
> Make way for me."

Then the fishermen were afraid and did not molest her. But one desirous of being the first to carry the news to the king, and obtain favour and a reward for it, hastened away to tell him that his daughter was coming to visit him.

The news plunged King Gumbi into a state of wonder, for as he had taken such pains to destroy all female children, he could not imagine how he could be the father of a daughter. Then he sent a quick-footed and confidential slave to inquire, who soon returned and

assured him that the girl who was coming to him was his own true daughter.

Then he sent a man who had grown up with him, who knew all that had happened in

his court; and he also returned and confirmed all that the slave had said. Upon this he resolved to go himself, and when he met her he asked – "Who art thou, child?"

And she replied, "I am the only daughter of Gumbi."

"And who is Gumbi?"

"He is the king of this country," she replied.

"Well, but I am Gumbi myself, and how canst thou be my daughter?" he asked.

"I am the child of thy wife, Miami, and after I was born she hid me that I might not

be cast into the river. I have been living with grandmamma, who nursed me, and by the number of banana-stalks in her garden thou mayest tell the number of the seasons that have passed since my birth. One day she told me the time had come, and she sent me to seek my father; and I embarked in the canoe with four servants, and the river bore me to this land."

"Well," said Gumbi, "when I return home I shall question Miami, and I shall soon discover the truth of thy story; but meantime, what must I do for thee?"

"My grandmamma said that thou must sacrifice a goat to the meeting of the daughter with the father," she replied.

Then the king requested her to step on the shore, and when he saw the flash of her yellow feet, and the gleams of her body, which were like shining bright gum, and gazed on the clear, smooth features, and looked into the wondrous black eyes, Gumbi's heart melted and he was filled with pride that such a surpassingly beautiful creature should be his own daughter.

But she refused to set her feet on the shore until another goat had been sacrificed, for her grandmother had said ill-luck would befall her if these ceremonies were neglected.

Therefore the king commanded that two goats should be slain, one for the meeting with his daughter, and one to drive away ill-luck from before her in the land where she would first rest her feet.

When this had been done, she said, "Now, father, it is not meet that thy recovered daughter should soil her feet on the path to her father's house. Thou must lay a grass-cloth along the ground all the way to my mother's door."

The king thereupon ordered a grass-cloth to be spread along the path towards the women's quarters, but he did not mention to which doorway. His daughter then moved forward, the king by her side, until they came in view of all the king's wives, and then Gumbi cried out to them – "One of you, I am told, is the mother of this girl. Look on her, and be not ashamed to own her, for she is as perfect as the egg. At the first sight of her I felt like a man filled with pleasantness, so let the mother come forward and claim her, and let her not destroy herself with a lie."

Now all the women bent forward and longed to say, "She is mine, she is mine!" but Miami, who was ill and weak, sat at the door, and said –

"Continue the matting to my doorway, for as I feel my heart is connected with her as by a cord, she must be the child whom the parrot carried to my mother with a banana stalk and two pieces of sugar-cane."

"Yes, yes, thou must be my own mother," cried the princess; and when the grass-cloth was laid even to the inside of the house, she ran forward, and folded her arms around her. When Gumbi saw them together he said, "Truly, equals always come together. I see now by many things that the princess must be right. But she will not long remain with me, I

fear, for a king's daughter cannot remain many moons without suitors."

Now though Gumbi considered it a trifle to destroy children whom he had never seen, it never entered into his mind to hurt Miami or the princess. On the contrary, he was filled with a gladness which he was never tired of talking about. He was even prouder of his daughter, whose lovely shape and limpid eyes so charmed him, than of all his tall sons. He proved this by the feasts he caused to be provided for all the people. Goats were roasted and stewed, the fishermen brought fish without number, the peasants came loaded with weighty bunches of bananas, and baskets of yams, and manioc, and pots full of beans, and vetches, and millet and corn, and honey and palm oil, and as for the fowls – who could count them? The people also had plenty to drink of the juice of the palm, and thus they were made to rejoice with the king in the return of the princess.

It was soon spread throughout Manyema that no woman was like unto Gumbi's

daughter for beauty. Some said that she was of the colour of a ripe banana, others that she was like fossil gum, others like a reddish oil-nut, and others again that her face was more like the colour of the moon than anything else. The effect of this reputation was to bring nearly all the young chiefs in the land as suitors for her hand. Many of them would have been pleasing to the king, but the princess was averse to them, and she caused it to be made known that she would marry none save the young chief who could produce matako (brass rods) by polishing his teeth. The king was very much amused at this, but the chiefs stared in surprise as they heard it.

The king mustered the choicest young men of the land, and he told them it was useless for anyone to hope to be married to the princess unless he could drop brass rods by rubbing his teeth. Though they held it to be impossible that anyone could do such a thing, yet every one of them began to rub his teeth hard, and as they did so, lo! brass rods were seen to drop on the ground from the mouth of one of them, and the people gave a great shout for wonder at it.

The princess was then brought forward, and as the young chief rose to his feet he continued to rub his teeth, and the brass rods were heard to tinkle as they fell to the ground. The marriage was therefore duly proceeded with, and another round of feasts followed, for the king was rich in flocks of goats, and sheep, and in well-tilled fields and slaves.

But after the first moon had waned and gone, the husband said, "Come, now, let us depart, for Gumbi's land is no home for me."

And unknown to Gumbi they prepared for flight, and stowed their canoe with all things needful for a long journey, and one night soon after dark they embarked, and paddled down the river. One day the princess, while she was seated on her cushions, saw a curious nut floating near the canoe, upon which she sprang into the river to obtain it. It eluded her grasp. She swam after it, and the chief followed her as well as he was able, crying out to her to return to the canoe, as there were dangerous animals in the water. But she paid no heed to him, and continued to swim after the nut, until, when she had arrived opposite a village, the princess was hailed by an old woman, who cried, "Ho, princess, I have got what thou seekest. See." And she held the nut up in her hand. Then the princess stepped on shore, and her husband made fast his canoe to the bank.

"Give it to me," demanded the princess, holding out her hand.

"There is one thing thou must do for me before thou canst obtain it."

"What is that?" she asked.

"Thou must lay thy hands upon my bosom to cure me of my disease. Only thus canst thou have it," the old woman said.

The princess laid her hands upon my bosom, and as she did so the old woman was cured of her illness.

"Now thou mayest depart on thy journey, but remember what I tell thee. Thou and thy husband must cling close to this side of the river until thou comest abreast of an island which is in the middle of the entrance to a great lake. For the shore thou seekest is on this side. Once there thou wilt find peace and rest for many years. But if thou goest to the other side of the river thou wilt be lost, thou and thy husband."

Then they re-embarked, and the river ran straight and smooth before them. After some days they discovered that the side they were on was uninhabited, and that their provisions were exhausted, but the other side was cultivated, and possessed many villages and plantations. Forgetting the advice of the old woman, they crossed the river to the opposite shore, and they admired the beauty of the land, and joyed in the odours that came from the gardens and the plantations, and they dreamily listened to the winds that crumpled and tossed the great fronds of banana, and fancied that they had seen no sky so blue. And while they thus dreamed, lo! the river current was bearing them both swiftly along, and they saw the island which was at the entrance to the great lake, and in an instant the beauty of the land which had charmed them had died away, and they now heard the thunderous booming of waters, and saw them surging upward in great sweeps, and one great wave curved underneath them, and they were lifted up, up, up, and dropped down into the roaring abyss, and neither chief nor princess was ever seen again. They were both swallowed up in the deep.

What is the object of such a story? Why, to warn people from following their inclinations. Did not the girl find her father? Did not her father welcome her, and pardon the mother for very joy? Was not her own choice of a husband found for her? Was not the young chief fortunate in possessing such a beautiful wife? Why should they have become discontented? Why not have stayed at home instead of wandering into strange lands of which they knew nothing? Did not the old woman warn them of what would happen, and point to them how they might live in peace once again? But it was all to no purpose. We never know the value of anything until we have lost it. Ruin follows the wilful always. They left their home and took to the river, the river was not still, but moved on, and as their heads were already full of their own thoughts, they could not keep advice.

Collected by Henry M. Stanley

The Adventures of Saruti

The Congo and Central Africa

THESE ARE AMONG THE THINGS that a young Mtongolè (colonel) named Saruti related after his return from an expedition to the frontier of Unyoro, the things that he had witnessed on his journey: Kabaka, I think my charms which my father suspended round my neck must be very powerful. I am always in luck. I hear good stories on my journey, I see strange things which no one else seems to have come across. Now on this last journey, by the time I reached Singo, I came to a little village, and as I was drinking banana wine with the chief, he told me that there were two lions near his village who had a band of hyenas to serve as soldiers under them. They used to send them out in pairs, sometimes to one district, and sometimes to another, to purvey food for them. If the peasants showed fight, they went back and reported to their masters, and the lions brought all their soldiers with them, who bothered them so that they were glad to leave a fat bullock tied to a tree as tribute. Then the lions would take the bullock and give orders that the peasant who paid his tribute should be left in peace. The chief declared this to be a fact, having had repeated proof of it.

At the next place, which is Mbagwè, the man Buvaiya, who is in charge, told me that when he went a short time before to pay his respects to the Muzimu (the oracle) of the district, he met about thirty *kokorwa* on the road, hunting close together for snakes, and that as soon as they saw him, they charged at him, and would have killed him had he not run up a tree. He tells me that though they are not much bigger than rabbits, they are very savage, and make travelling alone very dangerous. I think they must be some kind of small dogs. Perhaps the old men of the court may be better able to tell you what they are.

At the next village of Ngondo a smart boy named Rutuana was brought to me, who was said to have been lately playing with a young friend of the same age at long stick and little stick (tip-cat?). His friend hit the little stick, and sent it a great way, and Rutuana had to fetch it from the long grass. While searching for it, one of those big serpents which swallow goats and calves caught him, and coiled itself around him. Though he screamed out for help, Rutuana laid his stick across his chest, and clutching hold of each end with a hand, held fast to it until help came. His friend ran up a tree, and only helped him by screaming. As the serpent could not break the boy's hold of the stick, he was unable to crush his ribs, because his outstretched arms protected them; but when he was nearly exhausted the villagers came out with spears and shields. These fellows, however, were so stupid that they did not know how to kill the serpent until Rutuana shouted to them: "Quick! draw your bows and shoot him through the neck." A man stepped forward then, and when close to him pierced his throat with the arrow, and as the serpent uncoiled himself to attack the men, Rutuana fell down. The serpent was soon speared, and the boy was carried home. I think that boy will become a great warrior.

At the next village the peasants were much disturbed by a multitude of snakes which had collected there for some reason. They had seen several long black snakes which had taken lodging in the anthills. These had already killed five cows, and lately had taken to attacking the travellers along the road that leads by the anthills, when an Arab, named Massoudi, hearing of their trouble, undertook to kill them. He had some slaves with him, and he clothed their legs with buffalo hide, and placed cooking-pots on their heads, and told them to go among the anthills. When the snakes came out of their holes he shot them one by one. Among the reptiles he killed were three kinds of serpents which possessed horns. The peasants skinned them, and made bags of them to preserve their charms. One kind of horned snake, very thick and short, is said to lay eggs as large as those of fowls. The *mubarasassa*, which is of a greyish colour, is also said to be able to kill elephants.

I then went to Kyengi, beyond Singo, and the peasants, on coming to gossip with me, rather upset me with terrible stories of the mischief done by a big black leopard. It seems that he had first killed a woman, and had carried the body into the bush; and another time had killed two men while they were setting their nets for some small ground game. Then a native hunter, under promise of reward from the chief, set out with two spears to kill him. He did not succeed, but he said that he saw a strange sight. As he was following the track of the leopard, he suddenly came to a little jungle, with an open space in the middle. A large wild sow, followed by her litter of little pigs, was rooting about, and grunting as pigs do, when he saw the monstrous black leopard crawl towards one of the pigs. Then there was a shrill squeal from a piggie, and the mother, looking up, discovered its danger, at which it furiously charged the leopard, clashing her tusks and foaming at the mouth. The leopard turned sharp round, and sprang up a tree. The sow tried to jump up after it, but being unable to reach her enemy in that way, she set about working hard at the roots. While she was busy about it the peasant ran back to obtain a net and assistants, and to get his hunting-dog. When he returned, the sow was still digging away at the bottom of the tree, and had made a great hole all round it. The pigs, frightened at seeing so many men, trotted away into the bush, and the hunter and his friends prepared to catch the leopard. They pegged the net all about the tree, then let loose the dog, and urged him towards the net. As he touched the net, the hunters made a great noise, and shouted, at which the leopard bounded from the tree, and with one scratch of his paw ripped the dog open, sprang over the net, tapped one of the men on the shoulder, and was running away, when he received a wound in the shoulder, and stopped to bite the spear. The hunters continued to worry him, until at last, covered with blood, he lay down and died.

One day's journey beyond Kyengi, I came to the thorn-fenced village of some Watusi shepherds, who, it seems, had suffered much from a pair of lion cubs, which were very fierce. The headman's little boy was looking after some calves when the cubs came and quietly stalked him through the grass, and caught him. The headman took it so much to heart, that as soon as he heard the news he went straight back to his village and hanged himself to a rafter. The Watusi love their families very much, but it seems to be a custom with these herdsmen that if a man takes his own life, the body cannot be buried, and though he was a headman, they carried it to the jungle, and after leaving it for the vultures, they returned and set fire to his hut, and burnt it to the ground. When they had done that, the Watusi collected together and had a long hunt after the young lions, but as yet they have not been able to find them.

When the sun was half-way up the sky, I came from Kyengi to some peasants, who lived near a forest which is affected by the man-monkeys called nziké (gorilla?). I was told by them that the nziké know how to smoke and make fire just as we do. It is a custom among the natives, when they see smoke issuing through the trees, for them to say, "Behold, the nziké is cooking his food." I asked them if it were true that the nziké carried off women to live with them, but they all told me that it was untrue, though the old men sometimes tell such stories to frighten the women, and keep them at home out of danger. Knowing that I was on the king's business, they did not dare tell me their fables.

By asking them all sorts of questions, I was shown to a very old man with a white beard, with whom I obtained much amusement. It appears he is a great man at riddles, and he asked me a great many.

One was, "What is it that always goes straight ahead, and never looks back?"

I tried hard to answer him, but when finally he announced that it was a river, I felt very foolish.

He then asked me, "What is it that is bone outside and meat within?"

The people laughed, and mocked me. Then he said that it was an egg, which was very true.

Another question he gave me was, "What is it that looks both ways when you pass it?" Some said one thing, and some said another, and at last he answered that it was grass. Then he asked me, "What good thing was it which a man eats, and which he constantly fastens his eyes upon while he eats, and after eating, throws a half away?" I thought and considered, but I never knew what it was until he told me that it was a roasted ear of Indian corn.

That old man was a very wise one, and among some of his sayings was that "When people dream much, the old moon must be dying."

He also said that "When the old moon is dying, the hunter need never leave home to seek game, because it is well known that he would meet nothing."

And he further added, that at that time the potter need not try to bake any pots, because the clay would be sure to be rotten.

Some other things which he said made me think a little of their meaning.

He said, "When people have provisions in their huts, they do not say, Let us go into another man's house and rob him."

He also said, "When you see a crook-back, you do not ask him to stand straight, nor an old man to join the dance, nor the man who is in pain, to laugh."

And what he said about the traveller is very true. The man who clings to his own hearth does not tickle our ears, like him who sees many lands, and hears new stories.

The next day I stopped at a village near the little lake of Kitesa's called Mtukura. The chief in charge loved talking so much, that he soon made me as well acquainted with the affairs of his family as though he courted my sister. His people are accustomed to eat frogs and rats, and from the noise in the reeds, and the rustling and squealings in the roof of the hut I slept in, I think there is little fear of famine in that village. Nor are they averse, they tell me, to iguanas and those vile feeders, the hyenas.

It is a common belief in the country that it was Naraki, a wife of Uni, a sultan of Unyoro, who made that lake. While passing through, she was very thirsty, and cried out to her Muzimu (spirit), the Muzimu which attends the kings of Unyoro, and which is most potent. And all at once there was a hissing flight of firestones (meteorites) in the air, and immediately after, there was a fall of a monstrously large one, which struck the ground close to her, and made a great hole, out of which the water spurted and continued leaping up until a lake was formed, and buried the fountain out of sight, and the rising waters formed a river, which has run north from the lake ever since into the Kafu.

Close by this lake is a dark grove, sacred to Muzingeh, the king of the birds. It is said that he has only one eye, but once a year he visits the grove, and after building his house, he commands all the birds from the Nyanzas and the groves, to come and see him and pay their homage. For half a moon the birds, great and small, may be seen following him about along the shores of the lake, like so many guards around a king; and before night they are seen returning in the same manner to the grove. The parrots' cries tell the natives when they come, and no one would care to miss the sight, and the glad excitement among the feathered tribe. But there is one bird, called the Kirurumu, that refuses to acknowledge the sovereignty of the Muzingeh. The other birds have tried often to induce him to associate with the Muzingeh; but Kirurumu always answers that a beautiful creature like himself, with gold and blue feathers, and such a pretty crest, was never meant to be seen in the company of an ugly bird that possesses only one eye.

On the other side of Lake Mtukura is a forest where Dungu, the king of the animals, lives. It is to Dungu that all the hunters pray when they set out to seek for game. He builds first a small hut, and after propitiating him with a small piece of flesh, he asks Dungu that he may be successful. Then Dungu enters into the hunter's head, if he is pleased with the offering, and the cunning of the man becomes great; his nerves stiffen, and his bowels are strengthened, and the game is secured. When Dungu wishes a man to succeed in the hunt, it is useless for the buffalo to spurn the earth and moo, or for the leopard to cover himself with sand in his rage – the spear of the hunter drinks his blood. But the hunter must not forget to pay the tribute to the deity, lest he be killed on the way home.

The friendly chief insisted that I should become his blood-fellow, and stay with him a couple of days. The witch-doctor, a man of great influence in the country, was asked to unite us. He took a sharp little knife, and made a gash in the skin of my right leg, just above the knee, and did the same to the chief, and then rubbed his blood over my wound, and my blood over his, and we became brothers. Among his gifts was this beautiful shield, which I beg Mtesa, my Kabaka, to accept, because I have seen none so beautiful, and it is too good for a colonel whose only hope and wish is to serve his king.

I am glad that I rested there, because I saw a most wonderful sight towards evening. As we were seated under the bananas, we heard a big he-goat's bleat, and by the sound of it we knew that it was neither for fun nor for love. It was a tone of anger and fear. Almost at the same time, one of the boys rushed up to us, and his face had really turned grey from fear, and he cried, "There is a lion in the goat-pen, and the big he-goat is fighting with him." They had forgotten to tell me about this famous goat, which was called Kasuju, after some great man who had been renowned in war, and he certainly was worth speaking about, and Kasuju was well known round about for his wonderful strength and fighting qualities. When we got near the pen with our spears and shields, the he-goat was butting the lion – who was young, for he had no mane – as he might have butted a pert young nanny-goat, and baaing with as full a note as that of a buffalo calf. It appears that Kasuju saw the destroyer creeping towards one of his wives, and dashing at his flank knocked him down. As we looked on from the outside, we saw that Kasuju was holding his own very well, and we thought that we would not check the fight, but prepare ourselves to have a good cast at the lion as he attempted to leave. The lion was getting roused up, and we saw the spring he made: but Kasuju nimbly stepped aside and gave him such a stroke that it sounded like a drum. Then Kasuju trotted away in front of his trembling wives, and as the lion came up, we watched him draw his ears back as he raised himself on his hind feet like a warrior. The lion advanced to him, and he likewise rose as though he would wrestle with him, when Kasuju shot into his throat with so true and fair a stroke, that drove one of his horns deep into the throat. It was then the lion's claws began to work, and with every scratch poor Kasuju's hide was torn dreadfully, but he kept his horn in the wound, and pushed home, and made the wound large. Then the lion sprang free, and the blood spurted all over Kasuju. Blinded with his torn and hanging scalp, and weakened with his wounds, he staggered about, pounding blindly at his enemy, until the lion gave him one mighty stroke with its paw, and sent him headlong, and then seized him by the neck and shook him, and we heard the cruel crunch as the fangs met. But it was the last effort of the lion, for just as Kasuju was lifeless, the lion rolled over him, dead also. Had my friend told me this story, I should not have believed him, but as I saw it with my own eyes, I am bound to believe it. We buried Kasuju honourably in a grave, as we would bury a brave man; but the lion we skinned, and I have got his fur with the ragged hole in the throat.

The singular fight we had witnessed, furnished us all with much matter for talk about lions, and it brought into the mind of one of them a story of a crocodile and lion fight which had happened some time before in the night. Lake Mtukura swarms with crocodiles, and situated as it is in a region of game they must be fat with prey. One night a full-grown lion with a fine mane came to cool his dry throat in the lake, and was quaffing water, when he felt his nose seized by something that rose up from below.

From the traces of the struggle by the water's edge, it must have been a terrible one. The crocodile's long claws had left deep marks, showing how he must have been lifted out of the water, and flung forcibly down; but in the morning both lion and crocodile were found dead, the crocodile's throat wide open with a broad gash, but his teeth still fastened in the lion's nose.

Collected by Henry M. Stanley

The Search for the Home of the Sun

The Congo and Central Africa

MASTER AND FRIENDS. We have an old phrase among us which is very common. It is said that he who waits and waits for his turn, may wait too long, and lose his chance. My tongue is not nimble like some, and my words do not flow like the deep river. I am rather like the brook which is fretted by the stones in its bed, and I hope after this explanation you will not be too impatient with me.

My tale is about King Masama and his tribe, the Balira, who dwelt far in the inmost region, behind (east) us, who throng the banks of the great river. They were formerly very numerous, and many of them came to live among us, but one day King Masama and the rest of the tribe left their country and went eastward, and they have never been heard of since, but those who chose to stay with us explained their disappearance in this way.

A woman, one cold night, after making up her fire on the hearth, went to sleep. In the middle of the night the fire had spread, and spread, and began to lick up the litter on the floor, and from the litter it crept to her bed of dry banana-leaves, and in a little time shot up into flames. When the woman and her husband were at last awakened by the heat, the flames had already mounted into the roof, and were burning furiously. Soon they broke through the top and leaped up into the night, and a gust of wind came and carried the long flames like a stream of fire towards the neighbouring huts, and in a short time the fire had caught hold of every house, and the village was entirely burned. It was soon known that besides burning up their houses and much property, several old people and infants had been destroyed by the fire, and the people were horror-struck and angry.

Then one voice said, "We all know in whose house the fire began, and the owner of it must make our losses good to us."

The woman's husband heard this, and was alarmed, and guiltily fled into the woods.

In the morning a council of the elders was held, and it was agreed that the man in whose house the fire commenced should be made to pay for his carelessness, and they forthwith searched for him. But when they sought for him he could not be found. Then all the young warriors who were cunning in wood-craft, girded and armed themselves, and searched for the trail, and when one of them had found it, he cried out, and the others gathered themselves about him and took it up, and when many eyes were set upon it, the trail could not be lost.

They soon came up to the man, for he was seated under a tree, bitterly weeping.

Without a word they took hold of him by the arms and bore him along with them, and brought him before the village fathers. He was not a common man by any means. He was known as one of Masama's principal men, and one whose advice had been often followed.

"Oh," said everybody, "he is a rich man, and well able to pay; yet, if he gives all he has got, it will not be equal to our loss."

The fathers talked a long time over the matter, and at last decided that to save his forfeited life he should freely turn over to them all his property. And he did so. His plantation of bananas and plantains, his plots of beans, yams, manioc, potatoes, ground-nuts, his slaves, spears, shields, knives, paddles and canoes. When he had given up all, the hearts of the people became softened towards him, and they forgave him the rest.

After the elder's property had been equally divided among the sufferers by the fire, the people gained new courage, and set about rebuilding their homes, and before long they had a new village, and they had made themselves as comfortable as ever.

Then King Masama made a law, a very severe law – to the effect that, in future, no fire should be lit in the houses during the day or night; and the people, who were now much alarmed about fire, with one heart agreed to keep the law. But it was soon felt that the cure for the evil was as cruel as the fire had been. For the houses had been thatched with green banana-leaves, the timbers were green and wet with their sap, the floor was damp and cold, the air was deadly, and the people began to suffer from joint aches, and their knees were stiff, and the pains travelled from one place to another through their bodies. The village was filled with groaning.

Masama suffered more than all, for he was old. He shivered night and day, and his teeth chattered sometimes so that he could not talk, and after that his head would burn, and the hot sweat would pour from him, so that he knew no rest.

Then the king gathered his chiefs and principal men together, and said:

"Oh, my people, this is unendurable, for life is with me now but one continuous ague. Let us leave this country, for it is bewitched, and if I stay longer there will be nothing left of me. Lo, my joints are stiffened with my disease, and my muscles are withering. The only time I feel a little ease is when I lie on the hot ashes without the house, but when the rains fall I must needs withdraw indoors, and there I find no comfort, for the mould spreads everywhere. Let us hence at once to seek a warmer clime. Behold whence the sun issues daily in the morning, hot and glowing; there, where his home is, must be warmth, and we shall need no fire. What say you?"

Masama's words revived their drooping spirits. They looked towards the sun as they saw him mount the sky, and felt his cheering glow on their naked breasts and shoulders, and they cried with one accord: "Let us hence, and seek the place whence he comes."

And the people got ready and piled their belongings in the canoes, and on a certain day they left their village and ascended their broad river, the Lira. Day after day they paddled up the stream, and we heard of them from the Bafanya as they passed by their country, and the Bafanya heard of them for a long distance up – from the next tribe – the Bamoru – and the Bamoru heard about them arriving near the Mountain Land beyond.

Not until a long time afterwards did we hear what became of Masama and his people.

It was said that the Balira, when the river had become shallow and small, left their canoes and travelled by land among little hills, and after winding in and out amongst them they came to the foot of the tall mountain which stands like a grandsire amongst the smaller mountains. Up the sides of the big mountain they straggled, the stronger and more active of them ahead, and as the days passed, they saw that the world was cold and dark until the sun showed himself over the edge of the big mountain, when the day became more agreeable, for the heat pierced into their very marrows, and made their hearts rejoice. The greater the heat became, the more certain were they that they were drawing near the home of the sun. And so they pressed on and on, day after day, winding along one side of the mountain, and then turning to wind again still higher. Each day, as they advanced towards the top, the heat became greater and greater. Between them and the sun there was now not the smallest shrub or leaf, and it became so fiercely hot that finally not a drop of sweat was left in their bodies. One day, when not a cloud was in the sky, and the world was all below them – far down like a great buffalo hide – the sun came out over the rim of the mountain like a ball of fire, and the nearest of them to the top were dried like a leaf over a flame, and those who were behind were amazed at its burning force, and felt, as he sailed over their heads, that it was too late for them to escape. Their skins began to shrivel up and crackle, and fall off, and none of those who were high up on the mountain side were left alive. But a few of those who were nearest the bottom, and the forest belts, managed to take shelter, and remaining there until night, they took advantage of the darkness, when the sun sleeps, to fly from the home of the sun. Except a few poor old people and toddling children, there was none left of the once populous tribe of the Balira.

That is my story. We who live by the great river have taken the lesson, which the end of this tribe has been to us, close to our hearts, and it is this. Kings who insist that their wills should be followed, and never care to take counsel with their people, are as little to be heeded as children who babble of what they cannot know, and therefore in our villages we have many elders who take all matters from the chief and turn them over in their minds, and when they are agreed, they give the doing of them to the chief, who can act only as the elders decree.

Collected by Henry M. Stanley

Nunda the Slayer and Origin of the One-Eyed

Swahili-speaking Peoples, East Africa

ONCE UPON A TIME there was a Sultan, and he had seven sons, and he gave them ships, and they all went abroad to trade, and came back with much wealth, all except the youngest, who brought back only a dog and a cat, and he kept the dog and the cat till they grew and grew, and at last the dog died.

Then he kept the cat, and it grew and grew, till at last one day it ate a whole goat.

And it still grew, till one day the son said to the Sultan, "My father, give me an ox for my cat to eat," and he gave him an ox, and the cat grew and grew, till at last it finished all the camels and oxen of the Sultan.

So the Sultan said to his son, "You must turn that cat out of the town, as it has eaten all our wealth."

So that cat was turned out and went to live in the bush, and there it grew and grew, and it was called Nunda.

Till one day it came into the town and ate everybody in that town, all the people and the Sultan himself and all his sons; but the Sultan's wife was upstairs, and she shut the door and was saved, but everybody else in the town was eaten.

And when the Nunda thought that he had finished everybody he went again into the bush and there he lived.

And the Sultan's wife stayed in the upper storey, and there she gave birth to a son, and she called him Mohammed.

And Mohammed grew up, till one day he said to his mother, "How is it that we two sit alone and there are no other people here?"

And his mother said to him, "Go and open the window and look out." And he opened the window and looked out.

And she said to him, "What do you see?" And he said, "I see many houses."

Then she said to him, "All those houses were once full of people, but the Nunda has killed and eaten them all, even your father and brothers he has eaten."

So Mohammed said, "Did my father have any weapons?" And his mother said, "He used to go to war, and guns and spears and bows and arrows and shields were the weapons he had."

Mohammed said to her, "Bows and arrows are the weapons I want."

So he took a bow and three hundred arrows and set forth, and travelled through the bush, on and on, till one day he met a rhino.

He said to himself, "This must be the Nunda," so he shot his arrows and shot and shot till he had used all his three hundred arrows and the rhino fell dead.

Then he cut off a leg and set out for home, carrying it with him. When he got near the house he sung, "This is Nunda, this is Nunda who kills people."

And his mother, looking out from the upper storey, sang, "My child, that is not Nunda who kills people."

When he came into the house she said, "My son, that is not Nunda; it is a rhino."

So he said, "I will sleep here tonight, and tomorrow I will set out again."

In the morning he took seven bows and one thousand arrows and set out, and travelled and travelled, through forests and plains, till he came to a garden, and there he sat down.

Presently a great dust arose in the hills and came down into the plains.

So Mohammed climbed a tree and waited, saying, "This indeed must be Nunda."

Presently a great animal came out of the dust and came down to the garden to drink, and he drank from three o'clock in the afternoon to six o'clock in the evening.

And Mohammed, up in the tree, said to himself, "If I am to die I am already dead, and if I am to escape I have already escaped;" so he started shooting his arrows, and when he had shot five hundred the animal looked up from drinking, but he did not yet know that he was hit.

So Mohammed took his other five hundred arrows and shot and shot till he had used them all, and then he threw away his bow.

Then the animal arose and went to the tree where Mohammed sat, and jumped and bounded in his pain, but he did not reach him, and in the morning when Mohammed looked down he saw that the animal was dead. Then he descended and cut off a leg, and taking it started for home.

When he got near home he sang, "This is Nunda, this is Nunda who kills people."

And his mother looked out from the upper storey and sang, "My child, that is he, Nunda who eats people."

And she came down to meet him and said, "Hang the leg up in the verandah, and I will go and get you water to wash with."

So he hung up the leg and went inside to wash himself.

And the leg said, "By Allah, I feel cold here." And his mother called out, "Mohammed." "Yes, mother." "Why is the leg talking there in the verandah?"

So Mohammed came out from the bathroom and took the leg and hung it up at the top of the house, and went back to wash.

Presently the leg said, "I hear someone washing there." And his mother called out, "That leg is still talking upstairs."

And Mohammed came out again and said, "Give me my knife; I will cut it open and see what is inside."

So he took his knife and cut open the leg, and there he found his father and brothers and all the people of that town inside the leg; but in cutting it open he stabbed one man in the face and put out his eye.

And this man, when he came out from the leg, was very angry indeed and said, "Why have you put out my eye? See, you have let all the other people out quite whole; but me, you have put out my eye."

And Mohammed said, "I am very sorry. I did not know what was in the leg, and my knife slipped in cutting it open, so now be content that you have escaped and forgive me."

But the man said, "I will not forgive you. You have put out my eye and now you must let me put out your eye."

Mohammed said, "I do not agree."

The man said, "If you don't agree to my putting out your eye we must fight."

Mohammed said, "I don't want many words, so now listen to what I have got to say. Let one of us take a rifle and five cartridges and the other stones, and let us go down to the shore and fight. So now choose which you will take."

So One-eye chose to take the rifle and five rounds, and Mohammed took a cloth and filled it with stones, and they went down to the shore.

And Mohammed said, "Now, One-eye, you have the rifle, you begin."

So One-eye fired the first round and missed, and the second and missed, and so on all five rounds.

Then Mohammed came near with his bag of stones, and hit him here and there and all over, and came closer and stoned him, and hit him in the other eye, putting that out, till he went down on his knees and said, "I repent; I am satisfied."

And this is the beginning of all one-eyed and blind men in the world, and this is how they began.

Collected by Captain C.H. Stigand

Binti Ali the Clever

Swahili-speaking Peoples, East Africa

ONCE UPON A TIME there was a Sultan and his Wazir, and that Sultan had seven children, all sons, and that Wazir had seven children, all daughters.

Those daughters of the Wazir had no mother; their mother had died, and they were very poor.

The sons of the Sultan used to laugh at the daughters of the Wazir, saying, "You poor people, what do you eat? It is our father who pays your father his wages, and how do they suffice for you seven people who are in one house? You poor creatures, you have not even a brother to help you."

Now those girls used to plait baskets and sell them. They lived for many days like that, their work being to cry every day, and when they came out of school they used to plait and sell their baskets. Till one day the youngest daughter, who was called Binti Ali, was sitting with her father, and she said to him, "What advice have you to give us, father?"

Her father asked her, "Why, my child?"

She said to him, "We are only seven girls; we have neither husbands nor brothers. Should anything happen to you, who will be our headman? Father, you must arrange to have a ship built for me, and it must be ready in the space of three years."

Her father said, "All this wealth, where shall I get it from, that I may build a ship?"

She answered him, "God, the merciful, will provide."

In the morning the Wazir arose and went to the Sultan and said to him, "Give me help, for my youngest child wants a vessel built for her."

The Sultan brought out nine lakhs of rupees and gave them to his Wazir. Then the Wazir sought for workmen, and told them to build a ship and have it ready in three years' time.

Now that child, Binti Ali, was very beautiful, more beautiful than all her sisters. Many men had come to seek her in marriage, but she had refused them, saying, "I am poor; my father has not wealth to suffice for my wedding."

At the end of three years the ship was ready, and her father called her, "Eh, my child, Binti Ali." And she answered him, "Lebeka, father," which means "Here I am" in the language of today; but long, long ago, Lebek was the name of the god worshipped by the Phœnicians at the temple of Baal-lebek (Bal bek).

Her father said to her, "Your ship is finished and ready for you."

So she went to see it, and found that it was built in a wondrously fine way. When she returned she said to her father, "Now you must find me a captain and sailors, and you must put on the vessel enough food to last three years."

So he found a crew for her, and provisioned the ship and returned. Then she said, "Father, now you must buy for me fine raiment, a sultan's turban, a shirt and coat, and a sword and dagger. Also you must get for me sandals of gold braid and two men's gold rings."

So her father searched for one hour and half a second, and then returned and said, "My child, the things you want are ready."

Then he asked her, "My child, where are you going to? Tell me."

She said, "Father, have you no understanding? I am going to the country of the Sultan Makami."

Her father said to her, "My child, you are already lost. Do you not know that a woman may not go to the country of Sultan Makami? Any other than a male who enters the country is put to death."

Binti Ali said to him, "Father, have you no wits, you, a full-grown man, who rule all this land? Do you not see that all these clothes which you have bought for me are men's clothes? I want to go and see Makami's country."

Her father said, "I do not approve of this journey you are setting out upon."

His daughter replied, "What becomes of me is in the hands of God."

Then she entered the bathroom and washed herself, and when she came out she was dressed as a man. Now that girl had wisdom more than all her sisters, and she was well read in the Koran.

She took her dog, whose name was Atakalo, and she entered the ship and set sail.

She travelled day and night for three years, and there in the midst of the ocean she taught her dog till it attained great learning.

At the end of the third year she drew near to the country of Sultan Makami, and she ordered a salute to be fired, and the people on land replied also with a salute.

When her vessel drew near, the Sultan's son rowed out to meet her. He climbed on board, and there he saw a handsome Arab youth sitting on the deck.

Binti Ali arose, and they greeted one another after the fashion of men: "Peace be with you," "And with you peace."

She went ashore with that son of the Sultan, and they came to the palace.

When they came to the palace he said to his father, the Sultan, "How shall we see that this is a man and not a woman? Let us give him very hot gruel, and if it is a woman she will not be able to drink it, and then we will kill her."

So they ordered food to be brought, and slaves were told: "Take matting and platters, and very big trays and cups of gold, and place them ready for the feast."

When the food was ready they brought gruel for that foreign youth to drink, and it was very hot.

Binti Ali took it and threw it away, saying, "Am I a woman, that you bring me cold gruel like that?"

So they prepared fresh gruel, steaming hot, and gave it to her, and she said, "Ah, that is more fit for a Sultan's son to drink."

So she put it beside her, and her dog Atakalo blew on it, so that it quickly cooled, and she drank it.

Very good food was then brought, and they fed, and she returned to her ship.

The Sultan then said, "Tomorrow we must take this foreigner to my store of jewels and ornaments, and if it be a woman we will surely see, for she will take delight in women's jewellery."

All night long Binti Ali taught Atakalo what he should do, and in the morning the Sultan's son came to fetch her.

He said, "My father says that I am to take you to his store and show you his treasures."

So they went to the Sultan's treasure-house, where they showed her neck chains and nose pendants, anklets and bracelets, women's gold rings and ear ornaments.

She said, "Have you in this country no men's ornaments, that you should show me nothing but women's jewellery?"

So they brought her to the next store, wherein were gold-hilted daggers and all manner of arms, swords and pistols, guns and muskets. These she admired, and meanwhile Atakalo went and swallowed all the gold ornaments he could find and took them to the ship, till he had brought much wealth aboard.

Then the Sultan's son said to his father, "Now what shall we do, so that we may kill her if she is a woman?"

So the Sultan said, "Make him take off his turban, and then we will surely see by the manner in which he ties it whether it is a woman or not."

So the Sultan's son said, "Now will you not wash?"

Binti Ali said, "Thank you, I have already bathed on board."

So he said, "If it is only your face, I beseech you to wash."

So she said, "Certainly; but first you and your father must wash."

So they took off their turbans and began to wash, when suddenly there was a shout from outside: "The Sultan's house is on fire."

Behold, that dog Atakalo had brought a brand and set fire to the palace. Then the Sultan and his son and all the people in his house rushed out, with their turbans in their hands, to see what was the matter and help put out the flames.

Binti Ali went down swiftly to her ship and got on board, and meanwhile Atakalo had run round and bored a hole in the bottom of every boat and ship in the Sultan's harbour. Then Atakalo came back to her vessel and said, "Mistress, I have finished."

So she weighed anchor and changed into her woman's clothes. The Sultan and his son and all the people, when they saw that she was sailing off, rushed down to the beach and tried to row out and stop her, but every boat they launched sunk; and so they were not able to get to her.

Then they saw her come up on the deck.

Then, changing her clothes as a woman, she sings –

> "Makami, behold my bracelets and rings.
> See my anklets, Makami. Aha, behold!
> See the chain for my neck of beautiful gold.
> Behold now my ear-rings and nose-stud see.
> Lola, Makami, lola, look well at me.
> I'm Binti Ali, the Wazir's daughter;
> I came, Makami, from over the water.
> We are seven in all, the last born am I.
> Farewell, Makami, for I bid you goodbye.
> Lola, Makami, lola, farewell."

Then she said to the captain, "Set sail, and let us return home."

When she arrived home there in her town her father and sisters were holding a great mourning for her, for they said, "Our youngest one has now been away many years; surely she must be dead."

When they saw her their hearts were very glad, and a feast was made for her for the space of three days. And the riches she brought with her, which her dog Atakalo had taken from the Sultan's treasure house, were brought to land; and when he saw them her father rejoiced greatly.

After a space of ten days she said to her father, "I know that Sultan Makami's son is making a plan to get me. If he comes here and asks for me in marriage, do not refuse him, but agree. My cleverness, which I have in my heart, is that which will save me."

One day the Sultan of Makami's son arrived, and came to the Wazir and said, "I want your daughter, Binti Ali, in marriage."

So the Wazir agreed.

Binti Ali took a large pumpkin and filled it with honey and placed it on her bed, and she herself got under the bed.

That night the Sultan of Makami's son came into her room and said, "Ee, woman," and she replied, "Lebeka, master."

Then he said, "You, woman, you think that you can come to our country and cheat us, pretending that you are a man. Behold, today is your last, so make profession of faith quickly, so that you may be prepared for death."

Binti Ali said, "I testify there is no God but one God, and Muhammad is the prophet of God."

So he drew his sword and struck a blow which cut the pumpkin in two, and then he went out quickly and got on his ship and sailed away. When he came to look at his sword, to wipe the blood off, he found no blood, but only honey stuck all over it.

This is the end of the story. The tale comes from the Wazir and his daughter, the last born, who was called Binti Ali the Clever.

Collected by Captain C.H. Stigand

Lila and Fila

Swahili-speaking Peoples, East Africa

THERE WERE ONCE UPON A TIME two poor children, one was called Lila and one was called Fila, and they were great friends. Fila said one day to Lila, "Our mothers are poor; what can we do for a living, my friend? We have no money with which to repay them for the kindness they have shown towards us. We have now become full-grown lads, and have not yet earned any money to give them. I propose that we set out on a journey and see what we can find."

Lila agreed to the words of his friend, and so each one went to his mother and said to her, "Mother, make me seven ladu-cakes, for I am going on a journey to a very far country."

And each mother replied, "Where are you going, my beloved child?"

Lila's mother said to him, "Do not go with Fila."

Lila answered, "I am not able to leave my friend Fila for half a second."

His mother said, "It is he that will leave you, and it is you that will be lost."

He replied, "If a man is lost for the sake of his friend it is well."

So they had each one seven ladu-cakes made for him, and each one took a gourd of water, and on the next day they set out.

After they had gone a day's journey Fila said to Lila, "Bring out one of your ladus, that we may break and eat it. We will eat yours first, and when they are finished then will we eat mine."

So they ate one of Lila's ladus. On the second day they did likewise, and on the next and the next day, until, on the seventh day, all Lila's ladus were finished.

On the eighth day Lila said to Fila, "Bring out one of your ladus, my friend, that we may break and eat it, for all mine are now finished, and hunger is hurting me."

Fila replied, "You must give me that Kanzu shirt of yours first, and then I will give you a share of my ladu."

So Lila took off his Kanzu and gave it to Fila, and then Fila broke off a bit from one of his ladus and gave it to him.

On the next day Lila said, "My friend, I am hungry; bring out the second of your ladus, that we may eat it."

Fila replied, "Today if I am to give you some of my ladu you must give me your vest."

So Lila took off his vest and gave it to Fila, and received a piece of ladu for it.

On the next and the next day it was the same, till, on the twelfth day, Fila had taken away all Lila's clothes.

On the thirteenth day, when Lila asked for some ladu, Fila said, "You must let me put out one of your eyes if you are to have any ladu today."

Lila replied, "I cannot refuse, for I am very hungry."

So Fila put out one of his friend's eyes, and Lila said nothing; he put all his misfortunes in the hand of God.

On the fourteenth day Lila said to Fila, "My friend, have you not treated me evilly? Have you not done wrong? I left my mother to follow you, my friend, and you have deceived me. You have eaten my ladus till they were finished, and now you have taken all my clothes and put out my eye. Will you not today give me a piece of your ladu?"

Fila said, "Yes, I will give you a piece of ladu if you agree to me putting out your other eye."

Lila said to him, "Go on, put out my other eye."

So Fila put out his other eye, and then he sat him down under a tree and put his gourd of water and a piece of ladu beside him and went his way, leaving his friend blind and naked in the road.

Lila sat there awhile, and then he ate his piece of ladu, drank his water, gave praise to God and then slept.

When it was midnight two birds came and perched on the tree, one on one side and one on the other.

The first said, "Eh, my friend, I have a song which I will sing."

The other asked, "What song will you sing?"

Then the first bird looked down and said, "Look, there is a human asleep underneath."

The other said, "Oh, that son of Adam is lying just where those jars of money are buried; just opposite him is the tree whose roots are medicine for mad people, and he is leaning against the eye medicine tree."

Then they flew away; but Lila heard these words, and he groped and took some of the bark of that tree and rubbed it on his eyes, and behold, he could see; both his eyes were whole.

Then he went to the other tree and dug up some of the roots, and after that he dug down where he had been lying and found jars of money. He took a little money, and the rest he covered up and left.

Next day he took the road and journeyed on, and that day he arrived at a town, and there he heard the news that the daughter of the Sultan had been seized with madness.

He was told, "No one is allowed to come to this country unless he knows how to make medicine for the Sultan's daughter. This is now the seventh year since she became mad, and the Sultan has made a vow that he who cures her will marry her, and he who does not cure her will be killed."

So Lila entered that town, and he was at once taken before the Sultan, who asked him, "Can you cure my child?"

He replied, "Master, I do not know medicines, but I will try."

So he was taken in to the Sultan's daughter through seven doors, and he saw her where she had been put. She was fastened with chains on hands and feet.

He gave her of that medicine, and immediately she became cured.

Then the Sultan ordered a feast to be prepared, and he married Lila to his daughter. He himself descended from the throne and put Lila in his place. So Lila became the Sultan of that town.

One day, as he looked out of the palace window, he saw a man passing, and when he came near he recognised that it was his friend Fila.

He told his soldiers to fetch him and bring him before him.

When Fila was brought he said to him, "My friend, do you not recognise me?"

Fila replied, "I do not know you."

Then Lila said, "Is it not I whose eyes you put out?"

Then Fila was very afraid, and said, "Then it is you who will now put out mine."

Lila ordered his soldiers, "Take him out, put out his eyes and leave him in the way."

So they took him out and did as they were bid. After three days they went to look for him and found that he had died.

Lila and Fila, it was not possible for them to mix together, and even today, if there are two people who cannot agree, or two things which cannot go together, it is said of them: "They are like Lila and Fila."

Collected by Captain C.H. Stigand

The Wakilindi Saga:
Mbega, a Child of Ill Omen

Swahili-speaking Peoples, East Africa

MBEGA WOULD, IN ORDINARY CIRCUMSTANCES, have had short shrift, for he cut his upper teeth first, and such infants are, by most of the Bantu, considered extremely unlucky. Indeed, so strong is the belief that if allowed to grow up they would become dangerous criminals that in former times they were invariably put to death.

At Rabai, on the now forsaken site of the old fortified village on the hill top, a steep declivity is pointed out where such ill-omened babies were thrown down. It must have been the rarity of this occurrence that caused it to be regarded as unnatural, and so produced the belief. Mbega's parents, however, no doubt because his father despised such pagan superstitions (he must have been a Moslem, though his sons did not follow his faith), paid no attention to this custom, but on the contrary took every care of him, and he grew up strong and handsome and beloved by everyone, except his half-brothers, the sons of the other wives. Their hostility could not injure him as long as his father lived, but both parents died while he was still a youth. He had a protector, however, in his elder brother, "his brother of the same father and the same mother" – a tie always thus carefully specified in a polygamous society. But this brother died, and the rest took on themselves the disposal of his property, which – along with the guardianship of the widow and children – should naturally have passed to Mbega. They did not even summon him to the funeral.

When all the proper ceremonies had been performed and the time came for "taking away the mourning," which means slaughtering cattle and making a feast for the whole clan, at, or after, which the heir is placed in possession, all the relatives were assembled, but not the slightest notice was taken of the rightful heir. Mbega, naturally, was deeply wounded – the record represents him as saying, "Oh, that my brother were alive! I have no one to advise me, not one; my father is dead, and my mother is dead!" So he went his way home, and wept upon his bed (*akalia kitandani pake*), and was ready to despair.

Mbega Shut out from His Inheritance

THE BROTHERS CHOSE the son of a more distant kinsman to succeed to the property and marry the widow, and handed over to him the dead man's house and a share of his cattle, dividing the rest among themselves. Mbega, hearing of this, as he could not fail to do, consulted with the old men of the village, and sent them to his brothers and the whole clan, with the following message: "Why do they not give me my inheritance? Never once when one of the family died have they called me to the funeral. What wrong have I done?"

When the messengers had finished speaking, those brothers looked each other in the eyes, and every man said to his fellow, "Do you answer." At last one of them spoke up and said, "Listen, ye who have come, and we will tell you. That Mbega of yours is mad. Why should he send you to us instead of coming himself? Tell him that there is no man in our clan named Mbega. We do not want to see him or to have anything to do with him."

The old men asked what Mbega had done, that they should hate him so, and the spokesman replied that he was a sorcerer (*mchawi*) who had caused all the deaths that had taken place in the clan. Anyone might know that he was not a normal human creature, since he was a *kigego* who had cut his upper teeth first; but his parents had been weak enough to conceal the fact and bring him up like any other child. He went on to say that when Mbega's mother died he and the others had consulted a diviner, who told them that Mbega was responsible (a cruel slander on a most affectionate son), and they had represented to their father that he ought to be killed, "but he would not agree through his great love for him." Now that Mbega's parents and his own brother were no more they would take things into their own hands, since, if let alone, he would exterminate the whole clan. They did not wish to have his blood on their hands, but let him depart out of the country on peril of his life, and, as for the messengers: "Do not you come here again with any word from Mbega." They replied, with the quiet dignity of aged councillors, "We shall not come again to you." So they returned to Mbega, who received them with the usual courtesies and would not inquire about their errand till they had rested and been fed and had a smoke. Then they told him all, and he said, "I have heard your words and theirs, and in truth I have no need to send men to them again. I, too, want no dealings with them."

Mbega, a Mighty Hunter

NOW MBEGA, THOUGH hated by his near kinsmen, was beloved by the rest of the tribe, more especially the young men, whom he took with him on hunting expeditions and taught the use of trained dogs, then a novelty in the country. His father, no doubt, had brought some with him from Pemba. The name of Mbega's own favourite dog, Chamfumu, has been preserved. The chronicler adds : "This one was his heart." It does not seem clear whether this phrase merely expresses the degree of his affection for this particular dog, or whether there is some hint that Mbega's life was bound up with him.

The land was sorely plagued with wild beasts, which ravaged the flocks and destroyed the crops. We hear most of the wild swine, which still, in many parts of East Africa, make the cultivator's life a burden to him. Mbega and his band of devoted followers scoured the woods with the dogs, put a stop to the depredations of the animals, and supplied the villagers with meat.

When Mbega's messengers had reported the answer returned by his brothers he called his friends together, told them the whole story, and informed them that he would have to leave the country. They asked where he was going, and he replied that he did not know yet, but would find out by divination, and would then call them together and take leave of them.

We are given to understand that Mbega was highly skilled in magic – white magic, of course – and this may have lent some colour to his brothers' accusations. If the expression he used on this occasion ("I am going to use the sand-board") is to be taken literally it seems to refer to the Arab method of divining by means of sand spread on a board, the knowledge of which Mbega's father may have brought with him from Pemba.

The young men protested against the notion of his leaving them, and declared that they would follow him wherever he went. He was determined not to allow this, knowing it would cause trouble with their parents, but said no more till he had decided on his course. He then consulted the oracle, and determined to direct his steps towards Kilindi, where he was well known. Next day, his friends being assembled, he told them he must leave them. He would not tell them where he was going, in case they should be asked by his brothers. They were very unwilling to agree to this, insisting that they would go with him, but were persuaded at last to give way. He sent for all his dogs and distributed them among the young men, keeping for himself seven couples, among them the great Chamfumu, "who was his heart." He also gave them his recipes for hunting magic.

Mbega Goes to Kilindi

SO MBEGA WENT forth, carrying his spears, large and small, and his dog bells, and his wallet of charms, and, followed by his pack, came on the evening of the second day to the gate of Kilindi town. It was already shut for the night, and, though those within answered his call, they hesitated to admit him till he had convinced them that he was indeed Mbega of Nguu, the hunter of the wild boar. Then the gate was thrown open, and the whole town rushed to welcome him, crying, "It is he! It is he!" They escorted him to the presence of the chief, who greeted him warmly, assigned him a dwelling, and gave orders that everything possible should be done to honour him. So they gave him a house, with bedsteads and Zigula mats – about all that was usual in the way of furniture – and when all the people summoned for the occasion had gone their several ways rejoicing, Mbega rested for two or three days.

He remained at Kilindi for many months, and not only cleared the countryside of noxious beasts, but secured the town by his magic against human and other enemies. He possessed the secret of raising such a thick mist as to render it invisible to any attacking force, and could supply charms to protect men and cattle from lions and leopards. He seems also to have had some skill as a herbalist, for we are told that he healed the sick. In these ways, and still more "because he was he," he made himself universally beloved. The chief's son, in particular, who insisted on making blood brotherhood with him, worshipped him with all a youth's enthusiasm.

Death of the Chief's Son

AS TIME WENT on all the wild pigs in the immediate neighbourhood of Kilindi were killed or driven away, and the cultivators had peace; but one day it was reported that there was a number of peculiarly large and fierce ones in a wood two or three days' journey distant. Mbega at once prepared to set out, and the chief's son wished to go with him. Mbega was unwilling to take the risk, and his companions all tried to dissuade the young man, but he insisted, and they finally gave way, on condition of his getting his father's leave. The father consented, and he joined the party.

The pigs, when found, were indeed fierce: it is said they "roared like lions." The dogs, excited beyond their wont by a stimulant Mbega administered to them, were equally fierce, and when the hunters rushed in with their spears some of them were overthrown in the struggle and others compelled to take refuge in trees. A number of pigs were killed, but five men were hurt, and when the ground was cleared it was found that the chief's son was dead.

There could be no question of returning to Kilindi: Mbega knew he would be held responsible for the lad's death, and for once was quite at a loss. When the others said, "What shall we do?" he answered, "I have nothing to say; it is for you to decide." They said they must fly the country, and as he, being a stranger, did not know where to go they offered to guide him. So they set out together, fifteen men in all (the names of ten among them have been preserved by tradition), with eleven dogs – it would seem that three had perished in the late or some other encounter with the wild boars. Their wanderings, recorded in detail, ended in Zirai, on the borders of Usambara, where they settled for some time, and Mbega's fame spread throughout the country. The elders of Bumburi (in Usambara) sent and invited him to become their chief, and he ruled over the whole country and was renowned for his skill in magic, and his kindness, and the comeliness of his face, and his knowledge of the law; and if any man was pressed for a debt Mbega would pay it for him." He married a young maiden of Bumburi, and no doubt looked forward to spending the rest of his life there. But he had reckoned without the men of Yuga.

Mbega Called to be Chief of Vuga

VUGA, THE MOST important community of Usambara, had for some time been at war with the hillmen of Pare. The headman, Turi, having heard reports of Mbega's great powers, especially as regards war magic, first sent messengers to inquire into the truth of these reports, and then came himself in state to invite him to be their chief. He encamped with his party at Karange, a short distance from Bumburi, with beating of drums and blowing of war horns. Mbega, hearing that they had arrived, prepared to go to meet them, and also to give some proof of his power. Having put on his robe of tanned bullock's hide and armed himself with sword, spear, and club, he sent off a runner, bidding him say, "Let our guest excuse me for a little, while I talk with the clouds, that the sun may be covered, since it is so hot that we cannot greet each other comfortably." For it was the season of the *kaskazi*, the northeast monsoon, when the sun is at its fiercest.

The Vuga men were astonished at receiving this message, but very soon they saw a mist rising, which spread till it became a great cloud and quite obscured the sun. Mbega had filled his magic gourd with water and shaken it up; then taken a fire brand, beaten it on the ground till the glowing embers were scattered, and then quenched them with the water from the gourd. The rising steam formed the cloud, and the Vuga elders were duly impressed.

When, at last, they saw him face to face they felt that all they had been told of him was true, so comely was his face and so noble his bearing. Turi explained why he had come, and after the usual steps had been taken for entertaining the guests Mbega agreed to accept the invitation on certain conditions. These chiefly concerned the building of his house and the fetching of the charms which he had left in charge of his Kilindi friends at their camp in the bush. These were to be taken to Vuga by a trusty messenger and hidden at a spot on the road outside the town, which he would have to pass.

Everything being agreed upon, Mbega went to inform his father-in-law, and ask his leave to take away his wife – an interesting point, as indicating that the tribal organization was matrilineal. It should also be noted that the father-in-law, while consenting for his own part, said that his wife must also be consulted. She, however, made no difficulty, "but I must certainly go and take leave of my daughter."

Mbega than bade farewell to the elders of Bumburi, insisting that he did not wish to lose touch with them and enjoining on them to send word to him at Vuga of any important matter. He wanted his wife's brother to accompany him, so that she might not feel cut off from all her relatives; also four of the old men.

The party set out, travelling by night and resting by day, when Mbega sacrificed a sheep and performed various 'secret rites', which he explained to his brother-in-law.

On the following morning they reached the place where the charms had been deposited, and the man who had hidden them produced them and handed them over to Mbega, who gave them to his wife to keep. They camped in this place for the day, and when night came on a lion made his appearance. The men scattered and fled; Mbega followed the lion up and killed him with one thrust of his spear. When his men came back he gave most careful directions about taking off and curing the skin, for reasons which will appear later. They then set out once more, and reached Vuga by easy stages early in the morning. The war drum was beaten, and was answered by drums from the nearest hills, and those again by others from more distant ones, proclaiming to the whole countryside that the chief had come. And from every village, far and near, the people thronged to greet him. His house was built, thatched, and plastered according to his instructions, and when it was finished he had cattle killed and made a feast for the workers, both men and women. He then sent for the lion skin, which meanwhile had been carefully prepared, and had it made into a bed for his wife, who was shortly expecting her first child.

Soon after she had taken her place on this couch Turi's wife was sent for, and, she having called the other skilled women to attend on the queen, before long the cry of rejoicing, usual on such occasions, was raised. All the people came, bringing gifts and greetings, and Mbega had a bullock killed, and sent in some meat for the nurses. His first question to them was whether the birth had taken place on the lion skin; when informed that it had he asked whether the child was a boy or a girl. They told him that it was a boy, and he asked, "Have you given him his 'praise-name' yet?" They answered that they had not done so, whereupon he said that the boy's name was to be Simba, the Lion, and by this name he was to be greeted. Mbega's original name – the one first given him in his childhood – was Mwene, hence his son was to be greeted as Simba (son) of Mwene, which became a title handed down in the male line of the dynasty. But the name officially bestowed on the boy, at the usual time, was Buge.

As soon as the child was old enough his mother's kinsmen claimed him, and he was brought up by his uncles at Bumburi – another indication of mother-right in Usambara. Mbega afterwards married at least one other wife, and had several sons, but Buge's mother was the 'Great Wife', and her son the heir. When he had arrived at manhood his kinsmen at Bumburi asked Mbega's permission to install him as their chief, which was readily granted. The lad ruled wisely, and bade fair to tread in his father's footsteps. His younger brothers, as they grew up, were also put in charge of districts, ruling as Mbega's deputies; this continued to be the custom with the Wakilindi chiefs, who also assigned districts to their daughters.

Mbega's Death and Burial

NOW IT CAME to pass that Mbega fell sick, but no one knew it except five old men who were in close attendance on him. His failing to appear in public created no surprise, for he had been in the habit, occasionally, of shutting himself up for ten days at a time and seeing no one, when it was given out that he was engaged in magic, as was, indeed, the case. His illness, which was not known even to his sons, lasted only three days, and the old men kept his death secret for some time. They sent messengers to Bumburi by night to tell Buge that his father was very ill and had sent for him. He set off at once, and, on arriving, was met by the news that Mbega was dead. The funeral was carried out secretly – no doubt in order to secure the succession by having Buge on the spot before his father's death was known. First a black bull was killed and skinned and the grave lined with its hide; then a black cat was found and killed and a boy and a girl chosen who had to lie down in the grave, side by side, and stay there till the corpse was lowered into it. This, no doubt, was a symbolical act, representing what in former times would have been a human sacrifice. When the corpse was laid in the grave the two came out of it, and were thenceforth *tabu* to each other: they were forbidden to meet again as long as they lived. Then the cat was placed beside the dead man and the grave filled in.

All this was done without the knowledge of the people in the town. The elders agreed to install Buge as successor to his father, and his wife was sent for from Bumburi. She arrived in the early morning, and at break of day the drums were sounded, announcing the death of the chief, and Buge sacrificed two bullocks at his father's grave. Then he was solemnly proclaimed as chief, and his younger brother Kimweri took his place at Bumburi.

Mboza and Magembe

BUGE'S REIGN WAS a short one; when he died, Shebuge, the son of his principal wife, was still under age. He had, by another wife, a son, Magembe, and a daughter, Mboza, somewhat older than her brother. She was a woman of considerable ability and great force of character, as is apparent from the fact that the elders consulted her about the succession. She advised them to appoint Kimweri, keeping her own counsel as to further developments, for she was determined that her own full brother, Magembe, should succeed him.

Kimweri died after a reign of eight years, and was buried with the same rites as his father and brother, Mboza hurrying on the funeral without waiting for her brothers. Shebuge and Magembe, unable to arrive in time, sent cattle for the sacrificial feast. Mboza summoned a council of the elders, and gave her vote in favour of electing Magembe to the chieftainship, to which they agreed. She then said that in her opinion the mourning had lasted long enough, and they should now end it with the usual feast, after which she would go home to Mwasha and – when the proper number of days had passed – send the herald (*mlao*) with orders for the warriors to go and fetch the chief (*zumbe*).

Now word was brought to Shebuge at Balangai that Magembe was about to be proclaimed chief of Vuga by his sister Mboza. He made no protest, but contented himself with saying that he certainly intended to claim his share of his father's treasure, and to call himself, henceforward, not Shebuge, but Kinyasi. This he explained to mean : "I walk alone; I have no fellow."

When six months had passed Mboza sent word that the *kitara* (as the Zulus would say, "the King's kraal") was to be made ready, and messengers sent to fetch Magembe from Mulungui, where he lived. When she heard the signal – drums announcing his arrival she would set out for Vuga with her people. So far all her plans had worked smoothly, as no one dared oppose her, for she was a woman of a fierce spirit and feared throughout the country, because of her skill m magic. But now she met with a check: her messengers, on their way to Mulungui, were intercepted by Shebuge Kinyasi's maternal uncles, who induced them to delay while they themselves started for Balangai and conducted their nephew in triumph to Vuga. The messengers reached Mulungui, and set out on the return journey with Magembe, but always, without knowing it, a stage behind his rival. When, with the dawn, they reached Kihitu the royal drums crashed out in the town, and, marching on, they were further perplexed by hearing the shouts of *Mbogo! Mbogo!* ('Buffalo!'), with which the multitude were greeting the new chief. They were speedily enlightened by people coming from the town. Magembe, as soon as he knew that matters were finally settled, left Usambara in disgust, never to return; but this comes a little later in the story; for the moment the chronicler is more concerned with Mboza.

That princess left Mwasha as soon as the boom of the great drum was heard, and by midday had halted at the villages just outside Vuga, when she heard from some people returning from the town, who stopped to greet her, the name of the new chief. She at once sent for the elders and some of the principal men. "Let them come hither to the gate, that I may question them!" The men delivered their message to the Mlugu (a high official or prince), who asked: "Why so? Can she not enter the town and greet the chief?" Whereto the reply was brief and sufficient: "She does not want to do so." So they all went out and found her standing in the road, staff in hand, her sword girt about her and her kerrie slung over her shoulder, and they greeted her, but she answered not a word. At last she spoke and said, "Who is the chief who has entered the town?"

And the Mlugu answered, "It is Shebuge Kinyasi of Balangai." Said Mboza: "Whose counsel was this? When I called you, together with all the men of your country, and said to you, men of Vuga, 'Let us now all of us choose the chief,' we chose Magembe. Who, then, has dared to change the decision behind my back?"

Mboza Emigrates and Founds Another Kingdom

THEY EXPLAINED what had happened, and, once it had been made clear to her that Shebuge had already entered the *kigiri* (the mausoleum of the chiefs, which is placed in a special hut within the royal kraal – when the new chief has been introduced into this, in the course of his installation, his appointment is confirmed beyond recall), she knew the matter was past remedy, and shook the dust of Vuga from her feet, sending back to Shebuge's uncles a message which the bearers could not understand, but took to be a curse, and were filled with fear accordingly. Shebuge, however, paid no heed to it.

Mboza, with her husband, her three sons and two daughters, her servants, and her cattle, left at once for Mshihwi, the husband's home country. There she founded a new settlement, which she called Vuga, as a rival to her brother's town. The local inhabitants were very ready to welcome her, and to all who came to greet her she distributed cattle and goats and announced her intentions : "I set this my son Shebuge as chief in this my town, and he shall be greeted as 'Lion Lord', like as his uncle at Vuga." She thus founded a rival line, and when, in the course of years, she felt her end approaching she straitly charged all her children never to set foot in the original Vuga, or to be induced, on any pretext, to enter into friendly relations with their kinsmen there. To her eldest son she left all her charms, and imparted to him her secret knowledge, to be made use of in case of war – such as the magic for raising a mist and the charms for turning back the enemy from the town. Her last words to him were an injunction to keep up the feud forever, "you and your brothers, your sons and your grandsons."

Shebuge's Wars and Death

SHEBUGE KINYASI, for his part, was little disposed towards conciliation, and the two Vugas were soon at war, which continued till his attention was claimed in other directions. Unlike his grandfather, Mbega, who is not extolled as a warrior, but as a great hunter and a general benefactor to his people, Shebuge was ambitious to distinguish himself as a conqueror. He was successful for a time, making tributary, not only all the districts included in Usambara, but the Wadigo and other tribes as far as the coast at Pangani, Tanga, and Vanga. The Wazigula, however, refused to submit to him, and in a fight with them he was cut off with a few followers and overpowered by numbers. They let off arrows like drops of rain or waves in a storm. And Shebuge was hit by an arrow, and he died.

Next morning, when the Wazigula came to pick up the weapons of the slain, they found a man sitting beside Shebuge's body. He drew his bow on the first man who approached him and shot him dead, and so with the next and the next, but at last the rest surrounded him and seized him, and asked, "Who art thou?" And he said, "I am Kivava, a man overcome with sorrow and compassion." They said, "Wherefore are thy compassion and thy sorrow?" He answered, "In your battle yesterday my chief was slain." They asked him, "What chief?"

He told them: "In yesterday's fight Shebuge died. My fellows fled, but, as for me, I had sworn a free man's oath: this Shebuge who is dead was my friend at home; I bade farewell to my comrades; but, as for me, I cannot leave Shebuge. If I were to go back to Vuga, how should

I face Shebuge's children, and his wives? My life is finished today. I was called 'the Chief's Friend', I can no longer bear that name. It is better that I too should die as Shebuge has died."

They declared that they did not want to kill him, and turned to leave, but he, to provoke them, shot an arrow after them and hit the Zigula chief's son. Then at last they seized him, and he said, "Slay me not elsewhere, only on this spot where Shebuge is lying." So they slew him and left him there. And when they reached their village they told to all men the tale of Shebuge's friend, who kept troth and loved him to the death.

The fugitives of Shebuge's host, who meanwhile had reached the Ruvu river, heard the news on the following day; they gathered together and returned to the battlefield, which was quite deserted by the enemy. They made a bier and took up Shebuge's body and laid him on it, and so brought him back to Vuga for burial. And his son Kimweri succeeded him.

From thenceforth it was fixed that the chiefs of Vuga should bear the names of Kimweri and Shehuge in alternate generations.

Collected by Captain C.H. Stigand

How the Moon First Came into the Sky

Okun Asere of Mfamosing, of the Ekoi People, Nigeria and Cameroon

IN A CERTAIN TOWN there lived Njomm Mbui (Juju sheep). He made great friends with Etuk (antelope), whose home was in the "bush."

When the two animals grew up they went out and cut farms. Njomm planted plantains in his, while Etuk set his with coco-yams.

When the time came round for the fruits to ripen, Njomm went to his farm and cut a bunch of plantains, while Etuk dug up some of his coco.

Each cleaned his food and put it in the pot to cook. When all was ready they sat down and ate.

Next morning Etuk said, "Let us change. I saw a bunch of plantains in your farm which I would like to get. Will you go instead to mine and take some coco?"

This was arranged, and Etuk said to Njomm, "Try to beat up fu-fu." Njomm tried, and found it very good. He gave some to Etuk. The latter ate all he wanted, then took the bunch of plantains and hung it up in his house.

Next morning he found that the fruit had grown soft, so he did not care to eat it. He therefore took the plantains and threw them away in the bush.

During the day Mbui came along and smelt plantains. He looked round till he found them, then picked up one and began to eat. They were very sweet. He ate his fill, then went on, and later met a crowd of the Nshum people (apes). To them he said, "Today I found a very sweet thing in the bush."

In course of time Etuk grew hungry again, and Njomm said to him, "If you are hungry, why don't you tell me?"

He went to his farm and got four bunches of plantains. As he came back he met the monkey people. They begged for some of his fruit, so he gave it to them.

After they had eaten all there was, they in their turn went on, and met a herd of wild boars (Ngumi). To these they said, "There is very fine food to be got from Njomm and Etuk."

The Ngumi therefore came and questioned Etuk, "Where is coco to be had?" and Etuk answered, "The coco belongs to me."

The boars begged for some, so Etuk took a basket, filled it at his farm, and gave it to them.

After they were satisfied, they went on their way and next morning met Njokk (elephant).

To him they said, "Greetings, Lord! Last night we got very good food from the farms over there."

Njokk at once ran and asked the two friends, "Whence do you get so much food?" They said, "Wait a little."

Njomm took his long matchet and went to his farm. He cut five great bunches of plantains and carried them back. Etuk also got five baskets full of coco, which he brought to Elephant. After the latter had eaten all this, he thanked them and went away.

All the bush-beasts came in their turn and begged for food, and to each the two friends gave willingly of all that they had. Lastly also came Mfong (Bush-cow).

Now not far from the two farms there was a great river called Akarram (the One which goes round). In the midst of it, deep down, dwelt Crocodile. One day Mfong went down into the water to drink, and from him crocodile learned that much food was to be had near by.

On this crocodile came out of the water and began walking towards the farms. He went to Njomm and Etuk and said:

"I am dying of hunger, pray give me food."

Etuk said, "To the beasts who are my friends I will give all I have, but to you I will give nothing, for you are no friend of mine; "but Njomm said:

"I do not like you very much, yet I will give you one bunch
of plantains."

Crocodile took them and said, "Do not close your door tonight when you lie down to sleep. I will come back and buy more food from you at a great price."

He then went back to the water and sought out a python, which dwelt there. To the latter he said:

"I have found two men on land, who have much food." Python said, "I too am hungry. Will you give me to eat?"

So crocodile gave him some of the plantains which he had brought. When Python had tasted he said, "How sweet it is! Will you go back again and bring more?" Crocodile said, "Will you give me something with which to buy?" and Python answered, "Yes. I will give you something with which you can buy the whole farm."

On this he took from within his head a shining stone and gave it to crocodile. The latter started to go back to the farm. As he went, night fell and all the road grew dark, but he held in his jaws the shining stone, and it made a light on his path, so that all the way was bright. When he neared the dwelling of the two friends he hid the stone and called:

"Come out and I will show you something which I have brought."

It was very dark when they came to speak with him. Slowly the crocodile opened his claws, in which he held up the stone, and it began to glimmer between them. When he held it right out, the whole place became so bright that one could see to pick up a needle or any small thing. He said, "The price of this that I bring is one whole farm."

Etuk said, "I cannot buy. If I give my farm, nothing remains to me. What is the use of this great shining stone if I starve to death?" But Njomm said, "I will buy – oh, I will buy, for my farm full of plantains, for that which you bring fills the whole earth with light. Come let us go. I will show you my farm. From here to the water-side all round is my farm. Take it all, and do what you choose with it, only give me the great shining stone that, when darkness falls, the whole earth may still be light."

Crocodile said, "I agree."

Then Njomm went to his house with the stone, and Etuk went to his. Njomm placed it above the lintel, that it might shine for all the world; but Etuk closed his door and lay down to sleep.

In the morning Njomm was very hungry, but he had nothing to eat, because he had sold all his farm for the great white stone.

Next night and the night after he slept full of hunger, but on the third morning he went to Etuk and asked, "Will you give me a single coco-yam?" Etuk answered:

"I can give you nothing, for now you have nothing to give in exchange. It was not I who told you to buy the shining thing. To give something, when plenty remains, is good; but none but a fool would give his all, that a light may shine in the dark!"

Njomm was very sad. He said, "I have done nothing bad. Formerly no one could see in the night time. Now the python stone shines so that everyone can see to go wherever he chooses."

All that day Njomm still endured, though nearly dying of hunger, and at night time he crept down to the water, very weak and faint.

By the river-side he saw a palm tree, and on it a man trying to cut down clusters of ripe kernels; but this was hard to do, because it had grown very dark.

Njomm said, "Who is there?" and the man answered, "I am Effion Obassi."

The second time Njomm called, "What are you doing?" and EfBon replied:

"I am trying to gather palm kernels, but I cannot do so, for it is very dark amid these great leaves."

Njomm said to him, "It is useless to try to do such a thing in the dark. Are you blind?"

Effion answered, "I am not blind. Why do you ask?"

Then Njomm said, "Good; if you are not blind, I beg you to throw me down only one or two palm kernels, and in return I will show you a thing more bright and glorious than any you have seen before."

Effion replied, "Wait a minute, and I will try to throw a few down to you. Afterwards you shall show me the shining thing as you said."

He then threw down three palm kernels, which Njomm took, and stayed his hunger a little. The latter then called, "Please try to climb down. We will go together to my house."

Effion tried hard, and after some time he stood safely at the foot of the tree by the side of Njomm.

So soon as they got to his house, Njomm said, "Will you wait here a little while I go to question the townspeople?"

First he went to Etuk and asked, "Will you not give me a single coco to eat? See, the thing which I bought at the price of all that I had turns darkness to light for you, but for me, I die of hunger."

Etuk said, "I will give you nothing. Take back the thing for which you sold your all, and we will stay in our darkness as before."

Then Njomm begged of all the townsfolk that they would give him ever so little food in return for the light he had bought for them. Yet they all refused.

So Njomm went back to his house and took the shining stone, and gave it to Effion Obassi, saying:

"I love the earth folk, but they love not me. Now take the shining thing for which I gave my whole possessions. Go back to the place whence you came, for I know that you belong to the sky people, but when you reach your home in the heavens, hang up my stone in a place where all the earth folk may see its shining, and be glad."

Then Effion took the stone, and went back by the road he had come. He climbed up the palm tree, and the great leaves raised themselves upwards, pointing to the sky, and lifted him, till, from their points, he could climb into heaven.

When he reached his home, he sent and called all the Lords of the Sky and said, "I have brought back a thing today which can shine so that all the earth will be light. From now on everyone on earth or in heaven will be able to see at the darkest hour of the night."

The chiefs looked at the stone and wondered. Then they consulted together, and made a box. Effion said, "Make it so that the stone can shine out only from one side."

When the box was finished, he set the globe of fire within, and said, "Behold the stone is mine. From this time all the people must bring me food. I will no longer go to seek any for myself."

For some time they brought him plenty, but after a while they grew tired. Then Effion covered the side of the box, so that the stone could not shine till they brought him more. That is the reason why the moon is sometimes dark, and people on earth say "It is the end of the month. The sky people have grown weary of bringing food to Effion Obassi, and he will not let his stone shine out till they bring a fresh supply."

Collected by Percy Amaury Talbot

How Sun and Moon Went up to the Sky

Okun Asere of Mfamosing, of the Ekoi People,

Nigeria and Cameroon

OBASSI NSI HAD THREE SONS, named Eyo (Sun), Ejirum (Darkness), and 'Mi (Moon). The first two he loved, but the last he did not love. One day Nsi called to 'Mi and said:

"Go into the bush, catch a leopard, and bring him to me."

'Mi went sadly away, and as he reached the outskirts of the town began to weep. A man named Isse saw him and called "What is the matter?" 'Mi answered, "My father does not love me, and is sending me to catch a leopard in the bush, in order to destroy me."

The man said "Take comfort; I will give you a 'medicine 'which will make you successful." He went away, but soon returned with what he had promised, and rubbed the "medicine" on the boy's hands.

'Mi went into the bush, and almost at once saw a leopard lying down asleep. He cut strong lianes, and tied up the beast, so that it could not move, then dragged it along till he reached home once more, and stood before his father.

Nsi was astonished, but concealed his vexation, and said in a cunning way, "This my son is indeed a good son because he has done this thing."

Some time afterwards Nsi married another wife. Obassi Osaw came down to the wedding feast with his sons and daughters and a great retinue of sky people. These started to play with the earthfolk, who had also gathered together for the festival. After a while they took a cloth and tied it up in a bundle. To this a rope was fastened, and one of Nsi's sons caught the end, and began to draw it along the ground. All got sticks and tried to hit the bundle as it was dragged hither and thither. Ejirum also tried to hit it, but a splinter sprang from his stick as it struck the ground, and wounded the eye of one of Osaw's sons, so that the latter was blinded.

Osaw was angry, and said, "I myself will blind the eyes of Obassi Nsi."

The townspeople crowded round, and begged him to show mercy, but he would not relent. So they took Nsi and hid him away, where Osaw could not find him. After the latter had searched in vain he was still angry, and said:

"Now I am going back to my town, but Nsi will not escape me."

After two days he sent down ten men to fetch Obassi Nsi. They said, "We have been sent to bring you up," but the townsfolk said, "Here are great gifts of cows, bulls, and goats. Take them before your master, and perhaps he will not be angry any more."

When the men returned to the sky they said, "Here is a message from Obassi Nsi. He wants to beg you very much. He says, "It was not I who told anyone to hurt your son's eye."

Osaw would not listen, but sent down three other men, and said:

"Even if you yourself did not break my son's eye yet you must come up to me."

When Nsi heard this, he called his people together. To his son Eyo (Sun) he said:

"Here are forty pieces of cloth. Will you take them to Osaw and beg him for me?"

Eyo started on his journey, and had reached about half way when he saw five beautiful women standing at the entrance to a town. No sooner had he seen them, than he forgot all about his errand, and began to sell the cloth for plantains, palm oil and palm wine, with which he made a feast for the beautiful women. There he stayed for some weeks, then took what was left of the goods and went on a little further till he came to another town, where he found two more women, as beautiful as the first. For four years he stayed at one or other of the towns, journeying to and fro between them.

After four years, when Nsi found that Eyo did not come back nor send any message, he called to his son 'Mi and said:

"The case which I have before Obassi Osaw has taken a long time to finish. Go to Nsann (Thunder town) and fetch hence a cow which you will find. When you have brought it away take it as a gift to Obassi Osaw, and settle my case for me."

'Mi answered, "Very well;" and his mother called to him, and said:

"Do what you can for your father, who is guiltless as to Obassi Osaw, but take care for yourself when you reach Nsann town. Let no one know the place where you sleep, lest you should perish in the night time."

'Mi answered, "I will do what I can."

Next morning he set forth, and before evening had reached Nsann. The people asked him:

"Where will you sleep tonight?" He answered, "I will sleep among the goats." When all was still he left the goat pen in the darkness, and went to the Egbo house, where he lay down and slept.

At midnight a thunderbolt struck the shed where the goats were herded, and killed them all.

Early in the morning the people came together and opened the door. When they saw the dead goats, but could not find the boy they were much astonished. As they stood wondering 'Mi came forward and said:

"If I were not a smart boy, the bolt would have killed me. As it is, I have saved myself."

Everybody in the town was sorry for the lad, and said "Let us give him the cow to take to his father." So the boy set out homeward, well content.

When 'Mi reached his father's house and led the cow before him, Nsi said, very softly to himself, so that he thought no one could hear:

"What can I do to kill this son of mine?"

'Mi heard, and next morning took the gun which his mother had given him, and went into the bush to hunt. First he shot Ise, the little grey duiker, and next Ngumi (the wild boar). These he carried home, and brought before his father, but the latter said:

"I will not eat of them."

So 'Mi took his kill away sadly, and gave it to his mother.

The woman cooked the meat in a delicate way, and then took it to her husband, who ate gladly of what he had before refused; but when he learned what she had done, he said:

"From today take your son away from here. Neither of you shall live in my town any more."

When 'Mi learned this he also was very angry. He took his gun and his matchet and went to find his friend Isse, who had given him the "leopard medicine "years before. To his grief he heard that this good friend had died while he himself was away at Nsann. So he went sadly out into the bush to hunt, that his mother might not starve. After a while he saw an Ikomme (squirrel) standing between the thick branches. He raised his gun to shoot, but in a moment all the place grew dark. A voice called behind him out of the darkness, "'Mi 'Mi," and he answered, "Who calls?" The voice cried, "I am your dead friend. Tell me, now, which do you choose, to die or to live?" 'Mi answered, "I am willing to die. Why should I live when my father seeks to kill me?"

After he had spoken, a deep sleep fell upon him. When he awoke the whole place was clear of trees. The sun was shining brightly, and before him stood a long table, on which were set dried meat, biscuits, rum, and palm wine, and all kinds of gin. Then he saw Isse walking up and down as in life, and directing everything, while many people were busily working round about.

They worked hard, and as they worked more and more men came out of the bush, till in a little space the whole house was finished. Then Isse said:

"This is your house, and all these are your people. Now, your father's case is a very long one. I will give you goods so that you may go and arrange it."

'Mi agreed, and next morning called together seven companions. He gave them that Isse had provided, many heads of tobacco, and countless demi-johns of palm wine.

Then 'Mi himself set out at their head for Obassi's town.

When he reached the entrance he called a meeting of the townsfolk, and said to them:

"I have come to try to settle my father's case, which has already been a very long one. I wish to hear from you how many goods I must pay."

The people said, "Let us see what you have brought."

So he showed them all, and they went before Obassi and begged him to take the gifts in payment, and settle the affair. Obassi answered, "Good. I accept what you have brought. The case is finished."

Then 'Mi went back to his father's town to fetch his mother. He met her wandering about at the entrance to the town, and was about to lead her away, when Nsi himself came by.

"Whither are you going?" he asked.

'Mi answered, "I am leading my mother away to my own town, which is a long way from here, and is full of rich things."

On hearing this Nsi said, "I should like to see So he followed his outcast wife and son till they came to that part of the bush where the new town stood.

Nsi was amazed at what he saw, and still more so when he found that 'Mi had been to Obassi Osaw and arranged his case. On this he sent a great company of men to seize Eyo and bring the latter before him. When they returned Nsi called both his sons, and said:

"From today you, Eyo, are my unloved son. You are too hot; no one will like you any more. You are careless sometimes, and burn up all tender plants in the farms." But to 'Mi he said:

"You, 'Mi, are my good son. In the night you can shine softly, so that men may see to walk safely when they are away from home."

When Eyo heard this he thought, "Now my father will hate me as he used to hate 'Mi. Perhaps he will try to kill me also. I will not stay here on earth, but will go up to the sky to Osaw."

'Mi also thought, "Perhaps my father is deceiving me, or, at at any rate, he may grow to hate me again. It is better to go up to the sky and stay with Obassi Osaw. From thence I can see what passes both in his land and in that of my father. Also I can shine the brighter on high, so that heaven and earth will be full of my light." Thus Nsi lost both of these sons, and remained on earth alone with his third boy, Ejirum (Darkness).

Collected by Percy Amaury Talbot

How the First Rain Came

Okun Asere of Mfamosing, of the

Ekoi people, Nigeria and Cameroon

ONCE, LONG AGO, a daughter was born to Obassi Osaw, and a son to Obassi Nsi. When both had come to marriageable age, Nsi sent a message to say "Let us exchange children. I will send my son that he may wed one of your maidens. Send your daughter down to my town, that she may become my wife."

To this Obassi Osaw agreed. So the son of Nsi went up to the heavens carrying many fine gifts, and Ara, the sky maiden, came down to dwell on earth. With her came seven men-slaves and seven women-slaves, whom her father sent that they might work for her, so that she should not be called upon to do anything herself.

One day, very early in the morning, Obassi Nsi said to his new wife, "Go, work in my farm!" She answered, "My Father gave me the slaves so that they should work instead of me. Therefore send them." Obassi Nsi was very angry and said, "Did you not hear that I gave my orders to you. You yourself shall work in my farm. As for the slaves, I will tell them what to do."

The girl went, though very unwillingly, and when she returned at night, tired out, Nsi said to her: "Go at once to the river and bring water for the household."

She answered, "I am weary with working in the farm; may not my slaves at least do this while I rest?"

Again Nsi refused, and drove her forth, so she went backward and forward many times, carrying the heavy jars. Night had fallen long before she had brought enough.

Next morning Nsi bade her do the most menial services, and all day long kept her at work, cooking, fetching water, and making fire. That night again she was very weary before she might lie down to rest. At dawn on the third morning he said, "Go and bring in much firewood." Now the girl was young and unused to work, so as she went she wept, and the tears were still falling when she came back carrying her heavy burden.

As soon as Nsi saw her enter he called to her, "Come here and lie down before me…. I wish to shame you in the presence of all my people…." On that the girl wept still more bitterly.

No food was given her till midday on the morrow, and then not enough. When she had finished eating up all there was, Nsi said to her:

"Go out and bring in a great bundle of fish poison."

The girl went into the bush to seek for the plant, but as she walked through the thick undergrowth a thorn pierced her foot. She lay down alone. All day long she lay there in pain, but as the sun sank she began to feel better. She got up and managed to limp back to the house.

When she entered, Nsi said to her, "Early this morning I ordered you to go and collect fish poison. You have stayed away all day and done nothing." So he drove her into the goat pen, and said, "Tonight you shall sleep with the goats; you shall not enter my house."

That night she ate nothing. Early next morning one of the slaves opened the door of the goat pen, and found the girl lying within, with her foot all swollen and sore. She could not walk so for five days she was left with the goats. After that her foot began to get better.

So soon as she could walk again at all, Nsi called her and said:

"Here is a pot. Take it to the river, and bring it back filled to the brim."

She set out, but when she reached the water-side, she sat down on the bank and dipped her foot in the cool stream. She said to herself, "I will never go back; it is better to stay here alone."

After a while one of the slaves came down to the river. He questioned her:

"At dawn this morning you were sent to fetch water. Why have you not returned home?"

The girl said, "I will not come back."

When the slave had left her she thought, "Perhaps he will tell them, and they will be angered and may come and kill me. I had better go back after all." So she filled her pot and tried to raise it on to her head, but it was too heavy. Next she lifted it on to a tree trunk that lay by the side of the river, and, kneeling beneath, tried to draw it, in that way, on to her head, but the pot fell and broke, and in falling a sharp sherd cut off one of her ears. The blood poured down from the wound, and she began to weep again, but suddenly thought:

"My Father is alive, my mother is alive, I do not know why I I stay here with Obassi Nsi. I will go back to my own Father."

Then she set out to find the road by which Obassi Osaw had sent her to earth. She came to a high tree, and from it saw a long rope hanging. She said to herself:

"This is the way by which my Father sent me."

She caught the rope and began to climb. Before she reached half-way she grew very weary, and her sighs and tears mounted up to the kingdom of Obassi Osaw. When she reached mid-way she stayed and rested a while. Afterwards she climbed on again.

After a long time she reached the top of the rope, and found herself on the border of her Father's land. Here she sat down almost worn out with weariness, and still weeping.

Now, one of the slaves of Obassi Osaw had been sent out to collect firewood. He chanced to stray on and on, and came to the place near where the girl was resting. He heard her sobs mixed with broken words, and ran back to the town, crying out, "I have heard the voice of Ara. She is weeping about a mile from here."

Obassi heard but could not believe, yet he said:

"Take twelve slaves, and, should you find my daughter as you say, bring her here."

When they reached the place they found that it was Ara for true. So they carried her home.

When her Father saw her coming he called out:

"Take her to the house of her mother."

There one of the lesser wives, Akun by name, heated water and bathed her. Then they prepared a bed, and covered her well with soft skins and fine cloths.

While she was resting, Obassi killed a young kid and sent it to Akun, bidding her prepare it for his daughter. Akun took it, and after she had washed it, cooked it whole in a pot. Also Obassi sent a great bunch of plantains and other fruits, and these also they set, orderly upon a table before the girl. Next they poured water into a gourd, and brought palm wine in a native cup, bidding her drink.

After she had eaten and drunk, Obassi came with four slaves carrying a great chest made of ebony. He bade them set it before her, opened it and said, "Come here; choose anything you will from this box."

Ara chose two pieces of cloth, three gowns, four small loin cloths, four looking-glasses, four spoons, two pairs of shoes (at £1), four cooking pots, and four chains of beads.

After this Obassi Osaw's storekeeper, named Ekpenyon, came forward and brought her twelve anklets. Akun gave her two gowns, a fu-fu stick and a wooden knife. Her own mother brought her five gowns, richer than all the rest, and five slaves to wait upon her.

After this Obassi Osaw said; "A house has been got ready for you, go there that you may be its mistress."

Next he went out and called together the members of the chief "club "of the town. This was named Angbu. He said to the men:

"Go; fetch the son of Obassi Nsi. Cut off both his ears and bring them to me. Then flog him and drive him down the road to his Father's town, with this message from me:

"I had built a great house up here in my town. In it I placed your son, and treated him kindly. Now that I know what you have done to my child, I send back your son to you earless, in payment for Ara's ear, and the sufferings which you put upon her."

When the Angbu Club had cut off the ears of the son of Obassi Nsi, they brought them before Obassi Osaw, and drove the lad back on the earthward road, as they had been ordered.

Osaw took the ears and made a great Juju, and by reason of this a strong wind arose, and drove the boy earthward. On its wings it bore all the sufferings of Ara, and the tears which she had shed through the cruelty of Obassi Nsi. The boy stumbled along, half-blinded by the rain, and as he went he thought:

"Obassi Osaw may do to me what he chooses. He had never done any unkind thing before. It is only in return for my Father's cruelty that I must suffer all this."

So his tears mixed with those of Ara and fell earthward as rain.

Up till that time there had been no rain on the earth. It fell for the first time when Obassi Osaw made the great wind and drove forth the son of his enemy.

Collected by Percy Amaury Talbot

How All the Rivers First Came on Earth

Okun Asere of Mfamosing, of the

Ekoi people, Nigeria and Cameroon

IN THE VERY, VERY, VERY OLDEN TIME, an old man named Etim 'Ne (old person) came down from the sky; he alone with his old wife Ejaw (wild cat). At that time there were no people on the earth. This old couple were the very first to go down to dwell there.

Now up to this time all water was kept in the kingdom of Obassi Osaw. On earth there was not a single drop.

Etim 'Ne and his wife stayed for seven days, and during that time they had only the juice of plantain stems to drink or cook with.

At the end of that time the old man said to his old wife, "I will go back to Obassi Osaw's town and ask him to give us a little water."

When he arrived at the old town where they used to dwell, he went to the house of Obassi and said:

"Since we went down to earth we have had no water, only the juice which we sucked from the plantain stems. For three nights I will sleep in your town, then when I return to earth I hope that you will give me some water to take with me. Should my wife have children they will be glad for the water, and what they offer to you in thanksgiving I myself will bring up to your town."

On the third morning, very early, Obassi Osaw put the water charm in a calabash, and bound it firmly with tie-tie. Then he gave it to Etim 'Ne, and said, "When you wish to loose this, let no one be present. Open it, and you will find seven good gifts inside. Wherever you want water, take out one of these and throw it on the ground."

Etim 'Ne thanked Lord Obassi, and set out on his way earthward. Just before he came to the place where he had begun to cut farm, he opened the calabash, and found within seven stones, clear as water. He made a small hole and laid one of the stones within it. Soon a little stream began to well out, then more and more, till it became a broad lake, great as from here to Ako.

Etim 'Ne went on and told his wife. They both rejoiced greatly, but he thought, "How is this? Can a man be truly happy, yet have no child?"

After two days his wife came to him and said, "Obassi is sending us yet another gift. Soon we shall be no longer alone on earth, you and I."

When the due months were passed, she bore him seven children, all at one time. They were all sons. Later she became enceinte again, and this time bore seven daughters. After that she was tired, and never bore any more children.

In course of time the girls were all sent to the fatting-house. While they were there Etim 'Ne pointed out to his seven sons where he would like them to build their compounds. When these were finished, he gave a daughter to each son and said, "Do not care that she is your sister. Just marry her. There is no one else who can become your wife."

The eldest son dwelt by the first water which Etim 'Ne had made, but to each of the others he gave a lake or river – seven in all.

After one year, all the girls became enceinte. Each of them had seven children, three girls and four boys. Etim 'Ne said, "It is good." He was very happy. As the children grew up he sent them to other places.

Now the seven sons were all hunters. Three of them were good, and brought some of their kill to give to their father, but four were very bad, and hid all the meat, so that they might keep everything for themselves.

When Etim 'Ne saw this, he left the rivers near the farms of his three good sons, but took them away from the four bad boys. These latter were very sad when they found their water gone, so they consulted together and went and got palm wine. This they carried before their father and said:

"We are seven, your children. First you gave the water to all. Now you have taken it away from us four. What have we done?"

Etim 'Ne answered, "Of all the meat you killed in the bush you brought none to me. Therefore I took away your rivers. Because you have come to beg me I will forgive you, and will give you four good streams. As your children grow and multiply I will give you many."

After another year the sons had children again. When the latter grew up they went to different places and built their houses.

When these were ready Etim 'Ne sent for all the children and said, "At dawn to-morrow let each of you go down to the stream which flows by the farm of his father. Seek in its bed till you find seven smooth stones. Some must be small and some big like the palm of your hand. Let each one go in a different direction, and after walking about a mile, lay a stone upon the ground. Then walk on again and do the same, till all are finished. Where you set a big stone a river will come, and where you set a small stone a stream will come."

All the sons did as they were bidden, save one alone. He took a great basket and filled it with stones. Then he went to a place in the bush near his own farm. He thought, "Our father told us, if you throw a big stone a big river will come. If I throw down all my stones together, so great a water will come that it will surpass the waters of all my brothers." Then he emptied his basket of stones all in one place, and, behold! water flowed from every side, so that all his farm, and all the land round about became covered with water. When he saw that it would not stop but threatened to overflow the whole earth he grew very much afraid. He saw his wife running, and called to her, "Let us go to my father." Then they both ran as hard as they could toward the house of Etim 'Ne.

Before they reached it the other children, who had been setting the smooth stones in the bush, as their father had told them, heard the sound of the coming of the waters. Great fear fell upon them, and they also dropped what remained and ran back to Etim 'Ne.

He also had heard the rushing of the water and knew what the bad son had done. He took the magic calabash in his hand and ran with his wife to a hill behind their farm. On this there grew many tall palm trees. Beneath the tallest of these he stood, while his children gathered round one after the other as they got back from the bush. Etim 'Ne held on high the calabash which Obassi had given him, and prayed:

"Lord Obassi, let not the good thing which you gave for our joy turn to our hurt."

As he prayed the water began to go down. It sought around till it found places where there had been no water. At each of these it made a bed for itself, great or small, some for broad rivers, and some for little streams. Only where the bad son had emptied his basket it did not go back, but remained in a great lake covering all his farm, so that he was very hungry, and had to beg from his brothers till the time came for the fruits to ripen in the new farm which he had to cut.

After many days Etim 'Ne called all his children around, and told them the names of all the rivers, and of every little stream. Then he said, "Let no one forget to remember me when I shall have left you, for I it was who gave water to all the earth, so that every one shall be glad."

Two days afterwards he died. In the beginning there were no people on the earth and no water. Etim 'Ne it was who first came down to dwell with his old wife Ejaw, and he it was who begged water from Obassi Osaw.

Collected by Percy Amaury Talbot

When Angels Come Knocking

Drew Hayden Taylor, Curve Lake First Nations

ANGIE CONEB CURSED as the needle pierced her thumb for the fourteenth time that hour. By now she was used to the momentary but aggravating pain, but it was the frustration of not being able to properly bead the piece of leather in her hand. The young woman had been hoping to create at least a reasonable facsimile of a wild rose on the deer hide but at best, it more resembled a chipped car windshield. Even that summation was a rough approximation.

"Goddamnit" she muttered, not understanding her continued failure. After all, her grandmother had been able to do amazing things with just a needle, a thread, some beeswax, a small vial of multi-coloured glass beads, and her imagination. Great art from such humble ingredients it seemed. Hell, Granny Jay had even been half blind. Yet, creations of cultural beauty had somehow sprung from those old, decrepit but loving hands. And here sat Angie, in the prime of her life with a new bachelor of Indigenous Studies degree freshly framed, hanging on the wall, not being able to come close to that beaded brilliance she remembered from her childhood.

Maybe it was the fact she didn't wear glasses. She had been fighting the need for some time now, refusing to give in to advancing years... though those particular years added up to just over two decades. Still, there had to be a reason for the needle to ignore and even subvert her artistic intent. Yes she was aware that forty years of beading had been ingrained in those Anishnawbe hands two generations removed, but at the very least, it should mean there had to be at least a strain of cultural legacy passed down to her somewhere in that maternal DNA legacy.

Evidently not. Those fingertips, polished to a bright blue sheen by a Vietnamese manicurist, were more at home on a keyboard, not rearranging her thumbprint.

"Ah Christ..." Angie said again. That was prick number fifteen, complete with the accompanying blood droplets. Most bleeding beading beginners would have stuck the wounded finger into their mouth, sucking away all the evidence of needle assault, but for reasons of her own, that grossed the woman out more. Instead, she'd shake her thumb and accompanying hand three times. Her small Toronto apartment was dangerously close to looking like a crime scene. "What am I doing wrong?" she wondered.

Maybe it was the light. It was past ten in the evening and the desk lamp beside her did little to illuminate Angie's work area. The small glass table in front of her held bits and pieces of leather, a backup needle, two more vials of beads, a long-cold mug of tea, and various spatters of blood. What brightness there was from the desk lamp was supported by the shifting glow emanating from the television. Some reality show about cooking was helping her embrace an ancestral art form.

It had been a grand idea, to bead some slippers for her mother, to help remember the woman they both had loved who had passed away less than a year ago. Granny Jay had been the beader in the family: moccasins, vests, wall hangings, even a guitar strap for her brother. If it had a flat surface and could be punctured, it was not safe in the Coneb household. Though Angie was now officially well educated, she had concerns that talents beyond the academic were being lost in her family, and amongst her people. So, here she was, beading on a lonely Tuesday night, frequently using the best epithets known in the English language. Both her mother and father would have preferred her to learn the Anishnawbe language, but that had seemed a little taxing for the woman who, despite the fresh and sparkling degree on the wall, still did not know what a dangling participle was. Still, four years of university had taught her to reason out what was going wrong, to attack the beading travesty in front of her, like a test problem. A problem that could be solved. Maybe it was a depth perception problem, again going back to needing glasses... which of course she didn't.

"ANGIE CONEB."

The booming voice startled her, making her prick her thumb yet again. Her's was a small apartment, not used to such big voices. But where had the disproportionately loud utterance come from? She was most definitely alone. It was then that the woman noticed her television was no longer highlighting the best way to grill ahi tuna. Instead, it was an opaque colour, practically radiating a dull glimmering. Angie's first thought was perhaps it was an auditory hallucination of some sort. But why now, why here... if it was indeed an auditory hallucination... she wasn't sure. But there had indeed been an unmistakable and unignorable voice calling her name just a few seconds ago. Second reaction, it had done something to her television. "What the...?" She couldn't afford another television. Contrary to popular belief, Indigenous students didn't have reams of money thrown at them by the government to attend higher education. That television had been handed down. It was a family heirloom. This had...

"ANGIE CONEB."

There was the voice again. Louder. More insistent. Coming from the bathroom. Or the direction of the bathroom. Which up until now, she had not noticed how unnervingly close to the front door the bathroom was. Practically side by side.

"Yeah... Somebody there?" It was a stupid question because obviously somebody was there. It wasn't her toilet calling out to her. But Angie had been sitting there for three hours, ever since she got home, eating her dinner and beading. There should be nobody there. Angie put down her beading. This would require some serious investigation. "Hey! Where are you? How'd you get in my apartment?" The woman wasn't worried or frightened... just yet. Rapists or burglars don't usually announce her name in a big booming voice that could probably be heard several apartments over. Stretching her stiff back muscles, she leaned forward to get out of her padded chair. That's when she noticed her bathroom was also glowing. Or more accurately, something in front of her bathroom was glowing.

Minor irritation and surprise were fast turning into major puzzlement and an unwelcome concern. "Okay..." was Angie's assessment of the situation. The glowing got brighter. It seemed to take on a shape. Tall, cylindrical, with bumps, or things attached. Squinting, she leaned back down in her seat. Was it a fire? She felt no heat. She thought maybe somebody was beaming in from *Star Trek*. Whatever it was, it couldn't be good. Situations like this seldom were.

"ANGIE CONEB."

The imposing voice called her name a third time, loud enough so she could feel her hair practically being blown backwards. Beads were rolling everywhere on the coffee table.

"What!" Angie tried to respond as loud as the voice calling her but came in substantially short. Suddenly, there in front of her, standing in front of her tiny bathroom, stood a man. Of sorts. Though it had been several months since any XY chromosomes had entered her domain, she was fairly sure this was not an average kind of man. The figure standing a few feet away was a big man, easily over six feet tall. A glowing man. A glowing white man. A glowing white man with wings. And more problematic, he had a sword, and wore a toga of some sort. Her auditory hallucination had rapidly become a visual one. Perhaps on account of her loss of blood from the beading.

"What the fuck...?" This had swiftly become a serious issue. A tall white guy with a weapon and dressed very oddly was standing between her and the potential door to safety. He had a sword. Angie had a needle. It was a truly vexing situation.

"ANGIE CONEB. I BRING YOU GLAD TIDINGS."

Angie could feel His voice down to her very bones. The tone felt like something quivering and fluttering deep inside her. It seemed to emanate power. The good news was, He was bringing her glad tidings. The glowing man with the sword was in a good mood. So far, so good. Kinda.

"Good. Good. Glad tidings are good. Ah, how did you get in here?" On the table in front of her, the woman noticed her cell phone was also glowing, like the television. Might was well play for time, find out what's going on and how to deal with the situation. That's what Uncle Murray, the Rez cop, would tell her.

"I, LIKE OUR LORD GOD, AM EVERYWHERE."

Oh god, a religious nut! That both simplified and complicated the situation. Wonder if He knew her Aunt Julia. He'd have more in common with her than with Angie for sure.

"Okay. Why are you here? Carrying a sword, and wearing a toga?"

The man, if he could indeed be called a man… because of the wings… smiled. It was a beatific and reassuring smile. Again, she felt it down deep in her bones. Looking down, she noticed He was floating about a foot above the cracked, tiled floor. That was yet another mystery to contemplate once this was over.

"I AM THE ARCHANGEL GABRIEL. YOU HAVE BEEN CHOSEN. YOU ARE TO BECOME HIS VESSEL."

An Angel. The man was an Angel. Try as she might, Angie could not come up with another explanation. After all, there were the wings, and the levitation, and the toga, and the booming voice. All definite characteristics of what she knew of Angels. And what was that the Angel said…?

"I am? A vessel? I'm gonna need some more details… Gabriel. The Archangel Gabriel. What the hell are you talking about?" Flinching at the modest blasphemy, the floating man with the sword approached her, without moving His legs. Still smiling, the Angel hovered about two feet away from her. In the blinding light, Angie had to squint to see Him properly, but she did notice through the toga that Angel Man seemed pretty cut, and in excellent shape. Must be no carbs in Heaven.

"THE SON OF GOD WILL BE BORN AGAIN. THIS WILL BE HIS SECOND COMING. AND YOU, ANGIE CONEB, YOU SHALL BRING HIM FORTH UNTO THIS WORLD. YOU SHALL BEAR HIS CHILD. YOU HAVE BEEN BLESSED, PRAISE BE TO GOD."

The Angel waited for the woman to react with pious modesty and honour. After all, this was only the second time this had happened in history.

Unfortunately, Angie had another reaction in mind. "What? I'm going to … what?" All thoughts of beading had now evaporated. While tackling the thread and leather issue, she had also been pondering the possibility of maybe going for her Masters the following year. That too had become a distant memory, as was the fact that a few moments ago she had planned to use the Angel blocked bathroom for a pee break. All forgotten. Instead, she raised her hand as if in class. "Ah, a couple of questions if I may?"

"LIKE WHY YOU, ANGIE CONEB?"

By now, booming out her full name in such a loud speaker tone was beginning to annoy her. Secondly, in answer to His question, yes.

"Yeah. Why me? I mean, don't you usually need a virgin for this kind of thing?" How about that, all those years in Sunday school were actually paying off. As well as all those Christmas carols she'd sung as a child. As for the virgin thing… there had been four men in her life. Three she'd slept with. And only one that had any inkling of what to do with a woman's body. The Angel's smile faltered for a moment, as did his brilliance.

"THESE ARE COMPLEX TIMES. AND IN COMPLEX TIMES, YOU MAKE DO WITH WHAT YOU HAVE."

"So... I'm 'what you have?' I don't think I like that." The woman's wonderment was slowly being replaced with another, more confrontational attitude. The Angel had not been expecting this. Last time, the shepherds and simple folk had trembled before His majesty. This one was definitely not trembling. If anything, she seemed... angry.

"DO YOU NOT UNDERSTAND THE HONOUR GOD HAS BESTOWED UPON YOU?"

"To knock me up? That kind of honour?"

Once more, the Angel's beneficent demeanour wavered.

"UMM..."

For the first time in the encounter with the winged man, Angie got up from her chair, raising herself up to her full five feet six inches of indignance. "I don't think so. Look, my mother was a single mother. As were two of my aunts. It was incredibly hard for her and them. And in a perfect world, it would be pretty cool if I could have a partner before I start pumping out kids. Didn't Mary have that Joseph guy? Aren't YOU or Him going to even give me a Joseph?"

By now, the look of puzzlement on the Angel's face was inching its way back to being a smile. "YOU COULD ALWAYS GIVE GEORDI A CALL. YOU LIKED HIM."

So He knew about Geordi. The Angel fraternity and God had been privy to the mess involved with last year's breakup. Now that was both embarrassing and aggravating. Obviously Heaven hadn't been watching close enough. "Sure, I'll call him. When he apologizes!"

Angie spit that last word out at the floating man, making Him back up a few feet. "IT REALLY WASN'T HIS..."

This time she pointed her index finger directly at him with the fury of an arrow leaving a bow string. "Don't you dare take his side!" The Angel blinked. "And you didn't answer my question. Why me? Huh? Why ANGIE CONEB! Seven billion people on this planet, half of them women. Why me?" Angie tried to imitate his robust angelic vocal timbre, with limited success.

"GOD WORKS IN MYSTERIOUS WAYS. TO DIVINE HIS TRUE PURPOSE IS UNFATHOMABLE. HE..."

Angie rolled her eyes. Even in the celestial world, men still acted like men. "You don't know, do you?"

Gabriel's eyes darted back and forth. His floating body seemed to dip down a few inches.

"It's because I'm Indigenous, isn't it? Isn't it?"

"NO. OF COURSE NOT. THAT'S RIDICULOUS. WHY WOULD YOU SAY THAT?"

Angie stormed up to the Angel, preferring to respond face to face. Except the Angel was substantially taller than the woman. And floating. So it was more face to belly button. And why would an Angel need a belly button... but that was an issue best left to explore at a later time. The whole thing was beginning to make sense to the woman. After all, that degree on the wall wasn't just there to hide the scuffed paint where she'd thrown a copy of Thomas King's *The Inconvenient Indian* at Geordi and missed.

"Sure it is. I remember the story of when this first happened. What's her name... Mary. God picked Mary to give birth to Jesus..."

"AND YOU, ANGIE CONEB, WILL..."

"Yeah, yeah, I know. Things have changed since then, you know."

In His defense, the Angel tried to glow brighter, but with little success. "GOD IS ETERNAL. THE PASSAGE OF TIME MEANS NOTHING. HE IS THE BEGINNING AND THE END."

"Yeah, I know all that. The thing is... if I remember my Bible and history correctly, Mary... the first surrogate mother, was a Jew, a marginalized person in her own land which had been invaded and colonized by an invading force, the Romans. That's God's thing, isn't it?"

The Angel bit His lower lip. "AH... NO..."

"Impregnating women that live in what can be called fourth world conditions. I'm an Ojibway woman living in Canada." Angie's mind wrestled with everything that was occurring to her. "Wow! That's so weird."

For the first time in his existence, Gabriel found himself feeling nostalgic, which is very rare for Angels, what with existence being relatively unchanging and eternal. Two thousand years ago seemed like such a simpler, more manageable time. Having to explaining His actions and those of His Lord had not been part of His job description. He was just a foot soldier, granted a pretty high up one in the celestial ladder, but He still pretty much followed orders. And if on Earth a lowly Private or Sargent weren't allowed to question the commands of a mortal General, what chance did He have of getting a straight explanation from God. He just did what He was told. And that had worked up until now.

"ARE YOU QUESTIONING THE WISDOM OF THY LORD AND SAVIOR?"

At the moment, Angie was questioning everything. What had started out as a rather unusual and extreme evening had now developed into one of pretty important social and theological ramifications. With a substantial dash of life changing Angie Coneb issues thrown into the pot. Now, she had the opportunity to ask the questions that had plagued generations of Judeo-Christian scholars, including her Aunt Julia.

"Does this mean the Ojibway will become the Chosen People?"

By now, the toga around Gabriel's neck was getting a little tight. He wrestled with it as He wrestled with the woman's question. There had once been a deep and philosophical question: how many Angels can fit on the head of a pin? Or, in this particular case, a needle. At this moment, on the head of a needle sounded like as good a place as any to be.

Was it Angie's imagination or did the Angel's booming voice now sound a little less boomy?

"I DIDN'T SAY THAT. I DID NOT SAY THAT."

"What are you saying then?" Angie clinched and unclenched her hands as she waited for an answer. The Angel blinked His eyes for a moment. Normally gabriel was perceived as always carrying a trumpet, to loudly announce all the good news his Lord and Master wanted announced. Today, just for something different, he had decided to borrow Michael's sword. It was a little more imposing then a trumpet. Not used to gravity, it seemed to be weighing Him down.

"YOU DON'T SEEM TO UNDERSTAND. THIS IS A GREAT HONOUR. YOU WILL USHER IN THE SECOND COMING."

The woman shook her head. "I don't think so. As I remember, things didn't turn out so well the last time for the Jews. Death. Destruction. Pain. My people have had enough of that already. And you know, Christianity was a mixed blessing in most Indigenous communities. I don't know if we want to be at the forefront of another wave of that. We're just beginning to recover. Personally I don't have anything against you and your boss, the spirit of what he says is cool and amazing. The problem is… it's frequently the people who practice your message that make things difficult. You want to talk contradictory—"

Gabriel found himself in a position of not being able to argue. He knew of this human game where there was a line of people, and at one end somebody would whisper a sentence in an ear. The message would be whispered from person to person til the end of the line, then said aloud. More often than not, the message would be garbled and practically gibberish, losing something as it moved from person to person. Sometimes, when discussing shop in Heaven, that was the theory most frequently passed around concerning GOD'S message. At least, that was Raphael's notion.

"AH AH… YOU WILL USHER IN A NEW AGE OF ENLIGHTENMENT AND…"

"Have you met the human race?" Angie had always been taught that Angels were supposed to be fairly bright and knowledgeable. This one was beginning to sound like a broken record. Her Aunt Julia would be so disappointed. "I mean, looking at the history of the Jewish people is not exactly good publicity for what you're asking. They've had some pretty tough times. Look, if you and God are into finding some poor woman from an oppressed and marginalized people to have a baby, the Anishnawbe aren't interested. We have our own fish to fry."

Gabriel was silent. The woman had said no. He hadn't been expecting that. This was going to be difficult to explain back at headquarters. "YOU CAN'T SAY NO. IT'S... IT'S... NOT ALLOWED."

Angie sat down again, settling into the soft chair her mother had given her two Christmases ago. "Well, what are you going to do about it?"

Though the woman was unaware of the significance of what happened next, she did find it unnerving. For the first time in thousands of years, an Angel frowned. Both sides of Gabriel's mouth turned down, accompanied by a furrowed and troubled brow. In the old days, Michael would have probably slaughtered everybody on the street block, but times had changed. And Gabriel wasn't Michael. "O... O... OKAY. I'LL UHM ,,. I'LL PASS ON YOUR MESSAGE."

What with Gabriel appearing disappointed and a little unhappy, Angie found herself feeling somewhat sympathetic for the Angel. Obviously, this was going to cause some problems back where he came from. But better they were problems for Heaven rather than her. She was pre-diabetic, dyslexic, with only four days left to find another two hundred to top up her rent. Angie Coneb had her own problems. Being the mother of mankind's saviour would only complicate things.

"Look, there are lots of other downtrodden and oppressed people out there that would probably love the opportunity to give birth to the Son of God. I don't know, pick a refugee. There's a whole bunch in North Africa trying to find a new life. There are some Native people in Central America that could use some of the publicity. And don't forget the Rohingyans. I hear they might be interested in being the gateway to a new era."

By this point, Gabriel had lost all interest in speaking to the woman. Glancing out the window behind her, He could see a Tim Hortons and a gas station. This was Earth. He remembered the planet being substantially prettier and simpler. Didn't there used to be a lot of sheep? Amidst this contemplation, the Angel heard the woman's voice again, forcing Him back to this reality.

"You okay? I mean, sorry to pee in your rice crispies but I mean... Really... me? And another thing, what's all this with the 'Son' of God? Why can't it be the 'Daughter' of God? Huh? A woman can open the gates of Heaven just as easily as a man! In fact..."

The best Gabriel could muster was a wan smile. And with that, the Angel and the blinding light were gone. Looking around, the room and the woman's life were dark again. For a few brief seconds, Angie's mind was tumbling with what just happened. It was incredible. When she opened her diary tonight, this evening's events would definitely be a two-pager.

Presently, she picked up the needle and leather patch she'd been working on before Heaven had come knocking on her door. She carefully threaded six violet beads onto the needle. Most the rest were scattered all over the floor. Those she'd deal with later.

Wow, she thought. Wonder what Geordi would think of all this.

The Funeral Fire

Chippewa Tribe, Native American

FOR SEVERAL NIGHTS after the interment of a Chippewa a fire is kept burning upon the grave. This fire is lit in the evening, and carefully supplied with small sticks of dry wood, to keep up a bright but small fire. It is kept burning for several hours, generally until the usual hour of retiring to rest, and then suffered to go out. The fire is renewed for four nights, and sometimes for longer. The person who performs this pious office is generally a near relative of the deceased, or one who has been long intimate with him. The following tale is related as showing the origin of the custom.

A small war party of Chippewas encountered their enemies upon an open plain, where a severe battle was fought. Their leader was a brave and distinguished warrior, but he never acted with greater bravery, or more distinguished himself by personal prowess, than on this occasion. After turning the tide of battle against his enemies, while shouting for victory, he received an arrow in his breast, and fell upon the plain. No warrior thus killed is ever buried, and according to ancient custom, the chief was placed in a sitting posture upon the field, his back supported by a tree, and his face turned towards the direction in which his enemies had fled. His headdress and equipment were accurately adjusted as if he were living, and his bow leaned against his shoulder. In this posture his companions left him. That he was dead appeared evident to all, but a strange thing had happened. Although deprived of speech and motion, the chief heard distinctly all that was said by his friends. He heard them lament his death without having the power to contradict it, and he felt their touch as they adjusted his posture, without having the power to reciprocate it. His anguish, when he felt himself thus abandoned, was extreme, and his wish to follow his friends on their return home so completely filled his mind, as he saw them one after another take leave of him and depart, that with a terrible effort he arose and followed them. His form, however, was invisible to them, and this aroused in him surprise, disappointment, and rage, which by turns took possession of him. He followed their track, however, with great diligence. Wherever they went he went, when they walked he walked, when they ran he ran, when they encamped he stopped with them, when they slept he slept, when they awoke he awoke. In short, he mingled in all their labours and toils, but he was excluded from all their sources of refreshment, except that of sleeping, and from the pleasures of participating in their conversation, for all that he said received no notice.

"Is it possible," he cried, "that you do not see me, that you do not hear me, that you do not understand me? Will you suffer me to bleed to death without offering to stanch my wounds? Will you permit me to starve while you eat around me? Have those whom I have so often led to war so soon forgotten me? Is there no one who recollects me, or who will offer me a morsel of food in my distress?"

Thus he continued to upbraid his friends at every stage of the journey, but no one seemed to hear his words. If his voice was heard at all, it was mistaken for the rustling of the leaves in the wind.

At length the returning party reached their village, and their women and children came out, according to custom, to welcome their return and proclaim their praises.

"Kumaudjeewug! Kumaudjeewug! Kumaudjeewug! they have met, fought, and conquered!" was shouted by every mouth, and the words resounded through the most distant parts of the village. Those who had lost friends came eagerly to inquire their fate, and to know whether they had died like men. The aged father consoled himself for the loss of his son with the reflection that he had fallen manfully, and the widow half forgot her sorrow amid the praises that were uttered of the bravery of her husband. The hearts of the youths glowed with martial ardour as they heard these flattering praises, and the children joined in the shouts, of which they scarcely knew the meaning. Amidst all this uproar and bustle no one seemed conscious of the presence of the warrior-chief. He heard many inquiries made respecting his fate. He heard his companions tell how he had fought, conquered, and fallen, pierced by an arrow through his breast, and how he had been left behind among the slain on the field of battle.

"It is not true," declared the angry chief, "that I was killed and left upon the field! I am here. I live; I move; see me; touch me. I shall again raise my spear in battle, and take my place in the feast."

Nobody, however, seemed conscious of his presence, and his voice was mistaken for the whispering of the wind.

He now walked to his own lodge, and there he found his wife tearing her hair and lamenting over his fate. He endeavoured to undeceive her, but she, like the others, appeared to be insensible of his presence, and not to hear his voice. She sat in a despairing manner, with her head reclining on her hands. The chief asked her to bind up his wounds, but she made no reply. He placed his mouth close to her ear and shouted:

"I am hungry, give me some food!"

The wife thought she heard a buzzing in her ear, and remarked it to one who sat by. The enraged husband now summoning all his strength, struck her a blow on the forehead. His wife raised her hand to her head, and said to her friend:

"I feel a slight shooting pain in my head."

Foiled thus in every attempt to make himself known, the warrior-chief began to reflect upon what he had heard in his youth, to the effect that the spirit was sometimes permitted to leave the body and wander about. He concluded that possibly his body might have remained upon the field of battle, while his spirit only accompanied his returning friends. He determined to return to the field, although it was four days' journey away. He accordingly set out upon his way. For three days he pursued his way without meeting anything uncommon; but on the fourth, towards evening, as he came to the skirts of the battlefield, he saw a fire in the path before him. He walked to one side to avoid stepping into it, but the fire also changed its position, and was still before him. He then went in another direction, but the mysterious fire still crossed his path, and seemed to bar his entrance to the scene of the conflict. In short, whichever way he took, the fire was still before him – no expedient seemed to avail him.

"Thou demon!" he exclaimed at length, "why dost thou bar my approach to the field of battle? Knowest thou not that I am a spirit also, and that I seek again to enter my body? Dost thou presume that I shall return without effecting my object? Know that I have never been defeated by the enemies of my nation, and will not be defeated by thee!"

So saying, he made a sudden effort and jumped through the flame. No sooner had he done so than he found himself sitting on the ground, with his back supported by a tree, his bow leaning against his shoulder, all his warlike dress and arms upon his body, just as they had been left by his friends on the day of battle. Looking up he beheld a large canicu, or war eagle, sitting in the tree above his head. He immediately recognised this bird to be the same as he had once dreamt of in his youth – the one he had chosen as his guardian spirit, or personal manito. This eagle had carefully watched his body and prevented other ravenous birds from touching it.

The chief got up and stood upon his feet, but he felt himself weak and much exhausted. The blood upon his wound had stanched itself, and he now bound it up. He possessed a knowledge of such roots as have healing properties, and these he carefully sought in the woods. Having found some, he pounded some of them between stones and applied them externally. Others he chewed and swallowed. In a short time he found himself so much recovered as to be able to commence his journey, but he suffered greatly from hunger, not seeing any large animals that he might kill. However, he succeeded in killing some small birds with his bow and arrow, and these he roasted before a fire at night.

In this way he sustained himself until he came to a river that separated his wife and friends from him. He stood upon the bank and gave that peculiar whoop which is a signal of the return of a friend. The sound was immediately heard, and a canoe was despatched to bring him over, and in a short time, amidst the shouts of his friends and relations, who thronged from every side to see the arrival, the warrior-chief was landed.

When the first wild bursts of wonder and joy had subsided, and some degree of quiet had been restored to the village, he related to his people the account of his adventures. He concluded his narrative by telling them that it is pleasing to the spirit of a deceased person to have a fire built upon the grave for four nights after his burial; that it is four days' journey to the land appointed for the residence of the spirits; that in its journey thither the spirit stands in need of a fire every night at the place of its encampment; and that if the friends kindle this fire upon the spot where the body is laid, the spirit has the benefit of its light and warmth on its path, while if the friends neglect to do this, the spirit is subjected to the irksome task of making its own fire each night.

Collected by Charles John Tibbits

The Snail and the Beaver

Osage Nation, Native American

THE FATHER OF THE OSAGE NATION was a snail. It was when the earth was young and little. It was before the rivers had become wide or long, or the mountains lifted their peaks above the clouds, that the snail found himself passing a quiet existence on the banks of the River Missouri. His wants and wishes were but few, and well supplied, and he was happy.

At length the region of the Missouri was visited by one of those great storms which so often scatter desolation over it, and the river, swollen by the melted snow and ice from the mountains, swept away everything from its banks, and among other things the drowsy snail. Upon a log he drifted down many a day's journey, till the river, subsiding, left him and his log upon the banks of the River of Fish. He was left in the slime, and the hot sun beamed fiercely upon him till he became baked to the earth and found himself incapable of moving. Gradually he grew in size and stature, and his form experienced a new change, till at length what was once a snail creeping on the earth ripened into man, erect, tall, and stately. For a long time after his change to a human being he remained stupefied, not knowing what he was or by what means to sustain life. At length recollection returned to him. He remembered that he was once a snail and dwelt upon another river. He became animated with a wish to return to his old haunts, and accordingly directed his steps towards those parts from which he had been removed. Hunger now began to prey upon him, and bade fair to close his eyes before he should again behold his beloved haunts on the banks of the river. The beasts of the forest were many, but their speed outstripped his. The birds of the air fluttered upon sprays beyond his reach, and the fish gliding through the waves at his feet were nimbler than he and eluded his grasp. Each moment he grew weaker, the films gathered before his eyes, and in his ears there rang sounds like the whistling of winds through the woods in the month before the snows. At length, wearied and exhausted, he laid himself down upon a grassy bank.

As he lay the Great Spirit appeared to him and asked:

"Why does he who is the kernel of the snail look terrified, and why is he faint and weary?"

"That I tremble," answered he, "is because I fear thy power. That I faint is because I lack food."

"As regards thy trembling," answered the Great Spirit, "be composed. Art thou hungry?"

"I have eaten nothing," replied the man, "since I ceased to be a snail."

Upon hearing this the Great Spirit drew from under his robe a bow and arrow, and bade the man observe what he did with it. On the topmost bough of a lofty tree sat a beautiful bird, singing and fluttering among the red leaves. He placed an arrow on the bow, and, letting fly, the bird fell down upon the earth. A deer was seen afar off browsing. Again the archer bent his bow and the animal lay dead, food for the son of the snail.

"There are victuals for you," said the Spirit, "enough to last you till your strength enables you to beat up the haunts of the deer and the moose, and here is the bow and arrow."

The Great Spirit also taught the man how to skin the deer, and clothed him with the skin. Having done this, and having given the beasts, fishes, and all feathered creatures to him for his food and raiment, he bade the man farewell and took his departure.

Strengthened and invigorated, the man pursued his journey towards the old spot. He soon stood upon the banks of his beloved river. A few more suns and he would sit down upon the very spot where for so many seasons he had crawled on the slimy leaf, so often dragged himself lazily over the muddy pool. He had seated himself upon the bank of the river, and was meditating deeply on these things, when up crept from the water a beaver, who, addressing him, said in an angry tone:

"Who are you?"

"I am a snail," replied the Snail-Man. "Who are you?"

"I am head warrior of the nation of beavers," answered the other. "By what authority have you come to disturb my possession of this river, which is my dominion?"

"It is not your river," replied the Wasbasha. "The Great Being, who is over man and beast, has given it to me."

The beaver was at first incredulous; but at length, convinced that what the man said was true, he invited him to accompany him to his home. The man agreed, and went with him till they came to a number of small cabins, into the largest of which the beaver conducted him. He invited the man to take food with him, and while the beaver's wife and daughter were preparing the feast, he entertained his guest with an account of his people's habits of life. Soon the wife and daughter made their appearance with the food, and sitting down the Snail-Man was soon at his ease amongst them. He was not, however, so occupied with the banquet that he had not time to be enchanted with the beauty of the beaver's daughter; and when the visit was drawing to a close, so much was he in love, that he asked the beaver to give her to him for his wife. The beaver-chief consented, and the marriage was celebrated by a feast, to which all the beavers, and the animals with whom they had friendly relations, were invited. From this union of the Snail-Man and the Beaver-Maid sprang the tribe of the Osages – at least so it is related by the old men of the tribe.

Collected by Charles John Tibbits

⚡

The Three Sisters

Brigit Truex, Abenaki Nation, Native American

LONG AGO, IN THE TIME BEFORE our elders's elders were young, there were three sisters who lived in a village deep in the woods. The People who lived there had chosen the site wisely. They had everything they needed close by. Many Four-leggeds lived in the forest who could be hunted as game. Finned Swimmers crowded the streams and wide lake. Winged birds nested in the reeds and trees. Standing-still bushes and plants were heavy with berries and nuts. Their flowers, leaves and roots could all be used as well. The People were contented there, watching the seasons move around them. Among those in the village were three special elders. These sisters lived in the same lodge for so long, no one even remembered their given names. Each was simply called Grandmother, out of respect for their many years. Although they could not hunt or garden for themselves, the People made sure they were taken care of. Even if the children had to go deep into the forest to gather fire-wood, they always brought enough for these revered elders.

As close as the Sisters were, they looked nothing alike. Eldest Sister always seemed to have something of her favorite color on or at hand. It might be a stalk of wide-faced sunflower, or the dropped feather of the dawn-bright warbler. She might steep tiny seedpods with golden rod to bring out that tint, then turn them into necklaces. She might weave a cheery yellow thread of tree-bark into a basket. All these were gifts she hid in not-so-secret places for the villagers to find. There was always a smile on her round-as-the sun face. Her laughter sparked the passing of days and nights like a splash of warm sunlight in a cool shade forest.

Her next-older sister was quite the opposite. Where Oldest Sister was round, Middle Sister was lean. She was as thin and straight as a sapling. Her dark eyes sparkled like stars in her narrow face. All three sisters favored the lovely green color for their deerskin dresses. This was a special treat that Middle Sister worked on, using nettle leaves. So dyed so many pieces, her fine long fingers became stained with the color as well. Those hands also crafted the finest beadwork. The village women loved to watch how she did each piece. Inspired by the flowers and vines surrounding their homes, she brought these designs to life with each moccasin and jacket she worked on. The People often said she managed to fool other creatures with her work, it was so real. She would smile if a winged butterfly would land on her foot, seeking to gather nectar from a looks-like-a-flower stitched there. Other times, a hungry bird might peck at a beaded berry sewn on a winter hood, thinking they'd found a treat. More laughter shared and shared again, over the years.

Youngest Sister was somewhere in the middle, in her looks. Tall and dignified, she was neither plump nor skinny. This was an elder who studied the world about her with care and patience. Having lived so long, she had learned much. This wisdom was valued among the People. They often asked her advice. Hunters might ask about the Hunger Moon time, when food was scarce, when the game had burrowed deep in their lodges or flown far, far away until the warmth returned. Young mothers might have questions about their children, what to worry about, what to dismiss as a passing stage. The children themselves loved to gather around her when she sat before her lodge. She would wait until they quieted, then tell and retell their favorite stories.

When she walked along the village edges at dusk, her snow-colored hair stood out against her dark green dresses and always marked her location.

One winter, the hunting was especially bad. There were simply no four-leggeds at all. Moose and Deer disappeared. Beaver never left his tangled lodge of branches under the thick ice. The same water was shared by the silver-scaled finned Swimmers who barely wriggled their tails, dozing in the dark, chill lake. Frogs huddled in the heavy mud. Wingeds crowded together for warmth in their hollow trees. All the while, the snows fell, one after another. Some days, Sun never showed its face, hidden behind a thick robe of low, grey clouds. Moon might have gotten fat, but no one could tell. Hunting was useless. Walking was difficult. Even breathing was hard.

Spears of ice hung over the doorways. It draped the sides of lodges like animal hides, stiff and white. The People began to worry. Would there be enough food to last this long Starving Time?

Would the elders and children survive? They did as they always had – they prayed to Creator and continued to share what they had, making sure all were cared for. When the last rainbow-shaded fish was cooked, portions were set aside for the Sisters. When dried berries rattled in the birch-bark basket, a handful was taken to their lodge. The final piece of deer meat was divided so some would be set aside for the beloved elders.

After a very long time, Sun managed to push aside the cloud-robes. The snow began to shrink. Ice became water again, tumbling over itself rushing to the lake. A small brown bird appeared, singing when the shadows were just showing themselves at dawn. The People came out of their lodges and gave thanks to Creator for once again, letting them survive the harshest of times. They looked around, smiling at each other. Until, they realized something was wrong.

Someone was missing. Where were Grandmothers? Asking each, they realized it had been a while since the Elders had been seen. The People hurried to their lodge at the edge of the village. It was empty. Their sleeping robes were folded neatly. Stacked bowls sat on a ledge near the cold firepit. But where were the Sisters? No one knew what to think. What could have happened? The People began to worry. Hunters called deep in the forest. The women walked the fields. Children searched along the marsh. There was no sign anywhere. The daylight was fading. Soon, Grandmother Moon moved across the sky, spreading her white light onto the village. The Star People lit their campfires far overhead. Small, fat clouds drifted, dropping a fine gentle rain. It was the Breath of Life.

The next morning, Grandfather Sun rose brighter than ever. The People came out of their lodges, surprised by the brilliant light. Together, they walked toward the sunrise, reaching the lodge of the Sisters. Only there was no longer a lodge there. Instead, they found a clearing, filled with three new plants. In the center of the plot was a single tall stalk, with sleek, leaf-wrapped pods growing along its length. Fine white tassels, the color of Youngest Sister's hair, swayed from the ends of each. At the feet of this stalk sat plump yellow-orange squash, round as bowl, the favored color of Oldest Sister. And around the stalk and the melons, lush vines of green twined around and over, a net full of narrow pods like slim green fish. They reminded the People of Middle Sister, devoted to her sisters as each was to the other. This gift of the Three Sisters, Corn, Squash and Beans, had been given by Creator when they had so little, when even then, they shared and took care of each other. It was given in memory of their beloved elders, the Three Sisters who lived with them for so very long. And now they would be with them forever.

Beaver's Tail

Brigit Truex, Abenaki Nation, Native American

LONG AGO, before the two-leggeds were here, there were the Twins. One was Good, one was Evil. Because of this, they lived apart from each other. One day, Evil Twin was sitting in front of his lodge, bored. He looked for something to do, something to get into. He looked up and saw a gathering of grey clouds overhead. Not too far above, since they were giant Twins. He reached up and grabbed a handful of clouds and began to squeeze them. Water began to drip from the clouds. The tighter he squeezed, the more water fell. Soon they were all wrung out, white and dry. By then, puddles formed into ponds, then overflowed into lakes. Evil Twin kept on pulling down more clouds to squeeze. Rivers began to spill their banks. The earth began to flood. The rising waters worried the four-leggeds and the winged ones. They gathered their young and moved to higher ground, away from the water.

There was one special valley, high in the mountains, that was safe so far. It was the home of Awasos, the brown-robed Bear, and her furry new Cub. It was also the home of sky-colored Jay, Tidesso, and her fluffy nestlings. Shrewd Azeban, with his clever face mask, paced the forest, wondering what to do about the flooded valleys below. His raccoon-eyes widened with alarm as he saw the waters creeping up the hillsides towards their homes. He drummed on a hollow log, calling the other four-leggeds and winged ones together. Something had to be done, soon.

At last, the creatures gathered in a clearing. Last to waddle in was Tmakwa. Raccoon Azeban had his own name for this late arrival. He called him 'Beaver of Grand Entrances' and 'Braggart with the Fabulous Tail.' True, it was as large as a gourd. Proud Tmakwa used it for summer shade, as a snow-cover roof in winter. Tmakwa said Azeban was simply jealous of such a luxurious, follow-along-appendage.

While the animals all chittered and chatted among themselves, telling their tales of worry, Azeban was thinking. "What if?" the chief-thief-of-nighttime stealth, wondered – "*Could this halt the beaver's forever bragging? Could I stop him?*" Looking thoughtful, a plea squeaked from his tiny mouth.

"Who can sweep the sodden grey clouds away from Evil Twin? We need someone *clever enough, brave enough*, to outwit him," Azeban asked dramatically.

"All puzzled we are. We are *stumped*!"

The animals looked at each other, worried about the rising water. Shaking their heads, they returned to their homes, without any good ideas. Tmakwa mused as he headed to his pond. He murmured to the trees he passed. They rustled and nodded their answers to him. The next morning, he began his plan.

It seemed as nothing had changed. The white birch, dripping gold, was first to lay itself down. Next, the grey ash. Then the sturdy alder. Tree after tree offered itself to help save the animals. Using his scraper-wide teeth, Tmakwa chewed and chewed their trunks. The chips flew, rose higher than his fabled, fluffy tail. The trees leaned forward, fell into long piles beside the pond. All day, back and forth the beaver swam, carrying branches in his mouth. He wove limbs into a fence, a dam. Steadily, he kept at it all day, and into the night-darkness. Slowly, gradually, the rush of flooding waters became a slim wash, then a trickle. Then – nothing! Overhead, the clouds had shrunk to tatters of white. The only sound was the wind, sighing in relief.

In the far-off valleys, rivers began to settle back into their banks; streams narrowed into their usual paths. Drowned reeds could breathe again. Lakes became small ponds. Of course, by now, the Evil Twin also noticed the quiet. No more pelting rain, no more sheets of water flooding the hollows. He was puzzled, then angry. His footsteps sounded like thunder under the cloudless sky. He stomped across the land. Who had ruined his pastime, he fumed.

At last he came upon the secret mountain valley. He saw the plugged-up creek-bed, the dam that toothy, fat-tailed Tmakwa had made. The Twin was furious!

"I'll show that meddling pest!" he cried.

Overhead, Tidesso scolded a warning, flitting from branch to branch. Her safe and dry chicks stared, wide-eyed. Even brave Awasos urged her beloved Cub to climb higher up the tallest pine, away from the giant and his temper tantrum, bellowing through the woods. Tmakwa had just come ashore, to rest from his work. As soon as he saw the huge Twin, he knew he was in trouble. Evil Twin spotted the wet, waddling beaver at the same time and started waving his haunch-like hands in the air. Around and around the pond they ran, Tmakwa just inches away from his pursuer. But the beaver's little legs were no match for those tree-trunk legs of the Twin.

Evil Twin was gaining on him. Suddenly, the giant's huge foot came down on Tmakwa's wonderous, pride-full tail. It was squashed flat! All that beauteous, shiny fur was scraped away! Gone! All that was left was smooth and shiny, like the bottom of an old, trail-worn moccasin!

No matter! Tmakwa dove fast and deep into the water, paddling for his life. He headed straight to his mid-pond lodge and slipped inside. Beaver was safe and dry. Evil Twin pounded his feet, thrashing in the water, shaking leaves from the trees. He hadn't seen the hidden lodge behind the fallen trees. At last, he gave up in disgust. Muttering and waving his fists, he left. There were no more clouds left to squeeze anyway.

In the quiet, the animals climbed out of their hiding places. They gathered in the clearing, to exclaim over their success, to congratulate the hard-working beaver for his cleverness. Even sneaky Azeban had to blink his raccoon eyes twice when he saw his to-be-taught-a-lesson, four-leggged friend swimming towards them. Smiling as wide as the pond, here came Tmakwa, minus his fluffy fat tail, flashing front teeth big as a fist and turned gold as the sunset! Whatever had happened?

"Rewards for my labors," the beaver puffed out his chest. "And this," he said as he slapped his new now-deflated tail on the water, "this too. Smooth like a hand-drum. Listen! You can hear me from anywhere! Aren't I just fine?"

Off went Tmakwa to his secret underwater lodge, with a last *thwack*! *thwack*! of his tail.

Woodchuck Winter

Brigit Truex, Abenaki Nation, Native American

LONG AGO, the Animal People could speak to each other. One fall morning, mask-faced Azeban came out of his den to see his little friend Mikoa running up and down the oak trees, clutching as many acorns (anasaminal in the language of the Dawnland People) as he could carry. Chittering and waving his furry tail, the little gray squirrel dashed about, digging and burying his finds all over. So many, Azeban wondered if he'd ever find them again. He shook his head. Finally, the little climber stopped.

Azeban called out to him – "Greetings my friend! What are you doing, so busy this early in the day?"

"I'm worried about the coming Winter," he replied. "I don't know if it will be very cold. How many acorns I will need."

"Well," Azeban said, "it's too early for me to know. I SUPPOSE it will be cold, as it is every year."

"That's what I think too," answered Mikoa, "but will it be VERY cold?"

"Hmmm. Maybe you should ask old Akaskw the Woodchuck," Azeban suggested. "He's been through LOTS of winters. He's pretty wise, you know."

"That's a good idea," his friend said, "just as soon as I finish getting those last acorns!"

With that, the squirrel shook his furry tail and climbed back up the oak tree, running along the wide branches, breaking off acorns and stuffing them into his mouth. His cheeks bulged out on both sides like fat little full-moons.

Azeban smiled his toothy smile and went down to the stream to wash his little paws before he ate his first meal. He was very fussy about that.

He chuckled to himself as he saw Mikoa leaping from tree to tree, heading to where roly-poly brown Akaskw was sunning himself near his burrow in the meadow, moving very slowly from time to time to stay in the warmth.

Azeban wasn't called 'Trickster' for no reason.

Sure enough, the next day, Mikoa was hard at it. He had cleared the closest oak of all its acorns. Little tufts of dirt showed where he had hidden his winter store of food. Some even peeked through a small opening in a hollow log lying close by. They were packed in like kernels of corn, thought Azeban with a laugh.

Mikao headed off toward a new stand of spreading oaks, loaded with even more shiny acorns, fat and tempting. So many trips to make, so much food to hide.

"You never know," he whispered to himself. He was not going to worry.

But of course, that's what he did. He kept muttering and chittering, shaking his tail with each trip up and down the trees.

"Maybe I should ask again," he said to himself, "just in case Akaskw know more."

Azeban watched from across the meadow. He could have predicted this scene. In fact, he had. He knew what a worrier the squirrel could be. It was fun to watch.

The next day, when Azeban spotted Mikoa coming down the tree, the little squirrel hopped over and said,

"Azeban, what do YOU think about the coming winter?"

"Oh, I'm not at all sure! I was going to ask Akaskw myself. Do you want to come along?"

"Oh yes," his little friend said. "I would like that. I'm wondering if he know more this time. Let's go!"

So, off they went. They got there just as Akaskw was finishing up his meal of lilies he brought back from the marsh nearby.

"Greetings, my friends," Woodchuck called out as they approached him.

"How are you doing?"

"Greetings, Akaskw. We are good," said Azeban, being the elder of the two, spoke first. "Mikoa and I have a question for you," he continued. "We are wondering about the coming winter. Do you think it will be cold?"

"Cold? Indeed," Akaskw answered."

"HOW cold?" chirped the little grey squirrel anxiously.

"Oh, pretty cold," was the reply.

"I was worried about that!" Mikoa said quickly. He was twitching around, his tail flapping back and forth like a leaf in a windstorm.

"I better get more food!" he said and raced off, calling "Thank you!" over his shoulder as he disappeared into the woods.

"Well," said Akaskw, "that was interesting."

"He's a bit more wound up than usual," Azeban said with a smile. "He may be back."

After they chatted a while, they parted ways, each going to find more to eat on these days of shortened sunlight.

Four more times, Azeban saw his worried friend run zigzag across the meadow to where Akaskw had his burrow. Four more times, he came darting across the field and into the forest. When he asked the squirrel about what he found out, his answer from Woodchuck was always "oh yes, colder! MUCH colder!"

Azeban shook his head, hiding a small smile below his twinkling, masked eyes.

"Good to know," he said, thanking his nervous friend.

The poor little squirrel had almost worn himself out completely, running up and down the oaks, stuffing his cheeks with acorns. The ground around was full of little humps of dirt, hastily covered over with leaves and small twigs as if to disguise them. Few would be fooled, Azeban thought, but he didn't say anything.

At last, the weather did get cooler and cooler. It got darker much earlier in the day. Many of the winged ones, the birds, disappeared, calling goodbye as they flew towards the south. The leaves on the tall trees began to show different colors, more like the sunset each day – scarlets, oranges, bright yellow, deep reds and russets. One by one, they slipped off the branches and settled on the ground like many-colored robes spread out. Moose and deer could be seen moving through the forest now, among the bared tree-trunks. The tapping of red-headed Obasas wasn't heard as much either. Then, one day, it happened. The snow began to drift down, just as the beautiful leaves had earlier. Only this time, the robe was all white, like rabbit fur or the downy fluff from the cattails in the marsh.

Finally, Azeban went to see Akaskw before he entered his burrow for the season.

"My friend," Azeban called out, "it seems winter is indeed here. I know you will be warm inside, but I wanted to ask you about your warnings to Mikoa. Just how, if you don't mind telling me, how did you know it would be so cold?"

"Simple," said Akaskw in his wisest tone. "But don't tell everyone. Since we're alone here, I will tell you." He motioned with his fat little front paw for Azeban to come closer.

"I watched," he whispered, "I watched the squirrel to see how many acorns he stored away. The more he hid, the COLDER the winter is going to be! Isn't that smart of me?" he laughed and backed into his burrow for the long cold season.

Azeban just nodded his head wisely and went home, chuckling to himself. He'd have some laughs to get him through the winter himself. He was as clever as usual!

Confusion of Tongue

David Unaipon, Ngarrindjeri,

Aboriginal and Torres Strait Islander Peoples

KULE THOU OO (in the long ago) uoo goo nook (when) the coming of the many dawns and many sunrises, the sun shone on sea and land, kuk koo loon distributing its life and energy to Animal, Bird, Reptile, and Insect, Noop eel itch nungee, the sun continued its journey across the trackless sky over to Tolkami (the mysterious west) there was never a cloud of disappointment or sorrow, but eternal sunshine. Creation smiled, and Animal, Bird, Reptile, and Insect were linked up by one common language. For instance, the Kangaroo and Goanna were able to converse and exchange ideas; so would the Eagle Hawk and Platypus; and the Wombat and Dragon-fly. Each endeavoured to please and entertain and instruct the other, whilst following their individual vocations.

The food of the Animals, Birds, and Reptiles consisted of vegetable and fish. Once every year they would congregate and have great feasting and corroborees, and there would be giving in marriage. But on this occasion they were going to do something which would change the whole condition of affairs of the race. Some were desirous that they should give away in marriage the Kangaroo and Emu, the Dingo and Goanna, the Koala (Teddy Bear) and Lyre Bird. Whilst some were in favour of it, others were strongly opposed. Those in favour were strongly represented by the Kangaroos, Emus, Dingos, Goannas, Carpet Snakes, Koalas, Pelicans, Cockatoos, and Lyre Birds. Against them were the Tortoises, Frogs, and Crows. These three stood out against the whole of the tribes. The majority felt within themselves that they had a great and cunning antagonist in the Crow, for they knew that his wit and cunning would be sufficient to overcome their brute force.

Those in favour of the proposition set to work to consider what tactics they should adopt. The Dingo enquired of the Tontick nub bie (Tortoise), but he would not tell how or when the Crow would begin his campaign.

The Frog was next approached, but he too refused to give information.

Whilst they were preparing bann ka gee (boomerangs), yar na barrie (throwing waddies for killing animals or to do battle), key key (reed spears used in warfare) and other weapons, the three confederates, the Crow, Tortoise, and Frog, whose weapon was their mind, used to meet on top of a mountain or in the open country, on a great plain where there were no trees or shrubs, and they would sit and plan out a method of attack. The three were of one mind that if their opponents could be caused to have a great hunger, and to become angry with each other, they would be able to dispose of all their silly ideas.

Now there were three things which the whole of the tribes admired. First, the Crow was a great composer of native songs and an active dancer and impersonator; the Frog was one of the greatest dancers – more so than the Crow – and he was an artist and painted designs on his body that were unique with colouring that was much sought after and he was the possessor of a wonderful bass voice which could be heard for miles, and what was most remarkable, he was a ventriloquist. The Tortoise possessed neither voice nor agility.

The first act announced was a dance by the Tortoise in imitation of the Kangaroo. This aroused intense curiosity and wonder. Every Animal, Bird, Reptile, and Insect of the tribes turned out to see the

Tortoise dance. They were asked to sit in a semicircle, and no one was allowed to cross, because the Crow reserved the remainder of the circle for his performance. The Tortoise and Frog retired behind the scenes and Crow began to sing the song of the Kangaroo. Presently a figure approached the footlights. There was great shouting as the Tortoise came creeping slowly towards the audience, and at a sign from the Crow commenced leaping and bounding here and there just like a Kangaroo. They whispered amongst themselves how wonderful it was to see the slow-moving Tortoise acting the Kangaroo dance.

'Kay hey (Hurrah, hurrah),' they shouted.

The figure dancing was that of the Frog, wearing on his back a coolamon with a shield in front. The second dance, the Swan dance, was announced, and also that the Tortoise would sing the Swan song. Taking his stand in front of the audience, the Tortoise commenced singing, whilst the Crow danced to the song. The Animals, Birds, and Reptiles could not understand how it could be the voice of the Tortoise singing. Really it was the cunning Frog ventrilo quist.

The audience was carried away with enthusiasm by the marvellous performance of the slow-moving, voiceless Tortoise.

'Kay hey, kay hey! Mumgung! (Hurrah! Again! Encore)' they shouted, and for three days and three nights the performance lasted.

On the fourth morning everyone began to feel hungry, and the Kangaroo called out: 'Get the net, bring the net, and go fishing. The people are famishing with hunger.'

The Pelican set out and caught a number of fish, and the Crow was unanimously appointed by the various tribes to take charge of the distribution of them.

'Come, let us go to yonder point and cook the fish, ' he said. 'You know it is against the rules of the tribe to cook fish where they are caught. But there is not sufficient, try and get some more in yonder bay.'

And they dragged with their net and caught some.

'Come to yonder point, it is unlawful to make a fire and cook here,' he kept repeating, until the whole tribe became impatient.

They began abusing the Crow, and the cunning Frog threw his voice, making it appear that it came from the Kangaroo in support of the Crow.

Presently it appeared that the voice of the Kangaroo was insulting the Emu, then the Goanna commenced to insult the Koo ka ku, and the Wombat and the Dingo. They all grew angry with one another.

The Frog saw his opportunity and called: 'To battle! To battle!'

They were so angry that they all commenced calling and shouting and calling each other ugly names. Each challenged the other to battle, and there was hurling of spear and boomerang. There was a terrible pandemonium of sound.

The only tribe which stood aloof and took no part in using insulting words, and which strove to bring about a reconciliation, was the Lyre Bird, and no one would listen to his entreaties. That is why Animal, Bird, Reptile, and Insect tribes have adopted a language of their own, and that the Lyre Bird is able to imitate them all.

The Gherawhar (Goanna)

David Unaipon, Ngarrindjeri,

Aboriginal and Torres Strait Islander Peoples

THIS IS A story belonging to the Murrumbidgee River tribe, and they associate this locality as the first settled home of the Gherawhar (Goanna family) after leaving their temporary home at Shoalhaven, and before migrating to other parts of Australia. When they occupied this country there was no flowing Murrumbidgee River. The only river then was the Murray, which was formed by the ancient Pondi, a fish commonly called the Murray cod.

Now one of the laws agreed to by the Animals, Birds, and Reptiles, was that each tribe should marry not into their own tribe, but some other. For instance in the case of the Gherawhar, he would have to marry into the Muldarie family (the Magpie), so the wife of the Gherawhar was a Teal Teal, a little bird like the Magpie family in appearance, but a smaller type. At this time of the occupation of the Murrumbidgee district there lived on the Wolkundmia (north side) of the Gherawhar a great hunting family known as the Wandhillie (Porcupine) tribe, and at the Tolkamia (west side) lived another well known family, the Peenjullie (Emu) tribe. They too were hunters, but they did not attain to that perfection in bush craft as the Wandhillie.

After the landing of these Beings from their home in the sea of the birth of day, the change of place and climate and environment caused a change in each life, more so in the Gherawhar family. They were in their native land a very industrious family; they tilled and cultivated the soil, and grew vegetables and fruit. But since coming to Australia the climate had caused them to dislike vegetable food, and an uncontrollable craving for flesh food took possession of them. They became cannibals, and would slay and devour the smaller lizards of their species, and sometimes when it would happen that a young Wandhillie would wander from the care of his parents and become lost, and like little children would begin crying, perhaps a Gherawhar would hear the noise and would know at once that it was a cry of distress of a little Wandhillie, and he would hurry on towards the sound and pounce upon the helpless thing and devour it.

One thing noticeable when the Gherawhar changed their diet was that they became very lazy, indolent, and dishonest. They would steal food from their neighbours, the Wandhillie and Peenjullie, and it seemed strange that for many years the Wandhillie and Peenjullie could not find out the culprit. The Gherawhar were so cunning that they were able to cover up all clues leading to their discovery. Every surrounding tribe knew that the Gherawhar were lazy, and they also had a suspicion that they did steal their food, but were not able to sheath home the charge, until it came about in an unexpected way. One day the Wandhillie organised a hunting expedition and the Gherawhar heard of it, and on that day they went along and met the Wandhillie all prepared with their spears and Nulla nulla.

The Chief hunter of the Wandhillie was giving instructions. 'Ten shall go Wolkundmia (north), ten to Kolkamia (south), ten to Karramia (east), ten to Tolkamia (west). And you shall all walk straight along until you reach parties consisting of another who shall join, and then all shall spread out and walk in a circle, gradually coming towards the centre which you are now about to leave.'

And just as they were starting forth the Gherawhar, who were in hiding and listening to all that was said, suddenly made their appearance, looking as if they were surprised, and were sorry to interrupt them.

'Oh, that 's all right, we are just going to hunt for food.'

'Oh,' said a Gherawhar, 'will you allow us to accompany your party?'

'Will you pardon me, ' said a Wandhillie, 'but we think that you cannot help us in this matter, as you will admit that you are not competent to hunt the game, and in that case you may be a hindrance.'

'Yes, we are no hunters of game, we are aware of that, but supposing you allow us to come with you. There is no doubt we shall find honey. I am sure some of you know where there is some to be got; admitting that we are unable to hunt, you will also admit you are no tree climbers. Now you all are very very fond of honey. Come, let us accompany you. '

The Wandhillie were fond of honey. They would give anything that was in their possession for honey, and now here was an offer made to them by the Gherawhar, who were looked upon as expert climbers. The suggestion was such a tempting one that the Wandhillie would not let it pass, accepted the offer, and gave their consent that they should follow. Now they began the drive, and they were very successful. Those who were in front would come upon the game first and slay the Possums and hang them up in the limb of a tree, and those following would come and take them down and carry them to the centre. In the meantime the Gherawhar were busy; wherever they saw a bee, they would follow it until they discovered the hive. And they would climb the tree, and with their stone axes would chop and chop, just so that the Wandhillie were under the impression that it must be hard work for the Gherawhar to climb the tree, chopping footsteps as they climbed. But this chopping was only a sham, the Gherawhar were able to climb without steps cut into the bark of the tree.

Now when the Wandhillie and Cherawhar arrived at the starting point with their spoil, the Wandhillie were very tired and exhausted with running and chasing and carrying the game. Before resting, they made a large fire and began shearing the Possums before cooking them. After completing this first process the Gherawhar gave the hunters some honey to eat, so they sat down and enjoyed a good sweet meal. Then the Gherawhar suggested that they should lie down and have a sleep, and they would cook the food and wake them when it was done.

The Wandhillie agreed that it would just suit them and so they all lay down to sleep. One of the members of the Gherawhar went away to a large gum standing just on the boundary-line of the Gherawhar and Wandhillie hunting ground. This large gum tree was used as a place of refuge or vantage point, where the Gherawhar could take view of the doings of the Wandhillie.

Whilst the Wandhillie were sleeping one Gherawhar was removing all obstacles that were in the way leading to this tree, and the others were attending to the cooking of the Possums. Now the cook would place the head of the Possum into the midst of the fire with the tail out, the idea was that the tail would serve as a handle. Sometimes a Wandhillie would drowsily half-raise himself into a sitting position and enquire: 'Are they cooked?'

The Gherawhar would answer: 'No, a little while longer,' and the Wandhillie would lie down again. Then another would do the same and enquire: 'Are they cooked?' and the Cherawhar would reply, 'No, a little while longer.'

Now this was repeated by each Wandhillie, and they had the feeling that something was going to happen.

Now number two Gherawhar, who had climbed to the topmost limb of the gum tree, saw that everything was ready, and that there were no other Wandhillie about, and gave the signal. And the cook Gherawhar waited. Half-rising from his sleep a Wandhillie enquired: 'Are they cooked?'

'No,' said the Gherawhar. He waited a moment as the Wandhillie lay down to sleep, then suddenly rose to his feet and taking the Possums by the tail, made a dash for the gum. But when he did this a coal of fire fell upon the belly of a Wandhillie and burnt him so much that he jumped up with pain and trod upon a firestick, and scattered fire upon the other sleeping Wandhillie, who were burnt, some on the leg and other parts of their bodies. They rose, shrieking with pain. The first who rose came to himself, and looking into the fire, saw that the Possums as well as the cook were not there.

Turning sharply round he saw the Gherawhar running as fast as he could with the cooked Possums, and shouted: 'Look, there goes the Gherawhar.'

Seizing a firestick, which the others did also, he gave chase, and just caught up to the Gherawhar as he was about ten yards from the foot of the gum tree. A Wandhillie raised a firestick, and down it came swiftly upon the back of the Gherawhar, who ran around the gum tree. Just as the Gherawhar turned, out flashed a blaze of fire and it came into contact with his body. Round and round like a merry-go-round, with streaks of blazing stick, blow after blow was delivered at the body of the Gherawhar. One of the Wandhillie suddenly stopped and waited as the Gherawhar came round the tree. A flash of fire-light, and a blow upon his head, but still the Gherawhar clung to his prize. Then in desperation the Gherawhar made an upward move on the trunk of the gum tree, and climbed and climbed until he reached the hollow which was the resting place, and with the assistance of the other members of his race, packed the cooked Possums safely away and then sat down and enjoyed a meal. Down below the Wandhillie were shouting threat after threat, and strange to say it did not occur to them to burn the tree, but they attempted to throw a firestick into the hollow. They tried time after time, but met with failure, and in disgust as well as sadness, they went home, vowing to be avenged.

The Gherawhar who stole the Possums became very ill indeed. His body was covered with the marks caused by the blazing firesticks and these marks have been handed down ever since that day to all the Gherawhar as a reminder of their theft in the days long ago.

Now after some months of illness and suffering the Gherawhar became well, and they joined the great Waillarroomundi; that is, they went back to the great camping-ground, or what the modern boys and girls would say went back into town or city. Now, after this event a great drought visited the country; there was no rain and all the dams and rock holes became dry, and the Wandhillie and Peenjullie tribes did not know what to do. Because there were among members of their tribes many aged and infirm, some were sick, and a great many had little children, it was rather a difficult proposition. They had no means of taking them down to the River Murray. The drought did not affect the Gherawhar tribe, as they were in possession of a large reservoir which would last them for many, many years.

The cries of the little children and the distress of the aged and sick touched the hearts of the wives of the Gherawhar, and they would secretly go among them and do all they could to relieve their want and suffering. One day they enquired of their husbands the whereabouts of this great rock-hole, as they were anxious to go and get a supply to give to the aged and the sick and the children of the Wandhillie and Peenjullie. But the selfish Gherawhar refused to tell them, and what was more, they said to their wives: 'Since you are taking such an interest in the need of other Beings, we will not give you much water, but just sufficient to slake your thirst.'

And the Teal Teal, wives of the Gherawhar, found it useless to plead with their obstinate husbands. But they were determined that although they had given way to many objections before, and had willingly suffered the indignity of their refusals, they would not let this insult go by.

So they began their search, unknown to their husbands. They would take up their yam-sticks and make their husbands believe that they were going to dig yams and other roots of plants and shrubs, and they would track the footprints of their husbands, which led them into the mountains, but at the foot of the mountains they lost all trace of the footprints, so they returned to the valley and gathered a few yams and herbs, and went straight home to their mia mia. They would cook the yams in the hot ashes and then sit down with their husbands and family to a meal.

And the Gherawhar would ask questions where they had been so long, which was unusual.

'I noticed a speck of dirt that comes from the mountain. Have you been there?'

And the wives would say: 'What do you think you silly, we go hunting yams on the mountain top? We find and dig yams in the low flat country, not on rocky mountains. Now why do you ask such questions?' The Gherawhar without another word would lie down upon the Possum skins.

In the morning, just as the sun rose over the eastern range of the mountain, the Gherawhar were out looking for food. Their wives were up too, and gathered together and held a conference as to what steps to adopt to try and wrest the secret of the reservoir, and one more thoughtful than the others suggested that it would be a wise plan to go upon the mountain and make a mia mia and camp there, taking observations.

'Now who has courage among you? Let us sit awhile and think who will go.'

So they sat in silence a few moments, then up rose a figure, and all eyes were fixed on her. She was the wife of the Chief, and she spoke: 'Karroonnoo, Sister, I will take the responsibility. I volunteer to go. I consider it my duty as the wife of a Chief, and I am convinced within me that it is the wife of a Chief 's duty. Who will come and assist me to take my Now wondie (Camp, belongings, rug, etc.)?'

Up rose two young wives. 'We go with you.'

So they made haste and rolled up the belongings of the Chief 's wife, and hurried away to the mountain before the Chief and the other Gherawhar returned from their hunting expedition. Halfway up the side of the mountain was a spot which gave a go od view ofthe surrounding valley, especially the Gherawhar camping-ground. After making the mia mia the two returned home, leaving the Chief 's wife.

In the evening the young Chief summoned the Gherawhar to come before his mia mia and to give information whether anyone had seen his wife, or knew of any suspicious character that would lead to her disappearance. They were all ignorant about the matter, and expressed sorrow that they did not know of any reason that would cause her to leave the camp. They would do all in their power to assist him to try and recover her if she were taken captive to some other home.

And then the Chief summoned the Teal Teal, the female members and wives ofthe Gherawhar. They were closely questioned by the Chief and the elders, but they would not make any statement, and remained standing with their heads bowed. And the Gherawhar tried by threat to make them speak, but they shook their heads and remained silent. Then the Chief of the Gherawhar ordered that they should return to their mia mia. When the Teal Teal were safely home, the Chief spoke unto his people thus: 'I have a suspicion that the Peenjullie have come to our home whilst we were out hunting and taken my wife and given her to the young Chief of their tribe. So tomorrow before the sun rises beyond the mountain peak, every one that is able to fight, equip yourselves with three Kykie, four Rarrabarr, and four Pankuggee, and a Nulla nulla, and we will march into their land and seek my wife. Then, if she be not there, we shall return and march into the land of the Wandhillie. So tonight every on e to their mia mia, so you shall hear the cry "Par ruch ool low (Rise at once)".'

So every Gherawhar went straight home to bed and slept the sleep of the just, and they rose early and marched into the Peenjullie land.

Now as soon as the Gherawhar left home, the Teal Teal rose and met in conference as to what they should do, and one thought it would be wise that the two young ones that accompanied the Chief 's w ife should hurry away and tell her that her absence had caused a stir. And as the Chief with his army was marching into the Peenjullie land, thinking that they had captured his wife and made her the wife of the young Peenjullie Chief, the young Teal Teal girls ran away to the mountain to tell the Chief 's wife all that was taking place.

And she sat quietly listening to what they had to tell, and then in reply she said: 'Now is our deliverance; we have been given in marriage to these Beings who are not of our race and kind. I have made a discovery. At the dawn of day I was fast asleep, and one Tuckoonie (little men that live in thickly timbered country), came into the mia mia and sat beside the fire warming himself, and suddenly I awoke and saw him comfortably seated there. And I became so alarmed that I shrieked with fear, and he turned his eyes upon me and said: "Thou pulthook (Don 't be afraid)", I am your friend, and the friend of all that are in trouble and distress. I with my companions saw you and the other two come up from the plain and some members of our Beings have visited your camping ground and know all about you.' (I may say here that the Aborigines believe and are told very often of these queer little people, that they visit the camping-ground and become acquainted with all our ways.) 'You are in search of the water-hole of your husband, and you have been guided by the Mee well lum (the mind of my tribe), right to the spot. You slept upon it. If you will follow me I will show you the opening on top of this mountain.'

The wife of the Chief Gherawhar rose and followed the Tuckoonie up to the mountain and she was asked to sit down and rest herself. And the little man went a few paces away and gave a call somewhat like a 'Coo ee ', and like a flash somewhere out of space came many little men Tuckoonie, their bodies painted with stripes of red ochre and white pipe clay, with white Cockatoo feathers decorating their heads and tied round their wrists like bracelets, and holding in their hands small spears about the thickness of an ordinary lead pencil, about two feet long, and each wore a belt made of Possum skin round their waist, and into this belt were placed three tiny boomerangs and rarrabarr. They circled round their leader, eager to receive his instructions.

After a little palaver they made way, and he came from their midst to the Teal Teal, wife of the Gherawhar. They followed, and standing beside her he addressed his bodyguard thus: 'Hear, oh my Being, we have been appointed by the unseen forces that are about, the Spirit of the Good, the Spirit of Water, the Spirit of Food, the Spirit of Pleasure, the Spirit of Lightning and Thunder and Wind and Rainstorm, and lastly the Spirit of Sunshine. it is with their displeasure that the Gherawhar have withheld from the tribes that inhabit the country the longneeded water that is locked up in this mountain, and have used this gift for their selfish needs and have refused to give to the aged and infirm and children of other tribes. And what is more, they have refused to give and supply to their wives. Give this Meminie (woman) the help she requires to let loose from this mountain the water that there be within.'

The Tuckoonie turned to the Chief's wife and took her a few spaces father to a basin-like rock and commanded her to look in it, and she saw the sparkling water clear as crystal.

'Drink,' and she drank until her thirst was satisfied.

'Now you must descend, and when you reach the bottom of this mountain you shall meet the two young Meminan (women) and you must ask them to hurry back to their camp with this instruction to give to the others, that they must all stand on the Wolkundmurr (northern side) of the valley towards the Wandhillie boundary, and must await your coming.'

So she went and did as she was told. And the two young Meminan hurried back to give this strange order. But the other Teal Teal did just what they were asked to do, they stood on the Wolkundmurr of the valley. And the Chief's wife stood at the base of the mountain waiting for further instructions.

Presently the Tuckoonie stood beside her and said: 'Oh Meminie (woman), it is given to you by these good and great Spirits the privilege to let loose the waters that are anxious to be freed from the bonds that hold them prisoner these many, many years. Thou shalt be a blessing to all Beings, Animal, Bird, Reptile, and Insect life. And thou must keep in remembrance this great event. Teach thy children of the privilege the spirit of Pronhookie (Water) gave you. Take this.'

He handed her a grass-tree stick, and said: 'At a given signal thrust it to the mountain-side, and the water shall be let loose.'

Again the Tuckoonie disappeared, and she stood there alone, thinking of this strange happening; and she would pinch her arm and strike herself on the leg to see whether she was asleep and in a somnambulistic state. Yes, she felt the pinch and the blow.

'I am very much awake. What a wonderful experience.'

Then without warning a voice said: 'Thrust the stick into the mountain.'

She placed the stick to the mountain-side and pushed hard. It gradually went farther and farther, until its length was gone. Then the voice of the Tuckoonie said: 'Now flee for your life to where your sisters are.'

She sped away down into the valley as fast as her feet could carry; when she was gone half the distance, a loud noise broke the still air as if of a mighty wind. It was the water that leaped forth out of its prison and came thundering down the valley with a speed like that of a mighty wind.

And now the Chief 's wife arrived among her Teal Teal sisters and breathlessly told them that the water from yonder mountain would be flowing down the valley, and before she finished her sentence they saw the dust rising on the hillside in the valley and the water tearing its way through the valley, and huge trees were uprooted and carried along. And they looked with amazement as the water came by them onward to join the Murray. And when it reached the Murray it settled down to be a flowing river. And the Teal Teal came down to its bank and sat down in the shade of the trees, watching their children sporting and splashing in the water.

On the next day the Gherawhar returned and were making their way to the camp, and beheld with wonder that a river separated them from their wives and children. They were greatly annoyed. The Chief called across the river, asking where this flowing stream of water came from, and he was answered by the familiar voice of his wife: 'From the rock-hole that you and your Beings, the Gherawhar, have kept a secret from us and the other tribes. But I, oh Chief, your wife, have discovered your secret and have let loose the water that you have kept for your selfish purposes, this great gift and blessing that belongs to all Beings. So we who were your wives have decided that we shall no longer belong to you, we shall henceforth make our home in the trees. And we do not wish, or will not be your wives.'

So the separation of the husbands came about by the selfishness of the Gherawhar. Since that time the Teal Teal refuse to become the wives of the Gherawhar, and to keep in memory that long, long ago event, they make their homes in limbs and branches of the gum trees, and they construct their homes or nests with mud or clay designed after the shape of the mountain that contained the water. And in the miniature mountain-shaped homes they lay their eggs and when these are hatched and the little bird comes to see light and home, the mother in bird language tells them of the long, long ago time when another was in distress seeking water to quench their thirst, how a little man helped them and showed them where it was to be found, with the promise that they should ever throughout the generations of their kind, have a home and rear their children [in] such a memorial.

As for the Gherawhar, through their rough natures, stealing from others who endured the difficulties and hardships of hunting with its dangers so, they carry upon their bodies the mark received as a punishment for their misdoing; and also a much more grevious punishment, for their selfishness to all the surrounding Beings and more especially to their wives the Teal Teal, they have lost the great pride of their heart, the wonderful rock-hole which kept a lasting supply of beautiful refreshing and clear water. And what was more, that pride of theirs, their strictly guarded prize, now became a great barrier separating them from their wives and children for ever. And now in sorrow they have wandered to all parts of Australia, and in certain seasons of the year they dig a hole into the ground and bury themselves, with sorrow, and weep and weep during the dark cold wintery nights, until they fall into a deep sleep until the coming of Parr barrarrie calls them forth again to start their lives over once more. And in revenge for losing their wives the Teal Teal, they rob all their nests of their eggs, thinking that by devouring the eggs they may annihilate the existence of their former wives.

Whowie

David Unaipon, Ngarrindjeri,

Aboriginal and Torres Strait Islander Peoples

THE WHOWIE was the most dreadful animal in existence. It was a Being or Reptile like the Goanna, only much more or a great deal larger. Its length would be something about twenty feet. The funniest thing about this strange creature was that it possessed six legs, three on either side, something like the Goanna 's legs, and it had a tail. It had such an enormous head like a frog 's head. Now this animal was very treacherous and would attack anything that came in its way, and devour it. The people in those far-gone days would flee in terror from it, and it would take about thirty or sixty people to make a meal for it. It was not swift in its movements, but very slow. Sometimes it would come across a campingground when the people were fast asleep and without making a noise to show its presence, would swallow first one and then another, perhaps a mother and child together, and what it could not swallow it would take in his mouth to its den.

Now, the home of the Whowie was in the Riverina district, and it was about this locality that it lived and hunted. Its chief abode was on the bank of a river, a cave leading away from it for miles away. During the hot summer days, it would bask in the sunshine upon the bank of the river or among the sandhills. The sandhills were the result of the footprints of the Whowie; that is how they came to form in the Riverina district. Now, this dreadful animal was taking great toll on the people; the Itty itta (the Kangaroo Rat) were the greatest sufferers, so they held a meeting between themselves as to what step should be taken. And the Chief of the Itty itta said unto his fellow Beings: 'We are a very small race in stature, and we are gradually dwindling. There will be none of us left unless we clear out and take a journey into some distant country; to stay here means that we shall be all eaten up and none will be left to represent our race. So now I leave it to you all to decide what to do.'

So the Chief Itty itta sat down beside a log, waiting for his subjects to suggest a step to be taken. Then from among the assembly there arose an elder with long flowing beard, and he began to address the others of his race: 'Oh my children, I am far gone into years, and for me to think of taking a long journey would be out of the question. And it is not only that, but I have spent many, many happy days wandering up and down the Murray and in the surrounding country. Those were delightful days, plenty to eat, many mussels we gathered from the river, fishes were plentiful and so they are today. But we dare not go to the river side for fear of the Whowie, our great enemy. So I do not feel inclined to leave; let us think of some other means by which we shall overcome this great danger without a great loss to ourselves. We must endeavour to gain the assistance of three or more of the other tribes.'

So their Chief ordered that they should build many bonfires first thing after the rising of the sun. So they all retired that night, and whilst some were sleeping, others were on guard to give the warning cry should the Whowie appear in their camp. During the watching hours, one number of Itty itta would keep up for a time and that number would be released and go to sleep; this is how they kept guard whilst the family slept.

Now, after the sun rose, every Itty itta busied himself collecting wood and boughs and made many fires here, there, and everywhere. When the other surrounding tribes saw that there were many smoke signals, that was a sign that it was a message of distress and that it was also a call for help. There were smoking signals sent up all round-messages that all were willing and anxious to give whatever help was required. The messages also said that they would be there on the following morning, about the same time. So all the Itty itta set to work, hunted and captured as many fish as possible, and some gathered bags and bags of mussels; some were roasted upon the live coals, others baked in the oven holes dug into the earth. Oh, it was a very busy day among the Itty itta, making great preparations for the many tribes that would arrive in the morning, whilst some were away spying out the country to see the whereabouts of the Whowie, whether he was at large hunting food or basking in the sunshine. But that day he was nowhere to be seen, so some of the bolder Itty itta went away to the cave of the Whowie by the bank of the river and went quite close to the entrance of the cave for sign of footprints. And after a careful study they saw – or were convinced – that the footprints led into the cave. Now, it would take the Whowie a whole week before he came to the end of the cave, because it was such a long one and there were no other holes but this one.

Now, on the following morning, just at the time appointed, people came from all directions, marching with their spears, Nulla nulla, and some had their stone axes. Now the Animals, Birds, Reptiles, Kangaroos, Possums, Platypuses, Eagle Hawks, Crows, Magpies, Cockatoos, and every member of the feathered tribes, the Lizard and Reptile tribes, were represented in full force. When the spies returned to camp and told the others of the result of their scouting, that they felt sure that the Whowie had entered his home in the cave and would take a week to reach the terminus, they spent the day and night in entertaining themselves with dancing and corroborees, feeling safe.

This rejoicing lasted for a day and a night, and after that they set about to attack their great enemy, the Whowie. Now everybody set about gathering sticks and making them in small bundles, just large enough to carry into the cave, because they would have to carry them up into the cave a long way. And the people of various tribes began in earnest, beginning from the early hours of the morning till late in the evening. This was kept up until they thought that the Whowie would have reached the end of the cave, then they had stacked half of the length of the hole of the cave, and they stacked a great heap at the entrance and set fire to it, and the wood began to burn away into the cave and caused a great trail of smoke that filled the cave, which by now had made it rather uncomfortable for the Whowie, who began to force his way out, battling with the heat and smoke. And he began to roar like an angry beast, as if in deadly combat with some mighty foe.

This struggling lasted for six days and on the seventh the Whowie came out of the entrance, blinded and dazed in a stupor. And when he got free or right out of the hole, the Animals, Birds, and Reptiles began to attack him in earnest with spears, Nulla nulla, and stone axes, beating him all over the body, causing great wounds, with blood flowing freely; and with much beating and bleeding he fell to the ground, dying.

And now when the gentle night winds are blowing to the cave you will hear as it were the sighing of the Whowie. And when the little Aboriginal girls and boys are naughty and disobedient, mother will say: 'Look out, the Whowie is listening,' and the children will crouch up against their mother's bosom for safety, looking round with staring eyes expecting to see that Dread Dragon, the Whowie of the Riverina.

Why All the Animals Peck at the Selfish Owl: the Coming of the Light

David Unaipon, Ngarrindjeri,

Aboriginal and Torres Strait Islander Peoples

MY RACE, the Aborigines of Australia, has a vast tradition of legends, myths, and folklore stories. We delight in telling stories to the younger members of the tribe. These stories and traditions have been handed down orally for thousands of years. In fact, all tribal laws and customs are, first of all, told to the children of the tribe in the form of stories. Just as the white Australian mother first instructs her children by nursery stories, etc.

A legend I call 'The Coming of the Light' is a very old and popular one among my people. Of course, it must be understood that the mothers or the old men of the tribe, in telling these stories, drag them out to a great length, putting in every detail, with much gesture and acting. The story goes thus.

Long, long ago, before there was human life, there was only Animal life. There was the Bird tribe, the Animal tribe, and the Reptile tribe. Once a year, in the springtime, all these different tribes met and held a great festival called a 'Munmundi'.

The Bird tribe were great talkers. The Cockatoos cried: 'Come and let us prepare ourselves for this great Munmundi.'

So they retired into the bush and decorated themselves with leaves and bushes. When they came out again, they began to dance in their decorations before the Kangaroos, the Carpet Snake, the Goanna, and all the others of the Reptile and Animal tribes.

The Animal and Reptile tribes cheered and praised the feathered tribe's dancing. This admiration and praise made the feathered tribe very conceited. The Cockatoo, who was always a very cheeky fellow, went to the Eagle Hawk, Chief of the feathered tribe, and said: 'Oh Father Eagle Hawk, are not we feathered tribe, greater than the Kangaroo and Carpet Snake, the Goanna, and all the tribes? '

The Eagle Hawk answered: 'Oh my son Cockatoo, of course you are superior to all the other tribes.'

Now, the other tribes overheard all this, and it made them very angry. So after much wrangling, the feathered tribe challenged the other tribes to fight, and to prove who was the superior.

But there was one family, the Bat tribe, that stood alone and would not take any part in the dispute, nor would it consent to join forces with either party in battle. Now, the Chief of the Bat tribe called his family and told them that they were to stand by prepared for battle, and when they saw that one of the combatants was winning they must join in to decide the battle.

And how the battle raged. The Animals and Birds were throwing their spears and waddies, others were hand-to-hand fighting with Nulla nulla. Just when the battle was raging fiercely, it seemed as if the Bird tribe would win. They were pressing the Animal tribe so much that the Kangaroo and his army were driven back. At this moment the Bat shouted to his family: 'Come join the Eagle Hawk and his tribe. Onward, slay the Kangaroo and his army!'

So the Bat family stood side-by-side with the Cockatoo, Koo ka ka burra, Crow and Magpie. The Bats were experts in the use of the boomerangs, they threw their weapons so fast that the boomerangs about the armies resembled a huge cloud. But presently the Kangaroo called to his army and, speaking words of encouragement, stood waiting for the approach of the enemy. Now, when the Animals saw their Chief and General facing the foe, they fought with greater courage and drove the Bird tribe back.

Now the Bat saw that he had made a blunder, and called to his family: 'Retire from the ranks of the Bird tribe and quickly join the Animal tribe,' so the Bat joined the Animal tribe fighting against the Birds. Now the armies of the Animal and Bird tribes were swinging like a pendulum and the Kangaroo and Emu were in mortal combat.

'Oh Emu, why should we fight, it causes so much bloodshed, pain, misery and death. 'The Kangaroo, extending his hands, said: 'Come let us shake hands.'

So the Emu clasped the hands of the Kangaroo in friendship and said: 'Let us be friends.'

When the Animal and Bird tribes saw them shaking hands, the Cockatoos were shaking hands with the Dingos and the Koo ka ka burras were shaking hands with the Wombats, and there was a general shaking of hands among the Animal, Bird, and Reptile tribes which resulted in friendship. But the little Bat tribe did not know what to do, as they had been false to both parties. So the Bat tribe had to go and live with the wicked Owls, who always lived away by themselves and who delighted in the dark.

Now the Sun, the great ruler of all, saw this fighting and killing among the Animals. So the Sun became very angry and hid his face; and all the earth became dark. Now the Animals, Birds, and Reptiles were grouping in the darkness and life became a burden.

The Emu came to the Kangaroo and said: 'Oh Kangaroo, what shall we do? The children are unable to enjoy themselves and we find it difficult to provide food and clothing.'

The Kangaroo thought awhile; presently an idea came to him. He said to the Emu: 'Build bonfires, here, there and everywhere.'

So the Emu went and asked the Crows, Pheasants, Magpies, and Cockatoos to assist in bringing in a supply of wood to keep the fire burning. Now they were burning and burning the wood until there was a shortage of fuel. Once the Emu approached the Kangaroo with the seriousness of the position, again the Kangaroo thought and thought.

He quietly said to the Emu: 'Summon the whole tribe and let them meet me in conference and we shall discuss the problem of light.'

So the Emu went around to each camp and invited them to this meeting, so all the Animal, Bird, and Reptile tribes came and sat in conference to find some means of discovering a way of providing light or bringing back the sunlight. There was no one able to solve the problem. Now there was a little Lizard sitting beside the Kangaroo, and he was thinking hard.

Presently he addressed the Kangaroo: 'Oh Kangaroo, the Owl and Bat know how to give us light. I have heard a whisper that they are able to bring back the sunlight. '

So the Kangaroo said to the little Lizard: 'Will you go along and ask the Chief of the Owls and Bats to attend this meeting? I would like them to.'

The little Lizard went on his errand in search of the Owl and Bat and he found them, and he said: 'Oh Owl and Bat, the Kangaroo wishes that you should come along and attend a meeting; will you come?'

'Oh yes,' said the Owl and Bat, 'we are coming, we are coming.'

The little Lizard hastened back filled with joy that he was able to return to the Kangaroo with the great news; that he was able to procure the consent of the Owl and Bat.

When they arrived, the Kangaroo said: 'Owl and Bat, will you give us the light or bring to us the sunlight? '

'Oh,' said the Owl, 'I cannot do that because I love the darkness and my children delight in it. '

Then the Curlew called: 'Oh Uncle, you would not refuse me, thy nephew. Oh, for the sake of my children and the children of other tribes, give us the light.'

Once more the Owl refused: 'I will not.'

Then there arose a great cry among the Animals, Birds, and Reptiles: 'Oh, give us the light, Oh give us light.'

The cry was so pitiful that it smote the hardened conscience of the Bat and all the past wrongs that he did came before his vision, so he said within himself: 'Now I can atone for what I have done. '

So he shouted: 'I will give you the light, I will give you the light!'

So the Animals, Birds, and Reptiles ceased crying. Then the Bat asked: 'Has anyone a boomerang?' and the same Lizard that brought the Owl and Bat to the meeting answered: 'I have a boomerang, I will give it to you.'

So the Lizard gave the boomerang to the Bat. Once more the Bat spoke to the assembled crowd: 'I feel the great cost that I am making, I loved the darkness and my children delight to romp and skip and play in one continual darkness. But I know that when I make this sacrifice I shall have their approval.'

Then he took the boomerang and with a mighty force hurled it towards the north, and it travelled away north and came back from the south. Again the boomerang was sent on a mission towards the west; it travelled around the earth and came back from the east, and just as the Bat was about to throw the boomerang the Koo ka kee said: 'Wait a moment Bat, we do not want an exhibition of boomerang throwing, we require the light.'

'Yes, I know that you are all anxious to have the sunlight. But I am dividing that great darkness; I am going to give you light and I shall retain unto myself the darkness.'

And again with greater force he hurled the boomerang towards the east. It travelled around the earth and came back from the east and was hovering about his head. Then the Bat shouted: 'Look towards the east the light is coming, the light is coming!'

The Bird tribe looked and they became so excited they began chattering and twittering and whistling. At the approach of dawn, still the Bat shouted: 'The light is coming, the light coming!'

Presently, the boomerang touched the earth and the Sun arose. Oh, what a joy. The Kangaroo yelped with delight, the Dingos scrambled and turned somersaults and the Koo ka burras laughed with gladness. And the Bat returned to his home in the cave, waiting till the sun sank in the western sky. So now when the Owl ventures out into the daylight, all the feathered tribes will fly around seeking an opportunity to peck at him because he was so selfish in refusing to give them the sunlight. But if the Bat comes out at sunset, or on a dull evening before sunset, no Bird will ever attempt to molest him because he was willing to make amends for the wrongs he did by his act of kindness in bringing once more the glorious sunlight which all creation is so much depending on for life and energy.

As for the little messenger the Lizard, he still loves to sit and gaze at the Sun, and if you look closely at his neck you will see he still has there the Boomerang that the Kangaroo gave him.

The Water Rat Who Discovered the Secret of Fire and How it Was Taken from Him by the Eagle Hawk

David Unaipon, Ngarrindjeri,

Aboriginal and Torres Strait Islander Peoples

AMONG THE ANIMALS, Birds, and Reptiles that have made a name for themselves and their tribe are such names as those of the little Bat, with that wonderful boomerang which was invented by the Lizard; the Koala (Teddy Bear), the great astronomer, philosopher, discoverer, and navigator; the Pelican, the great manufacturer; and the Water Rat, the discoverer of fire for cooking and heating purposes. Now, before this wonderful discovery, all flesh and vegetable food was eaten raw and in cold climates during the winter season they suffered great misery. The little Dingos, Wombats, Kangaroos, and Bandicoots would always be crying and shivering, as their clothing was not sufficient to keep them warm.

One day a young Rat went seeking for a comfortable home spot for his wife, and his wife said to him: 'Nun kar wat pag ar rallin (Oh dear me, I had a most beautiful dream). You will remember the billabong where you used to come and visit me where those lovely water-lilies were blooming. I was sitting there on a log by the water thinking of our courting days, when presently out of the clear water came a dragon-fly, and, hurrying to a water-lily, sat upon it for a while, then hurried back to the spot from whence it came, hovering about the surface of the water. Presently a big clear bubble rose and floated towards the water lily, and the dragon-fly followed. Presently a great many dragon-flies came and gently raised the big bubble from the water, carrying it carefully and placing it upon the water-lily. I sat gazing in wonderment at this strange sight, thinking, when like a flash a clear beam passed before my vision. It was the spirit of the water-lily dancing around it and leaping skyward. At that moment the bubble burst. Oh dear, what a wonderful sight! A beautiful baby Retculdie (Water Rat) was lying peacefully in the bosom of the water-lily.'

The young Retculdie sat seriously thinking for a while, but presently he rose and, kissing his wife, hurried away to that little spot and walked round the bank several times in search of a suitable place to build a home for his wife. He selected a place over the pond and began digging under the roots of a large gum tree until he came to an obstruction. It was the root of the tree. He was annoyed and, not wishing to abandon a place that meant so much to him and his wife, he began to use his teeth as an implement to cut a way through. Biting and gnawing his way into the root, suddenly he kindled a spark. Again and again this occurred. After completing his work, the home furnished with soft grass, he hastened to his wife and invited her to follow him.

They wended their way silently to their new home. She walked inside and, sitting down by her bedside, a feeling of rest and comfort crept over her. She quietly went to bed and fell asleep. When she awoke, her husband told her of his wonderful discovery and performed before her the ceremony of producing fire, the much-needed blessing. Then he hastened away and told his father, mother, brother, and sister and they spread the news to other members of the Retculdie tribe. They all came and saw and felt the energising heat that came from the fire, and the Retculdie tribe vowed that they would endeavour to keep the secret to themselves and not reveal it to the Tortoise, Water-fowl, Kangaroos, Dingos, or any other tribe.

So the Retculdie tribe lived in comfort in all weathers and in all climates. Now the Kangaroos, Wombats, Goannas, and Tortoises could see the light through the weed, but the Retculdie were too wise for the Turtles, who would crawl through the grass, sneaking towards the home of the Retculdie to find out what it was. But the Retculdie would see them coming and hide the fire. Then they asked the Hawk tribe to approach the Eagle Hawk to wrest the secret from the Retculdie.

The Eagle Hawk consented, and on a sunny morning, when there was not a cloud to be seen, he began his mission. Up and up into the blue sky he soared until he appeared a mere speck, and still on and on beyond their vision. With telescopic eyes piercing the distance, scanning the river and every object, he saw the Retculdie rubbing the sticks and producing fire. Like a bolt from the sky, he sped on earthward, faster than an express train, with greater speed than an aeroplane, rending the air as he came with the noise of a mighty wind. All life was spellbound and even the Retculdie was paralysed. The Eagle Hawk swooped and, taking the Retculdie up in his mighty claw again, mounted in the sky, where he hovered for a while.

'Ask the Retculdie to give me your secret,' he said, 'or I will drop you to earth.'

The Retculdie preferred telling the secret to losing his life, and thus it was taken from his selfish tribe by the Eagle Hawk.

A Wonderful Bun Bar Rang (Lizard)

David Unaipon, Ngarrindjeri,

Aboriginal and Torres Strait Islander Peoples

AFTER A LONG time the Eagle forced the Retculdie (Water Rat) to give up his secret, telling him that it should become known to all the tribes Animal, Bird, Reptile, and Insect-for use in their cooking and lighting and to give warmth and comfort in their various homes. And then the Retculdie had demonstrated how to make fire: he rubbed two sticks and the striking of two pieces of flint produced a spark, and when the spark came in contact with fine grass which was rubbed and worked, pulled to pieces then rubbed again and rolled into a ball, it would then burst into flame, and all they needed to do was to place small twigs and sticks and later logs, and they would have a fire large enough to do anything. When he did this, each tribe took away a firestick and made other fires from this stick, which would continually be supplied with fire with sticks and large logs. So that when travelling from one hunting-ground to another they would have or appoint a member of their family and tribe to see that a fire was taken on their journey.

This custom was continued for a long, long while until one day there was a great thunderstorm and rain and wind. Those who lived in the plain country hastened away to the mountain and their fires were all extinguished; in fact all the tribes suffered the loss of fire, even the Water Rat. They became careless and after generations of generations, the children of the various tribes forgot how to produce fire because they had developed a habit of carrying firesticks.

Now all the Chiefs – Animal, Bird, Reptile, and Insect – were allowed to have two wives, who must be sisters. Now the Eagle Hawk made a very peculiar choice in this regard. Every other tribe expected that he would choose from the feather or Animal tribe. But what a surprise, he sent his messenger the Falcon to summon the two beautiful daughters of the Snake with a very red belly. So these two young ladies came along, escorted by their uncles, brothers of their mother. On the way, people were staring in wonderment and astonishment. When they came to the Hawk family camp, the Chief was sitting on his Mia mia and when they came very near, he came down and met them.

Then the uncle said: 'Oh Peewingie, Chief of the Bird tribes, we are proud and honoured that so great a tribe should con descend to choose wives from the camp of your humble servant. We willingly submit them to you. They shall become your servants for now and forever.'

The Eagle Hawk said not a word but held out his hand, taking hold of theirs, and received them unto himself. Now at this point we shall refer to these two sisters as they are known today: Kryang yartooka (Maiden Snakes). The members of their family were distinguished from others as they had a very, very red colour upon their bellies. Red to the Aborigines is symbolic of that fiery temper, warmth of hospitality, and healing effect. Their nature was all this .

At this time of the story all food was eaten raw. One day, whilst the Eagle Hawk was out hunting, these Yartookang kry, or Kryang yartooka, were just before midday basking in the sunshine and at this particular spot there were several Ant-beds, with the appearance of a stump of a tree thoroughly perforated with tiny holes, and they were deserted by the Ants. And on this summer day the sun was shining brilliantly with intense heat. These sisters were resting upon an Ant-bed each, and the heat of the sun and the heat from their red bellies caused a fire to be lit in these Ant-beds, and they both struggled and got off the beds and looked and saw a fire burning without smoke.

'Oh, wonders of wonders!' they both exclaimed, 'what a discovery. Throw sand upon the fire to hide it from the others.'

And from that day on they strictly guarded their secret. Then one day the Eagle Hawk came home with some food, and he equally divided the spoil and he went to sleep before having anything to eat. So the Kryang yartooka hastened to their fire heap, gently scraped the sand from the ant-bed that had already become their fire place, and began cooking their food. When this was done they covered up their fire again, sat down, and ate their meal. Then they returned to their Lord and Master, the King of Birds, and sat on either side of him.

The Eagle arose, and feeling hungry, asked that his meal should be served, so they both anxiously waited upon him. Whilst he was eating he said to his wives: 'It is strange that I smell cooked food. Have you been favoured with such?'

'Oh no,' they both replied, 'where do you think that we, thy wives, should be honoured above all others with such a long-lost favour?'

'Come now my wives, have I smelt aright, that you both have had cooked fish? Where is your portion? Let me see,' demanded the Eagle.

'We have eaten the allowance you gave us.'

But this is where they stopped speaking – they did not say whether cooked or raw.

The Eagle did not say any more but flew away in search of more food. He returned and divided the food and this time, he did not go to sleep, but sat up and ate his food straightaway. And he asked his wives that they should join him but in this they both declined, asking to be excused.

'Why?' said the Eagle, 'you have been accustomed to eat as soon as I give you your food but of late you eat in secret. Come now my wives, eat.'

But they still refused. Then the Eagle said: 'I go a-hunting. Goodbye wives!' and he flew away and travelled in a circle, coming back to where they were, thinking that he would find out their secret fire. But they were too cunning. They saw by his action that he began to be suspicious.

'Eat my wives, you are both looking hungry. Eat and be strong.'

'Not until you bring us some fish,' answered the wives.

So the Eagle Hawk flew away across the mountain until he came to a billabong. And he sat upon a limb of a large gum tree, with his keen eyes fixed upon the surface of the water. A perch feeding among the [reeds] rose a little, a whirr, the Eagle shot like an arrow straight upon its prey and struck its talon deep into the flesh of the fish, then rose and hastened back to his wives, who were sitting down sunning themselves.

When they heard the flap of the wings of their Lord and Chief they rose hurriedly to greet him, and he gave them the much sought-for food and asked them to have their meal.

'But,' said his wives,' we have just finished our meal and are feeling satisfied. We go to rest with your kind permission.'

The Eagle began to become uneasy about their conduct, since he smelt cooked food. So he went away and met the Magpie and told him about the suspicion he had about his wives.

'Now what shall we do to find out whether they really have the lost secret of fire? Would you mind going among the tribes and asking for volunteers?'

So the Magpie went and asked the Cockatoo. 'Oh yes, I shall endeavour to find out where they hide the fire.'

So he set off and spent days and days waiting round watching for signs of smoke. He said to himself 'Well, if they should make a fire I shall notice smoke rising.'

So he waited and waited and began to get uneasy. So he thought he would try another plan, and would follow after them when they received the allowance of food from their husband.

When the Eagle returned with the spoils, he gave them their portion and when the Eagle went to have his afternoon rest, the wives sneaked away to cook their food and the Cockatoo followed. And his clumsy feet became entangled in the boughs of the shrubs and he stooped and used his beak as a snip to cut his way through and they would click, a noise which would give a warning to the Kryang yartooka, who snuck away from their fireside and lay quietly among the bushes. Cocky would sit still, and after thinking that he had waited long enough, would begin to go forward. Again his feet became entangled in a creeper and he fell down scared, thinking someone had tripped him, so he screeched and, of course, the Snakes would just simply leave the place.

The Cockatoo returned to the Magpie and told him of his failure. Then the Magpie asked the Emu, thinking that he would, by having a long neck, see farther. He tried but failed.

'Now,' said the Magpie, 'this will never do. The King of Birds, the Eagle Hawk, will make a proclamation that should any fail in future, they shall be slain or put in prison. Now we must make a mighty effort. Let us form a circle round about them and draw closer and closer until we shall come upon them. Then someone must see them, surely.'

So they all agreed and set off on their mission. There were the Magpies, Cockatoos, Butcher-birds, Kookaburras, Emus, Wrens, Little Wrens, and Willy Wagtails, and a great many other members of the Bird tribe, forming a large circle, coming nearer and nearer. And the Cockatoo, with his clumsy feet gripping and falling, caused the Koo ka kee a great deal of amusement, and just as they got very near to the Kryang yartooka they could scent the smell of flesh cooking. All eyes were strained before them, stretching their necks and tip-toeing, when the Cockatoo slipped and fell. The Kookaburras could not resist it any longer and burst into laughter and spoilt the show. They sneaked off, feeling ashamed of themselves.

Then they called for the assistance of the Animal tribe but they were a greater failure than the Birds, because when they came within a certain distance their mouths would water when they smelt the appetising food that was roasting and they would hurry forward and come tumbling over twigs and sticks, and the Kryang yartooka would hear them coming and would disappear into the grass and bushes.

They began to become very desperate and threatened the Kryang yartooka that they must reveal the fire; if not, they would be killed.

The Magpie said: 'Why should you keep from all the tribes a much needed want?'

But the Kryang yartooka said to them: 'You forget we are wives of the great Bird Chief, and you cannot force us to tell. '

And they were all astounded at this reply, which they all recognised. And in shame of defeat, with heads bowed, they all disappeared to their own mia mia. As the Kookaburras were walking homeward enjoying jokes of their defeat, they came across a Lizard tribe, who had just returned from a hunting expedition with their great spoil of game and were making their mia mia to camp for the night. They asked the Kookaburras to spend the night with them, to which they willingly gave their consent. And as they were sitting down enjoying as best as possible their evening meal, one of the Bun bar rang – for that was the name of this little family of Lizards – said: 'Oh, if we could only have the long-lost fire, what a happy evening we should be spending-cooked food and light and warmth.'

'Well,' said a Koo ka ka, 'there is fire and we must make an effort to take it from the Kryang Marrallang, the Snake sisters, wives of the Eagle Hawk; they have the secret. We have tried all the smart hunters to wrest the secret but they all failed. We tried all in a body, formed a large circle around them but the Cockatoo at the last moment got his clumsy foot into something and fell. This happened to him and you know how excitable he is; he screeched and howled, and we thought that Muldarpie had him. Of course the noise warned the Kryang of our approach; and now perhaps you may be able to suggest means by which we shall procure the secret from them. '

The little Bun bar rang thought and thought all through the long hours of the night, and then he quietly went to bed and slept soundly. And in the morning some of the Bun bar rang began their journey homeward. But this one particular little Lizard expressed a desire to stay with the other tribe to try and help to procure the light. So he went out to the place where the two Kryang usually spent their time in the absence of their husband.

Now the little Bun bar rang came back to the camp and told the Cockatoo, Magpie, and others of that tribe, as well as the Animal and Lizard tribe, and asked that some of the picked men of each tribe, recognised hunters, should accompany him. He asked them to follow in his trail at a distance. So they all set off, the Bun bar rang leading about a hundred yards or more, winding his way in and out of the bushes and shrubs until they came to the spot that made every one excitable, because they could smell something like food cooking.

So the little Bun bar rang suggested that he should go by himself until he reached a certain spot where he thought it likely the Kryang would lie; on his way he would crawl flat upon his belly for a few yards, then stand upon his three legs and hold up the fourth one to beckon the others to follow or stop, just as the case may be. Then he would go forward through bush and grass, then take another glimpse to see how far away the Kryang were; in this he would hold up one of his front hands and beckon them to keep perfectly quiet, then he would put the hand down and raise the other-perhaps the right hand. He saw the Kryang busy cooking their food with fire that was cunningly hidden in the dis used Ant-bed and the Kryang sitting behind the Ant-bed enjoying their meal.

The Bun bar rang crept up cautiously, stopping now and again, beckoning first with the right and then with the left hand. All this while he carried a grass-tree stick and when he came near enough he poked the grass-tree stick into the Ant-bed and allowed it to remain a few moments, then withdrew it, and it was alight. W hen he saw that the grass-tree stick blazed he ran away towards where the others were waiting, and on his way he set fire to grass and bushes and the country was all ablaze.

The Kryang became very angry indeed when they saw that their secret was discovered; they swore vengeance upon all life that came within striking distance – they would inflict a wound that would cause death. They also became the most dreaded enemy of the Animal, Bird, and Lizard tribes since that day when the little Bun bar rang stole their secret and spread the fire all over the country, and they themselves were deprived. The Kryang were able to use fire only when it was embedded within the Ant-bed, and now since it was taken from the ant-bed the Kryang are unable to restore or use it.

Now the action the little Bun bar rang adopted on that day was so trying that, although many and many years have passed, you will see him anywhere among the bushes or rocky country crawling and stopping, and raising first one front leg and then the other, as if in the act of giving a sign to stop, or beckoning to come on. This is one of the peculiar habits of the little Bun bar rang that he still retains in memory of that far-gone day when his ancestor gave the then world or restored the gift of fire to become the property of all.

Mexpakinté: the Shadow Woman

Pedro Vázquez Luna, Tzotzil, Mexico

Mexpakinté (pronounced "mesh-pack-in-TAY") is a malevolent spirit of the highlands of Chiapas, southern Mexico. According to the indigenous Tzotzil tradition, she wanders the forests at night, feeding on the fear of human travelers.

IT ALL HAPPENED during the dark times, back when Grandfather Antonio was a young man.

Although this was only a few decades ago, in the 1970s, life in the highlands of Chiapas had not changed much since the colonial times. The native people of these mountains, descendents of the proud Mayan civilization, worked as virtual slaves on their own ancestral lands.

The descendants of those first Spanish invaders, known in the Tzotzil language as kashlanetik, treated the native workers as little more than beasts. Grandfather Antonio and the rest of his village sweated away under the hot sun, growing coffee and corn for the local kashlan landowner. They lived in fear of the whip and the rifle. They clung to the hope offered by their faith, a syncretistic blend of Catholic Christianity and the ancient Mayan ways.

It was during those dark days that Antonio encountered the spectre of Mexpakinté.

* * *

In his youth, Antonio worked six days a week on the plantation of the local kashlan. On Sundays, his only day of rest, he would make the long hike from his village to the large town of Pantelhó. He walked all the way from the hot, steamy lowlands where bananas grew, uphill through ocote pine forests, into the increasingly cold mountain air.

When he finally reached Pantelhó, he walked through the outdoor market to buy his family's groceries for the week. He packed his morral satchel with salt, lard, and chile peppers, along with candles and copal incense for their home altar. He often came across friends at the small wooden shack in Pantelhó whose owners sold glasses of posh, the homemade sugar cane liquor common in the highlands. Antonio and his friends would gather for a drink, share the local gossip, and enjoy a brief moment's respite from hard plantation life.

One particular Sunday, Antonio left town later than usual. The sunlight was already waning when he said goodbye to his friends, downed his last glass of posh, and headed out for home. He navigated the mountain trails by the light of the moon, shuffling along with his packed morral satchel at his right side. His machete hung in its leather sheath from his left shoulder.

He passed through a thick clump of trees where the branches blocked the moonlight. A light breeze rustled the leaves. From a distant treetop came the hooting cry of the tsurukuk, the owl, harbinger of death and misfortune. Antonio quickened his pace.

When he came to a small clearing, he stopped – something was moving toward him in the darkness. A shadow grew as it approached, meandering up the trail. He slowly reached for the handle of his machete. When the figure came within paces of Antonio, he stared in disbelief.

It was his wife.

"What are you doing out here, so far from home?" He asked. "Is something wrong? Is one of the children hurt or ill?"

"No," she replied calmly. "I just came to walk with you."

Although she spoke the Tzotzil language, her voice had a hollow, alien quality to it. As they walked side by side, Antonio noticed a strange cadence to the woman's gait. She moved like a person trying to walk backwards, with awkward and unsure movements. He tried to look her in the eyes, but she turned her face away from the moonlight. In the shadows, he could have sworn that her eyes were entirely black.

The woman reached out to embrace Antonio as they walked. When he put his arm around her shoulders, he found that her body was cold as ice. He shuddered, feeling as though all the warmth had drained from his body.

"You are so cold," he said with a tremulous voice.

"I recently washed my hair." She spoke with that same hollow, ethereal voice. Her clothes and skin were freezing, like a corpse freshly pulled from the cold earth. "I bathed and put on fresh clothes for you. I've been waiting for you."

She smiled. Her teeth shone in the moonlight, long and sharp and yellow.

An ineffable sense of dread washed over Antonio. He suddenly felt dizzy and nauseous. Overcome with terror, he pushed the woman away and sprinted down the mountain path. He ran through the misty forest, tripping over rocks and roots, until he saw the light glowing through the thatched roof of his home. He flung the wooden door open. There, by the open fire in the kitchen, stood his wife.

"You're here," Antonio said breathlessly.

"Of course I'm here." She flipped a tortilla on the comal griddle over the fire. "Where else would I be?"

"You didn't come out to meet me on the road?"

"Of course not. At this hour?"

Antonio felt that he was losing his mind. His wife, but not his wife. A human, but not human altogether. After he poured himself a shot of posh wish shaky hands, he calmed down enough to tell his wife what he had seen in the woods.

"That was not a person," she said, pulling her rebozo shawl tightly around her neck. "You have encountered Mexpakinté. The Shadow Woman. She came to trick you, to frighten you. Perhaps to death."

* * *

The following Sunday, Antonio went to market in Pantelhó once again. When he met up with his friends for a drink of posh, he told them what had happened that last week. Some of his friends crossed themselves. Others stared at the dusty ground.

Antonio tried to walk home by daylight, but the sun seemed to move at a rushed pace, dipping below the horizon as soon as he was alone in the woods. He walked the mountain trail in complete darkness.

Deep in the woods, the same strange figure came walking toward him. He recoiled as he recalled the icy chill of her skin, the deathly stare of her eyes. He fought against the dread and the fear, pushing through the panic, and summoned all his bravery.

"You will not fool me this time," he said with anger. "Your evil ends tonight!"

He pulled his machete from its leather sheath, raised it in the air, and brought it down onto the woman's skull.

The machete fell straight through the figure, like cutting through smoke. It clattered to the ground as the figure dissipated. A peal of spectral laughter filled the woods around him.

When Antonio came home to his wife that evening, he told her what happened. "I swear that she looked just like you. But she was not flesh and blood."

His wife stared into the embers of the fire with concern. "You must talk to my Uncle Lorenzo, he knows of such things. He can tell you how to fight her."

* * *

Antonio met Uncle Lorenzo after the following day's work on the kashlan's coffee plantation. "I attacked her with my machete," he explained, "but it did nothing. She just disappeared."

"That's the problem," the old man said slowly, tightening the straps of his morral as he walked. "You didn't attack the source."

"What does that mean?"

"You will never hurt Mexpakinté by attacking her body. What you see as a body is a mere reflection, a mirage. She is a being of darkness, and her essence lies in the shadow. Go to the source: attack the darkness."

The following week, the kashlan forced Antonio to work on Sunday. Two weeks later, however, he was able to walk to market to buy his wares. That evening, he walked back home down that familiar forest path. In the darkest part of the woods, the woman came shuffling slowly toward him.

"Hello, my love!" Antonio cried out, feigning calm. "What a pleasure to find you out here. Come walk with me!"

He lay a hand across her freezing cold shoulders and fell in step alongside her.

"Come, let's walk down this path where the moonlight shines clearly."

Although the woman struggled against him, Antonio led her toward a brightly lit clearing. As they walked, he slowly reached his other hand across his chest to grasp his machete. Slowly, he pulled it from the leather sheath. Slowly, he raised it above his head. He abruptly turned the woman around to face him.

"I know what you are," he said resolutely. "And I am not afraid."

The woman threw her head back and laughed. Antonio raised his machete higher. As Mexpakinté mocked him, he suddenly turned away from her body.

ZAZ!

He brought the machete down onto the earth where her shadow lay. The woman screamed like a wounded animal.

ZAZ!

He chopped the earth again. The two slash marks formed the sign of the Holy Cross, a sacred symbol of both the Catholic faith and the ancient Mayan ways. Mexpakinté screamed in agony. Antonio thrust his machete into the earth, right in the center of the cross. The woman fell to the ground, her face twisted into a hideous mask.

Then she was gone like smoke, leaving nothing but a black puddle of pitch behind.

* * *

Grandfather Antonio never came across Mexpakinté again.

As the years passed, things changed in the highlands of Chiapas. The native laborers overcame their fear of the plantation owners, came together, and organized. Together, they drove off the kashlanetik and took the land back, forming worker-owned co-ops throughout the region. The land finally belonged to those who worked it.

And yet, the shadows weren't dispelled entirely. Every now and then, a local farmer would swear that he came across the Shadow Woman again, walking those lonely mountain trails. When they did, they went straight to Grandfather Antonio for help.

"There is one very important thing that Mexpakinté taught me," he would explain. "Evil can take many forms, many faces. You must face it head-on, without fear. And when we are fighting evil, we must always fight the shadow. You can never fight evil by slashing at another human with your machete, for the essence of the evil is not inside other people. If we seek to fight evil, we must go to the source: we must attack the shadow. Not our neighbor."

Grandfather Antonio's teachings are just as true today as they were all those years ago, during the dark times, when he first fought Mexpakinté, the Shadow Woman.

* * *

As told to me by my friend Pedro "Pepe" Vázquez Luna, a young man of the Tzotzil ethnicity from the highlands of Chiapas, southern Mexico. Pepe heard this personal account from his grandfather Antonio, who swears that it happened exactly as conveyed here.

Recorded by David J. Schmidt

Glade of the Uncles

Jay Hansford C. Vest, Monacan Indian Nation

"GOOD MORNING SIR," remarked the Right Reverend Jones to the Governor, as frost crunched under his feet.

"Chilly enough for you, Right Reverend?" responded the Governor.

"It looks as though you have found a worthy steed for our journey. You need a good horse to visit the Indians at Junkatapurse. They will judge you by the horse you ride."

"It's called horse's neck, I understand, Sir."

"Sir, do you know the story… about the uncles?"

"I have heard tale of it, something about a wolf teaching them to hunt and all."

"They are so fond of their traditions. It seems every time I go there they are telling it over and over."

"But what of Jesus, Sir, do they tell his stories?"

"Not so entertaining for them."

"How did you sleep, Right Reverend?"

"Well enough, Sir, no pitching and swaying against a bulkhead, but the infernal cold has made my joints a bit stiff."

"The Saponi will have the cure for that, my friend. You'll be dancing the night away."

"Three months at sea and now this Godforsaken Virginia hell hole."

"The things we do for these savages!"

"You must certify the truth, your Worship. We are civilizing them."

"Right Reverend, this is Feather Jack, Chief of the Saponi."

"Thank you, Hicks."

"Chief Feather, there are children here laughing and playing in the middle of the day. Should they not be in school?"

"They are having lunch with their family."

"Take their lunch to the school."

"It is not our way."

"The parents get lonely for their children and the children cry for their parents. We try to keep them all happy."

"This will not do, my good man, we must educate these children in the ways of the Lord and righteousness."

"But they are happier this way and we are educating them to our ways."

"Hah!, without a teacher of the gospels sir."

"Their uncles teach our stories and traditions to them as it has been done since the beginning of life."

"Humph, I must see this charade."

"We will go to the school house and you will see for yourself."

"Get your horse, Right Reverend, and come along."

Hicks led the way with Chief Feather at his side as they rode to the glade of the uncles.

"The school is just there in that clearing beyond the glade."

Tethering the horses by the schoolhouse, they entered the building to find the children seated in a circle with the desks stacked in one corner. An uncle was telling the tale of Mother's Brother to the children. It was the tribal story most concerned with education so the Right Reverent listened intently while formulating questions for the teller in hopes to trip him up.

"Where are these uncles and what do they tell us, man?

"Is there anything within the tales that reveal the word of the one true God?"

"How are such yarns going to eliminate fear and ignorance among your children?"

"If a Christian tells a tale then stop up your ears," whispered someone in the room.

"Well there it is!" I dare say there is no respect among these children for the word of God."

"And this blasphemy is here at the school house in the words of babes."

"Uncivilized! I say, uncivilized."

"Just there, over by the commons outside, I saw a gruffy old trader – one of yours, Hicks? He was seated by the fountain, when a young girl, no more than eighteen approached him saying, 'Jog de log, nemaste?' What does it mean when young girls go about prostituting themselves in this manner Hicks?"

"She is none the worst for it, Sir. These Indians see it as a kind of freedom and do not look down on the girls who service our men. They are free to become respected wives and mothers without disgrace for their choices and actions."

"And good man, aren't you concerned about the cleanliness of these people?"

"Let me tell you, Sir. These people go to the river first thing every morning to bathe, they use a soap made of the agave plant, generously applying it to all parts of their bodies. They are among the cleanest people in the world. You will not find such devotion to personal hygiene of this kind anywhere in London, Sir."

"If a Christian crosses the road, he will kill you for a schilling." Softly murmured one of the children.

"It was a way of teaching the Rev. Griffith used to impress punishment and reward. By analogy so the children could better understand right from wrong. He felt it better served the childish imagination as they are steeped in reason by analogy and do not recognize our methods of rational thought."

"Now the children do it by force of habit."

"My God man, but what do they know of Jesus and the one true God?"

"Do you mean Tewas, Sir?" responded one of the children.

"Children what do you think of Jesus?"

"Tewas nemaste," they answered in a chorus.

"And what does that mean?"

"Jesus is love, Sir."

"They know, Sir but they just prefer these old stories from the uncles. You must come back tonight and you will see for yourself. There is a deer dance in the glade this evening."

Every one had gathered in the glade when the uncles arrived and began singing the deer songs. It was electric as the energy coursed through the darkness to fill the quiet air and pierce the still of the night.

Excited, the Rev's eyes appeared to pop out onto his forehead as he looked to the edge effect of the forest surrounding the glade.

"See there, he fairly well shouted behind those trees, "there are deer everywhere looking in on these doings. They seem to have faint smiles on their faces and a whimsical look in their eyes."

"Yes, they come out in droves when the uncles sing these songs at this time of year."

"But why, man? These uncles look like wolves to me."

"Hush, be quiet," whispered Hicks, "You must not say it and scare the deer away."

At the edge of the grove, a young buck remarked in the excitement, "Mother, I want to dance."

"Patience, child, you will get your chance. We all want to dance, it is our song… but we must wait until the uncles are ready."

Taking the measure of the crowd, the uncles began slowly building the song into a crescendo. It looked to the Right Reverend there were countless deer looking in on the glade from the fringe beyond the trees.

"I see them, Hicks, they are everywhere just beyond the glade."

"All the deer and shades of deer come in for this one, Sir."

It seemed as if a vortex developed, transporting everyone just above the glade as the deer began to dance below them in the field, while the uncles intensified their singing.

The Reverend was ecstatic having never enjoyed such an astral experience.

"How is it done Hicks?"

"The deer dance and we fly."

A doe replied, "You sing our songs, we dance in joyful thanks."

Another song caught the wind and the vortex began anew.

"Mommy, I want to dance all night."

"Good, child, it brings the life back to us and restores our kind."

"Are you sure Tewas loves us?"

"We know Mother's brothers do so."

"Nemaste uncles," shouted the young buck as an uncle turned to grin at him showing a mouth full of sharp teeth, fangs for tearing tender skin and flesh apart.

"Careful son, Mother's brothers will tear you to pieces and feed you to their young. We must be careful of them."

"Hicks, how is this teaching the children? Entertaining them, I concede, but what is to be learned from this spectacle?"

"It's the deer, your Worship, we are here to honor the deer. This entire community depends on the deer."

"We used to have dances like this for Jesus, but he never showed up and the people stopped coming to them."

"In the morning the mists drifted up from the glade as the Reverend searched about in the dawn light. There were deer tracks everywhere and he knew they had been real and all that he had seen was true.

"What will be your verdict, Right Reverend?"

"The school is doing just fine. Let it continue under the tutelage of the uncles."

Snow Blindness

Laika Wallace, Mi'kmaw and Passamaquoddy

THE RESIDENTS OF THE GWITNA'Q had been suspended in cryostasis for quite some time now, dreaming of lush landscapes and rivers flowing to the sea as their scrappy spacecraft drifted through the uncolor of empty space. It had been years since they had lifted off at their last spaceport, on Eleria, where even there life was scarce; just a struggling pitstop between solar systems. They were ready for a short lean period after being unable to pick up adequate supplies. What they were not ready for, though, was half a decade of crawling through a void that had not appeared on any of their maps.

At the console, surrounded by the seven flickering panels showing the vitals of hir friends and family, the Captain stared out into the absence of life at the one speck of hope sie had come across. A rogue planet, sie guessed, for there was no star and it wasn't transmitting any kind of signal. It was a few months away now, and had only been hir objective for about the same amount of time; it had just appeared one day and, not one to dismiss a boon, sie manually mathed out the course and had been hot on it ever since.

It was still out of reach, but it was something.

* * *

Watching the Captain watch the void, the girl could barely contain her excitement. To keep herself from touching stuff on the console that she knew she shouldn't, she kept her hands busy with her hair. It was long, dark, rich and beautiful, flowing freely almost to her waist. It had been out of her usual braids since her mother was put into the cryopod.

Looking over hir shoulder, the Captain said, "What is it, tu's?"

"We're so close now," she said, running up to hir and throwing her arms around hir waist. "I can't wait to see the new planet."

Sie smiled, putting one arm loosely around her shoulders. "We'll have to wait for a couple months more still."

"Can't we go faster?"

"Not while our family is asleep. We need the fuel to keep them comfortable in the cryopods."

She pressed her face into hir side, speaking into hir clothes as she moped, "And they need to be in the cryopods because we don't have enough food."

"That's right. This way, we will always have enough for you."

"Because I eat so much."

Sie laughed. "No, tu's, you don't eat too much. We just don't have enough resources to feed all nine of us right now." Sie kissed the top of her head. "And I don't want to even think about you going hungry."

She peeled herself away and leaned on the console to look out the window. "I wonder what will be on the planet."

"We will see, tu's. We will see."

* * *

Over the next couple weeks, the girl would ask the Captain every day for news about the planet. Often, there was nothing, so sie would indulge her fantasies about abundant food and water and safety for their family. But with six weeks left to go, they were finally close enough to clearly see the color of the planet.

It glowed white.

The girl and the Captain ate their breakfast of dehydrated meat and fermented fruit as they looked out the window at the planet. The Captain kept a neutral face as the girl gushed about how beautiful it was, like a beacon to tell them to come home, or a crack in the void.

"What do you think it is?" she asked with a dreamy sigh.

"Well, it's bound to be something in the atmosphere and something on the surface of the planet, but—"

"I know that," she interrupted, looking back at hir. "I remember the other planets we've seen. And I remember stories about Earth being blue from space because of all the water." Her eyes lit up. "Do you think it's all snow and ice?"

Sie smiled with the corners of hir mouth. "That would explain why it's white."

She hopped excitedly, putting her hands together and thinking. "Do you think it's like, um," she mimicked making and throwing a snowball, "wali'j?"

Not wanting to spoil her fun, sie said, "Maybe it is, tu's."

* * *

"Ge jugu'wa tu's?"

The girl heard the Captain calling her from the console room, but didn't want to leave her mother yet. She'd been in there all day. She had been reading off the logs of old radio transmissions and other communications, which was her mother's job before she went to sleep. Now, she was taking delight in describing the icy oasis she imagined they were headed towards.

But she admitted she was getting hungry by now, and that's probably why the Captain was calling her over. She kissed the glass of her mother's cryopod and slipped out of the cryostasis room, walking up the hallway past the storage room to where the Captain was sitting on the floor, back to the window, the glittering snowball watching them now.

"Did you want me to get us food?" she asked, seeing sie had nothing to eat.

Sie shook hir head. "Sit with me."

She did.

Sie pulled out a little metal box decorated with porcupine quills. Most of them had broken or fallen off and were replaced with bits of metal painted to resemble the brown, black, and white pattern on the quills.

"That's your…"

"Yes, tu's. I may be too sick to have long, lovely hair like yours, but I kept my favorite ties." Sie opened the box to reveal two leather braid ties. They were soft and brown, with little beads on the split tassels. Some of the beads had fallen off and almost all were discolored, but she knew they should be white, red, black, and yellow; she'd seen these before in old photos. They were well loved and old, not so old that they could be from Turtle Island, but old enough that the girl could dream. Sie used the other thing in the box, a fine comb, to brush her hair as sie spoke. "These were my mother's, and her mother's, and her mother's too. When I was around your age, maybe a little older, she gave them to me. She had no daughters, not until I realized who I really was. She was elated to have someone to pass this down to, especially with my brother's passing."

"Uncle died on Urdi… Urdish…?"

"Urditia, yes," sie corrected, gently twining her hair together. "That awful ocean planet swallowed his spacecraft when he tried to land, even with the correct landing gear deployed. We never found him."

She looked at her hands for a while, quiet, trying to enjoy her parent's careful braiding. She imagined her uncle, a man she had only met through photographs and a communication log she had found hidden in her mother's things, vanishing completely from the universe in the depths of some unknown water planet. She imagined her mother, asleep forever in her glass bed, not knowing she was sinking deep into the ocean floor.

"What's on your mind?" the Captain asked, moving from the first finished braid to the first twists of the second.

She waited for a moment before she spoke, twisting her thoughts together. "We will land on the ice planet and we will be okay."

* * *

"We'll gather the snow and melt it in here so it all doesn't melt under us. We'll have fresh water again. Not water that's been through so many recycling cycles. It tastes so weird now."

"We have seeds in stasis in the storage room. We'll have to test which ones will grow in these conditions, but I'm sure there will be something."

"There will be. Not just something. All of them will grow. We'll have a whole garden again. And we can hunt the wildlife. Oh, wow, do you think there will be animals like on Turtle Island? Like in the North. I remember caribou and wolves and polar bears and ptarmigans."

"There might be."

"There has to be. Maybe not exactly like the ones from Turtle Island, but there's gonna be animals. So many animals. And plants, too, to feed the animals. Like berry bushes and shrub trees."

"And lichen."

"Yes! Lichen for the caribou. I remember that, too."

They looked out at the planet, dreaming of their land of plenty as they ate cold, dry meat.

* * *

"We have to name the planet," the girl said one morning. It now took up quite a large amount of their field of vision. "There's no transmissions coming from it, right? It's not on any maps. We're the first people to get to it, probably, so we should name it."

"I suppose we could, at least so we can talk about it better."

"What should we name it?"

"Well, it was your idea to give it a name, so I think you should have that honor."

Her eyes lit up and she grinned. She twisted a braid through her fingers, thinking. It was easy to decide it would be a Mi'kmwei word. Even their ship was named the word for traveling by canoe in their old language from Turtle Island. So was the motto painted on the side of the hull: *Na'te'l gtu'lien, amujpa gwitna'mn.* If you want to go there, you must go by canoe.

It was her mother's most important mission in life to remember their language and culture from Turtle Island, so that wherever they may finally call home, and all the while in space, children born away from Earth will know the life their ancestors had. It was something so precious to know that was stolen from so many people. As her daughter, she knew she must make her proud.

She looked out the window at the planet throwing light towards them, bright, white light, cutting through the void and stinging her eyes like a lightbulb she had stared at for too long.

"Apuknapi," she said finally.

"'I am snowblinded'?"

"Yeah, because it's bright like sunlight reflecting off snow."

"Right. That's very smart." The Captain could only hope she was just remembering the times they'd landed on snowy planets. Looking out at the planet ahead of them, sie knew it would crush her dreams if she made the same connection sie had.

Hir daughter did not deserve that. Not now.

* * *

There wasn't much time left until they were to land, which was a blessing in disguise. Sitting in the storage room late one night, the Captain counted and recounted the bags of food they had left. If only the crew had gone into cryostasis sooner…

Sie stacked the bags back, folding some empty ones on top of each other behind the few full ones left. Hir hands trembled as sie sat back down, looking at the one row that should have been halved, should have been three. Sie couldn't help but feel sie had failed hir crewmates, hir family, hir friends. They didn't even have enough supplies to make lusqi'ni'qin; they were down to old, dry meat that nobody liked in the first place. Sie had almost sold it on Eleria to try to get something that at least tasted better, but hir wife had talked hir out of it. The protein was too important, she'd said. So sie had sold their frying pan, pot, and last bits and pieces of cutlery for a laughably low price just to buy a little more fuel.

It wasn't worth it anymore. Sie could hardly remember the last time they fired up the cooktop in the storage room and made lusqi'ni'qin together, as a family. The sickness, the hunger, the loneliness and stress were all eating hir memories away. Even if sie had just kept the pan, things might have been okay.

Sie sighed heavily, rubbing hir eyes with the back of hir hand. Before sie left, sie slipped hir dinner back into one of the bags.

This planet had to have something good for them. There wasn't another option. They needed this now, more than ever.

* * *

Only a few more days now. The planet was the brightest thing she'd ever seen. She'd have her face pressed to the glass if she could, taking it all in. This strange new place, glowing like a beacon, calling them home.

* * *

But it wasn't right. She knew that. Logically, she knew that. Apuknapi. How could it be reflecting the light of no sun?

"Tata't," she asked, curling her fingers around the Captain's arm as sie adjusted the trajectory for tomorrow's entry of the atmosphere, "should we really go towards it, if it's blinding us?"

Brown eyes steeled ahead, sie said barely above a whisper, "There will come a time in your life, too, where you have to take a risk, even if you don't understand the consequences."

* * *

She had woken up early to see the Gwitna'q break through the atmosphere. They both held their breath as the fire show subsided. Deep in her heart, she wanted the window to clear and show them an immaculate tundra, teeming with wildlife.

The Captain wanted so badly to take hir eyes off hir daughter, but sie couldn't. Sie couldn't.

The fire brightness turned up, ferocious, flashing off the window. It peeled away and rolled past the ship in huge angular shapes. Through the glare, she could just see that they were massive translucent crystals.

"Floating crystals?" she whispered, reaching to squeeze her parent's hand.

Sie worked hir jaw to speak but nothing would come out.

"They're glowing… They're glowing. That has to be what we saw."

The clusters of crystal whipped past them as though they were exploding outwards from one point on the surface of the planet. Sie couldn't tell if that was true or an illusion, and didn't know if sie should be comforted or concerned that none of them even got close to hitting the spacecraft.

Beyond the crystals, the surface of the planet still glittered like untouched snow. If sie squinted, sie could see it billowed like windblown snowdrifts, shadows dancing strangely from the bright light of the crystals, creating patterns unlike sie had ever seen. Sie imagined hir wife smiling up at the endless daynight that the crystals and the void fought to provide. Sie imagined hir wife, illuminated by the all too otherworldly light.

Sie squeezed hir child's hand as the ship stuttered, slowing to land. Sie opened her mouth to speak, hir shaky smile betraying her voice, "Oh, tu's, I think we're going to be—"

A rift in the snow opened up only a few hundred meters from where the ship was plotted to touch down. The landscape folded backwards like rumpled empty bags. A great white light, brighter than the beacon that brought them here, engulfed them. At the center, a vast black pupil took them in.

The Girls Who Wanted New Teeth

Banyarwanda People, Rwanda

A NUMBER OF YOUNG GIRLS agreed together to go and get teeth created for them. But one of their companions was unable to join the party. This girl's mother was dead, and she had a stepmother who kept her hard at work and otherwise made her life a burden, so that she had become a poor, stunted drudge, ill-clothed and usually dirty. As for going to ask for new teeth, this was quite out of the question.

So when her friends came back and showed her their beautiful teeth she said nothing, but felt the more, and went on with her work. When the cows came home in the evening she lit the fire in the kraal, so that the smoke might drive away the mosquitoes, and then helped with the milking, and when that was done served the evening meal. After supper she slipped away, took a bath, oiled herself, and started out without anyone seeing her.

Before she had gone very far in the dark she met a hyena, who said to her, "You, maiden, where are you going?" She answered, "I'm going where all the other girls went. Father's wife would not let me go with them, so I'm going by myself." The hyena said, "Go on, then, child of Imana!" and let her go in peace. She walked on, and after a while met a lion, who asked her the same question. She answered him as she had done the hyena, and he too said, "Go on, child of Imana!" She walked on through the night, and just as dawn was breaking she met Imana himself, looking like a great, old chief with a kind face. He said to her, "Little maid, where are you going?" She answered, "I have been living with my stepmother, and she always gives me so much to do that I could not get away when the other girls came to ask you for new teeth, and so I came by myself." And Imana said, "You shall have them," and gave her not only new teeth, but a new skin, and made her beautiful all over. And he gave her new clothes and brass armlets and anklets and bead ornaments, so that she looked quite a different girl, and then, like a careful father, he saw her on her way home, till they had come so near that she could point out her village. Then he said, "When you get home whatever you do you must not laugh or smile at anyone, your father or your stepmother or anyone else." And so he left her.

When her stepmother saw her coming she did not at first recognize her, but as soon as she realized who the girl was she cried out, "She's been stealing things at the chief's place! Where did she get those beads and those bangles? She must have been driving off her father's cows to sell them. Look at that cloth! Where did you get it?" The girl did not answer. Her father asked her, "Where did you pick up these things?" – and still she did not answer. After a while they let her alone. The stepmother's spiteful speeches did not impress the neighbours, who soon got to know of the girl's good fortune, and before three days had passed a respectable man called on her father to ask her in marriage for his son. The wedding took place in the usual way, and she followed her young husband to his home. There everything went well, but they all – his mother and sisters and he himself – thought it strange that they never saw her laugh.

After the usual time a little boy was born, to the great joy of his parents and grandparents. Again all went well, till the child was four or five years old, when, according to custom, he began to go out and herd the calves near the hut. One day his grandmother, who had never been able to satisfy her curiosity, said to him, "Next time your mother gives you milk say you will not take it unless she smiles at you. Tell her, if she does not smile you will cry, and if she does not do so then you will die!" He did as she told him, but his mother would not smile; he began to cry, and she paid no attention; he went on screaming, and presently died. They came and wrapped his body in a mat, and carried it out into the bush – for the BanyaRwanda do not bury their dead – and left it there. The poor mother mourned, but felt she could not help herself. She must not disobey Imana's commandment. After a time, another boy was born. When he was old enough to talk and run about his grandmother made the same suggestion to him as she had done to his brother, and with the same result. The boy died, and was carried out to the bush. Again, a baby was born – this time a bonny little girl.

When she was about three years old her mother one evening took her on her back and went out to the bush where the two little bodies had been laid long ago. There, in her great trouble, she cried to Imana, "*Yee, baba wee!* Oh my father! Oh Imana, lord of Rwanda, I have never once disobeyed you; will you not save this little one?" She looked up, and, behold! There was Imana standing before her, looking as kind as when she had first seen him, and he said, "Come here and see your children. I have brought them back to life. You may smile at them now." And so she did, and they ran to her, crying, "Mother! Mother!" Then Imana touched her poor, worn face and eyes dimmed with crying and her bowed shoulders, and she was young again, tall and straight and more beautiful than ever; he gave her a new body and new teeth. He gave her a beautiful cloth and beads to wear, and he sent his servants to fetch some cows, so many for each of the boys. Then he went with them to their home.

The husband saw them coming, and could not believe his eyes – he was too much astonished to speak. He brought out the one stool which every hut contains, and offered it to the guest, but Imana would not sit down yet. He said, "Send out for four more stools." So the man sent and borrowed them from the neighbours, and they all sat down, he and his wife and the two boys, and Imana in the place of honour. Then Imana said, "Now look at your wife and your children. You have got to make them happy and live comfortably with them. You will soon enough see her smiling at you and at them. It was I who forbade her to laugh, and then some wicked people went and set the children on to try to make her do so, and they died. Now I have brought them back to life. Here they are with their mother. Now see that you live happily together. And as for your mother, I am going to burn her in her house, because she did a wicked thing. I leave you to enjoy all her belongings, because you have done no wrong." Then he vanished from their sight, and while they were still gazing in astonishment a great black cloud gathered over the grandmother's hut; there was a dazzling flash, followed by a terrible clap of thunder, and the hut, with everyone and everything in it, was burned to ashes. Before they had quite recovered from the shock Imana once more appeared to them, in blinding light, and said to the husband, "Remember my words, and all shall be well with you!" A moment later he was gone.

Collected by Alice Werner

The Thunder's Bride

Banyarwanda People, Rwanda

IN THIS STORY we find Imana associated with thunder and lightning, so that we may suppose him to be a sky-god, or, at any rate, to have been such in the beginning. In story which follows, the Thunder is treated as a distinct personage, but he is nowhere said to be identical with Imana.

There was a certain woman of Rwanda, the wife of Kwisaba. Her husband went away to the wars, and was absent for many months. One day while she was all alone in the hut she was taken ill, and found herself too weak and wretched to get up and make a fire, which would have been done for her at once had anyone been present. She cried out, talking wildly in her despair: "Oh, what shall I do? If only I had someone to split the kindling wood and build the fire! I shall die of cold if no one comes! Oh, if someone would but come – if it were the very Thunder of heaven himself!"

So the woman spoke, scarcely knowing what she said, and presently a little cloud appeared in the sky. She could not see it, but very soon it spread, other clouds collected, till the sky was quite overcast; it grew dark as night inside the hut, and she heard thunder rumbling in the distance. Then there came a flash of lightning close by, and she saw the Thunder standing before her, in the likeness of a man, with a little bright axe in his hand. He fell to, and had split all the wood in a twinkling; then he built it up and lit it, just with a touch of his hand, as if his fingers had been torches. When the blaze leapt up he turned to the woman and said, "Now, oh wife of Kwisaba, what will you give me?" She was quite paralysed with fright, and could not utter a word. He gave her a little time to recover, and then went on: "When your baby is born, if it is a girl, will you give her to me for a wife?" Trembling all over, the poor woman could only stammer out, "Yes!" and the Thunder vanished.

Not long after this a baby girl was born, who grew into a fine, healthy child, and was given the name of Miseke. When Kwisaba came home from the wars the women met him with the news that he had a little daughter, and he was delighted, partly, perhaps, with the thought of the cattle he would get as her bride-price when she was old enough to be married. But when his wife told him about the Thunder he looked very serious, and said, "When she grows older you must never on any account let her go outside the house, or we shall have the Thunder carrying her off."

So as long as Miseke was quite little she was allowed to play out of doors with the other children, but the time came all too soon when she had to be shut up inside the hut. One day some of the other girls came running to Miseke's mother in great excitement. "Miseke is dropping beads out of her mouth! We thought she had put them in on purpose, but they come dropping out every time she laughs." Sure enough the mother found that it was so, and not only did Miseke produce beads of the kinds most valued, but beautiful brass and copper bangles. Miseke's father was greatly troubled when they told him of this. He said it must be the Thunder, who sent the beads in this extraordinary way as the presents which a man always has to send to his betrothed while she is growing up. So Miseke had always to stay indoors and amuse herself as best she could – when she was not helping in the house work – by plaiting mats and making baskets. Sometimes her old playfellows came to see her, but they too did not care to be shut up for long in a dark, stuffy hut.

One day, when Miseke was about fifteen, a number of the girls made up a party to go and dig *inkwa* (white clay) and they thought it would be good fun to take Miseke along with them. They went to her mother's hut and called her, but of course her parents would not hear of her going, and she had to stay at home. They tried again another day, but with no better success. Some time after this, however, Kwisaba and his wife both went to see to their garden, which was situated a long way off, so that they had to start at daybreak, leaving Miseke alone in the hut. Somehow the girls got to hear of this, and as they had already planned to go for *inkwa* that day they went to fetch her. The temptation was too great, and she slipped out very quietly, and went with them to the watercourse where the white clay was to be found. So many people had gone there at different times for the same purpose that quite a large pit had been dug out. The girls got into it and fell to work, laughing and chattering, when, suddenly, they became aware that it was growing dark, and, looking up, saw a great black cloud gathering overhead. And then, suddenly, they saw the figure of a man standing before them, and he called out in a great voice, "Where is Miseke, daughter of Kwisaba?" One girl came out of the hole, and said, "I am not Miseke, daughter of Kwisaba. When Miseke laughs, beads and bangles drop from her lips." The Thunder said, "Well, then, laugh, and let me see." She laughed, and nothing happened. "No, I see you are not she." So one after another was questioned and sent on her way. Miseke herself came last, and tried to pass, repeating the same words that the others had said; but the Thunder insisted on her laughing, and a shower of beads fell on the ground. The Thunder caught her up and carried her off to the sky and married her.

Of course she was terribly frightened, but the Thunder proved a kind husband, and she settled down quite happily and, in due time, had three children, two boys and a girl. When the baby girl was a few weeks old Miseke told her husband that she would like to go home and see her parents. He not only consented, but provided her with cattle and beer (as provision for the journey and presents on arrival) and carriers for her hammock, and sent her down to earth with this parting advice: "Keep to the high road; do not turn aside into any unfrequented bypath." But, being unacquainted with the country, her carriers soon strayed from the main track. After they had gone for some distance along the wrong road they found the path barred by a strange monster called an *igikoko*, a sort of ogre, who demanded something to eat. Miseke told the servants to give him the beer they were carrying: he drank all the pots dry in no time. Then he seized one of the carriers and ate him, then a second – in short, he devoured them all, as well as the cattle, till no one was left but Miseke and her children. The ogre then demanded a child. Seeing no help for it, Miseke gave him the younger boy, and then, driven to extremity, the baby she was nursing, but while he was thus engaged she contrived to send off the elder boy, whispering to him to run till he came to a house. "If you see an old man sitting on the ash-heap in the front yard that will be your grandfather; if you see some young men shooting arrows at a mark they will be your uncles; the boys herding the cows are your cousins; and you will find your grandmother inside the hut. Tell them to come and help us."

The boy set off, while his mother kept off the ogre as best she could. He arrived at his grandfather's homestead, and told them what had happened, and they started at once, having first tied the bells on their hunting dogs. The boy showed them the way as well as he could, but they nearly missed Miseke just at last; only she heard the dogs' bells and called out. Then the young men rushed in and killed the ogre with their spears. Before he died he said, "If you cut off my big toe you will get back everything belonging to you." They did so, and, behold! out came the carriers and the cattle, the servants and the children, none of them any the worse. Then, first making sure that the ogre was really dead, they set off for Miseke's old home. Her parents were overjoyed to see her and the children, and the time passed all too quickly. At the end of a month she began to think she ought to return, and the old people sent out for cattle and all sorts of presents, as is the custom when a guest is going to leave. Everything was got together outside the village, and her brothers were ready to escort her, when they saw the clouds gathering, and, behold! all of a sudden Miseke, her children, her servants, her cattle, and her porters, with their loads, were all caught up into the air and disappeared. The family were struck dumb with amazement, and they never saw Miseke on earth again. It is to be presumed that she lived happily ever after.

Collected by Alice Werner

Kwege and Bahati

Zaramo People, Tanzania

THERE WAS ONCE UPON A TIME a man who married a woman of the *Uwingu* clan (*uwingu* means 'sky') who was named Mulamuwingu, and whose brother, Muwingu, lived in her old home a day or two's journey from her husband's.

The couple had a son called Kwege, and lived happily enough till, in course of time, the husband died, leaving his wife with her son and a slave, Bahati, who had belonged to an old friend of theirs and had come to them on that friend's death.

Now the *tabu* of the Sky clan was rain – that is, rain must never be allowed to fall on anyone belonging to it; if this were to happen he or she would die.

One day when the weather looked threatening Mulamuwingu said, "My son Kwege, just go over to the garden and pick some gourds, so that I can cook them for our dinner." Kwege very rudely refused, and his mother rejoined, "I am afraid of my *mwidzilo* (*tabu*). If I go to the garden I shall die." Then Bahati, the slave, said, "I will go," and he went and gathered the gourds and brought them back.

Next day Kwege's mother again asked him to go to the garden, and again he refused. So she said, "Very well; I will go; but if I die it will be your fault." She set out, and when she reached the garden, which was a long way from any shelter, a great cloud gathered, and it began to rain. When the first drops touched her she fell down dead. Kwege had no dinner that evening, and when he found his mother did not come home either that day or the next (it does not seem to have entered into his head that he might go in search of her) he began to cry, saying, "Mother is dead! Mother is dead!" Then he called Bahati, and they set out to go to his uncle's village.

Now Kwege was a handsome lad, but Bahati was very ugly; and Kwege was well dressed, with plenty of cloth, while Bahati had only a bit of rag round his waist.

As they walked along Kwege said to Bahati, "When we come to a log lying across the path you must carry me over. If I step over it I shall die." For Kwege's *mwidzilo* was stepping over a log.

Bahati agreed, but when they came to a fallen tree he refused to lift Kwege over till he had given him a cloth. This went on every time they came to a log, till he had acquired everything Kwege was wearing, down to his leglets and his bead ornaments. And when they arrived at Muwingu's village and were welcomed by the people Bahati sat down on one of the mats brought out for them and told Kwege to sit on the bare ground. He introduced himself to Muwingu as his sister's son, and treated Kwege as his slave, suggesting, after a day or two, that he should be sent out to the rice fields to scare the birds. Kwege, in the ragged kilt which was the only thing Bahati had left him, went out to the fields, looked at the flocks of birds hovering over the rice, and then, sitting down under a tree, wept bitterly. Presently he began to sing:

> *"I, Kwege, weep, I weep!*
> *And my crying is what the birds say.*
> *Oh, you log, my tabu!*
> *I cry in the speech of the birds.*

They have taken my clothes,
They have taken my leglets,
They have taken my beads,
I am turned into Bahati.
Bahati is turned into Kwege.
I weep in the speech of the birds."

Now his dead parents had both been turned into birds. They came and perched on the tree above him, listening to his song, and said, "*Looo*! Muwingu has taken Bahati into his house and is treating him like a free man and Kwege, his nephew, as a slave! How can that be? "

Kwege heard what they said, and told his story. Then his father flapped one wing, and out fell a bundle of cloth; he flapped the other wing and brought out beads, leglets, and a little gourd full of oil. His mother, in the same way, produced a ready-cooked meal of rice and meat. When he had eaten they fetched water (by this time they had been turned back into human beings), washed him and oiled him, and then said, "Never mind the birds – let them eat Muwingu's rice, since he has sent you to scare them while he is treating Bahati as his son!" So they sat down, all three together, and talked till the sun went down.

On the way back Kwege hid all the cloth and beads that his parents had given him in the long grass, and put on his old rag again. But when he reached the house the family were surprised to see him looking so clean and glossy, as if he had just come from a bath, and cried out, "Where did you get this oil you have been rubbing yourself with? Did you run off and leave your work to go after it?" He did not want to say, "Mother gave it me," so he simply denied that he had been anointing himself.

Next day he went back to the rice field and sang his song again. The birds flew down at once, and, seeing him in the same miserable state as before, asked him what he had done with their gifts. He said they had been taken from him, thinking that, while he was about it, he might as well get all he could. They did not question his good faith, but supplied him afresh with everything, and, resuming their own forms, they sat by him while he ate.

Meanwhile Muwingu's son had taken it into his head to go and see how the supposed Bahati was getting on with his job – it is possible that he had begun to be suspicious of the man who called himself Kwege. What was his astonishment to see a good-looking youth, dressed in a clean cloth, with bead necklaces and all the usual ornaments, sitting between two people, whom he recognized as his father's dead sister and her husband. He was terrified, and ran back to tell his father that Kwege was Bahati and Bahati Kwege, and related what he had seen. Muwingu at once went with him to the rice field, and found that it was quite true. They hid and waited for Kwege to come home. Then, as he drew near the place where he had hidden his cloth, his uncle sprang out and seized him. He struggled to get away, but Muwingu pacified him, saying, "So you are my nephew Kwege after all, and that fellow is Bahati! Why did you not tell me before? Never mind; I shall kill him today." And kill him they did; and Kwege was installed in his rightful position. Muwingu made a great feast, inviting all his neighbours, to celebrate the occasion. "Here ends my story," says the narrator.

Collected by Alice Werner

The Tale of Murile

Chaga People, Tanzania

A MAN AND HIS WIFE living in the Chaga country had three sons, of whom Murile was the eldest. One day he went out with his mother to dig up *maduma*, and, noticing a particularly fine tuber among those which were to be put by for seed, he said, "Why, this one is as beautiful as my little brother!" His mother laughed at the notion of comparing a *taro* tuber with a baby; but he hid the root, and, later, when no one was looking, put it away in a hollow tree and sang a magic song over it.

Next day he went to look, and found that the root had turned into a child. After that at every meal he secretly kept back some food, and, when he could do so without being seen, carried it to the tree and fed the baby, which grew and flourished from day to day. But Murile's mother became very anxious when she saw how thin the boy was growing, and she questioned him, but could get no satisfaction. Then one day his younger brothers noticed that when his portion of food was handed to him, instead of eating it at once, he put it aside. They told their mother, and she bade them follow him when he went away after dinner, and see what he did with it. They did so, and saw him feeding the baby in the hollow tree, and came back and told her. She went at once to the spot and strangled the child which was 'starving her son'.

When Murile came back next day and found the child dead he was overcome with grief. He went home and sat down in the hut, crying bitterly. His mother asked him why he was crying, and he said it was because the smoke hurt his eyes. So she told him to go and sit on the other side of the fireplace. But, as he still wept and complained of the smoke when questioned, they said he had better take his father's stool and sit outside. He picked up the stool, went out into the courtyard, and sat down. Then he said, "Stool, go up on high, as my father's rope does when he hangs up his beehive in the forest!" And the stool rose up with him into the air and stuck fast in the branches of a tree. He repeated the words a second time, and again the stool moved upward. Just then his brothers happened to come out of the hut, and when they saw him they ran back and said to their mother, "Murile is going up into the sky!" She would not believe them. "Why do you tell me your eldest brother has gone up into the sky? Is there any road for him to go up by?" They told her to come and look, and when she saw him in the air she sang:

> *"Murile, come back hither!*
> *Come back hither, my child!*
> *Come back hither!"*

But Murile answered, "I shall never come back, Mother! I shall never come back!"

Then his brothers called him, and received the same answer; his father called him – then his boy-friends, and, last of all, his uncle (*washidu*, his mother's brother, the nearest relation of all). They could just hear his answer, "I am not coming back, Uncle! I am never coming back!" Then he passed up out of sight.

The stool carried him up till he felt solid ground beneath his feet, and then he looked round and found himself in the Heaven country. He walked on till he came to some people gathering wood. He asked them the way to the Moonchief's kraal, and they said, "Just pick up some sticks for us, and then we will tell you." He collected a bundle of sticks, and they directed him to go on till he should come to some people cutting grass. He did so, and greeted the grass-cutters when he came to them. They answered his greeting, and when he asked them the way said they would show him if he would help them for a while with their work.

So he cut some grass, and they pointed out the road, telling hill: to go on ill he came to some women hoeing. These, again, asked him to help them before they would show him the way, and, in succession, he met with some herd-boys, some women gathering beans, some people reaping millet, others gathering banana-leaves, and girls fetching water – all of them sending him forward with almost the same words. The water-carriers said, "Just go on in this direction till you come to a house where the people are eating." He found the house, and said, "Greeting, house-owners! Please show me the way to the Moon's kraal." They promised to do so if he would sit down and eat with them, which he did.

At last by following their instructions he reached his destination, and found the people there eating their food raw. He asked them why they did not use fire to cook with, and found that they did not know what fire was. So he said, "If I prepare nice food for you by means of fire what will you give me?" The Moon-chief said, "We will give you cattle and goats and sheep." Murile told them to bring plenty of wood, and when they came with it he and the chief went behind the house, where the other people could not see them. Murile took his knife and cut two pieces of wood, one flat and the other pointed, and twirled the pointed stick till he got some sparks, with which he lit a bunch of dry grass and so kindled a fire. When it burned up he got the chief to send for some green plantains, which he roasted and offered to him. Then he cooked some meat and various other foods. The Moon-chief was delighted when he tasted them, and at once called all the people together, and said to them, "Here is a wonderful doctor come from a far country! We shall have to repay him for his fire." The people asked, "What must be paid to him?" He answered, "Let one man bring a cow, another a goat, another whatever he may have in his storehouse." So they went to fetch all these things. And Murile became a rich man. For he stayed some years at the Moon's great kraal and married wives and had children born to him, and his flocks and herds increased greatly. But in the end a longing for his home came over him.

And he thought within himself: "How shall I go home again, unless I send a messenger before me? For I told them I was never coming back, and they must think that I am dead."

He called all the birds together and asked them one by one, "If I send you to my home what will you say?" The raven answered, "I shall say, *Kuruu! Kuruu!*" and was rejected. So, in turn, were the hornbill, the hawk, the buzzard, and all the rest, till he came to Njorovi, the mocking-bird, who sang:

> *"Murile is coming the day after tomorrow,*
> *Missing out tomorrow.*
> *Murile is coming the day after tomorrow.*
> *Keep some fat in the ladle for him!"*

Murile was pleased with this, and told her to go. So she flew down to earth and perched on the gate-post of his father's courtyard and sang her song. His father came out and said, "What thing is crying out there, saying that Murile is coming the day after tomorrow? Why, Murile was lost long ago, and will never come back!" And he drove the bird away. She flew back and told Murile where she had been. But he would not believe her; he told her to go again and bring back his father's stick as a token that she had really gone to his home. So she flew down again, came to the house, and picked up the stick, which was leaning in the doorway. The children in the house saw her, and tried to snatch it from her, but she was too quick for them, and took it back to Murile. Then he said, "Now I will start for home." He took leave of his friends and of his wives, who were to stay with their own people, but his cattle and his boys came with him. It was a long march to the place of descent, and Murile began to grow very tired. There was a very fine bull in the herd, who walked beside Murile all the way. Suddenly he spoke and said, "As you are so weary, what will you do for me if I let you ride me? If I take you on my back will you eat my flesh when they kill me?" Murile answered, "No! I will never eat you!" So the bull let him get on his back and carried him home. And Murile sang, as he rode along:

> *"Not a hoof nor a horn is wanting!*
> *Mine are the cattle – hey!*
> *Nought of the goods is wanting; Mine are the bairns today.*
> *Not a kid of the goats is wanting; My flocks are on the way.*
> *Nothing of mine is wanting; Murile comes today*
> *With his bairns and his cattle – hey!"*

So he came home. And his father and mother ran out to meet him and anointed him with mutton-fat, as is the custom when a loved one comes home from distant parts. And his brothers and everyone rejoiced and wondered greatly when they saw the cattle. But he showed his father the great bull that had carried him, and said, "This bull must be fed and cared for till he is old. And even if you kill him when he is old I will never eat of his flesh." So they lived quite happily for a time.

But when the bull had become very old Murile's father slaughtered him. The mother foolishly thought it such a pity that her son, who had always taken so much trouble over the beast, should have none of the beef when everyone else was eating it. So she took a piece of fat and hid it in a pot. When she knew that all the meat was finished she ground some grain and cooked the fat with the meal and gave it to her son. As soon as he had tasted it the fat spoke and said to him, "Do you dare to eat me, who carried you on my back? You shall be eaten, as you are eating me!"

Then Murile sang: "Oh my mother, I said to you, 'Do not give me to eat of the bull's flesh!'" He took a second taste, and his foot sank into the ground. He sang the same words again, and then ate up the food his mother had given him. As soon as he had swallowed it he sank down and disappeared.

Collected by Alice Werner

Biographies & Sources

Chukwu Sunday Abel

An Unwanted Two-Spirit
(Originally Published by International Human Rights Art Festival Awards on their website, after winning first prize for the Justice Literary Award essay category)
The Man Who Lost Himself
(First Publication)
Chukwu Sunday Abel is an Igbo-born writer whose forte is to explore the being of African society. He is a two-time winner of the Creators of Justice Literary Awards: 2020 and 2021, Short Story and essay categories respectively. Chukwu emerged the first runner-up in the 2019 Victoria Literary Festival, Canada, and was a finalist in Nigeria's END SARS National Poetry Competition in 2020. In 2021 he was shortlisted for the Professor Toyin Falola Literary Prize, and his literary works have appeared in anthologies and Magazines across four continents including in Rice University's reputable magazine, Texlandia. Chukwu Sunday Abel is currently unemployed, a sad truth about him. He can be reached on Twitter at @sunabel73.

Okun Asere

How the Moon First Came into the Sky
How Sun and Moon Went up to the Sky
How the First Rain Came
How All the Rivers First Came on Earth
(All Originally Published in I*n the Shadow of the Bush*, G.H. Doran, 1912)
Sadly, little is known of Okun Asere beyong that they were the source for many of the stories Percy Amaury Talbot translated and published in I*n the Shadow of the Bush.* Recorded as hailing from Mfamosing, Nigeria, they belonged to the Ekoi people.

Hartley Burr Alexander

The Creation Story of the Four Suns
Xolotl Creates the Parents of Mankind
Manco Capac Founds Cuzco
(All Originally Published in *The Mythology of All Races*, Marshall Jones Company, 1919)
Hartley Burr Alexander (1973–1939) was a philosopher, author, scholar, educator, iconographer, and poet. Born in Nebraska to a Methodist family, Alexander came to distrust Christianity and developed an interest in First Peoples of the Americas, their religions, and spirituality. Alexander wrote prolifically on the subjects of Native American philosophy, lore, mythology, and art. One of his best-known works is the poem 'To a Child's Moccasin (Found at Wounded Knee)', which stood in stark contrast to the prevailing negative views and treatment of Native Americans by the US government and American society of the time.

Laura Barker

Anansi, the World, and the Stories
(First Publication)
Laura Barker is a writer, artist, and facilitator. She runs an LGBT black writing group in London. Her

work has appeared in the *Guardian, Apparition Lit, midnight & indigo, The Other Stories, Planet Scumm, Free Black University, Middleground,* and *Love Letters to Poe.* She has guest edited for *Apparition Lit,* and her YA novel *Picnics* was shortlisted for the Faber Andlyn (FAB) Prize. Follow her at @LauraHannahBar. Laura's favourite crisps are Ready Salted and she is a no-dig orchard enthusiast.

Rosetta Gage Harvey Baskerville

Musoke the Moon-Boy
The Story of Nsangi and the Apes
(Both Originally Published in *The Flame Tree, and Other Folk-lore Stories,* Sheldon Press, 1900)
Rosetta Gage Harvey Baskerville, who wrote under the pen name of Mrs. George Baskerville, was an English author and ethnographer. Focusing her work mainly on Uganda, Harvey collected and published traditional stories, folk-lore, and mythology from the first peoples of Uganda. Her collection, *The Flame Tree and Other Folk-Lore Stories from Uganda,* was published in 1925.

George W. Bateman

Goso, the Teacher
(Originally Published in *Zanzibar Tales: Told by Natives of the East Coast of Africa,* A.C. McClurg & Co., 1901)
George W. Bateman (1850–1940) was the British-born author of the famous Zanzibar Tales: Told by Natives of the East Coast of Africa (1901), in which he presented stories, that he 'translated from the Original Swahili', told to him, in Zanzibar, by locals 'whose ancestors told them to them, who had received them from their ancestors, and so back.' Reportedly many of these tales were the inspiration for certain Disney stories such as Bambi, The Lion King and so on.

Shelley Burne-Field

Potter's Field
(First Publication)
Shelley Burne-Field (Ngāti Mutunga, Ngāti Rārua, Sāmoa) is from Aotearoa New Zealand and is a Māori writer of fiction and creative non-fiction. She is a graduate of both the Masters in Creative Writing (2020) at Auckland University and Te Papa Tupu Writing Programme developed by the Māori Literature Trust. Shelley's short stories have been published in anthologies and online – she is currently exploring the effects of colonisation on identity, loss of indigenous language, caste, and racism. Shelley was the only New Zealand finalist named in the Commonwealth Writer's Prize 2022.

Gina Cole

Sunset on Mars
(Originally Published in an Earlier Form in *Ora Nui 4, Māori Literary Journal,* Oranui Press Ltd, B.K Agency, 2020)
Gina Cole (fiction writer, poet) is Fijian (Koro, Levoni, Ono-i-Lau; Koro ni vasu, Culanuku, Serua), Scottish, and Welsh and lives in Auckland, New Zealand. She is the author of *Black Ice Matter,* which won Best First Book Fiction at the 2017 Ockham New Zealand Book Awards. Cole's work has been widely anthologised and has appeared in numerous publications. She is a barrister & solicitor, LLB(Hons), MJur, Auckland University. She has a Master of Creative Writing, Auckland University and a PhD in Creative Writing, Massey University. Her science fiction fantasy novel *Na Viro* (Huia Publishers, 2022) is a work of Pasifikafuturism.

Mabel Cook Cole

Mythology of Mindanao

(Originally Published in *Philippine Folklore Stories*, A. C. McClurg & Co, 1916)

Mabel Cook Cole (1880–1977) was born in Plano, Illinois. As an anthropologist focusing in ancient peoples and Filipino culture, Cole spent four years living with several tribes in the Philippines. She learned numerous folk tales and myths from these tribes, which she recorded down and eventually published in her collection *Philippine Folk Tales* (1916). Among her other published works is *The Story of Primitive Man* (1940).

Natalie Curtis

Legend and Song of the Daughter and the Slave

(Originally Published in *Songs and Tales from the Dark Continent*, G. Schirmer, c. 1920)

Natalie Curtis (1875–1921) was an American ethnomusicologist, born in New York City. Her scholarly work on ethnological studies in North America with a small group of other female researchers contributed significantly to the field in the early twentieth century. Curtis is known for her compilation and publication of a four-volume collection of African American music. She also held a strong fascination with Native American music, producing transcriptions, recording, and publishing the traditional music of the Hopi tribe, despite the US government's suppression of Native Americans' rights to practice and express their cultures.

Jeremiah Curtin

The Winning of Halai Auna at the House of Tuina

The Finding of Fire

(Both Originally Published in *Creation Myths of Primitive America*, Little, Brown, 1898)

Jeremiah Curtin (1835-1906) was a Detroit-born ethnographer and folklorist. While much of his work would focus on collecting myths and folktales from around the world, Curtin would also be renowned for his translations of works by Polish author Henryk Sienkiewicz. Between 1883 and 1891 Curtin's interests would focus closer to home when he worked as a field researcher recording the myths and customs of Native American people, which would later result in the publication of the book *Creation Myths of Primitive America* (1898).

Frank Hamilton Cushing

The Boy Hunter Who Never Sacrificed to the Deer He Had Slain

(Originally Published in *Zuñi Folk Tales*, G. P. Putnam's Sons, 1901

Born in 1857, Frank Hamilton Cushing was an American anthropologist and ethnologist who pioneered a new method of study – one which saw him actively participate in the cultures he studied, rather than merely observing from afar. Cushing's work was focused primarily on the Zuni Indians of New Mexico; he would live among them for a period of five years from 1879-84, and go on to write a number of books about them, including Zuni Folk Tales (1901). Cushing would continue to lead expeditions up to his death in 1900.

Elphinstone Dayrell

Of the Pretty Girl and the Seven Jealous Women

The Fate of Essido and His Evil Companions

(Originally Published in *Folk Stories from southern Nigeria,* Longmans, Green & Co., 1910)

Dayrell (1869–1917) collected his tales after hearing many first-hand from the Efik and Ibibio peoples of Southeastern Nigeria when he was District Commissioner of South Nigeria. His collections of folklore include Folk Stories from Southern Nigeria (1910) and Ikom Folk Stories from Southern Nigeria, the latter published by the Royal Anthropological Institute of Great Britain and Ireland in 1913.

Kylie Fennell

Finding Home

(Originally Published in Long Way Home's *Land/Marks* anthology, 2020)

Kylie Fennell has made a 25-year career out of wrangling words, working as a journalist, editor and author of speculative fiction. She is the author of *The Kyprian Prophecy* series and several other works. As an Australian writer of European and Aboriginal (Gumbaynggirr and Bundjalung) descent she likes to explore culture and identity through her writing, as well as magic…always magic! 'Finding Home' is set in Northern New South Wales, the Country of Kylie's ancestors, and is inspired by stories from her extended family. Kylie lives in Brisbane (Yuggera and Turrbal Country) with her husband, son and too many pets. Find out more at kyliefennell.com.

Dr. Marc André Fortin

Associate Editor, First Peoples, Shared Stories

Marc André Fortin is Associate Professor of English and Comparative Canadian Literature at l'Université de Sherbrooke in Quebec, Canada. His publications include research on Indigenous literatures, Postcolonial literatures, and Ecocriticism in collections and journals such as Canadian Literature and Cultural Memory (Oxford UP); Learn, Teach, Challenge: Indigenous Literatures in the 21st Century (Wilfred Laurier UP); Making Canada New: Editing, Modernism, and New Media (Toronto UP); Studies in Canadian Literature; English Studies in Canada; and Configurations. He is currently Member-at-Large for the Association for Literature, Environment, and Culture in Canada.

Pedro Sarmient de Gamboa

The Fable of the Origin of the People of Peru

(Originally Published in *History of the Incas,* printed for the Hakluyt Society, 1907)

Pedro Sarmient de Gamboa (1532–1592) was a Spanish explorer, writer, and historian. Gamboa first sailed across the Atlantic to New Spain (present-day Mexico) in 1555 and later moved to Peru. He joined an expedition with Álvaro de Mendaña de Neira, which resulted in the West's discovery of the Solomon Islands in 1568. Gamboa was commissioned in 1572 by the fifth viceroy of Peru to write a history of the Incas. Intended to portray the Incas as a violent people to justify Spain's colonisation, *The History of the Incas* focuses primarily on the Incas' conquest of the region, also featuring detailed accounts of their mythology.

Sophie Garcia

Sinking Cities

(First Publication)

Sophie Garcia is a writer, filmmaker, and astrologer born and raised in San Francisco. They've been writing since they were 4 years old. Nurtured by local creative writing programs such as 826 Valencia Pirate Supply Store and UC Berkeley's elementary program. Sophie has always gravitated towards short story fiction. Sophie has recently published nonfiction articles on housing justice, Mexican folklore, and astrology with organizations such as Resonance Network. They're also a scriptwriter, and their short documentary, *Otro Mundo Es Posible,* just premiered in LA in May. With this work, Sophie aims to restore the collective hope and access to information interrupted by colonial atrocities. Continuing the legacy as the great-granddaughter of a Zapatista and countless more unnamed Indigenous revolutionaries fighting for sovereignty and land back, Sophie's artistic practice comes with a deep commitment to home-making in cultural memory and preservation. Sophie's muses are currently the eclipses, makeshift altars, and their own life.

Owl Goingback
Grass Dancer
(Originally Published in *Excalibur*, Warner Books, 1995)
Owl Goingback has been writing professionally for over thirty years, and is the author of numerous novels, children's book, screenplays, magazine articles, short stories, and comics. He is a two-time Bram Stoker Award Winner, a Nebula Award Nominee, and the recipient of a Lifetime Achievement Award from the Horror Writers Association. His books include *Crota, Darker Than Night, Evil Whispers, Breed, Shaman Moon, Coyote Rage, Eagle Feathers, The Gift*, and *Tribal Screams*. Owl's stories are often inspired by his Native American heritage (Choctaw/Cherokee). In addition to writing under his own name, he has ghostwritten for Hollywood celebrities.

Edward Winslow Gifford
The First Tui Tonga
The Origin of the Magellan Clouds
(Both Originally Published in *Tongan Myths & Tales,* Bernice P. Bishop Museum, 1924)
Edward Winslow Gifford (1887–1959) was an anthropologist, ethnographer, and author born in Oakland, California. Fascinated with the indigenous peoples of California, Gifford focused much of his career on ethnography of the state's many tribes. He became an assistant curator at the Museum of Anthropology, within the University of California, Berkeley, and later joined the Bayard Dominic Expedition of 1920. During this expedition he conducted anthropological and archaeological surveys of the indigenous Polynesian people of Tonga. In 1945 he became a professor of anthropology at Berkeley, and he rose to the position of director at the Museum of Anthropology.

George Bird Grinnell
Scarface
Origin of the Medicine Pipe
(Both Originally Published in *Blackfoot Lodge Tales: The Story of a Prairie People*, 1892)
As an anthropologist, historian, naturalist and conservationist, George Bird Grinnell (1849-1938) did much to educate and inform about the Native American people during the latter part of the nineteenth and beginning of the twentieth centuries. His extensive studies of the Cheyenne and Pawnee tribes resulted in renowned works such as Blackfoot Lodge Tales (1892) and The Punishment of the Stingy and Other Indian Stories (1901) and Blackfeet Indian Stories (1913); Grinnell was also instrumental in the protection and conservation of the American wilderness and preservation of the threatened American Bison.

Shane Hawk
Imitate
(Originally Published in *Anoka: A Collection of Indigenous Horror*, 2020)
Shane Hawk, a member of the Cheyenne and Arapaho Tribes of Oklahoma, is a high school history teacher, writer, and editor. He entered the horror scene with his first publication, *Anoka: A Collection of Indigenous Horror*, in October 2020 via Black Hills Press. Hawk is also the co-editor of *Never Whistle at Night*, an anthology of Indigenous dark fiction that Penguin Random House will publish in 2023. You can find him in San Diego wearing his Support Indigenous Literature hat, alongside his beautiful wife, Tori. Learn more by visiting shanehawk.com.

Somto Ihezue
Whole
(Originally Published in *Cossmass Infinities*, 2022)
Somto Ihezue is an Igbo writer, filmmaker, and wildlife enthusiast. His story 'Whole' draws insight from a facet of the Igbo culture – one that interprets the five human senses as spiritual entities through which all life manifests. His works have appeared and are forthcoming in Tordotcom, Fireside, Cossmass Infinities, Flash Fiction Online, Afritondo, OnSpec, Omenana, and elsewhere. He is part of the editorial team of both Cast of Wonders, and Android Press. He lives with his sister, their dog, River; and their cats, Ify and Salem. He can be found on Twitter via @somto_Ihezue.

James Athearn Jones
The Mother of the World
The Wahconda's Son
The Origin of Women
(All Originally Published in *Traditions of the North American Indians,* Colburn & Bentley, 1830)
Born in the state of Massachusetts in 1790, James Athearn Jones would go on to work as a lawyer and editor. It is for his work collecting Native American legends that he is best remembered, however, beginning in 1820 with *Traditions of the North American Indians, or Tales of an Indian Camp,* which featured stories told to him by an Indian woman of the Gayhead tribe who was employed as his nurse. Jones would write three volumes in the *Traditions of the North American Indian* series prior to his death in 1853.

His Hawaiian Majesty Kalākaua
Hua, King of Hana: The Legend of the Great Famine of the Twelfth Century
Kelea, the Surf-Rider of Maui
Kaala, the Flower of Lanai
(All Originally Published in *The Legends and Myths of Hawaii*, Charles L Webster & Company, 1888)
His Hawaiian Majesty Kalākaua (1836–1891) was the last king and penultimate monarch of the Kingdom of Hawaii. Following the reign of his predecessor Lunalilo, Kalākaua was elected to the throne in 1874. Also called the Merrie Monarch, Kalākaua was known for his cheerful personality, entertaining guests with his singing and ukulele playing. Although he planned the creation of a Polynesian confederation, the United States' colonial machinations forced Kalākaua to sign a new constitution which greatly diminished the monarchy's power. He named his sister, Lili'uokalani, as his heir-apparent in 1877, and following his death she became Hawaii's final monarch.

D.K. Lawhorn
Little Pieces of Flint
(First Publication)
D.K. Lawhorn (he/him) has stories that have appeared in *Pyre Magazine, Haven Spec,* and *Ghost Orchid Press*. He is a citizen of the Monacan Indian Nation and lives on his ancestral land in Virginia with his legion of rescue cats. He is studying Native Speculative Literature at Randolph College's MFA in Creative Writing program. Follow him on Twitter @d_k_lawhorn or visit his website at dklawhorn.com.

J. William Lloyd
The Story of the Creation
The Story of the Flood
(Both Published in *Aw-aw-tam Indian Nights: The Myths and Legends of the Pimas of Arizona,* The Lloyd Group, 1911)

J. William Lloyd (1857–1940) was a writer, poet, and individualist anarchist. Born in Westfield, New Jersey, Lloyd moved to various states throughout the American South and Midwest, living occasionally on experimental colonies. His first book, a collection of poetry entitled *Wind-Harp Songs*, was published in 1896. He held a strong fascination with the Pima Native Americans of Arizona, publishing a collection of their myths and legends in 1911. He also wrote for numerous radical journals, including his own magazine *The Free Comrade*, basing his views on anarchism upon theories of natural law.

Tsitsi Mapepa
The Call of Ancestors
(First Publication)
Yeredzu River
(First Publication)
Tsitsi Mapepa is inspired by her dreams to write poetry and short stories and is a firm believer in the magic that is in the endless puzzle of the letters of all language. She studied at Manukau Institute of Technology, where she won an award of excellence in 2016 and the Kairangatira award in the BCA in 2018, before her MCW degree at the University of Auckland in 2020. Tsitsi's work has been published on *Ribcaged* (MIT Spoken 2017), *Little Treasures* (2018), *Black Creatives Aotearoa* (2020), and the *Ko Aotearoa Tatou Anthology* (2020), and *Radio New Zealand* (2021). The theme of *First Peoples, Shared Stories* has allowed Tsitsi to explore a side of her origins through words.

Sir Clements Markham K.C.B. (translator)
The Fable of the Origin of the People of Peru
(Originally Published in *History of the Incas*, printed for the Hakluyt Society, 1907)
Sir Clements Markham K.C.B. (1830–1916) was an English geographer, writer, and explorer. Serving as secretary of the Royal Geography Society from 1863 to 1888, and later the society's president for a further twelve years, Markham organised the British National Antarctic Expedition of 1901–1904. He is known for spurring the nineteenth-century revival of Britain's interest in exploring the Antarctic, as well as his prolific writings on geography, travel, and history. He also produced English translations of numerous Spanish works including Pedro Sarmient de Gamboa's *History of the Incas*.

Minnie Martin
Morena-Y-A-Letsatsi, or the Sun Chief
(Originally Published in *Basutoland: Its Legends and Customs*, Nichols & Co., 1903)
Minnie Martin was the wife of a government official, who arrived in South Africa in 1891 and settled in Lesotho (at that time Basutoland). In her preface to *Basutoland: Its Legends and Customs* (1903) she explains that 'We both liked the country from the first, and I soon became interested in the people. To enable myself to understand them better, I began to study the language, which I can now speak fairly well.' And thus she wrote this work, at the suggestion of a friend. Despite the inaccuracies pointed out by E. Sidney Hartland in his review of her book, he deemed the work 'an unpretentious, popular account of a most interesting branch of the Southern Bantus and the country they live in.'

C. Hart Merriam
How Ah-Ha'-Le Stole the Sun for the Valley People
The Birth of Wek'-Wek and the Creation of Man
(Both Originally Published in *The Dawn of the World: Myths and Weird Tales Told by the Miwok Indians of California*, Arthur H. Clarke Co., 1910)

Clinton Hart Merriam (1855-1942) was a zoologist, naturalist and doctor who conducted a number of expeditions to the American West in the latter half of the nineteenth century. Reliant on the knowledge of Native American guides in his surveys, Merriam would in later years become fascinated by their culture and abandon his zoological work to study the tribes of California, hoping to preserve their knowledge, language, customs and mythology before they were lost forever,. This would lead to the publication of his book *The Dawn of the World: Myths and Weird Tales Told by the Miwok Indians of California* (1910).

Arnoldo Millán Zubia

Buuts' Ka Luuk'
(First Publication)
Arnoldo Millán Zubia is a Mexican writer of Dark Fiction. His influences range from writers such as Edgar Allan Poe, Horacio Quiroga, and Gustavo Adolfo Bécquer to Richard Matheson and Stephen King. The history of mankind is a history of oppression, subjugation and annihilation of entire peoples. For academic interests, we have sometimes been shown the tyrants of the past in a flattering, undeserving light, disguising them as virtuous pioneers and pursuers of progress. In other words: wolves in sheep's clothing. Buuts' Ka Luuk', which translates from Mayan as 'Smoke that Swallows', shows us that sometimes even conquerors get conquered.

Paula Morris

Foreword, First Peoples, Shared Stories
Red Christmas
(Originally Published in *Forbidden Cities*, 2008)
Three Princesses
(Originally Published in *False River*, 2018)
Paula Morris MNZM (Ngāti Wai, Ngāti Whātua, Ngāti Manuhiri) is an award-winning novelist, short story writer, essayist and editor from New Zealand. She is the author of award-winning novels such as *Queen of Beauty* (2002) and *Rangatira* (2011), as well as fiction and nonfiction collections: *Forbidden Cities* (2008), *On Coming Home* (2015) and *False River* (2017). Paula holds degrees from universities in New Zealand, the UK and the US, including a D.Phil from the University of York and an MFA from the Iowa Writers' Workshop. She is the founder of the Academy of New Zealand Literature and Wharerangi, the Māori literature hub. She has been awarded numerous residencies and fellowships and since 2003 has taught creative writing at universities, including Tulane University in New Orleans, and the University of Sheffield in England. She is director of the Master in Creative Writing programme at the University of Auckland in New Zealand.

Weyodi OldBear

A Mother's Lament [(Justice and the Delusions of Power Part I)]
(First Publication)
Biter's Tale [(Justice and the Delusions of Power Part II)]
(First Publication)
Weyodi OldBear is a voting citizen of the Comanche Nation, living in her band's traditional range in New Mexico. Her work includes world building for the Nebula nominated table-top role playing game Coyote & Crow, as well as contributions to the anthologies *A Howl* and the Water Protectors Legal Collective Guide Comic. Her story 'Red Lessons' is co-winner of the 2017 Imagining Indigenous Futurisms Award. Raised listening to the strange tales of elders who were alive when her tribe was brought into captivity it seems only right that she should tell some unsettling allegorical stories of her own.

K. Langloh Parker

Goonur, the Woman-Doctor

(Originally Published in *Australian Legendary Tales*, Melville, Mullen & Slade, 1897)

K. Langloh Parker (1856–1940) was the pen name of Catherine Eliza Somerville Stow, an Australian author and ethnographer. Living in northern New South Wales, she was introduced to the culture of the Yuwaalaraay people and developed a strong affinity. Her work mainly involved the recording of the Yuwaalaraay's stories and mythology. Although her accounts are considered the most accurate and comprehensive of their time, they nonetheless reflect European views on the Aboriginal peoples of Australia and present their stories through a Western lens.

C.W. Peck

The Legend of the Pleiades

(Originally Published in *Australian Legends*, Stafford, 1925)

Born in 1875 in Woonona, a suburb of Wollongong in New South Wales, Charles William Peck worked as a student teacher from 1891 in the nearby suburb of Thirroul, which is known for being the place D H Lawrence wrote his novel *Kangaroo* in 1920. Little more is known about Peck apart from the fact that he served in World War I with the Australian Imperial Force and wrote *Australian Legends*, a compilation of legends telling the stories of the Indigenous Aboriginal people. His enduring love of botany prompted his enthusiastic but eventually unsuccessful campaign to get the national flower of Australia changed from the wattle to the waratah.

R. Sutherland Rattray (translator)

A Short History, Purporting to Give the Origin of the Hausa Nation and the Story of their Conversion to the Mohammedan Religion

How Brothers and Sisters First Came to Quarrel and Hate Each Other

(Originally Published in *Hausa Folk-lore, Customs, Proverbs, Etc.*, Clarendon Press 1913)

Robert Sutherland Rattray (1881–1938) was an Official anthropologist working for the British colonial government in Gold Coast, now Ghana, across the 1920s. His books on the Ashanti, or Asante, people have been characterised by some contemporary writers as 'thoughtful and nuanced', as his personal contact with the Ashanti helped him to develop an expansive and intimate knowledge of their culture. During his time in Africa he learned numerous local languages, enabling him to go on to translate Maalam Shaihua's *Hausa Folk-lore*.

Claudia Recinos Seldeen

A Mayan Story

(First Publication)

Claudia is a Florida native currently residing in Western New York. She is the author of the young adult novels *To Be Maya* and *Catch Me If I Fall*, and her poetry has appeared in *The Amphibian Literary Journal* and *MONO*. Claudia is a first-generation Guatemalan American. Though she makes her home in the US, she continues to nurture her Mayan roots through her work. When not writing, she's either spending quality time with her husband and son, or flying through the air on a trapeze. To find out more, please visit recinosseldeen.com.

A.W. Reed

Māui Tames The Sun

Creation

The Coming of Kūmara

Patupaiarehe
Taniwha
Denizens of the Sea
(All Originally Published in Two Volumes by Reed Publishing in *Māori Legends*, 1972 and *Māori Myth*, 1977)
Alexander Wyclif Reed (1908–1979) wrote over 200 books, many on the myths and culture of the Māori and Australian Aboriginal people. With his aunt, Isabel, and his uncle, Alfred Hamish Reed, he ran the publishing firm now known as Reed Publishing (NZ), which specialised in New Zealand literature. Hailing from a family of book lovers, Reed especially enjoyed researching and recording Māori stories, mostly from secondary sources, which he presented in an accessible way that appealed to many readers. His books include *Myths and Legends of Māoriland* (1946), *An Illustrated Encyclopaedia of Māori Life* (1963) and *Place Names of Australia* (1973).

David J. Schmidt (translator)
Mexpakinte, the Shadow Woman
(First Publication)
David J. Schmidt is an author, podcaster, and multilingual translator who splits his time between Mexico City and San Diego, CA. He is a proponent of immigrants' rights and fair trade, and works with worker-owned co-ops in Mexico to help them develop alternative, fair sources of income. Schmidt has published a variety of books, essays, short stories, and articles in English and Spanish. His books include *Three Nights in the Clown Motel*, a book of 'non-fiction horror', as well as the series *Gone Viral: Urban Legends of the COVID-19 Pandemic*. He speaks twelve languages (including three indigenous languages of Mexico) and has been to 33 countries.

Maalam Shaihua
A Short History, Purporting to Give the Origin of the Hausa Nation and the Story of their Conversion to the Mohammedan Religion
How Brothers and Sisters First Came to Quarrel and Hate Each Other
(Originally Published in *Hausa Folk-lore, Customs, Proverbs, Etc.*, Clarendon Press 1913)
Hailing from the Hausa people of West and Central Africa, Maalam Shaihua collected and transcribed scores of traditional Hasa folk-tales between 1907 and 1911. Published in his collection *Hasa Folk-Lore* (1913), his work preserves the culture and mythology of the Hasa people. Working closely with Africanist, anthropologist, and translator Robert Sutherland Rattray, Shaihua produced a pronunciation guide and some information on Hausa customs in addition to the stories. The significance of his work is due in part to the fact that it was first written in Hausa and then carefully translated, resulting in English versions that accurately reflect the originals.

Lewis Spence
Creation Story of the Mixtecs
The Mayan Creation Story
The Myth of Huathiacuri
A Story of the Rise and Fall of the Toltecs
The Creation Story of The Third Book
(Originally Published in *The Myths of Mexico & Peru*, Ballantyne & Company, 1913)
Scottish author and journalist James Lewis Thomas Chalmers Spence (1874–1955) founded the Scottish National Movement which campaigned for Scottish independence. He also edited various publications including The Scotsman and had a lifelong interest in folklore, traditions and the occult, specifically the

fabled lost city of Atlantis. Spence's interests ranged from the tales of his country of birth to Britain, Europe, Egypt, and North and South America, with his popularised version of the Popul Vuh, the sacred text of the K'iche Mayans (1908) written to share his love of ancient myths with the English-speaking world.

Henry M. Stanley
King Gumbi and His Lost Daughter
The Adventures of Saruti
The Search for the Home of the Sun
(Originally Published in *My Dark Companions and Their Strange Stories*, Sampson Low, Marston, & Co, 1893)
'Dr Livingstone, I presume?' Welshman Sir Henry Morton Stanley (1841–1904) is probably most famous for a line he may or may not have uttered, on encountering the missionary and explorer he had been sent to locate in Africa. He was also an ex-soldier who fought for the Confederate Army, the Union Army, and the Union Navy before becoming a journalist and explorer of central Africa. He joined Livingstone in the search for the source of the Nile and worked for King Leopold II of Belgium in the latter's mission to conquer the Congo basin. His works include *How I Found Livingstone* (1872), *Through the Dark Continent* (1878), *The Congo and the Founding of Its Free State* (1885), *In Darkest Africa* (1890) and *My Dark Companions* (1893).

Captain C. H. Stigand
Nunda the Slayer and the Origin of the One-Eyed
Binti Ali the Clever
Lila and Fila
The Wakilindi Saga: Mbega, a Child of Ill Omen
(All Originally Published in *Black Tales for White Children*, Houghton Mifflin Company, 1933)
Chauncey Hugh Stigand (1877–1919) was a British army officer, colonial administrator and big game hunter who served in Burma, British Somaliland and British East Africa. He was in charge of the Kajo Kaji district of what is now South Sudan, and was later made governor of the Upper Nile province and then Mongalla Province before being killed during a 1919 uprising of the Aliab Dinka people. During his time in Africa he managed to write prolifically, from Central African Game and its Spoor (1906), through *Black Tales for White Children* (1914), to *A Nuer-English Vocabulary*, posthumously published in 1923.

Percy Amaury Talbot
How the Moon First Came into the Sky
How Sun and Moon Went up to the Sky
How the First Rain Came
How All the Rivers First Came on Earth
(All Originally Published in *In the Shadow of the Bush*, G.H. Doran, 1912)
Anthropologist and academic, Percy Amaury Talbot (1877–1945) was a British colonial district officer who served in southern Nigeria in the early twentieth century. He authored several works chronicling the legends of the Nigerian, Ekoi and Chad people, including *In the Shadow of the Bush* (1912), which includes creation stories and animal fables. An enthusiastic anthropologist, Talbot donated to the British Museum and the Pitt-Rivers Museum. His story 'The Treasure House in the Bush' is thought to be a Nigerian version of Ali Baba and the Forty Thieves' from *One Thousand and One Nights*.

Drew Hayden Taylor

When Angels Come Knocking
(Originally Published in *Amazing Stories*, Fall/Worldcon 2018)
Drew Hayden Taylor (Anishinaabe) is an award winning playwright, novelist, journalist and filmmaker. Born and raised on the Curve Lake First Nation in Ontario, Canada, he has done everything from performing stand up comedy at the Kennedy Centre in Washington D.C, to serving as Artistic Director of Canada's premiere Indigenous theatre company, Native Earth Performing Arts. Next year, his 35th book, an Indigenous horror novel, will be released by McClelland & Steward and the second season of his documentary series, *Going Native*, will run on the Aboriginal Peoples Television Network.

Charles John Tibbits

The Funeral Fire
The Snail and the Beaver
(All Originally Published in Folk-lore and Legends: North American Indian, W.W. Gibbings, 1890)
Charles John Tibbits (1861–1935) was an English journalist, newspaper editor, and author. He attended Oxford university and married the novelist Annie Olive Brazier. Tibbits wrote prolifically on folk tales and legends, publishing extensive collections. One of his most popular works is the series *Folk-Lore and Legends*, which features numerous volumes of tales from cultures and societies around the world. These include folklore of Native American nations, Scandinavia, Russia, and Scotland, among others.

Brigit Truex

Beaver's Tail
(Originally Published in *Eye to the Telescope*, 2019)
The Three Sisters
(First Publication)
Woodchuck Winter
(First Publication)
Brigit Truex, an Abenaki/Cree writer and artist, lives in Kentucky after moving from the California Sierra Mountain foothills. Wherever she lives, the landscape figures prominently in her work. With her First Nations heritage, traditional story-telling is a timely and accessible means of passing on values and insights of Native peoples. Subtle humour often catches the audience's interest and teaches at the same time. She uses the same approach in her artwork as she celebrates her lineage. An internationally published poet, her credits include *Yellow Medicine Review, Native Literatures Generations, About Place, Reckoning, ImPress, Vallum*, and others. Anthologies include *I Was Indian* and *In Its Many Forms*. Her latest book, *Sierra Silk*, is available on Amazon. Her website is booksandsuchbybrigittruex.wordpress.com

David Unaipon

Confusion of Tongue
The Gherawhar (Goana)
Whowie
Why All the Animals Peck At the Selfish Owl: the Coming of the Light
The Water Rat who Discovered the Secret of Fire and How it was Taken from Him by the Eagle Hawk
A Wonderful Bun Bar Rang (Lizard)
(These Extracts are Reproduced from David Unaipon's *Legendary Tales of the Australian Aborigines*, Melbourne University Press, Carlton, 2001)
David Unaipon (1872–1967) was an author, inventor, and preacher of the Ngarrindjeri Aboriginal people. Travelling throughout Southern Australia, Unaipon gathered and published a wide-ranging

collection of myths and legends from Australia's Aboriginal peoples, reflecting the richness and diversity of their culture. Also penning numerous articles for the *Sydney Daily Telegraph* beginning in 1924, he was the first Aboriginal Australian writer to be published. He also gave lectures on Aboriginal rights and culture. Originally published under the name of anthropologist William Ramsay Smith, Unaipon's collection of stories were later republished, under his own name, as *Legendary Tales of the Australian Aborigines.*

Pedro Vázquez Luna

Mexpakinte, the Shadow Woman
(First Publication)
Pedro 'Pepe' Vázquez Luna is of the indigenous Tzotzil ethnicity of the highlands of Chiapas, southern Mexico. He has worked for years with the Fair Trade coffee farmers' co-op, Maya Vinic. Pepe heard this personal account from his grandfather Antonio, who swore that it happened exactly as conveyed here. He conveyed this story to translator David J. Schmidt in the town of Acteal, Chiapas, Mexico, in August 2011.

Jay Hansford C. Vest

Glade of the Uncles
(First Publication)
Jay Hansford Vest is a citizen of the Monacan Indian Nation; raised with the traditional tribal narratives that included 'Mother's Brother'; he was educated with a focus upon Native American religious traditions at the University of Montana and he drew upon this education to craft 'Glade of the Uncles' from the narratives of his childhood. He has taught American Insuan studies at several universities throughout the United States, Germany, and Canada; in a career of nearly 40 years. Recently he retired as a full professor from the University of North Carolina at Pembroke.

Laika Wallace

Snow Blindness
(First Publication)
Laika Wallace is a Two Spirit Mi'kmaw and Passamaquoddy author living in Ottawa, Canada with hir guinea pigs, ball python, and partners. Its work can be found in the *X/Y: A Junk Drawer of Trans Voices* and *Fear & Trembling* zines, and on his website, laikacore.neoticities.org. He writes YA fantasy, drawing from its experiences as a disabled, LGBT, indigenous wo/man. Aside from writing, sie loves speculative biology, reading, dreams, the history of soda production, and all sorts of animals.

Alice Werner

The Girls Who Wanted New Teeth
The Thunder's Bride
Kwege and Bahati
The Tale of Murile
(All Originally Published in *Myths and Legends of the Bantu*, George G. Harrap and Co., 1933)
Alice Werner (1859–1935) was a writer, poet and professor of Swahili and Bantu languages. She travelled widely in her early life but by 1894 had focused her writing on African culture and language, and later joined the School of Oriental Studies, working her way up from lecturer to professor. *Myths and Legends of the Bantu* (1933) was her last main work, but others on African topics include

The Language Families of Africa (1915), *Introductory Sketch of the Bantu Languages* (1919), *The Swahili Saga of Liongo Fumo (1926)*, *A First Swahili Book* (1927), *Swahili Tales* (1929), *Structure and Relationship of African Languages* (1930) and *The Story of Miqdad and Mayasa* (1932).

Dr. Eldon Yellowhorn
Introduction, First Peoples, Shared Stories

Dr. Eldon Yellowhorn is a member of the Piikani Nation and professor at Simon Fraser University where he teaches Indigenous Studies. He grew up on the Peigan Indian Reserve, attended the University of Louisville and later the University of Calgary where he completed his Bachelor of Science degree in Geography in 1983. After working at Head-Smashed-In Buffalo Jump he returned to the UofC in 1984 and completed a Bachelor of Arts degree in Archaeology in 1986. After he finished his degree, he was a Curator Intern at the Glenbow Museum until 1988. He was awarded a fellowship with the Smithsonian Institution in 1988 and worked on an archaeological site in Colorado. When he returned he started graduate school at Simon Fraser University, where he received a Master of Arts degree in 1993. He started his doctoral studies at McGill University in 1995 and received his PhD in 2002. He was recruited by Simon Fraser University in 1998 to develop the First Nations Studies Program. He established the Department of Indigenous Studies in 2012 and was the first Chair until 2017. His research combines archaeology, history and Blackfoot language revitalization. His published works have appeared in journals including *Native Studies Review* and *Plains Anthropologist*. Books he has co-authored include *Turtle Island: The Story of North America's First People* and *What the Eagle Sees: Indigenous Stories of Rebellion and Renewal*.

GOTHIC FANTASY

For our books, calendars, blog
and latest special offers please see:
flametreepublishing.com